THE
JAMES LEE BURKE
COLLECTION

CONTAINING

TO THE BRIGHT AND SHINING SUN

LAY DOWN MY SWORD AND SHIELD

THE LOST GET-BACK BOOGIE

PICADOR

To the Bright and Shining Sun was first published in 1970 in the United States
© James Lee Burke 1970

Lay Down My Sword and Shield was first published in 1971 in the United States
by The Countryman Press, Inc., Vermont
© James Lee Burke 1971

The Lost Get-Back Boogie was first published in 1986 in the United States
by Louisiana State University Press
© James Lee Burke 1978 and 1986

This collection first published in 1993 in Great Britain by Picador
an imprint of Macmillan Publishers Ltd
25 Eccleston Place, London SW1W 9NF
and Basingstoke

Associated companies throughout the world

ISBN 0 330 32118 8

This collection © James Lee Burke 1993

7 9 8 6

A CIP catalogue record for this book is available from
the British Library

Typeset by Cambridge Composing (UK) Limited, Cambridge
Printed and bound in Great Britain by
Mackays of Chatham PLC, Chatham, Kent

CONTENTS

TO THE BRIGHT
AND
SHINING SUN

This book is for my mother,
Mrs James Lee Burke, Sr,
of Houston, Texas,
and for my uncle and aunt,
Mr and Mrs Oran Burke,
of Baton Rouge, Louisiana

Come all you fellers, so young and so fine
Don't seek your fortune in the dark and dreary mine
It'll form to a habit and seep in your soul
Till the stream of your blood is black as the coal.

There's many a man I knowed in my day
Who lived but to labor his whole life away.
Like a fiend for his dope, a drunkard his wine,
A man can have lust for the lure of the mine

MERLE TRAVIS

ONE

Three men and a boy sat in the dark in a battered 1958 Ford on a shale road that wound along the base of the mountain. One of them smoked a hand-rolled cigarette in the cup of his hands, bending down his head below the level of the windows whenever he drew in the smoke. The first leaves were shredding from the trees, and they rattled dryly along the road in the wind. Around the curve of the road was the coal tipple, huge and looming over the railway tracks that led past the mine opening down towards the switch where the C & O made up the long freight cars that would eventually take the coal to Pittsburgh. The boy, Perry Woodson Hatfield James, sat in the back seat with one hand gripped tightly under his thigh and the other over his wrist. He could feel the sweat form under his arms and run cold down his sides. He believed that if fear had a smell it would already have soaked through his clothes and permeated everything in the car. He could smell it in himself every time he took a breath. It was a rancid odour, like something dead in the sun. Big J.W. and Little J.W. sat in the front, immobile against the glow of the moon except when little J.W. bent to smoke off the cigarette. They were half brothers, both fathered by a North Carolina moonshiner who was killed at the age of seventy-six in the dirt streets of Harlan while giving whiskey free to the miners when John L. Lewis first organized the coal fields and the National Guard was sent in by the state to shoot down a man who tried to stop a scab from crossing the picket.

Big J.W. wore a tin hat down low on his forehead, and his skin was grained with coal dust, rubbed so deep around the corners of his eyes that it looked like a burn. The faded pinstriped coat he wore over his overalls was stretched almost to tearing across his angular shoulders, and the knobs on his wrist looked like white bones sticking out of his sleeves. His teeth were yellow and long, and his fingernails were as thick and hard as tortoise shell, broken to the quick and coloured with blue-black half-moons. His wife cut his hair with a straight-edged razor, and it hung unevenly over the back of his neck like a girl's. Little J.W. was a small round man with a hard, little, round stomach that pushed against his work trousers. He was thought to be an invaluable man in the mines because he could go a half mile up and down a narrow shaft on his hands and knees like a groundhog. His soft, brown eyes and quiet mountain accent caused few people to pay any particular attention to him except when there was an explosion or cave-in down in the hole and somebody was needed to crawl through the fallen limestone and timbers to some gas-filled pocket deep in the earth where no sane person would go. But those who knew him well realized that he was a much more dangerous person than Big J.W., and when set in motion he would go at something or someone with the quiet rage of a hot iron scorched across wood. Once, he and an uncle argued while drinking, and after the uncle drew a knife, Little J.W. hit him six times in the head with a poker and threw him off the front porch of the company cabin into the yard. 'Pull a knife on me, will you,' he said, the poker still in his hand. 'Pull one against your own blood, will you. Well, if you get home tonight by yourself that's all right with me, and by God if you die out here in the lot that's all right with me, too.'

On the back floor of the car, under a blanket, were a lever-action 30-calibre Winchester, a double-barrelled twelve-gauge with the barrels sawed off two inches in front of the chambers, fourteen cans of dynamite, three primers, and a four-hundred-foot spool of cap wire. The boy also knew that each of the three men with him carried a .38, since they would no more leave home without it than they would without their trousers.

'It ain't we got to blow it,' he said. 'Maybe just set it up on the mountain and push some rock down on the hole.'

'I done told you, honey,' Big J.W. said. 'We're a-blowing that tipple right over on the moneyman's head. We didn't risk no year in Frankfort breaking open the shack just to move some rock around.'

'Moon's a-setting,' Little J.W. said.

'Get them charges out, Perry,' Bee, the man next to the boy, said. He was the boy's uncle, a tall man who had to stoop slightly so his head wouldn't hit the top of the car. Like Big J.W., he wore overalls, with a leather belt around his waist, and a suitcoat and a cloth slug cap on his head. Years ago he had lost his dentures, and his mouth was collapsed in rows of thick creases around his lips. His gums were blackened from the wad of snuff that was always under his tongue. During the forties he did two years in the Kentucky penitentiary for shooting a company deputy, and because he had refused to name any of the other men who shot three more company men in the same battle, he was made a business agent for the United Mine Workers when he was paroled. He rasped and coughed into his sleeve. He'd had silicosis since he was twenty-five from working in the mines before the companies had been forced to put ventilation systems in the shaft.

'What if them scabs is there?' Perry said.

'They're a-going right with it,' Big J.W. said. 'They can steal food out of a man's mouth down in hell if they've still a mind for it.'

Bee tore the blanket off the explosives and guns. 'Now you build them charges,' he said. 'By God, there ain't nobody saying a James or a Hatfield puts a scab before a working-man.'

The boy screwed the cans end to end, tightening each socket securely. He built the charges in cylinders of four cans each, with a primer on the butt end of each row. The sweat on his hands was cold against the metal. There's enough here to put half the mountain down in the holler, he thought. Them four hundred feet of wire ain't even going to give us running distance. We'll be a-setting here with rocks big as cars coming down on us. I seen them drop a charge like this on Black Mountain in Harlan once, and the trees and rocks burst all over the sun. The dust stayed black across the crest of the ridge until twilight when it started to rain. He wished he was back home in the cabin now, with the dry poplar logs and huge coal lumps burning in the blackened sandstone fireplace. He was too afraid to care whether he worked union or not. Maybe the operator ain't wrong, he thought. Maybe he can't afford to pay scale, and it ain't nothing but trouble to push union in the coal field. We was doing all right with what they was giving us. Twelve dollars a day is more than we're a-getting on the picket. There wasn't no shooting and no company men coming around the houses asking where the men was at the night before. We didn't have nobody cutting off our charge at the store. And on Saturday afternoon a feller had a hard dollar in his pocket to ride the bus into Winfro Valley for the Barn Dance that's over the radio.

Then he felt an old secret shame inside him at his fear. His people had been against the operator since his grandfather had had his mineral rights stolen out from under him for fifty cents an acre by a New York sharper – an eastern feller, with a gold watch that must have cost a hundred dollars hanging on his waistcoat, his grandfather had said. He set down at your table and told ye how good your fatback and greens was and how the half dollar would pay the country tax and said the land wasn't good for anything no way. Bought up the whole holler for no more than the price of that train ticket from New York. And didn't tell nobody that what ye signed give the operator the right to do whatever he wanted to the top of the land. They could tear away the mountain and let it slide all across your tobacco crop, there wasn't nothing ye could do about it except go to work for him.

Perry knew that no James or Hatfield in his family had ever been afraid of operators, company thugs, strikebreakers with their axe handles, or even the National Guard. His grandfather said he was related to Frank James, the outlaw who hid out in the Cumberland after robbing a bank with Jesse over in West Virginia, and his mother was a direct descendant of Devil Anse Hatfield, who killed McCoys all over Pike and Logan counties. His family had been union people even before John L. Lewis and the CIO organized the coal field. They had fought side by side with the organizers from the National Miners Union before the Great Depression, when the man who breathed the word 'union' was fired from his job, evicted from his company-owned cabin, maybe run out of the county by the sheriff, and sometimes shot and thrown down the hollow.

4

'It's dark enough now,' Big J.W. said. 'Hand baby brother up the shotgun.'

Perry gave Little J.W. the sawed-off double-barrel and watched him break open the breech and plop two shells into the chambers. Little J.W. rolled down his window and held the shotgun outside against the door.

The entrance to the mine was a dark, square gap in the face of the mountain. Farther down, a huge slag heap was smoking in the cold. Since the time he was a small child Perry could not remember ever having been near a mine without smelling the odour of burning slag. It was a fire that never went out because its source of fuel was never stopped, and the air around his home always had the same acrid stench to it. The coal from the tipple spilled across the road into a black slide and down the gulley into a stream. Next to the road a discarded sign on a wooden stick, left from the day's picketing, was propped at an angle against a rock. It read in crude, hand-printed letters: THIS MINE UNFAIR IT DON'T HIRE UNION MEN.

'They didn't leave no guard,' Little J.W. said.

'Watch that opening. Them scabs might be a-drawing right down on my windshield now,' Big J.W. said. 'Remember when they shot up Noah Combs? He never knew where they was at till he was right up on the shaft.'

Bee took the .38 special from the bib pocket of his overalls and let it rest in his palm against his leg. Big J.W. drove past the tipple a hundred yards and stopped the car under an overhang of pine trees. The base of the burning slag heap glowed red in the breeze. Down in the hollow Perry could hear the bats squeaking through the darkness as they swept in circles over the creek.

'Don't do no talking when we're out of the car,' Big J.W. said. 'And if you see a scab, drop him fast before he gets off a shot. He hits one of them primers and they'll have to scrub us off the mountain.'

The four of them got out of the car on to the road. The wind against the sweat on Perry's face made him cold. He and Big J.W. each carried two sticks of charges; they held the spool of cap wire between them with an iron pipe stuck through the centre. They moved up the mountain towards the tipple, over the scattered lumps of coal and slag. The rocks rolling down under the boots and hands sounded to Perry like an avalanche crashing into the hollow. There ain't no sense in it, he thought. You ain't got to blow half the country to let them know we wasn't working for no one-twenty-five. There ain't going to be no work anyhow when the tipple goes.

Before they got to the base of the tipple, Little J.W. and Bee dropped to one knee and pointed their guns to each side of the structure. Bee held his .38 straight ahead of him, with his left hand gripped around his wrist to steady his arm. The boy and Big J.W. moved up to the steel stanchions sunk in concrete that supported the weight of the tipple. Perry's fingers felt thick and uncoordinated as he and Big J.W. placed the charges around a stanchion on the downhill side of the mountain and wrapped them securely with bailing wire. Big J.W. pulled the end of the cap wire loose from the spool and carefully set the small, plastic tube of gelatin detonator across a primer head and wound it over with electrician's tape. Then he took the spool of wire and made two turns around the bottom of the stanchion and tied a sailor's bowknot in it so that the tube of gelatin would not pull loose when they strung the wire downhill.

Big J.W. grabbed the boy's arm hard and pulled him into a crouch beside him. Several rocks rolled past them from above. They waited in the dark, hardly breathing, while the bats squeaked and whirled above them. Little J.W. and Bee looked like carved soldiers, frozen in their positions. Run now, the boy thought. Drop the wire and take off across the road into the holler. It ain't cowardice to run from getting shot at. People in wars do it. They didn't say nothing about shooting. It ain't fair to get shot at when you ain't got a gun.

'Set, boy,' Big J.W. whispered fiercely, his hand tightening on Perry's arm.

'We can't even see them. They'll tear us up soon as we get in the open.'

'Shut.' This time the hand clenched so tightly over his arm that the boy thought his blood veins were pressed flat against the bone.

6

They waited five minutes under the tipple, each with his hand squeezed hard on the iron bar that held the spool of wire, the slag cutting into their knees. Perry felt that even if a small rock was set in motion by the point of his boot a volley of shotgun and rifle fire would open up that would blow him backwards like a pile of rags on to the road.

'Start stringing it,' Big J.W. said. They crawled down the mountain between the two other men while Big J.W. pulled the cap wire off the spool with one hand and laid it out evenly behind them. Bee's extended arm was as rigid as a thick piece of wood as he kept his pistol pointed towards the top of the rise, his jaws sucking slowly on the saliva-smooth lump of snuff in his mouth. He started to cough once and pressed his palm across his face, spitting tobacco juice all over himself in a dry rasp. Perry knew that somewhere up there in the dark a man had the V-sight of a carbine lined in on the nape of his neck, and involuntarily he kept touching the back of his head with his hand. I wouldn't be afraid if they give me a gun, he thought. Them company guards ain't likely to stick to a fight when they get shot back at. Big J.W. wouldn't be a-grabbing on to me like he was something unless he had that special in his pocket.

He felt that a gun would be like a piece of magic in his pocket. He knew the heart-pounding and heavy breathing would stop if he could feel a .38 stuck hard down inside his trousers with the hammer on half cock. A gun was something smooth and lovely that fitted into the curve of a man's palm as though it were an extension of his arm. You could hold scabs and company deputies at a distance with it, and you didn't have to be afraid of a man letting off a shot-gun at you from the dark opening of a mine shaft. Noah Combs wouldn't have been shot up if he'd had his revolver in his hand rather than in his glove compartment when the company guards hit him from both sides of the road.

Perry and Big J.W. made the road and strung out the last of the wire to the car. Big J.W. unlatched the bonnet, raised it carefully, and pulled the cap off of a sparking-plug. Little J.W. and Bee moved backwards down the mountain, with their guns still pointed in front of them. The mountains looked cold as iron. The black trunks of the trees and the sharp rock walls of the cliffs were beginning to coat with ice. The boy's feet felt like stone. J.W. opened his pocketknife and shaved off the insulation from the end of the cap wire. He pulled the wire apart in two sections and wrapped the exposed metal strands around the head of the sparking-plug and replaced the rubber cap.

It ain't too late, the boy thought. Run on down the road as far as you can get and it ain't a part of you no longer. Stringing the wire didn't hurt nobody. Get across the ridge into the next holler and it's them burning out the operator. You didn't have nothing to do with sending that spark up to the charge. They ain't going to send a feller to Frankfort for laying some wire down a mountain when it would have got done if you was there or not.

He put his chafed hands down deep inside his pockets and felt his fingers come out through the worn lining against his thighs. His long, straw-coloured coarse hair was damp with sweat, even in the wind. The women in his family said he looked like a Hatfield, because at sixteen he was already taller than most of the men in the hollow where he lived. They said his eyes were like a Hatfield's, too, washed-out and pale, as though he were looking at you from under water. The pupils looked like pieces of burnt cinder. He was always able to pass for several years older than his age, and he had been working in shaft mines since his fifteenth birthday. His hands and the hard, bone places in his face had already begun to take on the black discoloration from the coal dust. In a few more years his face would look like Big J.W.'s, with the grit from the coal seam ground deeply into the pores, and no amount of scrubbing with the hard, skin-blistering soaps they sold at the company store could get rid of it. His clothes, made of different fabrics and belonging to at least two generations of the James family, were faded and patched and without any resemblance of a crease in them from being washed in boiling water and left to dry over a rick fence behind the cabin. The old suitcoat his father had given him was too large for his shoulders and it hung limply against his back. The work shoes he wore were hard as brick from walking through water every day at the bottom of the hole, and they had rubbed a ring of callous around his ankles. He looked as though he were made of sticks; but his long arms could swing a pick harder than a grown man, and he could work two shifts in a row in the mine when other men wouldn't stay sixteen hours in the hole even for double time.

'What we got to blow it for?' he whispered. 'They'll find the charge and know we wasn't fooling with them.'

'Because the operator don't sign a contract till it starts costing him money,' Big J.W. said.

'There's somebody moving around on that ridge,' Little J.W. said, the sawed-off double-barrel hanging loosely by his side. 'Knock the fire out of their ass and let's get off this mountain.'

'Get ready to pull that wire, baby brother,' Big J.W. said. He got into the front seat to start the engine, and the other three crouched behind the far side of the automobile.

They ain't got no sense, Perry thought, his head pulled down between his knees. We'll get buried under all that coal and rock. There won't even be no way to tell who we was when they dig us out.

As Big J.W. turned the ignition and pressed the starter, the boy leaped to his feet and ran for the far side of the road, towards the slope that fell off into the hollow. He heard the car engine gun and looked over his shoulder to see the tipple explode in white and yellow flame. The noise was as if God had crashed every lightning bolt He owned into the side of the mountain. The roar of sound and the heat rushed over him and beat against the walls of the hollow. In that instant when the flame ripped over the black sides of the tipple, he saw a man's silhouette stand out sharply on top, and then the whole structure erupted in pieces of torn metal into the sky. Years later he would never know if he actually heard a scream in that ear-splitting second or if something inside him was screaming. Slag and coal and rock clattered down on the car and broke both front windows. Little J.W. and Bee were hunched over on the ground, with their hands over their heads. A twisted spar whistled through the air like a cannon ball, cutting through the tops of two maple trees. The air became black with coal dust. As the last echo of the explosion began to thin in the distance, the boy could hear the leaves from the trees settling to the ground around him.

Little J.W. ran to the hood of the car, pulled the cap wire loose from the sparking-plug, and threw it behind him on the ground.

'Get that boy out of there,' he yelled.

Perry felt a pair of hands on each side of him grab his arms and pull him towards the car. He choked on the coal dust when he breathed. It seemed that the mountain with the jagged hole torn in its side was spinning rapidly around him and was about to crash in an avalanche over his head. He thought he was going to be sick, as though he had drunk too much corn whiskey on an empty stomach. Then he felt the movement of the car jolt him against the seat, and he knew he was roaring down the mountain, because he could see the trees change shape in the moonlight through the spiderwebbed cracks in the front windows.

TWO

The hollow where Perry lived looked like any other in the Cumberland range. A creek wound out of a cut in the mountain and washed over the smooth pebble bottom and grew larger from the small drainages flowing into it from the springs up on the hillside. The walls of the hollow rose straight up into the clouds, with dark holes in the cliffs that were left from when eastern Kentucky was covered by an inland sea. Along the slopes above the creek were small, three-room cabins, the green and white paint blistered and flaking, and each had an identical small porch in front, a stone chimney, and an outhouse like an upended matchbox in the back. The hollow was the type of place the state tourist bureau would have photographed and put on the cover of a vacation brochure to advertise the scenic loveliness of the Cumberland Mountains and the simple life of the mountain people except that long streams of garbage were strewn down the front of the cabins into the creek, wrecked cars – some upside-down and gutted by fire – lay in front yards, and by the dirt road that led into the hollow were a school bus without wheels and several shacks made of crates, cardboard, logs and tarpaper. In front of each shack dirty children with mucus dried on their faces played with rusted barrel hoops and tin cans. The fences all had clothes laid over them to dry in the wind, and in some places rotted mattresses, bedsprings, piles of car parts and tyres, were heaped at the side of the house.

The mining company had once owned all of the hollow and the cabins and people in it; but through the years some had been able to buy their house from the company, others had been laid off or crippled in cave-ins and had been forced to leave and build a shelter out of whatever discarded material they could find. The property the company still held title to was not maintained, because a miner who didn't like what he was given could get out and look for a job driving a cab in Ohio. This hollow, along with almost every other settlement on the Cumberland plateau, had at one time or other been called a depressed area by either the state or federal government; but nothing ever changed greatly. More men were laid off the job because of automation or a decrease in the demand for coal; there was more garbage down the mountainside each year, more strip mines tore great pits in the top of the mountain, more tobacco crops were ruined from the yellow rainwater that seeped down over the exposed coal; and more people learned how to lie to the county relief worker when he made his monthly visit and asked if the man of the house was still gone and not contributing to his family's support.

In Perry's hollow a man had one of three kinds of support – if he had any at all. He could work in the mines, but it was getting harder every year to work union and get a decent scale. There were machines now that did the work of a hundred men with picks and mattocks, and the strip- and truck-mine operators could tear the earth away with bulldozers, explode the bared seam with dynamite, and pick up the great hunks of coal with machines, using only a handful of men as a crew. And if a man worked for the small operator, he crawled through badly ventilated shafts on his hands and knees, clawing the coal loose from the wall in a bent position, and the little money he made wouldn't pay the charge at the store at the end of the month. Also, he could have a shaft ceiling come down on top of him, and no one would be responsible for either his hospitalization or the support of his family, because he had no welfare card and no union disability fund.

So if a man didn't work in the mine, he made whiskey in a rock house, a shallow limestone cave in the base of the mountain, where he had a supply of water from a spring and there was a heavy cover of trees and brush over the entrance. If he made good whiskey that took its 'bead' from the corn and not from several sacks of sugar poured in the mash to hurry the fermentation, he could sell it in Detroit to the syndicate for as much as fourteen dollars a gallon; but he still had to split with the transporter, who had to run it across two state lines and risk not only arrest by federal law officers but by county deputies, who would stop a runner on his way back from the sale, take him before the local justice of the peace, and fine him every dollar they found taped under his dashboard. The moonshiner also knew that the ABC (Alcohol Beverage Control) would eventually get him, break up his cooker, thumping keg and mash barrels with axes, and chop his fifty-dollar condenser coil into pieces. The ABC used aircraft now, and they could spot a wisp of smoke from a rock house miles away or a trail worn by the mules through the trees where there should have been no trail.

If a man had no support at all, he could receive as much as two hundred and fifty dollars a month from the federal government as a 'happy-pappy' – an unemployed father. The happy-pappies in the hollow picked up paper and raked leaves for the Forest Service, cleaned the cinders from barbecue pits in recreation areas, and sometimes cut grass along the new interstate highway. Most of these men were either old or partly crippled. In the morning, when the sun broke over the edge of the mountain, an old army flatbed two-and-one-half-ton stake truck would grind down the road and pick up the men sitting on their front porches. They each carried a paper-sack lunch with pork chops and bread inside. When the truck was full, it would move back out of the hollow into the national forest, where the men spent most of their day. They always looked like part of an army of refugees, with their legs hanging over the tailgate of the truck and their scythes and shovels held in the crook of their arms.

Perry waited for the clerk to sack his groceries in the small clapboard company store and then asked for the charge slip to sign. The store smelled of the oil that was spread on the floor to collect the dust. The walls of the building looked as though they would cave inward from the weight of canned goods stacked on the shelves. The clerk was a balding man with thin grey hair above his ears who had gone to college a year at Richmond. He made seventy-five dollars a week to keep books and inventory, and to close a miner's account when the word came down from the company. People in the hollow treated him with the type of respect that comes from fear; he could use words they didn't understand, and anything he said was always backed by some power of money and authority down in Harlan or Sterns. He pulled open a drawer under the counter and thumbed through the stiff pieces of cardboard that separated the stacks of carbon charge tickets held together with rubber bands. He popped the edge of a file card with his fingernail and knocked the drawer shut with the flat of his hand.

'It says you're in arrears and you ain't working at the mine any more,' he said.

'There ain't nobody working at the mine now. It's shut down,' Perry said.

'I'm just going by the record. You didn't pay all of last month's bill, and the timekeeper ain't carrying you on the pay sheet.'

'I don't care about no pay sheet. They won't let us go down till we get an election.'

'Who won't let you go down? There's a full crew going into the hole every day.'

'That's them scabs from West Virginia. There ain't nobody from around here going through that picket.'

The clerk leaned against the counter.

'Your credit was good here while you were charging against your salary at the mine,' he said. 'You don't work there any longer. You already owe me money that you can't pay, and you can't buy groceries on money that you're not about to have. Do you understand that?'

'We was good enough to buy here till we ask for a white man's wage.'

'You can make twelve or fifteen dollars a day anytime you want to carry a shovel instead of a sign, son,' the clerk said.

Perry left the sack of groceries on the counter and walked out of the store on to the slanting wooden porch, where two other men from his mine were sitting on steps, chewing tobacco and spitting on the frozen ground.

'They taken away your charge, too?' one of them said.

'The bastard wouldn't give me two dollars' worth of pork chops and a loaf of bread.'

'He ain't a-giving anything to nobody,' the man said. 'They'd let that food go sour on the shelf before they'd give it to the likes of us.'

'Maybe somebody ought to spread a little coal oil on his place one night,' the second man said.

'It's too bad he wasn't up on the tipple with that scab when them boys blew it the other night,' the first man said. 'They couldn't find no part of that feller. They say that charge must have pushed the nails in his boots plumb up through his head.'

'I'll see you fellers around,' Perry said.

'Where you looking for work?'

'They say them truck mines over in Letcher is a-hiring,' he said.

'There ain't no operator taking men from our mine. They figure somebody might drop something extra down the hole one night.'

Both of the men laughed. Perry walked down the rutted road towards his cabin. The sky was covered with snow clouds, and there was a haze over the mountains in the distance. The first light snow from last night lay powdered in the pine and beech trees. As Perry started the climb up the slope to his cabin he felt the sharp air burn down in his lungs. A flight of geese flew high overhead in a V-formation. He could hear their faint honking through the cold. But they ain't going to set down around here, he thought. There ain't nothing good going to happen around here this year. Bee and J.W. seen to that. They're going to shut us out of work and starve us right out of this holler if they don't put us in the pen first.

The incline before his cabin was covered with tin cans, rusted tangles of wire, car parts and garbage. The green and white paint on the building had long since weathered to the dark colour of slag smoke. The rick fence had fallen down in places, and the clothes his mother had put out in the morning to dry on the rails had been blown to the ground by the wind. His younger brothers and sisters were playing inside the wheel-less wreck of a 1946 Chevrolet in the side yard. There were six children besides himself, all younger than he, and he had once had an older brother, who was killed in a bar-room knifing in Cincinnati. The children all had dirty faces and colds, and their clothes were more patched and wash-faded than his. The smallest one, Irvin, had had tuberculosis when he was two, and the doctor in Richmond, who had kept him in his clinic for two weeks without taking a fee, said the child needed to be in a hospital for several months; but Perry's father never had the money, and there was no charity hospital in any county close to their home. So Irvin was four now, and the fact that he had once had tuberculosis and had needed a hospital was something the parents pushed off into a dark corner of their minds, and in the cabin no one mentioned anything about it except that Irvin had once been 'sick'.

The front of the cabin was covered with broken bits of harness and rope hung on wooden pegs, dried coon skins, cane fishing poles stacked against the wall, tattered quilts that Perry's mother had laid across the porch rails to air in the wind, wagons for the children made out of apple crates and rollerskate wheels, and fish scales, dried like pieces of broken razor blade and ground into the wooden planking.

Perry's father sat in a straight-back chair in front of the fireplace, with his great square hands spread out on his thighs. His shoulders and back and the bend of his flat stomach were as rigid as the chair he sat in. His clear blue eyes and the sharp mountain features of his face made him look like a man in the prime years of his life, but on one side of his chest was a cavity that sunk back to the bone as though he had been struck with a sledge-hammer. Ten years ago he had been working across the line in Virginia in a hot coal mine where there was gas always in the shaft, and when somebody had lighted a cigarette during the lunch hour an explosion thundered through all the corridors and blew the elevator cage straight out of the hole. The pinning in his shaft gave way, and he lay two days in an air pocket under a mound of rock and coal before a rescue team got to him.

His hair had always been wavy and brown, and he had combed it straight back with a short bob on the nape of his neck. But now the hair had begun to thin and turn grey, and from his temple one lock always hung in the corner of his eye. But he was still a handsome man, with a high, straight forehead and a row of even teeth that looked like new enamel; and his wife said that as he grew older he looked more like the picture of Frank James he kept locked in a tin box on the top shelf of his closet. The picture had been given him by his grandfather, and it had a round gilt frame and showed Frank James with a Confederate tunic on his shoulders and a grey officer's hat above his pale, classic features. Once a man from the University of Kentucky offered Perry's father one hundred dollars for it, but he would no more have sold it than he would have sold part of his birthright.

Perry's mother looked older than her husband. Her skin had once had the smooth glow of a lilac petal, but now it was rough and creased around the eyes, and her hands were almost as calloused as a man's. Like most women on the Cumberland plateau, she came to flower before she was twenty, and by the time she had reached thirty, her hips were widened from child-bearing, there was a stoop to her shoulders, and the hours of work that started before sunrise and sometimes ended late the night had wasted her body. Once she had loved the square dances and dinners on the ground at the dollar fishing lake on Saturday night, when all the women talked about their children and traded jars of preserves and listened to the fiddle and banjo music coming over the lake while the men, in straw hats, stood around the bonnets of cars, chewing ten-cent cigars and drinking somebody's best corn whiskey; but with the years and the harder times she had settled into a resignation that was neither boredom nor determination, but an acceptance of her life as another mountain woman who would never have enough food to cook for the number of people at the table, never enough money at the end of the month for new clothes, or even a chance to see a place like

Cincinnati, where whole blocks stayed lighted all night and people never seemed to want for anything.

'Where's the groceries at?' Perry's father said.

'They won't give us no more charge,' he said. 'They ain't a-selling to nobody that don't scab for them. They ain't going to give nothing to anybody without work, and they ain't going to hire nobody from our mine.'

'They done it like that to me and Bee in 1930. Sent a company man down here with a pistol to run us out. By God, a dozen of us picked him and his little Ford up and throwed them both in the honey hole. They couldn't burn the smell out of that car with a blow torch.' The old man laughed, then pressed his hand to the cavity in his chest. 'He had it all over him. He tried to fire his pistol, but the barrel was clogged with it. The outhouse must have been setting thirty years over that hole.'

'You reckon there's any work over in Virginia?'

'I don't want you in none of them gas mines,' Perry's father said. 'My boy ain't a-getting buried five miles down because a fool wants to smoke or somebody jumps a spark off the wall. A man don't know what it's like to lay in the dark for days with the whole earth crushing in on you. There ain't no man should have to go through that. Rocks covering you all over till there ain't no feeling in your body. Just laying there sucking at the little bit of air you can get. Even God ain't got a right to do that to a man. You forget about anything over there in Virginia.'

'We ain't got any food, daddy,' Perry said.

'We got what the government give us,' his mother said. 'We'll make do with what we have.'

'That ain't enough. We couldn't hardly make do when I was working,' Perry said.

'We can't take no more loss in this family,' she said. 'Your brother run off just like you want to. He said there was big jobs up in Ohio. Then we didn't even know he was dead till the police sent us a wire.'

'The mines is going to open up again, anyway,' his father said. 'And they're going to put union men down in the hole working scale. They ain't beat the union here in ten years.'

'They ain't going to hire me. It don't matter if we win our election or not,' Perry said.

'There ain't a man working in this holler that ain't been on a job at sometime or other when somebody shot up some company men. They done their share of it to us, and we done it right back,' his father said. 'If they tried to keep out every man that worked around a blowed tipple, they wouldn't have nobody to bring up their coal.'

'What are we going to do when there ain't none of that government food left?' Perry said.

'We always got through before. The Lord ain't ever let us starve,' his mother said, almost believing the old Church of God axiom that she always told herself when times became so bad that she saw no way out of them. She went to the wood-burning stove and lifted the iron cover off the fire with a small handle. The flames leaped out through the open hole. She dropped a handful of dried twigs into the fire, replaced the cover, and pushed a cauldron of string beans and bit of ham over the heat. The water that had been carried from the well stood in a wooden bucket on the draining-board. She dipped water out of it with a ladle and poured it into the soup.

'It ain't going to end with cutting off our charge. They're going to do everything they can to run us out of the holler. I know it,' Perry said. 'I been feeling it all day.'

'They can't do nothing they ain't already tried,' his father said. 'They taken the land from your grandfather, and after that we learned the way they worked. They try to run Jameses or Hatfields off and there won't be no coal moved out of this country.'

'Daddy, it don't work that way no more. They got machines now that eat up a whole seam and dump it in the cars with just one man setting up on it. Twenty of us can't do the work in a day that them machines does in an hour.'

'Machines don't matter,' his father said. 'The union ain't a-going to let its men get run off to make more money for the operator. Them machines has got to have men to run them, ain't they? A machine can't set a charge and tamp it down so the whole mountain don't cave on your head. There's got to be men down in that hole.'

'That ain't the point,' Perry said. 'They just ain't got no use for us except working dollar and a quarter for the independents.'

'They taken care of Bee, didn't they? They give him a job in an office when he couldn't work no more.'

'That's because he could put a bunch of them in the pen if he told what he knowed about that shooting,' Perry said.

'Son, right or wrong, we ain't got no chance against the operator without the union,' his father said. 'They got our land for hardly nothing. They ruined the ground for growing anything. They give us shacks to live in, and they paid us in script so we couldn't buy from nobody excepting them. They taken all they could get and they never give nothing back. I put twenty-seven years in the hole, and I didn't get out with nothing except a check for part of the doctor bill.'

Outside, the winter sun began to set over the mountains. The rays struck across the crest and reflected bright scarlet against the snow clouds banked in the east. The creek was filmed with ice, and occasionally a wood duck would dip out of the twilight and hum low through the hollow and splash into the water. The wind blew cold down the mountain and beat against the walls of the shack.

One by one the children came in from playing inside the ruined car and sat down by the long plank table near the stove. The first ones in always sat on the bench closest to the warmth. Their cheeks were chapped from the wind. Their mother poured the soup of string beans and ham into their bowls and tore a piece of bread in half for each one of them. The largest portion of soup was given to Irvin, because his mother believed that enough food was cure for any type of sickness, and somewhere inside her she was never able to forget the voice of the doctor in Richmond who said the boy should be put into a hospital.

After supper Perry went into the small room where he and his brothers and sisters shared a large iron bed broken in the middle and a pallet on the floor. In the cold months Irvin and the two other small children slept next to Perry in the bed for his warmth, and the other three curled together on the pallet. On a wooden shelf nailed against the wall was Perry's Indian arrowhead collection. He had over one hundred spear and arrow points, tomahawks, hatchets, banner stones, pipes, awls, bits of pottery, beads, and part of a flintlock rifle with the inscription 'London England 1799' cut on the barrel. He picked up some arrowheads in his hand and felt the cool smoothness of the flint in his palm. He had dug them all from rock houses where the Cherokee and Shawnee used to camp when they followed the buffalo down the Warriors' Trail, which later became the Wilderness Trail, through Cumberland Gap into Virginia. He had found more Indian artifacts than anyone else in his hollow. He knew how to look for the smoke-blackened roof of a rock house, the few small pieces of broken flint on the surface of the soil, the smooth, hollow places in the bed of the rock where the Indians ground corn, and he would spend days sifting the dirt by the handful through a wire screen until he reached the charred cinders of a fire and knew that he had found the remains of an Indian camp.

The next day at sunrise the county sheriff's car stopped on the road at the bottom of the mountain in front of Perry's cabin, and the sheriff, a man of over three hundred pounds, with emphysema, toiled his way up the slope to the front porch. He was breathing hard, whistling down in his throat as though he were suffocating, when he knocked on the door.

'What you want him for?' Perry's father said.

'This ain't no arrest, Woodson,' the sheriff said. 'I ain't got a warrant and the boy don't have to come. We think we cotched one or two of them that done it, and I just want to talk to him if you'll let me.'

'I ain't saying I hold with killing a man, but that tipple wouldn't have been blowed if they'd paid them boys what was fair,' Perry's father said.

'Well, like I said, Woodson, I ain't going to do nothing to him.' The sheriff's short breath steamed off in the cold. 'I'll take him on down to the county seat to talk a minute, then I'll bring him home.'

'Who you brung in for it?'

'It might be one of the J.W. brothers. I ain't saying yet.'

'There ain't a court around here a-going to hold them guilty for it. Besides, my boy ain't got nothing to do with the J.W.s excepting he works at the same mine with them.'

'You know I don't take no sides in what goes on at the mine,' the sheriff said, 'and it ain't none of my business what the court does. Now you can let me have Perry for an hour, or I'll go back to the judge and get a warrant on him, even though I don't want to do it.'

Perry rode with the sheriff back down the bad, tar-covered road through the hills to the county seat. As he sat in the car he watched the beech and white oak trees sweep by overhead and wondered if it was not all a lie and the sheriff was going to send him off to Frankfort in manacles on the first train out of town. The steep cliff walls of the hollow loomed high above him like a prison. He wondered how many years they could give him in the penitentiary. They had put Bee away for two years just for wounding a man, and the company people even tried to have Noah Combs sent up after he was shot to pieces. I couldn't take no prison, Perry thought. It must be just like the mine caving in on you, with no air to breathe. I rather they set me in the electric chair than put me away in one of them places.

Almost every building in the county seat was painted green and white except the sandstone courthouse and jail and the company district manager's house, a blue and white mansion built among shade trees on top of a hill overlooking the town. The small, private clinic, run by a doctor who had received most of his education at a city college in Cincinnati, had broken windows and screens, and the foundation had settled at an angle. The store fronts along the main street were grimed with dirt, and men in overalls, brogans, cloth caps, miners' helmets and old army clothes stood on the corners in front of the saloons and pool halls. Because it was Saturday and the men were in town to drink up all the money they had, their women sat with the children in junker cars parked along the curb, and they would remain there all day and into the night, breast feeding, changing nappies, and rocking the infants to sleep until the men walked unsteadily back to the cars, telling how Jake McGoffin or Wilson Pruitt was cut up in the pool room; and then they would drive the fifteen or twenty miles back into the mountains.

The inside of the courthouse smelled strongly of urine. There was no bathroom in the building, and parents often let their children relieve themselves in a darkened corner. The finish was worn off the plank floors, the plaster had fallen out of the ceiling in places, and the glass windows in the office doors were filmed with dirt. The county had no full-time elected officials because the tax revenue was never enough to afford them, so the sheriff, the clerk of court, the county judge, the justice of the peace, and the tax assessor all worked two or three days at the most and made up the rest of their income in any way they could, which meant that every moonshiner, bootlegger, union agent, or company official usually delivered money in one form or another to the courthouse.

Big J.W. and Little J.W. sat on the straight-back wooden chairs inside the sheriff's office, smoking hand-rolled cigarettes. A deputy, without a uniform and wearing a World War I service revolver, sat on a window ledge, watching them. Big J.W. had his tin hat slanted down over his forehead, and he smoked bent over with his forearms propped on his knees. He cleared his throat and spat on the floor, then rubbed the saliva into the wood with his boot. Little J.W. looked as passive and immobile as a piece of dough. His soft eyes stared straight ahead, and he would do nothing more than nod when the deputy or his brother spoke to him. When he finished his cigarette he ripped the paper back along the seam and rubbed the tobacco between his palms into the waste basket, as though he were grinding some fierce energy out of his body.

Later, the sheriff and Perry came into the office. Perry sat on a bench against the wall, his cloth cap in his hands, and looked at the floor.

'All right, I ain't even going to talk about a murder,' the sheriff said. 'We'll put you down for illegal possession of dynamite and destroying property and say that man up there was an accident. Involuntary homicide. You didn't even know he was there. But you ain't walking off from it free.'

'We done told you. We wasn't nowhere near that mine,' Big J.W. said.

'And you don't know nothing about breaking into that dynamite shed, either, do you?' the sheriff said. He sat his huge weight on the corner of his desk. His face flushed with the effort of talking.

'That's right, sheriff. You just picked up the wrong boys,' Big J.W. said.

'Somebody seen four of you riding up towards that mine,' the sheriff said. 'You was one of them, Perry, and I have a notion that other one was Bee Hatfield.'

Perry felt something drop inside him. 'They give me a ride home the other night. That don't make me guilty of nothing,' he said.

'So the J.W.s is running a jitney service, is that it?' the sheriff said. 'You all was just riding up and down the mountain at night carrying people home.'

'Lookie, sheriff,' Little J.W. said. He peeled the dirt from under his fingernails with a small penknife. 'All you got is somebody seen us in a car up in the north part of the county. That don't mean nothing, and you know it and we know it. You could just as well bring in anybody that worked in that mine. So there ain't no use in us setting around here a-wasting your time.'

'I'll decide whose time you're wasting,' the sheriff said. 'Anybody could have blowed that tipple, but it was one of you and by God I'm going to prove it. This ain't the first time you been in on closing a mine. Three mines you worked in have been dynamited or somebody's got shot, and my county ain't going to turn into no war like Harlan or Pike. I don't know what part you had in it, Perry, but I guarantee you these men won't get you nowhere but on a cooling board or in the pen.'

Little J.W. folded his penknife in his palm and sucked his teeth.

'Now I give you an out,' the sheriff said. 'You can get off with maybe a year in Frankfort, but if you just set there and tell me you ain't done nothing I'm going to press for murder.'

'We got no more to say, sheriff. Either turn us out or put us in a cell,' Big J.W. said.

'What about you, Perry? Are you a-letting these men put you up in Frankfort with them?' the sheriff said.

'I don't have no hand in what they do,' he said. 'I told you they rode me home, and anything else they done ain't my business.'

'A dead man ain't your business?'

'Them scabs knowed what they was doing when they hired on that job,' Perry said.

'All right, I ain't holding none of you now,' the sheriff said, 'but that don't mean you and me is finished. J.W., you and your brother better not let me catch you even spitting on a pavement. You give me any cause and I'll put you in jail and leave you there, and the county judge ain't going to let you out on no habeas corpus. Perry, I'll take you home because I promised your daddy.'

'I reckon I'll stay around town a while.'

Perry walked out onto the square with Big J.W. and Little J.W. The pavements were crowded with people who had come into town for Saturday afternoon. Women, dressed in faded, old clothes, thin cotton coats, scarves, and some with men's shoes on, stood in front of the company stores looking at the cheap goods they could buy on credit if their husbands were working. There was a roar of noise from the taverns and pool halls on the side streets, and in places traffic was blocked because someone in a rusted Ford with smashed bumpers would stop his car and begin talking with people on the pavement. Next to the courthouse was the one-storey sandstone jail built in 1890; several men looked out through the bars and called to friends passing by. Farther down, people were lined up outside a tin warehouse, where they received their surplus government food – peanut butter, canned meat that tasted like paper, shortening, powdered milk and eggs, and flour.

'Honey, you just keep remembering there can't nobody shut that jail house door on you unless you open your mouth,' Big J.W. said.

'And that's something you ain't going to do,' Little J.W. said.

'I didn't tell him nothing, did I?' Perry said.

'He'll be back after you again when we ain't there,' Big J.W. said. 'Then you might reckon you can do better for yourself by testifying for the company.'

'I ain't that kind.'

'If you are, you better not let us catch up with you,' Little J.W. said.

'I ain't telling the sheriff nothing, because I ain't going to be around here,' Perry said.

'Where do you think you're going?' Little J.W. said.

'I might go over in old Virginia and get me a job where I ain't got to worry about pickets and sheriffs and going to the pen. So let me be.'

Perry crossed the street into the traffic and left the two men on the corner staring after him. He felt a relief at getting away from them. There was always something in Little J.W.'s voice that was like the edge of a well-honed knife. Perry walked across the square, past the taverns, the feed and hardware stores, the small Church of God tabernacle, which had been converted from an old barbershop, past the drunks in overalls and brogans who stood in front of the open pool room that always smelled of flat beer, talcum, tobacco spittle, greasy food and unwashed bodies. Next to the pool hall was the 'jenny-barn', a bar that had girls working upstairs. He could hear the music of the string band through the doorway. The fiddle, mandolin, bass, dobro, banjo and guitar blended together in an old Bill Monroe bluegrass song:

> *Run, ole Molley, run,*
> *Tenbrooks is going to beat you*
> *To the bright and shining sun.*
> *Out in California where Molley done as she pleased,*
> *Came back to old Kentucky,*
> *Got beat with all ease.*
> *Tenbrooks was an old gray mare,*
> *He rode that shaggy mane,*
> *Run all around Memphis,*
> *He beat the Memphis train.*
> *Go catch ole Tenbrooks*
> *And hitch him in the shade,*
> *We're going to bury Molley*
> *In a coffin ready made,*
> *In a coffin ready made, Lord, in a coffin ready made.*

The state employment service, along with the county welfare department, was located in a run-down clapboard office with a cracked front window. Perry had been there once before to apply for unemployment compensation, but he was told that he was ineligible because he was on strike and was therefore out of work by choice. Most of the people in the county thought of the state employment agency as a joke; there was no work outside the mines, and if the agency did not exist, the people who worked there would also be unable to find a job. The waiting chairs and all the desks were empty except for one, where a middle-aged woman sat filling out forms about non-existent job placements and filing them in a box for the state inspector. She was a stranger to the county, from somewhere up north, with an accent that no one could recognize or place.

'I don't want to take up none of your time,' Perry said. 'I'm looking for a job somewhere that ain't around here.'

'Fill out a card with your employment history and I'll help you in a minute,' she said.

'Is there any jobs or not?' he said.

'Well, there might be, but you do have to fill out the card.' She smiled at him pleasantly. She wore glasses tied to a ribbon around her neck, and her skin was smooth and white as though she had never had to boil clothes clean in a vat or cut wood by hand for her stove. She wore a woman's suit, something Perry had never seen before.

He printed his name in large, crooked letters on top of the card, then pushed it and the pencil towards her. His face reddened slightly.

'I can't write,' he said.

'All right. Then let's not worry about that now. What kind of work have you done before?'

'I cut tobacco for a half cent a stick, and I been down in the mine the last year. But I don't want no job here. I want to go over in Virginia or maybe up in Ohio. It don't matter what kind of work I do.'

'You know it's hard to find a job today unless you have some kind of skill or education. Did you ever think about finishing your schooling?'

'A feller don't make money while he's setting in a school-house,' he said.

'Did you ever hear of the Job Corps?' she said. Her strange, quiet accent made Perry drop his eyes to the desk when she spoke. She took a booklet with a blue, white and red shield on the cover out of the drawer. 'In Job Corps you can finish your education and learn a trade, and they'll pay you thirty dollars a month, put twenty-five in the bank for you, and send fifty dollars home to your family.'

'That's like them three-C camps where my daddy was. They don't do nothing but work on the forest.'

She leafed through the booklet and showed him pictures of boys studying in classrooms and welding shops, working on automobile engines, operating bulldozers and highway graders and printing presses, learning how to cook in large restaurants and how to repair electronic machinery. 'You can take up any of these things and maybe get a high school degree, too,' she said. 'They'll give you new clothes to wear, and they'll pay your travel home for vacation after six months.'

'There ain't nothing wrong with what I got.'

She reached over and touched his forearm with the softness of her palm. He felt the blood come to his face. He wanted to look over his shoulder to see if anyone was watching him and this strange woman.

'Son, there's nothing wrong with your clothes,' she said. 'You just give yourself a chance for a little better opportunity than your parents had.'

'Where's these camps at?' He avoided her eyes and held his cloth cap tightly in his hands between his knees.

'They're all over the United States. You might go to California or Texas or even up to Vermont.'

'I don't want to go to none of them places.'

'How about the Smoky Mountains in North Carolina?' she said. 'You wouldn't be too far from home in case you wanted to come back.'

'I ain't worried about that. How much is the bus fare to get there?'

'The government takes care of all your travel expense. You'll ride the bus to Lexington, and somebody will be there to put you on the plane.'

'I ain't getting on no airplane,' he said. 'You'll have to chloroform me before I get on one of them things.'

'You just sign your name on this card,' he said.

'All right. But by God they ain't putting me on no plane.'

THREE

From the aircraft window he saw the late sun reflected like pools of fire on the clouds above North Carolina. The land was flat and distant below him, cut into brown and green squares, with small red barns and white farmhouses close to the road. Over the plane's wing he could see the Smoky Mountains rise up against the brilliance of the sun's reflection in the east. It was the biggest range he had ever seen, much bigger than the Cumberland in Kentucky and Tennessee. There was a blue haze over the mountaintops, and in some places it was raining down in the hollows. It was a place so wonderful and huge that it could not have things like strip mines, smoking slag heaps, rivers filled with sulphuric acid, and whole mountainsides that had eroded into the hollows. Then the plane turned and dipped for the approach to the Asheville airfield. He grabbed the back of the seat in front of him, shut his eyes tightly, and felt his heart beat inside his chest.

'Do you feel ill?'

He didn't open his eyes, but he knew it was that stewardess again. She had tried to give him some type of pills twice before on the flight.

'No, I ain't sick. Why you keep asking me?'

'We'll be there in a few minutes,' she said.

He thought he was going to faint when the plane started its descent. The sweat broke out on his hands and face, and his lungs felt as though he had held his breath for two minutes. It's going to crash right into one of them mountains, he thought. That pilot said we was going over four hundred miles an hour. There ain't nothing that can touch the ground that fast and not tear us all apart. He opened his eyes and saw the countryside getting closer, flattening out before him, and the tops of the houses and trees rushing under the plane. Then he saw the long, white strip of concrete runway rise up suddenly from the ground, and he felt the impact reverberate through the plane as it touched down. He leaned back in the cushions of the seat and rubbed his wet palms against his work trousers.

Perry found eleven other Job Corpsmen waiting inside the airport, each wearing a blue, white and red card pinned to his coat. There were four Negroes, two Mexicans and an Indian in the group. A man in a Forest Service suit and two boys his own age dressed like soldiers were with them.

'This tall one must be the last of the bunch,' one of the boys in army clothes said. 'All right, you guys, everybody on the bus. Get moving, too, if you want to eat tonight. Where you been, anyway? We've been waiting for you two hours.'

'I was on the plane. Where's it look like I been?' Perry said.

Outside, they got into a green and white government bus, and the Forest Service man handed out sack lunches of ham sandwiches and fried potatoes. The bus moved off through the late afternoon traffic and then began the climb into the mountains. Perry walked to the back of the bus and looked out the window at the sprawling area of the city in the twilight. The buildings downtown rose out of the purple haze, huge green and red neons blinked on and off over large stores, and long lines of new automobiles stretched endlessly along the highway. Then as the sun set beyond the mountains, the city looked like a shower of light spread across the valley, and he smelled the cold air through the window and the scent of pine and spruce along the roadside. In the dark interior of the bus, he felt he was very far from the J.W.s, the county sheriff, the man on the coal tipple, and the company men who would be around his father's cabin – and there was no way they could touch him now.

One of the boys in army clothes stood up in the aisle with one hand against a metal bar for support. He had a dark, Latin face and black hair that was oiled and combed straight back over his head. There was a deep scar across his chin and part of his lip, and he had a cross with three rays emanating from it tattooed between the thumb and first finger of his left hand.

'We're glad to have all you guys in Job Corps,' he said. 'It's a straight outfit, and we've got the best guys and best camp in the states. If any of you are carrying a shank or anything else you're not suppose to have, you can drop it off at the administration building before you get your linen. If we catch you with it later, you'll get your bus ticket and sack lunch back home.'

'Who's that feller shooting off his mouth?' Perry said to the boy next to him.

'They say he's what they call a work leader,' the boy said. He was a thin, pale boy from Mississippi, with long brown hair over his ears. He wore a hand-knitted sweater that had holes at both elbows. 'They give a feller twenty extra dollars a month for getting up to leader, and he don't have to pull KP or work on clean-up.'

'Well, I ain't come here to be no janitor,' Perry said.

'Everybody gets along here,' the boy in army clothes said. He had a New York accent, hard and clipped. 'We don't allow no fighting, and any guy that don't work pulls extra duty on the weekend and loses his pass to town for two weeks. Play it straight and you get the best deal in the country.'

'Do all them fellers carry on like that when they give them some soldier clothes?' Perry said.

The camp was located high in the mountains, ninety miles from Asheville, near a blue lake that was frozen around the edges. The pines and silver-leaf aspens grew back beyond the sandy stretch of lake front, and the green camp buildings were set up on blocks in a large clearing in the forest. The buildings were all prefabricated and made of tin, and icicles hung from the eaves in the cold moonlight. Perry walked with the other Corpsmen over the frozen ground covered with pine needles to the administration office, where they were issued starched fatigues, leather boots that laced above the ankle, black Air Force dress shoes, Eisenhower jackets, Navy denims, slickers, long underwear, sheets, blankets and shaving kits. Perry carried all his issue piled in his arms.

Then they walked back out into the dark, along a worn dirt path through the trees, and into one of the barracks.

The barracks was a flat, oblong building separated by a single corridor and with rows of partitions on each side. Each partition had in it two bunks, foot and wall lockers, night stands and writing tables, and all the wood and metal gleamed softly from the light overhead. Perry and the boy from Mississippi were assigned bunks next to each other, and they set about putting their issue in their lockers and making their beds.

'You guys better learn how to stretch that blanket tighter than that,' a Negro boy said from across the hall. He was dressed in soiled pink slacks, tennis shoes with white athletic socks, a denim shirt with the sleeves cut away, and a white sailor's hat with the sides pulled down over his ears. 'If a quarter don't bounce on it at morning inspection, you'll be pulling extra duty tomorrow night.'

'What's this extra duty about?' Perry said.

'You get it for screwing off,' the Negro boy said. 'They give you all the dirty details, like scraping the ice off the sidewalks or cleaning the crapper.'

'I ain't a-cleaning no toilet,' Perry said.

'Man, where did you get that crazy accent?'

Perry closed his foot locker and straightened up. 'You got something to say about the way I talk?'

'Look, cool, you got to learn around here when another dude is just jiving you. We don't have no beefs. Everybody in this barracks is soul brothers. All the guys that thought they were bad ass have been kicked out.'

'I come here to go to school, not for no trouble,' Perry said. 'I had all I wanted of that back home.'

'You're talking soul now,' the Negro boy said. He put a thin cigar butt in a cigarette holder and lit it. 'You dudes get finished and I'll take you over to the chow hall. After you eat we got a movie in the rec room.'

The mess hall was immaculately white. The serving counter was made of glass and stainless steel, and the cooks and KPs wore laundered white uniforms and tall caps. Perry went through the serving line with the other new Corpsmen, who were all eating late, and filled his tray with steak, potatoes and gravy, a bowl of soup, string beans cooked with bacon and tomato sauce, ice-cream covered with pineapple, and milk and coffee.

'Soul, you eat like food's going out of style,' the Negro boy said to him.

Later that night after the movie was over, Perry lay in his bunk under the blankets in the dark, smoking a hand-rolled cigarette. His body was almost too long for the bunk. Through the frost-covered window he saw the full moon in the clear sky above the mountains. The wind scratched the tree limbs across the tin roof of the barracks, and somewhere in the distance he heard the thin whistle of a train echoing through the hollows.

'Put out that damn cigarette before the resident worker comes down here,' a voice said out of the darkness.

He dropped the cigarette into a butt can on his night table and lay back against the pillow. Maybe it ain't such a bad deal, he thought. That ranger said we could buy eighty-five dollars' worth of store clothes when we been here a month, and I can get into that welding and heavy equipment class. Six months of that and I can get one of them three dollar an hour jobs running a cat in Cincinnati. At least it's a lot better than working around the likes of the J.W.s. Then he felt himself pulled into sleep, and he thought once that his bunk dipped towards the earth like an aircraft.

The next morning, as the sun broke above the top of the mountain range, Perry lined up with two hundred other Corpsmen by the flag pole, while a man in a Forest Service uniform called muster. The boys who were attending class that week were dressed in street clothes, and the others had on their army issue jackets, snow boots, and fur-lined Korean War caps that tied around their ears.

Perry was assigned to the work crew that cleared trails and maintained the recreation areas on the forest. After one hour on the detail he threw his chain saw on the ground and refused to work until he was allowed to see the camp director.

'That ain't no different than the three C's,' he said. 'I can cut trees down back in Kentucky and get more money for it. I come out here to learn machinery, because that's where the good jobs is at.'

The director was a middle-aged man, an ex-forest ranger, with steel-rimmed glasses and a soft pink face. His collar was unbuttoned and his tie was pulled loose from his throat. The veins in his wrists were purple like a woman's.

'We don't put any of the Corpsmen into a vocational class until you've been here a month,' he said. 'That's because some of the boys leave during the first few weeks, and we don't have time or enough instructors to start teaching people who aren't going to stay.'

'They told me at the unemployment office I could go right into a trade.'

'Well, you can't. So you can go back to your crew and wait it out for three weeks or we can send you back to Kentucky.'

'I didn't say nothing about going home. I just didn't see no sense in doing the same work my daddy is and not getting nothing for it.'

'You go back to your crew and do what the work leader tells you, and I promise you'll be in the heavy equipment class,' the director said. 'But I'm going to give you four hours' extra duty for refusing to work this morning. Do you think that's fair?'

'No sir, I don't, but I'll pull it just the same as long as you put me in that class.'

Perry lost his first weekend pass and spent Saturday afternoon washing the camp buses in below-freezing weather. The water coated and froze on the windows even before he could rub the rag over them. By five o'clock he was numb with cold. There was a film of ice on his trousers where the water had splashed on them, and he had lost the feeling in his fingertips. He resolved that nobody was ever going to get him on the Saturday afternoon punishment detail again. It took him fifteen minutes under a hot shower before he felt the warmth begin to come back into his body, and then he fell into his bunk and slept until he heard the boys who had been into town weave through the corridor, carrying a drunk by his hands and feet.

The next week Perry went back to his work crew and felled trees with the chain saw, cut them into sections for burning, cleared brush off the trails, ripped roots loose with the pick, and cleaned out the soot and ashes from barbecue pits in the recreation areas on the forest. Most of the boys on the crew were either new in camp or ones who could not learn in a vocational class. There were also some who had been put out of vocational training by the instructor and were being considered for dismissal from the camp. During his first day on the crew Perry saw one Corpsman, a big Georgia cracker from Macon, turn the blade of his chain saw against a rock and tear out all the teeth so that he could take the truck back to the tool shed for another one. Instead, the work leader made him walk the six miles back to camp with the saw.

It was cold working out on the trail. Perry wore his long underwear, two pairs of trousers, an army flannel shirt and a sweater, boots with rubber snow shoes over them, and a fur-lined coat; but by noon the cold would always seep into his body, and his feet would become brittle and stay that way the rest of the day. The crew was too far from camp to return for the noon meal, and the cooks made up sack lunches for them; but the meat always froze in the sandwiches unless the boys put them under the bonnet of the truck for the heat.

During the first two weeks on the trail Perry gained six pounds. After a while he didn't mind the cold any more, and some days the sun would shine down out of a clear sky and reflect like gold off the mountaintops and off the snow on the branches of the evergreens. The shadows of the spruce and fir would fall blue on the ground. He loved the sweet, burning resin smell of the beech wood when the chain saw cut through it. There were deer, grouse, rabbit and bear tracks in the snow, and once when they were working by a natural rock bridge that arched over a stream, he could see rainbow trout lying in the swirling eddies behind the rocks, their tails fanning the water as they waited for food to come downstream.

Every other week Perry sat in the education building in a classroom that was decorated like the inside of an elementary school. There were geography maps on the wall, mathematic charts of basic addition and subtraction, the letters of the alphabet in bold, black print on individual cards, and reading machines that flashed cartoons and simple words on a white screen. Perry's first textbook was a cardboard primer with stickfigures and six letters of the alphabet. He felt ashamed in front of the other Corpsmen when he was assigned to the special class for non-readers, and he told the instructor that he could read as well as anyone in the camp.

'Read the title off the book in your hand,' the instructor said.

'I ain't interested in learning nothing but running them machines, mister,' Perry said. 'We had books like this in the first grade.'

'How can you operate a machine if you can't read the book that tells you how to do it?'

'I can tear down an air hammer, and I didn't learn it from no book.'

'Can you read an engineer's manual about a piece of equipment like that twenty-five-thousand-dollar bulldozer out there?' the instructor said. 'Or a blueprint that tells you how much grade and fill to cut on a highway job?'

'Double O Cool, you sweat everything too much,' the Corpsman in the next desk said to Perry. It was Popcorn, the Negro whom he'd met in the barracks his first night in camp. 'I been in this class three months, and I'll probably still be here when they kick me out after my two years. And, man, believe me when I say that half the studs in this place couldn't tell the difference between the men's and women's rest room unless somebody pointed them at it.'

Perry spent eight hours a day in the reading and maths classes, and filled his Big Chief notebook with simple words scrawled in his childish handwriting: *I am a pin, I am a man, I am an ant, I am a tin can, The tin can has an ant in it.* It always took him several minutes to write one sentence, squinting with one eye at each letter as he tried to hold the pencil correctly in his hand. He felt that writing words was the most difficult thing he had ever attempted. The words would never shape themselves the same way they looked in his primer, and his fingers would cramp and ache from the effort. But he worked hard every day, sometimes through part of his lunch hour, and at night he took his book of stick figures and simple captions to the barracks and read it in bed before the resident worker turned out the light. In a few weeks' time he went through eight books of the primer series, and he could recognize most of the words that the instructor flashed on the white screen with the reading machine.

After his first month on the trail crew the work leader recommended Perry for a five-dollar merit rise, and he was promoted to Corpsman first class, one step below an assistant work leader. Also, the director kept his word, and Perry was transferred to the heavy equipment class, where he began learning how to operate a bulldozer, a highway grader, a back hoe, a fork lift and a dragline. At the end of the day his clothes were always covered with grease from the engines. The instructor made the new boys in the class swamp the blade on the dozer, cleaning the dirt free with a shovel, and do all the lubrication on the other machines, which meant climbing under them on the frozen ground with a hand-soiled diagram of the bearings, and squeezing the hand pump into the sockets while the grease ran back into their faces. The worst detail was to change the oil, because as soon as the nut was unscrewed from the pan the oil would usually pour all over the Corpsman who was under it.

During his second week in the class the instructor told Perry to climb up into the double operator's seat of the bulldozer with him. Perry snapped the canvas safety belt over his waist, and they moved out along a flat stretch of red clay road through the forest. Perry learned how to control each of the treads with the levers and to turn the machine around by throwing one track into reverse while the other was in forward motion. Once, he lifted the blade too high so he couldn't see in front of him and ran into a thick pine trunk. His head banged into the side of the cab from the impact and his tin hat cut the bridge of his nose. He put his coat sleeve across his face to catch the blood and tried to back the machine off the tree. He gave it too much gas, pulled one lever too far back, and the bulldozer spun around in a half circle, the engine roaring and the treads ripping brush and small trees from the ground. Then Perry dropped the blade too fast and shattered a Forest Service trail sign into splinters.

'Look what you done,' another Corpsman yelled at him. 'You run over my chain saw. There ain't enough left of it to put in a paper bag.'

The saw was flattened into the clay, the parts twisted and smashed as though they had been beaten with sledge-hammers.

'What was it doing in the middle of the goddamn road?' Perry said.

'If I'd known you was running that dozer, I wouldn't be nowhere on this mountain,' the other Corpsman said.

'By God, you get up here and run it, then.'

'All right, you guys knock that crap off,' the instructor said. 'James, get over there and clean up all that brush and burn it in the stream bed. Then pick up what's left of the saw and throw it into the truck. Tonight we can explain to the director how we ran over the only chain saw laying on the ground in North Carolina.'

'Does that mean I don't get no more chance on the machine?' Perry said.

'No, it means that you try to do things on your own before you ask an older man a question.' The instructor had his machinist's goggles pulled up on his forehead. His face was red from the cold in the thin light through the trees. The skin around his eyes was white where the goggles had been. 'Once you learn a little patience and stop trying to do everything in one day, you'll be a good heavy equipment man. But I ain't going to let you tear up my machine because you have to show these other boys something. The next time you do something wrong, you pull the key on the ignition and let me get you out of it. We lost a chain saw this time, but it could have been some boy's foot, and I ain't going to spend three days making out accident forms for the Forest Service because somebody didn't have enough sense to know the difference between asking a question and being a fool.'

'I wasn't trying to show nobody nothing,' Perry said.

'Son, you've got an engine running in you all the time. You're the type that can't be second best at anything, and you're out to prove it even if you have to run over yourself doing it.'

'When can I get back on the dozer?'

'That's just what I mean,' the instructor said. 'You haven't asked me yet what you did wrong. All you can think about is making that machine do what you want it to without learning how to do it right.'

'All right, I ain't a-giving you cause to get on me again. You say frog and I'll say how high.'

'Go back to the oiling detail for the next two days and we'll talk about it then,' the instructor said.

'I already been on it a week.'

'Boy, I just said frog.'

That weekend Perry took his first town pass into Asheville. He had washed and starched his dress khaki uniform by hand in a tin tub of water in the shower and had pressed the creases in it as rigid and sharp as a knife blade. The barracks resident worker, a retired Navy enlisted man, had shown him how to spit shine his black shoes, and Perry spent all of Friday evening burning the old polish off the leather with a match and then rubbing wax and saliva into the rough grain with a woman's nylon stocking. He buffed the toes until he could see most of his body reflected in the shine. He stood in front of the full-length mirror in the shower and looked at the sharp cut of his uniform, his black tie tucked inside his blouse, the Job Corps shield sewn on his sleeve, and the pale area around his ears and the back of his head from the haircut one of the Negro boys had given him for a quarter. And he had fifteen dollars' pay in his pocket, money that he could spend in any way he wished, without having to worry about buying food or paying off the charge at the company store.

He ate eggs and sausage in the mess hall and signed out at the administration building. The leave bus was packed with Corpsmen, some dressed in uniforms and others in the street clothes they had been issued after their first month in camp. The day was cold and bright, and the fir trees were a violent green against the snow. The horses in the fields had ice in their manes and tails, and their breath fogged in the air. In the distance at the far end of the hollow Perry could see the small log cabins with wood smoke rising from the chimneys, and occasionally he would see deer tracks wandering through a clearing in the trees on the mountain.

The resident worker parked the bus at the YMCA in Asheville. In minutes the bus was empty and all the Corpsmen had disappeared into the busy traffic of Saturday afternoon. Perry and L.J., the boy from Mississippi, walked along a crowded pavement on a side street and looked at the rows of bars, secondhand stores, tattoo parlours, cafés that sold fried chicken and catfish, three-dollar hotels, and hillbilly dance halls. Many of the people on the path in that part of town were dressed like the mountain people Perry knew back in Kentucky. The men had on worn, shiny suitcoats over their overalls, and their women wore thin cotton-print dresses and hand-knitted sweaters that always looked shabby and never fitted them quite properly. Through the glass windows of a tavern Perry saw women sitting at the bar sipping beer and highballs, something that he believed women did only in the jenny-barn.

'Look at that feller getting a tattoo,' L.J. said. His uniform was too small for him, and his thin neck stuck up out of the collar like a turkey's. 'That needle is hopping up and down on his arm like a sewing machine.'

'Listen to that music across the street. Buddy, that sounds like home. Let's go over and get us a beer.'

'They ain't going to serve us. Besides, we won't get in nothing but trouble there, anyhow.'

'A twenty-cent beer ain't going to hurt you, is it?' Perry said. 'We'll get a table in back and I'll do all the buying at the bar. They give me my union card when I was fifteen because I looked twenty-one. These people can't tell no different.'

'There's always some feller cutting on somebody else in them places,' L.J. said.

'This ain't Mississippi. It's a city. We ain't going to have none of that here.'

'I'll wait outside. You go in.'

'No, we ain't a-doing it that way. Come on.' Perry took L.J.'s arm and they crossed the street through the line of cars. The noise was loud from the bar-room door as a drunk walked out into the street. 'Go get a place over in the corner and I'll be there in a minute,' Perry said.

'Let's get out of here, Perry.'

'They'll think you're a soldier. The whole town is full of them. Go set down now and stop a-worrying.'

He went to the bar and ordered two draughts in glass mugs that were filmed with ice. The tables were filled with men and women who drank straight shots of whiskey with beer chasers. On a raised wooden platform at the back of the dance floor was a country string band. One of the musicians lowered the microphone, and the fiddler played 'The Orange Blossom Special' directly into it. A man at the end of the counter passed out and shattered a bottle on the bar rail. Perry worked his way through the tables until he found L.J. sitting far back in the shadows, his face nervous and afraid.

'Look, Perry, my people is hard-shelled Baptists,' he said. 'If my daddy knew I was in a place like this and drinking, he'd wear me out with a belt. Once he caught my brother with some homemade wine, and he almost never turned loose of him.'

'Remember what they told us back at camp? You ain't a boy no longer with your daddy to tell you what to do. Drink your beer and we'll buy a big dinner.'

'I ain't throwing my money away in a place like this.'

'Well, I didn't work two weeks for fifteen dollars so I could waste it, neither,' Perry said.

Two hours later he was drunk. His tie was pulled loose from his collar, beer was spilled down the front of his shirt, and the colour had gone from his face. The whites of his eyes looked yellow in the bar-room light. He danced with several women, but he didn't know how to lead or make his feet follow any sort of pattern, and he backed one girl into a table and knocked over several glasses. He sat in his chair, a dull expression on his face; his shirt sleeve lay in a puddle of beer.

'You wore out all my patience,' L.J. said. 'Let's get out on the street and get something to eat.'

'Go on by yourself.'

'I can't leave you alone in here. Somebody'll tear you up.'

'I been drinking corn whiskey since I was fourteen, and there ain't nobody yet that had to take care of me.'

'You see all them fellers that just come in? They're just looking for somebody to grab hold of.'

'By God, they ain't running me off. My mother's people was Hatfields and the rest of us is related to Frank James. Back home we'd take fellers like that and stick their head in the honey hole.'

'Keep fooling with them women, and there ain't none of that going to help you,' L.J. said. 'If you was sober enough to see what you was dancing with, you wouldn't touch her unless you run castor oil and turpentine through it first.'

'Where's those fellers at that wanted trouble?'

'You're going to get us in jail, and then they'll throw us out of camp. You want that to happen to us?'

'We're on pass. What we do in town ain't any concern of theirs,' Perry said. 'What did them fellers say to you?'

'God darn it, I ain't setting still for any more of this. We're leaving.'

But Perry had already ordered another draught beer and a shot of whiskey. An hour later he vomited on himself in the men's room. His head was spinning and he couldn't walk straight. He walked unsteadily to the bar with his trousers unzipped and tried to buy a beer to get the bad taste out of his mouth, but the bartender refused to serve him. L.J. took him by the arm and guided him outside into the street. The sun had begun to set over the buildings, and the wind blew like ice against their faces. Perry slipped once on the pavement and fell into a parking meter. The side of his head struck the metal pole, but he felt only a dull numbness from the blow. The street and the store fronts looked dirty in the half-light of the late sun.

'Stand up straight. I can't hold you,' L.J. said.

'You ain't got to.' Perry pulled loose from him and stumbled out in the street through the traffic. He heard cars slamming to a stop and horns blowing as he tried to walk in a straight line. The vomit had frozen on his shoes and trousers. He tripped over the kerb and walked along the row of buildings, keeping one shoulder always close to a wall. I don't need nobody to take me home, he thought. They ain't seen the day that somebody had to pick up after me because of whiskey. The warmth of the alcohol began to wear off and he felt the cold reach inside his body, then he realized that he had left his coat in the bar; but he couldn't remember how many blocks he had walked down the street or even where the bar exactly was.

There was a policeman on the corner directing traffic. Perry began to wish he had stayed with L.J. He knew that he would never get across the street under the policeman's gaze without getting arrested. He stood in front of a tattoo parlour balancing himself on his feet, and he felt the eyes of the people passing on the path boring into his face. He opened the door of the tattoo parlour and almost fell inside. A muscular sailor with his shirt off sat on a stool while a man dressed like a horse tout worked on his arm with the needle. The walls were covered with brightly coloured designs of American and Confederate flags, knives dripping blood, dragons and snakes curled around Marine Corps and Navy emblems, nude women, inscriptions to mother, crosses and the face of Christ.

'I'll be with you in five minutes, soldier,' the man with the needle said. He wore a green and black checkered shirt buttoned at the throat without a tie, and pointed patent leather shoes. There were red and blue blood veins in his cheeks.

Perry sat in a chair against the wall and began belching. He reached into his shirt pocket and counted out his money. He had five soiled dollar bills left, which was all he would have until the next pay two weeks away. He tried to remember why he had come into the tattoo parlour, but his mind wouldn't clear and he looked at the designs through one squinted eye. He began to smell the odour from his clothes in the heated room. Then the sailor was gone and Perry was on the stool, pulling off his shirt.

'You sure you want a tattoo?' the man said. 'I don't like to work on a man while he's drunk and have him come around about it the next morning.'

'What do you think I come in here for? This don't look like the bus depot, does it?'

'OK, soldier, what do you want and where you want me to put it?'

'I ain't no soldier. Give me a tattoo just like that Job Corps shield on my shirt sleeve.'

'I got to have a pattern. Pick out something up there on the wall.'

'What's wrong with Job Corps?' Perry said.

'I've tattooed just about half of the marine base, and I have all the customers I need. I do the best work in Asheville, and if you want to argue with me you can go up the street to one of those parlours that'll give you blood poisoning in your arm.'

'Put one of them big Confederate flags on me with United Mine Workers of America under it.'

The man washed the upper part of Perry's arm with warm water and soap, and rubbed a cotton pad soaked in alcohol over his skin. His arm was cool as the alcohol evaporated, then he felt the needle go into him and burn as though someone held a lighted match to his body. The pain seemed to run up through his shoulder and into his groin. The blood broke to the surface in small drops and ran down his elbow. The man stopped for a moment, wiped his arm clean, and then continued. It took forty-five minutes for the man to finish the tattoo because he had to change ink three times to fill out the Confederate flag. By that time Perry's arm had gone numb. The man cleaned the tattoo once more with alcohol and rubbed ointment over it.

'It'll scab over and stick to your clothes a little bit the first week,' he said. 'Just don't pick at it and you'll have a good-looking tattoo the rest of your life.'

Perry tucked his shirt into his trousers and gave the man his last five dollars. He walked out into the dark street and felt his arm stiffen and begin to ache in the cold. The traffic had thinned and the policeman was gone from the corner, and Perry made his way across the street and walked towards the YMCA parking lot. Snow flurries spun through the air and stuck damply in his hair and shirt collar. He wanted to get another drink, but he didn't have a quarter in his pocket. He didn't know the time and he wasn't sure whether or not the bus had aleady left for camp. He began to feel a sense of fear at the thought of being left in the city with no money and nowhere to go. Just like L.J. said, he thought, they'll put me in the jail house and leave me there. Vagrancy and drunk, thirty days. The people at camp won't even know where I'm at. Then they'll put me down AWOL and kick me out of Job Corps.

Perry rounded the corner, his arms straightened out by his side in the cold wind, and saw the bus in the parking lot. There was nobody in it except one Corpsman in back. Perry pushed in through the folding doors and then slammed them shut with the big lever attached to the bottom of the dash-board. He walked down the aisle, holding on to the tops of the seats to keep his balance. It was cold even inside the bus. He could still see his breath in the air.

'All root, all reet, Double O Cool is back on the scene and balling,' Popcorn said from the back seat. He had on a lavender sports jacket and slacks, his frayed tennis shoes, and his sailor's cap pulled down over his ears. He drank out of a bottle of muscatel wine. 'Man, you look like a disaster area. Are they playing World War II down the street? Blue face, bloody arm, that good yellow vomit smell in the air. Baby, you have arrived in technicolor.'

'Let me have a drink.'

'Be careful with it, soul. They run airplanes on this stuff.'

Perry took a long swallow out of the bottle. The wine tasted like hair tonic and wood alcohol.

'Take it easy,' Popcorn said. 'You don't want to barf your groceries twice in one night. Who put the shank in you arm?'

'I got a tattoo. It cost five dollars.' Perry rolled up his sleeve carefully. The blood had frozen to his sleeve.

'That's what we call a bad news flag back in Cleveland,' Popcorn said. 'Like what all those studs wave around in the air down in Alabama while they're playing Dixie on a black man's head. What's that say under it?'

'United Mine Workers. I worked a year and a half under ground before I come here.'

'Don't go showing off that thing to any of the black guys tonight after they've been drinking.'

'Lookie, I don't show off nothing to nobody, and I ain't got any bad feelings towards any feller in this camp. We ain't got many coloured people around home, and I don't know much about them. So a flag like this don't have that kind of meaning to me.' Perry drank out of the bottle again and passed it to Popcorn.

'You know you got real innocence, Double O. You're so way out that the studs back in Hough wouldn't believe there's whites like you around. But you got something bothering you all the

44

time, and you're not going to make it in Job Corps unless you get that block of concrete off your head.'

'I ain't got nothing bothering me.'

'You're not talking to the heat on the corner. I've heard you saying things in your sleep. Then sometimes you stare at a wall like you've just fixed.'

'What did I say?'

'It don't matter to me what you've done. Back home the only thing we have for the law is a finger, because the law is Mr Skins with his blue uniform and a billy club.'

Perry took the bottle back and upended it. He felt himself begin to grow warm again. 'If I had the police after me, I wouldn't be a-setting in no government camp where they could come grab me whenever they had a mind to.'

'You're putting yourself on, not Popcorn. I know where you got those snakes. I was in on something once just like you were. When I was fourteen we had a rumble with some white hoosiers in the next welfare project. We told their warlord to come into our territory for a truce. I led him up the street behind a store, and the rest of the guys got him. He was the toughest stud they had. He put my brother's eye out with a chain and cut up two other guys the week before. I watched them while they stomped him all over the alley. That poor cat tried to run and they kicked his balls in. He even got down and begged before they all put their shanks in him. I was so scared and sick watching it that I puked all over myself and then got the dry heaves right there in the alley. I couldn't get rid of seeing that cat beg until my mother took me to the wig mechanic. Even then, it took me a year to put the snakes back in their baskets.'

'I didn't want to do it,' Perry said. 'We didn't know there was somebody up there on the tipple. Then I heered his scream come roaring out of the fire. He stood out like lightning was racing over his body. He wasn't nothing but a West Virginia scab, but we didn't have no need for a killing.'

'It happened, though, didn't it? And it could have been you that got it instead of him, or it could have been me in that alley instead of that hoosier. You didn't plan it, but that's the way it went. Man, don't you know that you can't pull the strings all the time?'

'That feller probably had people somewhere, even if he was a scab. They never found enough of him to tell who he was.'

'So you're going to worry about it until they put the net over you and carry you off to the monkey farm.'

'I don't want to talk about it no more.'

'All root, Double O.'

Perry looked out of the window and saw fifteen Corpsmen and the resident worker headed down the street towards the bus. The resident worker had rounded them up out of the bars during the last hour, and most of them were drunk to one degree or another. Their shirts were pulled from their trousers, their hair was down in their eyes, two of them had to be carried, and the Indian boys were yelling like Apaches in a grade-B movie. A Negro boy climbed up on a tall embankment and acted like a human sled with another Corpsman on his back. They swished down the slope through the snow and landed on their heads in the middle of the pavement.

After everyone was on the bus, the resident worker turned on the overhead light and stood at the front of the aisle. Some of the Corpsmen had already passed out in the seats.

'You guys are going to get it for this,' he said. 'I'll have each one of you chipping ice for the next two weeks. Close that window!'

'James is going to toss his cookies again,' Popcorn said.

FOUR

After they arrived back at Camp the resident worker and three other Corpsmen had to carry Perry to the barracks. He was sick all day Sunday with a hangover, and he lay in his bunk, shaking with nausea and a throbbing headache. He tried to eat at the evening meal, but he couldn't swallow any of his food and had to return his tray, still filled, to the KP window. Monday morning at roll call he was released from education and was told to report to the administration building for a board of review. Outside the director's office a dozen other Corpsmen sat on wooden benches waiting to be called in. They were either boys who had been drunk on the bus or ones who had already been assigned to the trail crew for disciplinary reasons. Ain't this a bunch to get yourself in with, Perry thought. There ain't one of them that's hit a lick since he's been here, and they got me right with them.

The director called Perry into his pine-panelled office that smelled of linseed oil and cigar smoke. Three other foresters and the head of the education programme sat in leather chairs, with note pads in their laps. Perry sat down in front of the desk and looked at the floor. He wished that he had put on his class-A uniform that morning instead of fatigues. He began to imagine that his tattoo was bleeding again and showing through his shirt sleeve.

'You know why you're in here, Perry?' the director said.

'Yes, sir.'

'I mean do you know that we're considering expelling you from Job Corps?'

'You give me warning the last time I was in here.'

'How do you feel about your conduct?' one of the other foresters said. His voice was level with no accusation in it.

'I done wrong and I didn't act no better than them people in the jenny-barn. I give my word to the director and the heavy equipment instructor that I wouldn't cause no more trouble. But I done it anyway. I'm sorry for it, and there ain't much more I can say.'

'Did you know that both your maths and reading teachers recommended you for assistant work leader?' the director said. 'Your vocational instructor told me that you'll be the best man on his detail once you learn that you can't be first in everything in a few weeks. You wouldn't be here unless we had something we could teach you.'

'I come here because I know I can't do nothing but common labour in the mine and cut tobacco. I don't want to go back to none of that. Mr Henson got on me for tearing up your trail sign

47

and running over the chain saw. He put me back on the oil crew, and he was right in doing it. But I worked hard for him, and he says he'll put me back in the dozer seat next week.'

'What about getting drunk in town?'

'I ain't a-touching no more whiskey or wine while I'm at this camp. I figure it's already cost me enough trouble.'

'Do you think you can start playing by our rules and not your own?' the director said.

'Yes, sir.'

'How do you feel about Job Corps?' the other forester said.

'I never had no better chance at anything.'

'All right, we're going to keep you,' the director said. 'But I'm giving you two weeks' restriction to camp. No football games, no trips to the roller rink, not even a hike in the woods. And eight hours' extra duty and a five-dollar fine for losing your jacket. Do you think that's too rough to take?'

'No sir, but I rather you gave me more extra duty instead of docking my pay. The fifty dollars the government sends home ain't enough to help my family as it is. My daddy's a happy-pappy, and what he brings in don't hardly pay the credit at the store.'

'You were willing enough to spend all your money on liquor.'

'That's because I was drunk and set on seeing how much of a fool I could make of myself. But I ain't going to have no more chance to waste my money in the saloon, because you ain't catching me in Asheville till I get my air ticket back home.'

The director gave Perry five more hours' extra duty instead of the fine. Perry worked the entire thirteen hours off in one week by trading KP duty with another Corpsman every night. He usually caught the pots and pans detail, the worst in the kitchen, and he would stand behind the receiving window, in the steam from the electric dish washer, and clean the spilled food and wet cigarette butts from the trays. During his restriction he was allowed no farther from camp than the front road, and he was not even allowed to go into town to buy his eighty-five dollars' worth of civilian clothes. He had no money for cigarettes, toothpaste or razor blades, and he spent his weekends in camp with the few other boys, shooting pool, ironing shirts for a dime apiece, or rolling cigarettes with a hand machine for two cigarettes a pack.

After his restriction was over he went on recreation trips only to the football game against the rural high school in a small town at the bottom of the mountain, or to the twenty-five-cent roller rink on Tuesday nights. He began sending half of his pay home, and he could usually earn two dollars on Saturday or Sunday by pulling someone's KP.

A month later a letter of commendation was put in his government file by the director. Perry received a carbon copy of it on Forest Service stationery with a large Job Corps seal under the letterhead, and he had to have one of the instructors help him read some of the long words.

One afternoon on a hike after Indian artifacts two Corpsmen had separated from the group and had crawled up on a flat ledge overlooking the hollow. They couldn't find their way back down and began calling for help; but no one could determine where their voices came from because of the echoes. Then one of them flashed a signal in the sun with a tin mirror. Both boys were two hundred feet straight up a cliff. They were pressed out flat on the rock, their white and drained faces sticking out over the edge. The resident worker tried to go after them, but he was an older man from New York, much out of condition, with a heavy roll of fat around his stomach, and he slipped on a loose rock twenty feet above the ground and landed on his back, scraping the skin off the side of his face. Perry took the rope from him, looped it crossways over his shoulders, and climbed up the face of the mountain. By instinct he always placed his foot in the right crevice and pulled his weight up on a root or protruding rock that would not give. He knew how to pause when the rocks rolled out from under his foot and showered down the mountain, and how to make his fingers dig into places where the only opening was a small split that had been caused by the expansion of the ice. Just before he reached the top of the cliff, there was a cave that cut back into the mountain and an area of completely smooth surface below it. He had both feet on a three-inch ledge. He jumped upwards with all his strength and caught the edge of the floor with his fingers and pulled himself inside. He strung out twenty-five feet of rope and tied a heavy oak branch to the end of it, then threw it on top of the cliff to the other two Corpsmen.

'Knot it around something that don't pull loose,' he said.

'I ain't going down on that thing,' one of the boys said.

'By God, you're going down or I'll leave you here and you can freeze to death before the ranger crew finds you. Now tie it down and get your ass moving.'

Perry threw the rope in a long arc down into the hollow. The other Corpsmen looking up at him were small figures against the late winter green of the brush and the patches of snow on the ground. The rope swung back and forth in front of the cave.

The first Corpsman came down past Perry hand over hand, his face bloodless with fear.

'Wrap your legs in that rope,' Perry said. 'If you slip, just hold on, even if you burn your hands off.' He watched the first Corpsman, who had his eyes shut, work his way down far below him. The heavily wooded hills and the creek that wound through the hollow looked miniature in the distance.

The second Corpsman would not leave the ledge. Once, he took hold of the rope and crawled backwards over the edge until just his feet protruded into space; then he climbed back again and lay out flat, shaking, against the rock shelf. He was a slight boy of sixteen who had been in camp one week, and his face had the frightened, empty expression of the retarded.

'I can't come up after you. There ain't no way for me to get over the ledge,' Perry said. 'Slide on down to me, and I'll get under you and we'll go down together.'

'We'll smash all over the rocks.'

'No, we ain't. Remember what they told you when you come into camp? This is a man's outfit and you got to act like one. Now get on down here.'

'I got sweat all over me. I can't hold on to the rope.'

'I can hold both of us if you let go. You can't get down no other way, and you might as well set your mind to it. Keep your eyes shut and let your legs come down on my shoulders. Goddamn it, boy, climb down off there and let's go get us some dinner.'

The second Corpsman inched backwards and began to slide

down the rope. Small rocks rolled out from under his body. The knuckles in his hands were as white as bone around the rope. Perry grabbed on to the slack, held it taut until the boy reached the opening of the cave, and then swung out and caught the boy's legs over his shoulders. They worked their way down together, the rope biting into their hands, while their own weight swung them hard into the face of the mountain. Both of Perry's elbows were bleeding, and he had a cut in his scalp just above his hairline. Later, the camp doctor picked out the pieces of rock from the wound with tweezers and put four stitches in his head.

A week after he received his letter of commendation, Perry was promoted to assistant work leader with a fifteen-dollar rise in pay. In the next three months he advanced to the regular reading programme and was able to read most of the words in a newspaper. He had gone through subtraction, addition and fractions and the instructor moved him up to decimals. As an assistant work leader he supervised a crew of trainees in the bulldozer class, checked out all the chain saws, picks and axes from the tool shack, and saw that the machines were oiled and gassed after morning roll call. His body had filled out and toughened, and his skin had the rough tan that comes from working outdoors in the reflection of the sun off the snow. He had his hair cut every two weeks, and even on the work detail he wore starched khakis.

The vocational instructor told him that in another three months he would know enough about heavy equipment to get an apprentice's book in the union, and Perry began to plan for the day he would go to Cincinnati and get a job that paid three dollars an hour. He could not imagine that a man could make twenty-five dollars a day, or even more if he worked overtime. He didn't believe anyone except coal operators could have so much money. It was enough money to have a house with plumbing, like at camp, or to take Irvin to a good doctor, a specialist, or to buy an electric icebox and fill it with more food than his family could eat. And there would be money left over for motion picture shows on Saturday afternoon, new clothes for his brothers and sisters, and maybe a car to drive down to the Winfro Valley Barn Dance. There would be no more company shack on the mountainside, no more string beans and ham stock every night for dinner, no more smell of the burning slag heap in the air.

Spring came to the Smoky Mountains with thunder showers every afternoon. The snow melted off the ground, except for the shaded areas under the timber, and the new grass was a light green against the hillsides. In the morning water ran down off the mountain and collected in pools on the blacktop roads, and then evaporated like steam in the sun's first light. One day the dogwood suddenly bloomed, and the blue-green of the spruce and the fir trees was broken by a spray of white flowers. The temperature still went below freezing at night, and the edges of the streams were coated with ice, but the days became warm and clear, and hawks flew high above the mountains in the bright sky. The farmers began ploughing in the hollows to plant their tobacco, and there was always a smell of new earth and guano in the air.

A rainstorm broke one afternoon when Perry was clearing a road through the woods with the bulldozer. He took his slicker from behind the operator's seat, slipped it over his shoulders, and pulled the machinist's goggles down over his eyes against the rain. In a half hour the ground was drenched, and the wet clay flew through the air from the dozer's treads. Perry lowered the blade and pushed a pile of stumps and tree limbs over the edge of the cliff into the riverbed below. He backed off, raised the blade, and two other Corpsmen cleaned it off with their shovels.

'Shut it down and let's go back to the truck,' one of the boys said. It was the big boy from Georgia, named Birl, whom Perry had seen turn his chain saw against a rock four months earlier. His wash-faded fatigues had turned dark olive from the rain. The water spilled down over the brim of his cap. He had been put on the brush detail for fighting, and he was scheduled for a board of review the next week.

'Mr Henson said we don't quit till five. He wants this road cleared down to the blacktop,' Perry said.

'I got enough sense to come out of the rain, even if he ain't.' One of his eyes squinted when he looked at Perry. He was powerful all over, and the muscles in his arms and thighs were tight against his clothes. His face was white with no tan, and there were deep pock marks in his cheeks. Red clay was splattered over his rubber boots and trousers. Some of the boys in camp said he carried an Italian switchblade inside his boot.

'I'm just telling you what Mr Henson said. If you want to holler about it, you can go on back there and talk to him,' Perry said.

'That work leader badge don't allow you to work us like niggers.'

Perry pushed the throttle in and cut the ignition. 'You ain't a-working for me. I'm just doing what I'm told. I don't like setting out in the rain no more than you do, but we're still going to run this road straight out to the blacktop.'

'Why don't you go fuck yourself, hillbilly?'

'Lookie, I ain't taking that from you or no other man. You got this detail because you beat up on a feller a foot shorter than you. I wouldn't give twenty-five cents for a bag full of your kind. Back in Kentucky you wouldn't even be a good scab. The likes of you stand in the welfare line and bitch about somebody not giving you a chair to set in.'

'Why don't we take it back in the woods?'

'You pull that knife on me and I'll whip it all over your head.'

'No knife. Just fists and feet,' Birl said.

'You better shut your mouth and start picking up that brush and throw it down the holler.'

'I think you got that yellow feeling down inside you, James.'

'You done it then, buddy.' Perry set the brakes on the bulldozer and jumped down from the cab. The mud and water splashed over his slicker. Birl stepped back, his one hand rolled into a fist by his side. 'No, there ain't going to be no fight,' Perry said. 'We're a-going to see Mr Henson.'

'You think you can take me down there?'

'I know I can.'

Birl reached down inside his rubber boot and switched open a long, double-edged Italian knife. The handle was made of bone. He held the blade out before him, moving it from side to side.

'I warned you, but you wouldn't pay me no mind,' Perry said.

He pulled a ballpeen hammer from the seat in the dozer cab and raised it up to the level of his shoulder. Lightning crashed across the sky and struck against the mountain on the far side of the hollow. The rain beat into their eyes. 'You know what I can do to you with this? Your head won't be nothing but a cracked flower pot. Throw it on the ground and get moving down the trail.'

'Look, James—'

'I mean now, goddamn it. Get rid of it. You taken enough of my time already. I ain't working after five on this road because of you.'

The boy dropped the knife on the road and walked back down the trail. Perry threw the hammer into the cab and followed him. The faint afternoon light glowed through the heavy timber and fell onto the pine needle-covered floor of the forest. Mr Henson was operating the back hoe with a crew of Corpsmen on a clay bluff high above the river. The hoe dug into a trench and lifted out a load of wet earth and broken tree roots. Some of the Corpsmen were shaking from the rain and the cold. Mr Henson put his machine in neutral and let it idle when he saw Perry and Birl come towards him.

'Why ain't you all back on that dozer?' he said.

'He don't want to work and he pulled a knife on me,' Perry said. 'I ain't going to have him on my detail no more.'

'Where's the knife?' Mr Henson said. There were beads of water on his goggles.

'It's a-laying back on the trail, but it don't matter because he won't have no chance to use it. I'm putting in my report with the director so they can pack his sack lunch and get his bus ticket ready.'

'He come at me with a hammer,' Birl said.

'I done it after he opened up that gut ripper. And I liked to split his head open, too.'

Mr Henson climbed down from the back hoe, pulled off his cloth gloves, and lighted a cigarette. The rain drops spotted the white paper. He smoked evenly for a few moments and spit the pieces of loose tobacco off his tongue. 'One of you other boys run back and find that knife and bring it to me. Perry, put the tarp over your machine and bring the truck around to pick up the crew. We ain't going to get anything done in this rain.'

'You ain't heard what I had to say,' Birl said. 'Do I get kicked out for having a shank when another man picks up a hammer at me?'

'Did you refuse to work?'

'I told him there wasn't no sense in standing out in the rain. You just said the same thing, didn't you?'

'But I didn't say it to you,' Mr Henson said. 'When one of my work leaders tells you to get on it, that's just like you're hearing it straight from me. I don't know for positive who pulled the hammer or knife first, but every time I've had you on my crew you've given me trouble, and I've had my fill of it.'

'You mean in this outfit a man gets a pay rise and one of them badges for copping out because he ain't got enough balls to step it off in the woods.'

'I'm going to do you a favour, son,' Mr Henson said. 'Get on the truck, set still until we get back to camp, and I'll make sure you're on your way back to Macon tomorrow. Keep bothering me and I'll put you and James in the woods by yourselves for fifteen minutes, and then I'll come pick you off the ground and carry you to the truck.'

Perry drove the canvas-covered van through the mud, and the Corpsmen threw their chain saws and tools inside and climbed up over the tailgate. A pool of water had collected in the centre of the tarp, and it sagged heavily between the wooden ribs that arched over the back of the truck. One of the boys pushed a hoe handle into the hard lump, and the water sluiced down in streams onto the trail. Perry got down from the cab and let Mr Henson get behind the wheel for the drive along the blacktop back to camp.

'You can ride up here, and one of the others can get in back,' Mr Henson said. 'I don't want to stop on the road and have to pull you boys apart.'

'There won't be no need for that,' Perry said. He pulled himself over the tailgate and sat back against the wood siding of the truck. The rain streaked in and spotted the boards. He unlaced the leather thongs on his work boots and rubbed the chafed area around his ankles, then he took out his package of Bugler tobacco and papers, and rolled a cigarette.

Most of the boys were exhausted. Their clothes were soaked through to their long underwear, their hair and faces were flecked with mud, and their hands were pinched and wrinkled from being wet all day. They smoked quietly, passing cigarette butts to each other, and occasionally one of the Indians spat a stream of tobacco juice over the tailgate. Birl sat against the cab, with his long legs spread out before him, and stared sullenly at Perry.

'I'm going to fix your ass for this, James,' he said.

Perry said nothing. He finished his cigarette, peeled the paper back along the seam, and let the tobacco spin out in the wind current.

The rain had washed down the mountain and covered the footpaths in camp with mud. Huge pools of water lay in the low areas, and the thunder rattled the tin buildings. The Corpsmen returning from their work details ran towards the barracks in the slickers and rubber boots. Lightning had struck a tree and dropped it across a power line, knocking out half the lights in camp. After the crew had unloaded from Perry's truck, he drove it a half mile down the shale road to the equipment shed, locked the ignition keys in the maintenance shack, and walked back through the driving rain to the administration building. It took him twenty minutes to write out a five-sentence incident report in large printed letters; then he took it in the director's office.

'Are you sure you didn't pick up that hammer first?' the director said.

'No sir, he pulled the frog sticker when I told him to take his bitching to Mr Henson.'

'Do you have a witness?'

Perry's clothes dripped water onto the carpet. His face was drawn with fatigue. 'Yes sir, but if you got to call him, this badge you give me don't mean much.'

'The other man has a right to a hearing, too.'

'He don't have no rights after he tries to cut on a man. The rule says a Corpsman caught with a weapon gets put out the same day. When you made me assistant work leader, you said you'd back me all the way as long as I kept straight. Well, I done it.'

'I don't think you ever forget anything that's said to you, do you?' the director said. 'I accept your word and I never doubted it. But there are things we have to go through that you don't understand before we put a boy out of camp. Go change clothes and get down to the mess hall before they close the line.'

Outside, Perry pulled his slicker up over his head and walked along the smooth clay trail through the pines to the barracks. He pulled off his wet clothes, wrung them in the washbasin, and stuffed them into his duffle bag. He showered with hot water, washed the mud out of his hair, and rubbed down his body with a towel. The Confederate flag on his arm was a brilliant blue and red against the paleness of his skin. He dressed in the brown slacks, soft wool shirt, and loafers that he had received with his civilian clothes issue; he slipped a transparent rain jacket over his shoulders and went to the dining hall. That evening they had ham steaks, rice and gravy, boiled corn on the cob, and ice-cream. Perry went through the receiving line twice, and then spent an hour in the library working on his reading book.

A movie was scheduled for that night, but the power line hadn't been repaired and the recreation hall had no electricity. The rain began to thin, and Perry walked back to the barracks, where the Corpsmen had lighted candles and melted them to the window sills. The rain looked like beads of crystal on the windows. Several boys were shooting pool, and Perry could hear the dice rattle across the tile floor in the bathroom. No gambling was allowed in the camp, but none of the assistant work leaders or the resident worker ever reported a crap game unless a fight broke out.

Popcorn had his battery-operated phonograph turned on full volume. He danced in the corridor by himself, the candlelight flickering on his dark face. He had on a long, striped housecoat, fur-lined slippers that came above his ankles, pyjamas with half-moons all over them, and a woman's nylon stocking rolled down tight over his scalp. He smoked with a cigarette holder between his teeth and spun around in circles.

'Listen to that sound,' he said. 'It's the hippy dippy from Mississippi. Yes indeed, Mister Jimmy Reed. And next we have that late and great secretary of state, Mister James Brown. He is out of sight and out of mind, and he turns your big daddy on. My head might be nappy, but ain't I beautiful?'

'Where you got the glue hid at?' Perry said.

'No glue, man. None of that scene any more. I can't take those big snakes crawling around behind my eyes the next day. I groove now only with that good spotioti that my soul brothers bring back from the dentist run. It's mellow and yellow, and it'll peel the paint off your walls.'

'Throw it out behind the barracks before the resident worker gets back,' Perry said.

'Cool, do you think I am going to give my good muscat to these North Carolina stumpjumpers? I didn't pay my hard-earned seventy-five cents to water this southern soil.'

'You're up for your merit raise. Don't do nothing to blow it.'

'Man, I ain't pulled an extra hour since I came to camp. That's because I don't lose my cool in front of the wrong people. In Hough you learn how to look like Sunday school all over when you deal with the Man. That's a good thing to know, Double O. You can blast and get high every day as long as you look good on the street for whitey.'

'It still ain't a-helping you none if the resident worker smells it on you at bed check.'

Popcorn reached inside the pocket of his coat and pulled out a bottle of synthetic wine. He unscrewed the cap and took a drink. 'What's the word, baby? It's thunderbird,' he said. The wine rolled down through the stubble of his beard.

'Put that goddamn bottle in your locker and get under the shower,' Perry said.

'You come on like gangbusters with that moral attitude,' Popcorn said. 'Have a drink of spotioti and stop letting that badge ruin your mind. What's this I hear about you playing on people's heads with the ballpeen hammer?'

'I didn't hit nobody with a hammer.'

'They say Birl looked like he'd crapped his pants when you brought him to Henson.'

'He didn't give me no choice when he come out with the knife.'

'Somebody should have fixed that stud a long time ago.'

Perry looked through the rain-streaked window and saw a man run bent over through the trees towards the front door of the barracks. The mountains looked like iron in the dark.

'The resident worker's back. Get rid of that bottle,' he said.

'Not your high rolling daddy. Popcorn will get under the sheets with sneaky pete and let the rest of you cats worry about the Man. Good night, soul brother.'

The Negro boy went to his bunk, took a flashlight and comic book off his night stand, and climbed under the covers with his bottle. He pulled the army blanket over his head, raised his knees to make a tent for himself, and flicked on the flashlight. Perry could hear him laughing under the blanket.

'This Plastic Man character stretches out like chewing gum,' Popcorn said. 'I bet he's got a dong thirty feet long.'

Perry took a thin hand-rolled Bugler cigarette from the tin on his table and lighted it. He breathed in the smoke and felt the day's exhaustion roll through his body. He took off his shirt and shoes, lay back in bed, and listened to the rain beat against the roof. He would get two hours' extra duty on Saturday if he was caught smoking in bed, but right now he didn't care. The light thunder echoed through the valley and rattled the window glass. Two Corpsmen had taken the boxing gloves out of the resident worker's quarters in the dark, and they boxed each other up and down the corridor, slapping the leather and loose strings into one another's faces. Perry was scheduled to call roll at muster the next morning, and he would have to eat with the KPs at four forty-five a.m. He put out his cigarette, pulled the pillow over his head, and tried to fall asleep, but the two boxers kept knocking into the walls, and the pool shooters in the foyer yelled every time someone made a shot.

Perry sat up on the edge of the bed and rubbed his face. His stomach was hard and lean under his T-shirt. 'You fellers ain't supposed to have them gloves out,' he said.

'We don't have nothing else to do. You want us to lay in the rack all evening?' one of the boxers said.

'You giving us an extra hour, Perry?' the second Corpsman said.

'No, I ain't. Just take them gloves and yourself down to the next bay, and you can punch on each other all night,' he said.

The boys went into the next section of the barracks, and Perry lay back down on his bunk and rested his arm across his eyes. In a few minutes the boys were back in the corridor slugging into one another, and a third Corpsman was with them, hitting at their heads with a leather chair cushion. Perry got up and walked barefooted into the foyer to watch the pool game until the resident worker would make bed check and force everyone to go to sleep.

The Corpsmen had set lighted candles in empty bottles on the four corners of the pool table. The shadows wavered across their faces as they bent to make a shot. The usual dime and quarter bets lay on top of the green apron. A Pima Indian from southern Arizona had won seven games straight, and he was trying to get someone to play him for a dollar a game.

'We'll make it nine ball, and I'll give you the break and two free shots afterwards,' he said.

'You run the table down to the last ball every time you shoot,' L.J. said.

'I'll shoot left-handed. You can't get better odds than that.'

'You're too good, man. There ain't nobody going to play you here,' a big Negro boy said. His face was so black that it was hard to see it in the dark. He wore the cloth liner from his work helmet over his head. 'Pass the stick and let's get back to a dime a game.'

'I got the stick as long as I win,' the Indian said. He had a large, square head and a flat nose, narrow shoulders, and a stomach that hung over his belt line. He was the best pool player in camp, and he had made his living by hustling games in Flagstaff before he came into Job Corps.

'Pick up a cue, James. Get rich in one night,' he said.

'I ain't no good at playing, and I got better sense than to pay for your weekends,' Perry said. Out of the corner of his eye he saw Birl sitting on a metal chair against the wall, watching him.

'I'll put a dollar to your fifty cents,' the Indian said.

'I don't know nothing about pool. I told you that.'

'Pass the fucking stick,' the Negro with the cloth cap said. 'We got bed check in thirty minutes.'

'Last chance around, pale faces. Who wants to beat the pride of the Pima reservation?' the Indian said. 'Write back to your family that you took on the best eight ball and rotation man in Flagstaff.'

'Let James shoot it. He's the big stud around here,' Birl said from the shadows.

No one spoke for a moment. The Indian chalked his cue and rubbed talcum on his palms, then rolled the cue on the table to see if it was warped.

'Go ahead and play him, kemosabe. The work leader gets extra pay every month for copping out on his crew,' Birl said.

'Cut that shit, man,' the Indian said.

'I got booted tonight because of this cock sucker. Don't tell me to cut it,' Birl said.

'I had my fill of this, Birl. You're starting to piss me off,' Perry said.

'Don't lose your cool, Double O,' the big Negro boy said.

'The director says I lost the fifty bucks a month they been putting in the bank for me because I got expelled,' Birl said.

'That's your doing. It ain't because of Perry,' L.J. said.

'You shut up, Missi'sip. I'm getting to Macon as broke as I come here and this fucker is the reason.'

'Go get the resident worker,' the Indian said to another Corpsman.

'We ain't going to need him,' Perry said. 'All right, Birl, any way you want it. You pushed me too much in one day, and I'm a-taking your goddamn head off.'

'Don't give up your badge for him,' L.J. said.

'He drew a knife on me and I didn't do nothing. He lied about me to Mr Henson and I didn't do nothing, either. By God, trash like this ain't going to spit on me again and walk away from it. You hear me, Birl? We can do it with fists and feet, or you can find us a couple of Coke bottles.'

'He's trying to get you kicked out with him,' L.J. said.

'He ain't going to be in enough pieces to see it. Get up, you sonofabitch,' Perry said.

'You guys quit that shouting and let us sleep,' somebody yelled from one of the bays.

'Cool it, Perry. That dude ain't worth it,' the Negro said, and took hold of Perry's arm. He was on the camp boxing team, and the knuckles in his hand stood out like quarters against the skin.

'Turn loose or I'll go over you to get to him,' Perry said.

'Hey man, what's all this shit out here? You cats are disturbing my high,' Popcorn said from the doorway. He had the wine bottle in his housecoat pocket.

'Go tell the resident worker to get his ass down here,' the Indian boy said.

'Why not give Double O his hammer and let him strum on the dude's head awhile?' Popcorn said.

'Let go. I ain't asking you again,' Perry said.

'You're pulling a bad news scene, soul,' the big Negro boy said, and released Perry's arm.

As Perry started around the pool table Birl stood up quickly in the shadows and lifted a cue stick with both arms high above his head. Perry tried to check himself and duck to one side, but the stick whipped down with a suck of air and hit him with the heavy-weighted end right between the eyes. Flashes of colour exploded in his brain, and he felt as though all the bone and cartilage in his nose had been crushed into his skull. He crashed into the wall and fell over the metal folding chairs, then he rose to his feet with his hands pressed across his face. The blood roared through his fingers over his shirt front. The room whirled about him and blurred, and he thought he was going to swallow his tongue. It was as though someone had fired a shotgun into the middle of his face. He collapsed across the pool table, with his arms spread out beside him, and watched the green velvet turn purple in front of him. His eyes were wide and staring, and he wanted to close them to make the flashes of light go away, but he felt that his eyelids were stitched to his forehead. Then he began to gag, and a dark yellow cloud slid over him. He rolled back onto the floor and thought he heard the ocean beating in his ears.

FIVE

Perry awoke the next morning in the county hospital. The tape and bandages, spread across his face in an X-pattern, felt like a pair of goggles around his eyes. The bridge of his nose was swollen tight against the gauze. The light outside the window reflected brightly off the patches of melting snow on the front lawn. He raised himself up on his elbows, and a pain as sharp as ice raced through his head. There were small, dried flecks of blood on his upper lip. The sunlight inside the room gave everything a hard, unnatural brightness that hurt his eyes. He tried to recall what had happened the night before; then he remembered the pool stick swinging out of the dark and Birl's murderous eyes behind it. He got out of bed in his nightgown and started towards the bath; but the room seemed to lift up sharply at an angle, and he pitched backwards on to the bed. The radiator hissed quietly. He wanted to pull the tape from his face, and he picked at the edge of the bandage until his eyes watered; then he felt himself go limp inside, and he drifted back into the cool brilliance of the sunlight through the window.

He dreamed of the man on the coal tipple, but this time he felt no guilt. The man looked like Birl, and the rage welled up inside Perry again. *They taken our jobs and credit away, and then they come at me with a knife.* He breathed heavily in his sleep. *There wouldn't be no trouble if they let us alone. We didn't ask for nothing more than that. We ought to take a turpentine can to all of them. They wipe their feet on us like we was a doormat, and then they try to cut on us and work us over. He deserved what he got up there on the tipple. He'd a done it to us unless we got him first.*

Perry awoke again in the mid-afternoon, his face sweating, and a shaft of sunlight pierced his eyes. He untangled the covers from around his legs and sat on the edge of the bed, his head spinning. After the sleep had cleared from his mind, he saw a fat nurse in a white starched dress watching him. She held a stainless steel container in her hands. The fat on her neck pressed out over her collar, and she wore her hair in tight curls against her head.

'My, but you must have bad dreams,' she said. 'I've had to come down here three times because of the noise you made.'

'How long I been here?'

'They brought you in last night and put thirteen stitches in your forehead and nose. Don't you remember?'

'I don't remember nothing.'

'You fought the doctor and broke a tray of syringes. That should cost the government a few dollars,' she said.

'Where's my clothes at?'

'You can't leave until you're checked out. Do you want to use the bedpan?'

'Get that thing out of here and find my clothes.'

'I'm sorry, but you have to wait for the doctor.'

'I ain't waiting on nobody. Does that highway out there go back to camp?'

'Sit down before you start bleeding again,' she said.

He stumbled across the room and pulled open the closet door. His trousers, undershirt, shoes, Popcorn's army jacket, and one cotton sock, all of them splattered with blood, lay in a pile on the floor. Perry took off his nightgown and sat on the floor in his shorts and began to pull on his trousers. He felt that something was dislocated in his head. He had no sense of balance, and he fell on his back several times before he could button his fly.

'You're not going to act like that in this hospital,' she said. 'Get off that floor right now.'

'I didn't ask to come here, and I sure ain't a-staying longer than I want to.'

'I'll put you back to bed with a shot if I have to.'

'No you ain't, because in five minutes I'm going to be down that road.'

He left his shoes untied, put on his shirt unbuttoned, and zipped up the army jacket over it. He stuffed the cotton sock in his pocket and got to his feet.

'You come back here,' the nurse said.

'I'm already gone, lady. Keep them bedpans for somebody else.'

The door swung open and a young intern in white clothes glared at Perry. His face was pale and antiseptic, and he wore large, black-framed glasses on his thin nose. He reminded Perry of the clerk at the company store.

'Was that you making all that noise?' the intern said. He'd had to leave another patient down the hall to come to Perry's room.

'He refused to get back in bed,' the nurse said.

'Where do you think you are?' the intern said. 'When you're in this hospital, you do what you're told.'

'I got the right to leave when I want, ain't I?' Perry held onto the door knob to keep his balance.

'You don't go anywhere until you're checked out. You're not on the street where you can push over people,' the intern said.

'I don't push over nobody, and them white clothes don't let you tell me what to do.'

'Should I call the orderlies, doctor?' the nurse said.

'No, a forest ranger is waiting for him now. Just get him out of here.'

'That makes a lot of sense, don't it?' Perry said. 'We go through all this, and you was fixing to turn me loose anyway.'

'Get out,' the intern said. 'And go to another hospital to have those stitches removed.'

Perry walked down the corridor to the waiting room. He couldn't shake the dizzy feeling from his head, and the yellow ceiling lamps reflecting off the cracked plaster made him blink his eyes. Mr Henson signed at the desk for Perry's medical bill, and they walked out into the cold, early spring day. The mountains were green and blue in the bright sun, and they seemed to stretch endlessly into the distance. Perry had to shade his eyes to look at the snowcaps on the ridges.

They drove back down the blacktop in a Navy carryall that jarred and rattled with each bump in the road. The melting snow had given the pines and spruce a deeper green, and the creeks that ran under the bridges were wide and sandy yellow. Perry saw a groundhog raise up in the grass by the side of the blacktop. It was a big, fat one, with a puffed tail like a rabbit's, and Perry remembered when he used to catch them with dried corn under an apple crate propped on a stick. In eastern Kentucky ground-hogs were called 'whistle-pigs' because of the high-pitched scream they made whenever they were trapped in their holes, and Perry had once kept four of them in a cage in his room for Irvin to play with until his father made him turn them out.

'The director wants to see you in his office,' Mr Henson said. His wind-chafed hands were brick red on the steering wheel.

'I reckon they're a-sending me home this time. I wouldn't have gone after Birl, but a feller can't keep taking it all day. Pulling a knife on me didn't get to me as bad as when he said I was to blame for him losing all his savings money.'

'It don't have anything to do with the fight,' Mr Henson said. 'Popcorn and the others told the director what happened, and he had Birl put in the county jail overnight and shipped him home this morning.'

'They ain't calling a board of review on me?'

'No.'

'What's he want me for, then?'

Mr Henson drove the carryall into the parking lot and cut the engine. His weathered, grey Stetson was pulled low over his sunburned forehead. He stuck a cigarette in his mouth and popped a match on his thumbnail.

'Did you eat lunch at the hospital?' he said.

'No, sir.'

'Go change your clothes and wash the blood off your face, then tell the cooks that I said to fix you a meal. Report to the director when you get finished.'

'Something's wrong, ain't it?'

'Get on down to your barracks.'

'You don't have to hold back on me. I rather hear it from you than the director.'

'That ain't my job, Perry. But you listen to me and remember what I say. You're a good heavy equipment man, and if you get yourself a couple more months' experience and training, they'll give you that union book. In time, you'll be as good an operator as I ever was. Just don't let anything make you quit, no matter how hard things seem to get.'

'It's somebody in my family. Something's happened that's going to pull me out of Job Corps, ain't it?'

'Just keep in mind what I said. Don't give up your trade because you take a hard punch now.'

'Was it Irvin again? Goddamn it, tell me.'

'I told you to go get changed, son.'

Perry walked through the trees to the barracks and put on a clean set of fatigues. The work crew had not returned yet, and his bay was empty. He washed the dried flecks of blood from his face in the basin and peeled part of the bandage off his nose. The stitches looked like raised black welts in his skin, and the bridge of his nose had two crooked, discoloured knots in it. He touched his fingertips lightly between his eyes and felt a sickening pain rip through his head. He held on to the washbasin until it passed, and then spread the bandage back across his face and pressed the tape flat against his skin.

He had no appetite, and he went directly to the administration building to see the director. A sudden gust of cold wind rippled the water standing in pools in the parking lot. The shale was a sharp white in the sun. It was all going too good, he thought. There ain't nothing that goes along this good for so long without something happening. Things just don't stay straight like that. At least not for us. There's always something that's going to shove a stick between your feet when you think you're almost there. It's like winning the wage election at the mine. You think you got something, and then they raise the charge at the store, and you know you didn't win nothing at all.

He waited on a chair in the administration building and listened to the static from the two-way radio until the director called him into the office.

'How do you feel?' the director said.

'I had worse happen to me.'

'Did you get the cooks to fix you something to eat?'

'I ain't hungry. What's wrong at home?'

'I have a letter from your mother. I guess she thought you still have some trouble with your reading.' He handed Perry a soiled envelope with the address scrawled and misspelled across the front. 'You can use our phone to call home if you want.'

'We ain't got electricity in our house.' Perry unfolded the single page of lined notebook paper and read the pencilled words slowly:

to the camp Director. Can you let Perry come home cause his daddy wants to see him. They blowed up the UMW meetin and hurt him real bad. He is old now and the Doctor dont no if he can make it. I didnt want Perry taken away from his trade but may be he will not be abel to see his daddy agin. we dont have money for his bus ride so can you send him for us. God bless you. Mrs. Woodson James.

Perry felt something tighten across his lungs, and the pain behind his eyes began to ache again. I told him they wasn't going to let us alone, he thought. We got one of theirs, and they was going to pay us back. Except they got him and he don't even belong to the union any more. Why'd he have to be there? Just to set around and talk about what they done to the operator thirty years ago. An old man that couldn't do nothing but happy-pappy for the government.

'How soon can I get home?' Perry said.

'We'll put you on a plane tonight, and you'll have a round-trip ticket.'

'I can't come back.'

'We'll give you two weeks' emergency leave. If that's not enough, we'll let you have more. I don't like to lose a good man.'

'I got to go back to work. We ain't going to have no income at all now.'

'Do you think you can help your family by going back to the same dollar-twenty-five job you had before? They'll never know anything better than what they have now.'

'Who's going to feed the kids and pay for daddy's doctor while I'm going to school? It won't stop with what they done to daddy, neither. They'll do everything they can to run us out of the holler. Once the company men shot into the cabins on the next ridge to us. It don't matter to them if they hit kids or old men. It ain't that I don't want to stay here. I told you before this is the best chance I ever had at anything, but I got no choice.'

'You know you have a place here if you decide to come back.'

'I owe you a lot for all the help you give me since I been here, and I thank you for it. Where do I check my gear in?'

'You've got your mind set on quitting the programme?'

'Yes sir.'

'I'll send the clerk down in an hour. So long, Perry. When this thing passes, give yourself a break and get out of those coal fields.'

Before supper Perry cleaned out his foot locker and folded his fatigues, dress khakis, work uniforms, rain slicker, socks and underwear neatly on his bunk, then laid out his shoes and work boots in a row on the floor. He changed into his slacks, sport shirt and loafers, and put the rest of his clothes into a cardboard suitcase that he had bought from another Corpsman for three dollars. The tip of the fading red sun showed above the rim of the mountain, and long blue shadows began to fall across the valley. The swallows dipped in circles out of the sky and spun over the tops of the buildings. In the distance a solitary star burned coldly in the twilight.

Later, after the clerk had checked off all his clothing, Perry sat on the edge of his mattress, smoked a hand-rolled cigarette, and watched the darkness gather in the pine trees outside. Most of the Corpsmen had returned from supper, and radios and record players blared, the showers roared against the tile walls in the bathroom, and someone at the far end of the corridor kept banging a locker door. The company must have brought in strikebreakers, Perry thought. There ain't none of them scabs brave enough to blow a union hall. The last time the coal field struck, they hired them wrestlers from Detroit to take the scabs through the picket. They caught Merle Flatt in the saloon and stomped on him till they broke all his ribs.

'What's this bad news about you splitting the scene?' Popcorn said.

'I got to go back to Kentucky.'

'Man, what you doing? Henson says they'll graduate you to a job in a few more months.'

'My daddy's dying. The company thugs blowed up the UMW meeting,' Perry said.

'Maybe it's not as bad as you think.'

'He ain't going to live.'

'Double O, I hear those gears turning in your brain. You're going back to get the studs that did it, aren't you? You didn't get enough of that shit before.'

'It ain't your business.'

'Man, I know that. But I don't like to see you eating grits in some hillbilly jail. You got too much soul for that. Forget about all those Little Abners back there. Finish up at Job Corps and you can really roll.'

'I don't feel like talking, especially about things you don't understand,' Perry said.

'Listen, I've been on this scene long enough to know the way you southern dudes think. I am hip to your mind, baby. A Confederate flag starts waving in your brain, and you set out to scramble some guy and you don't care if you get your ass shot off doing it. Tell me if I'm right or wrong.'

'My daddy didn't have nothing to do with the strike. He ain't been down in the hole in ten years. He couldn't hardly do the work for the Forest Service.'

'What can you do for him after you build a big rap in the pen?'

'I ain't worrying about that now.'

'No, you'll catch the cat at night with a shotgun, and then you'll wonder what you're doing out on one of those crazy road gangs. Those southern pens must be a great scene.'

'I got to get started. They're a-taking me to Asheville in a half hour.'

'You're really blowing your cool.'

Perry folded his blankets, placed them on top of his foot locker, and rolled up his mattress on the bedsprings. He put on his jacket and picked up his suitcase.

'So long, Popcorn. Don't go blind on that muscat.'

'Wait a minute. I got something for you to pour in the airplane tank in case you run out of gas. It's out of my best stock.' Popcorn went to his foot locker and pulled loose the plywood bottom on the inside. He had four bottles of wine and a pint of bourbon wrapped in pieces of newspaper. He took out his pocketknife and cut the seal from the whiskey bottle. 'I've been saving this for a special high. Here you are, cool.'

Perry took a drink and let the whiskey roll back into his throat. His stomach was empty, and he felt a warmth go through his body as the whiskey ran down inside him. He started to pass the bottle back to the Negro.

'Put it in your pocket, Double O. I can't drink sneaky pete later after good stuff. Get that heavy equipment job in Cincinnati, and I'll meet you at the ball game one Sunday and we'll crawl home on our elbows.'

'Take it easy, buddy,' Perry said.

'Don't go back to that mine bit, either. Leave all that shit for the groundhogs.'

Perry went into the recreation hall and shook hands with several other Corpsmen, and then walked through the purple dusk to the parking lot, where a carryall was waiting to take him to the airport in Asheville. There was a rain ring around the moon, and a black sparrow hawk floating motionlessly in the sky on the wind currents. The air was heavy with the smell of spruce and fir and the new sap in the pines. The last afterglow of the sun darkened over the mountain, and in the distance Perry thought he heard the thin roll of thunder.

SIX

Perry's father had been taken to the town's private clinic in the back seat of a deputy sheriff's car. The union meeting had been held in the wood-frame school building constructed by the WPA during the Depression. A Negro farm worker, who had been ploughing in the field across the road at dusk, said later that he had seen three men carry a cardboard box and an army jerry can around behind the building, but he had paid little attention to them at the time. At nine o'clock, when the building was filled, the explosion blew splintered boards through the roof, and the flame roared upwards as if pure oxygen had been touched with a lighted match. The gunny sack stretched across the windows burned in the heat like cobweb, and glass was imbedded in the tree trunks close to the building. Three miners were killed outright, and twelve more were drenched with burning gasoline. A woman holding a child in the back of the room was hit by part of a school desk and knocked unconscious. Men climbed through the windows, jammed the front door closed with the weight of their bodies, and some broke through one charred wall by wrapping their coats around their heads and throwing themselves against it. One man, a part time Church of God preacher, began to scream incoherently about the apocalypse. In minutes the building burned to the ground. The men who had been killed had been sitting right on top of the charge, and the sheriff and his two deputies put what remained of them in a canvas tarpaulin. A sickening odour, like that of burnt pork, arose from the canvas, and the sheriff had his deputies drag it into the trees. One man stumbled through the smoke, his hands over his ears, his mouth working without sound. His sleeves had been seared off to the elbows, and his forearms were covered with yellow and red blisters. Another miner, blackened from the fire, went back into the ruins and began lifting up charred timbers with his hands. The embers scorched his palms, and the frayed bottoms of his overalls sparked and then curled in flame. Three men dragged him to an automobile.

Woodson James lost all his fingers on one hand except the thumb, his face was badly burned, and a sliver of board was driven through his back into the lung. He lay pinned under a section of roofing and held the stump of his hand against his chest to stop the bleeding. The hot cinders burned into his face and scalp, and his chest felt as though someone had poured acid inside it. People were yelling, and feet trampled over the debris on top of his body. He tried to shout louder than the noise, but he coughed on the ashes and dust, and his eyes watered and filmed from the heat. The side of his head was pressed flat against the floor, and he could feel a nail penetrating into the small of his back each time someone stepped across him. He choked and almost vomited when he touched the place where his fingers had been. The blood on his hand had coagulated and turned black around the pieces of bone. After a few minutes he heard no sound except the pine boards bursting like firecrackers in the flame. You ain't got the right to do this to me twice, God, he thought. You buried me once, and you ought to taken me then if you was going to do it. There ain't no sin I ever done that could let you put me through this again. I been a Christian man as best I could, and I already paid three times over for anything I done against you. If you're set on doing this to me, bring the whole roof down and finish it quick.

He could smell his hair burning, and then he passed out. Two of his cousins couldn't find him in the crowd outside, and they went back into the fire and pried the debris off him with an iron bar. They carried him out just as a large section of roofing collapsed in a roar of sparks and flaming boards. The cousins put out the fire on Woodson's clothes with their hands, and took a handful of cobweb from an outbuilding and rubbed the wound in his back to stop the bleeding.

He almost died during his first night in the clinic because no one could find a doctor closer than Lexington who could treat anything more serious than colds and poison ivy. Woodson lay face down on the emergency table for eight hours and spit blood on a pillow, while the plasma ticked slowly into his arm. The next morning the union flew in a surgeon from Huntington, West Virginia. By mid-afternoon he had removed a nine-inch-long shaft of wood that was wedged in Woodson's back as though it had been hammered there. The doctor knew that the burns on Woodson's face would eventually require skin grafts, but he said nothing to Mrs James because he did not expect the old man to live more than a few days at the outside, since Woodson had already lost one lung and the other was left with a ragged wound inside. The following day the only ambulance in the county, a stationwagon with the back seats taken out, took him to the hospital in Richmond, where there were at least two doctors who had experience with respiratory cases.

The school was not the first building to be blown up in the last four months. Two operators' homes in Stern and Pikeville had been dynamited, and the union agent's office in Letcher County had been soaked with kerosene one night and set aflame. Strikes had shut down half of the truck mines in the state, and in Harlan and Perry counties the operators brought in out-of-state scabs rather than sign new union contracts. The UMW demanded a dollar-a-day wage increase in mines under contract, and mines put up picket lines around almost every coal tipple and C & O loading platform in eastern Kentucky and West Virginia. Four men died in a gun battle outside an auger mine in Floyd County after a truckload of scabs had tried to crash through a picket, and the sheriff and two of his deputies in 'Bloody' Breathitt resigned their jobs because they had been threatened by people from both the union and the operators' association.

Woodson James lay in a semi-coma for a week. Every time he became conscious he began screaming and the doctors had to give him heavy dosages of morphine. One eye and half of his face were covered with bandages. A nurse had shaved the hair from the burned places in his scalp, and a thin film of blood and spittle collected on his chin when he breathed. His feet were yellow and calloused, sticking out under the bed sheet. Once, the doctor had inserted a tube in Woodson's nose, but the old man pulled it out and fell off the bed.

In his morphine dreams he saw himself as a young man back in the hollow, when he had built his cabin for his new wife. He had hauled the white oak logs from the forest with mules and chains, working in the hot sun, with the leather reins wrapped tightly around his hands and the sweat bees swarming around his head. He split the logs with his axe and wedges, bevelled them, notched the corners, and shaped them level with a carpenter's plane. The wood shaved off evenly under the steady pressure of his arms, and he knew that he would not need much chinking when he set the logs across one another. He was as good a carpenter as he was a shaft miner, and he had a feeling for wood when he ran his rough hand across a board plank or put his axe with all his weight into the base of a tree trunk. Wood always had a good smell, like pine sap in the spring. It was something that belonged to the earth above the ground, where a man could see sky everyday and breathe air that wasn't filled with coal dust, where men didn't work six or seven at a time in a small pocket two miles back in the mountain, their picks striking into the limestone, to get at the seam while the carbide lamps on their helmets sent up dirty streams of smoke.

He had brought his wife into the cabin, after the wedding at the Church of God chapel in Jackson. Her skin was soft and smooth, the colour of a pink rose petal, and the blood flushed to her temples when he showed her their bedroom that he had covered with green wallpaper from Montgomery Ward's and furnished with a double bed – not a mattress stuffed with corn shucks, which most people in the hollow used. During the late 1920s, before the strip mines had ruined the soil with the yellow sulphuric drainage from the exposed coal seams, he grew tobacco on shares in the meadowland along the creek bottom. Even after he paid off the owner, he always cleared several hundred dollars in a season. The first year he was married he added another room on to the cabin for his first child and bought his wife a foot-operated sewing machine that had to be shipped all the way from Memphis.

During those first years of his marriage he worked in the mines only in the winter, after the tobacco had been cut, strung on sticks, and hung to dry in the barn for the dealers' auction in Winchester. In November he would go back in the hole again and make two to three hundred dollars a day loading coal by the ton. At that time no miner was paid any type of fixed wage, and if a man had the bad luck to work in a pocket where he couldn't reach the seam in his twelve hours underground, he received no money at the end of the day. Sometimes a miner would spend two shifts in the hole, tearing limestone and slag away from the coal, before he could start loading for pay.

But Woodson did well with his tobacco farming in the spring and summer, and his five months in the mine during the winter. He had no money in the bank, but his wife had two machine-made dresses to wear to church on Sunday, he bought a black suit and white shirt for himself, and he was one of the few people in the rural section of the county to own an iron stove with four lids on top. He planned to save his money and buy two acres of land in the next hollow near the south fork of the Kentucky River so he would no longer need to farm on shares; then the Depression cut back production in every shaft mine on the Cumberland plateau, and the tobacco buyers from Raleigh showed up in fewer numbers at the auction in Winchester and eventually stopped coming altogether. Many of the independent coal operators went broke and closed their mines; others tried to stay open by paying miners eighty cents a day for their maximum load, and the big corporations in the East began to make up their stockmarket losses by raising the rent in company-owned towns in Kentucky, West Virginia, eastern Tennessee and Virginia. Then John L. Lewis came to Harlan County and organized the first local in Kentucky of the United Mine Workers of America. Thousands of the rank and file began to carry union cards, and the worst gun battles, bombings, and burnings since the Civil War broke out throughout the eastern part of the state. In 1939 the governor called up the National Guard to protect scabs crossing picket lines, and many striking miners were shot down in the streets of Harlan.

It was at this time that Woodson James killed two soldiers in a battle outside a shaft on the Virginia line. On an early spring morning the Guardsmen had been given orders to clear away the pickets from the mine entrance. A miner was knocked to the ground with a rifle butt after he refused to move, and he slashed a soldier across the face with his knife. Other striking miners pulled their pistols, and in the battle three union men were killed. Later that day Woodson James, his brother-in-law Bee Hatfield, and ten other men crawled up on the mountain overlooking the mine with Winchester rifles that had been passed out by the union. Two soldiers were carrying a body to the back of a government stake truck. They wore World War I issue campaign hats, canvas cartridge belts, and leggings; their sleeves were rolled, and their shirts were damp with sweat. Somebody below saw a miner raise up over a ledge, a shot was fired, although no one ever knew by whom, and the explosions from the .30-30s and the Springfield .03s crashed through the hollow. The two soldiers dropped the body and ran for the cover of the truck. Woodson brought the V-sight of his Winchester down on the neck of one soldier, led him slightly, and squeezed off the trigger. The man struck the ground on his face as though he had been hit by a block of concrete. As Woodson worked the lever action and pumped another shell into the chamber, he could see the dark area spread from the base of the soldier's head into the coal dust on the ground. The second soldier's head was pinned down before he could make the truck. He crawled behind a small pile of rocks and huddled against them as bullets splintered the slag around his boots.

Woodson had never believed that he wanted to kill any man, but once the shooting started, he felt as cool inside as if he had been firing at a bear or a deer. He had no time to think about the fact that he had just killed a man. The rifle felt natural and easy in his hands, and the lever action seemed to work by itself. He fired shot after shot down on the man behind the rocks while bullets ricocheted off the ledge in front of him in a spray of limestone powder. His gun snapped empty, and he pulled back from the crest of the mountain and reloaded his magazine from the shells in his pocket. The brass shells had a good feel in his hand as he slipped them into the slot below the chamber. The blood beat in his temples and he felt a strange exhilaration that he'd never had before.

Kill union men because they want a decent wage, will you, he thought. Come in here from outside and shoot us down because we want more than eighty cents a day. You get government clothes and government pay for keeping us down in the hole twelve hours a day without enough money to show for it to buy groceries at the store. By God, you scab-loving sonofabitch, get up on your feet and catch it like a man.

Woodson slammed the lever on his rifle back into place and rested the end of the barrel across a rock. He aimed the top bead of his sight just above the exposed boot of the soldier to allow for the drop in the bullet's trajectory. This ought to bring you out, you company bastard, Woodson thought. He let out his breath slowly and squeezed the trigger. The bullet tore into the soldier's legging above the ankle. He jerked backwards, his foot in his hands, and exposed his body completely. His face was grey with pain, and his mouth was open wide, as though a silent scream were coming from it. Woodson raised up quickly on one knee and drilled a shot into the centre of the left pocket over the man's heart. Then they saw a truckload of more soldiers, armed with Springfields, grinding its way up the road to the mine, and Woodson ran with other men back down the mountain to the cover of the pine trees.

His heart beat as though it were going to burst inside him, and he felt the sweat rolling off his face. The sun was white over the timber line, and the colours of the forest and the cliff walls in the hollow seemed more brilliant than he had ever seen them before. Then he started laughing, although he didn't know why. He put his hand over his mouth to make it stop, but he laughed harder, choking on his own breath as he ran through the rust-coloured tree trunks in the woods, until he fell on his knees and had to hold his sides. He saw that the other men were laughing too, and he wondered if his face looked as horrible as theirs.

During the next few years Woodson felt a greater sense of guilt over his laughter than about killing the two soldiers, although after the shooting he kept no guns in his cabin and refused to have any part in the tipple bombings that were common through-out the forties. Sometimes in town he would see one of the men who had been with him during the gun battle, and he would sense a secret smile, a bright flicker of private knowledge in the eyes, and a feeling of shame would go through him. We didn't have no choice about what we done, he told himself. They gunned our men down on the picket and we give it back to them. We just ask to get treated fair, and they brought in outsiders to murder us. Maybe them soldiers didn't know what they was doing, but they was shooting down our men, anyway. But a man don't laugh over taking a life. It was something we had to do, and we fought them fair and it ain't something we got to walk around a-smiling about inside like we was ashamed of it. Because then we ain't no better than a man that would catch you on the road at night in the back with a shotgun. We ain't no better than them hired gun thugs that get drunk in the jenny-barn and talk about the miners they worked over on the picket.

As Woodson grew older he began to form in his own mind a type of fierce personal relationship between himself and God, about the nature of sin and atonement. He had an Old Testament vision of God as a wrathful person who was for the most part stern yet fair in His punishment; but nevertheless Woodson believed that God had to be corrected and defied sometimes because He had too much power on His side and often He forgot that He had made a deal and as a result He didn't honour it. Woodson had been raised in the Church of God, but he hadn't been to the Wednesday night or Sunday meetings since he was fifteen except for the day he was married. Right after World War II snake cults became common throughout the Cumberland Mountains. In clapboard schoolhouses and in big tents set up in fields, people listened for hours while preachers yelled incoherently about salvation through the test of faith. During the sermon women became hysterical, children cried out in fear, and some miners would light the carbide lamps on their tin hats, remove the glass cover, and hold the flame under their throats. On a table at the head of the congregation the preacher would set a cardboard box full of copperheads and rattlesnakes that had been caught in the woods during the day. Before midnight, when the congregation had lost all sense of reasoning, the preacher would call for the test of faith, and people would come down the aisle between the rows of folding chairs and plunge their arms into the cardboard box.

The state government passed a law against the snake cults, but their popularity spread. Several people died after their test of faith; however, the preacher usually explained later that the dead person had not truly believed in God's protection, and the congregation would pray to God that the deceased's lack of faith would not cause him to be punished in the afterlife.

Woodson had attended snake cult meetings six months before he went forward to give testimony and accept his salvation. He sat on a wooden chair in the back of the tent, his huge hands folded between his legs, and looked at the sawdust floor while the preacher spoke. He had just finished the four o'clock Sunday shift at the mine, and his face was black with coal dust except for the white area around his eyes where his goggles had been. His wife was next to him, wearing one of her machine-made dresses that she had laundered in boiling water and corn starch until the coloured design was almost completely faded from it. Her face had a fearful, serious expression, and she bit her lip as she listened to the preacher's words. She had always believed that the Church of God, or possibly even the Baptists, offered the only salvation, and she was fearful of Woodson's involvement with the snake cult, because she had the same distrust towards it as she did towards the Catholics and Hebrews.

The preacher, Father Clock, was a tall man, well over six feet, who wore a seersucker suit, a candy-striped necktie, and a large gold cross on his watch chain. He had a lean, ascetic face, black eyes that looked like chipped obsidian, and his thin, black hair was combed straight back to cover the bald spots in his head. His sweat-filmed face glistened in the light from the kerosene lamps. He was the most popular of the snake-cult preachers because he'd had a faith-healing radio show several years in Nashville on the same station as the Grand Old Opry. He was as well known in eastern Kentucky as Roy Acuff and Mother Maybelle Carter.

'How many of you out there have been saved?' he said. 'Which one of you is ready to say that you have taken God into your hearts and you don't fear His punishment because you have renounced your sins and you have faith in His mercy? Is it enough to set there and say you have been forgiven without coming forth to make your testimony and prove to yourself and the Lord that you have been cleansed? You answer me that one, brother.'

His voice began to rant, and he jabbed his finger in the air when he spoke. His face looked flushed with fever. His sermon would build to a point where he was screaming, and the congregation would shrink in their chairs and look at the floor with guilt-ridden eyes; and then suddenly he would lower his voice, push back his coat and place his hands on his hips, and speak softly as though to children.

'Yes, you are repentant, or you wouldn't be here. You've taken Jesus as your Saviour, and you've been baptized in the blood. You've put aside the lust of your youth, the ways of men that follow Mammon; you've stopped listening to the false prophets who deny the way of the cross. I know all of this, brothers and sisters, because I have gone through the same temptations, the same traps and snares that Satan lays before us. In the schools they tell us there is no God because science has proved it. Yes, they tell us God no longer exists. I went to schools where people were taught that science is even better than God. I had my faith tested, and I'm here today to tell you that it has not been shaken!'

His voice began to rise again, and his eyes burned even more brightly. He rested one hand on the box of snakes.

'Now I'm going to ask you to come give living witness to your faith. Not to just set and say that you believe, but to take up snakes and cast them down without fear like it says in the Bible. I want you to show God that right here in Perry County, Kentucky, we have continued his word. Can you do it, brothers? Do you have it in you to show God your love? I want to hear and see a testimony that will make God know that we haven't followed after the false prophets. That's right, get up from your chairs and come down the aisle. Yes ma'am, you go right ahead and weep in joy of your redemption. And the rest of you cry tears of happiness, too, because we're breaking through as witnesses to salvation tonight.'

Woodson rose, his face rigid and his eyes glowing hotly. He moved mechanically, as though he were walking in a dream. His wife held on to his sleeve.

'Don't do it, Woodson. Please. It's the devil he's preaching,' she said. He walked up the aisle with the others as she pulled after him. People began singing and clapping their hands, and one woman sank to the floor in front of the box of snakes and moaned and cried because of some dark sin in her youth.

'Lannie Dotson got killed doing it,' Mrs James said, her voice climbing higher now. 'We can't do without you at the house. You want me to raise the children by myself?'

'Get your hand off me, woman. I heered the calling,' Woodson said, and flung his wife's arm away from him.

He walked through the crowd and stood before the box. Brother Clock pulled off his seersucker coat, rolled up his sleeves over his elbows, and picked up a rattlesnake in each hand. The snakes coiled their bodies in the air and shook their rattles, their mouths and fangs yawning open at the congregation. Brother Clock's face looked as though he had been drugged.

'There it is, brothers and sisters,' he said. 'The proof that we have prayed through and the Holy Ghost has descended right down into this tent. We have given witness to the word.'

The people shouted and clapped their hands louder, and a miner stood up on a chair, lighted his carbide lamp, and let the flame lick over his arm. Woodson reached into the box and picked up a copperhead by the middle of its body. He looked up at the top of the tent and felt an ecstasy surge through him like a sexual orgasm. 'Great God, I been saved,' he yelled. 'I been to the river and I been baptized, and now I got redemption in the word.'

Then the snake coiled back in a loop, arched its neck, and its smooth metallic head struck through the air into Woodson's shoulder. He felt a burning sensation hit him, and he threw the snake high into the air above his head. He tore his overalls strap and shirt loose and saw two small punctures in his skin to one side of the collarbone. 'It got me, boys! I ain't got no chance now. It's a-pumping into my heart.'

He ran through the crowd, knocking people down in the aisle, and pushed through the tent flap into the night. He thought he could feel the green venom working its way through his veins. Two men chased after him and held him to the ground. Someone brought out a kerosene lamp, and in the flickering orange light a man cut an X with his pocket-knife on each one of the fang wounds, then kneaded the flesh with his fingers and sucked out the poison with his mouth. Another miner took a handful of string-cut tobacco, wet it in a pool of water, and pressed it down tightly on the wound.

Woodson lay in bed at home for three days in a sick coma until his system worked out the remaining poison in his body. He would have probably recovered sooner, except that Bee Hatfield brought him a gallon of corn whiskey, and they both got drunk every time Woodson became conscious again.

But what Woodson called his redemption never really came until he was trapped for two days under a pile of rock in a Virginia coal mine. In the first hours of darkness, with the great pieces of slag and limestone across his body, he listened for the sound of men moving about or for the distant shutter of air hammers cutting through the shaft wall. He knew that other miners had been working farther up the corridor, and some of them must have got out to tell the people above ground that he was still somewhere under the debris. He had seen other cave-ins, and he knew that miners didn't leave a man underground, even if they had to dig for weeks just to bring out his body. Eventually they would get to him. If they couldn't clear the corridor or get down through the shaft, they would sink an auger from the surface and break through the roof so that they could lower a team down on cables.

As the hours went by, his lung filled with blood and he passed out. When he awoke he didn't know if he had been unconscious for a few minutes or a day. He had relieved himself in his pants, and the air was much harder to breathe. The inside of his mouth and throat were filmed with coal dust, and he was so thirsty that his spittle was like string. Once he thought he heard picks and shovels scraping in the distance, and he listened for the sound to grow louder until his ears began to hum. Later, the silence made his head reel, and he realized that there was probably nobody alive within a mile of him. He remembered how the explosion had filled the corridor with an electric yellow flash and how some miners were blown along the floor like piles of rags. He had seen the pinning break loose in the ceiling, and the three men in the pocket next to him had been covered with tons of earth. He would have been killed outright, too, but he was under an overhang when the shaft caved in, and he was protected from the great pieces of rock that came down with the force of freight cars.

He was alone. The weight of all God's earth was resting on his back, and the people above ground had probably counted him off as dead. They would get to him sometime, but right now the rescue teams would be working their way to areas where they believed some men might still be alive. Then Woodson knew the way he was going to die. He would either suffocate slowly or starve. He remembered once in Pike County when a hot mine exploded and everyone in it was considered dead because the heat from the blast had melted the steel cables on the elevator cage. The rescue teams couldn't open up the shaft because of the fumes, and they had to put ventilator fans in the hole for a day before they could begin digging. Two weeks later they found a miner pinned upright in a wall crevasse; he had died from thirst and dehydration.

On the second day Woodson began to pray for death. The pain in his chest caused him to pass out periodically, and his bones ached in the damp cold. Each time he slipped into unconsciousness he felt a sense of relief and hoped that he wouldn't awaken again. Then suddenly his mind would come clear with more pain, and he knew that his death would take very long. The darkness seemed to seep into his eyesockets and fill his brain, and he felt the terror that a blind man feels when his sight is first snuffed out. He had always had a fear that after death a man was conscious of lying in the grave while people shovelled dirt over him, and many times at night he had awakened, sweating, after a dream in which he saw himself locked under the earth while people walked about overhead, deaf to his cries.

Towards the end of the second day he began to see different patterns of colour float before his eyes. You're finally coming for me, ain't you, Lord, he thought. I reckon things is set straight now for them men I killed and everything else I ever done. I don't hold it against you for this if you think it's right, but it can't go on no longer. I can't take it no more. If I ain't paid enough for what I done in the past, strike me dead now and send me straight to hell, because I don't want nothing more to do with you if I got to stay alive down here any more. I ain't defying you. I figure I made a bargain for punishment when I dropped them two soldiers, and now the bargain's complete, and you got to let me walk out of here or let the rest of the shaft come down on me.

Then the colour patterns before his eyes began to change, and he saw a brilliant square of yellow light open up in the corridor wall. He thought that the sun itself had exploded into the room. A light, warm feeling went through his body, and he felt that someone was pulling the great weight of rock off him. The cold ache left his bones, the fresh air went cool and deep into his lungs, and he was no longer thirsty. He knew that he could get up and walk now. The square of light was a stairway up to the surface. He just had to raise himself and walk up to the top of the earth, where his wife and children would be waiting for him. The dogwood was in full bloom on the mountainside, the sky was filled with summer rain clouds, and the wind was blowing across the meadows with the smell of horses and new tobacco. Tomorrow he and his wife would go to the county fair in Jackson, and he might spend an extra fifty cents to buy a pint of whiskey.

His skin seemed to glow with the radiance of ivory in the light.

The coal itself was a luminous blue in the aura from his body. You done it, God, he thought. You put me through my punishment, but you played fair and you're a-letting me go back up. I ain't giving you call to punish me again, and I'll keep my end of the bargain as long as you keep yours.

Then Woodson passed out. Six hours later a rescue team in gas masks cut a small hole through a wall of debris blocking the shaft, and one man saw Woodson's boot sticking out from under the pile of rock.

He saw figures silhouetted above him in a haze. There was a taste of ether in the back of his mouth, and a dull drumming sound beat inside his head. The eye that wasn't covered by the bandage hurt him as he tried to open it wide. There was a film of dried mucus over his eyelashes and lid. He expected to see the square of light in the wall shaft again, and he wanted the cool wind that smelled of the land above to blow over his body and take away the pain in his hand and lung. A bottle of white fluid, like clear syrup, hung from a metal rack over his head, and he could see the liquid run in bubbles through a tube into his arm. He didn't know where he was, nor could he remember what had happened to him. His mind was still back in the shaft, deep underground.

Someone held a glass with a plastic straw in it to his mouth, and the water washed that sickening ether taste down into his stomach. The dream about the light in the mine began to fade, and the figures around him became more clear. A doctor was writing on a chart at the foot of the bed. There were cracks like spiderwebs in the plaster ceiling, and a nurse had just opened the blinds to let light into the room. He tried to stir under the sheets, and then he saw that his arm was lying in traction and the tape wrapped around his chest. One side of the room remained dark to him, and he didn't know why his other eye wouldn't open. He heard a woman crying quietly, and he turned his head slowly to one side.

He saw his wife, her face drawn and lined from lack of sleep; the children were beside her, dressed in ragged overalls or in dresses made from Purina feed sacks. They stood in a row like stairsteps, and all of them had the classical features of the James family face – the high, pale forehead, the wide-set eyes, and the hard jawbone that came from the Indian blood in the family. He started to ask why they were not waiting for him outside the cabin to go to the county fair in Jackson, and then the memory of the explosion and fire at the union meeting came back to him, and he felt like a man who had painfully awakened from a long alcoholic binge. He saw the yellow belch of flame tearing through the floor and the boards shattering down on people's heads. He heard the screams and the men trying to kick down the wall, like horses trapped in a burning barn. Fear shot through him again, and he wanted to roll back under the cover of sleep. His chest convulsed and he coughed blood on his chin.

'It's us, Woodson. Your safe now. You ain't got to be afraid no more,' his wife said.

'Why can't daddy come home?' Irvin said.

'They left me under the boards. It was burning on my back.'

'That was two weeks ago. Put all that out of your mind,' she said. She twisted her handkerchief in her hands. 'The doctor don't want you to think about nothing except getting home.'

'I seen Ike Phelps and his brother blowed all to pieces. They just come apart right there in their chairs.' His voice was weak, as though somebody were talking outside himself.

'Don't talk no more about it or the doctor will give you another of them shots,' she said.

'I made a bargain with God. He shouldn't have done it to me twice.'

'Please, Woodson, don't talk that way. I been a-praying since they brought you in here.'

'He didn't have no right. I paid.'

'Daddy, do what mama tells you,' Perry said.

Woodson leaned his head sideways on the pillow and saw Perry sitting in a chair, dressed in slacks and a sport shirt, something which he had never been able to buy his son, and with a haircut and a good suntan on his face. He could not visualize Perry in anything but his wash-faded overalls, denim shirt, cloth cap, scuffed brogans, and the suitcoat that Mrs James had mended for him year after year.

'Why, it's you, boy,' Woodson said. The phlegm rattled in his throat. 'You're looking just fine. I ain't ever seen you look so fine. But why ain't you in school?'

'I come home when mama wrote the camp.'

'What they done to your face, son?'

Perry touched his fingers to the red S-shaped scar on the bridge of his nose.

'It ain't nothing. I got hurt out on the job.'

'You're going to be real proud of him when you get home and he tells you about all of what he done at that camp,' Mrs James said. 'He learned how to read and write, and they made him some kind of government leader. His teacher told him that he can get a job running a machine if he gets a couple of more months schooling.'

'I knowed you could do it,' Woodson said. 'There ain't a James yet that couldn't do a job better than the next man if he had the chance to. I want you to go on back to that camp and finish your schooling. Then you won't be a-running off to work in no hot mine in Virginia. You can operate a shovel at the strip mine and stay on top of the ground like God intended men to be.'

'I'm staying around here awhile till you get well,' Perry said. 'They give me leave at the camp and I can go back any time I want.'

'I ain't asking you to do it, son. I'm telling you to go back there to North Carolina so you ain't got to make your living the way I had to.' The effort of talking made him feel weak inside, and his head began to spin. Small grey dots appeared before his eyes. He breathed deeply and let his head sink back into the pillow. He felt that his skin was sagging against the bone. His body and mind were tired, as though a lifetime's energy had been sucked out of him.

'He ain't going against you, Woodson,' his wife said. 'The boy just wants to be around and help out till you're home again.'

'My daddy fought against them, and I did too, and it didn't do neither one of us any good. They ruined the land, they taken our homes, and they made good men take up guns to get back just part of what was theirs to begin with. I don't want no more of it for my children. One of our boys has got a chance now to be something better than a whistle-pig scratching up and down a shaft for barely enough to eat. By God, he ain't a-throwing that chance away to look after me.'

Woodson gagged and had to turn his face into the pillow to let the saliva drain out of his throat. He felt as if a big clot of blood was caught in his windpipe.

'We got to go. The doctor don't want you to talk long,' Mrs James said.

'I'm dying, woman. You know that. All the doctors in Kentucky can't change a man's time when it comes. I seen the sign in my sleep.'

'Why's daddy talking like that?' Irvin said.

'Hush up, child,' Mrs James said, her eyes beginning to water again. 'You others get outside and wait on me, and don't give me no cause to get a strap to you when we get home.'

'I should have died back in that shaft in Virginia. I know God was set on taking me then, and for some reason He must have changed his mind at the last minute. Maybe He thought I ought to be punished some more later. But He give me the sign last night, and I ain't going to be able to walk away from it this time.'

'I'm going to call the doctor back. It ain't good for you to talk so long,' Mrs James said.

'You ain't going to see me again after you leave this room, and I got something to say to this boy.'

'We got to go, daddy,' Perry said. 'They said we wasn't supposed to stay more than a few minutes.'

'Set still. I know what you come back for. I seen it in your eyes when I first looked at you. I know you too good. You come back to get even for what they done to me. It's Devil Anse Hatfield's blood running in your veins. You're set on revenge, and you won't rest till you kill a man. Hatfields was always that way. From the time they tied them McCoy boys to paw-paw trees and shot them down, they've paid everybody back in blood for anything that was ever done to them. You ain't going to grow up like that. I ain't going to have a boy for a murderer because of my death. Do you understand?'

'I ain't killing nobody.'

'You're a-lying to your daddy on his deathbed.' Woodson

reached his hand over and caught Perry by the wrist. His body had wasted until his fingers were like bone. The movement made his chest swell with pain. 'I can feel that Hatfield blood beating inside you. You got murder in your heart, son. I ain't going to be here to stop you from what you want to do, but I want you to remember that you're part James, too. We never gunned down no man unless they pushed it on us, and we never shot no man out of revenge. There's been people shot all over these coal fields, and there ain't anybody that was ever better off for it. We're just as poor as we always was, and a lot of our people and theirs got put in the ground for nothing.'

'You didn't do nothing to them. Maybe the J.W.s or the others got something coming, but you ain't been on a picket in ten years.'

'I done my share when I was younger, and I'm still a-paying. You get back in that school.'

Mrs James called the doctor, who filled a syringe to give Woodson another shot of morphine. As the doctor rubbed an alcohol-soaked pad on the skin, Woodson held up his hand weakly to push away the needle. Then the light began to grow fixed in his one uncovered eye, the muscles relaxed in his face, and his breathing became more shallow and even. He rested his head back on the pillow and looked up at the ceiling. A grey strand of hair stuck out from the bandage on his forehead. He felt a longing inside him for sleep and an end to the fury that had burned in him for a lifetime. A warm feeling, like a mild fever, began to glow inside his body, and a pink mist, the colour of blood diluted in water, seemed to circulate in the room. 'You ain't going to need it this time, doc,' he said.

The doctor drew the blinds, and everyone left the room. The stillness made the distant drumming grow louder in Woodson's head. The mist was so thick that he could feel it in his hand. It changed colour, to crimson and then to purple, and he knew that he was back in the mine shaft for the last time. He didn't have to worry about the clot of blood in his windpipe any longer. He could breathe the cool air through the pores in his skin. The burned wounds in his scalp had healed, his mutilated hand could grasp an axe handle with the strength of a man in his twenties, and he felt his darkened eye burn through the gauze until it could see the broken timbers hanging from the limestone in the top of the shaft. I'm going underground to stay this time, ain't I, God, he thought. I ain't got to fight with you or make no bargains any more. We're a-going home.

For the first time in his life he rested quietly, without heat or anger or struggling against that fierce, unknown enemy that had always tried to strike him down. A square ripple of fire broke through the rock wall, burning a great doorway in the shaft. The flame showered out in sparks like a welder's torch, and the room was again flooded with yellow light, but it was brighter this time. Then he felt himself being absorbed into the light and carried to its source. He seemed to rise from the floor without willing his body to move. As he went up through the earth towards the sky, he could smell the wind blowing in the white oaks and poplars, the new pine sap in freshly cut logs, and the sweat glistening on the horses. He rose faster to the surface now, closer to the light, and he saw that the sun had descended from the sky and spangled everything with a radiance that made him shield his eyes. He floated higher, feeling himself dissolve and become a part of all things, and he could see to the far reaches of the earth on both horizons. The oceans were blue and green, and the mountains rose up jagged against the sky behind them. He had never known the world so immense. He felt the light enter his mind and consume him, and the radiance became so bright that he was conscious of nothing else.

SEVEN

The day after his father died, Perry walked the seven miles from the cabin to town. The mountains were green from the spring rains and melting snow, and the leaves on the trees in the hollow glistened wetly in the morning light. The dogwood had broken out in a spray of white flowers, and new green vines had begun to crawl up the cliff walls. The rain had cleared the air of the smell from the burning slag heaps, and the creeks were flooded and rushing brown over big limestone boulders. From the shale road on top of the ridge Perry could see the Cumberland range stretch away in a long blue haze towards the West Virginia line. Hawks hovered high above the hollows, dipping occasionally out of the sky when they saw a groundhog or fieldmouse below. The winter leaves were still on the forest floor, piled around the tree trunks, and the first red and white flowers had begun to grow near the creek beds. High upon the next ridge a man was cutting wood in front of a poplar log cabin, and smoke curled from the stone chimney into the wind.

Perry was little aware of the spring changes around him. In his mind he continued to see his father's wasted form on the bed, the wounds in his scalp, the stubs of his fingers wrapped in gauze, the sunken chest, and he still heard the rattling sound of his dying voice. Perry's mind was pointed at revenge the way a man points a rifle at a target, and no other thought could enter his consciousness for very long. He knew that he would find the three men who had blown up the schoolhouse and kill them in any way he could. If he didn't find them today, he would catch them next week or next month or however long it would take him to make them pay. They ain't going to walk away from it this time, he thought. Them three thugs killed their last old man. We ain't a-taking it no more. I'll send them three men to hell or, by God, I'll go there myself. They can put me in the electric chair for it if they want to, but at least there ain't going to be as many men wanting to hire out to the operator to blow us up.

Perry took thirty dollars of his Job Corps discharge money to pay part of the credit at the company store down the road so they could continue to charge through the rest of the month. He still had seventy dollars left, and the government owed him another one hundred and fifty from his back savings. But the camp director had told him that his money wouldn't be sent to him for a couple of months, and Perry had to find a job soon. The rent on the cabin was thirty-five dollars a month, Irvin had to go back to the doctor in Richmond, and the children needed new clothes. The family had not been able to buy shoes for the last two years, and the youngest three children had one pair of shoes among them. Also, the woman at the health unit said that Irvin needed a better diet than the powdered milk, peanut butter and canned meat given out by the federal surplus food centre could provide.

A half mile outside town Perry caught a ride with a family in an old Buick. The inside was crowded with women and children, and he had to stand on the running board and hold on to the window jamb. They bounced over the ruts in the county road as they rolled down off the mountain slope into the town limits. Perry looked at the clapboard shacks with lumps of bulk coal piled outside, the junker cars parked in the yards, the farm equipment that had been left to rust, the barefoot children playing in the dirt, and the few cracked pavements that were overgrown with weeds. The Buick pulled into the centre of town by the courthouse, and Perry dropped off the running board on to the street.

Although it was the middle of the week, men stood around on street corners and in front of pool rooms. Most of the mines in the county were closed because the operators' association would not sign new contracts until the industrial referee from the National Labour Relations Board in Washington held a hearing. Some miners walked the picket line a few hours a day outside the shafts and then returned to town and got drunk on seventy-five-cent bottles of synthetic wine or moonshine whiskey that sold for two dollars in a Mason jar. Five years ago the mines had shut down throughout the state because of strikes, and the entire labour force had been laid off; but the strike had fallen in late summer, when the tobacco was ripe over in the bluegrass region, and many miners went to Winchester to pick tobacco for a half cent a stick. Now, there was almost no work to be had on the Cumberland plateau. Some men left for Cincinnati and Columbus to look for work as labourers on construction jobs, others caught two or three days a week cutting trees and cleaning picnic areas for the Forest Service. Most men sat on the kerb, spit tobacco juice on the hot cement, and put their change together for another bottle of white port. The sheriff arrested as least two dozen men a day on drunk charges or for fighting, and by the time the pool halls and taverns closed at two in the morning, there was usually one shooting or knifing. The one-room sandstone jail next to the courthouse was crowded with drunks. The sheriff brought charges against no one because he didn't have space for all the men he arrested during the day, and he kept a man in jail only four hours to give him time to get sober, and then put him out on the street again.

Perry walked down the tobacco-stained pavement past the hardware store. Groups of men in slug caps and tin helmets stopped their conversation and nodded to him as he passed. They shifted the toothpicks in their mouths in silence, with a knowing expression in their eyes. An elderly, fat woman with sagging breasts and varicose veins in her legs touched him on the arm as he stepped off the kerb. She wore a faded print dress and her teeth were rotted and stained with snuff.

'We was real sorry to hear about Woodson,' she said.

'Thank you.'

'My old man was there the night they blowed the building. I'll be out to see your mother and bring some soup this week.'

'That's mighty kind of you. She'll be grateful.' He started across the street towards the pawnshop. The sun was bright on the dirty store fronts.

'You keep your chin up, boy, and don't let this thing get you,' she called after him. 'Your mama's going to need you now.'

The window of the pawnshop was filled with rifles, pistols, brass knuckles, banjos, guitars, blackjacks, one dobro, fiddles, mandolins, switchblade knives, watches and sets of dice. Perry looked at the German Lugers, the .38 specials, the army .45 automatics, and the cheap nickel-plated mail-order revolvers that usually exploded after they had been fired a few times. He counted the money in his wallet and went inside. The interior was dark and smelled bad from lack of ventilation. The owner was a consumptive old man whose white shirt always looked soiled. For thirty years he had run his pawnshop in the same location, and almost every man in the county had borrowed money from him at one time or another, because few miners could get loans at the bank. He could have probably become rich in the pawn business, but his interest rates were lower than the finance company's, and he often gave out more money for a pawned item than it was worth. He slipped a tray of guns into the glass case and looked up at Perry over his rimless spectacles. His skin had a yellow tint to it.

'Well, lookie there. I thought you was off in the Job Corps somewhere,' he said.

'How do, Mr MacIntosh. I come to buy a pistol from you.'

'I saw Mrs James on the street the other day, and she said you was doing real good in your schooling.'

'I ain't in Job Corps no more. How much are those kind you got in the window?'

'She said they was awful proud of you. One of my nephews went off to the Job Corps last week. They flew him way out to California.'

'I got thirty dollars to spend on a pistol. I don't want to go no higher than that.'

'I rather see you come in here to borrow money from me, Perry. Your family could probably use it now, and I wouldn't push you about paying me back till you all get on your feet again. I knowed your daddy all my life, and I'll go out of my way to help you if I can.'

'That ain't why I'm here. How much you want for them Lugers?'

'Those are all in pawn. They ain't for sale.'

'What about these here in the case?'

'Your family ain't got the money for you to spend on guns. You take that thirty dollars and buy those kids some decent food. Get them some eggs and vegetables and whole milk.'

'I'm the one that's got to worry about what my family lacks. Let me see that Buntline revolver.'

'I know what you want it for, and I can't say that I blame you. Maybe if one of my kin was killed in that schoolhouse I'd go after somebody myself. But that won't do your daddy no good, and your people won't have anybody to look after them if you get yourself in jail. I know Woodson didn't keep guns in his house, and he wouldn't want you to do what you got in mind.'

'Every man that comes in here to buy a pistol ain't got but one thing in mind,' Perry said.

'Maybe that's right, but that don't mean you got to be like them. You give yourself a week to think about it, and you'll feel different. The sheriff's going to catch them men sometime, and they'll get punished the way they deserve. The trouble in the coal field's going to pass, and you'll be glad you didn't do nothing without thinking about it first. I seen it get a lot worse around here, but one day the mines always open up again and the shooting and the bombings stop. In a month or so men will be coming in here to get their banjos and fiddles out of pawn, and they'll want to sell me back every gun they bought.'

'I got to go see some people,' Perry said. 'The tag on that Buntline says thirty-five dollars, and here it is. Give me a box of magnum shells to go with it.'

'I hate to sell it to you, Perry.'

'My money ain't no different in colour than anybody else's, is it?' Perry laid a row of five-dollar bills out on the counter top. He felt a sense of guilt in spending money that his family needed, but he was intent upon carrying out what he had resolved to do when his father died.

'It's secondhand and I won't put no guarantee on it.' Mr MacIntosh set the blue Colt revolver down on the glass. It was a .22 magnum with a ten-inch barrel mounted on a heavy steel frame for balance, and it was accurate at fifty yards and could hit with the impact of a .38. The front sight had a gold bead on it, and the single-action and hair trigger worked as smoothly as a fine watch.

Perry cocked the hammer and snapped it twice on the empty cylinder. He felt the pistol had been made for his hand. The wood grips fitted into the curve of his palm, and the weight of the gun was balanced so perfectly that he could swing the sight on to a target in a second.

'I want you to keep it for me until this evening. I'll be back for it,' he said.

'I ain't ringing up the money on the register. You can pick up your thirty-five dollars any time you want it, and I'll keep the gun.'

'That's money you can take to the bank now, because I'll be here for my pistol before dark.'

Perry went out on the street again and into the bright sunlight. The cool spring air felt good to his face after the smell of the pawnshop. Parts of the mountains were shaded by clouds, and the treetops were dark blue in the distance. A battered pickup truck loaded with miners and picket signs pulled to the kerb in front of the men standing outside the pool hall. The truck was covered with UMW stickers and hand-painted inscriptions that read:

KEEP KENTUCKY UNION
VOTE AGAINST RITE TO WORK
SOLIDARITY FOREVER WITH UNITED MINERS
HOLD OUT FOR A FAIR WAGE
WE WANT SCALE

The men in the back of the truck piled out and went inside the pool room, and others took their place for the ride back to the picket lines outside the mine shafts. Most of the miners were drunk to some degree, unshaved, their clothes covered with dirt because they hadn't been home in several days; some of them didn't know if they were going on the picket or leaving it. A thin woman with skin the colour of old newspaper, holding a crying child in her arms, tried to get her husband out of the truck. She smiled weakly when she spoke, because in that part of Kentucky women didn't go against their husband's will in front of other men. She wore tennis shoes without socks, her legs were covered with hair, and her fingernails were broken to the quick. Her husband, tall and gaunt, with a wet, hand-rolled cigarette in his mouth, stood against the cab of the truck, holding a cardboard union placard in his hand. He sipped out of a whiskey bottle filled with corn liquor.

'We got to go to the food surplus, and I can't mind all the kids,' she said.

'Get on back to the house and stay there till I come home,' he said.

'Wilfred, I just can't—'

'Goddamn, you heard me, woman. I got to do my time on the picket.'

Perry went up the street to the tavern where he knew the J.W.s would sometimes be during the day. There was broken glass on the pavement in front of the door, and someone had knocked out a large triangular section from one of the windows with a pool ball. A barmaid in bluejean shorts and a sweater, with tattoos on her arms, leaned against the doorway and picked her teeth with her little finger. The rank smell of flat beer, cheap wine, cigarette smoke, sweat, bathroom disinfectant and chili breathed through the ventilating fan above the door.

'Where's the J.W.s at?' Perry said to the girl.

'How should I know? They don't punch no time card with me.'

'Have they been in here today?'

'No, they ain't. And if I had my way they wouldn't get back in here at all.' Her face looked as hard as plaster of Paris.

'What time do they come in off the picket?'

'You talk to the bartender about them two. I got no time for their kind.'

Perry went inside and stood at the end of the long, wooden bar. There were dirty spittoons by the brass foot rail, the mirror behind the bar was cracked and had turned the green of stagnant water from age, and empty beer cases and broken bottles were stacked against one wall. Clouds of smoke floated in the air, and several men were passed out on the tables. The UMW business agent had been buying beers since early morning for miners just off the picket. One man sat on a table with his feet on a rick chair and strummed a guitar with three steel banjo picks. Like every other man in the bar, his face was filmed with soot and covered with three days' growth of beard.

> *A miner's life is like a sailor's*
> *Aboard a ship to cross the waves,*
> *Everyday his life's in danger,*
> *Yet he ventures forth being brave.*

> *Union miners stand together,*
> *Heed no operators' tale,*
> *Keep your hand upon the dollar,*
> *And your eye upon the scale.*

The tune was to an old religious ballad called 'Life is Like a Mountain Railroad', and Perry had heard it sung on every union picket he'd ever been around. He waited an hour for the J.W.s to come in, then ordered a beer and ate a plate of pig's feet when he became hungry. Men who had known his father shook hands with him, and in their faces he could see the look of expectation. In the dried sweat he could smell their desire to see violence against the operator – but a violence that wouldn't involve themselves. The palms of their hands were moist, and their eyes shone dully with the same knowing expression he had seen in the faccs of the other men on the street.

'Every man here is with you,' they said.

'There ain't a man in the county that wouldn't take a gun to them three.'

'Even that's too good for them. They ought to get found in a burnt-up car.'

'There wasn't a scab on the street for a week after they blowed the school.'

'You want another beer, boy? The agent's a-buying.'

'The explosion knocked out my window glass. I run out on the porch and seen a car take off down the road. If I'd knowed what happened, I could have pumped holes all over them.'

'By God, we'll catch up to them one day, if we have to go through every town in Kentucky and West Virginia to do it.'

Perry drank two more fifteen-cent draught beers and spoke little to the men around him, because none of them knew anything except that they might eventually get to see another shooting. By mid-afternoon Perry had drunk too much, and the pig's feet had made his stomach vaguely sick. He started to leave when he saw the J.W.s come through the door, each of them framed in the sunlight outside, as though they were cut out of wood. Big J.W. had a hand-rolled cigarette in an empty space between his yellow, horse teeth, and he had a torn sign in his hand that read: *THIS MINE SUPPORTS RIGHT TO WORK*. Little J.W.'s hard, round stomach pushed against his suspenders, and he wore a crushed felt hat and a pair of overalls that had been cut away around the hips. His deceptive, quiet brown eyes looked straight at Perry without blinking. He pulled a piece of chewing tobacco off his lip and flicked it on the floor with his thumbnail. Perry had always had a sense of fear about the J.W.s since he had last seen them outside the sheriff's office before he went to North Carolina, but now he had no feeling at all towards them other than that they might be useful to him.

'Look what I had to tear off the tipple,' Big J.W. said, and waved the torn cardboard sign in his hand. 'I'd hate to have to feed this to that operator. Somebody put it out by the honey hole in case we run out of toilet paper.'

Everyone in the room laughed, and Little J.W. held up two fingers to the bartender. He and his brother looked like a comic Mutt and Jeff team in their worn, soot-stained trousers, bleached denim shirts and frayed suitcoats. Little J.W. took a bottle of corn whiskey from his pocket and poured it into an unwashed glass on the bar. He cleared his mouth of tobacco, spat it on the floor next to the spittoon, and drank the whiskey down in one swallow and then chased it with a draught beer. He looked at Perry with a flat expression, as though he had seen him only yesterday rather than five months ago.

'Well, just look who's there, baby brother,' Big J.W. said.

'I thought you was off in school with the coloured boys,' Little J.W. said.

'He wouldn't be around no coloured people with that Confederate flag on his arm.'

'Who done it?' Perry said.

'Scabs don't come talk to us,' Little J.W. said. 'You don't see none in here, do you? And you won't find none anyplace we're at.'

'We been a-looking for them. Three men nobody ever seen before bought dynamite over in Letcher the day before the bombing and some people saw an old Chevrolet come tearing down the mountain like it was burning alcohol right after the explosion,' Big J.W. said.

'That don't tell me nothing. Who were they?'

'If we knew that, they'd be down in the bottom of an old shaft now,' Little J.W. said. Perry could smell the odour of corn liquor and tobacco juice on his breath. 'Your daddy wasn't the only man killed in that building. My wife's cousin got a board drove through his head.'

'Which operator's a-paying for outside people?'

'Maybe the big one down the street, or maybe everybody in the association is putting in,' Big J.W. said. 'They got men with guns around every hole in the county. They call them special deputies, and every one of them is an ex-convict from Dayton or Detroit.'

'You run off before the real shooting started,' Little J.W. said. 'They was taking shots at union men like ground squirrels down in Harlan while you was riding airplanes.'

'They would have burned our agent out, but our boys caught them behind the building with the kerosene first.' Big J.W.'s wan, narrow face took on a greenish cast in the dim light of the bar.

'You ain't got to worry about it, anyway,' Little J.W. said. 'When it comes time we'll take care of them men for you.'

'You ain't going to do nothing for me,' Perry said. 'I don't want nobody else mixing in it.'

Little J.W. poured another glass of whiskey and sucked his teeth. 'The last time I seen you go up against something I believe I had to carry you to the car because you was too afraid to move.'

'I didn't wait here all afternoon to hear what you got to say about me,' Perry said. 'It don't interest me. If you find out where they're at, you tell me. And I ain't fooling when I say I don't want no help from either one of you all.'

Perry finished his beer and ordered another one. The glass was beaded with moisture, and under the foam the beer looked like amber light.

'You must have had your head in the jug too long today,' Little J.W. said.

'I just give you warning. Don't mix in it. It wasn't none of your blood kin that got killed in there.'

'I reckon you better pick every word you say pretty careful,' Little J.W. said. His eyes lost their quiet, doelike quality and became as sharp and bright as agate. His lips were a tight line across his face.

'You got no call to get in something that ain't your business.'

'A man don't talk to me like that more than once.'

'I ain't saying no more to you. Find out the ones that done it, and I'll be in your debt. But don't take up what's mine to do.'

'Baby brother's just telling you that one man can't do it by himself,' Big J.W. said. 'You got three of them up against you and maybe more. It don't hurt to have a couple more men with you.'

'You never done me no favours before, and I ain't asking you for one now.' Perry drank his beer glass to the bottom. He knew he was getting drunk, but he was already past the point of caring or remembering the long, sick weekend he had spent after the night he was tattooed in Asheville.

'Like Little J.W. said, there's more people than you that had somebody hurt in that schoolhouse. If my car hadn't broke down I might have been a-setting on top of that charge with them other fellers. So I figure that gives us the right to do what we want with them men.'

'What you got made up in your mind is one thing, but you heered what I said.' Perry clicked his glass on the bar for another beer.

'How long you figure you can keep talking like that, boy?' Little J.W. said. He had his bottle of whiskey half raised to his mouth. His face had grown ashen, and his jaws worked with each breath, as though he were chewing. His eyes seemed to shrink and recede into his forehead.

Perry paid the bartender and wiped the foam off the beer with the side of his hand. He said nothing and upended the glass. He could see the red, twisted scar on his nose in the mirror behind the bar.

'You ain't looking at me. Turn around,' Little J.W. said.

'Let it go, honey. The sheriff's set on putting us in jail now,' Big J.W. said.

'Look at me! Then open that mouth again. You set in a government camp and come back here and tell us what we're going to do and what we ain't. The man don't walk that tells me what to do.' His voice wasn't loud, but the heated intensity of it made other people in the bar stop talking.

'This ain't the place,' Big J.W. said. He rested his long, narrow hand over his brother's arm.

'Goddamn you boy, are you going to look at me or am I going to have to lay hold of you?'

The bartender moved down the counter and placed his hand on something under the bar; his face never changed expression and he looked straight ahead.

'I didn't come for trouble with you, but I ain't afraid of you no more, either,' Perry said. He turned and looked at the hatred in Little J.W.'s eyes and remembered the story about how Little J.W. had almost beaten his uncle to death with a fire poker and left him to die in the front yard.

'You ain't going to have the chance to be afraid.'

Perry couldn't see a sag in either one of Little J.W.'s pockets from the weight of a pistol, but he knew that Little J.W. always carried a short bowie hunting knife, filed sharp on an emery wheel, in a leather scabbard inside his overalls. Perry kept his hand on the handle of his beer mug in case he had to swing.

'We're a-going down the street, baby brother. Finish it another time,' Big J.W. said.

'It's getting done right now.'

'I done told you I don't want trouble,' Perry said. 'But do what you're a-thinking and your hand won't clear your pocket.'

'You young sonofabitch, you bought it now,' Little J.W. said.

'My place ain't getting tore up on account of you all again,' the bartender said. He was a big man with a granite head, a large pock-marked nose, and a thick ear. His scalp was shaved bald, and there was a deep blue scar that ran across his cranium. He had been a wrestler in Nashville until someone had hit him in the head with a metal chair. 'Take it outside or I'll pick up what I got in my hand.'

'Go ahead and draw it, you bastard,' Little J.W. said.

'Leave it where it's at, we're going,' Big J.W. said. He pulled his brother away from the bar.

'You're letting them wipe their feet on us,' Little J.W. said.

'I ain't giving the sheriff no excuse to put us in jail.'

'Just get the hell out,' the bartender said.

'You made a mistake sticking your face in this,' Little J.W. said. 'I hope you paid up your fire insurance.'

'I ain't waiting on you much longer,' the bartender said.

Big J.W. pulled his brother out the door on to the street. They argued for a moment in the square of light before the doorway, then climbed up on the union pickup truck that was headed back to the mines. Perry felt a drop of perspiration form on the corner of his eyebrow and run down the side of his face. He cleared his throat and spat dryly on the floor, and then drank down the rest of his beer. It felt like ice in his stomach. He wondered if truly he had not been afraid, or if the nervous twitch in his leg muscles and stomach were just a symptom of the anxiety that men felt when they were very near sudden violence. He knew that it had been close. If the bartender had not intervened, or if Big J.W. had not been there, the knife would have been out and it would not have been just a threat followed by more words; it would have flashed at Perry's stomach as quickly as a snake's head. He realized that his shirt was wet with sweat and his hand had left a damp print on the bar. The bartender drew another draught and set it before him.

People began talking again, and the guitar player rang the steel picks on the strings and sang:

> Watch the rocks, they're a-falling daily,
> Careless miners always fail.
> Keep your hand upon the dollar
> And your eye upon the scale.

Perry sipped the beer until the hard, tense feeling inside him began to fade. The barmaid came back from the front doorway and leaned against the counter in front of him. Her face had an unnatural shine in the light. She took a cigarette from a pack tucked inside her shorts and waited for him to light it.

'Ain't you got a match?' she said.

He handed her a book of matches from his shirt pocket. Her eyes were black in the flame.

'You're the first I seen to put one of them two in his place,' she said. 'I'd like to see them both laid out behind here some night.'

'I didn't put nobody in his place.'

'There ain't many men around here that's gone up against Little J.W.,' the man next to Perry said. He wore a dirty straw hat and there was a streak of chili on the side of his mouth. 'I seen him beat up on a feller with a chair leg once, just for looking at him the wrong way. Woodson would be proud of what you done.'

'I didn't do nothing,' Perry said. 'I don't want no more trouble with him. He'd a-cut me open if the bartender didn't stop him.'

'You wasn't backing off from him none, and we all seen it,' the man said.

'I didn't say nothing against him, and I ain't a-doing it now. If he's got it in him for trouble, that's his business. But I ain't the cause of it.'

'I've put up with that little sonofabitch since I come to work here, and I ain't seen another man talk back in his face yet,' the girl said.

Perry knew the stories that would spread about the bar-room incident with Little J.W. By that night people would say that he had backed down both the J.W.s, and they would remember little of what actually happened. In telling the story to other miners who came off the picket, they would say nothing of the sweated areas on his shirt, his moist palms, or that rigid, naked feeling in his stomach when he waited for Little J.W. to bring his knife out of his scabbard. The next day the story would be even more distorted, and then someone would stop Little J.W. on the street and casually mention that he'd heard something about a seventeen-year-old ex-Job Corps boy backing him down before a room full of people. Later Perry would have to face the J.W.s somewhere again. He would have to tell them that he had nothing to do with the rumour and then be accused of lying and cowardice, or fight both of them with any weapon he could get his hands on – neither of which he wanted to do. He was determined not to take any more abuse or threats from them; but even if he fought one or both of them and won, they would eventually catch him alone on a road at night, and the next day someone would find him lying in the weeds or thrown down the hollow.

'I got to find a job, and I ain't got time to worry about that pair,' he said.

'What did Little J.W. mean about carrying you to a car?' the man said.

'Go ask him. I don't know what goes on in his head.' He drank off his beer and had another. His head was starting to reel, and when he raised his glass he spilled part of the beer over his chin.

'You shut the little bastard's face up,' the girl said.

'Is there any strip work a-going on?' Perry said to the man in the straw hat.

'Buddy, there ain't no work anywhere around here,' another man said. He wore a tin hat, with a pair of coloured goggles pulled up on its elastic strap above the brim. There was a heavy, brown mole in the corner of his eye that made him blink constantly, and his mouth was discoloured from chewing snuff.

'A working man can't find no job except driving whiskey up to Ohio and Michigan, and the ABCs cotched half of the runners before they got to Lexington,' the man in the straw hat said. 'They give a man a year at Frankfort if they catch him with just a couple of drops in a bottle that ain't got a tax stamp on it. The federal people is even worse. Last January they got my uncle going over the Ohio bridge, and they sent him down to Atlanta for three years.'

'Ain't the Forest Service got any jobs?' Perry said.

'They won't hire no fire crews till it gets dry, and the happy-pappies is doing all the work on the trails.'

'It might pay a feller to string a couple of fires,' the man with the mole in the corner of his eye said. 'I reckon they'd be handing out some work if we burned up a couple hundred acres of their timber.'

'What they paying a runner now?' Perry said. There was another full glass of beer on the counter before him, and he couldn't remember if he had ordered it or if the union business agent was setting up the bar again.

'I heered fifty dollars, if you ain't got to go across the state line. I guess the fellers a-carrying it all the way to Detroit in their own car are splitting with the still. But the money ain't worth no three years in the pen.'

'It ain't like it used to be,' the man in the straw hat said. 'I never knowed them to give a feller more than thirty days on the honour farm his first time around. Now they fine you for every dime you got and lock you up for a big stretch, too.'

Perry was unsteady on his feet, and he held on to the bar with one hand when he drank from his glass. He couldn't remember how long he had been in the bar. Outside, the sun cast long shadows over the blue tops of the mountains, and the air had begun to chill. The pickup truck returned from the picket line, and more miners came into the bar. Their eyes were red with alcohol.

'What time is it? I got to pick up something at the pawnshop,' Perry said.

'Take some of this. Mr MacIntosh ain't going nowhere. I don't think he ever gets out of that place except to drop his britches out back.'

'I better not drink no whiskey.'

'It's good corn. It was kept buried in a charcoal barrel for five months. You can't tell no difference from it and red whiskey except for the colour.'

Perry took the bottle and drank. He could see small thread-like flecks of charcoal inside, and the taste was like turpentine and corn meal. He chased the whiskey down with a beer and had another swallow from the bottle. He shivered slightly when he felt the raw heat of the alcohol hit his stomach.

'Drink some more of that and you might try a little bit of that jenny-barner,' the man in the straw hat said. The girl in the shorts had moved farther down the bar.

'Where's the head at?' Perry said.

'Right in back. Don't fall in that honey hole. We couldn't find the last feller that dropped down in it.' Both men roared, but their laughter had a dry, phlegmy quality to it.

Perry walked unsteadily towards the back of the bar. He could feel his heart beating faster from the whiskey, and drops of sweat formed on his forehead. He pushed open the plank door that was held in place with a metal spring, and the odour that arose from the hole in the board seat made his eyes water. The small room had been built on to the back of the bar over a ten-foot drop to the slope below. An open pit, filled with creosote, had been dug in the ground, and the overflowing drainage ran into a creek down in the gulley. Through the cracks in the boards Perry could see piles of broken bottles in the creek bed, bags of garbage, a rusted bedframe, part of a car, and hundreds of beer cans. He buttoned his trousers and went back into the bar towards the front door. His face was flushed, and a noise like an electrical short kept humming in his head. It took all his effort to walk in a straight line on to the street.

The light was fading beyond the rim of the mountains, and dusk had settled into the hollow. The ridges had turned from dark green to purple, and in the east the sun's reflection was scarlet on the clouds. There was a sulphurous smell in the air, and Perry knew there would be an electric storm by nightfall. One of his uncles had been killed by lightning while leading a pair of mules along the mountain crest above his cabin. The force of the shock had blown off both his shoes. Perry thought about walking the half mile to the first hollow from town where Bee Hatfield lived; then he remembered that he had to go to the pawnshop before it closed, and he forgot about the storm. He felt the pavement tipping under his feet as he moved down the street through the groups of men putting change together with another bottle of white port.

Across the street Perry saw the office of the Lockwood Mining Company, one of the few in the area that had never signed a union contract. Two expensive new cars were parked outside, and a company deputy, with a badge and a revolver on his hip, stood by the front door. A leather-covered blackjack hung out of his back pocket. Two miners in raincoats with picket signs in their hands walked back and forth on the path. A man in a blue business suit, tie and white shirt walked out the door and through the pickets as though they were not there. As he got into his automobile, Perry saw the light gleam on his silver cuff links and polished black shoes. Perry didn't know his name, but he knew that he was a lawyer from somewhere up North who came to town and stayed at the association president's house whenever a big strike threatened the coal field. Once, when the union thought it had won a contract and a wage increase, this man had the case transferred for a later hearing before the Labor Relations Board in Washington, and nothing more was heard of the matter for nine months. Most of the miners couldn't hold out, and they went back to work at their old scale. Perry felt a sudden intense hatred of this Northern lawyer, his new car, the company deputy by the front door of the office, and the men inside who were devising ways to break the strike before their stock fell too far and their investors in New York pulled out on them. His father had been wrong when he said that fighting the operator had never helped the miner. Violence in kind was the only thing the association understood. They owned the courts, the special deputies, the tax assessors, and maybe even some of the industrial referees, and when a politician came to the plateau to campaign for Congress he always stayed at the association president's house on the hill. They had money that could reach all the way to the governor's mansion in Frankfort, or National Guard troops would never have been sent into Harlan to protect scabs and to break strikes. A company deputy never went to the penitentiary for shooting a miner, but union men were jailed for trespassing when they walked the picket in front of a shaft.

The rain began to fall evenly on the street. In the north lightning struck into the hollows, and a black thundercloud rolled over the top of the mountains. A white bolt split the sky apart and exploded in a ball of fire on the ridge above town. A few moments later flames were burning around several trees and spreading into the undergrowth with the wind. Perry pulled the peak of his cloth cap down over his eyes and walked under the eaves of the buildings to protect himself from the rain. In the west he could see the last afterglow of the sun fade beyond the mountains; then the storm seemed to spread from one horizon to another, and dark clouds swirled overhead like pieces of torn, black cotton.

The corn whiskey had made his mouth dry and he wanted another drink. He went into the first pool room he passed and drank two draughts in five minutes. He felt he could pour down every bottle of beer in the bar and still drink more. It seemed as though the energy in his body burned up the alcohol as soon as it hit his stomach. Before he left, two men asked him if the story was true that one of the J.W.s had backed off from him that afternoon.

'The man that told you it was a liar,' Perry said. 'You go get somebody else cut up.'

On the way to the pawnshop, he had another beer and two shots of wine at a bar farther up the street, his clothes were soaked through, and his shoes were full of water. He couldn't open the front door of the pawnshop, then realized that he was pulling it shut against the jamb. His eyes were glazed and his body had no sensation in it. The wind crashed the door back against the wall when he entered, and the rain swept across the floor.

'I want my gun,' he said.

'Shut that door,' Mr MacIntosh said. His shoulders were bent with the weight of two heavy ledgers in his arms.

'I got to get to Bee Hatfield's before the electricity starts.' Perry swayed back and forth on his feet.

Mr MacIntosh set the books down, came around the counter, and closed the door. The front of his dirty white shirt was splattered with rain drops.

'You must have drunk up every dollar in your pocket,' he said.

'Wrap up the shells in a paper bag so they don't get wet.'

'You won't ever make it to Bee's. You'll get hit by lightning or fall down on the road somewhere and get run over.'

'That's my lookout. Where's the gun at?'

'I can't let you have it when you're drunk. You can sleep on the cot in back tonight, or you can go home and come for it tomorrow,' Mr MacIntosh said.

'I paid for it. It ain't yours no more, and you ain't got the right to say when I can take it.'

'It will still be here in the morning. There ain't a lot going to change between now and then.'

'Goddamn it, you give me that pistol.'

'Who you got to shoot tonight? You want to blow holes in the

Lockwood office? Them three men that killed your daddy will like that. They won't have to worry about you for the next six months while you're in the county jail.'

Perry saw the long blue barrel of the Buntline revolver and the box of shells inside the glass case. He walked forward off balance, reached over the counter, and tried to slide back the glass door.

'You ain't going to do this in my shop, Perry. I'll call the sheriff on you,' Mr MacIntosh said.

'You do what you goddamn like.'

'Woodson was too good a friend of mine for me to have his boy put in jail. Don't push me into it.'

'I ain't made you do nothing. You wouldn't give me what's mine.' Perry wrapped his cloth cap over his fist and shattered the glass counter top. He felt a sharp pain slide across the inside of his palm, and he rolled his cap up in his hand and clenched it tightly to stop the blood. He reached inside the broken case with his left hand and picked up the pistol from among the splinters of glass.

'You don't know when a man's trying to help you,' Mr MacIntosh said.

'I'll be back tomorrow and pay for the case.' Perry slipped the box of magnum cartridges into his back pocket.

He walked out the door into the black rain while Mr Mac-Intosh dialled the telephone. Perry could hardly see to the other side of the street. He held the pistol loosely in one hand at his side and stumbled along the pavement. He was drunker than he had been in Asheville. The yellow light from inside the mining office reflected off the wet street. The deputy still stood by the front door with his raincoat pulled up over his head. Perry had little awareness of what he was doing as he sat down on the kerb and took six cartridges from the box in his pocket. He dropped his cap into the gutter and slipped the shells one by one into the cylinder. The blood from his cut palm diffused in the rain and ran in streams along the inside of his forearm. He fell back on the kerb when he tried to get up. Finally, he got to his feet and walked down the middle of the street towards the mining office. He could see the shadows of several men against the window glass, and he put the gun on half cock under his thumb.

'What in the hell are you doing, Perry?' Somebody called at him from the front door of a pool room.

'Mind your goddamn business.'

The deputy looked up from under his raincoat, and his hand went to the revolver on his hip. Farther up the street a car pulled away from the kerb in front of the courthouse and roared towards Perry. In the headlights the rain looked like spun glass. As the car neared him he thought he was going to be run down, but his legs wouldn't move under him. He pulled back the hammer of the pistol to full cock and raised it level with the windshield. Then he saw the red spotlight on the driver's door and the tall radio aerial whipping back and forth on the rear fender. The car slammed to a stop at an angle between him and the mining office, and the sheriff opened the door and lifted his huge weight out of the driver's seat.

'Lower the gun and let that hammer down slow,' he said.

'I didn't know it was you. I thought one of them scabs was trying to get me.' Perry used both thumbs to ease the hammer back into its place. He held the revolver sideways in his palm, with his fingers over the cylinder.

'Set it on the car.'

'I got no reason to go against you. You ain't got to worry about trouble from me.' He placed the pistol on the car fender. The sheriff picked it up, shucked out each cartridge on the street, and stuck the barrel down inside his belt.

'Mr Mac don't ever call me unless somebody gives him a real bad time, and you must have done just that. Get in the car.'

In the distance Perry saw the fire from the ball of lightning burning in the trees. He wiped the blood from his hand on the front of his shirt. The rain beat on his bare head and ran down into his shirt collar.

'You putting me in jail?'

'That's right.'

'I ain't broke no law on the street. I told him at the pawnshop I'd pay for his glass.'

'If I hadn't stopped you before you got to the mining office, I'd be arresting you for something else or picking you up off the street. Don't make me put you in the car, son.' The sheriff's khaki uniform was streaked from the rain.

'I can't spend no time in jail.'

'You'll get out in the morning, and maybe you'll have a little more sense then.'

Perry pulled open the car door and sat back in the seat. His wet clothes were like ice against his body. The sheriff backed the car around in the street and headed towards the courthouse. His stomach reached almost to the steering wheel. His great legs and buttocks spread over half the seat, and his breath expelled with a dry rasp while he drove.

'You had warning from me before Perry, and I don't reckon I have to tell you what I'll do if I catch you trying to carry out what you got in mind. I can't hold you for the gun because you didn't have it concealed, but I'll send you to Frankfort if I even hear you're in on blowing a tipple or burning out the operator. I ain't going to stand for no more of it in my county.'

'I ain't done nothing but get drunk. My daddy didn't do nothing, either, but they killed him, and they're still out there somewhere.'

'I had a lot of respect for Woodson, and if you give me time I promise you I'll get them three that did it.'

'I ain't seen a company man go to the pen yet for killing a miner.'

'You'll see it this time, even if I got to walk over everybody in the association to do it. But you try to do my job for me, and I'll put you away with them.'

The sheriff parked the car in front of the courthouse and cut the headlights. Thunder rolled through the hollows, and the poplars and white oaks shook in the wind. The courthouse lawn was already flooded, and wine bottles and beer cans floated in the gutters. Perry got out of the car and started towards the one-storey sandstone jail.

'Go into my office,' the sheriff said.

'You said you was putting me in jail.'

'You'll get there in due time. Don't worry about that. I just don't want you bleeding on my mattresses.'

Inside the office Perry soaked his hand in the washbasin. The cut on his palm was ragged and blue, like a wound from a rusted nail. The blood began to coagulate on the edges of the torn skin. The sheriff took Perry's Colt revolver from his belt and locked it in his desk drawer.

'Do I get my gun back tomorrow?' Perry said.

'You're set on making me come after you again, ain't you?'

'Any trouble we got was pushed on us. There wouldn't none of this started if they'd let us alone and treated us decent.'

'The best thing that could happen to you would be to get on the first bus back to that Job Corps centre. I already heered that you was almost in it with Little J.W., and that's the best way I know to get cut down in the back some night. He ain't a man to forget anything. He could kill you and drink a beer while he was doing it.'

'Are you going to give me my pistol back?'

'I'd be doing you a favour if I throwed it in the creek. But you'd probably spend the money your family needs on another one, because you're stubborn and you get your mind set on something till you can't think no other way, just like every one of the Hatfields. Stop dripping blood on my floor and wrap your hand in that towel.'

The sheriff put a piece of cotton over Perry's cut, and wound his palm with tape; then he took him through a side door to the jail. The rain drove at an angle to the ground, and the water on the lawn came over the tops of Perry's shoes. There was no window glass in the jail, and the men inside had propped pieces of cardboard behind the bars. A fire of newspaper and twigs, broken off the trees outside, burned on the concrete floor. The sheriff unlocked the chain on the barred front door.

'Out in the morning,' Perry said.

'I told you that, didn't I?' the sheriff said. 'And I keep my word. I ain't got enough room to keep anybody for more than a night, anyhow.' He closed the door behind Perry and fastened the lock back on the chain.

The inside of the jail was filled with smoke from the fire. Some men slept on dirty tick mattresses and others were still drinking from bottles in the firelight. A sickening smell came from a large bucket in one corner that was used for a bathroom. One man was going through the DTs, and he moaned loudly and rolled about on his mattress. He pulled his knees up to his chin and shook all over. Someone tried to give him a drink of wine, but his eyes stared wildly, and he struck at the man with his fist. Perry sat back against one wall as far away as he could get from the bucket in the corner. It must not have been emptied in days. The stone was hard and cold against his back, and he tried to stretch out on the floor and sleep; but his head spun from the beer and whiskey, a man stepped on his stomach, and one of the drinkers at the fire took some newspaper and went to the corner to relieve himself. Perry pulled a piece of cardboard off the window to let in the air, and the rain swept across the man sleeping in the concrete. Perry pressed his face against the bars and breathed the sweet smell of the spring storm and the new grass on the lawn.

'Close up that goddamn window,' somebody yelled.

Perry fitted the cardboard back in place and sat down again, with his arms folded across his legs. He felt the thick nausea of a hangover beginning to grow in his body. There wasn't enough heat in the room to dry his clothes, and his skin was pale from the cold. After an hour of the drunken voices and the rancid odour of unwashed bodies and tobacco spittle, he lost consciousness of time and kept expecting the sun's first light to break over the rim of the mountain and flood through the jail window. Then his head sagged on his chest, and he could not tell if the voices he heard were from inside himself or the men around him. During the night bottles were thrown at the windows, men fist fought, and someone overturned the bucket in the corner, but Perry lay on the floor in a sick stupor and dreamed nightmares about the schoolhouse exploding in flames and three men, with hideous, laughing faces, roaring down the mountain in an automobile through the moonless dark.

EIGHT

The brown leaves were deep on the forest floor, wet with dew, and the long white trunks of the beech trees rose high above Perry's head. In the light of the false dawn he could see the edges of the limestone cliffs on the far side of the hollow, silhouetted against the purple sky. There was little undergrowth because of the lack of sunlight and rainfall through the tall green canopy of trees overhead; and the great outcroppings of rock glistened faintly in the mist. The floor of the hollow dipped away from him to a creek that ran over a waterfall into the Kentucky River, and he could hear the water rushing from the springs farther up the mountain through the drainages into the creek bed. The rocks and cliffs seemed to change shape as the red strip of light on the horizon began to swell into the sky, and the vapour in the bottom of the hollow flattened and settled low over the stream. He smelled the oak logs burning under the still in the rock house and the coffee grounds boiling in the tin pot over the fire. As the first sunlight glowed through the trees he saw a whitetail deer and several groundhogs and rabbits drinking from the stream. The water was dark blue in the twisting current; then it changed to green, and he could see the pebbles washed smooth in the sandy bed.

The smoke from the fire in the rock house curled up around the fifty-gallon cooker, collected briefly on the ceiling, and strained off from under the ledge into the wind. One man fed logs into the flames, and another stirred the mash with a five-foot tapered branch from a poplar tree, shaved clean with a knife and wrapped with barbed wire at the fork to turn the corn meal, water, and sugar. The two mash barrels were pinned rectangularly with oak logs and shored with dead leaves to contain the heat and to hurry the fermentation. A metal extension ran from the cooker to the thumping keg, a small barrel that collected water from the vapour and allowed the alcohol to rise and condense in the coil. There was a hand-bevelled wooden plug in the bottom of the thumping keg for bleeding off the excess water.

The steam coughed and pumped through the metal arm and dripped off the coil on to a strip of peeled birch bark, which had been rolled into a funnel inside the neck of a gallon milk bottle to cut the taste of corn in the whiskey.

During the eighteenth and nineteenth centuries this particular area had been used by whiskey makers because there was a spring in almost every rock house in the hollow. The entrance through the cliff walls was right by the Kentucky River, down which they used to float their whiskey in kegs on big flatboats on to the Ohio and eventually down the Mississippi to New Orleans, where people had acquired a taste for Kentucky bourbon. At that time the mountaineer could take all the game and fish he needed from the forests and streams, the land was so rich that it grew almost any kind of crop, and he made whiskey so he could have a few hard dollars to buy shot and powder, and occasionally something from a travelling drummer. Then when most of the game was gone, the streams polluted, and the land ruined by the mines, whiskey making became his sole income. The hollow was still the best place in a three-county area to set up a still because there was no access to it except over a mountain that even mules had difficulty climbing. One rutted dirt road led to the base of the mountain, and a man on top of the ridge could see for miles in every direction. If someone from the ABC or a federal tax agent started up the steep incline towards the gap in the cliff wall, the still would be torn down in minutes and hidden, the mash barrels emptied into the creek, and the fifty-dollar copper coil buried in a rock house.

Perry knew every cave, rock formation, ledge and drainage in the hollow. The Warriors' Trail, which Daniel Boone had followed into the Ohio Valley after he opened Cumberland Gap, ran right by the hollow, and Perry had dug up handfuls of arrowheads and stone knives in the silt floors of rock houses where Indian braves had buried them. Since the time he was a small boy he had also searched here for the lost silver mine of John Swift, an English sailor who came to Kentucky through Pound Gap in 1761 and worked a vein of ore in a cave for eight years. Swift took his smelted silver back into Virginia each winter, but several times he was attacked by Shawnee Indians, who stole his horses, and he had to bury seventy thousand dollars' worth of silver on the trail. In 1769 he murdered his partners as they slept outside the mine, and he sealed the entrance with a rock the size of a salt keg, covered it with earth and locust branches, and left over two hundred thousand dollars in smelted ore inside the shaft. Later, he was imprisoned as a revolutionist by the British and during the years in jail he lost his eyesight and was never able to find the mine again, although he searched for it until his death in 1800. However, a map and part of his diary had been passed down through the generations, and Perry's aunt had read a copy of it to him so many times when he was a boy that he knew it by heart. He had found some of the Shawnee turkey tracks and crows' feet cut in rock that Swift described, and once he found part of an old smelter half buried in a cave. Swift had written of a window in the mountain close to the mine, and at the head of the hollow was a natural bridge that let in light through the cliff wall. Perry was sure that the mine was somewhere along one of the ledges, but the land had changed over the years, snow slides had brought avalanches of rock and earth down over the base of the mountains, and the wind had eroded away many of the Indian carvings.

The sun rose above the ridge, and the grey light thinned through the trees, and blue shadows from the trunks fell on the forest floor. Sitting on the damp leaves Perry felt a chill, and he went inside the rock house and sat by the fire under the still. The oak logs scorched up yellow and red over the rusted cooker. He picked up the tin pot from the fire, poured some coffee out over the rim to cool the metal, and drank. There were eight army jerry cans of whiskey, each containing five gallons, lined up against the back wall. They had loaded eight more on the mule in the dark hours before dawn and had taken them down the mountain to the 1953 Chevrolet, with the GMC truck engine, hidden in the trees by the river. A tall, old man with white hair bobbed on his neck, a hat with the brim pulled down all around his head, emptied the full milk bottle into one of the cans. His long underwear showed at his neck under the three shirts he wore, and his overalls were held on by one torn strap across his shoulder. His stubble of white whiskers was as coarse as wire, and the big knuckles on his hands almost stuck through his wrinkled skin. He was Lemuel McGoffin, and he had been making whiskey in this hollow as long as anyone could remember. He had been sent to the federal honour farm four times, fined for five hundred dollars twice, and once he had been sentenced to Atlanta for three years, but was released early because of his age. Most of the federal tax agents knew him well enough to stop and talk with him on the street in Richmond or Winchester, and the Forest Service had offered him a permanent job as crew leader on the trails if he would stop moonshining. But he had never done any other type of work; his Scottish ancestors had made whiskey with Daniel Boone when Kentucky was first settled, and he believed that he violated no moral law in continuing what his father and grandfather had done.

'That's the last of it,' he said, as he pulled the copper coil loose from the thumping keg. The coil was the most valuable piece of equipment on the still, and he couldn't afford to have it chopped into bits if an agent happened to find the rock house while he was gone and there was no lookout up on the ridge. 'Go catch up the mule and we'll move the rest of it down to the car.'

Noah Combs, bent and crippled from the bullet wounds he had received in front of a mine when he tried to dynamite the loading platform, shuffled off towards the bottom of the hollow, where the mule was tied by the creek. One of his arms stuck out stiffly in a crook at an angle to his side, there was a scar the size of a quarter in his cheek where a bullet had knocked out all his teeth in one side of his mouth, and a splinter of lead still lay imbedded in his spine, which caused him to walk as though he had a great block of concrete on his shoulders. He caught the mule by the reins and led him back up towards the rock house. Noah couldn't hold his head erect, and his eyes bulged from under his brow as he worked his way to the top of the incline. Half of his facial muscles were paralysed, and the skin along one jaw had deadened to a grey colour and had begun to peel in dry scales.

They heard the sound of an aircraft in the distance; then the droning of the engine came closer, and through the tops of the trees they saw the plane bank out of the sun and begin a low sweep over the hollow. The pilot cut back his speed and glided on the wind currents above the ragged cliffs. Perry could see the silver haze of the propeller spinning in the light and the black silhouette of the pilot in the cockpit. The plane arched up high in the sky like a crop duster, turned, and headed back for another pass over the hollow.

'It's the ABC!' McGoffin yelled. 'Get that mule in the rock house! Don't look up at the sky, neither. They can see the light on your face.'

He and Perry pulled back inside the limestone overhang and threw dirt on the fire under the cooker, while Combs laboured uphill with the mule. The animal was spooked from the noise of the aircraft and was jerking sideways. The dirt, moist from the spring in the back of the rock house, spit and hissed on the flames, and steam fanned out in the breeze.

'Hit that mule between the eyes and get him in here!' the old man said.

'I can't hold him,' Combs said. His crooked arm looked grotesque as he pulled at the reins.

'I ain't a-taking another stretch in Atlanta for no ten-dollar shithog of a mule.' McGoffin picked up a short, thin oak log from the pile of wood near the cooker and moved fast down the incline. His movements were stiff and awkward because of his age, but his body was still strong from years of toiling up and down the mountains. He jerked the reins out of Combs' hands and slashed the log down between the mule's ears. The mule's mouth convulsed and pulled back from his yellow teeth, and he tried to bolt to the bottom of the hollow. McGoffin struck him hard twice more in the same place, and Perry could hear the wood 'thunk' against the bone. The mule's eyes were wide with pain and fear. 'Now move, you sonofabitch, or I'll beat your goddamn skull in.' The mule thudded his hooves into the earth and struggled after McGoffin while Combs whipped his flanks with a switch.

'They'll see the smoke. The breeze ain't carrying it off,' Perry said.

'They ain't ever spotted me from the air yet,' McGoffin said, as he pulled the mule into the rock house, the log still in one hand. 'They got me before because they found a trail or they'd paid somebody to tell them where the still was at. But that ain't going to happen again because I don't come up through the hollow the same way twice and I don't stay set up in the same rock house more than a week. Put them branches across the opening.'

Perry picked up the green poplar limbs they had cut the night before and propped them against the roof of the rock house at the entrance. The old man and Combs kicked more dirt over the remaining embers in the fire, and ground the cinders under their feet. The plane dipped down over the ridge above their heads, the engine gunning in the updrafts, and roared through the hollow just a few feet higher than the canopy of trees. The leaves shook in the backwash from the propeller, and the mule reared sideways and kicked his hooves into the wall of the rock house. The plane was so low that Perry could see the metallic shine of the guy wires on the wings.

'You think he seen us? The smoke's still a-hanging in the trees,' he said.

'We ain't going to be here to find out. Get that mule loaded,' McGoffin said. 'They raid this time and they ain't going to get nothing for their trouble except a rusted-out cooker and two empty mash barrels.'

'They might get us going out,' Combs said. 'Maybe we ought to hide the load and pick it up later.'

'I don't dump five hundred dollars' worth of whiskey for some loggers to find. My boy's hid out on the ridge, and there ain't nobody getting into the holler without him seeing them first.'

The smoke from the dead fire collected behind the poplar branches over the entrance and hung in the air.

'I don't want to be around no more shooting,' Combs said. His body was twisted like a dwarf's in the shadows.

'Put the brace on the mule.'

'I ain't getting shot up again for all the whiskey in Kentucky.'

'You been paid for a full day's work and I expect to get it,' McGoffin said. 'I taken corn out of this hollow for thirty-five years and I ain't got shot yet. I reckon they know better than to draw a gun on a McGoffin. They do it once and I'll string fires all over their goddamn forest.'

Before the plane reached the end of the hollow it rolled

upwards and slipped sideways in the wind stream over the next ridge. The yellow wings flashed in the sun and then dipped out of sight beyond the timberline.

'Them federal men got scopes on their rifles. They could knock us down from a half mile,' Combs said.

'I'd say that would be a real mistake on their part.' McGoffin picked up a rifle leaning against the wall and slung it over his shoulder by the strap. It was an old bolt-action .30-.40 Kraig, with the box magazine on the right-hand side of the chamber.

'I still say dump the load. It ain't worth it,' Combs said.

'I put you on at the still because you couldn't get work any place else. Now if you ain't going to do what I say, you can get off the mountain and forget what you seen in here,' McGoffin said. 'I ain't got time to mess with you.'

'A man don't like to get shot up.'

'I can't hear the plane no more,' Perry said.

'Maybe he just let us think he didn't see us,' Combs said.

'That's right, or maybe he was taking a piss up there in a tin can and he wasn't looking down here at all. Get that goddamn jackass loaded. Perry, hide the thumping keg in them rocks across the creek.'

Perry pulled the bevelled wooden peg out of the bottom of the keg and drained the scalding water on the rock house floor; then he disconnected the arm from the cooker and lifted the keg up on his shoulder. The smell of distilled corn meal was strong in the air. He walked over the dead leaves, through the trees, to the creek bed. The light through the beeches and poplars was green on the forest floor, and the water was brown over the rocks in the stream. He put the keg between two limestone boulders, covered the crevice with branches and leaves, and then returned to the rock house.

Combs had laid two gunny sacks across the mule's back, and he set the pack brace over the sacks and pulled the cinch tight around the mule's belly. The mule drew air into his lungs to expand his body against the cinch, and McGoffin kicked him hard in the ribs. 'I ought to boil you down for glue, you sonofabitch,' he said.

'You don't want to move the cooker?' Perry said.

'Let them have it. It ain't worth a shit, no how. Pour the mash out and bury it with the sugar sacks. It won't look like nobody's made whiskey in here for months.'

Perry pulled the oak pinning loose from around the two mash barrels and kicked them over with his foot. The corn splattered out in a wet pile on the dirt and drained over the lip of the rock house floor into the hollow. His eyes burned from the smell. He took an army entrenching tool and threw most of the corn out into the undergrowth and covered the rest with earth. Then he folded up the shovel into the position of a hoe and chopped a hole in the ground to bury the sugar sacks. In the back of the cave was a squared poplar trunk, which loggers had hollowed out years ago to use as a trough for their animals. McGoffin had propped it under the flow from the limestone spring to collect water for the still. Perry flipped it over backwards with one hand and dragged it outside into some brush.

'I hear that plane again,' Combs said.

'You don't hear nothing,' McGoffin said. 'Grab up them cans and get them on the mule. We're a-running late now.'

Perry looked towards the top of the ridge near the entrance to the hollow for any sign from the old man's son.

'Boy, don't you think I got my eye on the same place?' McGoffin said. 'I'll be the first to tell you if there's anyone a-coming up from the river.'

They loaded the jerry cans of whiskey on the X-shaped wooden racks on the mule. The animal's legs splayed outward from the weight. They cleared the entrance of the branches and moved down the incline through the green shadows. Combs couldn't walk as fast as the others, and he held on to the mule's cinch.

'You can't see your boy now if he tries to warn us,' he said.

'He's got a shotgun pistol with him you can hear in the next county,' the old man said.

'We should have moved it out during the night,' Combs said.

'Go on back to the rock house and set there. The boy and me will take it out,' McGoffin said.

'I ain't said nothing about going back.'

'I know you ain't. But I'll leave you here if I hear any more from you.'

'It don't make sense moving it in full light.'

'Noah, I told you once already. I didn't go a-looking for you on this job. You knowed what you was hiring on for when you come to me.' The Kraig rifle was pressed flat on its sling against the old man's back.

They reached the creek bed and followed it downhill. In the heavy areas of shade there was moss on the rocks and lichen grew on the tree trunks. The breeze was cool through the shadows, and Perry could smell the dark, moist earth under the leaves. The mule tried to drink from the stream, and McGoffin jerked his head savagely with the reins. The incline became more steep and the hollow narrowed as they neared the entrance in the cliff wall. In the distance Perry saw the natural bridge in the mountain and the glow of the sun beyond it. On the top of the bridge was a Shawnee horse track, cut into rock, that pointed in the direction of John Swift's mine. The sunken marking, carved with flint tools, was as big as Perry's hand and three inches deep. Many times he had climbed to the top of the ridge, laid flat on the limestone ledge, and aimed a stick across the track towards every conceivable place on the opposite side of the hollow where the mine might have been. He knew that somewhere in the mountain a rock the size of a salt keg still lay plugged in the shaft opening, and beyond it were the remains of the men Swift had murdered.

'It ain't there. I'd have found it if it was,' McGoffin said. 'There ain't a place in this holler I don't know.'

'What are you talking about?' Perry said.

'Nothing, boy.'

'I got something better to do than chase after a mine nobody ever seen.'

'I reckon you do. It wouldn't hardly be worth a man's time to look for two hundred thousand dollars in silver.'

Perry's face reddened with embarrassment. 'Why ain't your son driving the load?' he said.

'Because every highway police between here and Michigan knows him. He got arrested once when he was driving his family to the ball game in Cincinnati.'

'I got to rest,' Combs said. His face was white, beaded with sweat, and his breath was laboured. He hung on to the side of the mule and wiped his forehead on his sleeve.

'We can't wait on you long,' McGoffin said. 'If you can't make it, you can set down here and walk out later.'

'I don't want to stay here. Give me a minute.'

'They can't put nothing on you for just being in the holler.'

'I wasn't expecting nothing when they caught me on that road in my car, neither. They opened up without giving no warning.' His wrist hung limply from his crooked arm. 'I was just at the top of the grade when I seen their rifles go off. Then the windshield broke and I felt the whole side of my face come half off.'

McGoffin's eyes strained through the trees towards the entrance to the hollow. His eyes were as grey and hard as shale under his white eyebrows.

'You ought to have let the union done its own dynamiting,' he said. 'What they done for you since you got shot up?'

'I don't hold that against them. They can't put a cripple man in the hole.'

'By God, they'd owe me something if I got my ass blowed off for them,' McGoffin said. 'Them union people up North cheats you out of as much money as the association does. They ain't in here because they like the way a miner smells. They make more money in a year than you do in a lifetime, without ever getting in the hole. I wouldn't give you a big mouthful of spit for the bunch of them.'

'We never got no wage till they organized the coal field,' Perry said. 'We couldn't get fifty cents an hour if it wasn't for the union.'

'What you got now?' McGoffin said. 'You can't work nowhere in Kentucky except scabbing. You're running whiskey and taking a chance on going to the pen for fifty dollars. Your daddy got his lungs crushed in over there in Virginia, and they never give him five cents for it. And I bet there ain't been no union people out to your mother's to see about taking care of them kids.'

'You ain't ever worked in the hole,' Combs said. 'You don't know nothing about the old days before the union, when we worked in gas without no fans.'

'I figure I got better sense than to get under the ground before my time, and I don't need nobody from up North to look after me.' He shifted the weight of the rifle on his back and stared out from under the down-turned brim of his hat towards the far end of the hollow. The dappled light through the trees caught in his stiff, white whiskers. 'We ain't got much time. Let's get it moving.'

'I ain't caught my breath,' Combs said.

'We can't hold up no longer. The plane might make another run on the holler, and we'll be setting here with our peckers hanging out.'

He slapped the mule against the flank and they moved off down the incline, the cans of whiskey banging against each other on the mule's sides. The blood had gone out of Combs' face from exertion. He hooked his hand inside the cinch again for support; then he let go and stumbled along behind them. Finally, he had to stop and prop himself against a tree trunk. There was a line of sweat down the front of his shirt.

'Maybe we ought to give him more time to rest,' Perry said.

'He ain't going to be in no trouble staying where he's at. Worry about yourself. If they catch us they'll put me back in Atlanta again, and they'll send you to the honour farm for a year.'

'They ain't getting me in no pen.'

'Keep dragging your ass because of Combs and you'll be a-working on them Forest Service trails with the happy-pappies, except you won't get no money for it and you won't go home at night.'

They reached the bottom of the hollow and started up a steep rise towards the entrance in the cliff walls. The opening was narrow and crooked through the mountain, and the rock sides rose up high above to the top of the ridge. The ground was worn bare and imprinted with mule and horse tracks. The sun never reached the bottom of the opening, and there was still a film of ice on the limestone. As they neared the top of the incline Perry looked back at the vastness of the hollow, the tall trunks of the trees, the hard line of cliffs against the sky, and the spray of mist over the waterfall at the base of the stream.

'Goddamn that sonofabitch! Here he comes again,' McGoffin said. 'Get that mule inside the cliff!'

Perry couldn't see the plane this time, but he heard the roar of the engine echo through the hollow. He picked up a knotted poplar branch from the ground and whipped it across the mule's scrotum.

'Someday when I ain't got nothing better to do I'm going to shoot one of them bastards down,' McGoffin said, yanking at the reins. The mule's hooves kicked dirt and leaves into the air.

Perry dug his boots into the soft earth and lunged uphill towards the crack in the mountain. He slipped on his face and grabbed on to some small bushes to pull himself erect.

'Hurry up! He's a-coming over the trees,' McGoffin said.

'He'll see Combs.'

'Shit on Combs. That pilot don't care about him. He's looking for somebody loaded down with whiskey.'

They led the mule back deep into the shadows between the cliff walls. The stone smelled cool and damp, and water dripped slowly down from the melting ice on to the ground. High above them they could see a long stretch of blue sky through the opening in the mountain. McGoffin turned one ear into the wind to listen for the plane while he filled the side of his mouth with loose-string Red Man chewing tobacco. He cleared his throat and spat.

'I don't know about you, but I got to drain the old pecker,' he said.

'Let's get on down to the car.'

'There ain't a better place to be than right here till that plane heads back to Winchester.' The old man urinated against a rock.

'Goddamn, he's flying right over the ridge. Where's your son at?'

'He's got a hole dug under a ledge. You ain't got to worry about him.'

'How did he get them three stretches in the pen?'

'He never done more than fifteen months, and that ain't bad for a man that run whiskey to Detroit over twenty years. Buddy, I tell you there ain't nothing better than a good piss.'

'Look back down the holler. Combs is still coming,' Perry said.

'I don't know which has caused me more trouble, him or this worthless shithog mule. I deserve to go back to Atlanta for hiring him. Get down, you dumb sonofabitch, before you bring them in on top of us!' he yelled at Combs.

'He can't hear you,' Perry said. Combs worked his way slowly up the incline and stared upwards at the plane.

'I have half a notion to shoot him and bury him right where he's at.'

'He's scared and he don't want to get left alone. His hands was shaking when we cleaned out the rock house. You can't hold it against him for being afraid after he got shot up like he did.'

'You goddamn right I can. I ain't got many years left, and I sure ain't a-spending them in jail because of somebody else screwing me up. They ain't going to do nothing to Combs because he's a cripple. He can walk out of court without even a fine, but by God they'll lay it on me and you. You hear me, Combs! Lay down on your face!'

'Here comes the plane,' Perry said.

'Get close against the wall. Look at the ground and don't move.' McGoffin pushed the mule flat against the cliff with his weight and held the rein close by the bit. The mule shuffled in the dirt and reared his head. The old man hit him in the head with his fist. 'Stay, you shithead, or I'll cut your balls out.'

They remained motionless in the blue shadows as the aircraft curved back out of the sky and flew low above the entrance. The noise from the engine was like the roar of a train between the cliff walls, and Perry thought he could feel the backwash of the propeller. After the sound decreased, he looked upwards and saw the plane bank at an angle against the clouds.

'I know he seen us then,' Perry said. 'He was flying sideways when he come over.'

'It don't matter if he did or not. In ten minutes that whiskey's going to be in the car with you on the way to Newport, and I'll be a-setting on the river with a cane pole in case anybody from the ABC wants to know how the fish are biting. Get it moving.'

'Maybe he'll make another run.'

'Piss on him. We been in this holler too long already. If we stay around any longer, that goddamn Combs will do something else, like set the woods on fire or climb up on the mountain so everybody from here to Virginia can see him.'

They led the mule through the narrow entrance towards the sunlight near the river. The breeze was cool from the river, and

Perry could see the green of the treetops on the slope that led down to the water. Heavy vines grew along the high portions of the cliff wall where the sun struck. On a flat outcropping above his head there was a deep crow's foot carved in the rock, weathered smooth at the edges, pointing back into the hollow. Perry rubbed his hand over it as he passed.

'It don't point to no mine, boy,' McGoffin said. 'I think them Shawnees had a jenny-barn back in a rock house somewhere, and they was just putting out their road signs.'

They came out of the gap between the cliffs and stared towards the river through the trees. The canopy overhead was much thinner than in the hollow, and the sunlight spangled on the cans of whiskey. Perry wished that he had taken sides with Combs and had argued for hiding the load until night. The tree trunks were spaced far apart, the ground was bare of undergrowth, and he knew they could be seen by anyone from a hundred yards. Their footsteps on the dead leaves were loud in the stillness of the forest.

'I hope your boy covered up the car good,' Perry said.

'You don't think he knows his business?'

'I didn't say that.'

'You see a car anywhere?'

'It's where we left it at, ain't it?'

'Look right straight in front of you about seventy-five yards and you'll see some beech branches laid over them two big boulders. If you can't see a car inside, you ain't got to worry about nobody else finding it.'

'You ain't told me yet where I drop the load at,' Perry said.

'You get off the interstate on the last street before the Ohio bridge and turn into the first filling station. There's a street map of Newport marked under the seat. When you get there you ain't got to say nothing to them. They know the car, and they'll take care of everything after that.'

'How much you pay a feller to drive it all the way to Detroit?'

'I don't have no one man ever make the whole run for me, any more. If a driver gets arrested after he leaves Newport, he don't have no idea what part of Kentucky that whiskey come from.'

'The police will trace the car right back to your son.'

'No, they won't, because it ain't got a number any place on the engine, and them plates come off a lot of different cars. Next week the boy will pick up his car and drive it back home empty with the right tags on it. We don't get as much money this way like we used to, but we don't run a big chance of going to the pen, neither.'

The incline became more steep, and the weight on the mule's back almost toppled him forward. Perry slid part way down the embankment to where the Chevrolet was hidden. The moisture on the great limestone boulders steamed faintly in the sun. The car had been backed between the two rocks and covered with branches and a large piece of army canvas camouflage. A federal agent would have had to walk right up on it to see the outline of the body under the leaves. Back through the trees Perry could see tire tracks on the ground; they ended where McGoffin's son had spread dead twigs and leaves over them.

'Clean it off and bring it out to load,' McGoffin said. He tied the mule to a tree and began lifting the heavy cans off the pack. The blood veins in his throat swelled as he worked.

Perry caught the canvas tarpaulin by one corner and pulled it off the car, then climbed up on one boulder and threw the branches off the roof. The sun reflected off the windscreen, and he looked up at the sky, waiting for the plane to reappear again over the crest of the mountain.

'Come on and get it out here!' McGoffin said. 'We ain't got time to screw around here. If they catch us, this is where they will do it. I ain't ever got busted in the holler before. I always got caught taking it out.'

Perry started the engine and drove the Chevrolet out from between the boulders. The twin exhausts roared when he touched the gas pedal just lightly. The car had a four-speed floor stick transmission, a new GMC motor with two carburettors, a modified cam, over-sized pistons, and a hot electric system. He had to keep the clutch depressed to stop the car from bolting forward.

The top portion of the back seat swung upwards on two metal springs, and the separating wall to the boot had been cut away. The lock on the boot had been deliberately smashed so that it couldn't be opened from the outside. Perry loaded the cans one by one into the car, distributed the weight evenly over the axle so the back end wouldn't sag noticeably, and replaced the seat. The day had grown warmer, and he began to perspire.

'You still reckon you can handle it?' McGoffin said.

'I'll tell you after you give me my fifty dollars.'

The old man took a wallet from inside the bib of his overalls and counted out the money with his thumb.

'It ain't much for the risk a man runs, but I don't get that much out of it myself after I cut with everybody between here and Detroit,' he said. 'I'd make it more if I could.'

'I ain't asking for no more than anybody else is a-getting.'

'There's a set of Ohio and Michigan plates stuck up under the dashboard. Tell them boys at the filling station I want them Kentucky tags off before they cross the river.'

'Does anybody at the toll station know this car?'

'You don't need to go through no toll station. Stay on the county road along the river and go up to Winchester through Boonesborough. I ain't got much else to tell you, except I seen you put that pistol under the seat this morning.'

'What's that go to do with anything?'

'My boy's got twenty-five hundred dollars in that car, and he don't want no holes in it. I don't want to see no holes in you, neither. If the ABC starts chasing you, pull over and let them take the load. Don't get shot for no corn whiskey that we can run off any time we got a mind to.'

'I ain't got that gun to shoot at the ABC.'

'I reckon I know what you got it for. I heered about the sheriff picking you up in front of the operator's office. That's your business and it don't concern me, even though I figure you got the right to get back at them men that killed Woodson. But I don't want you pulling no gun on a man while you're working for me.'

'The sun's over the mountain. Them log crews will be in here soon,' Perry said. 'I got to get moving.'

'All right, boy. Just make sure that pistol stays where it's at.'

Perry drove the Chevrolet out through the trees, avoiding the rocks and dead logs, and shifted into second gear as he started down the last part of the incline that led to the dirt road running along the river. The weight in the boot caused the car to hit high-centre several times. The trees began to thin, and he could see the river flowing green along its banks. Next to him on the seat was his canvas Job Corps overnight bag, packed with a change of clothes, two fried pork chops with bread, and a box of .22 magnum shells. The car bounced over the last of the incline on to the smooth, bare area by the river, and he floored the accelerator and headed down the dirt lane, with the exhaust pipes roaring.

Once on the blacktop, he shifted into fourth gear and passed every car he met. The sun was bright on the green meadows and mountaintops, and he let the wind rush through the window full into his face. The new tobacco in the fields had grown several inches high, and the farmers had strung cheesecloth across it on wooden stakes, to protect the plants from rain and occasional sleet. The air was sweet with the smell of spring, and in the distance he could see the mountains roll away and gradually become smaller near the edge of the Cumberland plateau. The light from the east cast dark shadows in the valleys, and the trees looked blue when the clouds passed overhead. His ears began to pop from the change in altitude, and he shifted down to third gear as the road sloped off towards the level country below the mountains.

He crossed the Kentucky River at Boonesborough. He looked through the spars of the great metal bridge and saw motor boats churning white wakes in the current far below; and people in wet bathing suits lay on the stretch of sandy beach by the water. Somewhere on the mountain high above were the rotted remains of Daniel Boone's fort, which he had built to protect the first white settlers from the terrible attacks of the Shawnee. Ahead was the even, rolling land of the bluegrass country. The road was lined with stone fences that had been built without mortar by slaves when they cleared the fields before the Civil War. The earth was rich here, and the grass was tall with a blue-green tint to it. Perry had never seen this area of Kentucky before. The streams were clear, there was no garbage on the hillsides, the stands of timber were untouched by the strip and auger mines, and the farmhouses were painted, the barns filled with hay, the gardens planted with mimosa trees and rose bushes, and in the fields there were fine race horses and rows of white beehives. He wondered how any man could have enough money to buy land like this, where tobacco paid two thousand dollars an acre and corn grew to seven feet within half the season.

A feller could work and save his money all his life and not be able to buy nothing like that, he thought. You don't get things like that for your sweat. They got it by stealing it from the Indians, and they held on to it by cheating other people out of their money and paying a man hardly nothing for planting and cutting their tobacco. A feller don't ever get anything worth keeping for the work he does. You don't have the chance to even get ahead of the charge at the store. You get this kind of land when you're smart enough to make other people work for you so they can pay their wage right back into your pocket. Them Northern mining companies knowed what they was doing when they come into the Cumberland.

Perry followed the narrow blacktop through the low green hills into Winchester. It was Saturday, and the streets were crowded with cars and people. Winchester was the only wet town on the edge of the plateau besides Mount Sterling and Richmond, and the bars and pool rooms were filled with men from the mountains, in overalls and tattered bluejeans, who had driven their junker automobiles over the twisting roads to drink, fight over three-dollar whores, and eventually pass out in a drunken stupor behind a tavern Sunday morning. There were several uniformed police-men directing traffic through the centre of town, and Perry felt drops of perspiration begin to form on his forehead and upper lip as he moved slowly through the line of cars. The engine idled too fast, and the Chevrolet's twin exhausts sounded like straight pipes off a diesel truck. He had no driver's licence, and if a policeman stopped him to check for a defective silencer, he knew he would be taken to jail and the car would be recognized as a transporter's and searched. He wiped the moisture off his brow into his hair with his palm. The traffic began to lessen after he had passed through the downtown area, and as he went by the last policeman on the stretch of road leading to the highway he depressed the clutch and let off the accelerator to deaden the roar through the exhaust pipes. He coasted as far as he could until he was sure he was out of the policeman's earshot, then he shoved the floor stick into second gear and pushed the gas pedal to the floor. The Chevrolet rocked back against its springs, the tires burning rubber, the front end uplifted, the two four-barrelled carburettors sucking air, and tore down the highway with the fence posts and telephone poles racing by like an accelerated film strip.

He got back on to the four-lane interstate and rolled towards Lexington. The engine hummed under the hood, the cool wind streamed through the window, and he rested one hand lightly on top of the steering wheel as the road signs flashed by. He'd had nothing for breakfast except coffee before dawn in the rock house, and he ate one of the fried pork chops and a piece of bread. Ahead, there was a car parked under the overpass, with the boot up and a spare tyre resting against the back bumper. He braked the Chevrolet slowly until he was under the speed limit, and as he went through the underpass he saw the police officer behind the wheel of the highway patrol car and the red light on top that was concealed by the open boot.

Perry reached the outskirts of Lexington by noon, and he turned north towards Cincinnati. On both sides of the road, racehorse farms stretched back over the blue meadows into the hills. The fences were white, the barns made of stone, and the stables were as big as two-storey houses. Shiny black horses that took up to twenty thousand dollars for a stud fee stood in the fields, and huge ante-bellum homes were set back in groves of oak trees. Negroes were grooming and shoeing thoroughbreds outside the stables, and Perry saw a woman in strange riding clothes and a peaked cap posting on a mare around a training track. He didn't know names like 'Spendthrift' or 'Calumet Farm' or 'Keeneland', and he had never seen anything that approached this type of wealth. The breeding barns were better than any house on the Cumberland plateau, and the money from the whiskey in his car couldn't even buy the paint on one of those big, columned plantation homes.

He entered the southern tip of the Ohio Valley, and gradually the land began to flatten on each side of the highway. The horse farms became small in the distance behind him, and now there were neat farms planted with corn, man-made brown lakes dug for irrigation, small clumps of locust trees on the rises, and grey outcroppings of limestone where the highway cut through the low hills. The wind was strong here, and it rippled the lakes in heavy gusts and buffeted his automobile. The sky was cloudless, and the young green leaves on the corn bent back against the wind. The grass in the fields still had a blue tint to it, and it waved back and forth as far as the eye could see.

The smell of spring and the soft haze of the sun on the meadows made Perry sleepy; then in the rearview mirror he noticed that a new Plymouth had stayed behind him for the last several miles. Slowly, he accelerated and increased his speed by ten miles an hour; the Plymouth did the same. He let off the gas, the silencers rumbling with the back exhaust, and watched the other car slow, also. In the mirror he could see two men in hats behind the Plymouth's windscreen. It ain't only the fellers at the filling station that know this car, he thought. The ABC's probably seen it through here so many times they don't even need to stop it to know what it's carrying.

He stayed at the same speed for the next fifteen miles, and the Plymouth kept at a distance behind him. The highway was being repaired near Cincinnati, and a flagman stopped the line of cars while a bulldozer moved a load of earth over the embankment. The traffic forced the Plymouth to pull almost abreast of Perry, and he turned and looked at the two men inside. They kept their faces forward, unconcerned, and one of them lighted a cigarette casually; but Perry saw the small pin aerial for the mobile radio on the back bumper. They're a-following me in till I make the drop, he thought. They figure to hit me at the filling station and get the other transporter and the still, too. Well, buddy, I hope you got a hot engine in that thing, because I ain't playing your kind of baseball game. While he waited for the flagman to release the line of cars he spread the road map out with one hand on the seat beside him and looked for the next exit before Newport.

Ten miles before the Ohio River he began to pass cars and put as many as possible between him and the Plymouth; then he saw the Erlanger exit sign and floored the gas pedal. In his mirror he could see the Plymouth weaving through the traffic that was bunching up for the one-lane crossing over the Ohio bridge. The

Chevrolet's tyres screamed as Perry went into the exit at seventy miles an hour. He shifted down, popped the clutch out, and hit the brakes momentarily just before he reached the stop sign, skidding sideways; then he double-clutched into second and burned across the intersection. An old truck stopped suddenly to let him pass, and a car slammed into its rear end, and for an instant Perry saw several pedestrians leap back to the curb, their mouths open and their eyes wide. The rows of brick homes, trees, and yards whipped by him, and people watering their grass and working in flower beds looked up quickly at him as his exhaust pipes echoed off the house fronts. He braked at the end of the street, cut a sharp right turn, the back end fishtailing with the weight of the whiskey, and shoved the gear stick into third.

He drove fifty miles an hour down the side street, running three stop signs, and he almost tore the door off a parked car. They'll wield that jailhouse shut on me if they catch me now, he thought. But by God they're going to earn their money before they get me there. He let the engine wind down against the transmission and cut into a narrow alley between two rows of houses. One bumper hit a rubbish bin and smashed it flat against the garage. An old Negro ragpicker, rooting through some cardboard boxes, jumped out of the way of the car as it passed. Perry bounced out of the alley and turned up another street, reducing his speed slowly. He knew that somebody had probably already called the city police after he had roared through this quiet neighbourhood section of town, and every patrol car in the area probably had his licence number and a description of the Chevrolet. He cut around several corners in a row, staying under the speed limit, and drove back towards the feeder lanes near the interstate highway.

Before he reached the entrance to the four-lane, he turned into a filling station and pulled his car into the empty grease rack. Now they can look up and down the road for me till their eyes cross, he thought. A fat attendant in a stained blue uniform with a lacquered-brim cap on his head and dirty rags in his pockets came out of the office.

'There's another car ahead of you. I was just going to bring it in,' he said.

'I don't want nothing but a grease job. It ain't going to take you ten minutes,' Perry said. Before the attendant could answer, Perry got under the Chevrolet and set the iron braces on the rack into place.

'That engine smells like it's burning,' the attendant said.

'The fan belt's slipping. You got a screwdriver? I ain't put on my new Ohio plates yet.'

'I think we have a fan belt that will fit it.'

'I ain't got time for that. Run it up on the rack,' Perry said. He reached under the dashboard and pulled out the Ohio licence plates.

'I'd put a new belt on it if I was you. There's steam whistling out of your radiator now.'

'Just give me the screwdriver.' Perry looked out through the gas pumps at the flow of traffic in the street. He saw the two men from the ABC cruise slowly past in the Plymouth. The driver was speaking into the microphone of his radio. Perry pulled his cap down over his eyes and turned his back. The attendant pushed down the hydraulic lever and raised the Chevrolet on the rack while the air compressor in the back of the station laboured from the pressure.

'You got them new kind of sliding doors. We don't see many of them back home,' Perry said. He pulled down the door part way, until it covered the back of the car from view.

'Open the door. It's too hot in here as it is.'

'It's stuck. Maybe you better do it.' Perry watched the Plymouth turn on to the entrance ramp of the highway and head back south towards Lexington.

He put the Ohio tags on his car and threw his Kentucky plate into a rubbish bin; then he rolled cigarettes, and smoked while he waited for the attendant to finish. In the next half hour two city police cars passed, but the men inside seemed unconcerned about anything, their arms resting easily in the open windows, and Perry knew they had probably stopped looking for him.

'You must have a big load in that boot the way it's sagging,' the attendant said.

'I'm hauling a load of bricks for a feller. You done with it yet?'

'Yeah, but you better watch that engine. I could feel the heat coming right through the oil pan.'

'I got to worry about that for only ten more miles, then it can catch fire and burn on down to the ground,' Perry said.

After he paid the attendant, he backed his car off the grease rack, shifted into first gear, and drove on to the interstate towards Newport. Great silver planes approaching the airfield came in slowly at a downward angle over the highway, the sun white on their wings, and fine hotels and restaurants sat up high on the hillsides. Billboard signs advertising German beer and Kentucky whiskey stood along the road, and cars were strung out in a long line before the Ohio bridge. He could see small, suburban towns with neat houses and green lawns and chestnut trees, and there were no clapboard shacks, log outbuildings, or wrecked cars piled one on top of another in dirty vacant lots.

The traffic began to slow as he went over a rise, and then through a cut in the hill he saw the wide sweep of the Ohio bridge, the long stretch of blue river winding through the green slopes, and the broken skyline of Cincinnati high above the valley. Along the riverbank, in the old section of town, narrow, brick German buildings, with chimneys on each side, stood in rows, pressed tightly together, almost like squeezed cardboard structures, and trees grew along every city block. On the hills above town there were more nineteenth-century European-style brick homes, with wood verandahs, set back in the oaks and poplars. Below the bridge a huge, white paddle-wheel boat churned down the river, the decks covered with people in canvas chairs, and the two, scrolled metal smoke stacks trailed off dark clouds in the wind. In the distance Perry saw the grandstands at Crosley Field, where the Reds were playing the Dodgers that weekend, and the white concrete ramps and overpasses were loaded with cars going into the ball game. The girders and spars of the bridge were like etched grey lines against the blue above the skyline, and wisps of torn clouds hung on the far horizon in the opulent green haze of the Ohio Valley.

Someday he would live here, after he had taken care of everything back home, he thought. He would get out of the coal fields, find a job that paid a living wage, and he would walk down those wide, tree-lined boulevards after work in the spring evening in a fresh pair of ironed khakis and a denim shirt and with a paycheck in his back pocket. It would just take time. Then he'd meet Popcorn at the ball game and they would crawl home on their elbows.

Just before the bridge he turned off the interstate into Newport, a dirty, run-down working-class area on the Kentucky side of the river. The old German buildings had turned into slum tenements, the streets were often littered with newspaper and beer cans, and there were rows of dingy bars and pool halls in which gambling, narcotics and prostitution were not recognized by the local police. There was supposed to be no liquor sold on Sundays or after two in the morning in that area of Kentucky, but the law hadn't been enforced in so long that it was considered a joke. Men, who looked much like people in the hills, stood on street corners, and there were dour women with dyed hair and big handbags in front of the bars. Most of the cars parked along the kerb had licence plates from counties back on the plateau, and the town itself was as grimed and depressed-looking as Harlan or Hazard.

Perry found the filling station where McGoffin had described it. He pulled around the side of the building and saw the attendant look up at the car over his newspaper through the window in the office. Perry took the pistol from under the seat and zippered it up inside his overnight bag. The attendant came out the side door, with a thin cigar stub in a gap between his teeth. His hair was long and covered with grease, and the skin on one side of his lower jaw was drawn and puckered where part of the bone was gone. His pinstriped uniform was frayed at the cuffs and sleeves, and his T-shirt was covered with dirt under his throat. His eyes were expressionless, but Perry could feel them examining him.

'What do you need?' he said, taking the cigar out of his mouth to spit.

'I thought I'd leave it with you.'

'Come back tomorrow if you want it serviced. I can't get to it today.'

'I was told to drop it here. I reckon you know what I'm talking about.'

'No, I don't mister.'

'Listen, I ain't got time for this. The other plates is under the dash.'

'You must be looking for somebody else.'

'I'm working for old man McGoffin. Does that name mean something to you?'

'What's he do?'

Perry picked up his canvas bag and got out of the car.

'I don't know who you was expecting to see, but I ain't waiting around here no more,' he said. 'I had people after me most of the way from Lexington, and I reckon it's somebody else's turn to play games with them. I done my part of the bargain, and I don't give a goddamn if you roll that car into the river.'

'Take it easy and come inside.' Perry followed him into the office, which was stacked with tyres and cases of empty pop bottles. 'What's this McGoffin look like?'

'I told you I didn't have time to waste here.'

'You don't have a private aircraft or something waiting on you, do you?' The attendant's mouth spread back over his bad teeth.

'He's got two heads and a hump on his back. What the hell do you think he looks like?'

'OK. Don't get pissed off. We just got to be careful. The ABC busted a transporter a few weeks ago and put one of their own men in the car. They arrested five guys over in Covington. Where did they spot you?'

'They followed me to Erlanger, and then I outrun them.'

'You sure you don't have a tail on you?'

'They never seen me after I cut off the highway, but I wouldn't move that stuff for a few days.'

Outside, another man from the station drove the Chevrolet into a tin garage in the back.

'We'll handle all that. Just forget you ever been in this filling station.'

'Buddy, I already forgot what you look like,' Perry said, and went out the door with his bag in his hand.

He walked down the street past the rows of honky-tonks and dollar-a-night flophouses. He felt good leaving the car, the jerry cans of rank-smelling whiskey, and the worries about the ABC behind him. He hadn't slept at all the night before, and the events of the last two days wouldn't stay straight in his head. His mind was tired, and it seemed like weeks ago that he had moved the whiskey downhill with McGoffin while the plane swept by overhead and Noah Combs toiled along behind them with his stiff, crippled movements. On the corner there was a barbecue stand and draught beer parlour, and his empty stomach ached when he smelled the hot sauce on the smoked pork and saw a waitress drawing cold mugs of beer for working men, with plates of ribs and links before them. He wanted to go inside and eat the buttered pieces of garlic bread and rare beef and wash it down with glass after glass of beer; but he had risked too many things for the money in his pocket to spend it on himself, and he still had feelings of guilt for getting drunk on part of his Job Corps savings after he bought the pistol.

The bridge across the river was high above his head, and he started up the steep, cobbled street that led to the walkway along the interstate. The day was warm now, and he took off his army field jacket with the big pockets and slung it over his shoulder. He could still smell the cooking in the barbecue stand, and he wanted to stop and eat the remaining pork chop and slice of bread in his overnight bag, but he would have nothing left for the trip back home. Cars going to the ball game were jammed along the entrance to the four-lane highway, and a Negro police officer stood in the middle of the intersection directing traffic. Perry walked out into the centre of the street and stood beside him.

'Where's a feller get a bus back to Richmond?' he said.

The policeman had a whistle clenched in his mouth, and his eyes were intent upon the cars.

'I want to get back home. Where do I catch a bus at?'

'Richmond where?' the Negro said, his face still turned towards the traffic and his hands gesturing rapidly in the air.

'Kentucky. There ain't no other except over in Virginia.'

'I never heard of it. Get out of the street before you get hit. Go ask somebody at the depot in Cincinnati.'

Perry started across the bridge, and his head swam when he

looked down at the water far below him. He could hear the wind sing in the girders and cables above him, and the long stretch of the bridge seemed to sway under his feet. He wondered how men could ever build something this wonderful and big across such a great span of water. Green and white eddies boiled around the concrete foundations below, and he could feel the force of the river vibrate through the handrail along the walkway. The skyline of Cincinnati loomed up even higher than before. The buildings looked as tall against the clouds as the top ridge of the Cumberland mountains, and there were restaurants that served food from all over the world, arbours of chestnut trees around newsstands, a big recreation park with Ferris wheels and roller coasters on the beach by the river, and the breeze through the valley had the smell of new grass and the first spring flowers.

For a moment he thought of forgetting the bus depot. He had almost fifty dollars in his wallet, and that would be enough until he could find some type of job. He could rent a room and find a job parking cars, working in a service station, or doing common labour out of the sweatshops. There was no work at all now back on the plateau, and his family would be better off if he stayed in the city and sent them part of his paycheque. There would be no J.W.s to worry about, no long evenings in the cabin while his mother stared blankly at the fire, and no more quiet hatred or that anticipation of sudden violence when he stood next to a scab or a company man on a street corner.

NINE

The bus trip back home that night took seven hours, and Perry was not able to go to sleep until just before daylight, when the sun broke above the mountains and shone directly into his face through the window. His body felt thick with fatigue and his face was lined and pale. In the Richmond depot he put his head under the tap and let the cold water splash over him.

The morning was cool as he walked out to the highway, and the air smelled clean after the seven hours in the bus. He caught a ride on the back of a flatbed truck into the next county, where he lived, and he lay back on the metal floor, put his canvas bag under his head, and watched the strips of cloud stream by overhead. He felt the hard outline of the pistol through the canvas, and he sat upright when he remembered that all six chambers in the cylinder were loaded. The truck climbed higher into the mountains, and the sun began to grow warm on the limestone cliffs. The narrow road wound through the hollows, crossed streams on one-lane wooden bridges, and eventually reached the crest of the plateau. As the truck pulled into the county seat, Perry banged on the cab with his fist and dropped off the back.

It was Sunday, the pool halls and taverns were closed, and the streets were almost deserted except for a few families dressed in their best clothes walking towards the clapboard Church of God building on the hill. The sound of singing and organ music was faint in the distance. The sheriff was opening the door to the sandstone jail, and the drunks who had been arrested the night before were crowded around the steel bars. They stumbled out into the bright sunlight, their faces drawn from hangovers. One man still couldn't walk straight, and the sheriff turned him around by one arm and walked him back into the jail.

Perry started across the street, then he heard the sheriff's voice behind him: 'Hold on a minute. I want to talk with you.'

He waited while the sheriff crossed the lawn towards him. He felt uneasy about the revolver in his bag, and he set it down by his foot and rolled a cigarette. The sheriff's great weight made him walk with his legs spread apart slightly, and although the day was still cool, his face was flushed as though he had been working under the summer sun.

'I got to get back to the house,' Perry said.

'A minute of your time ain't going to hurt you none. Noah Combs got drunk in town last night and I had to drive him home.'

Perry folded the cigarette paper around the tobacco and licked the glue on the edge.

'He was talking about a lot of things that he probably don't remember this morning,' the sheriff said.

'That ain't got nothing to do with me.'

'It does if you're a-working for old man McGoffin.'

'I ain't working for nobody.'

'Combs said some whiskey got moved yesterday and you was the transporter.'

'You don't see me driving no car, do you? I ain't even got a driver's licence.'

'You reckon fifty dollars is worth going to jail for?'

'I can't tell you nothing about what Combs told you. I been looking for a job in Lexington.'

'And you didn't happen to drop off a load of whiskey while you was at it?'

'If you're sure I been working with Combs and old man McGoffin, why ain't they in jail?'

'I know McGoffin's got a still somewhere in that holler, and I know that half the moonshine in this county comes out of it. If I was set on arresting him, I could do it without much trouble. But I figure the ABC gets paid for that sort of thing, and I got enough to do without having to sleep all night in a rock house to put an old man and a cripple in jail.'

'I got to go now. There's a feller up the street I can get a ride home with.'

'You wait till I'm finished. The ABC or them federal people ain't going to just talk with you. They don't care what happens to your family if you get put away in Atlanta. It don't mean five cents different to their paycheque. Or if they got to put a couple of holes in you, they'll do it faster than you can spit, because enough of their people have got shot down around here to make them a little nervous when they walk up on a still.'

'Tell me where you expect a man to get any money today? The association's got us locked out of all their mines, and there's a picket in front of all the independents'. The tobacco won't be ready to cut till the end of summer, and the Forest Service ain't a-hiring because the happy-pappies is doing all the trail work.'

'You can get on the welfare. There's plenty of people drawing it now.'

'My family ain't. You ever knowed my daddy to line up at that welfare office?'

'Sometimes you ain't got a choice about things, Perry.'

'By God, I still do. We can take care of ourselves without no help from anybody else.'

'There ain't much use in trying to talk with you, is there?' the sheriff said. 'You can't understand nothing outside of what you've got made up in your own mind. Get in my car and I'll drive you home.'

'Thank you. I feel like walking.'

'All seven miles. Just because you're so damn fond of walking,' the sheriff said.

Perry flicked the stub of his cigarette into the street, picked up his canvas bag, and slung his army field jacket over his shoulder. He didn't think that he had ever been so tired before, not even after working two straight eight-hour shifts in the mine. His back and neck were stiff from trying to sleep on the bus, and his legs felt weak and awkward, as though he had been standing in one position a long time. He walked to the edge of town and started up the rural road that led to his ridge. There had been a shower the night before, and the hardwoods in the forest had taken on a deeper green and blue. Two miles up the road his legs began to ache, and he sat down in a grove of maple trees that overlooked a deep chasm below. The sun had moved into the south, and it shone down through the trees and spangled the ground with areas of light and shadow. He lay down on the cool grass, his jacket under his head, and watched the squirrels racing across the limbs overhead. The light began to diffuse through the leaves, and in moments he was asleep.

In his dreams he saw the man on the coal tipple again. He was framed against the black horizon, his face transfixed in terror and his skin white as bone, then Big J.W. started the car engine, the spark jumped through the cap wire, and once more the flame and smoke exploded across the face of the mountain. The screaming continued in Perry's mind until he rolled his face down in the grass. Then he was standing on a street corner in town in the violet twilight just before dark. The air was hot and still, and even the pavements radiated heat. The billiard balls clicking together in the pool hall sounded metallic in the dry air, then the door crashed open and the three men who had murdered his father walked out on to the street. Each of their faces looked alike, twisted and sallow, the teeth rotted, eyes with the insane glimmer of chipped glass. He felt the heavy weight and even balance of the pistol in his palm. He put his thumb over the hammer, cocked it into place, and aimed at the face of the first man. None of them seemed to pay any attention to him. 'I'm Woodson James' boy and I'm putting you in hell tonight,' he said. Still they took no notice of him. He steadied the revolver, the metal cool in his hand, and fired directly into the first man's face. The explosion of the magnum shell was deafening, and the recoil kicked his forearm upwards. Then he cocked the action again and fired shot after shot into their faces. He smelled the burnt gunpowder, and the blue smoke drifted in a haze before his eyes; and he knew that the hollow-point shells had ripped through the flesh and bone of those awful faces and he would never have to look at them again. But when the smoke cleared, he saw them grinning at him obscenely. He chucked the empty hulls out on the pavement with the ejection rod and began pushing in fresh cartridges through the loading gate. The three men started laughing at him, at first slowly, their faces creasing like dry paper, then they roared, tears came down their cheeks, and they had to hold their sides. 'Boy, you don't know when to leave things alone,' one of them said. 'We might have to cut out your balls now.'

Perry awoke suddenly. He was sweating, his hair was matted with grass and twigs, and he saw that his hand was clenched on the revolver through the canvas bag. At first he wasn't sure where he was, and he looked about him for the three men, the pavements and dirty buildings, and kept thinking that it should have still been twilight. Slowly things became fixed in his head, and he realized that he was on a ridge overlooking a huge hollow where spring was in full flower and squirrels raced through the new maple leaves.

He walked another mile up the road before he caught a ride the rest of the way home. There was a new car parked at the bottom of the hill below his cabin. At first Perry thought someone from the mining company was on the ridge again to collect back rent or credit bills at the store, but then he saw the official licence plate on the back. He walked up the crooked dirt trail through the litter of rusted cans, unmoulded feed sacks and broken glass. The ABC got on to me somehow, he thought. They must have hit the filling station after I left or maybe they got old man McGoffin. But they still can't put nothing on me. They got to catch a feller with the whiskey before they can put him in jail.

Two of his younger brothers, both barefoot and in overalls, ran around the side of the cabin. Their hands and faces were covered with dirt, and their long hair hung over their eyes. Even though they were over a year apart, they looked enough alike to be twins. Their straw-coloured hair, the same texture and shade as Perry's, had started to bleach from the sun.

'Why they got to go, Perry?'

'Who?'

'They're a-taking Irvin, Mae and Collie.'

'What are you talking about?'

'Mama says they got to go somewhere in Richmond.'

'You ain't making no sense. Get in the house,' Perry said.

'Mama won't let us come in till them people leave.'

'What people's in there?'

'I don't know. Let go of my arm.'

'Where do they come from?'

'Richmond, I reckon. Turn loose of me.'

Perry crossed the porch and opened the battered screen door. Inside, he saw Irvin and two of his sisters eating quietly at the table, their faces turned down into their plates. They were dressed in their best clothes, which their mother never put on them except to go to the Church of God meeting once or twice a month. A man and woman whom Perry had never seen before sat uncomfortably in the wooden chairs, shifting their weight occasionally against the stiff boards. Perry felt the instinctive distrust towards these people that he felt for all strangers. Also, their clothes were expensive, they were too out of place in his cabin, and he knew that they were there for some reason that would cause trouble for his family. Few people from outside the county ever came on to the ridge unless they represented the law, the association or a finance company. The man was thin, balding across the top of his head, and the clip-on bowtie he wore didn't match his tweed coat. There was a business satchel by his foot. The woman was in her fifties, with a blue tint to her grey hair, and her chest swelled out like a robin's against her blue suit.

Mrs James took a pot from the wood stove and ladled spoonfuls of grits on to the children's plates. Her face was tired, and there was a lacklustre quality in her eyes.

'This is Mrs Lester and Mr Call, son,' she said. Her eyes didn't meet Perry's. 'They come up from Richmond.'

The man rose to shake hands and the woman smiled pleasantly, but Perry did not look in their direction.

'What's this about somebody a-taking Irvin and the girls away?' he said.

'Set down at the table and I'll get your dinner.'

'I ain't hungry.'

'You didn't have nothing to take with you except them two pork chops.'

'Why ain't Irvin and the girls outside playing with the rest of them?' he said.

'These people come from the welfare, and they got a home where the children will get taken care of like they should.' She looked at the table and bit her lower lip.

'The programme can be a pretty good deal for kids,' Mr Call said.

'I ain't talking to you.'

'It's a good home, Perry,' Mrs James said. 'The children get the food they need, and they got doctors to take care of them.'

'We don't need no welfare people.'

'I don't think you'd feel so badly about this if you saw our home,' Mrs Lester said.

'I got no plans about seeing it, and my brother and sisters ain't going to see it, either. So you all can get in your car and head right back to Richmond.'

'It ain't right to talk like that to people in our house,' Mrs James said.

'They ain't got to stay.'

'We don't treat people that way in this house.'

'You can't support all these children without a job,' Mrs Lester said.

'I got fifty dollars, and the Job Corps still owes me money.'

'Would you like to go back to the Job Corps?' the man asked.

'You ain't got to do nothing for me. If I want to go back, all I got to do is call the camp collect and my ticket will be in the next mail.'

'What are you going to do when your money is gone?' the man said.

Perry sat down in a chair by the table and rolled a cigarette between his fingers. He felt the fatigue rush through his body. 'I can't see how that's any of your business, mister.'

'We'd like to help your family, if you'll let us,' Mrs Lester said. 'Our programme can make things a little better for your mother as well as the children.'

'I don't reckon you been a-listening to anything I said. This family's staying together, and you burned up a few gallons of petrol for nothing.'

'We're not trying to break up your family,' the woman said. 'You can visit the children whenever you want, and it won't be long before you'll be able to take them back.'

'You think your money lets you come in here and tell us we got to change our lives. You all don't like setting in a cabin like this for even ten minutes. You ain't ever lived in a house that didn't cost less than ten thousand dollars, but you figure you got the right to make us live like you want.'

'I won't let you talk like that no more, Perry,' his mother said.

'I ain't going to have to, because they're a-leaving.' He popped a kitchen match on his thumbnail and lighted his cigarette.

'Do you know Irvin needs to be in a hospital? He might have active tuberculosis, and every one of you has been exposed to it,' Mr Call said.

'If you people are so goddamn charity minded, why ain't you ever done anything for him before?'

'Because we don't always have the facilities we need, but I guarantee you that boy will receive treatment,' the man said.

'There ain't a hospital on the plateau where he can get taken care of,' Perry said.

'We have places in Lexington,' Mrs Lester said.

'I'll be the one to take him if he needs it. Now, I'm through talking with you.'

'I'm afraid you're not,' Mr Call said. The blue veins in his temples pulsed as he pulled some papers from his business satchel. 'I don't like to use this, but we have your mother's signed permission to take the children to our home, and she's the only legal adult in this house.'

Mrs James lowered her eyes to the floor and clenched her hands until the fingernails made white marks against her palms. Perry stared at her.

'You done this?' he said.

'I don't reckon we got much choice, son. There ain't enough to eat for all the children, and I don't look for things to get much better.'

'The mines will open up sooner or later, and the union says after we get an election they'll raise our wage,' he said. 'It ain't like I'm always going to be out of work.'

'I've heered the same thing for twenty-five years, and it ain't ever got better. At least when Woodson was alive we had his happy-pappy money, but we ain't even got that now.'

'Bee Hatfield said a man's coming down from Washington in two weeks, and they're going to make the mines open up. There won't be no more strikes and the association can't lock us out. With all them empty coal cars lined up on the spurs, we'll be a-working overtime every evening.'

'Bee don't know nothing but what other people tell him, and he don't hear that right half the time,' she said. 'Even if the mines open, you'll spend more time on the picket than in the hole. I seen it too many years. The union never done nothing for your daddy, and it ain't going to do nothing for us now, except take part of your wage.'

'By God, they still ain't taking the kids,' Perry said. 'Mister, that paper in your hand don't mean nothing to me. Stick it back in your satchel and get on down the road.'

'Perry, I can't set still no more for that kind of talk,' his mother said.

'Look at the kids. You think they want to leave?'

'These things are hard, but your brother and two sisters will be better off for it,' Mr Call said.

'Go on and get out of here. I ain't telling you again.'

'You don't have this right,' Mr Call said.

'Yes sir, I do. Now see how fast you can drive down that ridge.'

'I'm going to leave because Mrs Lester is with me, but I'll be back later.'

'You ain't going to get in this house again, and you can study on that all the way back to Richmond.'

Later, after Perry had watched the two people step gingerly down the steep incline towards their car, he sat on the porch in the sunlight and smoked another cigarette. In the distance the dust from the automobile hung in the air above the ridge. Far off in the hollow the trunks of the birch trees were white against the green hillside. Farther down the road a family from the bottom of the mountain walked towards their home, built of boxes, logs and tar paper. The man was in the lead, and his wife and five children were in single file behind him. The woman's back was stooped, and the children were dressed in clothes made from feed sacks or cut-down denims. They lived in a settlement called Rachel's Hollow, where no one was sure who held title to the land and the men all made their living by moonshining, bootlegging or stealing parts of automobiles and farm machinery. People from North Carolina, West Virginia and Tennessee who were usually wanted by the law moved in and out of the cabins regularly, and because shootings were common in that hollow, the sheriff and the ABC seldom went into it. Them welfare people ought to take their goddamn charity down there, Perry thought. Except they'd get their tyres cut to pieces and maybe get throwed in the honey hole, besides.

His mother opened the screen door and set a plate of grits and a piece of ham next to him without speaking.

'I'm sorry for cussing in front of you and the kids,' he said.

She wiped her hands on her dress and started to go back inside.

'It's just I ain't got no use for them kind of people,' he said. 'They look down on us, and they don't have no more real feeling for the kids than they do a dog they feed on their back porch.'

'You reckon it's easy for me to let my own children go?' she said.

'You wouldn't have signed them papers unless they talked you into it.'

'I can't look at them every day and know there ain't enough to feed them. A person don't have the right to keep children when things is like that.'

'It ain't ever going to be so bad that we got to give part of our family away.'

'You can't hold back what's got to happen, son. We just wasn't meant to have things go like we want them to.'

'There ain't nothing going to happen, at least not from the likes of them people.'

But one hour later the deputy sheriff's old sedan sped up the ridge with the shale flying from under the tyres, and Mr Call sat next to the driver with his business satchel on his lap. Perry watched them toil their way up the trail in the afternoon sun. The deputy, Bud Winston, worked part time in the sheriff's office, and on Friday and Saturday nights he played banjo and fiddle in a bluegrass band at Mount Sterling. His face was young and lean, red with sunburn, and his tall, narrow frame always looked awkward in his clothes. For a uniform he wore his old army khakis with the corporal insignias torn off the sleeves. The heavy, officer's model double-action .45 revolver hung in a holster on his belt. His blue eyes were intent, but he didn't look straight at Perry when he neared the porch.

'I didn't figure you to come out here with him,' Perry said.

'I do what the sheriff tells me, Perry. This feller's got some papers that says he's supposed to take three of the little ones to a home in Richmond,' Winston said. He looked aside when he talked.

'I already seen them.'

'Then you know he's got the legal right.'

'I reckon I should have torn them papers up before I run him out of the house,' Perry said.

'That wouldn't make no difference. Mrs James give her consent.'

'Would you let him take your brother and sisters?'

'I don't like coming out here this way. In fact, I told the sheriff I didn't want nothing to do with it.'

'Then tell this man he ain't got any business in this county. He don't pay your salary,' Perry said.

'There's not much point in going through this again,' Mr Call said. His face was perspiring from the uphill climb, and the blue veins in his temples were swollen against the skin.

'You ain't even here, mister,' Perry said.

'He's from the state government, and he's got the authority to take the kids,' the deputy said. He spit tobacco juice into the dust.

'Who give it to him? I ain't ever seen him before, and neither have you. He come in from outside with a bunch of paper, and now he can bring the law out to our house.'

'The fifty dollars a week I get for this job ain't hardly worth it, and if I'd knowed I'd have to do this today I might have gone looking for another job,' Winston said. 'But you're going to have to let them kids come out.'

'They'll be out soon as he leaves.'

'That ain't the way it's going to be.' His eyes looked directly at Perry's.

'You got no part of this. It ain't your people he's trying to take away.'

'I got to do what I'm told, even if I don't like it. I reckon you know that by this time.'

'It don't change what I already said.'

'Bring them outside, Perry,' the deputy said. His jaw bone stood out in a stiff line against his cheek.

'That's something I ain't going to do.'

'Buddy, you're putting me between a rock and a hard place. I don't want to have to go inside and take them out myself.'

'You have to make up your mind about that. But I'd say you'd be doing the wrong thing,' Perry said.

'The sheriff told me he took a pistol off you once, and I know you're either carrying it or you got it right close by. If you're a-figuring on stopping me that way, you won't ever get up off that step again.'

Perry heard the screen door slam behind him.

'There ain't going to be nothing like that around this house,' Mrs James said. 'I've lost my husband and one boy already, and I ain't going to see Perry shot down or go to the penitentiary. You take the children.' She pulled Irvin and the two girls through the door on to the porch.

'Get them back in there,' Perry said.

'I don't want no more grief in this family, and I won't let you cause it,' she said. 'Take them, Bud. He won't get in your way.'

'Stay where you're at,' Perry said.

'Years ago I stood at the depot and watched them take your brother's body off the train in a box. Part of my life slipped right out of my soul then, like I could feel it draining away into the air. The same thing happened when I looked down at your daddy in his coffin. I ain't got much more to give now, and if you put me through it again there won't be nobody left to look after none of the children.'

The deputy stepped up on the porch and took the children by their hands. His eyes were bright, and there was a line of sweat down the front of his shirt where it buttoned. Perry started to his feet.

'You set right there,' Mrs James said. 'If you raise your hand to Bud, you'll have to do it to me first.'

'Daddy wouldn't let you do this. He wouldn't care how bad times got.'

'I meant it, son. Stand out of his way.'

'You can't do nothing about it, Perry,' the deputy said. 'Even if you could run me off or shoot me, there would be somebody else out here.'

'He ain't a-shooting nobody,' Mrs James said.

Bud Winston led the children down the steps past Perry. His face was sweating heavily now. He watched Perry out of the corner of his eye. The children's heads were twisted back towards their mother on the porch.

'You people done more harm to us than even them company gun thugs,' Perry said.

'You won't feel that way later,' Mr Call said.

'Mister, I better not ever see you on the same side of the street as me,' Perry said.

'Where they taking us?' Irvin said.

'It's a good place, like I told you,' Mrs James said. Her eyes were wet and she brushed them with the palm of her hand. 'Go with Bud and I'll be down to see you all Sunday. Pretty soon you can come home again, and Perry's going to take you down in the holler to find arrowheads.'

'I don't want to go.'

'Get them in your car and off this mountain, Bud,' Mrs James said. Her grey eyes were filmed, and the thin flesh at the sides of her mouth was pinched in a tight line.

'I won't forget what you people done,' Perry said.

But the deputy and the welfare worker were already part way down the trail and they did not turn around. Perry looked dumbly at the faces of the children, who continued to stare at him, and he knew that regardless of what he did in reprisal against Bud Winston, Mr Call or Mrs Lester, they still had the world of paper, legal signatures and authority on their side, and they could affect his family's life in any way they wished whenever they desired. In his exhaustion, he saw them holding the same power as the mining association, which, on a whim, could suddenly evict his family from the cabin, shut off their supply of food at the store, fire him from his job, blacklist him at every mine on the plateau, kill his father, and finally take his brother and two sisters from home.

He sat on the porch the rest of the afternoon in the still heat and looked out across the great expanse of the hollow below. At twilight he walked down the shale road to Rachel's Hollow and bought a pint of corn whiskey for fifty cents from a bootlegger who lived with his wife and three children in a dirt-floor shack covered with Montgomery Ward brick. There was a yellow sediment in the bottom of the whiskey, and the taste of the corn meal was so raw that it sickened his stomach. The purple dusk began to darken over the ridges, and the swallows spun in the air above the treetops. Later, after the last glow of the sun had diminished in the distance, the full moon rose above the limestone cliffs and reflected off the white road. He walked along in the dark to his cabin, sipping from the bottle and listening to the night birds calling to one another far below. The air was cool, and he could smell the water rushing over the rocks in the stream bed. At the top of the road he finished the bottle and threw it whistling end over end to the bottom of the hollow.

By the time he reached his front porch his heart was pumping hard, the whiskey spun in his brain, and although he didn't remember it later, he took his revolver from his canvas bag and stumbled down the incline behind the cabin to the creek. The openings to the rock houses were black in the moonlight, and green vines grew along the overhanging ledges. The limbs of the white oaks and beech trees were spread overhead against the sky, and in places the water in the creek flashed like quicksilver over the smooth stones. He cocked the revolver, aimed with both hands unsteadily at a rock house, and pulled the trigger. The flames exploded through the barrel and from the sides of the cylinder, the bullet ricocheted and whined off the walls of the cave, and the noise crashed down the creek bed. He splashed through the water and fell on his face. The cold rushed inside his clothes and work boots, and he rolled over in the wet dirt on the bank. His hair hung in front of his eyes, and the earth, trees, and rocks began to spin around him. He wiped the mud off of the revolver's cylinder, propped his elbows on the ground, and fired the remaining five shots at the rock wall across the creek. The roar of the magnum shells thundered in his ears, and he felt particles of lead shave off the back of the barrel and scald his face. His aim was low and two bullets struck the surface of the creek and blew water to the treetops. He kept cocking the action and squeezing the trigger even after the gun had clicked empty; then he passed out with one arm under his face. He did not wake until the sun came up white in the sky above the ridge.

TEN

For three more weeks the picket lines stayed up at the union mines, and the independents continued their lockout rather than sign contracts. There were several shootings, one attempt to dynamite a C&O loading platform near the coal tipple, and the union agent in Hazard was almost beaten to death behind his office by two company deputies. Then the National Labor Relations Board in Washington issued an order for all the mines on the plateau to open again, and industrial referees were sent into every coal-mining county in eastern Kentucky and West Virginia to supervise the union elections. Within hours of the order the Brotherhood of Locomotive Trainmen, who had honoured the UMW picket lines, reported back to work, and the first full C&O coal cars to leave the Cumberland in months were on their way north to Dayton and Pittsburg. The bars and pool rooms in town were suddenly empty, and men stood in long lines outside the company office shacks to sign on for the first eight-hour shift in the hole.

The sun had not risen above the mountain yet, and there was a chill in the grey dawn when Perry arrived, two hours early, at the mine. He took his place in the line that began at the locked door of the company office. He wore his hard hat, army field jacket and steel-toed boots, and he carried his lunch pail in his hand. The mist glistened on the coal pile by the tipple, and the clouds hung low on the great scarred areas across the face of the mountains. The ground was strewn with pulverized slag and limestone, and the smoke from the slag heap drifted back in the wind over the line of men. During the strike most of the windows in the office shacks had been broken with rocks, and misspelled picket signs were still nailed to some of the doors.

An hour later, after the sun had climbed above the mountain's crest and cast deep shadows into the hollow, no one from either the company or the union had arrived. The miners drank coffee from thermos jugs and passed around pint bottles of corn whiskey in paper sacks, and if a man had to relieve himself, he unbuttoned his trousers and urinated on the ground rather than chance losing his place in the line. Nearly half of the men there were out-of-state scabs and strip-mine workers, and Perry knew that the company would probably try to pack the election with non-union votes. The scabs stayed grouped together, silent, their faces blank; and their eyes always managed not to meet another man's stare. Perry could hear Big J.W.'s voice at the head of the line and the phlegmy laughter that made him think of something obscene. Little J.W. stood beside his brother, his face hard and impassive, and worked the point of his bowie knife under his fingernails. He had a small lump of tobacco in his cheek, and occasionally he sucked his teeth and spit a drop of brown spittle off the tip of his tongue. There were three scabs from Tennessee behind the J.W.s, and they stayed several feet away from them in the line and looked at the ground or the side of the mountain.

At seven thirty the company foremen, the timekeeper and the operator drove up the shale road to the shack in three auto-mobiles. Four company deputies, in soiled grey uniforms and with pistols on their hips, followed in a surplus navy carryall. Perry had seen them before when he was on the picket line, and two of them had once beaten three miners with axe handles after the miners had been caught pouring sand into the gas tanks of company trucks. The timekeeper opened the office and brought out a wooden table and chair and a ledger. The cuffs of his white shirt were rolled back over his thin arms, his slacks bagged at the rear, and he smoked one cigarette after another. His face always looked irritated, like the clerk's in the company store by Perry's cabin, and he spoke with the same clipped accent of authority. Two deputies stood behind him like twins, with their heavy, leather pistol belts stretched across their stomachs and their big hands on the hips.

'You reckon you got enough fire power there to watch over all these scabs?' Big J.W. said. 'I heered somebody say some of them West Virginia boys might get around up for dog food.'

'Do you want to work in this mine?' the timekeeper said.

'Buddy, I'll load the first car that comes out of that hole this morning. You just put my name down there,' Big J.W. said.

'You better get something straight, then. There ain't any such thing as a scab in this mine. There's a job open for any man that wants to work.'

'Them three behind me sure look like scabs. I bet they taken jobs away from union men all over the plateau. What do you fellers say about that?'

The three men from Tennessee looked away nervously. One of them had a film of perspiration on his forehead, although the morning was still cool.

'I don't guess they got anything to say,' Big J.W. said. 'They're probably a-thinking about the way they're going to vote this evening – if they come out of the hole.'

'Get out of the line,' the timekeeper said.

'Listen to that, baby brother. That white shirt lets him tell us to get out of line.'

'There's fifty men behind you, and I ain't got the time to waste on you,' the timekeeper said.

'I bet they pay you plenty of money for setting behind a desk with a couple of gun thugs to back you up against union men. You probably get twice as much as us without ever getting that white shirt dirty.'

'Stop talking with these sonsofbitches and get on with it,' Little J.W. said. He pared off the edge of his thumbnail and didn't look up when he spoke.

'You write Big J.W. and Little J.W. Sudduth's name down in that book. After our election I reckon you'll know how to watch that smart company mouth.'

The two J.W.s walked past the table and the two company deputies to the open shaft and climbed into an empty coal car behind the motorman. The sun climbed higher in the sky, and the breeze blew the smoke from the slag heap up the hollow. Perry waited in line until it was his turn to sign the book.

'Can you write your name?' the timekeeper said.

'Yes sir, I sure can. Here's my union card.'

'That don't mean nothing around here.'

'What's the scale?' Perry said.

'That's another word we don't have here. You get a dollar and a quarter like everybody else.'

'They said we would get two dollars.'

'Get your name down there if you want to work.'

'Why ain't we getting what the foreman told us in town?'

'There's ten men for every job in this hole. You can go right back to town, and we won't miss you.'

Perry signed his name on the ledger. The timekeeper looked at it and ran his finger down a list of names on a printed sheet.

'You were working in Blue Belle Number Two when somebody dynamited the tipple, weren't you?' he said.

'Half the fellers in this line has worked in that hole.'

'But I think you were one of them that got pulled in by the sheriff.' The timekeeper tapped his pencil on the desk. He felt his sense of advantage.

'I didn't get arrested for nothing. He just talked to me. That don't mean anything,' Perry said.

'He took you in to pass the time of day. Is that right?'

'Go ask him.'

'I'm talking to you now,' the timekeeper said.

Perry felt his temper begin to rise inside him.

'Them two fellers at the head of the line was taken in with me. You didn't say nothing to them.'

'They ain't on this list.'

An official from the company had come out of the office shack, and stood behind the two deputies. He wore yellow leather gloves, and his bright, print tie was blown over the shoulder of his white shirt.

'Let him go by or he'll run to the industrial referee and charge discrimination,' he said.

'I don't run to nobody,' Perry said.

'You're a real pistol, ain't you?' the timekeeper said. 'In a few days we won't have to take your kind down here any more. Get on down to the hole.'

'What do you mean my kind?' Perry said.

'Don't worry about that, and just give us a good eight hours,' the man with the yellow gloves said.

'I put out as hard a day's work as any man in this coal field.'

'You're blocking the line,' the timekeeper said.

'What's your name?' Perry said.

'I've seen them come and go like you by the hundreds. You don't bother me, James.'

'You people treat a man like he ain't nothing because he needs a job.'

'Strike his name if he says anything else,' the man with the yellow gloves said.

Perry walked to the coal cars and climbed inside with two other men. His face was hot, and his hands shook when he rolled a cigarette. He glared at the backs of the timekeeper, the deputies and the company official, and the rage inside him was like a piece of rope twisted across his chest. He smoked one puff after another until he felt the ash close to his lip.

'Take it easy,' the man next to him said. 'We'll catch that shithead in town one night.'

'We ain't got to do that,' the other man in the coal car said. 'After our election we'll get him fired and run him out of the county.'

'I reckon the J.W.s got something even better planned for him,' the first man said. 'Maybe they might catch him in that shack one night and set fire to him and it, both.'

The line of men passed by the timekeeper's table until all the jobs were filled, and fifty men were told that they could report back the next day in case there were more openings. The string of coal cars was filled with miners in hard hats with battery-operated head lamps, picks and loading shovels and tamping rods for the explosives. The motorman started the engine and the cars moved down the track into the black opening of the mine. The limestone had been blasted away on the face of the mountain, and great oak timbers shored up the roof around the entrance. Perry felt the cool, dank air of the shaft hit his face as they moved under the limestone ledge, and he could smell the stagnant water that was down at the bottom of the shaft. Under the string of generator-powered light bulbs, the corridors seemed to reach back endlessly into the mountain, and he felt something drop inside him as he looked at the winding course of the tracks between the rock walls. The ceiling was pinned with steel rods set two feet apart; Perry had once seen a square of rock slip out neatly between the pins and break a man's back. In the year and a half he had worked in the mines, he had never grown used to going into the hole; each trip was always like the first. The quiet fear was always there in his stomach, and there was an unnatural feeling inside him that he could never describe. In some ways the mine had the smell of an opened grave, and something primeval in him rebelled against his entering the earth. The weight of the ground above seemed to crush upon his head, and the spiral cut of the corridor made him lose his sense of equilibrium, as though he were rushing straight downwards towards the centre of the world. After an hour of loading coal and driving the air hammer into the seam, the fear would begin to disappear; but the next day at the eight-o'clock shift that terror would have to be overcome again as he sat quietly against the hard metal side of the coal car.

The fear was in the other men's faces, also, even though many of them had spent half of their lives underground. They chewed tobacco dryly, smoked hand rolled cigarettes away in a few puffs, rubbed the backs of their wrists against their foreheads, and sometimes talked in loud, strained voices. Someone threw an empty pint bottle out of a car against a wall, and the sound of breaking glass was like an explosion in the corridor. All the miners laughed, and the echo rolled up and down the side tunnels and deserted rooms, where the seam had ceased to pay. The cars clicked over the tracks deeper into the mountain, and Perry felt a drop of sweat form on his temple and run down the side of his face.

'Some of these cars sure do smell bad,' Big J.W. said. His skin was yellow under the lights, and the ingrained coal dust around his eyes and forehead looked purple, like a bruise. 'I bet some of them scabs didn't wash the jenny-barn off themselves last night.'

The three non-union men from Tennessee sat silently in the car, behind the J.W.s.

'In fact, it smells just like rut off a whore, don't it, baby brother?' Big J.W. said. 'We might have to give some of them boys a bath in that flooded room at the bottom of the hole.'

'I told you not to waste your time on these sonsofbitches,' Little J.W. said. 'They ain't a-working in this mine much longer.'

'Look at these three behind us,' Big J.W. said. 'They come a long way to scab. I reckon they figure on staying a while.'

'They'll stay down here permanent if they try to work scab after our election,' Little J.W. said. He never looked up while he pared his fingernails.

'We ain't done nothing to you people,' one of the men from Tennessee said. He was taller than his two friends, lean, with the same hard mountain features as other men throughout the Cumberland. His arms rested on top of his pick helve. His green and brown flecked eyes looked straight at Big J.W.'s.

'You don't reckon it's nothing to take a man's job?' Big J.W. said.

'We hired on like everybody else. It don't matter to me if this hole is union or not. I just go where the work is.'

'You been crossing picket lines three months getting strike-breaker wages,' Big J.W. said.

'They never give us more than a dollar and a quarter. And we ain't no strikebreakers. I got people to support back home, and if I don't work they don't get nothing to eat.'

'What do you figure our families eat while we're on the picket?' another man said.

'That ain't my concern,' the man from Tennessee said. 'I got my own family to look out for. It don't have nothing to do with you people.'

'You make money while we go without, and it don't have nothing to do with us?' Big J.W. said. 'You were brought in from outside to take our jobs, and we're going to run your kind off. If that's all that happens to you.'

'I ain't ever been run off a job, and there ain't a man here that can do it. I didn't say nothing to you fellers outside, but you better forget about threatening me any more. I won't set still for it much longer.'

'There's a lot of dark rooms at the bottom of this hole,' Big J.W. said.

'Buddy, I'll promise you one thing. You'll be the man left down here if you push me.'

'Shut your face, scab,' Little J.W. said. 'You won't do nothing, except maybe get your bus ticket back to where you come from. You're lucky somebody ain't got you already.'

'If you want to ever try it, you better get an apple box to stand on,' the man from Tennessee said.

Little J.W. looked up quickly. His knife rested in his hand, and the calloused tip of his thumb lay across the base of the blade. His eyes were dark and hardened, and his round features became rigid.

'You want to walk out of here this afternoon?' he said.

'I don't reckon you'll be the one to stand in my way.'

'I'm real close to laying your face open right now.'

The man from Tennessee set the point of his pick on the edge of the coal car and clenched the butt end with one hand. His blood veins were tight across the bones of his wrist.

'You can try, but they'll carry you out of that car,' he said.

'That ain't going to do you much good with one eye,' Little J.W. said.

'It's up to you, buddy.'

'That's enough of that shit back there,' the motorman, who was a union foreman, said. 'We got our election tonight, and then we won't need no more of this. These cars got to be loaded and out by ten o'clock, and there ain't going to be no fighting to hold it up.'

'You working to get a white shirt in that company shack?' Little J.W. said.

'When I make a run it comes out on time,' the motorman said. 'At ten o'clock I'm a-making my drop, and the man that makes me late is going to be looking for another job.'

Little J.W. put his knife back in its scabbard and dropped it inside the bib pocket of his overalls. The rest of the way down the corridor he stared rigidly at the man from Tennessee.

They started loading coal one mile back in the mountain. There was an inch of water along the bottom of the corridor, and the water in some of the side rooms went up to the men's knees. The tunnel was narrow, the ceiling low, and moisture had formed on the outcroppings of limestone. The cold began to soak through Perry's boots, and he wished he had spent three dollars to buy a pair of rubber overshoes. As he shovelled the coal and slag into the empty cars, he felt the fear of the earth's interior begin to grow in him again. There was too much water seepage through the rocks, there were no ventilator fans to draw gas and bad air out of the rooms, pieces of limestone had fallen loose from the overhead pinning, the ceiling seemed to groan above him, and after the men had been working a while he could feel the coal dust down in his lungs. He remembered the stories about the explosions that roared through the corridors and deafened men a half mile from the blast and left them with brain concussions. Once, he had seen a non-union mine that had collapsed in Letcher County. The miners were paid ten dollars for an eight-hour shift, and they spent most of the time in narrow pockets on their knees, digging low-grade coal out of the seam. The pinning had not been set properly in the roof, and when the mine caved, a long V-shaped sink hole settled on top of it across the mountain's incline. No one was ever able to reach the men inside, and later people believed they either died from lack of air or from starvation.

Perry knew other stories of blow-outs and cave-ins, men drowned in flooded corridors, flash gas explosions that incinerated whole crews; but the worst story he had ever heard was of two men who were buried alive two weeks in a Virginia shaft. Water broke through the side of the tunnel at the end of the first week, and both miners were given up for dead. When the blockage was finally cleared, the rescue team found them sitting against a wall, with water up to their chests. Their skin had faded and wrinkled like wet paper, and their minds were totally insane.

Perry's crew finished loading the slag into the coal cars, and the motorman backed the string up the tracks towards the entrance. Perry picked up the air drill, propped its heavy weight against the coal seam, and thudded the bit into the wall. The hammering vibrations made his tin hat bang against his forehead, and he had to clench his teeth to keep them from chattering against each other. In minutes his palms were sore through his metal-beaded gloves. The dust clouded up around him and stuck to his damp skin. The coal broke away from the wall and fell into the water by his feet. He worked steadily for a half hour, and then he had to stop and wipe the film from his goggles.

'Don't knock down that wall all at one time,' the man from Tennessee said. 'They ain't pinned this ceiling yet.'

'That's because it's a scab mine, and it don't follow safety regulations,' Big J.W. said.

'It don't matter what kind of a mine it is if it comes down on your head.'

'We wouldn't be worried about no ceiling if the union inspection team was down here,' Big J.W. said. 'They ain't ever been in this hole because the company could always bring in outside scabs like you, and a scab don't care where he works.'

'Like I told you before, buddy, I never had no choice about where I worked,' the man from Tennessee said. 'They never asked me to vote in no election, either, and I didn't ask them nothing about it. I figure a dollar and a quarter is better than having nothing.'

Perry filled his fingers with loose, string tobacco and put it in the side of his mouth. He pulled his goggles down over his eyes, spit into a pool of water by his feet, and set the drill into the wall again.

'Don't knock no more down,' another miner said. 'That drill sounds like a train against this dead end. They ain't a-paying enough to work us that hard or bring one of them walls in on us.'

'The foreman said he wants the seam cleared back to the next room,' Perry said.

'Piss on him,' Big J.W. said. 'He won't be here if this mountain folds in. He's drinking coffee above ground, and all he'll hear is a big crunch down in the hole.'

'I signed on to do a day's work,' Perry said. 'You all can get back around the corner if you figure the wall's a-coming down.' He pushed his weight against the drill handle and triggered the air pressure. He didn't look up at Big J.W. or the other men, although he felt them watching him. He hadn't worked an air drill in a long time, and his hands had grown soft. At one time there was a ridge of thick callous across each of his palms, but now the throbbing cut into his hands as though he had deep stone bruises under his skin. The coal shaled away from the wall until it stood in piles up to his knees. Finally, he couldn't support the drill's weight any longer against the seam, and he cut the air pressure and pulled his hard hat and goggles off his head. His hair was wet with sweat, and water blisters the size of quarters had formed on his palms.

After the motorman had picked up the next load, the men sat on top of the piles of slag and ate their lunch. Their fingers left dark creases in their sandwich bread, and the dust settled out of the air into their thermos cups. There was a damp smell of sweat in the corridor, and most of the miners' clothes were soaked with water. Little J.W. sat across from Perry and neatly pared the skin off an orange. The knife was sharpened on both sides, and there was a thumb guard at the bottom of the blade. Little J.W. had been stringing lights in a flooded room during the morning, and his overalls were dark up to his chest.

'What are you watching me for?' he said.

'I wasn't paying you no mind,' Perry said.

'You was looking at me like you had something to say.'

'I ain't talked to you this morning, and I wasn't figuring on it.'

'I heered you said plenty in town, though. Something about backing the J.W.s down. Is that right?'

Perry dropped his eyes and put a piece of ham and bread in his mouth. He chewed slowly and wiped the grease off his fingers on to his trousers. Don't let it get started now, he thought. He's just talking. He won't pull nothing with this many people around.

'Somebody said you run us out of the bar-room,' Little J.W. said.

'I ain't talked about you with nobody. What people say ain't my business.'

'By God, it's mine when somebody can say a Sudduth was run off by a kid.'

'I ain't done nothing to you. What you got against me is in your own head.'

'Who do you reckon told all them people that the J.W.s backed down?'

'Go ask them in town. I didn't have nothing to do with it. You started trouble with me without no call, and I told you once I just wanted you to let me alone.'

'I think you're a goddamn liar that talks behind a man's back and can't face up to it.'

Perry felt something jerk inside him, and involuntarily he set the flat of his hand on top of his pocket where his knife was. He looked at the hatred in Little J.W.'s eyes, the tight mouth, and the lines of sweat through the coal dust on his face.

'A man don't call me that,' he said.

'You got another name for it?'

'I'll walk out of this hole before I'll have trouble with you, but you ain't going to say that to me again.'

'What do you have in that pocket? Take it out and let's see if you're any good with it.'

'I ain't got to prove nothing to you. I ain't bothered you in no way, I didn't start no rumours in town, and if I'd knowed you all was working in this hole I wouldn't be down here. So don't fool with me no more.'

'Your face is sweating,' Little J.W. said.

'It ain't because of you.'

'I don't think you got the balls to back up that big mouth.'

'Leave him be. He didn't start nothing with you,' the man from Tennessee said.

'Keep clear of it, scab,' Little J.W. said.

'I been a-hearing you order people around all morning. You ain't no foreman, and I'm fed up listening to you threaten us.'

'I reckon you might not get to take that bus ride back home after all,' Little J.W. said.

'I'll be working this mine as long as they'll hire me, and when I decide to catch air, it won't have nothing to do with you,' the man from Tennessee said.

'This boy and me got something to settle, and when I get finished with him I'll give you some of it, too,' Little J.W. said.

'I ain't settling nothing with you, because I ain't working around you no more,' Perry said. He put his lunch back in his pail and started down the coal car tracks on the floor of the corridor. His boots splashed in the pools of water.

'He run off quicker than I expected,' Big J.W. said.

'I ain't a-quitting this job or no other on account of you all,' Perry said. 'I'm just getting on another crew where I don't have to be near you.'

'We'll see you again when you come out of the hole. You ain't getting away from us,' Little J.W. said.

Perry followed the winding tunnel up to the next level, where he found the foreman eating lunch with another crew. The coal dust was heavier here because there was less moisture in the air and less seepage through the walls, and the men's faces were completely black except for the area around their eyes, where they wore their goggles.

'I don't want to work in that back pocket no more,' Perry said.

'You work where you get dropped. That pocket ain't no more dangerous than any other.'

'It don't have nothing to do with the pocket. I want on another crew.'

'Is there anything else you want? Maybe a pay rise or a vacation,' the foreman said. The other men sitting against the wall laughed.

'I signed on for a day's wage, not for no trouble. I ain't pulling another shift with the J.W.s.'

'Has that shit started again? By God, I'm going to see a half dozen men fired by this evening if I hear any more of it. Now get on back down where you belong and tell them others to get their ass busy.'

'You better fire me now, then, because I ain't taking no more from the likes of them. I'll run the air drill for you and I'll load as many cars as any man here, but the job don't pay enough to put up with them two all day.'

Normally, the foreman would have fired Perry for speaking back to him, but the election was that night and he knew the union couldn't afford to lose any votes against all the scabs who went down into the hole that morning.

'All right, you can stay with this crew, but you'll be a-filing your unemployment if there's any more of this crap.'

Perry worked on the upper level the rest of the day. The blisters on his hands broke, and the tender skin peeled back from his palms as he dug his shovel into the piles of slag. The small of his back began to ache from working stooped over, and the coal dust became so bad that he could taste it in his throat. Some of the older men coughed fitfully, with the deep chest rattle of silicosis, and one man set his shovel down and walked back towards the entrance with a handkerchief over his mouth. The day's tedium wore on, and Perry stopped thinking about the weight of the mountain above his head, the cracks in the ceiling around the steel pins, and the possibility of a soft wall suddenly collapsing. He thought only of the pain in his hands and back, the fetid smell of men's bodies and stagnant water in the flooded rooms, and the click of the coal cars coming down the tracks for another load. By the end of the day his blisters were bleeding and he could hardly remove the gloves from his hands. The heat from his body steamed in the damp air, and his wet work boots had rubbed his ankles raw. When the five o'clock whistle blew outside and echoed faintly through the corridors, he was too tired to care if the J.W.s would be waiting for him above ground or not.

The afternoon sunlight was bright on the poplars and red maples across the hollow when he rode out of the hole in the string of cars with the rest of his crew. He shielded his eyes until they adjusted to the light. The cool wind in the shadow of the mountain blew against his face, and he felt his sweat dry against his skin. He cleared his throat and spit the coal dust taste out of his mouth, and breathed in the good smell of the summer air. The mountains were green and blue in the distance, and he could see white water rushing over rocks in the stream beds. Strips of purple rain clouds had formed across the horizon, and the slanting rays of the sun struck like gold on the white oaks along the ridges of the cliffs.

The industrial referee from the National Labor Relations Board had set up two tables by the company office for the election, and the lines of blackened men waiting to vote already stretched back to the mine entrance.

Perry went to the water tap by one of the tool shacks and turned it on full force. He took off his hat and shirt, knelt down on his knees, and let the water pour over his head. The coal dust ran off his hair and face on to his T-shirt and trouser legs. He found a used bar of soap and tried to scrub the grime out of his pores, but he knew he could never get it all off even with a wire brush. He turned his palms upwards under the tap to wash the pieces of cotton lint and grit out of his broken blisters, then he dried his face and arms on the inside of his shirt and walked back to the voting line.

Each man was given two slips of paper, one of which stated 'union' and the other 'open shop'. The miners were told to fold one and place it in the ballot box as they passed, but many of them could not read the words on the paper, and the UMW agent went down the lines with a union ballot outstretched before him in his fingers until the industrial referee said that he was trying to influence the vote and ordered him to stop. There were six more company deputies on duty, each with a pistol and blackjack on his leather belt, and although they didn't speak to any of the miners, they walked up and down the lines and often looked hard into a man's face. The scabs and strip-mine workers stayed in groups to themselves, and as Perry glanced at the faces around him, many of them unfamiliar, he wondered if the union would have enough votes to carry the election. He had heard that if the mine went non-union, the scabs would receive all the jobs, along with a pay rise, for staying loyal to the company, and no man with a union card would be allowed down in the hole. Some of the union miners rolled cigarettes, cut slices of chewing tobacco with finely honed pocket knives, and talked in voices loud enough for the scabs to hear:

'I heered they shot a couple more scabs over in Letcher. Somebody cotched them on a road at night and blowed them all over the side of a rock house. They say you couldn't even tell who they was by looking at their faces.'

'They say a scab down at Sterns stole so many chains he couldn't swim across Cumberland Lake. They couldn't find him for three days until somebody waved an association cheque over the water and his hand come up a-looking for it.'

'What about that feller that got burned up on the tipple at the Blue Belle? There wasn't enough of them charred pieces left to fill up a Bull Durham sack. That fire must have covered him up like he'd been soaked in gasoline.'

'I don't figure nothing like that could happen in this hole. Every man here looks like he knows which way to vote if he don't want to worry about walking on the street after dark.'

Once, a fight broke out in the line between a scab and a union miner. They rolled in the dirt, clubbing each other with their fists, and before they could be separated by the company deputies, the union man picked up a flat rock and knocked the scab unconscious. He lay still on the ground, his mouth wide open, with a large skinned lump above one eye. After two other scabs had picked him up and carried him between them to the water tap, the industrial referee climbed on top of a wooden chair and said that he would close the election if there were any more fights or if any deputy or union agent even came near the lines.

Perry waited his turn to drop his union vote into the box, then he began the long walk up the mountain road in the evening twilight towards his cabin. There was a car headed up the gravel in his direction; but Perry saw both of the J.W.s in the back seat, and he waved the driver on when he slowed to give him a ride. 'We'll see you in the hole tomorrow morning,' Little J.W. said out of the back window. He spit into the wind stream as he passed.

As Perry walked along and looked at the dust of the car he thought of the next day and the one after that and the endless weeks to follow. Every day in the mine would be the same. The J.W.s would always be somewhere near, with their threats and hatred, the fear would lie cold in his stomach every time he went back down the dark entrance, the dust would coat the inside of his mouth, his boots would be hard and stiff from the pools of water on the corridor floors, and each day the cracks along the ceiling would look wider from the tons of rock crushing down overhead. He thought of Cincinnati in the spring sunlight, the rows of maple trees in front of the narrow, German houses, and the beautiful sweep of the steel bridge above the river. He wondered if he would ever get back there, away from the mines, the slag heaps, the smell of men crowded together deep underground, the boredom of work that never changed from day to day, and the fears inside him that he could never admit to anyone. There was no way to tell how long it would take him to find the men who murdered his father, and after he did, he would probably be faced with years, or even death, in the state penitentiary. It's like you don't have nothing to say about the way any of it turns out, he thought. The law and the company and the J.W.s got you between them, and there ain't nothing to do about it except run, and you can't do that. So you got no choice about any of it.

On Friday night all of the election votes were counted, and almost every major mine on the plateau, including Perry's, had gone union. The association was forced to sign contracts, pay union scale, allow safety inspection teams to visit the mines, pay into a welfare fund for injured miners, install ventilator systems in shafts where there was gas, and guarantee time and a half pay for work over forty hours. Hundreds of miners had come into town directly from their jobs to hear the vote count read in front of the union office, and by ten o'clock all the bars and poolrooms were filled with drunken men, many still covered with dust from the mines. Those who had no money borrowed from the union agent on their next cheque, and the sheriff had to put on four extra deputies to protect the scabs, who were often shouldered off pavements, knocked about in the saloons, or had their car tyres cut on the streets. Men broke bottles on the concrete, windows were shattered, a miner was shot in the leg by a prostitute inside the jenny-barn, and the sheriff's jail was crowded before midnight. Men staggered along the pavements from one bar to the next, and a moonshiner from Rachel's Hollow sold clear whiskey in half-pint bottles on the street. Five scabs were forced to leave a café by union men, and as they tried to drive out of town, their car was surrounded by drunken miners, who at first made only insults and threats; then they began to rock the car until the underside of the body was hitting the pavement. One man spider-webbed the driver's window with a beer bottle, another cut the air valves off the tyres, and someone poured dirt into the gas tank. The men's faces inside were strained with fear. They pulled away from the windows and held onto the dashboard and seats. The driver got the engine started, and the car lumbered down the street on its metal rims while the tyres split into ribbons. The union men laughed and threw more bottles against the back window and boot.

Perry had also come into town to find out if the union had carried his mine. He had intended to return to the cabin early, but as he stood in the crowd of men in the velvet light before the union office, he took a drink from Bee Hatfield's bottle, then another. The whiskey was warm inside him, and it took away the long day in the mine and dull fatigue in his body. He bought a bottle of corn liquor from a bootlegger who was selling out of his truck cab, and in a short while Perry was as drunk as any of the other men in town. The clock above the bank read ten o'clock, and he promised himself that he would start home by eleven. It seemed as though he was watching the time constantly, but then it was suddenly midnight and he couldn't remember what he had been doing for the last hour. There was a half-empty bottle of cheap wine in the side pocket of his field jacket, the fiddler and banjo player on the platform in the bar-room were playing into the microphone, and Bee Hatfield was standing next to him, waving a full beer bottle in the air and yelling at people around him. The foam splattered on the floor. Bee's eyes were red, and his voice rasped above the hillbilly music.

'By God, every union man's a-making twenty-two dollars a day,' he said. 'The union come through for us, boys. We beat them scabs and strikebreakers, and the association ain't ever going to step on us again. Goddamn, let's have another drink.'

Perry upended the bottle of wine and passed it to his uncle. A man collapsed over a table filled with drinks, and one of the sheriff's deputies dragged him by the arms across the floor to the doorway.

'I been a-working for the union all my life, and I always knowed one day we'd lock this coal field up,' Bee said. 'There ain't going to be a scab left on the plateau Monday.'

'There ain't going to be no live ones,' another man said.

'Bring them goddamn drinks down here,' Bee yelled.

Perry steadied himself and looked at three men who were drinking at the end of the bar. Through the drunken haze he saw their brutal faces grinning at him. Their expressions were like death above their jiggers of whiskey. He had seen them many times in his dreams, and he knew that these were the men he had been searching for. He could smell their rotted breath and the acrid odour of exploded dynamite that still clung to their clothes. In the reflections of their eyes he could see the school building roaring in flames at night on top of the mountain. His elbow knocked Bee's bottle of beer over on the bar.

'You got to take me home to get my pistol,' he said.

'What?' Bee said.

'That's the ones that done it.'

'What are you talking about, boy? Done what?'

'Them three at the end of the bar blowed the schoolhouse.'

'That's the Caudill brothers. They're a-working in the same hole you're at.'

Perry's breath was coming hard and something was trembling inside him.

'I know the Caudills. You drive me home.'

'Set down in that chair. You must have bought some real bad moon this evening,' Bee said.

'I'll take them with my knife if I can't get my pistol.'

'You hush up. I ought to taken that corn away from you. Everything they sell out of Rachel's Holler has got bleach poured in the mash.'

'Who's he talking about cutting up down there?' one of the Caudill brothers said.

'He's drunk. He don't even know where he's at,' Bee said.

'By God, it sounded like he was talking about us,' the same Caudill brother said. His whiskey-inflamed eyes looked out from under his hard hat. His sleeves were cut off at the elbows, and he had tattoos of nude women on both arms.

'You goddamn murdering company sonofabitch,' Perry said.

'Buddy, that was the wrong thing to say,' Caudill said. He rose from the bar stool and walked around the side of the bar towards Perry.

'You stay where you're at,' Bee said. 'He don't mean nothing against you all. He thinks you're somebody else.'

'That don't matter. He ain't talking to me like that.'

'I'm a-taking him out. His daddy got killed and it don't ever get off his mind. He just got too much of that bad Rachel whiskey tonight.'

'He's a-staying till I say he can go.'

'No, sir, he ain't. Don't try to do him no harm, either, or I'll have your union card tore up by tomorrow morning.'

'Goddamn, they're the ones that—'

'You shut up and don't open your mouth again,' Bee said, and pulled Perry past the Caudill brothers. Perry knocked over a chair and stumbled into a table before Bee could get him outside.

'I got it under my bed.'

'Get in the car,' Bee said. He pushed Perry into the front seat and slammed the door.

The neon lights above the bars glittered off the broken glass on the pavements. A miner was passed out on the kerb and a girl from the jenny-barn was bargaining with two men in the doorway of the only hotel in town. Perry rested his head on the dashboard and felt the blood spinning in his brain. The car pulled out on the street and headed for the gravel road outside town. His head rolled back and forth on his arm, and he thought the motion of the car was going to make him sick. The wind blew through the open vane into his face. Bee coughed as he drove, and wiped the spittle off his lips with his shirt sleeve.

'Ain't you got enough problems without fooling with the Caudills?' he said.

Perry tried to speak, but his mouth wouldn't work and in his mind he still saw the three grinning faces at the end of the bar. The moon was blue over the trees on the mountain, and the shale road stretched out white under the headlights as they drove through the limestone hollows and over the hills. He fell sideways against the door and his head banged against the window jamb. Then the darkness of the hills seemed to enclose about him as though he were dropping down through the shaft into the bottom of the mine.

Two weeks later Perry received his first union scale paycheque. As the men filed out of the hole, the timekeeper called each man's name and handed out the brown envelopes. Perry noticed that the timekeeper seemed nervous and avoided looking directly into anyone's eyes. The sun was warm on Perry's back, and the light was yellow above the line of shadow on the limestone cliffs. He planned to use part of his money to take his mother on the bus the next day to see Irvin and his two sisters at the state children's home in Richmond, and he wanted to get home and scrub the coal dust off his body in the stream behind the cabin.

'What the shit is this?' a miner next to him said. The man had opened his pay envelope, and he held a slip of mimeographed paper in his hand. He stared at it as though he didn't understand the words.

Perry was too exhausted from the day's work to pay any attention to him, and he put his own paycheque in his back pocket and buttoned the flap down on top of it. He slung his field jacket over his shoulder and started through the groups of men towards the road.

'This says I ain't working here no more,' he heard the miner say. 'Who the hell put this in my envelope?'

Then Perry saw that other men also had slips of paper in their hands, and their faces all had the same dumbfounded expressions. He took out his envelope, tore it open across the end, and looked at an identical slip clipped to his cheque. It read, *Due to the introduction of new machinery in your mine and a cut back in production orders, you are temporarily discharged. Until there is a request for an increase in the work force, your membership in the United Mine Workers of America is also temporarily voided. We regret that circumstances have brought this situation about – UMW Local 442.*

'Where's that goddamn timekeeper?' a miner said.

'What's it mean?' someone else said.

'They're canning us,' Perry said, still looking at the paper with the same disbelief as the others.

'We got our contract. They can't fire us.'

'Get that goddamn timekeeper out here,' the first man said.

'This don't come from the company. It's signed by the local,' Perry said. 'They a-taking our cards away.'

'They can't take no union man's card away. Tell that time-keeper to get his ass out of the shack.'

The miners who had not been laid off walked towards their automobiles. Most of them looked at the ground and didn't speak to the angry men forming in groups.

'Some of them scabs has still got their jobs, and we ain't,' a man said.

'They ain't running me off this hole. I waited four months for it to open up. My family ain't going hungry no more.'

'I'm going to tear that shack down unless that goddamn timekeeper gets himself out here. You hear that, you sonofabitch! Come outside and tell us we're fired!'

'Lay one of them bricks through his window.'

'I'll do you one better than that, buddy. I'll drag him outside and stomp his head good.'

The door to the company office opened, and the timekeeper walked out with two uniformed company deputies behind him. He had taken off his tie, and his shirt was damp under the arms. There was fear in his face as he looked at the fifty men who stood before him. The deputies had unsnapped the leather holding straps on their pistols. One man wadded up his lay-off slip and threw it at the timekeeper's feet.

'You tell me to my face I ain't a-working this hole no more,' he said.

'The lay off is temporary. We might have full crews back on in a few weeks,' the timekeeper said. His voice almost cracked when he spoke.

'That's a goddamn lie. You're bringing in more machines to take our jobs because we're making scale now.'

'He looks like he's fixing to turn his britches brown, don't he?' another miner said.

'I work here just like you men,' the timekeeper said. 'I don't have nothing to do with laying anybody off.'

'I seen you get union men fired before we got our contract.'

'You people have been laid off before. You know you always get work again,' the timekeeper said. His voice was strained and his hands were awkward at his sides.

'This says our union cards is cancelled,' Perry said.

'The association don't have anything to do with that,' the timekeeper said. 'That came down from the business agent at your local.'

'The union don't turn against its own people. You sonsofbitches are behind this shit,' another man said.

'Go find your agent and ask him who took away your cards. You wouldn't have this trouble if you'd stayed with the company.'

'Why don't we take him down to that last flooded room and teach him how to swim?'

'Them deputies look pretty dirty, too. I know a deep hole they might fit in at the bottom of the second level.'

'You can't blame the company for what happened to you,' the timekeeper said. The deputies had set their hands on their revolvers. They shifted their weight and looked uncomfortably at the crowd of miners. 'This mine can't stay open and at the same time pay scale for all you men. The company just ain't got the money. You can work a dollar and a quarter forty hours a week and put a paycheque in your pocket every Friday night, or you can get nothing at all. The union didn't hire you, and the union don't make out your cheque. See if that business agent is interested in your problems now. They carried the election, and they don't need you all no more. Your card ain't worth a bubble gum wrapper down at the hall.'

'You lying bastard. You all had this planned since the hole opened.'

'Let's see the agent,' Perry said.

'I think we ought to fix this feller first.'

'That won't do no good. He ain't nobody. They wind him up every morning and tell him when to open his mouth and when to shut it,' Perry said. 'We been a-paying our dues to the union, and the agent's got to answer about taking away our cards.'

'That's right, by God. This sonofabitch can't tell us nothing. He's too scared now to know what he's talking about.'

'Everybody get in your cars and meet down at the local,' someone said.

'We'll see you at the first shift tomorrow morning, timekeeper,' another miner said. 'Them deputies of yours ain't going to keep us out of the hole, either.'

The miners crowded into their battered old cars and pickup trucks, and some men stood outside on the running boards, with their arms wrapped around the window jambs. The cars headed down the shale road through the hollow and a cloud of white alkali dust rose above the treetops. Perry sat between two other men in the back seat of a Ford coupé. The rocks rattled under the bumpers, and the dust from the other automobiles poured back through the open windows. One man opened a bottle of corn whiskey and passed it around, and as each man took a second drink, some of the fatigue seemed to leave his face, and his eyes became more bright and intent. The cars reached the bottom of the hollow and turned on to the blacktop towards the town. The old Ford and Chevrolet engineers roared through broken silencers off the surface of the road, and some of the cars careened around the curves at the base of the mountains. The men on the running boards were bent down inside the windows, their arms pressed tightly against the door panels.

There was already a line of cars double parked on the main street when the men from Perry's mine pulled into town. At least a hundred miners were standing on the pavement in front of the union office, and others were walking towards the office from the side streets where they had left their cars. Some of the men still had their discharge slips in their hands. The late sun reflected off their tin helmets and head lamps, and perspiration glistened thought the coal dust on the backs of their necks. There was a rank odour in the air of men pressed against one another, and as Perry worked his way into the crowd he could smell the sweat, the hot tar on the street, the slag smoke in their clothes, and the cheap whiskey and wine on their breaths.

The door to the union office was locked and the shades were drawn across the windows.

'There's somebody in there. Beat on that goddamn door till they come out,' a man yelled from the back of the crowd.

'We been a-waiting for the agent a half hour.'

'Maybe they shut down early when they knowed we was coming.'

'They ain't gone nowhere. They're probably hid out in the back.'

One man walked up the concrete steps to the entrance and knocked on the door. When there was no answer, he hammered on it with his fist.

'A couple of you fellers up front kick it open. We ain't standing out in this sun no more.'

'Tear it right off the frame. They're a-making their salary right out of what we pay them, and they ain't locking no doors on us.'

Two other men climbed the steps and began kicking the door with their steel-toe work shoes. A wood panel splintered out of the bottom.

'Stand back, boys, and I'll put that sonofabitch right through the back of the building,' one man said. He set himself, raised his foot, and slammed the sole of his boot into the wood. The door flew back on its hinges and crashed against the side wall.

The union agent and a man dressed in a business suit stood just inside the entrance. The agent's name was Bert Ramey, and he always wore starched khaki working-man's clothes and a Lima heavy equipment badge on his watch fob, although no one had ever known him to work on a construction or mining job. He was short and overweight, and his head was bald through the centre of his hair. He wore a brown rain hat whenever he was outdoors, and there was a line of faint pink sunburn across his forehead. The man in the business suit was a stranger to Perry. His thin, greying hair was oiled and combed straight back, and he wore a silk tie with a gold pin through his white collar. His manner was relaxed and confident as he looked out over the heads of the men in the street.

'I been on the phone talking long distance, boys. You all didn't have no need to kick my door in,' Bert Ramey said.

'We don't care what you been doing. Who had this slip put in our envelopes?' one miner said.

'We can explain that to you if you give us time,' Ramey said.

'You better start doing it pretty fast, then.'

'Mr Hendricks here is from the main office in New York, and he's got a statement to read,' Ramey said.

'Goddamn, we ain't stood out here this long for no shit like that. What about our cards?'

'This thing ain't happening just here in our county,' Ramey said. 'They're a-cutting back men all over the plateau and in West Virginia, too.'

'You ain't said nothing yet. Who sent out these slips?'

'The association's putting in new machinery in every big mine around here, and there just ain't that much work for everybody no more,' Ramey said. 'The union don't want to drop you, but they can't send men out to jobs where there ain't none.'

'Our welfare cards ain't no good, either, then.'

'The welfare fund's been broke a year,' Ramey said. 'You all know that. There's more men drawing disability now than we got money for.'

'I been in the union sixteen years, and I ain't giving up my card,' the miner who had smashed the door open said.

'Every man here has walked pickets all over Kentucky for you,' another man said.

'I done two years in Frankfort penitentiary for the union, and by God I don't figure the UMW's going to tear up my card now.'

'Look, it ain't me that done it,' Ramey said. 'The order come down from New York. I've worked with all you fellers on every strike around here, and I don't like to see none of you get dropped.'

'You taken our dues out of today's cheque. You're a-drawing your money right out of our sweat.'

'It ain't that way. They might drop me just like they done it to you,' Ramey said.

'That's why you and this New York feller had yourself locked in the office together.'

'I can't tell you all no more. None of the locals around here would have taken your cards away. We just didn't have no say about it,' Ramey said.

'You made a deal with the association. You carried us till all the mines was union, and then you locked us out.'

'That ain't true,' Ramey said.

'Shit, it ain't. You better have your ass out of this county tonight.'

'As Bert told you, the union doesn't like to reduce the labour force, but there's almost a quarter million dollars of new machinery going into every major mine in the association, and there is no way to stop automation and its effects on labour,' Hendricks said. His clean-shaven cheeks shone in the sunlight.

'Who the hell are you, anyway?'

'I represent the southern region of UMW. You men have seen this cut back coming for a long time. All of the miners out here can't do the work of three new auger drills. We don't like it, but there's nothing the union can do about it.'

'Why don't you shut that smooth Yankee mouth? There wasn't nobody talking to you.'

'I bet you ain't ever been in the hole.'

'This isn't doing any of us any good,' Hendricks said. 'You men have to understand that we had no other recourse.'

'I spent thirty years underground, and you're a-telling me I can't work no more.'

'We can't do nothing now except scab or work truck mines for eight dollars a day.'

'My family lives in a company cabin, and they'll put us out just as soon as I miss one month's rent.'

'Our charge ain't no good at the store unless we're working.'

'That don't bother you, does it? You're a-staying in an air-conditioned motel down in Richmond, and tomorrow morning you'll have your plane ticket back up North.'

'You men stay back. Hurting me won't help you,' Hendricks said.

'You think you can tell us we got to scab for a living?'

'We been on the picket six months waiting for this election. You ain't a-taking away what we won.'

'All of you stand away. This won't change your situation,' Hendricks said.

'Pull that sonofabitch off there.'

As the crowd pressed forward, the union agent ran for the back of his office. A big miner in a hard hat and overalls, with no shirt on, pushed Hendricks off the steps on to the pavement. The crystal on Hendricks' wristwatch broke, and his coat sleeve tore at the elbow. The walk was covered with tobacco spittle, and there were brown stains on his trousers and the palms of his hands. He got to his feet and backed against the wall of the building. 'It won't restore your jobs. You'll just have something to regret tomorrow,' he said. His collar had broken loose, and his oiled hair had fallen down on his temples. Someone threw a wine bottle through the office window, and other bottles crashed inside the doorway. The miner with no shirt shoved Hendricks to the pavement again, then knelt beside him and ripped his coat up the back. 'I don't reckon you'll come down here again and tell us we ain't got jobs,' the miner said. The white sun reflected off the pavement, and the miner's eyebrows were heavy with sweat. He pulled Hendricks by the shirt into a sitting position and threw him back against the wall. A siren echoed off the building fronts at the end of the street. The miner looked over his shoulder as the sheriff's car braked to a stop at the edge of the crowd, then he stood up and stared down at Hendricks. 'You're a pretty lucky sonofabitch, mister,' he said, 'and you can think about that all the way back to New York.'

ELEVEN

The late July heat settled on the plateau and shimmered on the ridges in waves. There was no breeze in the hollows, and the hardwood trees remained motionless in the humid air. The creeks and streams went dry, and the sandy beds were covered with swarms of sweat bees. Copperheads and rattlesnakes slithered through the burnt grass looking for water, and the tobacco in the fields began to wilt and turn yellow under the sun. In town unemployed miners who had hoped to get work cutting tobacco sat under the canvas awnings in front of the saloons and pool halls, cursing the heat and wiping the sweat off their foreheads on to their shirt sleeves. No one could remember when drought had lasted so long on the plateau, and as the weeks passed and the plough rows began to harden and crack, the farmers marked off their crops as lost. The corn stalks withered and rattled dryly in the fields, and crows fed off the new ears lying parched on the ground.

Perry worked one or two days a week at a strip mine, where he had to report every morning at seven o'clock before he could find out whether or not he had a job for that day. He sat hours at a time in the Richmond employment office, only to have the window closed at four thirty without his name being called. He applied for work cleaning out bars and filling station rest rooms, washing cars, scrubbing the insides of oil drums, and picking chickens for a nickel a piece on a poultry farm. In the afternoon he walked aimlessly around town and listened to other men talk about their unemployment claims that had been disallowed, the work to be had in Ohio, the ten-dollar-a-day jobs in the truck mine, and the county welfare allotment that was never enough to feed a family.

For two weeks the company cut off Perry's credit at the store because he hadn't paid last month's bill and was no longer employed. There was nothing in the cabin that could be pawned or sold except his pistol; and the manager at the finance company in Richmond wouldn't even accept his application for a loan. His mother made corn bread from the powdered milk and meal given out at the federal surplus food centre, and in the early morning Perry killed rabbits by the red pools of water in the bottom of the creek beds. He cleaned and skinned the rabbits and hung them upon the front porch to let the heat and blood drain from their bodies in case they carried summer fever. At night his mother boiled them in a stew and poured it over pieces of old bread that the store sold at half-price. At breakfast they ate the same stew again, but the grease and fat lay thick on their plates, and the stale bread was harder to chew and swallow. Then there were fewer rabbits in the creek bed as the remaining water evaporated or seeped into the dry cracks, and some days the James family ate three meals of grits mixed with powdered milk.

Perry thought about transporting whiskey for old man McGoffin again, but the ABC had caught seven more runners in the last three months, and all of them had received at least a year in jail. Also, the federal agents had smashed stills all over the plateau and had sent several moonshiners to Atlanta. Even the bootleggers in Rachel's Hollow were afraid to move their whiskey, regardless of the high prices paid by the syndicate in Detroit. There were more men each morning at the strip mine shape-ups, and eventually Perry was not able to get even one day's work a week. Finally, he applied for relief to the welfare office.

The waiting room was crowded and hot, and the air was heavy with smoke that drifted towards the single window fan in back. Women sat stiffly on the straight-back chairs, holding crying children in their laps, while their husbands spat tobacco juice on the wooden floor and ground it into the grain with their boots. There were only two social workers to interview all the people in the room, and a family usually had to wait five or six hours before it was called to one of the desks. The toilet in the rest room was broken, and often a woman took her children across the street to the filling station and returned to find that her name had been called and she would have to wait until everyone else had been interviewed. At noon the social workers and the typist left for an hour, but the people in the waiting room ate sack lunches of fried potatoes and pork chops rather than chance losing their place in line. By mid-afternoon the air was fetid, the floor was littered with paper, orange peels and cigarette butts, and children slept stretched out on the chairs, their faces flushed from the heat.

Perry sat on the back row and wiped the sweat off his neck with his cap. A child on the chair in front wet his pants, and the urine ran down his legs on to the floor.

'It ain't right to make us wait this long,' a man next to Perry said. He was a miner, and there was still a pale line around his eyes where his goggles fitted. A boy of four slept in his lap. There was a damp imprint of perspiration on the miner's shirt where his son's head pressed against it. 'I been in here six hours and the boy ain't had nothing to eat.'

'How much can you get on the welfare?' Perry asked.

'We come down here three times, and they ain't give us nothing but a two-dollar grocery order so far. We had to go all the way to Richmond to cash it because the company stores don't take them.'

'I ain't ever done this before,' Perry said.

'I never had nothing to do with these sonsofbitches, either. But I ain't worked in a month, and the union's got us locked out clear over to old Virginia. My welfare card ain't no good, and I had to give our last thirty dollars to some shithead doctor in Richmond when the boy was sick. If they don't give us nothing today, I'm going to pull that feller over his desk and stick his head in that broken toilet.'

At four o'clock one of the social workers called Perry's name. She was a thin woman, and she wore her straight black hair on her shoulders with a ribbon in it like a young girl. Her face was covered with white powder, and across the desk Perry could smell her perfume and the odour of cigarettes on her breath.

'Are you applying just for yourself?' she said.

'It ain't for me. I come here because of my mother and the kids.'

'Are they here?'

'I didn't see no reason to make them set in this office all day.'

'Your mother will have to sign an affidavit of need,' the woman said.

'What's that mean?'

'It's just a rule the agency has.'

'I been in that chair since seven-thirty this morning.'

'I'm sorry, but you'll have to come back with the rest of your family.'

'There ain't no food in our house, and my mother ain't up to setting in a hundred degree heat for seven hours,' he said. 'We ain't ever asked you all for nothing before, and I wouldn't be here now if I could go anywhere else. But by God I ain't spent all this time for nothing and I ain't leaving till I know the kids are going to have something to eat besides grits everyday.'

The woman looked at the clock on the wall and lighted a cigarette. She blew the smoke out and coughed, holding her hand over her mouth. A child began crying loudly in the waiting room.

'Let's fill out this form and I'll have a social worker make a home call at your house,' she said.

'What's that for?'

'It's the only way your case can be certified.' She wrote Perry's name on the top of the welfare application. 'How many people are there in your family?'

'Seven besides me, but three of the little ones are in the state children's home,' he said.

'You should have told me that before. You probably already have an ADC case opened.'

'I told you I ain't been here before.'

'If anyone in your family is receiving state aid, we have a record of it,' she said. 'I'll have to pull your case history tomorrow.'

'When can I get something for the kids?'

'The social worker will be out next week, and then we can make a determination.'

'They can't wait a week. There won't be nothing left to eat by then,' Perry said. 'We can't get no more surplus food till the end of the month.'

'There's not much more I can do. You'll just have to manage the best you can.'

'What are the kids supposed to eat till you all get finished fooling with them papers?'

'I'll arrange a home call for next Thursday,' she said. 'That's the earliest I can make it. Have all your family at home that afternoon.'

'This place don't help nobody,' he said. 'People wait in here all day so you all can tell them to go home and wait some more.'

She turned sideways in her chair and dropped his application into a metal file drawer. Perry put his cloth cap on his head and walked back out through the waiting room. The broken toilet had overflowed on to the floor, and cigarette butts and paper wrappers floated in the water. Some families still sat on the hard chairs, hoping that their names would be called before the office closed in five minutes. Perry stepped outside into the bright sunlight and felt the moisture on his face dry in the hot breeze.

Two days later Perry received a government cheque in the mail for the remainder of his Job Corps savings. He paid his charge at the company store and gave the clerk twenty-five dollars for credit on next month's account. He bought screening for the windows on the cabin, to keep out the mosquitoes that swarmed up in clouds from the creek bed at night, and he spent five dollars on shoes for the children at the second-hand store in town. After he paid for the patent medicine nerve tonic that his mother had been charging at the drug store, almost all of his money was gone and he still needed to buy new work gloves and boots for himself in case he caught a day's work at the strip mine.

The days passed into August and the heat continued. Perry sat on the front porch in the stillness of the twilight evening and looked off at the purple haze above the mountains. The crickets and cicadas were loud in the breathless air, and occasionally a bullfrog croaked at the bottom of a stream bed. The children played on the broken wagon in the dusty front yard, and Mrs James sat in her rocker, gazing at them with no expression on her face. Perry felt the tedium of the long evening begin to settle upon him. But he had no money to shoot pool in town or buy whiskey from Rachel's Hollow, and it was too hot to sleep. His mother seldom spoke, except to ask if he or the children were ready for their dinner, and their evenings were usually spent in listless silence. Tomorrow he would go to all the strip mines again, then he would stand on the street corner for a couple of hours in town until he had to return home once more and sit on the porch and listen to his mother's rocker creak back and forth on the wood boards. Mrs James' head nodded on her chest and her hands went limp in her lap. Her grey hair was wet around the temples. In the distance Perry saw an old coupé driving fast up the road, with a cloud of white dust behind it. On the turns the car showered rocks into the hollow far below. The rusted bumpers and running boards shook and rattled, and wisps of steam rose from the engine. He must be drunk, Perry thought. He's going to put one of them pistons through the hood or go over the cliff.

'Who's that?' Mrs James said. She raised her head up abruptly from her chest. Her eyes were dazed with sleep.

'It's Bee Hatfield.'

'What's he up here for? He don't come by except when there's trouble. The last time I seen him he took your daddy to the union meeting at the schoolhouse.'

Perry watched the car slow into second gear on the last curve and stop at the foot of the hill.

'He's probably drinking. I'll go talk to him,' he said.

'You tell him he don't need to stop by here no more. We already had our share of his kind of trouble.'

Perry stood up and walked down the trail towards the road. The dirt was dry and hard under his bare feet. Half of the red sun still showed above the ridge, and the dark shadow of the cliffs fell across the treetops in the bottom of the hollow. All the windows in the coupé were rolled up and filmed with dust. Perry could smell the hot odour of the tyres and engine. He stepped out softly on the rock road as Bee rolled down the driver's window. He wore a cloth, duck-bill cap and a soiled, striped shirt, and his face was beaded with perspiration from the heat inside the closed car. Perry could smell whiskey on his breath.

'We got them. Go get your gun,' Bee said.

'Got who?'

'All three of them. Hurry up and get that pistol.'

'Wait a minute. What do you mean you—'

'Goddamn it, boy, we ain't got time to wait.'

'Where are they at?'

'Listen, I didn't almost pile this junker up so I could come out here and argue with you. You been talking about getting them three men ever since they blowed the schoolhouse. Now if you want to go back and set on the porch, that's all right with me, because I'll let the others finish it for you.'

'What others?' Perry said.

'I'm starting this engine, boy. You better move it if you're a-coming.'

Perry headed back up the trail in a half run. The sun had set lower behind the cliff, and over the mountains the early moon was pale in the fading light. Mrs James had fallen asleep in her chair. The magazine she used to fan herself lay at her feet, and her flat breasts rose up and down with her heavy breathing. Perry opened the screen door quietly and went into the bedroom. He slipped his shoes on over his bare feet and took out the long-barrelled, Buntline special revolver and the box of magnum shells from under his mattress. He unwrapped the oil cloth from the pistol, pushed it down inside his work trousers, and covered the butt with his shirt. The metal was cold against his body. Two of the children began fighting in the front yard, and through the thin board wall he heard his mother's rocker scrape on the porch. He stuck the box of shells in his pocket and went back outside.

'Why is Bee still down there?' she said.

'He knows about a job in Jackson.'

'I don't want you going with him.'

'I ain't going to be long. Go inside and lay down. It's cooler now.'

'He don't have a job for you, son. He ain't been around work since he come out of the penitentiary.'

'I got to go. He's a-waiting.'

'Turn around here. You got that pistol under your shirt.'

'We might jump a rabbit along the road.'

'You ain't telling me the truth. I can see it in your face.'

'Don't fix no dinner for me. I'll eat in Jackson.'

'Woodson would have never let you keep that gun in the house. I ought to have throwed it down the holler. Now you're going out to use it on someone. You're acting just like all the Hatfields, and I can't take it no more, Perry.'

'I'm going now. Drink some of that tonic and go lay down.'

He worked his way back down the trail to the road and got inside Bee's car. He pulled the pistol out of his trousers and set it and the box of cartridges beside him on the seat. There was a layer of white dust on the dashboard. The last slanting rays of the sun struck the front of the cabin, and he saw his mother motionless and small in her chair. Bee put the car in first gear and roared off down the road, spraying rocks against the bumpers. There was a half-empty bottle of whiskey in his lap.

'All right, where you got them?' Perry said.

'Down by that flooded shaft at the far end of Rachel's Holler.'

'How'd you find them?'

'You know that company deputy that looks like he's half nigger? He was drunk in the bar-room, and he was telling them whores he'd educated some union men in a schoolhouse. We got him outside in the alley and sweated him good till he told us who the other two was. We found both of them upstairs in the jenny-barn. One of them was in a room with his pecker out when we grabbed hold of him.'

Perry opened the loading gate of his revolver and inserted the shells into the cylinder. His heart was beating fast and his hands felt uncoordinated. He eased the hammer back into the safety position on one empty chamber and snapped the loading gate shut.

'Who all's with you?' he said.

'The J.W.s and some others that's been waiting to catch them sonsofbitches.'

'They got no part in this.'

'They figure they have. They wanted to kill them three and

throw them off the ridge soon as we got out of town. But I told them not to do nothing till I got you.'

'I already had it out once with Little J.W. I warned him about fooling in my business.'

'Look, you'll get your chance at them men. They're locked up in Big J.W.'s boot, and there ain't nobody going to bother them till we get there. All you got to do is line them up and finish it. Just leave the J.W.s alone. I don't feel like pulling you out of no more trouble.'

Bee drove with one hand on the top of the steering wheel and drank out of the whiskey bottle with the other. They neared the bottom of the road as the last light faded in the hollow. The car bounced over a wooden bridge that spanned a dry stream bed, and the dark trees and cliffs rose up ahead. The road through Rachel's Hollow was corrugated and baked hard as concrete by the sun. There were a few clapboard shacks and log cabins set back in the trees, and occasionally a cigarette glowed in the shadows on a front porch. The car banged over the ruts, and the whiskey in Bee's hand spilled out on his shirt. They drove deeper into the hollow, and the maples and white oaks towered above the road like a canopy under the moon.

'I didn't want nobody else in on it,' Perry said. 'You should have come for me when you first heered that deputy talking in the bar.'

'Boy, everything can't be like you want it. You'd have never cotched them men without us helping you. Goddamn this heat. There ain't no air at all down here.'

'What do the other two look like?' Perry said.

'They probably don't look like much at all after riding ten miles in that boot. It must be two hundred degrees in there.'

'I didn't want it like this.'

'Are you backing out? By God, if you are I'll set you on the road right now.'

'I ain't a-backing out of nothing. You just get me there and keep them J.W.s out of it.'

Perry's breath became more rapid. He unbuttoned his shirt and let the hot air from the vane blow against his chest. The gun metal on the pistol was warm in his grip. He put a plug of tobacco in the side of his jaw, but his mouth was so dry that he could not chew.

The road ended at the base of a limestone cliff on the far end of the hollow. Bee turned off into the trees and followed an abandoned logging trail through the dense scrub brush and briar thickets. The beech trees were white in his headlights, and water ticked out of a rock house and glistened on the grey boulders at the foot of the cliff. The night was strong with the smell of the woods and of the dead leaves piled around the tree trunks. Then the undergrowth began to thin, and ahead Perry saw a clearing, where a Coleman lantern burned on the ground beside a parked car. The shadows of six men grouped in a circle stood out in the light. One figure raised something in his hand above his head and slashed it down murderously, then someone screamed out in pain.

'Let's get it over with quick. That whiskey's making me sweat like a whore,' Bee said. He braked the car on the edge of the clearing and cut the headlights.

Perry got out and stuck his pistol down his trousers. He felt the muscles tremble in the back of his legs as he walked towards the lantern's white glare. Three men lay on the ground, and Perry wanted to turn his head aside after he had looked at them. They had been beaten with chains. Their faces were swollen and streaked with blood, and their shirts had almost been ripped from their backs. Two of them had their arms over their heads, and the company deputy's shoulder sagged as though his collarbone were broken. His eyes were glazed with fear, and his mouth shook convulsively when he tried to speak. His hair was matted with sweat and dirt, and his exposed, soft stomach bulged out over his trousers. He tried to push himself away from the group of men, but his arm folded under him and he fell against his bad shoulder. One of his shoes had come off, and his sock had slipped down over his hairless, pink ankle.

Perry had seen the other two men before in the pool room. They were both sallow and thin, their hair was uncut, and they had crude tattoos on their arms. They made their living shooting dice, hustling the pool tables, and sometimes driving company coal trucks through union picket lines. Their sharkskin slacks were torn at the knees and covered with grease from the trunk of the car. Little J.W. stood above them with a double length of chain in his hand. He wore his tin hat at an angle on his head, and his denim shirt was rolled up neatly over his short, muscular arms. His jaw bone was tight against his cheek. He let the chain swing loosely against his pants leg, and he chewed on a match stick in the corner of his mouth. Perry looked at the other faces reflected in the lantern's light. Big J.W. stood tall and lean by his brother, with a hand-rolled cigarette between his long, yellow teeth. Next to him was Foley Rankin and three of his cousins, all of whom had belonged to the Ku Klux Kian when it had existed briefly in southeastern Kentucky after Negroes from Alabama had been hired to scab in the mines. Perry remembered the story his father told about how Rankin had led a caravan of cars filled with men in peaked hats and bed sheets to the company shacks where the Negro workers lived. One cabin was burned, several Negroes were forced to kneel in the dust, and a company bus was turned over into the hollow.

Rankin walked behind the car and picked up three heavy cement cinder blocks and dropped them by the three men on the ground. His narrow eyes glinted, and the blood had drained from his lips. He pulled a coil of thin rope from his back pocket and cut it into three sections with his knife.

'You know what this is for, boys?' he said. 'I'm going to tie them blocks around your neck, and in a few minutes you're going all the way to the bottom of that hole.'

The deputy twisted his neck and looked at the flooded mine opening set back in the trees. Broken timbers were scattered around the sink hole, and rotted twigs and leaves floated on top of the stagnant water.

'I reckon it's a hundred feet straight down,' Big J.W. said. 'I hope you fellers can hold your breath a long time.'

'Maybe they might find somebody down there to talk with,' Rankin said. 'Didn't somebody throw a nigger in there once?'

'That's the one that swole up till he floated all them bricks to the top,' one of Rankin's cousins said.

The deputy put one hand over his eyes and began to cry softly. His fingers trembled on his forehead.

'He looks like he's going to piss all over himself, don't he?' Big J.W. said.

'I just drove. I didn't know they were going to blow the schoolhouse when anybody were there,' the deputy said. His breath came in spasms.

'You was bragging on it in the bar, you sonofabitch,' Little J.W. said. He raised the chain and whipped it down on the deputy's back with all his weight three times. The deputy writhed in the dirt under each blow. His eyes protruded from his head, a dry scream caught in his throat, and his body arched backwards as though his spine had been broken. 'Here, you want some more? I can do it all night if you want to open your mouth again.'

Good God, Perry thought. *Not like this*. The heat seemed to gather in the clearing like steam off a forge, and he felt the perspiration run down his face and neck onto his shirt. He smelled the stagnant water in the mine shaft, the dried sweat of the men around him, and his head began to spin. The cruel faces in the light and the figures on the ground didn't look real to him. Heat lightning flashed above the ridge, and he heard a clap of thunder echo in a distant hollow.

Rankin tied a section of rope through the hole in a cinder block, then knotted the other end in a loop. He swung the weight back and forth in his hand to test the strength of the rope.

'Let's get on with it,' he said.

'They ain't in no hurry. Sweat them a little more, baby brother,' Big J.W. said.

'We spent too much time on this trash already,' Little J.W. said. 'Throw that little one in there first. We'll save something special for this loudmouth deputy.'

One of the pool-room hustlers dragged himself backwards and tried to get to his feet. Big J.W. kicked him hard in the small of the back and knocked him into the dust.

'Don't do it, mister. Please,' the hustler said. His face had gone white, and a line of spittle ran from the corner of his mouth. His puffed eyes were dilated with fright. Then he began to shake all over.

'He's a yellow sonofabitch, ain't he?' Big J.W. said.

'Please, for God's sake,' the hustler said. 'You beat us enough already. Don't kill us.'

'Tie it tight around his neck and shut off his air,' Little J.W. said.

Rankin knelt beside the man on the ground and tried to force the rope over his head. The man curled into a ball and clenched his arms across his face. Rankin pulled him upright by his hair and struck him in the mouth.

'Hold your head up straight, you bastard, or I'll take your eyes out with that chain,' he said.

'Wait a minute,' Bee said. 'Let Perry finish it. I reckon he's got more right than anybody else.'

'It don't matter to me,' Rankin said. 'I don't like putting my hands on them, no how. They all smell like piss.'

'Just do it and let's get moving. It's too goddamn hot down here,' one of Rankin's cousins said.

'You figure that boy's got it in him?' Big J.W. said.

'He don't look too good, does he?' Little J.W. said. 'In fact, he looks just like he did when we run him out of the hole.'

'Goddamn, throw them in the shaft and let's get back to town,' Rankin's cousin said.

'Lay it on them, Perry,' Bee said.

Perry felt the veins grow tight in his head, and the line of treetops seemed to shift against the mountain's dark outline. His shirt was soaked through. The pulse pounded in his wrists, and his eyes filmed and burned in the light.

'Let them go,' he said. His voice almost broke when he spoke.

'What did you say?' Little J.W. said.

'Get that goddamn gun out, boy,' Bee said.

'We ain't going to kill them,' Perry said.

'Why'd you bring this little sonofabitch down here?' Big J.W. said.

'You listen, Perry. Them men never give your daddy no chance,' Bee said. 'Now, you get that gun out quick.'

'Get him out of here,' Little J.W. said.

'No, by God. He's going to finish it,' Bee said.

'I ain't going to do it. Nobody is. I told you all before not to mix in it.'

'I ain't a-waiting on this kind of shit,' Big J.W. said. 'Pull the rope over the little one's head. If he fights back again, I'm going to cut his throat.'

He opened his knife blade against his trousers and stooped his long frame over the man on the ground. He held the point of the blade under the hustler's chin while Rankin widened the loop in the rope.

'Stand away from him,' Perry said.

'You shut your face,' Little J.W. said.

'I ain't fooling. Turn loose of him.'

'Rap him across the head with that chain,' Big J.W. said.

'I'm just about to do it, and once I start I ain't stopping,' Little J.W. said.

'You ain't going to do nothing.'

'I been putting up with you too long, boy,' Little J.W. said. His words were slow and measured.

'You and your brother ain't no better than a pair of shithogs,' Perry said. 'You ain't good for nothing except burning people out or beating a man to death while you hold a gun on him.'

Little J.W. raised the chain over his shoulder and came towards him. He breathed heavily through his nostrils, and his eyes looked insane. Perry pulled the revolver from his trousers and pointed it at arm's length directly into Little J.W.'s face. He cocked the hammer back with his thumb and felt the cylinder click into place.

'It's got magnums in it. They'll tear half your head off,' he said.

Little J.W. stopped, his mouth tight, and remained motionless. There was no sound in the clearing except his hoarse breathing.

'Throw the chain down,' Perry said.

'Your life ain't worth nothing now. You won't ever get out of this holler.'

'Throw it down, or I swear to God I'll kill you where you're at.'

Little J.W. released the chain and let it drop to the ground. Perspiration rolled down through the ring of dirt on his neck.

'You do this against union men?' Bee said.

'Stay out of it,' Perry said.

'We cotched them for you, and you pull a gun on us,' Bee said.

'I told you to keep clear of it.'

'You ain't no kin of mine. I wouldn't let you in my back door.'

Perry moved out into the light by the three men on the ground and kept his pistol pointed at the J.W.s. Rankin stepped back from him and tripped on one of the cinder blocks. The hard lines in his face had gone slack, and he rubbed his fingers up and down his trouser leg.

'You three sonsofbitches get up and run,' Perry said.

'I can't make it. They broke something inside me,' the deputy said.

'Buddy, your luck's pretty good right now. Get moving.'

'I won't have no chance.'

'I ain't going to give you long. Pick him up,' Perry said.

The other two men rose slowly to their feet, watching the circle of faces in the shadow. Their legs were weak under them, and they couldn't straighten their backs. They stumbled forward, off balance, and lifted the deputy up by his arms. He winced in pain at the pressure on his bad shoulder.

'Goddamn you, run,' Perry said.

'Take us out with you, mister. They'll find us again,' one of the hustlers said. He swayed on his feet.

'Then you just ain't got no more luck. I'm a-turning them loose in about one minute, and you better start finding a rock house to hide in.'

The three men stepped backwards across the clearing, still watching the J.W.s; then they turned and crashed into the briar thickets. The thorns scraped across their faces and tore their skin; they slashed at the branches with their forearms, tripped over rocks and dead logs, fell to the ground, then plunged forward again.

'How do you figure on getting out of here?' Little J.W. said.

Perry heard the thrashing in the underbush grow more distant.

'You don't worry about it. You ain't even going to move,' he said. He edged around the group of men, reached inside Big J.W.'s car window and pulled the keys from the ignition. He threw them as far as he could into the trees.

'You're going to sweat harder than them others for that,' Big
J.W. said.

'I'm taking your car, Bee,' Perry said. 'You can pick it up in
front of the courthouse.'

He kept the gun pointed in front of him while he retreated
towards Bee's coupé. His knuckles whitened from his grip on the
pistol.

'Kick over the lantern,' Little J.W. said.

'I'll dump all six shells right in the middle of you,' Perry said.

'He can't hit nobody in the dark. Kick it over, Rankin. He
ain't going to walk away from us like this.' But no one moved.

Perry opened the car door and steadied the pistol across the
window jamb. He leaned inside, flipped the gear stick into neutral
and turned the ignition, then depressed the gas pedal and floor
starter at the same time with one foot. The engine throbbed under
the hood, and he eased into the seat sideways, with the door still
open and the pistol levelled across the window. He waited a
moment for any movement from the J.W.s, then he threw the
pistol on the seat beside him, shoved the car into reverse, and
popped out the clutch. The coupé spun around in a half circle,
the tyres whining on the hard earth, and the door sprang back on
its hinges into a tree trunk. For an instant he saw the group of
men break up in the light and head towards him. He double-
clutched the transmission, slammed the gear stick into first, and
pressed the accelerator to the floor. The car roared through the
brush and weeds, and he heard the silencer hit a rock and tear
loose from the frame. A tree limb smashed the right front window.
He turned on the lights and wound up the transmission in first
until the gear lever was shaking in his palm. He swerved around
the chuck holes in the road, bounced across logs at thirty miles
an hour, and scraped the entire side of the car against a white oak
tree.

He could smell the tyres and engine burning when he turned
out of the woods and headed back through the hollow. He had
knocked the front end out of alignment, and the car swayed from
side to side over the ruts. He knew that it would take the J.W.s
only a few minutes to cross the wires on their ignition, and then
they would be down the road after him. He was breathing fast, as

though he couldn't catch his wind, and he wiped his face with the front of his shirt. Heat lightning flickered above the ridge again, and a black thunderhead had begun to move across the moon. Up ahead he saw lights in a cabin through the poplars, and the road became more even and started to climb towards the far cliff.

The exhaust fumes from the broken tail pipe rose up through the floor boards and made his eyes water. He worked his shirt off his shoulders with one hand, rubbed it over his chest and neck, and opened the air vent on the hood. He watched the rearview mirror for any headlights behind him, but the road was empty and the bottom of the hollow was dark. As he climbed higher, a thin breeze began to bend the treetops and the air felt suddenly cool. Then he saw the moonlight on the wood bridge across the stream bed and the limestone boulders in the dry sand.

He kept the car in second gear up the gravel lane along the ridge. Below him he could see the flat expanse of black-green trees, the dry washes, and the logging roads pale and yellow under the moon. More clouds had formed on the horizon, and gusts of wind swept across the cliffs and spun dead leaves through the air. He heard the pines creak in the breeze, then a bolt of lightning ripped through the sky in a brief, crooked white line and struck a mountain top in the distance.

Perry felt spent inside, as though all the fury and heat in his blood had been drained from him in a few minutes' time. The strain and violence of the last hour had left him exhausted. His hands were thick on the steering wheel, and the skin of his face felt dead to his touch. In the beating of the air stream through the window, he thought he could still hear the voices of the J.W.s and the screams of the men on the ground, then he forced them out of his mind and looked ahead at the ragged line of maples on the ridge, the steep cliffs, and the black clouds that rolled and twisted over the hollow. A solitary raindrop struck his windscreen as he turned on to the blacktop towards town.

The store fronts in town were darkened, the streets almost deserted, and the wind blew the dust in clouds along the worn brick paving. He could hear the banjo and fiddle music in the tavern and the drunken laughter that always continued until early morning. There was a smell like scorched copper in the air, and a rubbish bin rolled loudly down a pavement. The light in the sheriff's office fell out on the courthouse lawn. Perry parked the car at the curb, unloaded the revolver and stuck it in his belt. He put on his shirt, without buttoning it, and walked across the grass to the courthouse entrance.

The sheriff sat behind his desk with an electric fan blowing in his face. His brown uniform was rumpled and stained darkly around the collar, and the papers under his huge arms stuck to his skin when he moved. There was a pitcher of ice water by his elbow. He stopped writing and looked up at Perry, then dropped his eyes to the revolver.

'You must have lost your goddamn mind,' he said. His breath wheezed down in his throat when he spoke.

'Them three men that killed my daddy are at the back of Rachel's Holler. They ain't going nowhere, either.'

'By God, I warned you what would happen if you—'

'I didn't do nothing to them. The J.W.s worked them over with chains. They're hid out in a rock house somewhere.'

The sheriff stood up from his chair, opened his drawer and took out an automatic pistol and a blackjack with a spring handle. He slipped one in each of his back pockets.

'Get in the car,' he said.

'You don't need me for nothing. Just drop this gun at the pawnshop and tell Mr Mac to give the money to my mother.' Perry pulled the revolver from his belt and set it on the desk top.

'Where are you going?'

'I ain't got to stay here no more.'

'Wait a minute.'

'I'm gone, sheriff.'

Perry left the courthouse, crossed the street, and walked past the coal bins to the edge of town. He followed a dirt road lined with clapboard shacks and junker cars, then climbed through a barbed wire fence into a meadow, and headed towards the C & O railway embankment on the far side. The wind was blowing harder now, and he could smell the rain in the distance and the ferns in the stream beds. The moon had turned blue overhead. Cows were bunched together in the field, and he heard them chewing at the grass and dandelions in the dark. He jumped across an irrigation ditch by the water tower and climbed the railway grade to the track. Weeds grew between the gravel and wooden ties, and the rails stretched off between two black mountains where the grade made a bend.

He followed the track to the curve and sat down on the edge of a tie. The rain began to fall evenly on the mountain top, and a white mist moved through the hollow and settled in the base of the trees. Then he felt the rail vibrate under his palm, and a train whistle echoed on the other side of the ridge. A few moments later the headlamp on the engine swept around the bend, and he saw the rain spinning in the light and the line of freight cars that stretched back a half mile. He slid down the embankment and waited as the locomotive drew closer. The chains on the couplings banged and sparked against the gravel, the earth trembled from the weight of the cars, and the weeds along the side of the road bed were knocked flat by the blast of hot air from the wheels. The engine thundered past Perry, and he began running over the rocks in an even line with the string of box cars and tankers. The train was starting to pick up speed again at the end of the curve. All of the doors were locked and sealed, and none of the flat cars had handrails on them. He was running short of breath, and over his shoulder he saw the green and red lights on the caboose coming up behind him. He leaped upwards and grabbed the iron rung on the side of a refrigerator unit and pulled his legs up over the wheels. For a moment he thought he would lose his grip and be sucked under the car. The ties and road bed sped by below his feet, and when the train made the curve he had to hook both of his arms around the iron rung. The rain beat in his face, and the mist between the mountains was so thick that he couldn't see the tree trunks. He climbed to the top of the car and sat on the wooden walkway with his knees pulled up in front of him and his back to the wind.

In a few hours he would be out of the Cumberland Mountains, rolling through the bluegrass country towards Lexington. Then he would hop another C & O freight to Cincinnati, and by dawn he would see the great bridge across the Ohio River, the white paddle-wheel pleasure boat churning in the current below, and the sunlight on the narrow, German buildings and trees along the boulevards. He'd find a job somewhere, and on Sunday afternoons he would go to the ball games and drink beer and eat sausage at Crosley Field. In the evening dusk he would walk along the water-sprinkled streets, and maybe, if he had enough money, he would go out to River Downs where the best thoroughbred horses in Kentucky raced. The train gathered speed as it roared down the grade on the far side of the mountain, and he held onto the walkway tightly with both hands. The purple silhouette of the hills stood out against the sky when lightning crashed into a hollow, and he could smell the sweet odour of wet earth in the tobacco fields and meadows. Part of the moon shone from behind a cloud, and the rain in his hair reflected like drops of crystal.

LAY DOWN MY
SWORD AND SHIELD

This book is for my father,
James L. Burke, Sr,
who taught me most of the good things
I know about

ONE

Almost ninety years ago during the Sutton-Taylor feud, John Wesley Hardin drilled a half dozen .44 pistol balls into one of the wooden columns on my front porch. My grandfather, Old Hack, lived in the house then, and he used to describe how Wes Hardin had ridden drunk all night from San Antonio when he had heard that Hack had promised to lock him in jail if he ever came back into DeWitt County again. The sun had just risen, and it was raining slightly when Hardin rode into the yard, his black suit streaked with mud, horse sweat and whiskey; he had a shotgun tied across his saddle horn with a strip of leather and his navy Colt was already cocked in his hand.

'You, Hack! Get out here. And don't bring none of your Lincoln niggers with you or I'll kill them, too.'

(My grandfather was sheriff and justice of the peace, and the Reconstruction government had forced him to take on two Negro federal soldiers as deputies. Of the forty-two men that Hardin eventually killed, many were Negroes, whom he hated as much as he did carpet-baggers and law officers.)

Hardin began shooting at the front porch, cocking and firing while the horse reared and pitched sideways with each explosion in its ears. Wes's face was red with whiskey, his eyes were dilated, and when the horse whirled in a circle he whipped the pistol down between its ears. He emptied the rest of the chambers, the fire and black powder smoke roaring from the barrel, and all six shots hit the wooden column in a neat vertical line.

Hack had been up early that morning with one of his mares that was in foal, and when he saw Wes Hardin through the barn window he took the Winchester from the leather saddle scabbard nailed against the wall and waited for Wes to empty his pistol. Then he stepped out into the lot, his cotton nightshirt tucked inside his trousers, blood and membrane on his hands and forearms, and pumped a shell into the chamber. Wes jerked around backwards in the saddle when he heard the action work behind him.

'You goddamn sonofabitch,' Hack said. 'Start to untie that shotgun and I'll put a new asshole in the middle of your face.'

Hardin laid his pistol against his thigh, and turned his horse in a half circle.

'You come up behind me, do you?' he said. 'Get your pistol and let me reload and I'll pay them nigger deputies for burying you.'

'I told you not to come back to DeWitt. Now you shot up my house and probably run off half my Mexicans. I'm going to put you in jail and wrap chains all over you, then I'm taking you into my court for attempted assault on a law officer. Move off that horse.'

Wes looked steadily at Hack, his killer's eyes intent and frozen as though he were staring into a flame. Then he brought his boots out of the stirrups, slashed his spurs into the horse's sides, and bent low over the neck with his fingers in the mane as the horse charged towards the front gate. But Hack leaped forward at the same time and swung the Winchester barrel down with both hands on Hardin's head and knocked him sideways out of the saddle into the mud. There was a three-inch split in his scalp at the base of the hairline, and when he tried to raise himself to his feet, Hack kicked him squarely in the face twice with his boot heel. Then he put him in the back of a vegetable wagon, locked his wrists in manacles, tied trace chains around his body and nailed the end links to the floorboards.

And that's how John Wesley Hardin went to jail in DeWitt County, Texas. He never came back to fight Hack again, and no other law officer ever got the better of him, except Johyn Selman, who drove a pistol ball through his eye in an El Paso saloon in 1895.

As I stood there on my front porch that hot, breathless July day, leaning against the column with the six bullet holes, now worn and smooth, I could see Hack's whitewashed marker under the pin oaks in the Holland family cemetery. The trees were still in the heat, the leaves filmed with dust, and the shade was dappled on the headstones. Four generations of my family were buried there: Son Holland, a Tennessee mountain man from the Cumberlands who came to Texas in 1835 and fought at the battle of Sam Jacinto for Texas' independence, was a friend of Sam Houston, later received twelve hundred acres from the Texas Republic, and died of old age while impressing horses for the Confederacy; Hack's two older brothers, who rode with the Texas cavalry under General Hood at the battle of Atlanta; Great Uncle Tip, who made the first drive up the Chisholm Trail and married an Indian squaw; Sidney, a Baptist preacher and alcoholic, who always carried two revolvers and a derringer and killed six men; Winfro, murdered in a brothel during the Sutton-Taylor feud, his body dragged on a rope back and forth in front of the house by drunken cowboys; Jefferson, who had two years' business college in Austin and decided to compete with the King and XIT ranches in the cattle market and lost six hundred acres of Holland land as a result; and Sam, my father – Hackberry's son – a genteel man with a rheumatic heart, a one-time southern historian at the University of Texas and later a United States congressman during the New Deal, and finally a suicide.

Out beyond the cemetery the low, green hills sloped down towards the river, which was now low and brown, and the crests were covered with blackjack, live oak and mesquite. The cotton in the fields was in bloom, the rows evenly spaced and stretched out straight as a rifle shot, and the tomatoes had come out big and red in the early summer showers. The sun flashed brilliantly on the windmill blades, now idle in the still air, and in the distance the clapboard and shingle homes of the Mexican farm workers looked like flattened matchboxes in the heat. My three natural-gas wells pumped monotonously up and down, the pipes on the well heads dripping moisture from the intense cold inside, and occasionally I could smell the slightly nauseating odour of crude gas. The wells were located in the middle of the cotton acreage, the derricks long since torn down, and the cotton rows were cut back from the well heads in surgically perfect squares, which always suggested to me a pastoral reverence towards the Texas oil industry.

The front lane was spread with white gravel, the adjoining fields planted with Bermuda grass, and white wood fences ran both the length of the lane and the main road where my property ended. The lawn was mowed and clipped, watered each day by a Negro man whom my wife hired to take care of the rose gardens, and there were magnolia and orange trees on each side of the porch. The main portion of the house had been built by Hackberry in 1876, although the logs of Son Holland's original cabin were in our kitchen walls, and it had changed little since. My wife had added a latticework verandah on the second storey, with large ferns in earthen pots, and a screened-in side porch where we used to eat iced-tea dinners on summer evenings. After we began to take our meals separately, the porch was used as a cocktail bar for her lawn parties, complete with a professional bartender in a white jacket who shaved ice into mint julep glasses for the Daughters of the Confederacy, the Junior League and the Texas Democratic Women's Club.

But regardless of the Sunday afternoon lawn parties, the political women with their hard eyes and cool drinks, the white boxes filled with roses, the air-conditioning units in the windows, it was still Old Hack's place, and sometimes at night when I was alone in the library the house seemed to creak with his angry presence.

I suppose that's why I always felt that I was a guest in the house rather than its owner. Even though I was named for Hack, I never had the gunfighter blood that ran in the Holland family. I was a Navy hospital corpsman during the Korean War and spent three months in Seoul passing out penicillin tablets for clap until I was finally sent up to the firing line, and I was there only six days before I was shot through both calves and captured by the Chinese. So my one attempt at Hack's gunfighter ethic was aborted, and I spent thirty-two months in three POW camps. However, I'll tell you more later about my war record, my wound and purple heart, and my testimony at a turncoat's court-martial, since they all became part of my credentials as a Democratic candidate for Congress.

I lit a cigar and walked down the glaring white lane to where my car was parked in the shade of an oak tree. I had showered and changed clothes a half hour before, but already my shirt and coat were damp, and the sun broke against my dark glasses like a hot green scorch. I sat back in the leather seat of the Cadillac and turned on the ignition and the air conditioner, and for just a moment, as the stale warm air blew through the vents, I could smell the concentrated odour of the gas wells, that scent of four thousand dollars a month guaranteed income from Texaco, Inc. I dropped the car into low, pushed slowly down on the accelerator, and I felt all three hundred and fifty horses throb up smoothly through the bottom of my boot. The gravel pinged under the bumpers, and I rumbled over the cattle guard on to the main road, then pushed the accelerator to the floor and listened to the tyres whine over the soft tar surfacing. My white fences whipped by the windows, clicking like broken sticks against the corner of my eye, and I steered with three fingers at ninety miles an hour around the chuck holes and depressions, biting gently down on my cigar and watching the shadows on the fields race with me towards San Antonio and Houston. Several times when drunk I had driven one hundred and twenty miles an hour at night over the same road, hillbilly and gospel music from Del Rio thundering out of the radio, and the next morning I would sweat through those whiskey hangovers and see yellow flashes of light in my mind, the Cadillac rolling over in the field, the white fence gaping among the shattered boards, and I would be inside, bleeding blackly between the steering wheel and the crushed roof.

But sober I drove with magic in my hands, an air-cooled omnipotence encircling me as the road sucked under the long frame of my car.

As I neared Yoakum I unscrewed the cap of my whiskey flask and took a drink. The white ranch houses and the barns, the cattle and horses in the fields, the acres of cotton and the solitary oak trees rolled by me. The sun reflected in a white flash off the bonnet of the car, and ahead the road seemed to swim in the heat. A thin breeze had started to blow, and dust devils spun along the dry edge of the corn fields. On the top of a slope the blades of a windmill turned into the breeze and began spinning rapidly; then the water sluiced out in a long white spray into the trough. At the edge of town I passed the rows of Negro and Mexican shacks, all alike even though some of them were built decades apart, all weathered grey, the porches collapsing, tarpaper nailed in uneven shapes on the roofs, the dirt yards littered with broken toys, tangled wire, dirty children, plastic Clorox bottles, and rubbish set out to rot in boxes. In the back, old cars with rusted engines and spider-webbed windows sat among the weeds, faded overalls and denim shirts hung on the washlines, and the scrub brush that grew in the gravel along the railway bed was streaked black by passing locomotives.

I sipped again from the flask and put it in the glove compartment. It was Saturday, and Yoakum was crowded with ranchers and farmers, women in cotton-print dresses, Mexican and Negro field workers, pickup trucks and battered cars, and young boys on the corner in lacquered straw hats and starched blue jeans that were as stiff as cardboard. On Main Street the old high footpaths had iron tethering rings set in them, and the wooden colonnade, built in 1900, extended over the walk from the brick storefronts. Old men in white shirts with clip-on bow ties sat in the shade, spitting tobacco juice on the concrete and looking out at the traffic with their narrow, sunburned faces. At the end of the street was the stucco and log jail where my grandfather had locked up Wes Hardin. It was set back in a lot filled with weeds, and the roof and one of the walls had caved in. The broken timbers and powdered stone lay in a heap on the floor, and kids had smashed beer bottles against the bars and had left used contraceptives in the corners. But on one wall you could still read the worn inscription that an inmate had scratched there with a nail in 1880: *J. W. Hardin says he will kill Hack Holland for nigger meat.*

I had always wondered if Hack ever worried about Hardin breaking out of prison, or about Hardin's relatives catching him in the back with a shotgun. But evidently he was never afraid of anything, because when Hardin was released from prison after fourteen years Hack sent him a telegram that read: '*Your cousins say you still want to gun me. If this is true I will send you a train ticket to San Antonio and we can meet briefly at the depot.*'

Through law school at Baylor I used one of Hack's .44 Colts as a paperweight. The bluing had worn off the metal, and the mahogany grips were cracked, but the spring and hammer still worked and the heavy cylinder would rotate properly in place when I cocked it. After I started law practice with my brother in Austin, I hung the pistol on my office wall next to a 1925 picture of Hack as an old man, with my father in a white straw hat. I had my law degree and Phi Beta Kappa certificate framed in glass on the wall, also; but the gun, Hack's creased face and long white bobbed hair dominated the office.

It was almost two o'clock and over one hundred degrees when I reached San Antonio. The skyline was rigid in the heat, and on the hills above the city I could see the white stucco homes and red-tiled roofs of the rich with their terraced gardens and mimosa trees. I turned into the Mexican district and drove through blocks of second-hand clothing stores, Baptist missions, finance companies and pawnshops. Slender pachucos in pegged slacks and maroon shirts buttoned at the cuff, with oiled hair combed back in ducktails, leaned idly against the front of pool halls and wino bars.

I pulled into the Mission Motel, a dirty white building constructed to look like the Alamo. There were arches and small bell towers along an outer wall that faced the street. Cracked earthen jars, containing dead plants, stood in an imitation court-yard in front of the office. The bricks in the courtyard had settled from the rains and Johnson grass grew between the cracks. I took a room that I'd had before, a plaster-of-Paris box with a double bed (an electric, coin-operated vibrating machine built in), a threadworn carpet, walls painted canvas yellow, and a bucket of ice and two thick restaurant glasses placed on the dresser. I cut the seal on a bottle of Jack Daniel's and poured a glass half full over ice. I sat on the edge of the bed, lit a cigar, and drank the whiskey slowly for five minutes. The red curtains were pulled across the window, but I could still see the hot circle of the sun in the sky. I finished the glass and had another. Then I felt it begin to take me. I had always liked to drink, and I'd found that during the drinking process the best feeling came right before you knew you were drunk, that lucid moment of control and perception when all the doors in your mind spring open and the mysteries suddenly reduce to a simple equation.

I dialled an unlisted number given to me three years ago by R. C. Richardson, a Dallas oilman whom I'd kept out of prison after he defrauded the government of fifty thousand dollars on a farm subsidy. He had written out a ten-thousand-dollar cheque on my office desk, his huge stomach hanging over his cowboy belt, and handed me his business card with the number pencilled on the back.

'I don't know if lawyers like Mexican chili, but you won't find none better than this,' he said.

He was crude, but he was right in that it was one of the best call-girl services in Texas – expensive, select and professional for that ethic. I always felt that the money and organization must have come from the Mafia in Galveston, because none of the girls or the woman who answered the phone seemed to be afraid that the client might be a cop.

The woman on the phone sounded like a voice from an answering service. There was no inflection, accent or tonal quality that you could identify with a region or with anyone whom you had ever met. I used to imagine what she might have looked like. She must have answered calls from hundreds of men in motel rooms and empty houses, their voices nervous, slightly drunk, hoarse with embarrassment and passion, cautious in fear of rejection. I wondered if those countless confessions of need and inadequacy had given her a devil's insight into the respectable world, or if she was merely a mindless drone. I couldn't identify her with the image of a fat, bleached madam with glass rings on her fingers, who would be altogether too human for the voice over the phone. Finally, I had come to think of her as a hard, asexual spinster, thin and colourless, who must have developed a quiet and cynical sense of power in her ability to manipulate the sex lives of others without any involvement on her part.

As always she was discreet and subtly indirect in asking me what type of girl I wanted and for what services. And as always I made a point of leaving my motel registration name – R. C. Richardson.

I hung up the phone and poured another whiskey over ice.

Thirty minutes later the girl arrived in a taxi. She was Mexican, tall, well dressed in expensive clothes, and she had a delicate quality to her carriage. Her black hair was combed over her shoulders, and her white complexion would have been perfect except for two small pits in one cheek. She had high breasts and a good ass, and her legs were well formed against her tight skirt. She smiled at me and I saw that one of her back teeth was missing.

'You want a whiskey and water?' I said.

'It's too hot now. I'm not supposed to drink in the afternoon, anyway,' she said. She sat in a chair, took a cigarette from her purse, and lit it.

'Have one just the same.' I poured a shot into a second glass.

'It won't make me do anything extra for you, Mr Richardson.'

'People in Dallas call me R.C. You can use my name in the Petroleum Club and it's better than a Diners card.'

'I don't think you'll get your money's worth if you drink much more,' she said.

'Watch. I'm a real gunfighter when I get loaded.'

I stood up and took off my shirt and tie. The whiskey had started to hum in my head.

'You should pay me before we start,' she said. She smoked and looked straight ahead.

My white linen coat hung on the back of a chair. I took my notecase from the inside pocket and counted out seventy-five dollars on the dresser top.

'Does any of your organization come out of Galveston?' I said.

'We don't learn about those things.'

'You must meet some of the juice behind it. An occasional Italian hood wearing sunglasses and a sharkskin suit.'

'Your date is for two hours, Mr Richardson.'

'Take a drink. What about that voice on the phone? Has she ever been laid herself?'

The girl set her cigarette on the dresser edge, slipped her shoes off, and rolled her hose down. I drank a long swallow from my glass.

'Maybe she's Lucky Luciano's grandmother smoking a reefer into the receiver,' I said.

'You must not get a chance to talk much.'

She stood up, put her arms around my neck, and pressed her stomach hard against me. I could smell the perfume in her hair. She moved the flat of her hand down my back and bit my lip lightly with her eyes closed.

'Don't you think we should start?' she said.

I kissed her mouth and could taste the whiskey on my own breath.

'Why don't you have a drink?' I said. 'I don't like a woman to wither under me because of Jack Daniel's.'

'You're married, aren't you?' She smiled and worked her fingers under my belt.

'I just don't enjoy women who look like they're in pain when you bend over them. It's part of my R. C. Richardson genteel ethic.'

'You must be a strange man to live with.'

'Give me a try sometime.'

She pushed her stomach into me again, then dropped her arms and finished undressing. She had a wonderful body, the kind you rarely see in whores, with high breasts and brown nipples, long legs tanned on the edge of some gangster's swimming pool, a flat stomach kept in form by twenty-five sit-ups a night, the buttocks pale right below the bathing-suit line, and a small pachuco cross with three rays tattooed inside one thigh.

I took off my trousers and pants and laid them across the top of the chair. I picked up my cigar from the ash tray and looked into the full-length mirror on the closet door. At age thirty-five I had gained fifteen pounds since I played varsity baseball as a sophomore at Baylor. I had a little fat above the thigh bones, the veins in my legs were purple under the skin, and my hair had receded a little at the part; but otherwise I was as trim as I had been when I shut out almost every team in the Southwestern Conference. There was no fat in my chest or stomach, and there was still a ridge of muscle in the back part of my upper left arm from two years of throwing a Carl Hubbell screwball. My shoulders had grown slightly stooped, but I still stood over six feet barefooted, and the bit of grey in my sand-coloured hair made me look more like a mature courtroom lawyer than an ageing

man. Then there was my war wound, two holes in each calf, white
and scarred over, placed in an even, diagonal line as though they
had been driven there by an archer's arrow.

We made love on the bed for an hour, stopping only for me to
pour another glass. My head was swimming with whiskey, my
heart was beating, and my skin felt hot to my own touch. The
floor was unlevel when I walked to the bottle on the dresser, and
my breathing became heavier and more hoarse in my throat. We
went through all the positions which she knew and all the
experiments I could think of, re-creating the fantasies of adolescent masturbation. She was a good whore. She affected passion
without being deliberately obvious, and she tensed her body and
widened her legs at the right moment. After the third time when
I didn't think I could go again she bent over my stomach and
kissed me and used her hands until I was ready to enter her. She
was soft inside, and she hadn't been at her trade enough years yet
to enlarge too much. She raised herself on her elbows so that her
breasts hung close to my face, and constricted the muscles in her
stomach and twisted one thigh sideways each time we moved
until I began to feel it swell inside me, then build in force like a
large stone rolling downhill over the lip of a canyon, and burst
away outside of me with the empty tranquillity of an opium
dream.

Then I fell into an exhausted whiskey stupor. The dust in the
air looked like weevil worms turning in the shaft of sunlight that
struck against the Jack Daniel's bottle. The girl got up off the bed
and began dressing, and a few moments later I heard the door
click shut after her. I was sweating heavily, even in the air
conditioning, and I leaned my head over the edge of the bed to
make the room stop spinning. There were flashes of colour behind
my closed eyes, and obscene echoes of the things I had said to the
girl when the stone began to roll downhill. My throat and mouth
were dry from the whiskey and heavy breathing, the veins in my
head started to dilate with hangover, and I wanted to get into the
shower and sit on the floor under the cold water until I washed
all the heat out of my body; but instead I fell deeper into a
delirium and then the dream began.

I had many dreams left over from Korea. Sometimes I would

dig a grave in frozen ground while Sergeant Tien Kwong stood over me with his burpgun, occasionally jabbing the short barrel into my neck, his eyes flat with hatred. At other times the sergeant and I would return to the colonel's interrogation room, where I sat in a straight-backed chair and looked at nothing and said nothing until the sergeant brought my head down on his knee and broke my nose. Or sometimes I was alone, naked in the centre of the compound, where we were allowed to wash under the water spigot and scrub the lice out of the seams of our clothing once a week. And each time I went there and turned the rusted iron valve I saw the words embossed on the surface – *Manufactured in Akron, Ohio*.

But this afternoon I was back in the 'Shooting Gallery', a very special place for me, because it was there that my six days on the firing line ended. That afternoon had been quiet, and we had moved into a dry irrigation ditch that bordered a two-mile plain of rice farms with bare, artillery-scarred foothills on the far side. In the twilight I could see the shattered trees and torn craters from the 105s, and one hill, from which the North Koreans had started an attack, had been burned black with napalm strikes. We had heard that the First Marine Division had made contact with some Chinese at the Choshin, but our area was thought to be secure. They had two miles of open space to cross before they could reach us, and we had strung wire and mines outside our perimeter, although it was considered unnecessary because the North Koreans didn't have enough troops in the hills to pull a straight-on offensive. At seven thirty the searchlights went on and illuminated the rice fields and devastated slopes; then the nightly bugles and megaphone lectures against American capitalism started. The reverberating cacophony and the unnatural white light on the hills and corrugated rice fields seemed like an experiment in insanity held on the moon's surface. Sometimes the North Koreans would fail to pick up the phonograph needle and the record would scratch out static for several minutes, echoing down off the hills like someone raking his fingernails across a blackboard. Then the searchlights would change angle and sweep across the sky, reflecting momentarily on the clouds, and settle on another distant hilltop pocked with brown holes.

I sat with my back against the ditch and tried to sleep. My blanket was draped around me like iron in the cold, and my feet ached inside my boots. I had got wet that afternoon crossing a rice paddy, and grains of ice had started to form inside my clothes. Even with my stocking cap pulled low under my helmet, my ears felt as though they had been beaten with boards. In the distance I heard one of our tanks clanking down a road; then a .30 calibre machine-gun began firing far off on our right flank. 'What's that fucking asshole doing?' a corporal next to me said. He was a tall hillbilly boy from north Alabama. His blanket was pulled up over his helmet, and he had cut away his glove around the first finger of his right hand. I had a small bottle of codeine in my pack, and I started to take it out for a drink. It didn't taste as good as whiskey, but it warmed you inside like canned heat. The machine-gun fell silent a moment, then began firing again with longer bursts, followed by a BAR and the irregular popping of small-arms fire. 'What the hell is going on?' the corporal said. He raised up on his knees with his M-1 in his hands. Suddenly, flares began bursting in the sky, burning in white haloes above the corrugated fields. The corporal's face was as pale as candlewax in the light, his lips tight and bloodless.

The first mortar rounds struck outside our wire and exploded the mines we had strung earlier. Yellow and orange flames erupted out of the earth and flicked around the strands of concertina wire. I could feel the suck of hot hair from the vacuum, my ears roared with the thunder of freight trains crashing into one another, and the wall of the ditch slammed into my head like a sledge-hammer. The rim of my helmet had cut a neat slit across my nose, and I could taste the blood draining in a wet streak over my mouth. Somewhere down the line, among the shower of rocks and frozen earth, the tremors reverberating through the ground, the locomotive engines blowing apart, I heard a Marine shout, a prolonged voice rising out of a furnace, 'DOOOOOOOOOOOC!' I started to crawl along the floor of the ditch on my hands and knees, then the Chinese corrected their angle of fire and marched the barrage right down the centre of our line.

Somehow I had believed that if I ever bought one it would come as a result of some choice I had made; that I would be

killed after some positive act of my own – no matter how
unconscious or reckless – but there would still be a type of control
in my death. However, now I knew that I was going to die in the
middle of a fire-storm. I had no more chance of resisting my death
than if God crashed His fist down on top of me. The shells burst
in jagged intervals along the ditch, blowing men and weapons in
every direction. The corporal was suddenly frozen in an explosion
of light and dirt behind him. His mouth and eyes were wide, his
helmet pitted and torn with shrapnel. He seemed to pirouette in
slow motion, the weight of his tall body resting inside one boot,
then he fell backwards across me. The blood ran from his stocking
cap like pieces of string over his face. He opened and closed his
mouth with a wet, sucking sound, the saliva thick on his tongue.
He coughed once, quietly and deep in his throat; then his eyes
fixed on a phosphorescent flare burning above us.

Moments later the fire-storm ended, almost too quickly,
because it seemed that nothing that intense and murderous could
ever end, that it would perpetuate itself indefinitely with its own
cataclysmic force. I pushed the corporal off me, my ears ringing
in the silence (or what seemed like silence, since automatic
weapons had begun firing again on both sides of us). The
corporal's helmet rolled off his head, and I saw a long incision,
like a scalpel cut, across the crown of his skull. The dead were
strewn in unnatural positions along the ditch, some of them half-
buried in mounds of dirt from the caved-in walls, their bodies
twisted and broken as though they had been dropped from
aircraft. The faces of the wounded were white with shock and
concussion. Down the line a man was screaming.

'Are you hit, Doc?' It was the first lieutenant. He carried his
carbine in one hand. His left arm hung limply by his side.

'I'm all right.' Our voices sounded far away from me.

'Get ready to move the wounded out of here. The right flank is
getting their ass knocked off. We're supposed to get artillery in
five minutes and pull.'

'You're bleeding pretty heavy, Lieutenant.'

'Get every man moving you can. We're going to have gooks
coming up our ass.'

However, the artillery cover never came, and we were overrun fifteen minutes later. Our automatic weapons men killed Chinese by the hundreds as they advanced across the rice fields. We packed snow on the barrels of the .30 calibre machine guns to keep them from melting, and the bottom of the ditch was littered with spent shell casings and empty ammunition boxes. The dead lay in quilted rows as far as I could see. They moved forward and died, then another wave took their place. The bugles began blowing again, potato mashers exploded in our wire, and every time a weapon locked empty or a Marine was hit they moved closer to the ditch. Our only tank was burning behind us, the lieutenant was shot through the mouth, and all of our NCOs were dead. We fired our last rounds, fixed bayonets in a silly Alamo gesture, and then the Chinese swarmed over us.

They ran along the edge of the ditch, firing point-blank into us with their burpguns. They shot the dead and the living alike, in the hysterical relief that comes with the victory of living through an attack. Their weapons weren't designed for accuracy, but they could dump almost a full clip into a man who was closer than twenty feet. For the first time in my life I ran from an enemy. I dropped the handles of a stretcher with a wounded Marine on it and ran across the bodies, the ammunition boxes, the bent bazookas, the knocked-out machine-guns, the lieutenant spitting blood and parts of teeth on his coat, and suddenly I saw a young Chinese boy, not over seventeen, his thin, yellow face pinched with cold, standing above me in tennis shoes and quilted clothes. I guess (as I remember it) that I threw my arms out in front of me to prevent that spray of flame and bullets from entering my face and chest, but the gesture was unnecessary because he was a poor marksman and he never got above my knees. I felt a pain like a shaft of ice through both legs, and I toppled over as though a bad comic had just kicked me deftly across the shins.

My Korean recall, born out of Jack Daniel's and sexual exhaustion, ended here. I awoke at six thirty, sweating, my head thick with afternoon whiskey. For a half hour I sat on the shower tile under the cold water, chewing an unlit cigar. The white indentions in my calves felt like rubber under my thumb.

TWO

The Shamrock-Hilton Hotel in Houston was crowded that night with Democrats from all over Texas. They came in party loyalty almost seven hundred strong – the daughters of forgotten wars, the state committee from Austin, the AFL-CIO fat boys, the oil-depletion wheelers, manicured newspaper publishers, slick public relations men, millionaire women dressed in Neiman-Marcus clothes with Piney Woods accents, young lawyers on their way up in state politics (each of them with a clear eye, hard grip, and a square, cologned jaw like Fearless Fosdick), the ten-percenters, the new rich who bought their children's way into Randolph-Macon, the ranchers with a bright eye on the agriculture subsidy, a few semi-acceptable Mafia characters from Galveston, several ex-hacks, doormen, flunkies and baggage carriers from Lyndon's entourage, three Hollywood movie stars who had been born in Texas, an astronaut, one crippled commander of the Veterans of the Spanish-American War who sat in a wheelchair, an alcoholic baseball player who used to pitch for the Houston Buffaloes before he went up to the Cardinals, some highly paid prostitutes, an Air Force general who has probably won a footnote in military history for his dedication in the fire-bombing of Dresden, and United States Senator Allen B. Dowling.

I had driven from San Antonio in two and a half hours, highballing wide-open like a blue shot through small towns and farm communities, while drunken cowboys drinking beer in front of saloons stared at me in disbelief. I pulled into the white circular drive of the Shamrock and waited in the line of cars for the band of uniformed Negro porters to take over my luggage, my Cadillac, and even my attempt to open a door by myself. They moved about with the quick, electric motion of rubberbands snapping, their teeth white, their faces black and cordial, obsequious and yet confidently efficient. I imagined that they could have cut all our throats with pleasure. They reminded me of Negro troops in Korea when they were dealing with Mr Skins, a white officer. They could go about a job in a way that deserved group citations, and at the same time insult an officer and laugh in his face without doing anything for which they could be reprimanded unless the officer wanted to appear a public fool.

I idled the car up to the glass doors at the entrance; one Negro pulled open the car door for me, another got behind the wheel, and a third took my suitcase from the boot. I handed out one-dollar tips to each of them (with the stupid feeling of an artificial situation that you have when you pay a shoeshine boy), and followed the third porter into the hotel. And I wondered, looking at his grey, uniformed back, the muscles stiff and flat under the cloth, *Would you really like to tick a razor across my jugular, you uprooted descendant of Ham, divested of your heritage, dropped clumsily and illiterate into a south Texas cotton patch, where you could labour and exhaust yourself and kind through the next several generations on tenant shares? Yes, I guess you would, with a neat, sharp corner of the blade that you would draw gingerly along the vein.*

But I still had a fair edge on from the Jack Daniel's, the Mexican girl and the dream, and I imagine that is why I suddenly had such strange insights into that black mind walking before me.

I gave my name at the desk and was told that my wife had taken a suite of rooms on the tenth floor. She and my brother Bailey had come to Houston yesterday when the convention started, and I was supposed to join them today at noon for lunch on the terrace with several of the oil-depletion boys who had all types of money to sink into a young congressman's career. However, I didn't have to speak before the convention until ten that night, and I didn't think that I could take a full day of laughing conversation, racial jokes, polite gin by the swimming pool, and powdered, middle-aged oil wives who whispered banal remarks like slivers of glass in my ear. I had met all of them before in Dallas, Austin, Fort Worth and El Paso, and they were always true to themselves, regardless of the place or occasion. The men wore their same Oshman western suits and low-topped boots, the diamond rings from Zale's that looked out of place on their fat hands, the string ties or open-neck sports shirts that directed attention away from the swift eyes and the broken veins in the cheeks. They spoke of huge finance with indifference, but I knew that their groins tingled with pleasure at the same time.

Their women liked me because I was young and good-looking, successful as a lawyer, tanned from playing in fashionable tennis courts, and with an inner steeled effort I could clink the ice in my glass and look pleasant and easy while they told about all the trivial problems in their insipid lives (in this respect I was very self-disciplined, because I always knew when to excuse myself and walk away before the inner rigidity broke apart).

Besides, I really didn't need them to be elected congressional representative from my district. The Holland name and my father's reputation would assure almost any member of my family a political position if he wanted it. Also, people still remembered when I returned from the war as a wounded hospital corpsman, dressed in Marine tropicals with a walking stick, an ex-POW who had resisted brainwashing for thirty-two months while other American troops were signing confessions, informing on each other, and defecting to the Chinese.

Finally, my Republican opponent was a seedy racist, so fanatical even in his business dealings that his insurance agency failed. At different times he had belonged to the John Birch and Paul Revere societies, the Independent Million, the White Citizens League and the Dixiecrat Party. He was a mean and obnoxious drunk, a bully towards his wife and children, and I don't know why the Republicans let him run, except for the fact that he could always raise money from fools like himself and they hadn't won an election in DeWitt since Reconstruction, anyway.

Verisa had taken a five-room suite with a cocktail bar, deep rugs, oil paintings on the walls, potted rubber plants, and a porch that overlooked the swimming pool far below. The porter set my suitcase down and closed the door behind me. I could see the anger in Verisa's eyes. She sat on the couch in a white evening gown, her legs crossed tightly, with the tip of one high-heeled shoe pointed into the coffee table. Her auburn hair was brushed to a metallic shine, and her skin looked as bloodless and smooth as marble. If I had been closer to her I could have smelled the touch of perfume behind her ears, the powdered breasts, the hinted scent of her sex, a light taste of gin on her breath. She looked at me briefly, then turned her eyes away and lit a cigarette.

The toe of the shoe flicked momentarily into a carved design in the side of the table. She was always able to hold her anger in well. She had learned part of that at Randolph-Macon and the rest from living with me. She could reduce flying rage to a hot cigarette ash or a few whispered and rushed words in the corner of a cocktail party, or maybe one burst of heat after we were home; but the pointed flick of the shoe was a fleshy bite into my genitals for seven years of marriage, broken young-girl dreams, her embarrassment when I brought oil-field workers or soldiers from Fort Sam Houston to the country club, my drunken discussions in the middle of the night about my Korean War guilt, and for the stoic and futile resignation she had adopted, out of all her social disappointments, in hopes of becoming the wife of a Texas congressman on his way to the Senate and that opulent world of power which goes far beyond any of the things you can buy or destroy with money.

'Hack, don't you give a goddamn?' she said quietly, still looking straight ahead.

'What did I miss?'

'A day of my making excuses for you, and right now I'm rather sick of it.'

'Lunch by the pool with the Dallas aristocracy can't be that awful.'

'I'm not in a flippant mood, Hack. I don't enjoy apologizing or lying for you, and I don't like sitting three hours by myself with boorish business people.'

'Those are the cultured boys with the money. The fellows who oil all the wheels and make Frankenstein run properly.'

I went to the bar and poured a double shot of whiskey over ice. It clicked pleasantly on the edge of the afternoon drunk, and I felt even more serene in the sexual confidence which I always had towards Verisa after whoring.

'I don't know where you've been, but I suspect it was one of your Okie motel affairs.'

'I had to meet R. C. Richardson in Austin.'

'How much do you pay them? Do they go down on you? That's what they call it in the trade, isn't it?'

'It's something like that.'

'They must be lovely girls. Do they perform any other special things for you?'

'Right now R.C.'s working on a deal to patent hoof and mouth disease. He has federal contracts for Viet Nam that run in millions.'

'Your girl friends probably have had some nice diseases of their own.'

'Let it go, Verisa.'

'Oh, I shouldn't say anything to you? Is that it? I should spend a day of congenial conversation with people who chew on toothpicks, and then meet you pleasantly at the door after you return from screwing a Mexican whore.'

Something inside me flinched at her accuracy. I poured a short drink into the bottom of the glass.

'I bet you've gone to bed with me, not knowing whether they had given you one of their diseases,' she said.

She was really tightening the iron boot now.

'Do you want a highball? I'm going to change clothes.'

'Oh Christ, you've probably done it,' she said, and put her fingers over her mouth.

'I never did that to you.'

'You probably don't even remember. You have to wait two weeks to know, don't you?'

'You're letting it walk away with you.' But she was right. I didn't remember.

'It happened to a girl I knew in college, but she was a dumpy thing who did it in the back seats of cars with Marines and sailors. I didn't believe it ever happened with your husband.'

'Pull off it. You're working towards a real bad conclusion.'

'I wonder that you didn't give me sulpha tablets.'

I fixed her a drink with a squeeze of lemon and set it on the table in front of her.

'I'm sorry that you got strung out today,' I said. 'I thought Bailey would take you to lunch if I didn't make it.'

'Tell me if you really did it to me.'

'Look, it was a shitty day for you. I should have been here to eat lunch with those bastards, or I should have called Bailey and told him to take care of it. But I'm going to change clothes now. We should go downstairs in a few minutes.'

'You must have a very special clock to go by. It starts to work correctly when you feel the corner at your back.'

'You ought to drink your highball.'

'Why don't you drink it? It makes you more electric and charming in public,' she said.

'You've got it out pretty far in a short time.'

'I might stretch it out so far that you ache.'

'Isn't this just spent effort? If you want to believe that you've won the ballgame in the ninth inning, go ahead. Or maybe you would like me to kiss your ass in apology.'

'You've done that without a need for apologizing. An analyst would have a wonderful time with you.'

'I won't go into embarrassing descriptions, but as I recall you enjoyed every little piece of it.'

'Yes, I remember those sweet experiences. You tried to enact all the things you had learned in a Japanese whorehouse while you slobbered about two boys who died in a Chinese prison camp.'

'You better shut it off in a hurry.'

'What was the boy's name from San Angelo and the Negro sergeant from Georgia?'

'You don't listen when I tell you something, do you?'

'It's just a little bit of recall from things you brought up. Didn't you say they were buried in a latrine? In your words, to lend more American fertilizer to the Korean rice crop.'

'You're fucking in the wrong direction.'

'My, Captain Marvel with his favourite drunk word.'

'This isn't your style. So step back real quick before you find yourself in a bad place.'

'Are you going to hit me? That would make a perfect punctuation mark in my day.'

'Just don't bend it any more.'

'Don't walk away, Hack. If you blow this for us, I'll divorce you and sue for the home. Then I'll repay you in the most fitting way I can think of. I'll cover that historical cemetery of yours with concrete.'

I took the bottle of whiskey and my glass from the bar and slammed the bedroom door behind me. I could feel the anger beating in my head and the veins swelling in my throat. I seldom became angry about anything, but this time she had reached inside me hard and had got a good piece between her nails. I drank out of the bottle twice and started to change clothes. My face was flushed with heat in the mirror. I kicked my trousers against the wall and pulled off my shirt, stripping the buttons. I stood in my underwear and had another drink, this time with measured sips. The whiskey began to flatten out inside me, and I felt a single drop of perspiration run down off an eyebrow. Hold it in, sonofabitch, I thought. The Lone Ranger never blows his Kool-Aid. You just give the sheriff a silver bullet and let Tonto pour you a drink. But Verisa had really been off her style this time. She had collected a valise of surgical tools during the day for an entry into all my vital organs. In fact, I didn't know whether to mark this to her debit or credit. As I said, in the past she could always load all of her outrage into a quiet hypodermic needle, thrust subtly into the right place (her best probe, the one she used after I had done something especially painful to that private part of her soul, was to go limp and indifferent under me, her arms spread back on the pillows, during my disabling moment of climax).

I had one more drink, just enough to go over the back of the tongue, then brushed my teeth, took three aspirins and two vitamin pills, and rinsed out my whiskey breath with Listerine. I dressed in an Italian silk shirt, a dark tie, a pressed white suit, and rubbed the polish smooth on my boots with a damp towel. I lit a cigar and breathed out the smoke in the mirror. You're all right, Masked Man, I thought.

I heard Verisa open the front door, then the voices of Bailey and Senator Dowling.

'Hack,' Verisa said, tapping her fingernails lightly on my door. I knew she had already gone into her transformation as the pleasant wife of a congressional candidate. It was amazing how fast it could take place.

I stepped out of the bedroom and shook hands with the Senator.

'How are you, Hack?' he said, his face healthy and cheerful. He was fifty-five years old, but his handshake was still hard and his wrist strong. He was six inches shorter than I, solidly built, his shoulders pulled straight back, and his white hair trimmed close to the scalp. His acetylene-blue eyes were bright and quick, impossible to penetrate, and you knew after he glanced confidently into your face that his lack of height was no disadvantage to him. He had the small, hard chest of a professional soldier, and his tailored suit didn't have a fold or a bulge in it. He wore dentures, and they caused him to lisp slightly with his Texas accent, but otherwise he was solid. Also, Senator Dowling had managed to remain a strong southern figure through five administrations. He had been on many sides over the years, and he always walked out of the ballpark with the winning team (and therein lay his gift, the ability to sense change before anyone else got a whiff of it). He was put into Congress by a one-million-acre southwest Texas corporation ranch in 1940, and in the next two years he paid off his obligations by sponsoring large subsidies for growing nothing on arid land. Then he represented the oil interests, the franchised utility companies, and the Houston and Dallas industries up on antitrust suits. He assured his constituents that he was a segregationist until the Kennedy administration, then he backed one of the first civil rights bills. In the meantime he acquired a three-thousand-acre ranch in the hill country north of Austin, and stock in almost every major corporation in Texas with a defence contract.

'Fine, Senator. How have you been?' I said.

'Good. Relaxing at the ranch. Fishing and playing tennis a little bit before the campaign.'

'Hack, fix the Senator a drink,' Verisa said.

'Thank you. A half jigger and some soda will be fine,' he said.

'You should try the bass in Hack's ponds,' Bailey said. He sat in one of the tall bar chairs with his arm over the back. Good old Bailey, I thought. He could always come through with an inane remark at the right time. He looked like my twin, except five years older and fifteen pounds heavier, with wrinkles in his forehead and neck. Bailey was a practical man who worried about all the wrong things.

'I'd hoped to talk with you earlier today,' the Senator said, and looked straight into my face with those acetylene-blue eyes.

'I had to stop over in Austin with a client. Maybe we can talk after my speech,' I said.

'Verisa says you're having people up for drinks later. I'd rather we have some time between ourselves.'

'Hack, we're invited for breakfast at the River Oaks Country Club in the morning,' Bailey said. 'Maybe the Senator can join us. You all can talk, and then we'll play some doubles.'

'That sounds fine,' the Senator said. 'I could use a couple of sets against an ex-Baylor pitcher.'

The sonofabitch, I thought.

'My opponent hasn't somehow organized his ragtail legions, has he?'

'Oh no, no. I don't think we need to spend too much time on this gentleman.' He laughed with his healthy smile. 'I wanted to talk with you about several things that will come later in Washington. Your father helped me a great deal when I was first elected to Congress, and I learned then that it's invaluable to have an experienced friend.'

I handed him his highball glass with the half jigger and soda. He had learned to be a cautious person with liquor, and I knew he wouldn't finish the glass I had given him.

'Well, I appreciate it, Senator. But I don't know how good my Baylor arm will be on the court,' I said, biting down inside myself.

'Hack is defensive tonight,' Verisa said.

'He should be,' the Senator said. His eyes took on a deeper blue with his smile.

'I have a weak serve, but I'm hell on defending the net,' I said. 'One flash of the wrist and I drive tennis balls into concrete.'

'We had better go downstairs pretty soon,' Bailey said. His face was flat, but his discomfort showed in the nervous tic of his fingers on his trouser leg.

'I don't expect that our audience will disappear,' the Senator said. 'They usually have their way of waiting, as a US Senator sometimes does.'

Sorry, you bastard. I'm all out of sackcloth and ashes tonight, I thought. I set my cigar in the ashtray and poured an inch of Jack Daniel's into a glass. Bailey's face began to tighten in the silence. Verisa's eyes waited on me, her lips pinched slightly, but I held out. I sipped the whiskey and drew in on the cigar as though the conversation were far removed from me.

'Would you like to drive with us out to the country club in the morning?' Bailey said.

'Thanks. I'll find my way there. From what I understand, Hack drives like he's trying to put A. J. Foyt back in the grease pit,' the Senator said.

'I wouldn't try to beat a Texas boy at his own game, Senator.'

'It depends on what type of game.' His eyes crinkled at me.

'I have a pretty good shutout record in my field.'

'I remember, Hack. I watched you pitch twice. But as I recall you used to have a little trouble with a left-handed batter.'

'Sometimes you have to bear down a little more.'

He took a thin swallow of his highball and placed the glass on the bar, his expression assured and pleasant, then looked casually at his watch.

'Bailey's probably right. We should go downstairs. I'll drop up later for a few minutes and say hello to your guests,' he said, and put his hand on the small of my back. 'Then tomorrow we'll see what type of tennis game we can work out.'

I saw the ease come back into Verisa's face, and Bailey stood up stiffly as though he had just been unstrapped from an electric chair. I took my typewritten speech in its leather folder from my suitcase, and we walked down the carpeted corridor towards the lift like an amiable family of four.

The dining tables in the Shamrock Room were filled. The silver, the crystalware, the white tablecloths, the spangled evening gowns and decanters of wine reflected softly under the lights. The Senator introduced me from the rostrum, and the rows of faces became hushed and polite. Even the fat boys from the oil interests, in their string ties and cowboy boots, looked quietly deferential. I read them my twenty-minute speech of non-language and they applauded thirteen times. Whenever I approached some vague conclusion, pointed at nothing, I could see their eyes grow more intent, their heads nodding slightly, as some private anger with the nation, the universe, or themselves found a consensus in my empty statements, then the hands would begin clapping. They had found a burning spokesman to represent all the outraged good guys. I was tight enough to be unconscious of my speech's stupidity, and after a while I even felt that I might be saying something meaningful. They rose to their feet when I finished. I shook dozens of hands, smiled with country boy humility at the compliments, and invited half the dining room to Verisa's cocktail party.

The party was a success in every way. Verisa was able to become the radiant wife of a congressional candidate, moving with detached pleasantness between groups of people (the society editors from *The Houston Post* and *The Chronicle* both agreed the next day that Mrs Holland was one of the most lovely hostesses to appear in Texas politics in a long time). And I was able to make a doubleheader out of the evening: I managed to get drunk twice in one day. The Negro waiters put a fresh whiskey and water in my hand every time I flicked my eyes in their direction, and within two hours Mr Hyde had begun to prowl obscenely through the hallways of my mind. The room was so crowded by midnight that the air conditioning couldn't clear the smoke, and the noise brought complaints from the floors above and below us. People whom I had never seen before drank three cases of bourbon and Scotch, ate four hundred dollars' worth of catered food, burned cigar holes in the carpet, charged thirty-minute long-distance calls to my room, and threw glasses and bottles off the terrace into the swimming pool. Someone wheeled in the commander from the Veterans of the Spanish-American War, who sat stupefied in one corner, staring out at the bedlam from his atrophied, withered face, until a sentimental WW II veteran decided to take him on a careening ride through the corridor. The alcoholic baseball pitcher and I argued about how to throw a crippling beanball, one of the society editors threw up in the bathroom and had to be put in bed by Verisa, and the firebomber of Dresden unzipped the back of a woman's evening dress.

I insulted the astronaut and his wife, who left after a polite five-minute interval, then two of the Negro bartenders quit when an oil broker made a racial remark to them. I took over the bar and poured all the remaining bourbon, gin and Scotch into a punch bowl, and insisted that everyone in the room have a drink. This resulted in four more people passing out, a clogged toilet, and a group plan to open up the dining room for steak and eggs. Someone brought in a hillbilly singer from a nightclub, who propositioned Verisa, and the Air Force general drank six glasses from the punch bowl and urinated off the balcony. By four a.m. the room was totally destroyed. All the furniture was either burned or broken, the floor was littered with cigar and cigarette butts, the French doors were smashed, the potted plants over-turned, and the electric plug in the drink mixer had short-circuited and melted into the wall socket. (Later, I received an eight-hundred-dollar repair bill from the Shamrock-Hilton, and I kindly forwarded it to the Texas Democratic Committee in Austin).

At five a.m. the last of the guests supported each other out of the door, while Verisa accepted their incoherent compliments and told them to visit us at the ranch (she was still radiant, even through her fatigue). I lay down on the bed next to the society editor, and as the false dawn glowed on the horizon and touched the room with its grey light, she rolled her head towards me, her mouth wide with snoring, her face oval and white, and I thought *Good night, good night, sweet Desdemona,* and I fell once more into Mr Hyde's world.

The clay tennis courts at the country club were green and freshly chalked under a hot, blue sky. I sat at a marble-topped table with Bailey under the shade trees, sipping a glass of tomato juice and vodka, while Verisa and the Senator whocked the ball back and forth across the net. Behind the courts the sun shattered off the swimming pool, and children in dripping swimsuits lined up on the diving board. In the distance the smooth green contours of the golf course arched away through the oak trees, and the sandtraps looked like ground white crystal in the light. My hangover was bad. I was sweating unnaturally, shaking inside like a tuning fork vibrating to the wrong chord, and I felt a hard pressure band across one side of my head. My tennis shorts and polo shirt were already wet, although I hadn't been on the court yet, and the vodka wouldn't take hold. Bailey kept talking about our law practice in Austin, my failure to come into the office regularly, and my rudeness to the Senator. His words were like pieces of broken china in my head. He spoke from some abstraction inside himself, looking into my eyes occasionally, his face earnest with the dumb innocence of a non-drinker talking to a man with a bleeding hangover. I lit a cigar, tried to concentrate on the tennis game, and had another vodka and tomato juice.

'It's insane to do these things to yourself,' he said. 'You're hungover three days out of seven, you go into court with your fingers shaking, and in the meantime other people are picking up after you.'

'Are you picking up after me, Bailey?'

'What do you think I did yesterday? And last night you insulted a half dozen people within fifteen minutes.'

'I thought I only got the astronaut.' I wiped the sweat off my forehead on my sleeve and drained the vodka and tomato juice.

'You want to get blasted again?'

'I might unless the conversation changes.'

'It's goddamn insane. You can be in office in a few months. The youngest congressman from the state. After one or two terms you can do anything you want in Texas.'

'I know those things.'

'Then why don't you act like you have a goddamn mind?'

I held up my glass to the waiter for another drink.

'You count on too much from people,' Bailey said.

'Will you go to hell or shut up for about five minutes?'

'You can get angry, but I'm right in what I say.'

'Bailey, would you get away from me a few minutes?'

'You see what that booze does?'

'Goddamn it, go swimming or chase golf balls if you like. Believe me, I'm up to my eyes with it.'

He stood up, his face slightly hurt and angry, and walked across the clipped grass to the clubhouse. I knew that in a half hour he would be back as though nothing had been said, and then later he would start to bore in again. Bailey was a good boy, but he was simply unteachable.

The Senator moved about the court like a man twenty years younger than his age. I have to admit that he looked good out there. The matted grey hair on his chest and his thick, muscular shoulders glistened with sweat, and he whocked the ball in a white streak across the net. For a short man he had a fine driving serve, and his backhand was always accurate and strong. He had a good eye for court distance, and most of his shots just skimmed the top of the net and hit in a low bounce on the clay. Verisa was a good tennis player, but he took her in two easy sets. The Senator was a competitor, and his gentlemanly affection ended when he entered the games.

They joined me at the table, and the waiter served us a cold lunch of picked shrimp on cracked ice. For the next hour I listened to the Senator's advice on my campaign, the forthcoming year in Congress, and contributions from several oil companies (the cheques, which already amounted to over sixty-five thousand dollars, had all been deposited by Bailey in a special account in Austin). Then I was told indirectly, with compassion, to avoid public statements on civil rights, at least while in Texas, and that I shouldn't lean too far towards labour, since as a Democrat I could already count on their vote. I nodded my head and listened as intelligently as possible, but my hangover wouldn't let go and few of his sentences seemed to have any relationship to one another. Actually, more than any instruction in Texas politics, he wanted to exact penance from me because of yesterday, and I was in the perfect condition for it – a mental cripple.

'Next week I plan to visit the wounded Viet Nam veterans in Walter Reed,' he said. 'I think it might be good for you to come along.'

'Why's that?'

'You were wounded yourself in Korea. I think the boys like to know that they have congressmen who understand what they've been through.'

'I'm afraid I had enough of VA hospitals, Senator,' I said.

'We'll be there an hour or so. Then you'll be back home the same night.'

'I better pass.'

'Go on, Hack. Bailey will be at the office,' Verisa said.

'No, I don't—'

'You need a trip. Enjoy it,' Bailey said. He had come back from the clubhouse fresh with resolve.

'I spent two months in the VA in '53 and I really—' I was smiling in my best convivial way.

'This type of exposure is important to you, Hack,' the Senator said.

Fuck it, I thought. 'All right, Senator. I'll be glad to.'

We finished lunch and played a set of doubles. Verisa and I stood the Senator and Bailey, and the sweat rolled down my face and chest in rivulets. My timing was bad, my movements uncoordinated, and I drove most of my serves into the bottom of the net. My head was thundering from the heat and exertion. The air seemed so humid that it was like steam on my skin. If Bailey hadn't been such a bad player we would have lost the set six games straight, but Verisa managed to keep us only one game behind. I was even proud of her. In her short white tennis skirt and cap with a green visor she was the loveliest thing on the courts. Her legs and shoulders were freckled with suntan, her auburn hair wet and shining on the back of her neck, and you could get a good look at her fine ass when she bent over with her serve.

We went into the final game five to four, and I wanted to beat the Senator very badly. He played confidently, controlling the backline with an easy sweep of his racket in either direction. His thick eyebrows were heavy with perspiration, and his blue eyes refracted a mean success every time he drove the ball into my shoelaces.

However, I soon learned that the Senator's revenge for yesterday wasn't complete yet. I moved up to the net for the final point, Verisa served, and Bailey returned the ball in an easy, high-arching lob. I whocked it with all the strength in my shoulder straight into the Senator. The game should have been over and the set tied, but the Senator caught my drive with one short, forearm chop of the racket, and smashed the ball murderously into my face. My sunglasses broke on the court, my eyes watered uncontrollably, and I felt the blood running from my nose.

Through the tears I could see him walking quickly towards me, his face gathered in concern, but there was victory in his eyes.

Later, Verisa drove us back to the hotel while I held a blood-flecked towel filled with ice cubes to my nose. The bridge was already swollen, and there was a sickening taste in the back of my throat. I tilted my head back on the seat and looked with one eye out of the window at the stream of angry traffic along South Main. At the court the Senator had apologized in his most empathic manner, the tennis pro arrived with a first-aid kit and tried to push cotton balls up my nose, a Negro waiter put another vodka and tomato juice on the table and left, and now Bailey sat in the back seat talking about going to the hospital for an X-ray.

'Do you think it's broken?' Verisa said.

'No, he just flattened it a little. A warning,' I said. My words were nasal and smothered under the towel.

'It was an accident,' Bailey said. 'You cut the ball right into him.'

'Why don't you get off the goodguymanship ethic? Leave the Boy Scouts for a while, at least till we get to the hotel,' I said. 'He was out to tear my head off.'

'That's hangover paranoia.'

'Oh, shit,' I said.

'How many US Senators would spend their time trying to help a thirty-five-year-old lawyer's political career?'

'Don't you know a sonofabitch when you see one?'

'You're constructing things to fit some strange frame of reference in your own mind.'

'You're an amateur, Bailey. You better learn to recognize sophisticated viciousness.'

'You're really thinking foolishly.'

'I don't care if you want to look at the world like Little Orphan Annie. But right now I feel like someone took a shit in my head, my nose is full of blood, and if you say anything more I'm going to call the Senator from the hotel and give him my best delivery.'

'You better take us to Herman Hospital,' Bailey said.

'I've had my nose broken before and I know what it feels like. Just turn it off for a few more blocks.'

'I'll have the hotel doctor come to the room,' Verisa said.

'Forget that, too,' I said. 'I'm driving down to the Valley this afternoon. Just as soon as I can get six aspirins down and a double shot of Jack Daniel's.'

'You're going to the Valley!' Verisa said. Her head turned sharply at me.

'I got a letter from a Mexican fellow I was in Korea with. He got involved in some trouble with this farm labour union, and he's in the county jail waiting to go up to prison on a five-year sentence.'

'What am I supposed to do in the meantime?' she said.

'Ride back home with Bailey or take a flight. You don't like to drive with me, anyway.'

'So I'm left with the pleasant experience of explaining the condition of the room to the management. Is that it?' she said. 'I imagine that by this time the cleaning woman has run down the hall in hysterics.'

'Ignore them. We didn't do the damage. They know what to expect when they contract for a convention. Particularly when it's composed of lunatics.'

'It's lovely of you to leave me with these things.'

'All right. I'll talk with the manager on the way out. I'll drip a few drops of blood on his desk, talk with him cordially, and then I'll tell him to go to hell.'

'You do what you want, Hack,' she said. 'Get drunk for a week in the Valley, go across the border and find a sweet two-dollar girl, indulge all your disgusting obsessions.'

She turned the car into the hotel drive, and a doorman stepped out to the edge of the walk under the canopy. I rubbed the dampness of the towel over my face.

'I have to go see this man,' I said. 'He was a good friend to me when I went on the line. I was so goddamned scared I couldn't paste a Band-Aid on a scratch.'

'Just don't talk about it,' she said. 'Drive down the road and forget anything else. That's the way you do things best.'

'Listen a minute. I don't enjoy driving three hundred miles in one-hundred-degree heat with a hangover and a bloody nose. But this man has five years' hard time to do because of a scuffle on a picket line. He doesn't have a goddamn cent and he can't get a white lawyer to file an appeal for him. Next week he'll be chopping cotton on the prison farm and there won't be a thing I can do for him.'

'We can call the ACLU. You don't have to go down there today,' Bailey said.

'No, you go on, Hack,' she said. 'It would be too terrible for you to live through one day of putting things together without beginning another adventure.'

'OK, piss on it,' I said. 'I'll catch air in a few minutes, and you can go back to the ranch and serve cocktails to the DAR. Then next week we can take a trip to Walter Reed and shake hands with the basket cases. A war-time VA ward should be included on all bus tours. You can meet the dummies in their wheelchairs and the guys without human faces. It's a balling scene.'

Bailey lit his pipe in the back seat and Verisa's eyes were brilliant with anger as the doorman stepped around the front of the car. I lowered the window and dumped the cracked ice in the towel on to the concrete.

People stared at me in the lobby as I walked towards the elevator with the towel under my nose. I still wore my tennis shorts and canvas shoes, with a sports coat over my blood-streaked polo shirt. Verisa and Bailey walked on each side of me as impervious as granite. Upstairs, I showered and changed into a pair of cream slacks and a soft, maroon shirt, ordered a bottle of Jack Daniel's from the bar, and ate a half dozen aspirin in the bathroom. I could hear Verisa making reservations on an afternoon flight to San Antonio. I looked in the mirror at my swollen nose, a slightly puffed upper lip, and the white discoloration in my face, and I decided to leave the whiskey doubleheaders to Grover Alexander or some other better left-hander than I. A bellboy brought the bottle; I took one drink out of it and closed the suitcase. I started to speak to Verisa, but she put a cigarette in her mouth and looked out through the smashed French doors at the oil wells pumping in the distance.

THREE

The late sun was red on the hills above the Rio Grande. The river was almost dry in places, dividing around bleached sandbars, and in the twilight the water had turned scarlet. On the other side, in Mexico, there were adobe huts and wooden shacks along the banks, and buzzards circled high in the sky. I turned off the air conditioner, rolled down the windows, and let the warm air blow through the car. In the first quick rush of wind I could smell the sweet ripeness of the whole Valley: the citrus groves, the tomato and watermelon fields, the rows of cotton and corn, the manure, and pastures of bluebonnets. The windmills were spinning, and cattle moved lazily towards the troughs. A single scorch of cloud stretched across the sun, which now seemed to grow in size as it dipped into the hills. The base of the pin oaks and blackjack trees grew darker, then the bottom rim of the sky glowed with flame.

I had mended from my hangover during the long drive, and I felt the numb serenity of a longtime dying man who had just received an unexpected extension of life. Then, in that cool moment of reflection, I wondered why I always drank twice as much when I had to make ritual appearances, or why I had gone to Houston in the first place, since my talk before a few hundred semiliterate oil men had little to do with my probable election, anyway; or lastly, why I had ever entered politics and the world of Senator Allen B. Dowling.

I could guess at the answers to the first two questions, which weren't of particular consequence, except that I didn't want another hangover and defeat at the tennis court like I'd had this morning; but the answer to the third question worked its way through the soft tissue and dropped like an ugly, sharp-edged black diamond into a bright space in the centre of my mind. Inside, under all the cynicism, the irreverence towards the icons and totems, my insults to astronauts and country club women, I wanted a part of the power at the top.

I tried to believe that my motive was to atone for Verisa's spent dreams, or that I wanted to equal my father in his law and congressional career, or at least that I was simply an ironic man who felt he could do as good a job as comic-page segregationists; or maybe at worst I was just a pragmatist with knowledge of the money to be made in the dealings between the federal government and the oil interests. But that black diamond had blood crusted on its edges, and I knew that I had the same weaknesses as Verisa and the Senator; I wanted power itself, the tribal recognition that went with it, and that small key to its complexities carried secretly in my watchpocket.

I accelerated the Cadillac through the low hills towards Pueblo Verde. The evening had started to cool, the sky deepened to dark purple, and the last of the sun's afterglow burned into itself in a gathering fire at one small point on the horizon. I didn't care for these moments of reflection, even though they came with the cool release from hangover, and I had learned long ago that solitude and introspection always bring you to Mr Hyde's cage. Every jailer knows that an inmate would rather take a beating with a garden hose than go to solitary, where the snakes start coming out of hibernation and the voices from years ago thunder through long tunnels. The North Koreans and the Chinese knew the same trick, too. The broken noses and smashed finger tips, or even digging your own grave under Sergeant Tien Kwong's burpgun, weren't nearly as effective as six weeks in a dirt hole with an iron sewer grate over your head. There you could concentrate on your guilt for forgotten sins, your inadequacy as a man, your lack of courage when you dropped a wounded Marine on a stretcher and ran, your resentment towards a dying Australian who was always given the largest portion of rice in the shack; or you could look up through the iron slits in the grate at the Chinese sentry who watched you while you squatted like a dog and defecated into a helmet.

So Socrates and his know-thyself ethic were full of shit, I thought, or he never spent time in solitary before he drank the hemlock or drove down a south Texas road on a clear summer evening with Mr Hyde sitting in the passenger's seat.

The main street in Pueblo Verde was almost empty, the wood frame buildings along the high pavements locked and darkened. A few old cars and pickup trucks were parked in front of a beer tavern with an insect-encrusted neon sign buzzing above a broken screen door. In the Sunday night quiet I could hear the hillbilly music from the jukebox and the laughter of half a dozen high school kids smoking cigarettes under the oaks in the courthouse square.

The hotel was a two-storey wooden building with flaking white paint and a latticed verandah. The letters on the ROOMS FOR GUESTS sign were blistered and faded, and the small lobby, with a plastic television set in one corner and wilted flowers in dime-store vases, smelled like dust and old wallpaper. I signed the register while the desk clerk looked over my shoulder at my Cadillac parked in front, then I could feel his eyes become more intent on the side of my face.

'Will you have somebody wake me at seven in the morning?' I said.

'You're getting on the road early, huh?'

'No, I'll be in town.'

'Oh.' His narrow grey face continued to watch me as I followed the Negro hired man with my bag towards the staircase.

My room overlooked the street and the trees on the courthouse lawn. I sent the Negro to the tavern for six bottles of Jax, pulled off my shirt, and turned on the overhead wooden fan. It was probably too late to visit the jail, and also I was too spent to argue with night-duty cops. I sat in a straw armchair with my feet in the open window and pried the cap off a beer with my pocketknife. The foam boiled over the top and ran down cold on my chest. I tilted the bottle and drank it straight to the bottom. I could still feel the highway rushing under my car, the mesquite and blackjack sweeping behind me, and I drank two more beers, tasting each cool swallow slowly. Then a breeze began to blow through the window, a train whistle echoed beyond the dark hills, and I fell asleep in the chair with a half-empty bottle held against my bare stomach.

At first I felt only the swaying motion of the freight car and the vibration of the wheels clicking across the points. Then I heard my own voice, loud with urgency, telling me to wake up before it started. But it was too late, or that alter-self inside was inept in turning off the right valve, because I now saw the drawn faces of the other men crowded in the freight car with me. Outside in the night the snow was driving almost parallel to the ground, there was a slick of ice on the floor of the car, and some of the men had already been stripped of their boots by the Chinese. Their feet were beginning to discolour with the first stages of frostbite, and by morning the skin would be an ugly yellow and purple, the toes swollen into balloons. I watched a Greek urinate on his feet, then dry them carefully and rewrap them with his scarf. The wounds in my calves throbbed with each pitch of the car, and the blood had run down into my socks and frozen. But I had been lucky. The Chinese had machine-gunned all our wounded before we were loaded on the train, and I would have been shot, too, except that I had managed to keep limping forward in the line between two Marines. Before the guard slammed the freight car door and bolted it, I looked out into the snow at the bodies of the men who had been thrown begging in front of the burpguns. Their mouths and eyes were still wide with disbelief and protest, their hair flecked with snow like old men.

In the next fifteen hours the train stopped three times, and each time we heard a freight car door slide open, hysterical shouts in English and Chinese, and the firing of burpguns. Whenever the train slowed we became a community of fear as each of us listened, motionless, to the decreasing metallic clack of the wheels. Once, while pulled off on a siding, we heard several guards crunching outside in the snow, then they stopped in front of our freight car. They talked for a minute, laughed, and one of them slid back the iron bolt on the door. I looked dumbly into the black eyes of the Greek who had urinated on his feet, and the heart-racing fear and desperate question mark in his face seemed to join us together in a quick moment of recognition. Then another train roared by us a few feet away, its whistle screaming in our ears, and our freight car jolted forward, knocking us backwards into one another. We heard the bolt slam into place and the guards running towards the caboose.

By morning the car was rancid with excrement and urine. We had no water, and several men broke ice from the floor with their boots and melted it in a helmet over a dozen cigarette lighters. It tasted like wheat chaff, sweat and manure. The snow had stopped blowing and the sun shone through the cracks in the walls. The light broke in strips on our bodies, and the stench from the corner began to grow more intense. During the night I had been unable to stand up and urinate through a crack in the car wall, and I had to let it run warmly down my thighs. My own odour sickened me. I wondered if the Jews who had been freighted to extermination camps in eastern Europe ever felt the same self-hating, cynical disgust at their condition, lying in their own excretions, or if they tried to tear the boards out of the walls with their fingernails and catch one SS guard around the throat with probing thumbs. My feeling was that they went to their deaths like tired people lined up before a movie which no one wanted to see, revulsed by themselves and the human condition, their naked bodies already shining with the iridescence of the dead.

I woke into the hot morning with a dark area of warm beer in my lap. Two Negro trusties from the jail, the white letter *P* Cloroxed on the backs of their denim shirts, were watering the courthouse lawn. The wet grass was shiny with light, and the shade of the oaks was like a deep bruise on the footpaths. At the edge of the square there was an open-air fruit market, with canvas stretched on poles over the bins, and Mexican farmhands were unloading cantaloupes and rattlesnake melons from the bed of a stake truck. The sky was clear blue, and the shadows from a few pink clouds moved over the hills.

I dressed in my linen suit with a blue silk shirt and walked down the main street to a café. I had a breakfast steak with two fried eggs on top, then smoked a cigar and drank coffee until the courthouse opened. Even though I could feel the July heat rising, it was still a beautiful day, the orchards at the foot of the hills were bursting with green and gold, I was free from the weekend's whiskey, and I didn't want to visit the jail. Most people think that the life of a criminal lawyer is a romantic venture, but it's usually a sordid affair at best. I had never liked dealing with redneck cops, bailbondsmen, county judges with high school educations, or talking with clients at two a.m. in a drunk tank.

I crossed the street to the courthouse and went to the sheriff's office in the back of the building. By the office door there was a glass memorial case filled with junk from the World Wars and

Korea – German helmets, bayonets, a Mauser rifle without a bolt, an American Legion medal, canteens, a .30 calibre machine-gun with an exploded barrel and a Chinese bugle. A deputy in a khaki uniform sat behind an army surplus desk, filling out forms with a short pencil. He was lean all over, tall, and his crewcut, glistening head was pale from wearing a hat in the sun. His fingers were crimped over the pencil as he worked out each sentence in printed and longhand letters. His shirt was damp around the shoulders, and his long arms were burned brown and wrinkled with veins.

'Can I help you?' he said without looking up.

'I'd like to see Arturo Gomez.'

He put the pencil down and turned his face up at me. His green, yellow-flecked eyes were flat, his face expressionless.

'Who are you?'

'My name's Hackberry Holland. I'm a lawyer.'

'You ain't his.'

'He's a friend of mine from the service.'

'Well, visiting hour is at two o'clock.'

'I have to go back to Austin this morning. I'd appreciate it if I could talk with him a few minutes.'

The deputy turned the pencil in a circle on the desk top with his finger. There was a hard knot of muscle in the back of his arm.

'You working with these Mexican union people?'

'No.'

'You just drove down from Austin to see a friend in jail?'

'That's right.'

'It won't help him none. He's going up to the state farm Wednesday. And I expect there might be a few more with him soon.'

'I wouldn't know about that.' I bent over and tipped my cigar ashes into the spittoon, then waited for the deputy to continue the statement which he had prepared long ago for strangers, slick lawyers, and nigger and Mexican lovers.

'You can take it for what it's worth, Mr Holland, but these Mexicans was stirred up by agitators from the outside. They can make fair wages in the field any time they want to work, but they

245

stay drunk on wine half the time or sit in the welfare office.' His yellow-flecked eyes looked into my face. 'Then those union organizers started telling them they could get twice as much money by shutting down the harvest. Just let the cotton and grapefruit rot and they're all going to be nigger-rich. People around here is pretty fed up with it, and it's lucky that a couple of them California Mexicans haven't been drug behind a car yet.'

'As I said, I'm not representing anyone.'

'It's against the rule, but I'll take you down to see Gomez a minute. I just thought you ought to know we ain't pushing these people into a corner they didn't build for themselves.'

I followed him down a staircase into the basement of the building. The rigid angles in his body, the rolled khaki sleeves, and the flush of anger in his neck reminded me of several drill instructors whom I had met at Parris Island. They all had the same intense dedication to perverse abstractions which had been created for them by someone else.

The basement of the courthouse, the jail, had been constructed with large blocks of limestone, sawed and chiselled and set with mortar in uneven squares. The corridor was lighted by two bulbs screwed into sockets on the ceiling, and the cells looked like caves cut back into the rock with iron doors on them. The stone was damp with humidity, and the air was rank with disinfectant, DDT, urine and tobacco smoke. Each of the iron doors had a row of holes perforated in the top, and a slit and apron for a food tray. At the end of the corridor was a large room, with two wide barred doors that swung open like gates, and overhead on the rock in broken white letters were the words *Negro Male*. I could see the spark of handrolled cigarettes in the dark, and smell the odour of stale sweat and synthetic wine. There was a wire-screen cage built against one wall, with a small table and two wooden chairs inside. The deputy unlocked the door and opened it.

'Wait in here and I'll bring him out,' he said. He walked back down the corridor and slipped the bolt on one of the cells. He had to use both hands to pull the door open.

Art stepped out into the light, his pupils contracted to small black dots. His denim jail issue was too big for him and his hair hung down over his ears. He was barefoot, his shirt and trousers were unbuttoned, and his thin frame was stooped as he walked towards the cage, as though the rock ceiling was crushing down on him. He had a cigarette in an empty space where a tooth had been, and there was a cobweb scar on the edge of one eye. He had started to get jailhouse pallor, and the two pachuco tattoos on his hands looked like they had just been cut into the skin with brilliant purple ink. I hadn't seen him in five years, when he was contracting tomato harvests in DeWitt County, but it seemed that everything in him had shrunken inwards, hard and brittle as bone. The deputy closed the cage door on us and locked it.

'You can talk ten minutes,' he said, and walked back down the corridor. The light gleamed on his shaved head.

'What about it, Hack? You want to play Russian roulette with me?' Art said, and smiled with the cigarette in his teeth. His long fingers were spread out on the table top.

'How in the hell did you go up for assault because of a picket-line arrest?'

'What happened and what I got tried for ain't the same thing. The Texas Rangers moved in on our picket line because they said we wasn't fifty feet apart. They knocked a couple of our people down, and when I yelled about it they put the arm on me. I pushed this one fat bastard on his ass, and he got up and beat the shit out of me with a blackjack. Man, they're real bad people when they turn loose. I can still see that guy swinging down on me. His eyes was sticking out of his head. He must have saved it up for a long time.'

'What did your lawyer do in the trial?'

'He was appointed by the court. He lives right here in the county and he wanted me to plead guilty. I told him to go fuck himself, so he chewed on his pipe for three days, cross-examined one witness, and shook hands with me after the judge gave me five years.

'Look, Hack, I know I'm leaning on you for a favour, but I want to beat this shit. Our union's got a chance if we don't get broke up. We got a few people in Austin on our side, and some of the locals are afraid enough of the chicano vote that they might come around if we stay solid. But our treasury's broke and I got nobody but kids to organize the pickets and boycotts while I'm in the pen. And I'll tell you straight I don't want to build no five years. Four cents a day chopping cotton ain't good pay.' He smiled again, and took the cigarette from his lips and put it on the bottom of the table.

'All right, I'll try to file an appeal. It takes time, but maybe with luck I can spring you on bond.'

He took another cigarette from his shirt pocket, popped a kitchen match on his thumbnail, and lit it. The scar tissue around his eye was yellow in the flame. 'A year ago I was ready to charge the hill with a bayonet in my teeth. Corporal Gomez going over the top like gangbusters with a flamethrower. I was ready to build life in the pen for our union, but three months in lockdown here, man, it leaves a dent. Every night when that bastard sticks a plate of grits and fried baloney through the slit I say hello to his fingernails.'

'You know what you're doing is crazy, don't you?'

'Why? Because we're tired of getting shit on?'

'These people have lived one way for a hundred and fifty years,' I said. 'You can't make them change with a picket sign.'

His face sharpened, and his yellow-stained fingers pressed down on the cigarette.

'Yeah, we been eating their shit for just about that long. But we ain't going that route no more. We got more people than the anglos, and this land belonged to us before their white ass ever got on it.'

'You can't alter historical injustice in the present. You're only putting yourself and your people up against an executioner's wall.'

'You can jive about all that college bullshit you want, but we been picking your cotton for six cents a pound. You ever do stoop labour? Your back feels like a ball of fire by noon, and at night you got to sleep on the floor to iron out your spine. All you anglos are so fucking innocent. You got the answers counted out in your palm like pennies. You march off every Christmas and hand out food baskets to the niggers and greaseballs, and then for the next twelve months you congratulate yourself on your Christianity.'

He drew in on the cigarette and pushed his long black hair out of his face. He looked at the table and breathed the smoke out between his lips. 'OK, man, I'm sorry. I sit in my cell all day and think, and I don't get to talk with nobody except the hack. So I just make you my dartboard.'

'Forget it,' I said.

'But learn something about our union before you start to piss on us.'

'All right.'

'Like maybe we ain't just a bunch of uppity niggers.'

'The deputy's going to be back in a minute.'

'Look, watch out for that motherfucker. The other night one of the blacks started screaming in the tank with the d.t.'s, and he kicked him in the head. I think he's a Bircher, and the guys in here say he's got a bad conduct discharge from the Corps for crippling a guy in the brig.'

'OK, let's finish before he gets back. Were there any Mexicans on the jury?'

'What world do you live in, man?'

'We can use jury selection in an appeal, even though I'd rather hang them on the charge itself. I'll have to get a transcript of the trial and talk with your lawyer.'

'Don't fool with him. I told you he wouldn't pour water on me if I was burning. He's a little fat guy with a bald head, he owns five hundred acres of blackland, and he thinks I was brainwashed in Korea. When I asked him about an appeal he chewed on his pipe and farted.'

'What's his name?'

'That's Mister Cecil Wayne Posey. His office is right across the street.'

'Why didn't you write me before the trial?'

'I don't like to bruise old friends.'

'Well, you sure picked a shitty time to bring in a relief pitcher.'

'You're a good man, Hack. I trust your arm.'

I heard the stairway door slam and the deputy walking down the stone corridor in his brogans.

'I'll be back tomorrow,' I said. 'You want anything?'

'No, just watch after yourself in town. They're pissed, and that southern accent of yours won't help you none when they find out you're working with our union.'

'I don't think they'll roll a congressional candidate around too hard.'

'I mean it, Hack. They don't give a damn who you are. We stepped on their balls with a golf shoe. There ain't been any Klan activity here since the 1920s, and last week they burned a cross on an island in the middle of the river. You better keep your head down, buddy.'

Art lit another cigarette off the butt while the deputy unlocked the cage.

'Tomorrow,' I said.

'Yeah, stay solid, cousin.'

I looked at the black soles of his bare feet as the deputy led him back to his cell. The deputy clanged the door shut, shot the bolt, and stared at me with a fixed gaze while I tore the cellophane wrapper off a cigar. I bit the end off and spit it on the floor. I could feel his hot eyes reaching me through the wire screen. He rattled his change in one pocket with his hand.

'You want to get out of here this morning, Mr Holland?' he said.

Upstairs by the office door a girl leaned against the wall with a carton of cigarettes in her hand. She wore sandals, bleached blue jeans, and a maroon blouse tied in a knot under her breasts. She had on large, amber sunglasses, hoop earrings, and a thin strand of Indian beads around her neck. Her skin was brown, her body lithe and relaxed, and her curly brown hair was burned on the ends by the sun. Her eyes were indifferent through her glasses as she looked at me and the deputy.

'Would you give these to Art Gomez, please?' she said. Her voice was level, withdrawn, almost without tone.

The deputy took the carton of cigarettes and dropped it in his desk drawer without answering. He sat down in his chair and began to sharpen a pencil with his pocketknife into the waste-basket. I knew that each stroke of that knife was cutting into his own resentment at the restraint his job forced upon him in dealing with a hippie girl and a slick, outside lawyer. He bent over his traffic forms, his knuckles white on the pencil, and began to print out his report as though we were not there.

The girl walked back towards the entrance. There was a pale line of skin above the back of her bluejeans, and her ass had the natural, easy rhythm that most women try to learn for a lifetime. Everything in her was smooth and loose, and her motion had the type of cool unconcern that bothers you in some vague place in the back of your mind.

'Hello,' I said.

She turned around, framed in the square of yellow light through the entrance, and looked at me. She wore no make-up, and in the black shadow over her face she looked like a nun in church suddenly disturbed from prayer.

'I expect you work with Art's union. My name's Hack Holland. I'm trying to file an appeal for Art before he goes up to prison.'

She remained immobile in the light.

'I'd like to meet some of the people in your union,' I said.

'What for?'

'Because I don't know anybody in this town and I might need a little help.'

'There's nothing we can do for you.'

'Why don't you give me a chance to see?'

'You're wasting your time, man.'

'I'd like to see Art out in the next light-year, and from what I understand so far I can't expect any help from his lawyer, the court or the clerk of records. So I can either wander around town a few more days and talk with people like the deputy in there or cowboys in the beer joint, or I can meet someone who'll tell me what happened on that picket line.'

'We told what happened.'

'You told it in a local trial court that was prejudiced. I'm going to take the case to the Court of Criminal Appeals in Austin.'

'What's your thing with Art?'

'We were in Korea together.'

'You can't do any good for him. The ACLU has had our cases in Austin before.'

'Maybe I'm a better lawyer,' I said.

'Believe it, man, you've got a bum trip in mind.'

'I believe in the banzai ethic. At least I'll leave a dark burn across the sky when I go down.'

'You ought to find a better way to pay back army debts.'

'I was a Navy corpsman, and I paid off all my debts in Band-Aids before I was discharged.'

She turned back into the light to walk outside.

'Do you want a ride?' I said.

'I'll walk.'

'You don't want to miss a good experience with the most arrested driver in Texas. Besides, I need some directions.'

'Stay away from our union headquarters if you want to help Art.'

'I don't expect that we'll all end up in the penitentiary if I drive you home.'

We walked down the courthouse pavement under the shade of the oak trees to my car. The sun had risen high in the sky, and the tar surfacing on the street was hot and soft under our feet. The heat shimmered off the concrete walk in front of the hotel.

We drove into the Negro and Mexican section back of town. The dirt roads were baked hard as rock, and clouds of dust swept up behind my car. The unpainted wood shacks were pushed into one another at odd angles, the ditches strewn with garbage, and the outhouses were built of discarded boards, R.C. Cola signs, and tarpaper.

'I have to see Art's lawyer after I drop you off, but I'll come back a little later,' I said.

'I thought you didn't expect any help from him.'

'I don't, but maybe I can use inadequate defence as a reason for appeal.'

She took a package of cigarettes from her blue-jeans pocket and lit one. I glanced at the smooth curve of her breasts as she pushed the package back in her pocket.

'You're pretty sure I've got a loser, aren't you?' I said.

'I just don't think you know very much about the county you're working in.'

'So you're up against some cotton growers who don't want to

pay union scale, and a few part-time Klansmen. And you've met a redneck deputy sheriff who probably rents his brains by the week. That doesn't change the law or trial procedure.'

'Wow. You must walk into court with a copy of *The National Review* between your teeth.'

'I've had eight years of law practice, babe, and I haven't lost many cases.'

'I don't believe you've dealt very much with union farm workers, either.'

'I've spent all my life in Texas. I don't expect to find out anything very new about it in this case.'

'Don't you realize the rules in your court don't apply to us? Art's jury brought in a guilty verdict in fifteen minutes, and later the foreman said it took them that long because they sent out for some cold drinks.'

'All right, I can use things just like that in the appeal.'

'I'm not kidding you, man; lose some of those comic-book attitudes if you want to do anything for him,' she said.

'You really know how to turn on the burner, don't you?'

'I'm just telling you about the bag you're trying to pick up.'

'You're a hard girl.'

'Do I get that free with the ride home?' The sunlight through the window was bright on the burned ends of her hair. She had her arm back on the seat while she smoked, and I could see the whiteness at the top of her breasts.

'You're not from Texas. What are you doing here, anyway?'

'Would you like to flip through the celluloid windows in my wallet?'

'It's just a question.'

'It seems like an expensive trip home.'

'Maybe I should put on my chauffeur's cap, and you can sit in the back seat and I'll close the glass behind me.'

'I was a graduate student in social work at Berkeley. I got tired of writing abstract papers about hungry people so I joined the Third World and came out to your lovely state.'

I hit a chuckhole in the road and felt the car slam down on its springs. The dust was so heavy that it had started to filter through the air-conditioning system. Two Negro children were running along the edge of a ditch, throwing stones at an emaciated dog scabbed over with mange. The road reached a dead end in front of a converted general store with a sign above the door that read: *United Farm Workers Local 476*. The glass display windows were yellow and pocked with BB holes, and filmed with dirt on the inside and outside. Strips of Montgomery Ward brick had been nailed over the rotted boards in the walls, the steps had collapsed, cinder blocks were propped under one side of the building to keep it from sagging, and I could almost hear the flies humming around the outhouse in the back. A boy of about nineteen, barefoot and without a shirt, sat on the front porch playing a twelve-string Gibson guitar.

'Don't wrinkle your eyes at it, man,' she said. 'We're lucky we could rent anything in this town.'

'I didn't say a thing.'

'I could hear the tumblers click over in your head. You've got the middle-class hygiene thing. Anything except green lawns and red brick sends you running up the street.'

'That's a lot of shit.'

'OK. Thanks for the ride.'

She closed the door and walked down the dusty path to the building. I watched the motion of her hips and her full thighs as she stepped up on the porch, then I turned the Cadillac in a circle and headed back towards town.

I went to Mister Cecil Wayne Posey's office and was told by his junior partner that I could find him at home. His ranch was all blackland, lined with rows of cotton and corn and orange trees. A dozen Mexicans and Negroes were hoeing in the cotton, and horses stood in the groves of live oak trees on the low hills. The large, one-storey house had new white paint and a wide screened-in porch, and poplar trees were planted along the front lane. There were two great red barns in back with lightning rods and weather vanes on the peaks, a windmill pumping water into a trough, and rolls of barbed wire and cords of cedar posts stacked against a tractor shed.

As I walked up the lane I heard a woodpecker rattling against a dead limb in the heat. Mr Posey rose from his round-backed wicker chair on the porch and shook hands. The lower portion of his stomach was swollen all the way across the front of his trousers. His skin was soft, pudgy to the touch, and his head was almost completely bald except for a few short grey hairs. His eyes were colourless, and his voice had the bland quality of oatmeal. He reminded me of a miniature upended white whale. When he sat down the watch in his pocket bulged against the cloth like a hard biscuit.

A Negro maid in a lace-trimmed apron served us iced tea with mint leaves and slices of lemon on a silver service, then I began quietly to press Mr Posey for his reasons in not filing an appeal for Art. Actually, my questions, or even my presence there, would probably be considered a violation of professionalism among attorneys, since I was indirectly implying that he had been negligent in the case; but the flicker of insult never showed in his eyes, and if his tone or the pale expression around his mouth indicated anything, it was simply that I was an idealistic young lawyer who had embarked on a fool's errand. He lowered his face into the tea glass when he drank, and momentarily the moisture gave his lips a streak of colour.

'I didn't feel there was basis for appeal, Mr Holland,' he said. 'I originally advised Art to plead guilty in hopes of a reduced charge, but he refused, and I doubt if the Court of Criminal Appeals will consider the case of a man who was convicted on the testimony of four Texas Rangers and two bystanders. He did hit the officer twice before he was restrained, and that's the essential and inalterable fact of the case.'

'Who were these bystanders?'

'Two country workmen who were operating a grading machine on the road when the arrests were made.'

I looked at him incredulously.

'Did you feel these men were objective witnesses?' I said.

'They had no interest in the issue. They merely stated what they saw.'

'I understand that most of the people on the picket line testified, also.'

'Unfortunately, most of them have been in local court before, and I'm afraid that their statements were overly familiar to the jury. One young man admitted to the district attorney that he'd been three hundred yards away from the arrest, but he was sure that Art hadn't struck the officer. It's difficult to contest a conviction on evidence of that sort, Mr Holland.'

His face bent into the iced tea glass again, and a drop of perspiration rolled off his temple down his fat cheek. He shifted his buttocks in the wicker chair and crossed his legs. His massive, soft thighs stretched the crease in his slacks flat.

'Art's been organizing a farm workers' union in this county for the past year. Do you believe any members of the jury had preconceived feelings towards him?'

'None that would affect the indictment against him. He was tried for assaulting a Texas Ranger, not for his involvement in a Mexican union.'

I borrowed a match from Mr Posey and lit a cigar. I looked at him through the curl of flame and smoke and wondered if he had any conception of his irresponsibility in allowing his client to be sentenced to five years in a case that would be considered laughable by a law school moot court.

He put his empty pipe in the centre of his teeth, drew in with a wet rattling sound, and farted softly in the back of the chair. I finished my tea, shook hands and thanked him for his help, and walked down the gravel path to my car under the trees. Behind me I heard him snap the metal latch into place on the screen door.

I drove back to town and had lunch and two beers at the café, then spent an hour in the clerk of records office while an aged secretary made a Xerox copy of the trial transcript for me. There was no breeze through the windows, my sunglasses filmed with moisture in the humidity, and the electric fans did nothing but blow drafts of hot air across the room. The deputy sheriff came in once to drop a pile of his pencilled reports on the clerk's desk, and as he walked past me he stared into my face without speaking.

I spent the rest of the afternoon in the hotel, with my feet propped in the window, reading the transcript and sipping whiskey poured over ice. The flies droned dully in the stillness, and occasionally I would hear the hillbilly music from the beer tavern. Across the square the sun slanted on the rows of water melons and cantaloupes in the open-air fruit market.

The transcript was an incredible record to read. The trial might have been constructed out of mismatched parts from an absurd movie script about legal procedure. There had been no challenge of the jurors, each of the Texas Rangers contradicted the others, a Baptist minister testified that many of the union members were Communists, and the two county workmen said they had seen a Mexican attack a Ranger, although they had been eating their lunch in the back of a truck half a mile down the road at the time. The three witnesses for the defence were sliced to pieces by the district attorney. They were led into discrediting statements about their own testimony, forced into stumbling admissions about their involvement in revolution, and referred to sixteen times as outside agitators. And Cecil Wayne Posey never raised an objection. Normally, any two pages torn at random from such a comic scenario would be grounds for appeal, but under Texas law the appeal has to be made in local court within ten days of sentencing, unless good cause is shown for an extension, and since Mr Posey's refusal to continue the case had virtually guaranteed that his client would go to prison, I would have to start the whole process over again in Austin.

It was dusk outside now. I threw the transcript in my suitcase, took a cold bath, and shaved, with a glass of whiskey on top of the lavatory. As a rule I didn't try to correct the inadequacies inherent in any system, but in this case I thought I would send a letter to the Texas Bar Association about Mr Posey. Yes, Mr Posey should receive some official recognition for his work, I thought, as I drew the razor blade down in a clean swath through the shaving cream on my cheek.

I ate a steak for supper and drove back to the union head-quarters in the Mexican district. There were thunderclouds and heat lightning in the west, an electric flash all the way across the horizon, and then a distant, dry rumble. The air tasted like brass in my mouth. Parts of the dirt road had been sprinkled with garden hoses to wet down the dust, and the cicadas in the trees were deafening with their late evening noise. Fireflies glowed like points of flame in the gathering dusk, and across the river in old Mexico the adobe huts on the mud flat wavered in the light of outdoor cookfires. High up in the sky, caught in the sun's last afterglow, a buzzard floated motionlessly like a black scratch on a tin surface.

I parked the car in front of the union headquarters and walked up the path to the wooden steps. The boy with the Gibson twelve-string still sat on the porch. He had three steel picks on his fingers and a half-gallon bottle of dago red next to him. His bare feet were covered with dust, and there were tattoos on each arm. He chorded the guitar and didn't turn his head towards me.

'She's inside, man,' he said.

'Do I knock or let myself in?'

'Just do it.'

I tapped with my knuckle on the screen and waited. I heard dishes rattling in a pan in the back of the building.

'Hey Rie, that guy's back,' the boy shouted over his shoulder.

A moment later the girl walked through a back hallway towards me. Her arms were wet up to the elbow. She had splashed water on her blouse, and her breasts stood out against the cloth.

'Man, like you really want to meet us, don't you?' she said, pushing open the screen with the back of her wrist.

'I decided against watching television in the hotel lobby this evening.'

'Come in the kitchen. I have to finish the dishes.'

The flowered wallpaper in the main room was yellowed and peeling in rotted strips, coated with mould and glue. United Farm Workers signs, pop art posters of Che Guevara and Lyndon Johnson on a motor cycle, and underground newspapers were thumbtacked over the exposed sections of boarding in the walls. A store-window manikin lay on top of the old grocery counter with an empty wine bottle balanced on her stomach. A mobile made of beer-bottle necks clinked in the breeze from an oscillating fan that rattled against the wire guard each time it completed a turn. The single lightbulb suspended from the ceiling gave the whole room a hard yellow cast that hurt the eyes.

I followed her through the hallway into the kitchen. Her brown hips moved as smoothly as water turning in the current. Two young girls, a college boy, and a Negro man were scraping dishes into a rubbish bin and rinsing them under an iron pump. Through the back window I could see the last red touch of the sun on a sandbar in the middle of the Rio Grande.

'We had a neighbourhood dinner tonight,' the girl from Berkeley said. 'There's some tortillas and beans in the icebox or you can get a dish towel.'

'You have a charge account with the supermarket?'

'We get the day-old stuff from the Mexican produce stands,' she said.

'I think I'll just have a whiskey and water if you'll give me a glass.' I took my silver flask from my coat pocket.

'Help yourself,' she said.

I offered the flask to the other.

'You got it, brother,' the Negro said.

He picked up a tin cup from the sideboard and held it in front of me. His bald, creased head and round black face shone in the half light. Four of his front teeth were missing, and the others were yellow with snuff. I poured a shot in his cup and then splashed some water in my glass from the pump. I could taste the rust in it.

'So what would you like to find out about the United Farm Workers?' the girl said.

'Nothing. I read the trial transcript and talked with Mr Posey this afternoon. The conviction won't hold.'

The Negro laughed with the cup held before his lips. The college boy straightened up from the rubbish bin and looked at me as though I had dropped through a hole in the ceiling.

'You believe that?' the Negro said. He was still smiling.

'Yes.'

'I mean, you ain't bullshitting? You're coming on for real?' the college boy said. He wore blue jeans and a faded yellow and white University of Texas T-shirt.

'That's right, pal,' I said.

The Negro laughed again and went back to work scraping plates. The two young girls were also smiling.

'Who you working for, man?' the boy said.

'Judge Roy Bean. I float up and down the Pecos River for him on an inner tube.'

'Don't get strung out,' the girl said.

'What am I, the visiting straight man around here?'

The girl dried her hands on a towel and took a bottle of Jax out of the icebox. 'Come on out front,' she said.

'We wasn't trying to give you no truck. We ain't got bad things here,' the Negro said. He grinned at me with his broken, yellow teeth.

In the front room the girl sat in a straight-backed chair, with one leg pulled up on the seat, her arm propped across her knee, and drank out of the beer bottle. Behind her on the wall was a poster with a rectangular, outspread bird on it and the single word *HUELGA*.

'They're kids, and they don't know if you're putting them on or if you're a private detective working for their parents,' she said. 'The black guy has been in the movement since the Progressive Labor Party days, and he's heard a lot of jiveass lawyers talk about appeals.'

'I guess I just don't like people to work out their problems on my head.'

'I told you this afternoon about coming down here.'

'Maybe I should have worn my iron helmet and flak jacket.'

'They don't have any bad will towards you. They're good people.'

'I'm paranoid and suspicious by nature.'

'That's part of the middle-class syndrome, too. It goes along with the hygiene thing.'

'Goddamn, I picked a hell of a ballgame to relieve in. Between you, Cecil Wayne Posey, and that deputy at the jail I feel like I'm standing ten feet from the plate and lobbing volley balls at King Kong.'

She took the bottle from her lips and laughed, and her almond eyes were suddenly full of light. She touched away the foam from the corner of her mouth with two fingers.

'I should have put on my Groucho Marx clothes this evening,' I said. 'You know, an hour or so of Zeppo and the gang throwing pies while your people go up to the pen.'

I finished my drink, and the minerals and iron rust in the water tasted like a gladiator's final toast in the back of my throat.

'You're out of sight,' she said.

I poured a thin shot over the orange flecks in the bottom of the glass and drank it down. The smoky, charcoal-filtered taste of undiluted Jack Daniels, born out of Tennessee limestone springs and rickyards of hickory, rolled down inside me with the lightness of heated air, then I began to feel the amber caution signal flashing somewhere behind my forehead.

'Yeah, I'm a walking freak show. The next time I'll appear with my whole act. Seals blowing horns, monkeys riding unicycles, jugglers, clowns with exploding bombs in their pants.'

'Wow, you really let it hang out,' she said. Her wet eyes were bright with refractions of light.

'It comes free with the ride home.' I poured the rest of the whiskey into my glass. 'Come on, let's drink.'

'What do you do when you're not defending ex-Korean War buddies?' she said.

'I work for the money boys. Oil corporation suits, swindles against the government, the Billy Sol account. I also run for Congress part time.'

'You're putting me on.'

'Buy a copy of *The Austin American* November 5. I'll be smiling at you on the front page.'

'If you're not jiving, you must be an unbelievable guy.'

'You want to talk about my geek act some more?' I said.

'I mean what do you expect? You drop in here from outer space and come on like H. L. Hunt and W. C. Fields at the same time.'

'I was put together from discarded parts.' I finished my glass, and the amber light flashed red and began to beat violently.

'Tell me, really, why did you come here tonight?'

'I already told you. Television ruptures the blood vessels in my eyes.'

The Negro, the two girls and the college boy walked out from the kitchen.

'There's a man who likes to drink,' I said.

'You been reading my mail,' the Negro said.

'How about a case of Jax and a bottle of Jack Daniels?' I took a twenty-dollar bill from my wallet.

'We got a few more people coming over tonight,' he said.

'Get two cases. Take my car.'

'It's just down the road. I'd get busted for grand auto in that Cadillac, anyway.'

He took the twenty-dollar bill and stuck it in the pocket of his denim shirt.

'You ain't going to tip me later, are you?' he said.

'I left my planter's hat in the car.'

He laughed and his round black face and brown eyes glistened with good humour. 'You're all right,' he said, and went out the screen door with the college boy.

'You always do this on a case?' the girl said.

'No. I usually don't drink with the people I know. Most of them belong to the ethic of R. C. Richardson and the Dallas Petroleum Club. They like to throw glasses and urinate off hotel balconies. They also like to feel waitresses under the table. R. C. Richardson is a very unique guy. In the last fifteen years he's taken the state and the federal government for a little less than one million dollars. He wears yellow cowboy boots, striped western pants, a string tie, and he has a one-hundred-pound stomach that completely covers his hand-tooled belt. Three days a week he sits in the Kiwanis and Rotary and Chamber of Commerce luncheons and belches on his boiled weenies and sauerkraut, and then rises like a soldier and says the pledge of allegiance with his hand over his heart. But, actually, the guy has class. The others around him are clandestine in their midnight dealings and worm's-eye view of the world. They don't have his sincere feeling for vulgarity.'

'He must be an interesting man to work for,' she said.

'Do you have another beer in the icebox?'

'This is the last one. Take it.'

'I never take a girl's last drink. It shows a lack of gentility.'

'You are from outer space.'

I could feel the blood tingling in my hands and face. My scalp started to sweat from the whiskey.

'What's your name, anyway?' I bit the end off a cigar.

'Rie Velasquez.'

'You're not Mexican.'

'No.'

'So what are you?' I reached over and took the beer bottle out of her hand.

'My father was Spanish. He came from Spain during the Civil War.'

I let the beer and foam roll down my throat over the dry taste of the whiskey and cigar smoke.

'Hence, you joined the Third World Liberation Front. The petrol and dynamite gang.'

'You ought to change your brand of bourbon.'

'Right or wrong? Didn't they incinerate a few college buildings in the last year?'

'Don't you think that sounds a bit dumb?'

'Bullshit. Ten of those people could have a whole city in flames within twenty-four hours.'

She took a cigarette from the pack in her blue jeans and lit it. She pinched the end between her lips as she drew in on the smoke.

'What type of bag do you think we operate out of, man?' she said. 'Did you see any kerosene rags and coal oil hidden under the porch? You believe we all came down here because of your tourist brochures about the scenic loveliness of the Texas desert?'

'I just don't buy that revolution shit.'

'Why don't you read something about the United Farm Workers? They don't have anything to do with revolution. They're tired of being niggers in somebody's water-melon patch.'

'Yow!' the Negro yelled, as he kicked open the screen door with a case of beer on one shoulder and a block of ice wrapped in newspaper on the other. 'Man, we got it. Spodiodi and brew. We're in tall cotton tonight, brothers.'

The college boy carried the second case of beer, and the boy with the guitar had already cut the seal on the bottle of Jack Daniels. They put the two cases on the old grocery counter, and the Negro chopped up the ice with a butcher's knife and spread it over the bottles. He opened the first bottle by putting the cap against the edge of the counter and striking downward quickly with the flat of his hand. The white foam showered up over his head and splattered on the floor. He covered the lip of the bottle with his mouth and drank until it was almost empty. The beer streamed down his chin into the matted black hair on his chest.

'Lord, you can't beat that,' he said.

I took the whiskey and poured three inches into my glass.

'You'll drive nails through your stomach like that. Put a little brew on top of it,' the Negro said. He slapped another cap off on the edge of the counter and handed the bottle to me.

'Use this and avoid the slashed hand shot,' Rie said, and threw an opener to the college boy.

Eight Mexican field hands, all dressed in faded denim clothes, overalls, straw hats and work shoes, came through the screen door in single file as though they had been lined up at a bus stop. They were pot-bellied and short, thin and stooped, tattooed with pachuco crosses and hung with religious medals, scarred and stitched, some of them missing fingers, sunburned almost black, with trousers bagging in the rear and their Indian hair wet and combed straight back over the head.

They had a pint of Old Stag and a gallon milk bottle filled with blackberry wine. The Negro began passing out the Jax, and an hour later the room roared with mariachi songs and Apache screams.

'Let me try that guitar, buddy,' I said to the boy from the front porch. He sat on the floor with his back against the wall and a glass of wine and whiskey between his legs. His face was bloodless and his eyes couldn't fix on my face. I put the strap of the twelve-string around my neck and tried to pick out 'The Wreck of Old '97', but my fingers felt as though a needle and thread had been drawn through all my knuckles. Then I tried 'The Wildwood Flower' and 'John Hardy', and each time I began over again I hit more wrong notes or came up on the wrong fret. I smoked somebody's cigarette out of an ashtray, finished my drink, and then started an easy Jimmie Rodgers run that I had learned to pick when I was sixteen. It was worse than before, and I laid the guitar face down on the counter among the scores of empty beer bottles.

'I bet you blow a good one when you're cool,' Rie said. She was sitting in the chair next to me with a small glass of wine in her hand. Her legs were crossed, and the indention across her stomach and the white line of skin above her blue jeans made something drop inside me.

'Give me an hour and I'll boil them cabbages down,' I said.

'Do it tomorrow morning.'

'I'm going to streak out of here like the fireball mail tomorrow morning. My Cadillac and I are going to melt the asphalt between here and Austin.' Someone put the whiskey bottle in my hand, and I took two large swallows and chased it with beer.

'You must have a real dragon inside,' Rie said.

'No, I deal with Captain Hyde. That bastard and I have been together almost fifteen years. However, when he starts acting like an asshole I unscrew my head and throw it in the Rio Grande a couple of times.'

'No kidding, pull it back in, man,' she said.

'I thought you were a hip girl. You're giving me the concerned eye of a Baptist reformer now.'

'I think you're probably a madman.'

'You ought to see me and John Wesley Hardin drunk in the streets of Yoakum. He rides on the bumper of my Cadillac, busting parking meters and spotlights with a revolver in each hand.'

The noise became louder. All the beer, whiskey and wine were gone, and I gave one of the Mexican field hands another twenty dollars to go to the tavern. The twelve-string guitar was passed from hand to hand, tuned in half a dozen discords, two strings broken, and finally dropped in a corner. Someone suggested a knife-throwing contest, and a bread cutter, two bowies, a rippled-bladed Italian stiletto, my pocket knife, a hand axe and a meat cleaver were flung into the wall until the boards were split and shattered and knocked through on the ground outside.

The room was beginning to tip and blur in front of my eyes. I was smoking a dead cigar butt that I had frayed under my boot heel a few minutes earlier.

'Spodiodi, man. It's the only thing. You got to put them snakes back in the basket,' the Negro said in my face. His eyes were red, and his breath was sour with wine.

'I don't deal in snakes.'

'Man, they're crawling through your face.'

I knew that I had an answer for him, but the words wouldn't rise out of the echoes and flashes of light in my head.

'Shit, let's go down to the river. This place is hotter than a brick kiln,' I said.

'It's all that corn,' the Negro said.

'Come on, Judge Roy Bean is holding court in his inner tube,' I said, and pulled Rie up from her chair by the hand.

'Hey, man,' she said.

I carried the bottle of whiskey by the neck and pulled her through the hallway into the kitchen. The Negro followed us with a beer in each hand and half a dozen bottles stuck down in his trousers.

We walked down the bare slope towards the mud flat. The moon was full and white as ivory in a breathless sky. A rusted Ford coupé with no glass in the windows sat half-submerged in the river. The current eddied and swirled through the gaping window in the back and coursed over the top of the seats and the steering wheel. The moon's reflection rippled across the water's brown surface, and I could see the sharp backs of garfish turning by the sandbars. Behind us the Mexican field hands were still singing. The Negro finished one beer and threw the bottle arching high over the river.

'Yow!' he yelled.

'Goddamn, look at it. There's Mexico,' I said. 'Fifty yards and you can drop right through the bottom of the twentieth century.'

Rie sat down on a rotted log with her bare feet in the water. The moonlight turned the burned tips of her hair to points of silver.

'A whole land full of bandit ghosts and Indian legends,' I said. 'You just step through the hole in the hedge, and there's Pancho Villa splashing across the river with pistols and bandoliers hanging all over him. Zapata cutting down *Federales* with his machete. Illiterate peasants executing French kings. Cortez destroying an entire culture.'

'There's diphtheria in the well water of the adobe huts, too,' Rie said.

'You're like every goddamn Marxist I ever met. No humour or sense of romance.

'Quit shouting.'

'Isn't that straight?' I said. 'It's the revolutionary mind. You can't realize that man is more a clown than a Satan. You approach everything with a sullen mind and try to convert buffoons into Machiavelli.'

'Oh for God's sake, man.'

I took a drink out of the bottle. The whiskey splashed over my mouth.

'You goddamn people don't know what human evil is. One of these days you and I are going to have some Chinese tea and talk about the Bean Camp together. I'll also give you a couple of footnotes on Pak's Palace and No Name Valley.'

I felt the ground shift under my feet, and I thought I was going to fall. I put my arm on her shoulder to keep my balance.

'There's mudcat nesting in that car. I know how to get them, too,' the Negro said. He took off his shirt and shoes, and laid the remaining bottles of beer in an even line on the bank. 'You just swim your hand under the water and back that shovel-mouth into a corner and catch him real fast inside the gill. Come on, brother. I'm going to teach you how to fish like black people.'

He waded out into the river up to his hips and pulled open the rusted door with both hands. The moon's reflection off the water made his black body glow.

'He does this when he gets drunk,' Rie said. 'You can do it, too, if you want me to take both of you down to the county hospital tonight.'

'That's just what a Yankee would say. Don't you know that coloured people catch fish when white people couldn't bring them up with a telephone crank?'

I sat down on the mud flat and pulled off my boots. I felt the water soak through the seat of my trousers.

'He had eight stitches the last time he handfished in that car,' she said.

'I don't believe it. That sounds like more Marxist-Yankee bullshit.'

I walked out into the river, and the warm, muddy current swirled round my waist and my feet sank into the silt. The Negro was bent over the top of the front seat with both his arms submerged to the shoulder. His face was concentrated, his eyes looking into nothing, as though his fingers were touching some vital and delicate part of the universe.

'She's backed up and fanning right next to the trunk. She's got young ones under her,' he said.

'Watch her fins.'

'She'll open up in a minute to get a piece of my finger, then I'll grab a whole handful of meat inside her gill.'

He ducked forward, the surface of the water shook and quivered momentarily, and then he drew one hand back with a ragged cut between the thumb and forefinger. The drops of blood squeezed out through the bruised edges of the skin and ran down his wrist. He closed his eyes in pain and sucked the cut.

'I told you to—' Then I heard the sirens rolling in a low moan down the dusty street in front of the union building.

'Shit,' Rie said from the river bank.

I turned around and saw the revolving blue and yellow lights on top of three police cars, winking and flashing in the dark.

'The Man done arrived,' the Negro said, with his cut hand still held before his mouth.

Sheriff's deputies and city police went through the front door of the building, walked around the sides with flashlights, looked in the outhouse, and then focused two car spotlights on us in the river. The electric white glare made my eyes water.

'You people walk towards me with your hands on top of your head!' a voice shouted from behind the light.

'Them dudes can reach out from a long way, can't they?' the Negro said. He flopped both his arms over his bald head and started wading out of the river. The light broke around his body as though he had been carved out of burnt iron.

For some drunk reason I closed the car door carefully in the current and lifted the handle upward into place.

'On your head, punk!' The voice shouted.

'Fuck you,' I said.

Suddenly, both of the arcs were turned directly into my face, and the Negro disappeared from my vision in one brilliant explosion of light.

'Don't screw with them, Hack. Get out of there,' Rie said from the darkness.

I waded out of the shallows with one hand over my eyes. My face burned with the heat from the light.

'I give you warning. Get them over your head.'

'I told you to go fuck yourself, too.' I tripped on the mudbank and fell on my elbows. My forearms and one side of my face were covered with wet sand. Rie tried to pick me up by the back of my shirt.

'They'll kill you, Hack. Get up and walk. It's just a disturbing the peace bust. We'll be out in the morning,' she said.

A sheriff's car, with both spotlights burning, drove down the embankment on the hard ground, bounced over a log, and turned to a stop in front of me. As the beams of light changed angle I saw the Mexican field hands lined up against the building, with their arms outstretched before them and their legs widespread, while two policemen shook them down.

The whip aerial on the car rocked back and forth, and the deputy from the jail opened the driver's door and walked towards me. I stood up and put a wet cigar in my mouth. My clothes were filled with sand and mud, and my hair felt like paint on top of my head. His .357 Magnum and the cartridges in his leather belt glinted in the moonlight. There was a line of perspiration down the front of his shirt, and his packet of cigarettes stuck up at an angle under the flap of his pocket, which struck me at the time as an odd thing for a military man. His jawbones were as tight as his crewcut scalp.

'I figured that you was you, Mr Holland, and I didn't want nobody dropping the hammer on you for some wetback crossing the river,' he said.

'What have you got? Disturbing the peace? Disorderly conduct?'

'We got all kinds of things. I expect if we look around here a while we might find some dope.'

'Why don't you let these people alone? There wasn't any complaint from this neighbourhood.'

'Get in the car, please, miss,' he said to Rie.

'Look, she was out here. She didn't have anything to do with that drunk party.'

He opened the back door of the automobile and took Rie by the elbow.

'Just keep your peckerwood hands in your pockets a minute,' I said.

'What?'

'You heard me, motherfucker.'

'Mr Holland, you can drive out of here tonight in that Cadillac of yours and I'll forget about that. The next time you want to help out the niggers and the wetbacks you just write out a cheque to the Community Chest and stay out of this county.'

'I'll be all right. Go to Austin tomorrow and put it in for Art,' she said. She sat in the back seat behind the wire-mesh screen.

'Let her out,' I said.

'You really want to push it, Mr Holland?'

'Yeah, I do. From what I understand you have a b.c.d. from the Marine Corps and you do most of your law enforcement on helpless winos in a drunk tank. So why don't you get off the bad ass act?'

'You're under arrest. I don't expect you're going to get out of our jail very soon, either.'

'You're fucking with the Lone Ranger, too, peckerwood,' I said.

He brought his billy out of his back pocket and caught me right above the temple. A shotgun shell exploded in my head, and I fell against the car door and hit the ground on my hands and knees. He kicked me once in the stomach, and my breath rushed out of me as though someone had opened a large hole in the middle of my chest. The inside of my mouth was coated with sand, my eyes bulged and I started to vomit, then his boot cut across the back of my head with the easy swing of a football player kicking an extra point.

FOUR

Sometime in the early morning hours I woke up on the stone floor of a cell in the bottom of the courthouse. The cell was almost completely black, except for the dim circles of light through the row of holes in the top of the door. Moisture covered the walls, and the toilet in the corner had overflowed. I pulled myself up on the iron bunk and touched the huge swelling above my temple. It was as tight as a baseball, and the blood had congealed in my hair. My head was filled with distant bugles and claps of thunder, and I felt the cell tilt on its axis and try to pitch me off the bunk into the pool of water by the toilet. Then I vomited between my legs.

I raised my head slowly, my eyes throbbing and the sweat running down my face. I found a dry kitchen match in my shirt pocket and popped it on my thumbnail. I held the flame over my wristwatch and saw the smashed crystal and the hands frozen at five past one. My white slacks were still wet and streaked with mud, and my shirt was torn off one shoulder. I stumbled against the door and leaned my face down to the food slit.

'Hey, one of you sons of bitches better—' But my voice broke with the effort of shouting. I tried again, and my words sounded foolish in the stillness.

'Cool that shit, man,' a Negro voice said from down the corridor.

I lay back on the tick mattress with my arm across my eyes. I could smell the urine and stale wine in the cloth, and I imagined that there were lice laying their strings of white eggs along the seams, but I was too sick to care. I slept in delirious intervals, never sure if I was really asleep or dreaming, and my nightmare monsters sat with spread cheeks on my feet and grinned at me with their obscene faces. They appeared in all shapes and sizes of deformity: hunched backs, slanted eyes, split tongues and lipless mouths. Major Park was there with his fanatical scream and the electrician's pliers in his clenched hand, the guards in the Bean Camp who let our wounded freeze to death to save fuel, and then

Sergeant Tien Kwong leaned over me and inserted the end of his burpgun into my mouth and said, smiling, 'You suck. We give you boiled egg.'

A deputy slipped the bolt on my cell and pulled open the door. I winced in the light and turned my face towards his silhouette. His stomach hung over his cartridge belt. Behind him a Negro trusty was pushing a food cart stacked with tin plates and a tall stainless-steel container of grits.

'You can go now, Mr Holland, but the sheriff wants to talk with you a few minutes first,' the deputy said.

'Where's the man who brought me in?'

'He's off duty.'

'What's his name?' My head ached when I sat up on the bunk.

'You better talk with the sheriff.'

I got to my feet and stepped out into the corridor. The Negro trusty was ladling spoonfuls of grits and fried baloney into tin plates and setting them on the iron aprons of the cell doors. The uneven stone on the floor hurt my bare feet, and my right eye, which had started to stretch tight from the swelling in my temple, watered in the hard yellow light. The deputy and I went down the corridor and up the stairs to the sheriff's office. The fat in his hips and stomach flopped inside his shirt each time he took a step. His black hair was oiled and pasted down flat across his balding pate, and he used the handrail on the staircase as though he were pulling a massive weight uphill.

The sheriff sat behind his desk with a handrolled cigarette between his lips, and my notecase, pocketknife and muddy boots in front of him. He wore steel-rimmed glasses, and his ears peeled out from the sides of his head. His face was full of red knots and bumps, a large brown mole on his chin, and his grey hair was mowed right into the scalp, but his flat blue eyes cut through the rest of it like a welder's torch. He put the cigarette out between his fingers in the wastebasket, and started to roll another one from a package of Virginia Extra in his pocket. The tips of his teeth were rotted with nicotine. He curved the cigarette paper under his forefinger and didn't look at me when he spoke.

'My deputy wanted to charge you with attempted assault on a

law officer, but I ain't going to do that,' he said. He spread the tobacco evenly in the paper and licked down the edge. 'I'm just going to ask you to go down the road, and that'll be the end of it.'

'Your man is pretty good with his feet and a billy.'

'I reckon that's what happens when you threaten a law officer, don't it?' He put the cigarette in his mouth and turned towards me in his swivel chair.

'I don't suppose that I could bring a charge against him here, but I have a feeling the FBI might be interested in a civil rights violation.'

'You don't seem to understand what I'm saying, Mr Holland. I got my deputy's report right here, co-signed by a city patrolman, and it says you were drunk, resisted arrest, and swinging at an officer with your fists. Now maybe you think that don't mean anything because you're an Austin lawyer, but that ain't worth piss on a rock around here.'

'You're not dealing with a wetback or a college kid, either.' My head felt as though it were filled with water. Through the window I could see the sun striking across the treetops.

'I know exactly what I'm dealing with. I been sheriff here seven years and I seen them like you by the truckload. You come in from the outside and walk around like your shit don't stink. I don't know what you're doing with them union people, and I don't really give a goddamn, but you better keep out of my jail. The deputy went easy with you last night, and that's pretty hard for him to do when he runs up against your kind. But the next time I'm going to turn him loose.'

'You might also tell your trained sonofabitch that he won't catch me drunk on my hands and knees again, and in the meantime he ought to contact a public defender because I have a notion that he'll need one soon.'

The sheriff struck a match on the arm of the chair and lit his cigarette. He puffed on it several times and flicked the match towards the spittoon. The knots and bumps on his face had turned a deeper red.

'I'm just about to take you back to lockdown and leave you there till you find some other smart-ass lawyer to get you out.'

'No, you're not, because you've already been through my wallet and you saw a couple of cards in there with names of men who could have a sheriff dropped right off the party ticket.'

'I'll tell you something. Tonight I'm going out on patrol myself, and if I catch you anywhere in the county you're going to get educated downstairs and piss blood before you're through. Pick up your stuff and get out of here.'

'What's the bail on the others?'

'Twenty-five dollars a head, and you can have all the niggers and pepper-bellies and hippies you want. Then I'll get my trusties to hose down the cells.'

I picked up my notecase from his desk and put four one-hundred-dollar bills before him.

'That ought to cover it, and some of your water bill, too,' I said.

He figured on a scratch pad with a broken pencil for a moment, smoking the saliva-stained cigarette between his lips.

'No, we owe you fifty dollars, Mr Holland, and we want to be sure you get everything coming to you.' He opened his desk drawer and counted out the money from a cash box and handed it to me. 'Just sign the receipt and you can collect the whole bunch of them and play sticky finger in that union hall till tonight, then I'll be down there and we can talk it over again if you're still around.'

'I don't believe you'll be that anxious to talk when you and your deputy and I meet again.'

'I'm going to let them people out myself. Don't be here when I get back,' he said. He stood up and dropped his cigarette into the spittoon. His flat blue eyes, staring out of that red, knotted face, looked like whorls of swimming colour without pupils. He stuck his shirt inside his trousers with the flat of his hand and walked past me with the khaki stiffness of a man who had once more restored structure to his universe.

I sat down in a chair and put my boots on. They were filled with small rocks and mud, and when I stood up again I felt the dizziness and nausea start. I wiped the sweat off my face with my shirt and I wondered how in God's name I could have ever become involved in a fool's situation like this. I was glad there were no reflecting windows or glass doors or mirrors in the sheriff's office, because I was sure that the present image of Hackberry Holland – ripped silk shirt, mud-streaked trousers, swollen temple and blood-matted hair, and face white with concussion and hangover – wouldn't help me resolve my torn concept of self.

I walked outside into the sunlight to wait for Rie. The sun and shadow sliced in patterns across the lawn, and a warm breeze from the river carried with it the smell of the fields. I sat on the concrete steps and let the heat bake into my skin. My clothes and body reeked of the jail, and the odour became stronger as I started to perspire. Two women passing on the pavement looked at me in disgust. 'Good morning. How are you ladies today?' I said, and their eyes snapped straight ahead.

A few minutes later Rie and the others came out of the front door. The faces of the Mexicans were lined and bloated with hangover, and the guitar player and college boy looked like definitions of death. Their faces were perfectly white, as though all the blood had been drawn out through a tube. Rie carried her sandals in her hand, and she looked as lovely and alive as a flower turning into the sun.

'Thanks for going the bail,' she said.

'I'll mark it off on my expense account as part of my expanded education. Right now I need to pick up my car, unless our deputy friend set fire to it last night.'

'Rafael's brother has a truck at the fruit stand. He'll take us back.'

'Yeah, I don't think I could walk too far this morning,' I said.

'Say, man, you really took on that bastard, didn't you?' the college boy said. His face was so wan that his lips moved as though they were set in colourless wax.

'Afraid not,' I said. 'It was a one-sided encounter.'

We started walking across the lawn towards the open-air market. My head ached with each step.

'No, man, it takes balls to go up against a prick like that,' he said.

'Stupidity is probably a better word,' I said.

The shade was cool under the trees, and mockingbirds flew

through the branches overhead. Across the street a Mexican was wetting down the rows of water melons in the bins with a hose. Their fat green shapes were beaded with light in the sun. We crossed the street like the ragged remnant of a guerrilla band, and people in passing cars twisted their faces around and stuck their heads out of the windows at this strange element in the midst of their tranquil Tuesday morning world.

One of the Mexicans and Rie and I got into the cab of a pickup truck and the others climbed in the back, and we headed into the poor district. The driver pulled out a half-pint of Four Roses from under the seat and took a drink with one hand on the steering wheel. His face shook with the taste. Then he took three more swallows like he was forcing down hair tonic, and offered the bottle to me.

'Not today,' I said.

He screwed the cap on and passed the bottle out of the window of the cab to one of his friends in the back. The bottle went from hand to hand until it was empty, then the Negro banged on the roof when we passed the first clapboard beer tavern on the road. He and the Mexicans piled out and went in the screen door, pulling nickels, dimes and quarters from their blue jeans. Before the truck started up again I could already hear their laughter from inside.

The driver dropped the rest of us off at the union hall. My Cadillac was powdered with white dust so thick that I couldn't see inside the windows.

'Come in and I'll put something on your head,' Rie said. The truck rattled back down the road towards the tavern.

'Unless I figured that sheriff wrong, he's already been to the hotel and my suitcase is waiting for me on the front step.'

'Your eye is starting to close.'

'I keep a couple of glass spares in my glove compartment.'

She put her arm through mine and moved towards the porch.

'All right, no protest,' I said.

'I thought he'd killed you.'

'I don't believe you're a hard girl after all.'

'Your eyelid's turned blue. I even cried to make that asshole take you into emergency receiving, and he shot me the finger.'

'Don't worry. I'm going to make this fellow's life a little more interesting for him in the next few weeks.'

'I didn't think you believed in charging the barricade.'

'I don't. There's always ten others like him who'll crawl out of the woodwork to take his place, but you can't fool with the Lone Ranger and Tonto and walk away from it.'

We went inside, and I sat in a chair while she washed the lump on my head with soap and water. The tips of her fingers were as light as wind on the bruised skin.

'There's pieces of rock and dirt in the cut. I'll have to get them out with the tweezers,' she said. 'You should go to the hospital and get a couple of stitches.'

'Do you have a quart of milk in your icebox?'

She went into the kitchen and came back with a carton of buttermilk and a pair of tweezers in a glass of alcohol. I drank the carton half empty in one long chugging swallow, and for just a moment the thick cream felt like cool air and health and sunshine transfused into my body, then she started picking out the pieces of rock from the cut with the edge of the tweezers. Each alcohol nick made the skin around my eye flex and pucker.

'Goddamn, what are you doing? I don't need a lobotomy.'

'You probably don't need poisoning, either.' Her eyes were concentrated with each metallic scratch against my skin.

'Look, let me have the tweezers and give me a mirror. I used to be a pretty fair hospital corpsman.'

'Don't move your head. I almost have it all out.' She bit her lip and squeezed out a splinter of rock from under the cut with her finger. 'There.'

Then she rubbed a cotton pad soaked with alcohol over the lump.

'Listen, goddamn it, there's other ways to clean a cut. They ought to give first-aid courses in the Third World before you kill somebody with shock.'

'Wait a minute,' she said, and went into the kitchen again and returned with a piece of ice wrapped in a clean dish towel. She held it against my head, her almond eyes still fixed with a child's concern.

'A cold compress can't do any good after the first two hours,' I said.

'What was that Bean Camp stuff about last night?'

'Nothing. I create things in my head when I try to run up Jack Daniel's stock a couple of points.'

'Were you in a prison camp during the war?'

'No.'

The whiskey edge was starting to wear off, and grey worms and spots of light swam before my eyes when I tried to stand up. She pressed her hand down on my shoulder.

'You ought to pull the fish hooks out. You're all flames inside,' she said.

'I feel like I've been dismantled twice in three days, and I'm not up to psychoanalysis right now. It seems that every goddamn time my brain is bleeding someone starts boring into my skull with the brace and bit.'

'OK, man, I'm sorry.'

'I've got a brother that can make you grind your teeth down to the nerve with that same type of morning-after insight. There's nothing like it to send me right through the goddamn wall.'

'So I won't say anything else,' she said.

I felt myself trembling inside, as though all the wheels and gears were starting to shear off against one another at once. My palms were sweating on my knees, and I realized that my real hangover was just beginning.

'Let me have one of your cigarettes,' I said.

She laid the ice compress down, lit a cigarette, and put it in my mouth. The smoke was raw in my throat, and a drop of sweat rolled off my lip on to the paper.

'Does it always take you like that?' she said.

'No, only when I'm stupid enough to get my head kicked in by a redneck cop.'

I smoked the cigarette and exhaled slowly, while my temple and eye beat with pain, then pushed the sweat back into my hair with one hand.

'Look, you're not a drinker, so you don't know the alcoholic syndrome,' I said. 'I'm not a shithead all the time.'

'Sit down. Your cut is bleeding.'

'I'm going down the road. I'll take a couple of those hot beers with me if you don't mind.'

My legs were weak, and the blood seemed to drain downward in my body with the effort of standing.

'You can't drive anywhere now.'

'Watch.'

'You're pulling a dumb scene.'

I started towards the counter where the remaining bottles of Jax stood, and a yellow wave of nausea went through me. The sour taste of buttermilk and last night's whiskey came up in my throat, and I felt a great throbbing weight on my forehead. My cigarette was wet down to the ash from the sweat running off my face.

'Goddamn, I really got one this time,' I said.

'Come in the back,' she said, and put her arm around my waist. My shirt stuck wetly against my skin.

We went down the hallway through a side door into a small bedroom. The shade on the window was torn, and strips of broken sunlight struck across the floor. An old crucifix was nailed against one wall above a Catholic religious calendar with two withered palms stuck under the top edges. I drew in on the dead cigarette and gagged in the back of my throat. You've just about made the d.t.'s this time, I thought. Work on it again and you'll really get there.

My body felt as rigid as a snapped twig. She pressed me down on the edge of the bed with her hands and turned on an electric fan. The current of air was like wind blowing over ice against my face.

'Lie down and I'll put a dressing on your cut,' she said.

Something was rolling loose inside me, and my fingers were shaking on my knees.

'Look, you don't need—'

'Lie down, Lone Ranger.' Then she leaned over me with her breasts heavy against her blouse, her brown face and wild curly hair a dark silhouette above me, and pressed me back into the pillow.

She rubbed ointment on the cut in a circular motion with her fingers and taped a piece of gauze over it. I could feel the heat of the sun in her skin and hair, and her eyes were filled with a dark shine. I touched the smoothness of her arm with my hand, then the light began to fade beyond the window shade, the fan blew cool over my chest and face, and somewhere out in the hills a train whistle echoed and beat thinly into a brass sky. I heard her close the door softly as on the edge of a dream.

It was afternoon when I awoke, and the wind was blowing hard against the building. The shade flapped back from the window, rattling against the woodwork, and dustdevils spun in the air outside. The boards in the floor quivered from the gusts of wind under the building, and there were grains of sand on my skin. My head was dizzy when I stood up, my face tingling, and I could taste the hot dryness of the air in my mouth. I tripped over the fan and opened the door to the hallway. The sudden draught tore the religious calendar and withered palms from the wall, and the mobile made from beer bottles clattered and twisted in circles on the ceiling in the main room. I leaned against the doorjamb in the numbness of awaking from afternoon sleep. Through the front screen I could see the clouds of dust blowing along the street into the trees. I heard Rie walk out of the kitchen towards me. She held a tall glass of ice water in her hand, and she had put on a pair of white shorts and a navy denim shirt. There were freckles on the tops of her bare feet.

'How do you feel?' she said.

'I'll let you know in a minute.' I took the glass of ice water from her hand and drank it down to the bottom. I didn't believe that I had ever been so thirsty. The coldness ached inside my empty stomach.

'You have bad dreams,' she said.

'Yeah, I've got a whole wheelbarrow full of them.' I walked past her into the kitchen and put my head under the iron pump. I worked the handle, and the water poured over my neck and shoulders and inside my shirt. I wiped my face slick with the palm of my hand. Down the slope the Rio Grande was rippled and dented by the wind. The brown current was turning white around the wreck of the submerged car.

'You can stay here. You don't have to go back today,' she said.

'I'd better hit it.'

'Wait until the wind storm passes.'

'They don't pass this time of year. That's a three-day affair out there.' The water dripped off my clothes on to the floor.

'You can't see out of your eye.'

'I sight with one eye over my Cadillac hood just like a pistol barrel,' I said.

'I'll ride to the hotel with you.'

'No, the sheriff will probably be hanging around there some-where. I think you've had enough innings with a left-handed pitcher for one day.'

The building shook in the wind, and pieces of newspaper blew by the window. Across the river two Mexican children were leading a flat-sided, mange-scarred cow off the mud bank into a shed. Her swollen, red udder swung under her belly.

'I don't want to see you get busted again,' Rie said.

'You take care, babe.' I put my hands on her shoulders and kissed her on the cheek. For just an instant the nipples of her breasts touched me and I turned to water inside. Her mouth and eyes made my heart race. 'I expect I'll be back here eventually and try to do something for that Yankee mind of yours.'

'Be careful with yourself, Hack.'

I walked out into the dust and drove to the hotel. Leaves were shredding from the trees on the courthouse lawn and blowing along the footpath. An empty tomato basket bounced end over end in the middle of the street, and the wooden sign over the hotel slammed back and forth on its iron hooks. The fat deputy who had let me out of the cell that morning sat in the swing on the verandah with his feet propped against the railing. He looked off casually at the yellow sky when I passed him, his huge stomach bursting against his shirt buttons.

'Mr Holland, we'll be needing your room tonight,' the desk clerk said inside. His eyes were focused about three inches to the side of my face, then they would flick temporarily across the bridge of my nose and back again to a spot on the far wall.

'By God, that's right, isn't it?' I said. 'The Cattlemen's Association is holding its world convention here this week.'

My room had been cleaned, the bed made, the empty beer bottles carried out, as though I had never been there, and my suitcase was packed and closed and sitting just inside the door, ready to be picked up in one convenient motion. Someone had even put a Gideon Bible on the dresser top.

I paid my bill at the desk, and the clerk managed to show me nothing but the crown of his head while he marked off the ticket and counted out my change.

'You don't sell cigars in here, do you?' I said.

He fumbled in the middle of his counting, his eyelids blinking nervously, and I thought I had him, but he regained his resolve and kept his eyes nailed to the counter. 'No sir, but you can get them right next door,' he said, and turned away to the cash register.

I started down the steps to my car, then I heard the swing flop back empty on its chains and the boards of the porch bend under the deputy's massive weight. Shit, what a time not to have a cigar, I thought.

'Mr Holland, the sheriff wanted me to give you this road map,' he said, pulling it out of the back pocket of his khaki trousers. The paper was pressed into an arc from the curve of his buttocks. 'He don't want you to get lost nowhere on that highway construction before you get into the next county.'

'I guess that would be easy to do unless I had a map. Say, you don't smoke cigars, do you?' I said. 'Let me get a Camel from you, then.'

His eyes looked at me uncomprehendingly out of his white volleyball face. His greased black hair, combed over the balding pate, had grains of sand in it. He pulled a cigarette out of his shirt pocket with two fingers and handed it to me.

'This is goddamn nice of you and the sheriff, and I appreciate it.' I borrowed his lighter, which had a Confederate flag on the side of it, and lit the cigarette. 'Look, I've got two lifetime World Rodeo Association passes that I never use. They're good for box seats at any livestock show or ass-buster in the state. Here, you take them.'

I pulled the two thick, cardboard passes from my notecase and stuck them in his shirt pocket.

'Well, thank you, Mr Holland,' he said.

I went next door to the tavern, bought a box of cigars and a six-pack of cold Jax, and headed down the road in the blowing clouds of dust, the corn stalks rattling in the wind, the gold of the citrus exposed among the swelling green trees, and each time I made a curve between two hills at ninety miles an hour I felt the old omnipotence vibrate smoothly out of the engine through the steering column into my hands. The fields of cotton, water melons and tomatoes flashed by me, and the late sun splintered in shafts of light through the dust clouds and struck on the tops of the hills in soft areas of pale green and shadow. Then the country began to become more level, the twilight took on all the violent purple and yellow colours of an apocalypse, and I felt the wind driving with me eastward down a narrow blacktop highway that stretched endlessly across empty land towards the gathering darkness on the horizon.

FIVE

The poplar trees along my front lane were bent in the wind when I got back to the ranch that night. Under the full moon their shadows beat on the white gravel, and the air was full of swirling rose petals from Verisa's gardens. Someone had forgotten to chain the windmill by the barn, and the blades were spinning in a circle of tinny light while the water overflowed from the trough on to the ground. I could see the dark shapes of ruined tomatoes lying in the rows, and some of the cotton had started to strip. Then I saw Sailor Boy, my Tennessee walking horse that I had bought from Spendthrift Farm for six thousand dollars, knocking against the rails in the lot. His nostrils were dilated, his black head shiny with moonlight and fear, and he was running in a broken gait against each of the rick fence corners, rearing his head and kicking dirt and manure in the air. I climbed into the lot with him, worked him back easy against the rails with both my arms outspread, and got a halter over his head. There was a four-inch cut in one flank, and he had broken a shoe and splintered part of a hoof against the barn wall. I led him into a stall, slipped an oats bag over his ears, pulled the rest of the shoe, and dressed the ragged split in his skin. Then I went into the house, my blood roaring.

Verisa was reading a book under a lamp in the living room. She wore her nightgown, and she had two curlers set in the front of her hair. A cigarette was burned down to its filter in the ashtray. She had the nocturnal, isolated composure of a woman who might have lived by herself all her life.

'Question number one: who in the hell left Sailor Boy out in the lot?' I said.

She turned and looked at me, and her face whitened under the lamp.

'What—' I saw her eyes trying to adjust on the swollen side of my head.

'Who left my goddamn horse out in a wind storm?'

'Hack, what in God's name have you done now?'

'I want to know which idiot or combination of idiots left my horse to tear himself up in the lot.'

'I don't know. Why don't you stay home and take care of him yourself?'

'The perfect non-think answer. If his gait is thrown off I'm going to set fire to somebody's hair.'

'You'd better not be talking about me.'

'Read it like you want. It takes a special type of fool to do something that stupid to a fine horse.'

'You just stop your shouting at me.'

'I'll crack the goddamn ceiling if I want. And as long as we're on it, question number two: who forgot to chain the windmill? Which might strike you as a minor thing to consider between book pages, but right now our water table is almost dry and there are some crops that have a tendency to burn when they're not irrigated.'

'I'm getting sick of this,' she said.

'I'm not asking you to walk around in the manure with a cattle prod in your hand. I'd just like you to stick your head out of the door occasionally and make sure the whole goddamn place hasn't blown away.'

'I don't know where your present adventure took you, but you must have damaged some of the brain tissue. I'm going to bed. If you want to shout some more, either close the door or go down the road to your tavern.'

'Don't you know what it means to hurt a horse like that?'

'Good night, Hack.'

She set her book down with a marker between the pages and walked past me in her best remote fashion. Her blue nightgown swirled around her legs in a whisper of silk, then she closed the door behind her. I had a drink out of the decanter on the bar, while my chest rose and fell with my breathing. Outside, the trees scratched against the house, and the door on the barn loft kept slamming like a tack hammer in the wind.

In the morning I went to the office in Austin and began work on Art's appeal. I was supposed to help Bailey that week on two large insurance suits, but after he had recovered from staring at my bandaged head and the swollen corner of my eye under my sunglasses, I told him that he would have to carry it alone for a few days. He was still angry from the weekend, and now his exasperation with his younger brother almost made his eyes cross. He sat with one thigh over the corner of my desk, his hands folded, straining like a stoic to retain his patience, while each word tripped out like an expression from a peptic ulcer.

'This is a two-hundred-thousand-dollar deal, Hack,' he said. 'We waited on it for six months.'

'So I'll pick it up next week.'

'We're going to try to settle next week.'

'They're not going to settle. Forget it. We'll be in court a year.'

'Give that case to the ACLU. They handle them all the time.'

'I just want three goddamn uninterrupted days.'

'Even if you win appeal, you won't get him out of prison on bond.'

'I might if I can get some work done and be let alone for any random period of time.'

'What happened in Pueblo Verde?'

'You won't buy a car accident, will you? All right, a pecker-wood cop kicked the hell out of me and I spent a night in a drunk tank. I was also indirectly presented with a map from the sheriff so I could find my way out of the county. In the meantime I managed to get a dozen other people arrested. Lastly, I'm going to write off their bail on my expense account. Now you can worry about the wire services picking up a sweet piece of interesting journalism on a congressional candidate. Does that make your day any better?'

'I don't believe you.'

'I have a receipt for the bail if you would like to look at it.'

His stomach swelled as he drew in on his dead pipe. It made a sound that hurt something in the inner ear. His vexed, almost desperate eyes focused out of the window. Then his control began to slip, the anger and impotence rose in his face, and he ranted for fifteen minutes in clichés about responsibilities, major accounts, a judge who said that he never wanted me in his chambers again, my career in politics (and its profitable effects on our law practice), and my pending trip to Walter Reed Hospital with Senator Dowling.

'Oh, that's right,' I said. 'We view the Claymore mine and AK-47 cases this weekend. Why don't you come along, Bailey? You missed the Korean show. These guys are a blast.'

He slammed the door behind him, and I lit a cigar and looked up at the picture of Old Hack and my father on the wall. In the faded photograph, now yellow around the edges, his black eyes still burned from his face, which had begun to grow soft and childlike in his old age. His eyes turned directly into mine as I moved the swivel chair in either direction. They were like shattered obsidian, filled with fire and the quiet intensity of a levelled rifle. His bobbed hair was as white as his starched shirt, and his stiff black coat looked as though a pistol ball would flatten out against it. Next to him, my father's gentle face and straw boater and summer suit made me think of two strangers who had met in the middle of an empty field and had decided to have their picture taken together.

I worked the next three days on the appeal with an energy and freshness that I hadn't felt in years. In fact, I even felt like a criminal lawyer again rather than an expensive manipulator for the R. C. Richardson account. My bottle of Jack Daniel's stayed in the desk drawer, and I came to the office at seven in the morning and stayed until dusk. As I said before, the appeal should have been a foregone conclusion, but I began to wonder if any judge in the Austin court would believe that so many absurdities could have actually taken place in one trial. Moreover, each time I went through the transcript I didn't believe it myself. Thursday afternoon, after I'd had the secretary in my office for five hours of dictation and typing, Bailey's patience cracked apart again and he came suddenly through the door, his face stretched tight with anger. (The air conditioner was broken, and we had the windows over the street open. The hot air was like warm water in the room.)

'All right, you can let two hundred thousand dollars go to hell, but I'm still paying half the overhead around here,' he said.

'Bailey, look at this goddamn thing, then tell me that I ought to let this guy sit it out in the pen while some kid lawyer from the ACLU plays pocket pool with himself.'

'I don't want to look at it. I have a desk covered with twice my ordinary load of work.'

'Then have a drink of water. You look hot.'

'Goddamn it, Hack, you're putting me over the edge.'

'I just want you to glance at what can happen in a legal court without one voice being raised in protest.'

'What did you expect to find down there? Those union people knew the terms when they came in here.'

'I think I heard a deputy sheriff say about the same thing while he was pouring his mouth full of chewing tobacco.'

And once more Bailey slammed out the door, a furious man who would never understand the real reasons for his anger.

I spent Friday night in an Austin motel, and Saturday morning I met the Senator's private plane at the airport. I stood on the hot concrete by the terminal in my white suit, and watched the plane tilt across the sky and approach the runway, its wings and propellers awash with sunlight. One wing lifted upward momentarily in the wind, then balanced again, and the wheels touched on the asphalt as smoothly as a soft slipper. The heat waves bounced off the fuselage, and the sun turned the front windows into mirrors exploding with light. At the end of the runway the pilot feathered one engine and taxied at an angle towards me, and I saw the Senator open the back door and wave one arm, his face smiling.

I walked to the plane, and the backdraught from the propeller blew the tail of my coat over my shoulders. The Senator was grinning in the roar, and he extended his hand and helped me into the compartment. I pulled the door shut after me, locked the handle down, and the plane began to taxi out on the main runway again. The Senator was dressed in slacks, a Hawaiian sports shirt, and calfskin loafers. There was fresh tan on his face and a few freckles along the hair line of his white, crew-cropped head. In the opposite seat, with a drink resting on his crossed knee, was a man whom I didn't know, although I sensed at the time that I probably would never forget him. He wore a charcoal business suit, silk shirt with cuff links, a grey tie, and his face was pale and expressionless behind his sunglasses. The mouth was small and compressed, as though he never spoke except with a type of quiet finality, and his manicured, half-moon fingernails and confident reserve reminded me of a very successful corporation executive, but there was something about the hue of his skin and the trace of talcum powder on his neck that darkened the image.

'Hack, this is John Williams, an old friend from Los Angeles,' the Senator said.

We shook hands, and I felt the coldness in his palm from the highball glass.

'How do you do,' he said. Only the mouth moved when he spoke. The face remained as immobile as plastic. He pushed his smoky, metallic hair back on one temple with his fingertips.

The plane gained speed, the engines roaring faster, then it lifted off the runway, and I felt the weightless, empty feeling of dropping unexpectedly in an elevator as the countryside spread out below us and the blocks of neat houses and rows of trees seemed to shrink away into the earth.

John Williams, I thought. The name. Where?

'What happened to your head?' the Senator said. 'I hope you haven't run into another tennis player with a bad aim.'

'A minor car accident.' *You shithead*, I thought.

'Well, John, this man is going to be the youngest congressman from the state in November.'

Williams nodded and took a sip from his drink. I tried to see his eyes through his sunglasses. John Williams, goddamn, where did I see it?

'John's not from Texas, but he's a good friend to the party.'

'I see,' I said.

'I've had him at the ranch for a few days of shooting. I'm trying to convince him that the only place to build industry today is in the Southwest.'

'A beautiful state,' Williams said. His face was turned to me, but it was impossible to read his meaning or intention.

'Do you mind if I have a drink?' I said.

'I'm sorry, Hack. I usually don't drink this early myself, and I forget that other people don't have my same Baptist instincts.' The Senator opened the cabinet door to the bar and folded out a small table from the wall. He picked up three cubes from the ice bucket with the tongs and dropped them into a tall glass and poured in a shot of bourbon.

'I was glad to see you at the airport,' he said. 'I thought maybe we were too forceful last Sunday in getting you to come along.'

'Oh, I keep my promises, Senator.'

'We'll only be there a short while. A couple of the state news services will meet us at the hospital, and then we'll have dinner and take off again this evening.'

'News services?' I said.

'Yes, the local ones. They usually like to cover this sort of thing for the state television stations.'

'I didn't know about that.'

'I see you're a bit new to politics,' Williams said. There was just a touch of a smile at the corner of his mouth, a faint wrinkle in the plastic skin.

'No, no, Hack's father was a congressman. In fact, a very fine one. It's just that Hack had some private reservations at first about visiting Walter Reed.'

'Why's that, Mr Holland?'

'I suppose it's connected with superstition. You know, bad luck,' I said.

'Really?' The skin wrinkled again at the corner of his mouth, and he clinked the ice in his glass. I felt the pulse begin to swell in my neck.

'Probably a silly thing, but I never found much pleasure in visiting a veterans' ward,' I said.

Williams' face remained opaque as he looked at me, but I saw one finger tighten on his glass.

'Maybe it's something about the smell of a dressing on a burn. I really couldn't tell you,' I said.

He continued to stare at me, and I knew that behind those sunglasses his eyes were burning into mine.

'How about another drink, John?'

'I'm fine.'

'I suppose I shouldn't have brought it up. Actually, Hack was wounded in Korea and spent some time in the VA after the war.'

'Is that right, Mr Holland?'

'It wasn't of much consequence. A flesh wound. The John Wayne variety,' I said.

'It was a little more serious than that,' the Senator said.

'I'd like to talk with you about your experiences sometime,' Williams said. His voice was as dry as paper.

'They're not very interesting, but anytime you're passing through DeWitt County on your way between Washington and LA, we'll sure crack a couple of bottles.'

'You'll see John at my ranch. He visits often,' the Senator said. 'Your glass is empty, Hack.'

I wouldn't have believed it, but the Senator was uncomfortable. His acetylene-blue eyes were bright, and his easy laugh had a fine wire of strain in it. He poured another shot in my glass and pressed the stopper hard in the bottle neck with his thumb. And I began to feel that John Williams was a much more formidable person than I had realized.

'If you continue in politics I'm sure we'll see a lot more of each other,' Williams said. I could almost taste the bile in his teeth. 'It looks like your career is going to be a very good one.'

'I expect that's one of those things you never know about.'

'I wouldn't say that.'

Again, I couldn't tell if there was a second meaning in what he said, or if he used deliberate vagueness to keep his opposition full of unspoken question marks. But I did know that the Senator was still sitting a bit forward in his seat, and his thigh muscles were tensed under the crease of his trousers. Yes, there's a real lesson in this, I thought. Even the predators sometimes have to lie under the reef while the shadows of much larger fish move through the dark waters overhead. I lit my first cigar of the day and squinted at the Senator and Williams through the smoke, and I wondered what umbilical cord connected them.

I didn't say anything else that would test that delicate pattern of membrane behind the Senator's healthy smile, and Williams sensed that the match was over. He set his drink on the table, folded his hands on his knee, and looked out of the window like a withdrawn demiurge at the pools of fire in the clouds.

Three hours later I was on my fourth bourbon and water as we began our approach to Dulles Airport.

The air in Washington was humid and hazy with smog. There had been rioting in the Negro district off Pennsylvania Avenue during the week, and from the plane I had seen plumes of smoke blowing across the blocks of red-brick tenement buildings towards the Capitol and the Lincoln Memorial, that island of green and marble and blue water in the centre of a colossal slum. Now, standing on the drive among the potted plants in front of the terminal, I could smell just the hint of burned wood in the air, and my eyes watered in the yellow pall that hung over everything in sight.

The Senator's chauffeured Cadillac limousine picked us up, and on the way to Walter Reed I fixed another drink from the portable bar built into the back of the driver's seat. The Senator didn't like it, but he confined his objection to a steady look at the amount of bourbon in my glass. Williams sat silently on the fold-out seat, his back straight and his face turned indifferently to the window; however, I could feel his sense of superiority in the knowledge that I was starting in heavy on the whiskey. That's all right, motherfucker, I thought. Wes Hardin and I will kick your ass any day in the light-year you want to choose.

Two television newsmen from Houston and Fort Worth were waiting for us by the information desk in the main room of the hospital. They were both young, dressed in narrow-cut suits and knitted neckties and button-down collars, and their hair looked as though it were trimmed every day. They had been leaning against the counter with their cameras hanging loosely in their hands, and when they saw the Senator they snapped into motion and came towards us with their leather soles clicking on the marble floor. Their college-boy faces showed the proper deference and energetic respect, and I thought, *ahhh*, there are two young men who will never live within breathing distance of the Fort Worth stockyards.

Three hospital administrators joined us, and we began our tour of the wards holding the Viet Nam wounded. I had a fair edge on from the whiskey, but now I wished that I had made a bigger dent in the bottle. The beds, with high metal rails on the sides, stretched out in long rows, and the afternoon sun slanted across the bodies of the men under the sheets. I had made a cynical remark to Williams about the smell of a dressing on a burn; but that was only part of it. The astringent odour of the antiseptic used to scrub the floors mixed with the reek of the bedpans, the sweaty and itching flesh inside the plaster casts, the urine that sometimes dried in the mattress pads of the paraplegics, and the salve oozing from bandages that covered rows of hard stitches. There was another odour in the air, too, one that might be called imaginary, but I could smell the distant rain forests and the sores that formed on men's bodies from living in wet uniforms and in boots that hardened like iron around the feet. The stench of terror and dried excrement on the buttocks was there, also, and if you wanted to think hard on it you could fill your lungs and catch the sweet-sour grey smell of death.

The Senator shook hands cheerfully from bed to bed, and each time he found a man from Texas he made several banal remarks while the cameras whirred away. A few of the men were bored or irritated at seeing another politician, but the majority of them grinned with their boyish, old men's faces, propped themselves up on their elbows with cigarettes between their fingers, and listened to the Senator's thanks about the job they were doing. Only one time did he have trouble, and that was with a Negro Marine who'd had an arm amputated at the shoulder. The Negro's eyes were bloodshot, and I saw a bottle of paregoric sticking out from under his pillow.

'Don't thank me for nothing, *man*,' he said. 'When I get out of here you better hide that pink ass behind a wall.'

The cameras stopped whirring, and the Senator smiled and walked to the next bed as though the Negro and his anger were there only as the result of some chance accident not worth considering seriously. Then the cameras started working again, the two newsmen were back to their coverage, and the Marine pulled out his bottle of paregoric and unscrewed the cap by flipping it around with one thumb. His bloodshot eyes continued to stare into the Senator's back.

At the end of each ward the Senator made a speech, and I wondered how many times he had made it in the same wards during World War II and the Korean War. He had probably changed some of the language to suit the particular cause and geographic conquest involved, but the content must have been the same: The people at home support you boys. We're proud of the American fighting man and the sacrifices he's made to defend democracy against Communist aggression. You've taken up the standard that can only be held by the brave, and we're not going to let anyone dishonour that standard. It's been bought at too dear a price . . .

And on and on.

As I watched him I remembered sitting in a similar ward in 1953 after the last pieces of splintered lead had been removed from my legs, and listening to a state representative make almost the same speech. I didn't remember his name, or even what he looked like, but he and the Senator were much alike, because in the intense emotional moment of their delivery they believed they had fought the same battles as the men lying before them, felt the same aching lung-rushing gasp when they were hit, bled into the same dark soil, and had fallen through the same endless morphine deliriums in a battalion aid station.

But the Senator had one better. After all the hackneyed patriotic justifications for losing part of one's life, he outdid himself:

'I bet you boys aren't burning your draft cards!'

And they replied in unison, one hundred strong:

'NO SIR!'

The Senator went through the doorway with three hospital administrators, who all the time had been smiling as though they were showing off a nursery of hot-house plants, and one of the newsmen turned his camera on me.

'Get that goddamn thing out of my face,' I said.

He didn't hear me over the electric noise of his machine, or he didn't believe what he'd heard, and he kept the lens pointed at the centre of my forehead.

'I mean it, pal. I'll break it against the wall.'

He lowered his camera slowly with his mouth partly open and stared at me. He didn't know what he had done wrong, and all the reasons for his presence there in the hospital were evaporating before him. I don't know what my face looked like then, with the cut on my temple and my slightly swollen eye, but evidently it was enough to make a graduate of the Texas University School of Journalism wince. He dropped his eyes to the camera and began adjusting the lens as though the light had changed in the last ten seconds.

'I had a car accident this week and I don't want any of the guys at the country club thinking my wife hit me in the head with a shoe,' I said. I laughed and touched him on the arm.

He smiled, and I saw that his pasteboard frame of reference was secure again. He walked into the next ward after the Senator, and I thought, I hope that thirty-thousand-dollar house in the Fort Worth suburbs will be worth it all, buddy.

Later, back in the Cadillac, with the sun steaming off the bonnet, I poured a half glass of straight bourbon and took two deep swallows. The yellow haze outside was worse now, and the air-conditioning vents were dripping with moisture.

'That Negro soldier should be brought to the attention of his commanding officer,' Williams said.

'He was a Marine,' I said.

'Regardless, there's no excuse for a remark like that,' he said.

So you're a propriety man as well, I thought.

'It's nothing,' the Senator said. 'His attitudes will change back to normal with time. I've seen many others like him.'

'I didn't like it,' Williams said.

'Maybe he doesn't care to be part of the science of prosthesis,' I said. 'Provided they can fit something on that stub.'

Williams looked at me steadily with his opaque, pale face. For just a second his finger tips ticked on his thigh. I knew that if I could have looked into his eyes I would have seen flames and grotesque mouths wide with silent screams.

'Do you like that brand of bourbon, Mr Holland? I'd like to send you a case of it,' he said.

'Thanks. I'm a Jack Daniel's man myself, and I get it on order straight from Lynchburg.'

'You must have a very good relationship with the whiskey manufacturers, then.'

I smoked a cigar and finished my drink in silence while we moved through the late traffic towards the downtown district. When I noticed that Williams was irritated by the smoke I made a point of leaving the cigar butt only partly extinguished in the ashtray. Originally, the Senator had planned for the three of us to have dinner together, one of those charcoal steak and white linen and pleasant conversation affairs that the Senator was fond of; but now it was understood between us that Williams should be dropped off at the Hilton, where he kept a permanent suite.

He stepped out of the car on to the pavement and bent over to shake hands with me through the open door. In the hot air there was a a tinge of his perspiration mixed with the scent of talcum and cologne. The shadow of the building made his skin look synthetic and dead. His sunglasses tipped forward a moment, and I caught a flash of colour like burned iron.

'Another time, Mr Holland.'

'Yes, sir,' I said.

We drove to the airport and I waited for the Senator to begin his subtle dissection. I was even looking forward to it. I felt the whiskey in my head now, and I would have liked an extension of last week's tennis match. But he surprised me completely. His attack came down an entirely different street, and I realized then that he probably disliked Williams even more than I did, although for different reasons.

'You weren't in a car accident last week, Hack. You were put in jail with several members of that Mexican farm union.'

I had to wait a moment on that one.

'The sheriff could have charged you with attempted assault on a law officer.'

'Your office reaches much farther than I thought, Senator.'

'You might also know that I made sure the story wouldn't reach the wire services.'

'As a long time friend of our family you probably also know that I've had other adventures of this sort.'

'Another one like it could end your career in Texas.'

'I don't think either one of us believes that, Senator.'

'I'm not talking about a drunken escapade. If you involve yourself with a radical movement, you'll find yourself on the ticket as an independent. The party won't support you. I don't think your father would enjoy the idea of your associating yourself with people who are trying to destroy our society, either.'

He was after the vulnerable parts now.

'It always seemed to me that my father's work with the New Deal was considered pretty radical at the time,' I said. 'However, I don't have any connections with the United Farm Workers. I was trying to help a friend from the service.'

The sun was starting to set among the purple clouds on the horizon, and through the car window I could see aircraft approaching Dulles with their landing lights on.

'I think you should turn over your friend's case to someone else.'

'Well, in eight years of practice I haven't lost a criminal case, Senator, and I'm usually a pretty good judge about what clients our firm should handle.'

'I hope you are, Hack, and I hope that we don't have this same kind of discussion again.'

The chauffeur pulled into the terminal drive, and I went into the restaurant and had a dozen steak sandwiches made up while the Senator waited for me at the passenger gate. His plane taxied out of the hangar and rolled along the apron of the runway towards us, and in minutes we were back aboard and roaring towards the end of the field.

We lifted off sharply into the sun, the city sparkling below us in the twilight, and the interior of the plane was filled with a diffused red glow. My glass of bourbon and ice rattled on the table with the engines' vibration.

'Who is he, anyway?' I said.

'John Williams? He owns the controlling stock in two of the government's largest missile suppliers.'

SIX

I spent the next week working on Art's appeal while the July days grew hotter and my broken air conditioner cranked and rattled in the window. The temperature went to one hundred degrees every afternoon, and the sky stayed cloudless and brilliant with sun. The pavements and buildings were alive with heat, and sometimes when the air conditioner gave out altogether I'd open the window and the wind would blow into my face like a torch. In the street, below, people walked under the hot shade of the awnings away from the sun's glare, their faces squinted against the light and their clothes wet with perspiration. The humidity made your skin feel as though it were crawling with spiders, and when you stepped off a kerb into the sun the air suddenly had the taste of an electric scorch.

In the evening, when the day had started to cool, I would drive out into the surrounding hills with the windows of the car down. (I had taken a hotel room in town so I could come to the office early each morning, and also Verisa was holding two cocktail parties at the house that week, and I wasn't up to another round of drinking, and the disaster that always followed, with empty-headed women.)

In the mauve twilight the oak trees and blackjack took on a

deeper green, and deer broke through the underbrush and ran frightened across the blacktop road in front of my car, their eyes like frozen brown glass. The air was sweet with the smell of the hills and woods, and jackrabbits and cottontails sat in the short grass with their ears folded along their flanks. I remembered as a boy how I used to flush them out of a thicket and then whistle shrilly through my teeth and wait for them to stop and look back at me, their ears turned upward in an exact V. A slight breeze blew through the willows growing along the river bank, and I could see the bass and bream breaking the water among the reeds and lily pads. Fishermen in rowing-boats with flyrods glided silently by the willows, casting popping bugs into the shadows, then the water would explode and a large-mouth bass would climb into the air, shaking the hook in the side of his mouth, and the sun's last rays would flash off his green-silver sides like tinted gold.

One evening, after a flaming day and a one-hour harangue from Bailey about all my deficiencies, I drove down to the Devil's Backbone, a geological fault where the land folded sharply away and you could see fifty miles of Texas all at once. On the top of the ridge, there was a Mexican beer tavern built entirely of flat stones, and as I looked out over the hills at the baked land, the miniature oak trees in the distance, the darkening light in the valleys, and the broken line of fire on the horizon, I felt the breath go out of me and the ground move under my feet. In the wind I could smell the shallow water holes, the hot odour of the mesquite, the carcass of a lost cow that was being pulled apart by buzzards, the wild poppies and bluebonnets, the snakes and the lizards and the dry sand, the moist deer dung in the thickets of blackjack, and the head-reeling resilience of the land itself. I knew that if I stood there long enough, with the shadows spreading across the hills, I would see the ghosts of Apache and Comanche warriors riding their painted horses in single file, their naked bodies hung with scalps and necklaces of human fingers. Or maybe the others who came later, like Bowie and Crockett and Fannin and Milam, with deerskin clothes and powder horn and musket and the self-destructive fury that led them to war against the entire Mexican army.

The stone tavern was cool inside, and the cigarette-burned floor, the yellow mirror behind the bar, the shuffleboard table, and the jukebox with the changing coloured lights inside the plastic casing were right out of the 1940s. Cedar-cutters and Mexican farmhands sat at the wooden tables with frosted schooners of beer in their hands, the bartender set down free plates of tortillas, cheese and hot peppers, and the long-dead voice of Hank Williams rose from the jukebox. The last cinders of the sun faded outside, bugs beat against the screen door, and a brown moon sat low over the hills. I ordered a plate of tacos and a draught beer and watched two cedar-cutters sliding the metal puck through the powdered wax on the shuffleboard. For some reason the Mexican farmhands kept toasting me with their glasses every time they drank, so I bought a round for three tables, and that was the beginning of a good beer drunk.

The next morning I drove to the state penitentiary with my head still full of beer and jukebox music. The blacktop highway stretched through the rolling hills of red clay and cotton and pine trees, and my tyres left long lines in the soft tar surfacing. The smell of the Piney Woods was sharp in the heat, and thin cattle grazed in the fields of burned grass. The rivers were almost dry, the sandbars like strips of bleached bone, and flocks of buzzards turned in slow circles over the woods. The corn had started to burn on the edges, and in two more weeks, with no rain, the stalks would wither and the ears would lie rotting in the rows.

As I approached the city limits I saw all the familiar warning signs for this world and the next posted along the roadside:

DO NOT PICK UP HITCHHIKERS
STATE PENITENTIARY NEARBY

PREPARE TO MEET THY GOD

SAVE AMERICA AND IMPEACH EARL WARREN

JESUS DIED FOR YOU HAVE YOU BEEN SAVED

DON'T WORRY
THEY'RE ONLY NINETY MILES AWAY.

And farther on, in a happier mood,

DON'T FAIL TO SEE THE HOME OF
SAM HOUSTON
AND JACK'S SNAKE FARM

I stopped at the main gate of the prison and showed my identification to the guard. He wore a khaki uniform and a lacquered straw hat, and his hands and face were tanned the colour of old leather. One jaw was swollen with chewing tobacco, and after he had looked at my Texas Bar Association card he spat a stream of brown juice through the rails of the cattleguard, wiped the stain off the corner of his mouth, and handed me a cardboard visitor's pass with the date punched at the bottom.

'Don't try to drive out till the gate man goes through your car,' he said.

The main complex of buildings was at the end of a yellow gravel road that wound through acres of cotton and string beans. The inmates, in white uniforms, were chopping in the rows, their hoes rising and flashing in the sun, while the guards sat on horseback above them with rifles or shotguns balanced across their saddles. The sun was straight up in the sky, and I could see the dark areas of sweat in the guards' clothes and the flush of heat in the inmates' faces. Except for the motion of the hoes, or a horse slashing his tail against the green flies on his flanks, they all seemed frozen, removed, in the private ritual that exists between jailer and prisoner. Sometimes a trusty, sharpening tools in the shade of the cedar trees at the edge of the field, would carry a water bucket out to the men in the rows, and they would drink from the dipper with the water spilling over their throats and chests, or a guard would dismount and stand in the shade of his horse while the men sat on the ground and smoked for five minutes; but otherwise the static labour of their work day was unrelieved.

The dust clouds from my car blew back across the fields, and occasionally an inmate would raise his head from his concentration on the end of his hoe and look at me, one of the free people who drove with magic on the way to distant places. And as one of the free people I was the enemy, unable to understand even in part what his microcosm was like. From under his beaded forehead his eyes hated me, and at that moment, looking at my air-conditioned car and the acrid cloud of dust that blew into his face, he could have chopped me up with his hoe simply for the way I took the things of the free world for granted – the women, the cold beer, the lazy Saturday mornings, the endless streets I could walk down without ever stopping.

But I did know his world, maybe even better than he did. I knew the sick feeling of hearing a cage door bolted behind you, the fear of returning to solitary confinement and the nightmares it left you with, the caution you used around the violent and the insane, the shame of masturbation and the temptation towards homosexuality, the terror you had when a cocked gun was aimed in your face, the months and years pointed at no conclusion, the jealousy over a guard's favour, and the constant press of bodies around you and the fact that your most base physical functions were always witnesed by dozens of eyes. I knew how the weapons were made and where they were hidden: a nail sharpened on stone and driven through a small block of wood; a double-edged razor wedged in a toothbrush handle; barbed wire wrapped around the end of a club; spoons and strips of tin that could open up wrists and jugular veins; and all of it remained unseen, taped between the thighs, carried inside a bandage, tied on a string down a plumbing pipe, or even pushed into the excrement in the latrine.

The reception building was surrounded by trees and a green lawn. Three trusties were trimming the hedges, edging the footpaths and weeding the flower beds. They looked right through me as I walked past them to the entrance. I didn't know why, but I always felt a sense of guilt when I was around prison inmates, as though I should apologize for something. I knew the sequence of absurdities that often put them there, and I knew, also, that the years of punishment and the debilitating ethic that went with it had almost nothing to do with correction; but if I thought too long on any of that I would have to fold my law degree into a paper aeroplane and sail it out of my office window. I looked directly at the Negro clipping the top of the hedge (he was so black that his white uniform looked like an insult on his skin), and he moved the clippers at a downward angle on the side of the hedge so that his face turned away from me.

In the distance I could see one of the crumbling grey block-houses left over from the last century, and I wondered if that was the one where John Wesley Hardin spent years chained to the wall of a dark cell. They fed him gruel and water, and whipped him every day with a leather strap to break him, and when he was finally taken out to work in the fields they manacled an iron ball to one ankle, and two guards always stood over him with shotguns. He served his hard time like that, fourteen years in chains with the whip and horse quirt laid across the buttocks.

And I remembered the songs that Leadbelly had sung on the same farm: 'The Midnight Special', 'There Ain't no More Cane on the Brazos', and 'Shorty George', and the lines about the 'black Betty', a four-inch-wide razor strop, three feet long, nailed to a wooden handle.

I sat in the scrubbed reception room and waited for the guard to bring Art from the fields. The room was divided by a long, low-topped counter, and the inmates sat on one side and the visitors on the other, their heads bent towards one another in a futile attempt at privacy. There was a sign on the far wall that read: DO NOT GIVE ANYTHING TO THE PRISONERS; CIGARETTES CAN BE LEFT WITH THE PERSONNEL. At one end of the counter a huge guard, with rings of fat across his stomach, sat in a wooden chair that strained under his weight. There was a dead cigar in his mouth and a filthy spittoon by his feet. Most of his teeth were gone, and he licked his tongue across the strings of tobacco on his gums. His face was like a pie plate, and the washed-out eyes wouldn't focus in a straight line. Occasionally, he looked at his watch and pointed one thick finger at an inmate to tell him that his visiting time was over, then he would suck on the flattened end of his cigar. I could almost hear the digestive juices boiling in his stomach.

Art came through a back door with a guard behind him. His black hair was dripping sweat, and the cobweb scar in the corner of his eye was white against his tan. His palms were grimed and his forearms filmed with dirt and cotton lint. There were black rings in the creases of his neck, and his clothes were rumpled and stained at the knees. He had lost more weight, and the veins in his hands stood out like knotted pieces of cord.

'How long we got, boss man?' he said, taking a package of Bugler tobacco from his shirt pocket.

'Fifteen minutes,' the guard said.

Art sat down and curled a cigarette paper between his fingers. He didn't speak and his eyes remained downcast until the guard had walked back to the door.

'What do you say, cousin?' he said.

'I think we'll get a new trial.'

'Half the guys in here live on new trials. They don't talk about nothing else. They write letters like paper is going out of style.'

'The difference is that you're not guilty of anything.'

'You know that don't have nothing to do with serving time.'

'Listen, as soon as the appeal goes through I'm going to have you out on bond.'

'That ain't good-guy jive, is it?'

'I don't bullshit a client, Art.'

'All right, you don't. But I'm hanging by my ass in here. This is a rough joint, man.'

'What's happened?'

He rolled the cigarette and folded down the wet seam with his thumb, watching the guard at the end of the counter.

'A couple of the hacks are laying it on. They know I'm with the union, and they're getting off their rocks while they got me in the field. Three days ago the hack said I was dogging it in the cotton and they gave me the apple-box treatment. They take you down to the hole without supper, and all night you have to stand on an unended apple crate, even though you piss your pants. If you fall off, the hole boss gives you a few knots to get your attention.'

He took a book of paper matches from his shirt, split one longways with his thumbnail, and lit his cigarette. He breathed the smoke out through the empty space in his teeth.

'The field boss already told me I'd have to wear out a hoe

handle a week if I wanted to earn good time from him,' he said. 'He stays so close on my ass that horse is shitting and pissing all over me. They're going to make me build the whole five, man, and I'll run before I do another month.'

'Don't do that.'

'I'll run or I'll ice one of those bastards. I'm through with that pacifist shit. When I was standing on that box with the hole boss looking down at me from the cage, it hit me what a dumb sonofabitch I've been for the last five years. The anglos want us to be pacifists, just like they taught us that blessed are the poor crap in church. Man, we never knew how blessed we were. They want us to keep our hands in our pockets while they knock the piss out of us.'

'Forget about that running stuff, you hear?'

'It's not something you plan. You start thinking about all that time and your clock gets wound up, and you're ready to go through the wall with your fingernails.'

Art's voice had risen, and the guard was looking at us with his crooked eyes. The fat tissue of his mouth was pressed in a small circle around his dead cigar.

'I spent a little time in a prison compound, too,' I said.

'Then you know what that patience shit sounds like.'

'Give it another couple of weeks and I'll turn every handle I can to have you on the street.'

'I tell you, buddy, if I make the street they'll never get me back in again. New trial or not, they better bring the whole goddamn army with them.'

'You'll walk out of it clean, and I have a feeling that Cecil Wayne Posey's ass is going to get barbecued, at least if I have anything to do with it. Also, the deputy at the jail is going to have a few interviews with the FBI.'

'Say, you cats really pulled a scene, didn't you? I heard them bring you in that night. Something hit the cell floor like a sack of cement, and one of the blacks in the drunk tank told me it was a tall blond guy in ice-cream slacks. You didn't believe me when I told you to keep your head down.'

'I'm learning. I haven't made a career of getting my head beat in.'

'So I have, huh? The greaseball who always gets his ass caught in the water-melon fence.'

'I met some of the people you have to deal with. I know it's bad.'

'Man, you didn't see nothing. You never got closer to a migrant camp than the highway.'

'I had a small taste of the local law enforcement.'

'I got two purple hearts in my trunk and you can have both of them.' He put out his cigarette, peeled the paper back carefully along the seam, and poured the unused tobacco in his Bugler pack.

'Do I get to be the dart board again?' I said.

'The next time you're in Pueblo Verde get Rie to give you a tour of the farm worker camps. Stick your head in a few of those stinking outdoor toilets, or talk with the kids sitting in doorways with flies swarming over their faces. Have dinner with a few of the families and see how the food sits on your stomach. Get a good breath of the dead rats under the houses and the rubbish rotting in the ditches. Check the scene out, man. It really comes alive for you when you breathe it up both nostrils.'

'It looks like I have to stay white when I talk with you, doesn't it?'

'You're a good friend, Hack, but you're a straight and your mind is white as Clorox.'

He got to me with that one.

'What should I be?' I said. 'You want me to apologize because I was born me instead of you?'

'No, man. You still don't see. It's mind style, something you grew up with. Your people go through life like they're looking down a long tunnel and they never see anything on the edges. You roar down the highway a hundred miles an hour and never remember anything later except a motel billboard because everything on the other side of the fence is somebody else's scene. It don't belong to you. It's painted by some screw who lost his brushes and forgot what he was doing.'

'I don't like to tell you that you're full of shit.'

'Take the tour, buddy.'

'I've been on the tour. I grew up around it.'

'No point, cousin. You're right in the middle of the pipe.'

'Another gringo, right? One of the oppressors. A dickhead with the liberal tattoo.'

The guard heard me, and he took the cigar out of his mouth between his fingers and leaned forward, with his stomach folding over his gunbelt. The chair legs splayed slightly under his buttocks, and his crossed eyes were fixed in the smooth fat of his face.

'Look, Hack, if I make the street we're going on a sweet drunk together. We'll hit every chicano joint in San Antonio. We won't have to pay for nothing, either. We'll slop down the booze and ball with brown-skin chicks till our eyes fall out. Yokohama on a three-day pass. A real wild one.'

'You're cooking with butane now,' I said.

'I ain't kidding you. I'm going to wash this jailhouse stink off me in the Guadalupe and buy my own beer truck. We'll just tool around the roads drinking and slinging bottles at the highway signs. Then when I get back to Pueblo Verde they're going to learn what real shit smells like.'

'You want to go back for some more?'

'The ballgame's just starting. We're going to hit them with a strike in August. I don't know if we can win, but a lot of cotton is going to burn in the rows if we don't.'

'Our defence will work like piss in a punchbowl if you have a half dozen new charges against you.'

'I can't sweat that.'

'You'd goddamn better, unless you want to end up here again with another five to do.'

'The only thing we got on our side is us. The cops, the legislature, the farm bureau, the whole fucking bunch – we got to bust them the only way we can, and that's to shut down the harvest until they recognize our union and start to negotiate.'

'You can't make a strike work in the fields. There's ten people standing in line for the job you walk off of.'

'They're going to win in California. We'll win here, too, as long as they can't scare us or turn us against each other. You see, man, that's what their real bag is all about. We twist the screws because of the shacks they give us and the seventy-dollar rents, and they throw out twenty or thirty families and tell them they got to do it because the union's forcing standards on them they can't meet. But people ain't buying that shit any more.'

The guard looked at his watch and pointed a fat finger at us, then cleared his mouth of tobacco spittle and spat it into the spittoon.

'I left two cartons of cigarettes for you at the desk,' I said.

'Yeah, thanks, man. Look, you were straight when you said two weeks, weren't you?' His dark eyes were concentrated into mine, and one hand opened and closed on his forearm.

'I can't set it on the day.'

'I know that. I ain't dumb about everything.'

'I'll start on the bond as soon as the appeal goes through.'

'OK,' he said, and smiled for a moment. 'I just don't want to go on the nutmeg and coffee kick and start flogging my rod in the shower like most of the stir freaks in here. Take care, cousin, and look around for that beer truck.'

I walked back outside into the hard light, and I was perspiring before I reached my car. The trusty gardeners were sweeping the cut grass from the footpath, their faces turned downward, and a crew of men from the fields were walking in file along the road, four abreast, their hoes over their shoulders in military fashion, with two mounted guards on each side of them. The sun had moved farther into the west, and the shadows from the cedar trees fell to the edge of the cotton field. The sunburned faces and necks of the men ran with sweat, and the guards had their hats slanted over their eyes against the sun.

I drove back down the dusty road and stopped at the gate while two guards looked through my car and in the boot. As I rumbled over the cattleguard and turned on to the highway I felt a strange release from that confined world behind those high walls. The oaks along the road were greener, the sky a more dazzling blue, the hot wind heavier with the smell of the pine woods, the murderous sun less of an enemy. The billboard signs advertising charcoaled steaks and frosted bottles of beer penetrated the eye with their colour, and even the weathered farmhouses and barns with metal patent-medicine signs nailed on their sides looked like an agrarian romanticist's finest dream. There's a line of separation between the world of free people and the confined which you never realize exists until you discover yourself on the opposite side. Once there, behind the barbed wire or mesh screens or concrete walls, all objects and natural phenomena have a different colour, shape, angle and association from anything you have ever known previously. And no one who hasn't been there can understand the light-headed opulent feeling of walking back into the free world.

Fifty miles up the road I stopped at a tavern and steak house built on stilts above the edge of a green river. The board walls were grey and peeling, and the open windows were covered with screens to keep out of the clouds of mosquitoes in the shadows of the willow trees along the bank. A screened eating porch shaded by a tall cypress tree extended over the water, and I sat at one of the checked-cloth tables and ordered a steak and a pitcher of beer. The bottom of the river was soap rock, a type of smooth grey sandstone that the Indians had used to bathe with, and in the middle, where the current had eroded deeply into the rock over thousands of years, you could see the dark shapes of huge catfish and carp moving in and out of the light and shadow, then the surface would ripple with the wind and they would break apart and dissolve in the sun's refraction. I cut into the steak and soaked up the hot grease with bread, and washed it down with beer. The pitcher and mug were crusted with ice, and the beer was so cold that it made my throat ache. Cowboys and oilfield roughnecks in hardhats were bent over the bar with dozens of empty bottles before them, and the barmaid, in shorts and a sun halter, was opening more bottles as fast as she could pull them from the beer case. Across the river a group of Negroes were cane fishing with worms in the shallows, their black faces shaded with flop straw hats, and the moss in the cypress tree straightened and fell like silk in the wind.

In two more hours I would be back at the ranch, and then Verisa and I would begin to enact our ritual that usually worked itself towards one of three conclusions. The least unpleasant would be a pointless and boring conversation about the office, a new account, a cocktail party at the Junior League, or one of Bailey's trite suggestions for the campaign. Each of us would listen to the other with feigned interest, the head nodding, the eyes flat and withdrawn. Then, after a careful period, I would change clothes and go into the horse lot, or Verisa would remember at that moment that she had planned to invite people to the ranch from Victoria for the weekend.

More unpleasant was the possibility that the control wouldn't be there – the Mexican girl had burned everything on the stove, the gardener had dug out the wrong plants from the flower bed, the odour from the gas wells had made the house smell like a Texas City refinery – and the conversation would quickly deteriorate into a sullen silence and a door slammed sharply in another part of the house.

The last alternative was the worst: nothing would be said when I came into the house until we were forced by geographical necessity to be in the same room together for sixty seconds, and then our exchange would have the significance and intensity of two people talking at a bus stop. I'd spend my time in the library with the door closed, drinking bourbon and playing my guitar, and finally when I was in a drunken fog, my fingers thick on the guitar neck, with the house humming as loud as my own blood and Old Hack's angry ghost walking the front porch, the seams would start to strip and Mr Hyde's bloody eyes would look into mine, and Verisa would have to lock the bedroom door until the next morning.

However, Verisa wasn't always like the person I've described here. When I met her at a country club dance in San Antonio eight years ago she was Verisa Hortense Goodman, the only daughter of a millionaire stock financier, a hard-shell Baptist who never drank or smoked and kept his hard body trim with fifty press-ups a day until he dropped dead from a heart attack. That night on the terrace under the mimosa trees the moon-sheen tangled in her auburn hair and her white skin glowed in the light from the Japanese lanterns. Her face was cool and pale, the small mouth achingly beautiful as she looked up at me. There were always men around her, and when she moved across the terrace, her legs like grace in motion against her tight silver gown, the men would follow her, eager, smiling, their own dowdy women left at the drink table. I took her away from her date that night, and we went on a wild ride with a magnum bottle of champagne through the hill country to an open-air German dance pavilion in San Marcos. I had a Porsche convertible then, and I kept it wide open through the black-green hills, drifting across the turns, while she poured the wine in two crystal glasses for us. Her face was happy with adventure and release, her voice loud above the roar of the engine and the wind, and she told me she was sick of country club men and beaux who hadn't outgrown Kappa Sig, and I knew then that I had her.

The next four months were all green and gold days and turquoise evenings, fried chicken picnics on the Guadalupe River, a burning hour under a willow tree in an afternoon shower, tennis and gin rickeys at the club, horseback riding into the hills and swimming in the black coldness of the Comal under the moon. We spent weekends at the bullfights in Monterey, with breakfasts of eggs fried in hot sauce and chicory coffee and boiled milk, and our mornings were filled with sunshine and mad plans for the rest of the day. We danced in beer gardens, hired a mariachi band at a street party in the San Antonio *barrio*, went to cowboy barbecues, and always kept a bottle of champange in an ice bucket on the back seat of the Porsche. She never tired, and after another furious night of roaring across the countryside from one wonderful place to the next, she would turn her face up to be kissed, her eyes closed and the white edge of her teeth showing beween her lips, and I would feel everything in me drain like water poured out of a cup. I'd leave her at her front door, the mockingbirds singing in the grey stillness of first light, and the road back to the ranch would be as lonely and empty as a stretch of moonscape.

We were married in Mexico City and spent the next three weeks fishing for marlin in the Yucatan. I rented a villa on the beach, and at night the waves crested white in the moonlight and broke against the sand and the Gulf wind blew cool with the smell of salt and seaweed through the open windows in our bedroom. In the mornings we raced horses in the surf, and I taught her how to pick up a handkerchief from the sand at a full gallop. Her skin darkened with tan, and in bed I could feel the heat in her body go into mine. While we ate lobsters in a pavilion on the beach after the afternoon's fishing, her eyes would become merry, flashing at me privately, and I would already see her undressing before our closet mirror.

But later, as the months went by at the ranch, I began to see other things in Verisa that I had overlooked previously. She was conscious of class, and underneath her rebellion towards country club romance and the pale men with family credentials who had courted her, she was attached to her father and the strict standard he had followed and expected in other men. He was the son of a small grocery-store owner, and after he became wealthy he learned, with some pain, the importance of having family lineage as well as money, and he never failed to remind Verisa that she belonged to a very special class of people who did not associate with those beneath their station. She had learned the lesson well, although she was probably never aware of it. She simply didn't recognize the world of ordinary people, those who lived on salaries, rode Greyhound buses, or carried drinks from behind a bar; they were there, but they moved about in another dimension, one that existed in the centre of hot cities, drab neighbourhoods and loud, working men's taverns.

Also, she didn't like drunkenness. Although she considered herself an agnostic, a good deal of her father's devotion to the Baptist church had been left in her (he attributed his financial success to his early redemption at a Dallas revival and the fact that he practised the teaching of Christ in his business; once he stared me straight in the face and told me that the Jews in the stock market were afraid to deal with a truly Christian man; he also believed that FDR was a Jew). I never liked her father, and I always made a point of serving highballs, filling the room with cigar smoke, and drinking too much when he was at the house. He was glad to have Verisa married into the Holland family, and privately he asked her to name a child after him; so he was always restrained when I poured double shots of whiskey or asked him if he knew a Baptist minister in Dallas who was a grand dragon in the Ku Klux Klan. At first Verisa was indulgent towards my performances with her father, and occasionally, after he had left the house with his face disjointed in concern, she would say something mild, a quiet reproof, in hopes that I would be tolerant of him.

But I couldn't stand his bigotry, his illiterate confidence in the reasons for his success, and his simplistic and sometimes brutal solutions for the world's problems. Also, I resented the influence he'd had on Verisa's mind, that early period when he had infected her with the stupidity of his class. As she grew older I knew she would become more like him, much more sophisticated and intelligent, but nevertheless marked with the rigid social attitudes of the new rich. Worse, as my dislike for him became more open and his weekly visits turned into embarrassing periods of silence in the living room and then finally stopped altogether, I pushed her closer to him and she began to make comparisons between her father and other men who had been *given* everything. Sometime later, after I had come in drunk from a duck-hunting trip, she commented that heavy drinking was a symptom of the weak who couldn't stand up under competition.

I paid my bill at the steak house and took two cans of Jax with me for the drive home. Evidently, I was confused about Verisa's schedule for the week, because one of her afternoon lawn parties was underway when I arrived. The Negro bartender was shaving ice for mint juleps on the screened porch, and blue-haired ladies in sundresses sat around tables on the lawn under the oak trees. *Goddamn, here we go*, I thought. Two men from the state Democratic committee were there, neither of whom I wanted to see, and somebody had ridden Sailor Boy and had left him thirsty in the lot with the saddle still on. I went around the far side of the house and entered the library through the side door, but an insurance executive from Victoria and his wife were there, staring at my gun case with drinks in their hands. They turned their flushed faces at me, smiling. 'Hello. Good to see you,' I said, and went straight through and into the kitchen. Cappie, an old Negro who lived on the back of my property and sometimes barbecued for us, was chopping green onions and peppers with a cleaver on the draining board. His grey hair was curled in the thick furrows on the back of his neck.

'Cap, get that goddamn saddle off of Sailor Boy and turn him out.'

'There some young ladies been riding him, Mr Holland.'

'Yeah, I know. Nobody thinks he drinks water, either.'

'Yes, sir.'

I started up the staircase to the bedroom, and then one of the Democratic committee men called from behind me and I was caught in the centre of it. I drank mint juleps under the oaks with the blue-haired ladies, listened with interest to their compliments about my wife and ranch, explained politely to a mindless co-ed that Sailor Boy was a show horse and shouldn't be ridden into barbed-wire fences, and laughed good-naturedly with the two committee men at their Kiwanian jokes. People came and left, the sun started to set beyond the line of trees on the horizon, and the bartender moved among the groups with a tray of cool drinks, and at dusk Cappie served plates of barbecued links and chicken and potato salad. My head was drumming with the heat, the whiskey and the endless conversation. Verisa stood next to me with her hand on my arm, accepting invitations to homes that I would not enter unless I was drugged and chained. Finally, at nine o'clock, when the party moved inside out of sheer exhaustion, I took a bottle of bourbon from the bar and drove down the back road to one of the ponds that I'd had stocked with bass. One of Cappie's cane poles was leaned against a willow tree, and I dug some worms out of the wet dirt by the bank and drank whiskey and bottom-fished in the dark until I saw the last headlights wind down my front lane to the blacktop.

During the next ten days I spoke at a free Democratic barbecue in Austin (it was crowded with university students and working people, most of whom stayed at the beer kegs and didn't know or care who was giving the barbecue), addressed two businessmen's luncheons in San Antonio (the American and Texas flags on each side of me, the plastic plants forever green on the linen-covered tables, the rows of intent faces like expressions caught in a waxworks), talked informally at a private club in Houston ('Well, Mr Holland, regardless of the mistake we made in Viet Nam, don't you think we have an obligation to support the fighting men?' 'Granted that coloured people have a grievance, do you believe that the answer lies in destruction of property?' 'Frankly, what *is* your position on the oil-depletion allowance?'), and spent one roaring drunk afternoon in a tavern with two dozen oilfield roughnecks and pipeliners who all promised to vote for me, although almost none of them came from the district.

The appeal came through at the close of the second week since I had seen Art. The judge who had reviewed the trial record, a hard old man with forty years on the bench, wrote in his decision that 'the conduct of the local court was repugnant, a throwback to frontier barbarism,' and he ordered Art's release from the state penitentiary on appeals bond pending a new trial. I set down the telephone, took a bottle of Jack Daniel's and a glass from my desk drawer, and poured a large drink. On my second swallow, with a fresh cigar in my mouth, Bailey walked through the door and hit the broken air conditioner with his fist.

'Why don't you turn the goddamn thing off so the building can stop vibrating a few minutes?' he said. It had been a bad two weeks for Bailey. The heat bothered him much worse than it did me, and we had lost one of our big accounts, which he blamed on me. He believed that he was developing an ulcer, and each morning he drank a half bottle of some chalky white medicine that left him nauseated for two hours.

'Just turn the knob, Bailey, or you can hit it some more.'

'I see you're getting launched early this afternoon.'

'No, only one drink. Do you know where I can buy a beer truck?'

'What?' A drop of perspiration rolled down from his hair line like a thick, clear vein.

'I tell you what, buddy. Let's lock up the office in about an hour, and I'll take you on a three-day visit to all the Mexican beer joints in San Antonio.'

'Put up the whiskey.'

'Come on. For one time in forty years of Baptist living, close the office early and tie on a real happy one.'

'Did you look at our calendar for this afternoon between drinks?'

'Yeah, R. C. Richardson is about to get burned again, and he needs us to clean up his shit.'

'You accepted him as a client. I don't like the sonofabitch in the office.'

'You don't understand that old country boy, Bailey. He's not a bad guy, as far as sons of bitches go. Anyway, his ass can burn until Monday. Get a glass and sit down. The only ulcer you have is in the head, and you're going to have a few dozen more there unless you let some cool air into that squeezed mind of yours.'

'If you want to get into the bottle and blow half our practice, do it, but shut off that patronizing crap. I've pretty well reached my level of tolerance in the last two weeks.'

'Look, I won appeal today on Art Gomez and the judge has set bond, and you have to admit that we haven't sprung many of our clients from the state pen. So take a drink and lower your blood rate, and I'll pick up Richardson's case early Monday morning.'

'I can't get it through to you, Hack. You've got cement around your head. The office isn't a tennis club where you play between drinks.'

'All right, goddamn, forget it,' I said, and picked up the telephone and dialled the number of a bondsman we dealt with. I turned my eyes away from Bailey's vexed face and waited in the hot stillness for him to leave the room.

The bondsman was named Bobo Dietz. He was a dark, fat man, who always wore purple shirts and patent-leather shoes and a gold ring on his little finger. He had moved to Austin from New Jersey ten years ago, set up a shabby office next to the county jail, and in the time since then he had bought two pawnshops and three grocery stores in the Negro slum. He considered avarice a natural part of man's chemistry, and you were a sucker if you believed otherwise; but he was always efficient and you could count on him to have bail posted and the client on the street a half hour after you set him in motion.

He assured me over the phone, in his hard Camden accent and bad grammar, that the ten-thousand-dollar bond would be made before five o'clock and Art would be released by tomorrow morning. For some reason Bobo liked me, and as always, when I went bail for a client on my own, he wouldn't charge me for anything except expenses. Many times I wondered if there was some strange scar in my personality that attracted to me people like Bobo Dietz and R. C. Richardson.

I turned off the air conditioner and opened all the office

windows. The stale afternoon heat and noise from the street rose off the yellow awnings below me. My shirt stuck to my skin, and the odour of petrol exhaust and hot tar made my eyes water. In the middle of the intersection a big Negro in an undershirt was driving an air-hammer into the concrete. The broken street surfacing shaled back from the bit, and the compressor pumped like a throbbing headache. I sipped another straight drink in the windowsill, sweating in the humidity and the heat of the whiskey, then I decided to give Bailey and his Baptist mentality another try. I took a second glass from the drawer, poured a small shot in the bottom, and walked into his office.

He was dictating to our secretary, his eyes focused into the wall, and I could see in the nervous flick of his fingers on his knee that he expected an angry exchange, profanity (which he hated in front of women), or a quick thrust into one of his sensitive areas (such as his impoverished bachelorhood, the empty weekends in his four-hundred-dollar-a-month apartment). I leaned against the doorjamb, smoking a cigar, with a glass in each hand. He faltered in his dictation, and his eyes moved erratically over the wall.

'Hack, I'll talk to you later.'

'No, we have to shut it down today. It's Friday afternoon and R. C. Richardson will appreciate us a lot more Monday morning. Mrs McFarland, my brother needs to direct me into the cocktail hour today, so you can leave early if you like.'

The secretary rested her pencil on her pad, her eyes smiling. Her hair was grey, streaked with iron, and her face was cheerful and bright as she waited for the proper moment either to stop work or resume the dictation.

I set Bailey's drink down before him.

'I'd like to finish if—'

'Sorry, you're unplugged for the day, brother.' I said. 'Go ahead, Mrs McFarland. There's a slop chute down the road where I need a warden.'

Bailey saw that I had the first edge of a high on, and he let the secretary go with an apology. (He was the only Southerner I ever knew who could have been a character in a Margaret Mitchell novel.)

'That's too goddamn much,' he said. 'I've had it with this type of irresponsible college-boy shit around the office. When you're not loaded you're coming off a drunk, or you're spending your time on a union agitator's appeal while our biggest account gets picked up by a couple of New York Jews. You've insulted everybody who's tried to help you in the election, you got yourself put in jail because you were too goddamn drunk to know what universe you were in, and you had the balls to file a civil rights complaint against the man who arrested you.'

'Bailey—'

'Just shut up a minute. Senator Dowling kept that story off the wire services, but since you felt so outraged that you had to file a complaint with the FBI we should have some real fine stuff in the newspapers before November. In the meantime you haven't been in a courtroom in three months, and I'm goddamned tired of carrying your load. If you want out of the partnership, I'll sign my name to a cheque and you can fill in the amount.'

'I started off to have a drink with you, brother, but since you've brought the conversation down to the blood-letting stage, let's look at a couple of things closely. Number one, the criminal cases we've won in court have been handled by me, and our largest paying accounts, keeping Richardson and his kind out of the pen for stealing millions from the state, have been successful because I know how to bend oil regulation laws around a telephone pole. Number two, you haven't been pumping my candidacy for Congress just because you want to see your brother's sweet ass winking at you from Washington, DC. I don't like to put it rough to you like that, Bailey, but you don't understand anything unless it comes at you like a freight train between the eyes. You have all these fucking respectable attitudes and you heap them out on everybody else's head and ask them to like you for it. You better learn that you have a real load of shit in that wheelbarrow.'

On that note of vicious rapport I received the call from Bobo Dietz. Bailey's face was white, the veins swollen in his neck, his eyes hot as he raised the whiskey to his mouth and I picked up the receiver.

'I don't know what kind of deal this is, Mr Holland,' Dietz said.

'What are you talking about?'

'That man's dead.'

'Look, Dietz—'

'I called the warden. He said a couple of boons chopped him up with bush axes yesterday afternoon.'

SEVEN

It took me a half hour to get the warden on the phone. He didn't want to talk with me, but after I threatened to see him in his home that night he read me the guard's report about Art's death and added his own explanations about the unavoidable violence between the Negro and Mexican inmates.

Two Negroes had hidden a paper bag full of Benzedrex inhalers in the tractor shed, and they had been drinking bottles of codeine stolen from the pharmacy and chewing the cotton Benzedrine rings from at least two dozen inhalers when Art went inside the shed to get a lug wrench. A few minutes passed; a mounted guard working a gang in the cotton field heard a single cry, and by the time he rode to the shed and threw open the door the Negroes had disembowelled Art, torn the flesh from his back like whale meat, and severed one arm from his body.

There wasn't much more to the report. Art had probably been killed with the second or third blow. The Negroes were so incoherent they couldn't talk, and the guard had no idea why they had attacked Art instead of a half dozen other men who had been in and out of the shed earlier, although the warden added that 'a doped-up nigger isn't a human being no longer.' The Negroes had been put in solitary confinement and refused to talk about killing Art, if they even remembered doing it, and Art's body was to be buried in the prison cemetery unless his family was willing to pay for shipment back to Rio Grande City.

I hung up the receiver and sat numbly in the chair with my eyes closed and my fingers trembling on my forehead. So that was it. Just like that. Two crazed men single out another man, for no reason other than the fact that he walked into their bent, angry minds at the wrong time, and then they tear all the thirty-six years of life and soul from his body in seconds. My right hand was still sweating from the heat of the phone receiver and my ears burned with the casual language of the guard's report and the warden's footnotes. I couldn't shut out the vision of the two Negroes dismembering a man who had nothing to do with their lives, their brains boiling in a furnace of satisfaction, just as sometime in the future several other madmen would seat them in a wooden chair fitted with leather straps and buckles and metal hood and place a cotton gag in their mouths and burst every cell in their bodies with thousands of volts of electricity. Bailey poured a drink in a glass and placed it in my hand. I watched the brown light shimmering in the whiskey. My arm felt too weak and lifeless to raise the glass to my mouth.

'I'm sorry, Hack,' Bailey said.

I stood up and set the glass on the desk. My movements seemed wooden, disconnected from one another, as though I had just awoke in the centre of a vacuum. I could feel the beat of my pulse swelling into my eardrums. For just a moment the room looked unfamiliar, the ordered arrangement of chairs and desk and file cabinets foreign to anything that was me. I began putting on my coat.

'Where are you going?' Bailey said.

'I'm going to try to explain how a—'

'Sit down a minute and finish your drink.'

'I said I'm going down to the valley and try to explain how a good man was murdered in a prison where he shouldn't have been in the first place. And then I'll explain how I won appeal on a man twenty-four hours after he was dead.'

'Don't let it take you like this, Hack.'

'How should we take it, Bailey? Maybe if I go to work fast I can arrange to have his body shipped home before he's buried in a prison cemetery with a wood marker. And if I'm too late to prevent that, I can always work on a court order to have the body exhumed. And while we're doing all that, we can consider that a lynch court had this in mind for him when he was first charged.'

'Here, drink it, and I'll go with you.'

'You wouldn't like it.'

'I'll rent a plane and we'll fly down tonight.'

I drank from the glass, but the whiskey had no taste. I had started to perspire under my coat, and the shapes and late afternoon shadows in the room were as strange as the distorted lines in a dream. Outside, the air-hammer thudded into the asphalt. I felt the sweat dripping off my hair down the back of my neck. The glass was empty in my hand.

'They wouldn't like you, either,' I said.

'Goddamn it, Hack, you can't drive like this.'

'They don't buy that work-with-the-system shit. And I don't feel like telling them the system is all right, except for those twenty-four-hour differences that you have to take into allowance. And I don't like to tell them that I was having drinks with the DAR ladies and shaking hands with the paraplegics while Art's clock was one day behind the court's. Give me another one.'

He put his arm on my elbow and tried to turn me towards the chair.

'Just get the goddamn bottle, Bailey. Pour youself a super one while you're at it.'

He went to the desk and came back with the bottle of Jack Daniels. He held the stopper in one hand.

'All right, sit down, and I'll call the airport.'

'Would you listen to me just for one goddamn time?' I said. 'I'm not going down to meet with a Rotarian luncheon, and number two I'm not a fucking lunatic who needs his older brother to strap a control harness on his back.'

I took the bottle out of his hand and drank from the neck. I swallowed until the muscles in my throat closed and the whiskey backed up in my mouth.

'There, goddamn. That glues everything a little tighter,' I said.

'Hack.'

I left him standing in the open door with the bottle in his hand, his lined face covered with pinpoints of moisture.

*

On the four-lane highway west of town I opened up the Cadillac, lowered the windows, and passed long strings of late afternoon traffic, hitting the shoulders and showering gravel over the asphalt. The red sun burned across the tops of the hills and lighted the dark edges of the post oaks and blackjack, and the shadows of the cedar-post fences along the road broke silently against my bumpers like a blinking eye. Although I had driven that same highway hundreds of times, the sunset gave a different cast and colour to the land than anything I had seen there before. The windmills were motionless in the static air; the cattle in the fields were covered with scarlet, their heads stationary in the short grass, and the neat white ranch houses seemed as devoid of life and movement as an abandoned film set; the irrigation ditches were dry and cracked with drought, the thickets of mesquite like burned scratches against the hillsides, and the few horses in the pastures looked as though they had been misplaced.

The shadows deepened over the hills, the traffic thinned, and I kept the accelerator to the floor for the next fifty miles. The sign boards, the oil rigs and the three-dollar Okie motels sped past me in the twilight, but none of it would click together as a stable piece of geography that I had lived around all my life. It was removed, unconnected, and the whiskey from my flask made it even emptier and more disjointed. As a Southerner I had been brought up to believe that through conditioning and experience you could accept with some measure of tranquillity any of the flaws in the human situation. But death is one flaw that always lands like a fist in the centre of the forehead. No matter how many times you see it, or smell its grey rotting odour, or come close to buying it yourself, each time is always like the first. No amount of earlier experience prepares you for it, and after it happens the world is somehow unfairly diminished and bent out of shape.

It was night and just the horn of the moon shone above the hills when I reached Pueblo Verde. Lights glowed inside farm-houses beyond the dark fields and orchards of citrus trees, and the river was as black as gun metal under the starless sky. Everything was closed on the main street except the hotel and beer tavern, and I turned down the rutted road into the Mexican district, wondering what type of inadequate words I would choose to tell Rie and her friends that Art's death had come about in the same way that a stupid fool steps on your foot aboard a crowded bus. I understood why Western Union offices always kept a pamphlet of prepared condolences on their counters. Death is the one occasion when words have as much relevance as a housewife talking across her back fence about a broken washing machine.

My flask was empty. I stopped in the Mexican tavern for a fifth of Jack Daniel's and had two drinks from the bottle in the car before I pulled up in front of the union headquarters. Bugs flicked against the screen door and turned in the yellow square of light on the porch. One of the windows had a large, spider-webbed hole in the centre, and someone had taped a piece of cardboard over it from the inside. *Okay, doc, let's go*, I thought.

I walked up the dirt path and knocked on the door. The Negro and two Mexicans in cowboy shirts and blue jeans were talking at a table piled with cardboard picket signs and bumper stickers. Only the Negro turned his head towards the door when I knocked; the other two kept talking, their faces calmly intense with whatever they were saying, their hands and fingers gesturing in the air with each sentence.

'Say, hello,' I said.

The Negro looked back at the door again, then pushed back his chair and walked towards me with a beer in his hand, his cannonball head shining in the light. He squinted at the screen with his red-rimmed eyes.

'That's my whiskey brother out there, ain't it?' he said. 'Come on in, home. You ain't got to knock around here.'

He pushed open the door for me and put out his large, calloused block of a hand.

'Is Rie here?'

'She's laying down. I'll get her.'

'Maybe I should come back tomorrow.'

'No, she'll want to see you. Get yourself a beer off the counter.'

'Look—'

'No, man. It's all right.'

He went into the back of the building, and a few minutes later Rie walked out of the hall into the light. She was barefoot and wearing blue jeans and a flowered shirt, and her curly, sunburned hair was uncombed. I looked once at her face and realized that she already knew about Art's death.

'How you doing, babe?'

'Hello, Hack.'

'I started to call first.'

The skin around her eyes was pale and there was no colour in her mouth. I felt empty standing in front of her.

'Do you want to go for a drive?' I said.

Her eyes blinked a moment without really seeing any of us.

'There's a meeting tonight,' she said.

'That's them church people coming tonight,' the Negro said. 'They don't offer us nothing but prayers. You all go on.'

'I know a place to eat across the river,' I said. 'Come on. I might run into a Carta Blanca sign by myself.'

I had peeled off the cellophane wrapper from a cigar and I couldn't find an ashtray to put it in. It seemed that every word I spoke and every movement I made was somehow inappropriate.

'That's right. Go on out of here,' the Negro said. 'I'm going to run them church people off, anyway. Every time they come here they start sniffing at my wine breath.'

She pushed her hair back with her fingers and slipped on a pair of leather moccasins. She was too strong a girl to have cried much, but her face was wan and drawn and the suntan on it looked as though it didn't belong there.

We walked out into the dark, down the path, and I put my arm around her shoulders. When I touched her and felt the trembling in her back I wanted to pull her into me and press her head against my chest.

'I spent three hours thinking of the wrong words to say,' I said.

'You don't need to, Hack.'

'Yes, I do. A man's death deserves an explanation, but I don't have it. Every time I saw a guy buy it in Korea I tried to see some rational equation in death, but it had no more reason or meaning than those faded billboard signs out on the highway.'

323

'Art's brother phoned this afternoon and told me how he died. It didn't have anything to do with anybody. There's nothing to say about it.'

So I didn't try to say anything else. I turned the Cadillac around in the dust, and we drove back down the corrugated road between the rows of clapboard shacks and dirt yards to the main street. The slip of moon had turned yellow and risen above the hills in the dark sky. The air was hot, motionless, and the oak trees on the square looked as though they had been etched in metal. The deputy who had given me the road map out of town stood under the neon sign in front of the beer tavern, talking with two men in overalls. His khaki shirt was dark around the neck and armpits with perspiration. He took the toothpick out of his mouth and stared hard as the car passed.

'Have they been bothering you?' I said.

'We had three arrests on the picket last week, and two nights ago somebody burned a cross in the front yard. It's strange to walk out on the porch and see something that ugly in the morning light. They'd nailed strips of tyres to the wood, and I could still smell the melted rubber.'

'Well, by God, we can do something about the Klan. The FBI wants to nail them any way they can.'

'The local fed thinks it was high school kids, even though some chicanos in the tavern saw half a dozen men in the back of a pickup with the cross propped against the cab.'

'Rie, we have civil rights statutes that can get those men one to ten in Huntsville.'

'We don't care about them.'

'Listen, those men are dangerous and violent people, and they should be in the penitentiary.'

'We've given the farm companies until Monday to sign, and then we shut it down. We have enough people organized now to do it, too.'

'Do you know what's it going to be like when the cotton starts burning in the rows and the citrus goes soft because it wasn't picked in the first week? Those farmers are going to lose their ass, and those KKK bastards will have chains and baseball bats next time.'

'They won't stop the strike.'

'Goddamn, I don't want to see them pouring kerosene on your house, either.'

'Let's don't talk about it any more, Hack. I'm really tired.'

And then I felt that I had selected almost every bad sentence possible in the three hours of driving from Austin to the Valley. I followed the blacktop south of town and crossed the concrete bridge over the Rio Grande. The low, black water rippled through the trash caught in the pilings, willow trees and scrub brush grew along the sandy banks, and the windows of the adobe huts on the Mexican side glowed with candle light and oil lamps. I stopped at the port of entry, and a tired Mexican immigration official in a rumpled khaki uniform and plastic-brim hat told me not to go farther than fifteen miles into the interior without a tourist's permit. Rie's face had the shine of ivory in the light from the official's small office. If I touched my fingers to her cheek I knew the skin would be as cool and dry as stone. All the pain was way down inside her, and it would stay there without ever burning through her composure. Somewhere she had learned how to be a real soldier, I thought. Either in those insane billy-swinging, head-busting campus riots, or maybe in a Mississippi jail where they put cattle prods to civil rights workers, but somewhere she had earned her membership in a private club.

I drove down the bad tar-surfaced highway between tall rows of cedar and poplar trees. The evening star flickered dimly above the bare hills in the west, and a hot breeze had started to blow across the flatland from the Gulf. Most of the adobe houses by the roadside were in ruins, the mudbricks exposed and crumbling, the roofing timbers hanging inside the doorways like long teeth. I could never drive into old Mexico at night without feeling the presence of Villa and Zapata in those dark hills, or the ghosts of Hood's Texas cavalry who chose exile in a foreign country rather than surrender when the Confederacy fell. Even on my drunken excursions to meet three-dollar Mexican whores, the wild smell of the land and the long stretch of burned hills and all the mystery in them cut through my sexual fantasies. Even now, with Rie beside me, her drawn face painfully beautiful as she held a match unevenly to her cigarette, I still heard the jingle of sabres and the cock of rifles, pointed by the thousands down a hill at some forgotten army.

Ten miles from the port of entry there was a small town of flat, adobe buildings, cobbled streets caked with horse manure, whorehouses, two or three dangerous bars, a rural police station, and a cemetery against the hillside with a stucco wall around it. High up on the hill and formed with whitewashed fieldstones were the words PEPSI-COLA. The adobe houses were as brown as the land, but the doors were painted blue, fingernail-polish red and turquoise to prevent spirits from crossing the threshold. Most of the people in the town were poor Indians, but the whorehouses and the bars were run by either the police or marginal gangsters from Monterey. Oilfield workers sat in the open-front cantinas with fifteen-year-old girls, the jukeboxes blaring with mariachi horns, and farther up the narrow main street two policemen in dirty uniforms stood in the lighted doorway of the town's largest whorehouse. One of them beckoned to me as I passed, then he saw Rie and turned his attention to the car behind me.

The *cervezería* and café was across the small square from the church. The owner had hung lights in the mimosa trees over the outdoor tables, and the shadows flickered in webbed patterns on the flagstones and the white oilcloth table covers. In the middle of the square was a weathered bandbox, with a round, peaked roof, and I could see the altar candles burning in the darkness beyond the open door of the church. We sat under the trees, with the dappled shadows breaking across us, and I ordered dinner and two bottles of Carta Blanca.

'Could I have a tequila?' Rie said.

'The stuff they sell here is like pulque. It's a yellow and you can see the threadworms swimming in it.'

'I'd like one just the same.'

The waiter brought us a quart bottle with a cork in it, two slender shot glasses, and a plate of sliced limes and a salt shaker. I poured into our glasses, and she drank it neat, without touching the limes or the water chaser, her eyes fixed on the darkened square. She winced a little with the bitter taste, and for just a moment there was a flush of colour in her cheeks.

'That's not the way to do it,' I said.

'Let me have another one.'

'You can burn holes the size of a dime in your stomach with that stuff.'

'I would like for you to pour me another one.'

'All right. Hold the lime in your left hand and put some salt between your thumb and forefinger, then sip it.'

I watched her tilt the glass to her lips and drink it down in two swallows. She choked slightly in the back of her throat and sucked on the lime.

'It's better the second time,' she said. Her eyes had already gone flat.

'If you like I'll pour some in the ashtray and touch a match to it, and you'll get some idea of the raw alcohol content.'

'I don't think it's as bad as you say.' She drank out of the Carta Blanca bottle and looked past me into the square.

'I've invested a good deal of time in it,' I said.

'It makes you feel quiet inside, doesn't it?'

'Then it pulls open all kinds of doors you usually keep shut.'

'Why don't you teach me how to drink it, then?'

I gave the waiter my best American tourist look of irritated impatience, and he nodded in return and went to the kitchen window to hurry the cook.

'Give me another one,' she said.

'You're not a drinker, Rie. Don't try to compete with the professionals.'

'Here, I've finished the beer and I don't like it. I want you to show me how to drink tequila.'

'The best way is to fill your glass and pour it in your petrol tank.'

'Hack.'

'No, goddamn it.'

'Maybe we should go. It's hot, anyway, isn't it?'

'I don't like to go out on abortive missions.'

'Yes, you do, even to make one point about your knowledge of drinking.'

'OK, Rie. You nailed me to the wall with that one.' I filled her shot glass and lit a cigar.

'Do you enjoy being angry?'

'No, but I'll be goddamned if I'll take on my idiot brother's role with somebody else.'

'I believe you enjoy it when the blood starts beating in your head.'

'I'm all out of fire tonight, babe. My white flag is tacked to the masthead.'

She sipped out of her glass and fixed her flat eyes on my face. I drew in on the cigar and waited for it.

'Was there anything we could have done?'

'No.'

'Anything at all so he wouldn't have been in that tool shed?'

'It was all done.'

'I visited him the day he was transferred to prison. I watched them take him down the courthouse path in handcuffs, then I went back on the picket the same afternoon, just like nothing had changed.'

'I turned every lock I could. We were almost home free. It was one of those dumb things that nobody can do anything about.'

She raised the glass again, and her almond eyes looked electric in the light from the trees.

'But it had to be black men who killed him. Not a sadist or a racist guard. Two spades who probably lived everything he did.'

The waiter placed our dinner before us, holding the plates by the bottom with a folded napkin, and looked quickly at Rie, then at me.

'*Dos mas Carta Blanca*,' I said.

'*Si, señor*,' he said, and drew his curiosity back inside himself.

'I don't think I'm hungry now,' she said.

'Eat a little bit.'

'I don't want it. I'm sorry.'

'Be a doll.'

'Let's go, Hack.'

'I'll have the waiter wrap it in waxpaper.'

'Please, let's just go.'

I paid the bill inside, and the waiter looked offended because we hadn't eaten, until I explained that my wife was ill and told him to keep the rest of the tequila for himself. We drove back down the cobbled street past the loud bars, and a barefoot Indian child in ragged clothes ran along beside my window with his hand outstretched. The two policemen in front of the whorehouse were helping a drunk American in a business suit from his car. He leaned against a stone pillar, his face bloated and white with alcohol under the Carta Blanca sign, and gave each of them a note from his wallet. I shuddered with the recollection of stepping unsteadily out of taxicabs on similar streets and walking through other garish doorways under the slick eyes of uniformed pimps, and I wondered if my face had looked as terrible as the man's under the neon sign. I accelerated the Cadillac past the last cantinas and turned back on to the dark highway. The moon broke apart in the branches of the tall cedar trees sweeping by me.

'Why did you say we were almost home free?' she said.

Goddamn you, Hack.

'I thought I could have him out with some more time.' I kept my eyes on the highway and didn't look at her when I spoke. 'It's one of those things you can't tell about. You do everything you can and wait for the court to act.'

I could hear her breathing in the dark.

'It could have gone in the other direction,' I said.

'Oh goddamn, Hack,' she said, and put her face against my chest with her hands clenched around my arm. Her tears wet the front of my shirt, and she held on to me tighter each time she tried to stop crying. I pulled her close into me and rubbed the back of her neck and her curly hair; her forehead felt feverish against my cheek and she trembled inside my arm like a frightened girl. I could smell the sun in her hair and the raw tequila on her breath, and I wanted to pull on to the side of the road and press her inside me.

Her face was as white and smooth as alabaster in the light from the dashboard, and when she had stopped crying and tried to sit up straight I held her close against me and pushed my fingers up through her hair. Her eyes were closed, her breasts stopped rising, and I felt the muscles in her back tense once more and then go loose under my palm. She breathed slowly into my neck, and by the time we reached the border she was asleep.

I rolled across the bridge over the Rio Grande, and an

immigration official in a Stetson hat looked once at my Texas Bar Association card and waved me through. The hot night air was sweet with the ripe citrus and water melon, and there was just a taste of salt in the wind from the Gulf. The moon had risen high above the hills now, and a strip of black storm cloud hung off of one yellow horn. I drove slowly over the ruts and chuckholes through the Mexican and Negro district and parked along the broken fence in front of the union headquarters. The light was still on in the front room, and a man was silhouetted behind the screen door with a bottle in his hand. I eased my arm from behind Rie's neck and rested her head against the seat. Her eyelashes were still damp, her cool face caught the softness of the moon, and when she parted her lips slightly in her sleep I felt the blood sink in my heart. I leaned over and kissed her lightly on the mouth. The screen door slammed, and the Negro walked out on the porch. I went around to the other side of the car and picked Rie up carefully in my arms and carried her up the front path. Her eyes opened momentarily, then shut again, and she turned her face into my neck. The Negro held the door back for me, and I laid her down on the bed in the back room and switched on the electric fan. Her hair moved on the pillow in the breeze, and the alabaster colour of her face was even more pale and cold in the half light. I heard the Negro opening two bottles of beer in the front room, and I closed the door behind me and went back through the hallway.

'Sometimes people got to get high and boil it out,' the Negro said. He put a bottle of Jax in my hand.

'I'll get some vitamin B and aspirin out of my car. Give it to her if she wakes up before you go to bed.'

'I been on that spodiodi route a long time, man. You ain't got to tell me how to fight it.'

'I guess we went to the same school.'

'There you go,' he said. 'Look, I'm glad you taken her out tonight. Some dudes come by and wanted to give us some shit. For a minute I thought they was really going to get it on.'

'What happened?'

'A couple of carloads of young studs come down the street throwing firecrackers at the houses. Then they parked out front, drinking wine and rolling them cherry bombs up on the porch. I figured they'd get tired of it after a while, but three of them come up to the door and said they wanted to skin out a nigger. Yeah, they said they ain't hung a nigger up on a skinning hook in a long time. They was blowing wine in my face, and I could smell lynch all over them, just like piss on fire. One of them started to pull open the door, and then a dude in the car blew the horn and hollered out, 'Don't waste it on a jig. Let's find them hippie freaks.' Two of them cut, but this stud with the door in his hand wanted a pair of black balls. If the chicanos hadn't started coming out of their houses, the shit would have gone right through the fan, and I'd be up for icing a white kid. Because I tell you, whiskey brother, I give up on the days of letting white people shove a two-by-four up my ass until the splinters are coming out of my mouth.'

I drank from the beer and looked at the Negro's face. For the first time since I had met him I saw the hard glass quality in his eyes, the flicker of humiliation in them, the thin raised scar, now as colourless as plastic, on his lower lip. His gleaming head was covered with drops of perspiration, and the lumps of cartilage behind his ears pulsed as though he were chewing angrily on something down inside himself.

'What the hell are you doing here, anyway?' I said.

'I got a bad habit, man. I picked it up in the army digging latrines all over Europe for sweet pink assholes. I figure a yard of white shit went into the ground for every shovelful of dirt I turned. When I got out I decided I paid my dues to Mr Charlie's bathroom and I ain't applying at the back door no more for my mop and pail. You know what I mean, man?'

He licked his tongue over his bottom lip, and the scar glistened like a piece of glass. For the second time that day I felt I had nothing to say. Outside, the cicadas were singing in the stillness. I finished my beer and left him at the table, lighting one of my cigars.

I didn't believe that I would be welcome again at the rooming house, so I drove thirty miles to the next town on the river and checked into a motel. I lay on the bed in the air-conditioned darkness with my arm over my eyes, and each time that I almost made it into sleep, broken images and voices would click together in my mind like the edges of a splintered windowpane, and I would be awake again with the veins drawing tight against my scalp. The highway rolled towards me out of the twilight, then the bush axes were raised high in the air once more, glinting redly in the gloom of the toolhouse, and a Chinese private leaned his face down to the sewer grate and spat a long stream of yellow saliva on my head. I sat on the edge of the bed in my underwear and drank half the bottle of Jack Daniels before I fell asleep in the deep whiskey quiet of my own breathing.

The next morning I dressed in a pair of khakis, my old cowboy boots, and a denim shirt (all of which I carried in a suitcase that always stayed in the boot of the Cadillac), had my hangover breakfast of a steak with a fried egg on top and a slow cup of coffee and a cigar, then started down the road for Pueblo Verde. The sun was white on the horizon, and the washed-out blue sky hurt your eyes to look at it. The green of the citrus orchards, the fields of corn and cotton, and the sear hilltops floated in the humidity and heat. Water melons lay fat in the rows, shimmering with light, and the cucumber vines were heavy with their own weight. Even with sunglasses on I had to squint against the glare. Hawks circled over the fields, and on some of the cedar fence posts farmers had nailed dead crows, salted and withered in the sun, to keep the live ones out of the corn. In the middle of an empty pasture, far from the roadside, a sun-faded billboard warned that THE COMING IS SOON, LISTEN TO BROTHER HAROLD'S NEW FAITH REVIVAL ON STATION XERF.

Outside Pueblo Verde I pulled into a clapboard country store shaded by a huge live oak. There was an old metal patent-medicine sign nailed to one wall, three pickup trucks parked on the gravel in front, and on the wood porch was a rusted Coca-Cola cooler with bottle caps spilling out of the opener box. The inside of the store was dark and cool and smelled of cheese and summer sausage and cracklings in quart jars. I bought a wicker picnic basket, a tablecloth, two bottles of California burgundy, some peppered German sausage, white cheese, a loaf of French bread, and six bottles of Jax pushed down in a bag of crushed ice. A small barefoot Negro boy, with blue jeans torn at the knees, helped me carry the sacks to the car. Then I turned back on to the highway into the white brilliance of the sun above the Rio Grande.

The high pavements in town were crowded with people, and the beer taverns and pool halls were filled with cowboys and cedar-cutters who had come into town to drink every piece of change in their blue jeans. I was always struck by the way that all small Texas towns looked alike on Saturday morning, whether you were in the Panhandle or the Piney Woods. The same battered cars and farm trucks were parked at an angle to the pavements; the same sun-browned old men spat their tobacco juice on the hot concrete; the young boys in crewcuts and Sears Roebuck straw hats with health and blond youth all over their faces stood on the street corners; and the girls with their hair in curlers and bandannas sat in the same cafés, drinking R.C. Cola and giggling about what Billy Bob or that crazy Lee Harper did at the drive-in movie last night.

I drove down the dusty street of the Mexican district with the lisping voice of a local hillbilly singer blaring from my radio:

> I warned him once or twice
> To stop playing cards and shooting dice
> He's in the jailhouse now.

Rie was sitting at the table in the front room of the union headquarters with a cup of coffee in her hand. She was barefoot and wore a pair of white shorts and a rumpled denim shirt, and her face was pale with hangover. I went through the screen door without knocking.

'Get in the car, woman. I'm going to do something for that Yankee mind of yours today,' I said.

'What?' She looked at me with her hair in her eyes.

'Dinner on the ground and devil in the bush, by God. Come on.'

'Hack, what are you talking about?' Her words were slow and carefully controlled, and I knew she really had one.

'I'm going to introduce you to my boyhood. Goddamn it, girl, get up and stop fooling around.'

'I don't think I can do anything today.'

'Yes, you can. Never stay inside with a hangover. Charge out into the sunlight and do things you never did before.'

'How much did I drink?'

'You just did it with bad things in your mind.'

'I'm sorry about last night. I must have seemed like a real dumb chick.'

'You could never be that.'

She smiled and pushed the hair out of her eyes.

'I'm sorry, anyway,' she said.

'Right now there's a green river about seventy miles from here, and under a big grey limestone rock there's an eight-pound bass with one of my flies hanging in his lip, and unless you get your ass up I'm going down the road by myself.'

'You're a real piece of pie, Hack.'

'No, I ain't. I'm shit and nails and all kinds of bad news. You ought to know that by this time. If you need any references you can contact my brother. I left him yesterday with his ulcer bulging out of his throat.'

She put her fingers to her forehead and laughed, and that wonderful merry flash of light came back into her eyes.

'I'll be out in a minute. There's some chicory coffee and cornbread on the stove,' she said.

'Well, goddamn, for a Yankee girl you may be all right after all,' I said, and watched the smooth curve of her hips against her shorts as she walked into the back of the house.

We drove north through the hills and flat farmland of string-bean and corn fields and cow pasture to a wide, green, slow-moving river lined with willow, redbud and juniper trees, where I had fly-fished as a boy with my father. The river was low from the drought, and the surface was covered with seeds from the juniper trees, but there were still eddies and deep holes behind the boulders in the current, and I knew that I could take all the crappie, bream and bass that I could put on a stringer. The mudbanks were covered with the sharp, wet tracks of deer and racoons, and mockingbirds and bluejays flew angrily through the hot shade of the trees. The sunlight reflected off the water, and farther down, where the river turned by a grove of cypress trees, the sandbars gleamed hard and white in the middle of the current. Dragonflies flicked over the reeds and lily pads near the bank, and the bream were feeding in the shade of the willows, denting the water in quiet circles, like raindrops, when they rose to take an insect.

I took my three-piece Fenwick flyrod in its felt cover and the small box of number-eighteen dry flies from the boot, and we walked through the trees and dead leaves and twigs to the river. Comanche and Apache warriors used to camp here on the banks to cut and shave arrow shafts from the juniper wood, and for a moment my eyes became twenty years younger as I looked for the place where they had probably built their wickiups and hung their venison in the trees over smoking fires. I knew that if I looked long enough I could find their old camp: the fire line a foot or so below the soil, the flint chippings from a work mound, the bone awls and shards of pottery. Since I was a boy I always felt that the land breathed with the presence of those dead men who had struggled on it long before we were born, and sometimes as a boy, particularly in the late evening, I almost felt that they were still living out their lives around me, firing their arrows from under the necks of war ponies at pioneer cabins that had long since decayed into loam. Once when I was ploughing a field that we had always used for pasture, I felt something hard and brittle snap against the share and grind into pieces over the mouldboard. I felt it right through the vibration of the tractor, and before I had shut off the engine and turned around in the metal seat I already knew that I had scraped across a warrior's grave. The shattered skull and bits of white vertebra were scattered in the furrow, and all of his rose quartz arrowpoints gleamed among his ribs like drops of blood.

We sat under a cypress tree close to the water, and Rie opened the beer and made sandwiches of sausage and cheese while I tied a new tapered leader with one-pound test tippet. I waded out into the warm water and false-cast under the overhang of the trees, pulling out the line from the reel easily with my left hand, and shot the small brown hackle fly into a riffle on the far side of a boulder. The Fenwick was a beautiful rod. It was as light as air in my palm, and it was tapered and balanced so perfectly in its design that I could set the hook hard with one flick of the fingers. The fly drifted through the riffle twice without a strike, but on the third cast a large-mouth bass rose from the bottom of the pool, like a green air bubble floating slowly upwards, and broke the surface in an explosion of light. He took the fly in the corner of his lip, shaking his head violently, his dorsal fin and tail boiling the water, then he dived deep again towards the heavy current. I kept the rod high over my head with my right arm outstretched and let the line run tightly between my fingers. He sat on it once, deep, pointed downstream, and the tip of the rod bent downward until I knew that he was about to break the leader and I had to give him more line. I waded with him in the current, working him at an angle towards the bank, then he rose once more, the hook now protruding close to his eye, and hit the water sideways. He tried to turn his head back into the current, but he was weakening fast, and I started pulling in the line slowly with my left hand. He waved his tail in the shallows, clouding the water with sand, and each time I lifted the rod to bring his mouth to the surface he sat on it again and bent the tip in a quivering arch. I let him spend his last strength against the spring of the rod, then I worked my hand down the leader and caught him carefully under the stomach. He was heavy and cold in my hand, and I slipped the hook out of his mouth, watching the eye, and placed him back in the water. He remained still for a moment, his gills pulsing, then he moved slowly off through the shallows and dropped into the green darkness of the current.

I leaned the rod against the cypress trunk and drank a bottle of Jax with a sausage and cheese sandwich. The Spanish moss overhead looked like wisps of cobweb against the sun, and I could smell the dark, cool odour of the rotted stumps and worm-eaten logs back in the woods. Rie had waded on the edge of the river while I fished, and her bare, suntanned legs were coated with sand. She sat with her arms behind her, looking at the sandbars and stretch of willows on the far side of the river, and I had to force myself from dropping my eyes to her breasts.

'How did you find such a wonderful place?' she said.

'My father used to take me here when I was a boy. In the spring we'd fish the riffle from that rosebud tree down to where the river turns in the shade. Then we'd dig for an old Indian camp. I found my first bannerstone in the bottom of that wash.'

I sat down beside her on the tablecloth and drank from the beer. A shaft of sunlight struck inside the amber bottle.

'It must be fine to have a father like that,' she said.

'Yeah, he was a good man.'

'Was he a lawyer?'

'He taught southern history at the University of Texas, then he was in Congress two terms during Roosevelt's administration. He took me deer hunting once on John Nance Garner's ranch in Uvalde, but I was too small then to believe that the Vice-President of the United States could chew on cigars and spit tobacco juice. My father had to convince me that Mr Jack really did work in an important capacity for the government.'

'Gee, what a great story,' she said.

'I shook hands with Roosevelt once at Warm Springs, too. I wanted to look at the metal braces on his legs, but his eyes were so intense and interested, even in a boy's conversation, that you couldn't glance away from them. I was full of all kinds of pride and sunshine when I realized that my father was a personal friend of this man. I watched them drink whiskey on the verandah together, and for the first time I knew my father had another life that I'd never imagined before.'

I drank the foam out of the bottle and looked at the summer haze on the river. It was a wonderful place. The juniper seeds on the water turned in swirls past the sandbars, and stray seagulls that had wandered far inland dipped and hovered over a dead gar on the mudbank.

'Go on,' she said. Her face was happy and so lovely in the broken shade that I had to swallow when I looked at her.

'I don't like people who show home movies,' I said.

'I do, especially cowboy lawyers that dig up old arrowheads.'

'I told you I'm shit and nails, didn't I? The Lone Ranger with a hangover.'

'You just think you're a bad man.'

'There are probably several hundred people who will disagree with you.'

'You're not even a good cynic.'

'You're taking away all my credentials.'

'Go on. Please.'

'The old man knew Woody Guthrie, too. He stayed at the house once during the war, and every evening I'd sit with him on the front steps while he played that beat-up old Stella guitar and his harmonica. He always wore a crushed felt hat, and when he spoke his words had a cadence like talking blues. He could never talk very long, at least while he had a guitar in his hands, without starting another song. He played with three steel banjo picks on his fingers, and he had the harmonica wired to a brace around his neck. He played Negro and working men's beer-joint blues so mean and fine that I didn't want him to ever leave. When we drove him to Galveston to catch a merchant ship my father asked him what the migrant farm workers thought of the movie *Grapes of Wrath*, and he said, "Most of the people I know ain't going to pay a quarter to see no more grapes, and I don't expect they need any more of this here wrath, either."'

'Wow, did your father know anybody else?'

'Those were the best ones. And I'm all out of stories, babe.'

'Your father must have been an unusual man.'

'Yes, he was.' I bit the tip off a cigar and looked at the haze on the water and the line of willows beyond, and for just a moment, in the stillness and heat of the summer morning, in the time that the flame of my match burned upward in one sulphurous curl, I saw my father lying half out of the chair in the library, the circular explosion of gunpowder on the front of his cream-coloured coat, with his mouth locked open as though he had one final statement to make. The pistol had flown from his dead hand with the weight of its own recoil, and his arm had caught behind him at a twisted angle in the chair. His eyes were receded and staring, and his grey hair hung down on his forehead like a child's. As I stood in the doorway, unable to move towards him, with the shot still loud in my ears and Bailey running down the stairs behind me, I thought: *It was his heart. He had to do it. He couldn't let it kill him first.*

'Hey, come in, world,' Rie said.

'The old man had rheumatic fever when he was a kid. All of the things he loved to do put his heart right in a vice.'

She touched the back of my hand with her fingers and looked quietly into my face. Her strands of sunburned hair were gold in the broken light through the cypress tree.

'All right, goddamn, how about opening another beer?' I said.

'You're a special kind of guy, Hack.'

'How did we get on this crap, anyway? Come on, girl. Get the beer open.'

'OK, kemosabe.' Her eyes went flat, and she reached inside the sack of crushed ice.

'I mean, you're hurting my badass identity.'

She worked the opener on the bottle cap without answering.

'Say, Rie. Come on.'

'You kick doors shut real hard,' she said.

'Look, I behave like a sonofabitch so often that sometimes I don't think about who I'm talking to.'

'You don't like anyone to get inside you, and maybe that's cool, but you ought to hang out a sign for dumb chicks.'

'I'm sorry.'

'It's a swell day and you're still a piece of pie.'

I leaned over her and kissed her on the mouth. I felt her heavy breasts against me, and I slipped my arms under her back and kissed her forehead and her closed eyes and put my face in her hair. She breathed against my cheek and ran her hands under my shirt.

'Oh, Hack,' she said, and moved her whole body into me.

My blood raced and I could feel my heart clicking inside me. Each time I kissed her my head swam, my breath became short, and I felt myself dropping through her into the earth.

She put one leg in mine and held me closer and ran her fingernails up my neck through my hair. When she moved her body against me the dark green of the trees and the summer haze on the river seemed to spin in circles around me.

'I felt you kiss me last night. I didn't want you to stop,' she said. 'All night I wanted to feel you around me.'

'My southern ethic wouldn't let me take advantage of a bombed girl.'

'You have so many crazy things in your head, Lone Ranger.' She moved her lips over my cheek and bit me on the neck, and then I couldn't stop it.

I put my hand under her shirt and felt her breasts. They swelled out each time she breathed and I could feel her heart beating under my palm. I unzipped her white shorts and touched her thighs and her flat stomach.

'I'm sorry for the woods. I should take you up the road, but you really got down inside me, babe,' I said.

She smiled and kissed me, and her almond eyes took on all the wonderful colour and mysterious light that a woman's eyes can have when they make you weak with just a glance.

That evening we drove back through the hills and the baked fields of string beans and corn, and stopped at a roadside restaurant and beer tavern north of Rio Grande City for Mexican food. On the broken horizon the sun was orange behind clouds that looked as though they had been burned purple. The sky seemed so vast and empty in its darkening light that my head became dizzy in looking at it. (Sometimes, at moments like this, I felt a south Texas sunset was so hard I could strike a match against it.)

We finished dinner and drank bottles of Carta Blanca while two drunk cowboys played the jukebox and arm-wrestled with each other at the bar. We had chicory coffee, and I brought in my flask of Jack Daniel's from the car and poured a shot into our cups. On the jukebox Lester Flatt and Earl Scruggs rolled out a Blue Ridge song, in their mournful southern accents, of ancient American loves and distant mountain trains:

> I can hear the whistle blowing
> High and lonely as can be
> Each year is like some rolling freight train
> Cold as starlight upon the rails.

I don't know if it was the whiskey (I eventually drained the whole flask into my cup), the events and emotional fatigue of the past two days, or my need to confess my guilt of fifteen years ago, or a combination of the three, but anyway I began to talk about Korea and then I told her all of it.

EIGHT

My legs were on fire as we marched the five miles along a frozen dirt road from the freight train to a temporary prison compound. The sky was lead grey, and the dark winter brown of the earth showed in patches through the ice and snow that covered the fields and hills. The few peasant farmhouses, made from mud-bricks mixed with straw, were deserted, and at odd intervals across the fields there were old craters left from a stray bombing. Our Chinese guards, in their quilted uniforms and Mongolian hats, walked along beside us with their burpguns slung on straps at port arms, one gloved finger curled inside the trigger guard, hating us not only because we were Occidentals and the enemy but also for the cold and misery in their own bodies. When a man fell or couldn't keep pace with the line or find someone to help him walk he was pushed crying (or sometimes white and speechless in his terror) into the ditch and shot. The Chinese were thorough. Two and sometimes three guards would fire their burpguns into one shivering, helpless man.

By all chances I should have bought it somewhere along that five miles of frozen road. My trouser legs were stiff with dried blood, and each step sent the flame in my wounds racing up my body and made my groin go weak with pain. I had never known that pain could be as prolonged and intense and unrelieved. I saw the guards kill six men and I heard them kill others behind me, and I knew that I was going to fall over soon and I would die just as the rest had, with my arms across my face and my knees drawn up to my chest in an embryonic position. But a Marine major from Billings, Montana, a huge man with lumberjack arms, caught me around the waist and held me up, even when I felt my knees collapse entirely and the horizon tilted quickly as in a feverish dream. His right ear was split and crusted with black blood, and his eyes were bright with control of his own pain, but it never showed in his voice and his arm stayed locked hard around my waist.

'Stay up, doc. We're going to need all of our corpsmen,' he

said. 'Just throw one foot after another. Don't use your knees. You hear me, son? These bastards won't march us much farther.'

And for the next four miles we went down the road like two Siamese twins out of step with each other. That night the guards put us in a wooden schoolhouse surrounded by concertina wire, and in his sleep the major cried out once and tore open his mutilated ear with his fingernails.

Several months later I heard that he died of dysentery in the Bean Camp.

I was in three camps while I was a POW. Whenever the complexion of the war changed or a new offensive was begun by one side or the other, the Chinese moved us in cattle cars or Russian trucks or on foot to a new camp where there was no chance of our being liberated, since we were an important bargaining chip at the peace talks. I spent two months at the Bean Camp, a compound of wretched wooden shacks used by the Japanese to hold British prisoners during World War II, and for reasons unknown to me, since I had no military knowledge worth anything to the North Koreans or the Chinese, I was singled out with twelve others, including two deranged Greeks, for transfer to Pak's Palace outside Pyongyang. Major Pak conducted his interrogations in an abandoned brick factory, and each morning two guards led me across the brick yard covered with fine red dust to a small, dirty room that was bare except for two straight-backed chairs and the major's desk. A rope with a cinched loop in one end hung from a rafter, and when everything else failed the major would tie the hands of a prisoner behind him and have him drawn into the air by the arms and beaten with bamboo canes. It was called Pak's Swing, and the screams that came from that room were not like human sounds.

Major Pak's personality was subject to abrupt changes. Sometimes his eyes burned like those of a religious fanatic or an idealistic zealot who revelled in the pain of his enemies. His tailored uniform was always immaculate, as though he were born to the professional military, but the wrong answer from a prisoner would make his face convulse with hatred and his screaming would become incoherent. Then moments later his eyes would water, his constricted throat would relax, and his voice would take on the tone of a tormented man who was forced to do things to people who couldn't understand the necessity of his job or the historical righteousness of his cause. The two Greeks suffered most from him, because he was sure that their insane, pathetic behaviour was an act. Each night they were returned to our building streaked with blood and moaning in words that we couldn't understand.

The major also had fixations. He threatened to tear out my fingernails with pliers unless I told him where the 101st Airborne planned to drop into North Korea. I infuriated him when I answered that I was a Navy corpsman and that I had spent only six days on the line before capture. He believed that all Americans lied instinctively and looked down upon him as an Oriental of inferior intelligence. He struck me in the head with the pliers and cut my scalp, and as I leaned over with the blood trickling across my eye I waited for him to order the guards to draw me up on the rope. However, he threw a glass of water in my face and pulled my head up by the hair.

'Americans are weak. You can't accept pain for yourselves. You only expect others to bear it,' he said.

Then I realized that it really didn't matter to him whether or not I knew anything about the 101st Airborne. He hated me because I was everything which he identified with the young American archetype portrayed in *The Saturday Evening Post*: I was tall, blond, good-looking, unscarred by hunger or struggle or revolutions whose ideology was just rice. So Major Pak's interest in me was personal rather than of a military nature, and he soon tired of interrogating me in favour of a British commando who had been caught behind their lines, and I was sent back to the Bean Camp in a captured US truck loaded with Australian prisoners.

But my recall deals primarily with Camp Five in No Name Valley, where I spent the greater portion of the war until I was exchanged at Freedom Village in 1953. Also, it was here that I learned that men can live with guilt and a loathsome image of themselves which previously they didn't believe themselves capable of enduring.

The Yalu River was north of our camp, and in the winter the ice expanded against the banks and rang in the cold silence at night, and sometimes we would hear it break up and crash in great yellow chunks at a turn in the current. The wind blew all the time, sweeping out of the bare hills across the river in China, and when there was no fuel in our shack we slept on the floor in a group, breathing the stench of our bodies under the blankets, the nauseating odour of fish heads on our breath, and the excretions of men with dysentery who couldn't control themselves in their sleep.

We were always cold during the winter. Even when we had fuel to burn in our small iron stove the heat would not radiate more than a few feet, and the wind drove through the cracks in the boards and would drop the temperature enough to freeze our jerrycan of water unless we kept it close to the fire. During the day the sun was a pale yellow orb in the sky, and the light was never strong enough through the grey winter haze to cast a hard shadow on the ground. Three men were taken out with a guard once a week to forage for wood, but the landscape was largely bare and the sticks and roots that hadn't already been picked up were now covered by ice and snow. We had one pair of mis-matched knitted mittens in our shack, and when the wood detail went out one man would take the mittens and be responsible for gathering the largest share of fuel, as our fingers would often be left cut and swollen or discoloured at the tips from frostbite after a day of ripping frozen sticks out of the snow.

There were oil stoves in the camp, but these went to the progressives, those who had signed peace petitions, confessions to participating in germ warfare, or absurdly worded statements denouncing Wall Street capitalists. The progressives were kept in two oblong buildings on the far side of the compound, separated from the rest of us by a barbed-wire fence and a wooden gate that stayed locked with a chain. Many of them were informers, or 'snitches', and they would have been killed had they been forced to live with the rest of the prisoner population. In the morning they exercised in the yard behind the wire fence, their faces averted so they wouldn't have to look at the rest of us. They received the same diet as we did, bean cakes, millet and boiled corn, but much more of it, and occasionally they were given some greens and hardboiled eggs, and they didn't have to worry about beriberi and diarrhoea that left your entrails and rectum burning day and night. I should have hated them for the weight on their bodies and the flush of health in their faces, the Red Cross packages they were given by the guards, but I was always too sick, cold or afraid to care what they did on their side of the fence. Like most of the others I didn't believe that we would ever be liberated or exchanged. New prisoners told us that the Chinese had poured into South Korea, the ROKs had thrown down their weapons and run, and our forces were being pushed into the sea. So even the most optimistic and strong knew that freedom was probably years away, and our death rate in the camp averaged a dozen men a day.

Some died quietly in their sleep under their blankets, and in the morning we found them white and stiff, the skin hard as marble, and we dragged them outside the shack like pieces of stone and left them for the burial squad. Others died delirious with agony, their eyes feverish and rolling white in their heads, their inflamed entrails bulging out the colon like inflated rubber. There was nothing to do for them – no medicine, no priest, not even the option of killing out of mercy.

There were fifteen enlisted men in my shack (the Chinese kept the officers, NCOs, and enlisted men separated from one another so there would be no system of military order or authority among us). We spent our days in boredom or listening to ridiculous lectures by Colonel Ding and a 'group monitor', one of the progressives whom Ding always brought with him. Ding was a small, thin man, with a harelip and a face that was as lifeless as wax. There were spaces between his front teeth, and when he ranted about imperialism and the American bombing of Pyongyang his disfigured mouth gave his face the appearance of a lunatic's. He was fond of telling us that he had attended the University of California for a year in the thirties, and also that he had been with Mao on the Great March. Many times he would digress from his tirades on the evils of the Western world and slip into a history of his own career, which seemed to give him a special pleasure. Sometimes he would ask where each of us was from, and then show the knowledge that he had of that area, although he often referred to such places as 'San Antonio,

Missouri'. The group monitor was usually even more pathetic. He would stand behind the colonel, embarrassed, his gloved hands never able to find a pocket more than a few moments, and sometimes he would light a cigarette nervously, then pinch it out and put it back in the pack when our eyes looked into his. After the colonel had finished, the monitor would read to us from his journal, his self-deluding confession of guilt, and tell us that American troops were waging a war against innocent people and that we were as much victims of the defence industrialists as the people whom we killed. But his face always stayed buried in the notebook, as though he couldn't read his own handwriting, or he stared above our heads at the distant hills. Many times his words faltered and he would look helplessly at the colonel, who would only nod for him to go on. I suppose that I felt more pity towards the progressives than anger. They were cared for and would live, and eventually they would have to face some of us after the peace came.

However, our classes weren't merely an exercise in Marxist buffoonery. The Chinese knew a great deal about the effect of compromise on the individual. The progressives did not end up on the other side of the wire fence simply because they knew that the rations were better there. It was a gradual process, much like the irreversible stages of seduction portrayed in a stag movie. Most of us knew that it was a matter of time before we died of hunger or any of the diseases that accompanied it, and if we volunteered for Ding's classes, although it was never stated, we knew that the guards would put extra bean cakes in our shack's food bucket at night. And once we were in the classes all we had to do was sign a non-political peace petition, asking in the most general terms for an end to the war (supposedly these were sent to the United Nations), and our millet would include fish heads, which we could boil into broth with roots and give to those who had the worst cases of dysentery. Then if we wanted an occasional hardboiled egg or a package of tobacco for the shack, we could say a couple of sentences against war into a tape recorder without identifying ourselves. Many nights we sat close to the small stove in silence, the honey bucket reeking in the corner, and thought about the next stage in the progression. Sometimes we would

discuss the morality of signing a peace petition or whether or not
it was all right to do it if you misspelled your name or gave your
serial number incorrectly, since someone would surely know that
you didn't mean it after all and you had beaten the Chinese at
their own game, and I thought of Chaucerian monks debating the
virtue of their fornication.

'Fuck it. I'm going to sign what the bastard wants,' one man
would say. 'Nobody believes that shit, anyway. It probably don't
even go out of camp. Ding gets his rocks off and we get some
more chow. It's just a piece of paper. He probably wipes his ass
with it.'

We wrote journals for Colonel Ding, confessing imaginary sins
and describing the poverty of our lives in America (many times
this was done as much to relieve our boredom as it was to earn
extra rations). He particularly liked descriptions of slums and
sweatshops. Often we would collaborate on one journal and
invent accounts of social injustice that would make Charles
Dickens pale. Orphans were beaten with whips by Catholic nuns,
virtuous young girls were forced into prostitution and infected
with venereal disease by fat bankers, southern policemen fired
their pistols from car windows into Negro homes, a dismal pall of
despair and political oppression hung over the tenement buildings
of the working classes while Zionists with faces like sleek pigs
filled their bank accounts with the profits of war. We all had
committed every type of sin, from sodomy and incest to fornication with sheep. In the candle light at night we revelled in our
iniquity and wrote detailed histories of axe murders, arson,
screwing a dead woman, and male rape in the shower at the
YMCA. No group of men had ever been guilty of greater crimes,
and the more depraved the confession the more generous Ding
became towards his captives.

We all grew to know each other in the intimate and physical
way that men do when in confinement. There was no secret
shame or weakness that one of us could conceal from the others
for very long. We shared our love affairs, our nights of depravity
in Japanese brothels, our memories of a beating by a bully on the
elementary school ground, our failures with wives and company
bosses. We knew each other's smell, latrine habits, particular

nightmares, or when one man was masturbating under the blanket. Through hunger and fear our virtues and inadequacies burned just below the skin. When one man in the shack died and was replaced by a new prisoner, we knew him within a week as well as we had the lifeless piece of stone we had dragged out into the compound for the burial detail.

We were of every background and mental complexion: the helpless who already had the smell of their dying in their clothes; the strong ones, the gladiators, with iron in their bodies, who knew they could live through anything and boiled their fish heads into broth for the sick; the brave and the terrified, the cowards and the Shylocks, the hoarders, the dealers, the religious, and those whose self-sacrifice made them glow, in the hush of their deaths, with the aura of early martyrs. There was Joe Bob Winfield from Baton Rouge, a redneck hillbilly and an ex-convict at nineteen, with leg-iron scars on his ankles and a story about every type of crime and prison caper; Bertie Fast, the house mouse, our one roaring homosexual, who was raped his first week in camp and liked it so much that he went professional; a Sears Roebuck shoe salesman from Salt Lake who wrote endless letters to his wife and children which Ding threw in the garbage can; O. J. Benson from Okema, Oklahoma, a bootlegger who used to run whiskey from Joplin in a bookmobile before the war; a reactivated World War II paratrooper, the oldest man in the shack, who had spent two years in a German concentration camp; Cigarette Williams, the other Navy corpsman, from Mount Olive, Alabama, a six-foot-five country singer who hanged himself during the night because his feet were so frostbitten he couldn't put boots on them; the Australian miner who called Ding a bloody yellow nigger and was strung up all day on a rafter by his hands; and the wild Turk who knew no English, a man on fire, a killer with insane eyes and a bricklayer's trowel hidden in his tick mattress.

There were many others who came and died or were transferred for interrogation, but only two of them from my shack are important in this brief account of my Korean experience. Pfc. Francis Ramos from San Angelo had Indian-black hair, wide-set intense eyes, hard bones in his face, and hands and wrists that could break boards in half. He used to drive a beer truck before he was drafted, and the muscles in his shoulders and chest were as taut and hard as concrete from years of loading and stacking metal beer kegs. There were white scars on his knuckles where they had been mashed on a warehouse ramp, and another thick, raised scar that he had received in a whorehouse brawl ran back in a crooked line through his hair. He had an obsession with escape. He had spent six months in a city stockade once for non-support, and he was released only after the jailer became convinced that he was mad, and solitary confinement and beatings with rolled newspapers would not make him less of a threat to the guards and the rest of the prison population. He had been Golden Gloves middleweight champion of Texas in high school, and sometimes when I looked at his huge fists and the swollen veins in his wrists I had nightmarish images of what he must have done to his opponents in the ring.

He couldn't sleep at night. After Sergeant Tien Kwong handed us our food bucket and locked the chain on the shack door, Ramos's eyes flicked wildly across the walls and ceilings, his breathing became deeper, and then he would set about doing dozens of unnecessary things with the frenetic energy of a man on the edge of hysteria. He put fuel into the stove when we were trying to conserve every twig, boiled water to make soup when we had no fish heads, shook out his blankets and folded them so he could unfold them again, restrung his bootlaces, tried to teach the wild Turk English, and eventually sat alone in the darkness after the rest of us had gone to sleep. He would be so tired the next day that sometimes his head would fall on his chest during one of Ding's lectures, which meant one night in the hole under the sewer grate.

Then there was Airman First Class Lester Dixon, captured when the Chinese overran Seoul, a teenage hoodlum from Chicago, one of the dealers, a ten-per-center, a pool-room hustler and reefer salesman on the South Side, slick, a kid with a venal mind and an eye for the profit to be made from free enterprise, blue movies, dope and fifteen-year-old Negro prostitutes. He had tattoos of skulls and snakes' heads on his arms, and his hair had grown out long enough to comb back in ducktails. His colourless face was like the edge of a hatchet. He thought of charity as naïveté, bravery as stupidity, and honesty with others, even in a prison of war compound, a fool's venture.

He shared nothing. He stood first in line for his bean cakes and millet, and ate alone from his tin plate in one corner while the rest of us put small bits of our food into the soup pot on the stove for the Australian who was dying of beriberi. He was never ashamed of not sharing, or at least he didn't show it; he ate with his face in his plate, his chopsticks scraping against the metal, as though his whole being were concentrated into one scrap of bean cake that he might miss.

It was a cold, windswept grey morning with hailstones on the ground, and Dixon had just left the shack with the wood detail.

'I think he's a snitch,' Ramos said. 'I seen him eating some vitamin pills in the dark last night.'

We were hunched around the iron stove, bent forward towards the heat. Our breaths steamed out like ice in the silence.

'Are you sure?' I said.

'He took three of them out of his pocket and swallowed them dry.'

'I don't know about no vitamin pills,' Joe Bob, our ex-convict, said, 'but I got something in my pecker that goes off when I get near a snitch, and that boy gives me a real bone.'

'If you're right, what are we going to do with him?' another man said.

'For openers, you better start shutting up about running,' Joe Bob said. His sandy red hair stuck out from under his stocking cap, and he chewed on the flattened end of a matchstick in one corner of his mouth.

'We ice him,' Ramos said.

'Hey, cut that shit, man,' Joe Bob said. 'Ding'll waste the whole shack.'

'No, he ain't,' Ramos said. 'I'll tell Kwong that Dixon's been spitting blood and ask him for some eggs, and then we wait a few days and smother him.'

'I tell you, buddy, they ain't that stupid,' Joe Bob said.

'We got to take him out one way or another,' O.J., the bootlegger from Okema, said. 'If Ding's greasing him, he's got to burn somebody.'

'Yeah, you don't fuck around with guys like this.'

'There's other ways to get a snitch out of the shack,' Joe Bob said. 'We can turn the Turk loose on him, and he'll ask Ding to transfer over with the pros.'

'You're not sure about him, anyway,' I said. 'He could have gotten those pills off of somebody else in the yard.'

'You know that's a lot of crap, too, Holland. He smelled like a snitch when he first come in here,' Ramos said.

'He's a pimp and a wheeler, and that's all he's been his whole life. That doesn't mean he's working for Ding,' I said.

'I'll do it in the middle of the night,' Ramos said. 'There won't be no sound, and he'll look just like every other guy we drug out in the yard.'

'I ain't telling you what to do,' Joe Bob said, 'but you got some pretty amateur shit in your head for this kind of scene. Ding might be a harelip dickhead, but he ain't dumb and he's going to fry our balls in a skillet before you get done with this caper.'

'The sonofabitch has to go. What else are we going to do with him?' O.J. said.

'If you got to ice him, use your head a minute and do it out in the yard,' Joe Bob said. 'Catch him in a bunch during exercise time and bust him open with the Turk's trowel. You'll probably get shot, anyway, but maybe the rest of us won't get knocked off with you.'

'If you don't want it, just stay out of my face,' Ramos said.

'Like I said, I ain't trying to grow any hairs in your asshole. You just don't know what you're doing. Like this escape caper. I chain-ganged in the roughest joint in the South, and I started to run once myself, but you got to be out of your goddamn mind to try and crack a place like this. You got two fences to cut through, there's a hundred yards of bare ground between both of them, and them gooks up on the platform ain't going to be reading fortune cookies while you're hauling for Dixie. You better get your head rewired before Ding lays you out in the yard like he done to that Greek that took off from the wood detail.'

'If I get nailed I'll buy it running on the other side of that wire,' Ramos said. 'I ain't going to stay here and shit my inside out till somebody rolls me into the yard like a tumblebug. There's a coloured sergeant with a compass and some pliers for the fence, and he figures if we can make it to the sea we can steal a boat and get out far enough for one of our choppers to pick us up.'

'Goddamn, if that ain't a real pistol, Ramos. I once knew a guy that climbed into the back of a rubbish truck with chains on, buried himself in the trash, and rode down the highway with the hacks looking all over for him. Except he almost got fried when they unloaded the truck in the county incinerator. But you got him beat, buddy. Running across North Korea with a nigra. Now that's cool. You guys ought to stand out like shit in an ice-cream factory.'

Ramos didn't say anything more. He glared at the grey ash in the grate a while, then paced around the shack, beating his arms in the cold. He didn't have the intelligence or prison experience to argue with Joe Bob, but we knew that he planned to kill Dixon, regardless of what anyone said.

And it wasn't long before Dixon knew it, too. He came in from the wood detail late that afternoon, his face red and chafed with windburn, and dropped a load of sticks and roots by the stove. There was snow in his hair, and his quilted trousers were wet up to the knees. In the silence we heard Kwong lock the chain on the door. Dixon pulled off his mittens with his teeth and stuck his hands under his armpits.

'Somebody else is going on that bastard next time,' he said. 'That whole goddamn field's picked clean. I broke two fingernails digging down to the ground.'

No one answered.

'Shit, look at them.'

We turned our faces away or found things to do that would remove us from the eventual meeting of eyes between Ramos and Dixon. But instead it was O.J. and Bertie Fast, the drag queen, who tore open the wrapper and let Dixon look for just a moment inside the box.

'What is this crap, anyway?' Dixon said. 'Maybe I didn't wipe my ass clean this morning or something. Don't I smell sweet enough to you, house mouse?'

'I didn't say anything,' Bertie said, his voice weak and his eyes searching for a spot on the far wall.

'House mouse, you better not hold out on me.'

'Fuck off, man,' O.J. said. He was sticking twigs into the fire grate, and his jawbones were flat against the skin.

'What's the deal, then?' Dixon said. 'You want me to kick in part of my chow for the soup? OK. No sweat. Is everybody cool now?'

'Where did you get vitamin pills?' O.J. said.

'Vitamins? You must have a wild crab loose in your brain.' But he was surprised, and there was a flicker of fear in his face.

'Yeah. Like those little red ones Ding gives to the pros,' O.J. said.

'You better see a wig mechanic when you get out of here. You got real problems.'

'You're holding a hot turd with both hands, buddy,' Joe Bob said. 'This ain't the time for none of that smart-ass Yankee jive.'

'You guys have been flogging your meat too much or something. I mean, what kind of joint is this, anyway? I spend the whole day digging in the ice with Kwong jabbing me in the ass, and I come back and you guys got me nailed for a pro.'

'How did you get the pills?' I said.

Everyone was looking at him now. The snow in his hair had melted, and his face was damp with water and perspiration. He held his two bruised fingers in one hand and glanced at the locked door.

'I traded them off a spade in the yard for some cigarettes. All right, so I didn't share them. Big deal. You going to tear my balls out because I want to stay alive?'

'Which spade?' O.J. said.

'I don't know. He's with the NCOs.'

'There ain't but one over there,' Ramos said.

'Maybe he's an enlisted man. What difference does it make? All those boons look alike.'

'Get it straight, cousin. That turd is melting in your hand,' Joe Bob said.

'You guys already want to fry me. It don't make any difference what I say. You've been pissed ever since I come in here because I wouldn't put in my chow for guys that were already dead. All of you got a purple heart nailed right up in the middle of your forehead because you keep some poor sonofabitch alive a few extra days so he can shit more blood and chew his tongue raw. If I buy it I hope there ain't a bunch like you around.'

'OK, you got the pills off a coloured sergeant,' Ramos said. He sat cross-legged on his blanket close to the stove, rubbing his dirt-caked bare feet with his hand. 'That's all we wanted to know. Next time you share anything you get in the yard.'

Dixon stared into Ramos's face, and then realized that he was looking at his executioner.

'Not me, buddy,' he said. 'You're not going to stick my head down in the mattress. None of you pricks are. You find some other cat to hang a frame on. How about Bertie here? He don't keep his ass soft and fat on bean cakes.'

'Quit shouting. There ain't anybody going to bother you,' Ramos said. 'Just don't try to bullshit us next time.'

'No, you're going to ice me. You been wanting to do it a long time, you spick, and now you got those other bastards to go in with you. Hey, Kwong!' He began beating against the wooden door with his fists and kicking his feet into the boards. The chain and padlock reverberated with the blows.

'You get down here. You hear me? I want to see Ding!'

O.J. and Ramos started for him at the same time, but Joe Bob jumped up in front of both of them and stiff-armed them with all his weight in the chest.

'The shit already hit the fan. Just ride it out and stay cool,' he said.

We heard Kwong running through the frozen snow outside. Dixon's face was white with fear, and he brought his knees into the door as though they could splinter wood and snap metal chain after his feet and fists had failed. Kwong turned the lock and threw open the door, with his burpgun slung on a leather strap around his neck and the barrel pointed like an angry god into the middle of us. His squat, thick body was framed against the grey light and the snow-covered shacks behind him, and his peasant face was concentrated in both anger and anticipation of challenge. He grabbed Dixon by his coat and threw him into the snow, then flicked off the safety on his gun.

'Crazy,' Joe Bob said, pointing to his head. 'He had the shits all week. *Shea tu*. Blood coming out his hole.'

We were all frozen in front of the burpgun, each of us breathing deep in our chests, our hearts clicking like dollar watches. I couldn't look at the gun. Dixon got to his knees in the snow and started crying.

'He needs medicine,' Joe Bob said, and held his head back and pointed his thumb into his mouth. 'Shits all the time. Got shit in his brain.'

'You fucked,' Kwong said, and kicked the door shut with his foot, then locked the chain.

He must have hit Dixon with the stock of his burpgun, because we could hear the wood knock into bone, then the two of them crunched off in the snow towards Ding's billet on the other side of the wire.

The next morning at dawn Kwong was back with two other guards. They opened the door and motioned us against the far wall of the shack with their guns before they stepped inside. The fire in the stove had died out during the night, and the room temperature must have been close to zero. We stood in our socks, shivering under the blankets we held around our shoulders, and tried to look back steadily at Kwong while his eyes passed from face to face. He already knew the ones who had been chosen for the first interrogation, but he enjoyed watching us hang from fishhooks. Then he motioned his burpgun at five of us: O.J., Bertie Fast, Joe Bob, the Turk and me. We sat down in the middle of the floor and laced on our boots, then marched in single file across the yard with the guards on each side of us. The pale sun had just risen coldly over the hills, and as I looked at our dim shadows on the snow I felt that my last morning was now in progress, and that I should have bought it back there in the Shooting Gallery and whoever shuffles the cards had just discovered his mistake and was about to set things straight.

The wounds in my legs had never healed and had become infected, and when I slowed my pace in the snow Kwong jabbed the barrel of his gun into my scalp. I felt the skin split and I fell forward on my hands and knees. Kwong kicked me in the kidney and pulled me erect by my hair.

'You walk, cocksuck,' he said.

I put my arm over Joe Bob's shoulder, my side in flames, and limped along with the others to the yellow brick building that Ding used for his headquarters. Bertie Fast's eyes were wide with terror, and I could see the pulse jumping in his neck. He looked like a child in his oversized quilted uniform and all the blood had drained out of his soft, feminine face. Even Joe Bob, with scars from the black Betty on his butt, was afraid, although he held it down inside himself like a piece of sharp metal. But the wild Turk showed no fear at all, or possibly he didn't even know what was taking place. His hot black eyes stared out of his white, twisted face, and I wondered if he had the trowel hidden somewhere inside his clothes. His tangled black hair had grown over his shoulders, and he breathed great clouds of vapour, as though he had a fever, through his rotted teeth. He stood immobile with the rest of us while Kwong knocked on the door, and I thought that beyond those hot black eyes there was a furnace instead of a brain.

Ding sat behind his desk in his starched, high-collar uniform with a tea service in front of him. Dixon stood in our corner by the oil stove, his face heavy with lack of sleep, and there was a large, swollen knot above his right eyebrow. His eyes fixed on Ding's desk when we entered the room, and drops of sweat slid down his forehead in the red glow of the stove.

Ding finished his tea, flicked a finger for a guard to remove the tray, and lit a Russian cigarette. He leaned forward on his elbows, puffing with his harelip, his eyes concentrated like BB's into the smoke, and I knew that we were all going to enact a long and painful ritual that would compensate Ding in part for his lack of a field command.

'I know there's a plan for an escape,' he said, quietly. 'It's a very foolish plan that will bring you hardship. There has never been an escape from a Chinese People's detention centre, and you're hundred of miles from the American lines. Now, this can be very easy for you, and it will also help the men who would be shot in trying to escape. Give me their names and you can return to your building, and nothing will be done to the men involved.'

We stood in silence, and the snow melted off our clothes in the warmth of the room. I looked at Dixon, and for a moment I wished that Ramos had killed him as soon as he had come back from the wood detail. The cut in my scalp was swelling and drawing tight, and my legs felt unsteady from fear and the pain in my calves.

'You're not in a cowboy movie,' Ding said. 'None of you are heroes. You're simply stupid. I don't want to punish you. I don't want to see the other men shot. There's no reason for it. This war will be over someday and all of you can return to your families. It's insane for you men to die in trying to escape.'

Our eyes were flat, our faces expressionless, and the room was so quiet that I could hear Kwong shifting the weight of his burpgun on its strap.

'Do you want me to punish all of the men in your building?' Ding said. 'Do you want to see the sick Australian punished because of a stupid minority? All of you grow up on silly movies about Americans smiling at death. You think the Chinese are busboys in restaurants and laundrymen for your dirty clothes. You believe your white skin and Western intelligence reduces us to fools in pigtails grovelling for your tips.'

'We don't know about no escape, Colonel,' Joe Bob said. 'Nobody can crack this joint. Dixon give you a lot of shit last night.'

'You do think we're stupid, don't you?'

'No, sir, we don't. I done time before, Colonel, and I don't want to get burned because some jerk wants to run. Believe me, there ain't no break planned.'

'What do you have to say, airman?' Ding said, and turned towards Dixon.

Dixon's face blanched and he swallowed in his throat. He hadn't thought it was going to be this tough. His eyes looked up at us quickly and then fixed on the desk again. His words were heavy with phlegm.

'It's like I told you, Colonel. They been planning it a long time.'

'How long?'

'I heard them whispering about it in the corner the other night after they blew out the candle.'

'Which ones?' Ding drew in on the cigarette and looked at Dixon flatly through the smoke. He was really tightening the rack now, and he enjoyed tormenting Dixon as much as he did us.

'All of them, I guess. It was dark.'

'You haven't told me very much to earn all those extra gifts.'

Dixon's face flushed and drops of sweat began dripping from his hair.

'You should move away from the stove,' Ding said. 'It's bad for you to become overheated.'

'Colonel, we ain't trying to con you,' O.J. said. 'We got on Dixon because he wouldn't share nothing and he was eating vitamin pills, and he thought we was going to knock him around. He went off his nut and started beating on the door and screaming for Kwong. There wasn't no more to it.'

'Would you like to say something, private?'

'No, sir,' Bertie said. I had to turn and look at him. His voice was high with fear, but I didn't believe the resolve that was there, also.

'Do you want to suffer with these other men?'

'They told you the truth, Colonel. There ain't any break.'

'You haven't spoken. Would you like a turn?' Ding said to me, and at that moment I hated him more than any other human being on earth, not merely for his cruelty but also for the mental degradation that he could continue indefinitely with his physical power over us.

'There's nothing to say, sir. Dixon lied.' I wouldn't let my eyes focus on his face, but he sensed my hatred towards him, anyway, and he smiled with that crooked harelip.

'So the corpsman believes me stupid, too. What are we going to do with you American fighting men? That's how you're called at home, isn't it? What would you suggest if you had my position? Intelligent Western men like you must have suggestions. You're a Texan, aren't you, corpsman? You must have learned many lines from cowboy movies.'

'They gave it to you straight, Colonel.'

'He was one of them last night,' Dixon said. 'They were going to smother me in my sleep.'

(At the time I would have never guessed that the terrified man in the corner, sweating in the heat of the stove, would one day have his picture on the front page of newspapers all over the world as one of the twenty-two American turncoats who chose to remain in Red China after the peace was signed. However, the photograph would show him with full, clean-shaven cheeks, his cap pointed neatly over one eye, a red-blooded enlistee fresh out of the Chicago pool rooms.)

'Then maybe we should begin with you, corpsman,' Ding said, and motioned Kwong with his hand.

The sergeant slammed me down in the wooden chair in front of the desk. Ding lit another cigarette and dropped the burnt match into a butt can. The room was now close with the smell of our bodies and the cigarette smoke. I could almost feel the cruel energy and expectation in Kwong's body behind me.

'Do you want this to be prolonged, or do you want to talk in an intelligent manner?'

I stared into nothing, my shoulders hunched and my hands limp in my lap. I could hear the Turk breathing through his teeth in the silence. Kwong slapped me full across the face with his callused hand. My eyes watered and I could feel the blood burning in the skin.

'Do you think you're in a movie now, corpsman?' Ding said. 'Are the Flying Tigers going to drop out of the sky and kill all the little yellow men around you?'

I stared through my wet eyes at the wall. The lines in the room looked warped, glittering with moisture, and the oil stove burned brightly red in one corner of my vision. Ding nodded to the sergeant, an indifferent and casual movement of maybe an inch, and Kwong brought my head down with both hands into his knee and smashed my nose. The blood burst across my face, my head exploded with light, and I was sure the bone had been knocked back into the brain. I was bent double in the chair, the blood pouring out through my hands, and each time I tried to clear my throat I gagged on a clot of phlegm and started the dry heaves.

'He don't know nothing, Colonel,' Joe Bob said. 'Sometimes the guys bullshit about escape, but he don't even do that. He knows they're bullshitting and he always walks away from it. He don't have no names to give you.'

'Would you like to give me some names?'

'It ain't nothing but guys setting around shitting each other about a break, Colonel. Anybody in a joint does the same thing, or you start beating your rod with sandpaper after a while. Dixon's a goddamn fish and he couldn't cut it, so he sold you a lot of jive.'

'Your corpsman hasn't been hurt at all. The sergeant can do many other things to him.'

'I know that, sir,' Joe Bob said. 'It just won't do no good. He can't tell you nothing.'

'Then I think you should take his chair,' Ding said.

My hands were covered with blood and saliva, and I was still choking on my breath, but I wanted to go over Ding's desk and get my thumbs into his throat. However, I never got the chance to learn if I was that brave or desperate with pain and hatred, because the Turk suddenly stopped breathing a moment, his white face filling with dark areas of rage, and his hot, black eyes glared insanely. Then he shouted once, a bull's roar that came out of some awful thing inside him, and he started for Ding with his huge hands raised in fists over his head.

Kwong stepped quickly in front of him and swung the stock of his burpgun upwards into the Turk's mouth. I could hear his teeth break against the wood. He reeled backwards on the floor, his lips cut open in blue gashes, then Kwong raised his foot back, poised himself, and kicked him in the stomach. The Turk's breath rushed out in a long, rattling gasp, he drew his knees up to his chin, and his face went perfectly white. His mouth worked silently, the veins rigid in his throat, and his eyes were glazed with pain like a dumb, strangling animal's.

Ding was on his feet, shouting in Chinese at Kwong. His waxlike face was enraged, and he kept stabbing one finger in the air at some point outside the building.

'He's crazy, Colonel,' Joe Bob said. 'A stir freak. He probably don't even know where he is.'

'You wouldn't behave intelligently,' Ding yelled. 'You stand there with your confident faces and think you're dealing with comical peasants. You're stupid men that have to be treated as such.'

Kwong pulled me out of the chair by my collar and pushed me towards the door, then he began kicking the Turk in the spine. The Turk's breath came in spasms, and when he tried to suck air down into his lungs the blood bubbled on his lips.

'Pick him up and carry him!'

Joe Bob and O.J. lifted him between them by the arms. His dirty, black hair hung over his face, and his chest heaved up and down.

'Look, Colonel, we ain't to blame for what some nut does,' Joe Bob said. 'He ain't much better than that with us. We got to watch him all the time.'

Ding spoke again in Chinese to Kwong and the other two guards, and they levelled their burpguns at us and motioned towards the door.

'They're going to kill us,' O.J. said.

'Colonel, it ain't fair,' Joe Bob said. 'We never give you no trouble out of our shack.'

'I told you it could have been very easy for you.'

'There wasn't nothing to tell you,' O.J. said. 'Do we got to lose our lives because we give it to you straight?'

'Fuck it,' Joe Bob said. 'They're going to waste us, anyway.'

Kwong hit him in the ear with his fist and pushed us outside. It had started to sleet, and the ice crunched like stones under our feet. The sun was a hazy puff of vapour above the cold hills, and then we saw a lone F-86 bank out of the snow clouds and begin its turn before it reached the Yalu River. It dipped its wings once, as all our planes did when they passed over the camp, and then soared away into a small speck on the southern horizon. We stopped at the work shack, and each of us was given a GI entrenching tool. The Turk dropped his in the snow, and Kwong picked it up and punched it hard into his chest.

'You hold, cocksuck,' he said.

Kwong chained the door shut, and we marched across the compound, past the silent faces of the progressives who watched us from their exercise yard, past the few men who had stopped scrubbing out the lice from their clothes under the iron pump, past our own shack and the men inside who were pressed up against the cracks in the wall, and finally into the no man's land between the two fences that surrounded the camp.

'Here. You dig hole,' Kwong said.

'Oh, my God,' Bertie said.

'You dig to put in shit.' He kicked five evenly spaced places in the snow, and then raised his burpgun level with one hand.

We folded our entrenching tools down like hoes and started chopping through the ice into the frozen ground. The bridge of my nose was throbbing and the blood had congealed in my nostrils. I had to breathe through my teeth, and the air cut into my chest like metal each time I took a swing. The Turk knelt in a melted depression around him, thudding his shovel into the ground, while large crimson drops dripped from his mouth into the snow. I raised my eyes and saw the compound filling with men. The guards were unlocking all the shacks while Ding delivered a harangue through a megaphone. He had his back to us and I couldn't understand the electronic echo of his words, but I knew the compound was receiving a lesson in the need for cooperation between prisoner and captor. Hundreds of faces stared at us through the wire, the steam from their breaths rising into the air, and I began to pray that in some way their concentrated wills could prevent Kwong from dumping that pan of bullets into our bodies.

He walked back and forth in front of us, his eyes bright, his hand rubbing the top of the ventilated barrel. His face was as tight and flat as a shingle, and when one man slowed in his digging he jabbed the gun hard into his neck. Some of the prisoners said Kwong had been a train brakeman in North Korea before the war and that all of his family had been killed in the first American bombings. So he enjoyed his work with Americans. And now he was at his best, in his broken English, with the loading lever on the magazine pulled all the way back.

'Deep. No smell later,' he said.

We were down two feet, the mud and broken ice piled around us. I was sweating inside my clothes, and strange sounds lifted in chorus and disappeared in my mind. The wind polished the snow smooth in front of me, rolling small crystals across Kwong's boots.

His leather laces were tied in knots across the metal eyes. The sleet had stopped, and the shadow of my body and the extended shovel moved about as a separate, broken self on the pile of dirt and ice that grew larger on the edge of my hole.

'I ain't going to buy it like this,' O.J. said. 'I ain't going to do the work for these bastards.'

'You dig deep,' Kwong said.

'You dig it.'

'Pick up shovel,' Kwong said.

'Fuck you, slope.' O.J. breathed rapidly, and the moisture from his nose froze on his lip.

'All stand, then.'

'Mother of God, he's going to do it,' Bertie said.

The sun broke from behind a cloud, the first hard yellow light I had seen since I had come to the camp. My eyes blinked against the glaring whiteness of the compound and the hills. The ice on the barbed wire glittered in the light, and the hundreds of prisoners watching us beyond the fence stared upward at the sky in unison, their wan faces covered with sunshine. The stiff outlines of the buildings in the compound leaped at me and receded, and then Kwong turned his burpgun sideways so that the first burst and recoil would carry the spray of bullets across all five of us.

'You stand!'

We got to our feet slowly, our clothes steaming in the reflected warmth of the sun, and stood motionless in front of our graves. My body shook and I wanted to urinate, and my eyes couldn't look directly at the muzzle of his burpgun. I choked in my throat on a clot of blood and gagged on my hand. Joe Bob's face was drawn tight against the bone, and Bertie was shaking uncontrollably. O.J.'s arms were stiff by his sides, his hands balled into fists, and there were spots of colour on the back of his neck. The Turk's heavy shoulders were bent, his ragged mouth hung open, and the blood and phlegm on his chin dripped on the front of his coat.

'You want talk Ding now?' Kwong said, and smiled at us.

No one spoke. The line of men behind the fence was silent, immobile, some of their heads turned away.

'Who first?'

'Do it, you goddamn bastard!' O.J. shouted. Then his eyes watered and he stared at his feet.

'You first, then, cocksuck.' Kwong raised the burpgun to his shoulder and aimed into O.J.'s face, his eyes bright over the barrel, a spot of saliva in the corner of his mouth. He waited seconds while O.J.'s breath trembled in his throat, then suddenly he swung the gun on its strap and began firing from the waist into the Turk. The first burst caught him in the stomach and chest, and he was knocked backward by the impact into the grave with his arms and legs outspread. The quilted padding in his coat exploded with holes, and one bullet struck him in the chin and blew out the back of his head. His black eyes were dead and frozen with surprise before he hit the ground, and a piece of broken tooth stuck to his lower lip. Kwong stepped to the edge of the grave and emptied his gun, blowing the face and groin apart while the brass shells ejected into the snow. When the chamber locked open he pulled the pan off, inserted a fresh one in its place, and slid back the loading lever with his thumb. The other two guards began to kick snow and dirt from the edge of the grave on top of the Turk's body.

'You next, corpsman. But you kneel.'

The wire fence and the empty faces behind it, the wooden shacks, the yellow brick building where it had all begun, Kwong's squat body and the hills and the brilliance of the snow in the sunlight began to spin around me as though my vision couldn't hold one object in place. My knees went weak and I felt excrement running down my buttocks. The wind spun clouds of powdered snow into the light.

Kwong shoved me backwards into the hole, then leaned over me and pushed the gun barrel into my face. His nostrils were wide and clotted with mucus in the cold.

'You suck. We give you boiled egg,' he said.

I clinched my hands and put my arms over my face. There were crystals of snow, like pieces of glass, in my eyes, and he brought his boot heel down into my stomach and forced the barrel against my teeth. My bowels gave loose entirely, a warm rush across my genitals and thighs, and my heart twisted violently in my chest.

'Good-bye, prick. You no stink so bad later,' and he pulled the trigger.

The chamber snapped empty, a metallic clack that sent all the air rushing out of my lungs.

Kwong and the other two guards were laughing, their faces split in hideous grins under their fur caps. Their bodies seemed to shimmer in the brilliant light. Kwong pushed his boot softly into my groin, pinching downward with the toe.

'I put new clip in and we do again. Each time you guess.'

He spoke to one of the other guards, who handed him a second clip, then he pulled the empty one loose from his burpgun and held them both behind his back.

'Which hand you like, corpsman?'

'You fucking Chink. Get it done!' Joe Bob said.

The guard who had given Kwong the clip struck him back and forth across the face with his open hand. Joe Bob's arms hung at his sides while his head twisted and his skin rang and discoloured with each slap.

'I pick for you, then,' Kwong said, and he dropped one pan into the snow and snapped the second one into the magazine.

He stood above me, his gun balanced on its strap against his waist, and we went through it again, except this time I curled into a ball like a child, my hands over my face, a sickening odour rising from my clothes, and when the firing pin hit the empty chamber I vomited a thick yellow residue of millet and fish heads out of my stomach.

Then I heard Ding speak in Chinese through the megaphone on the far side of the fence. Kwong's boots stepped backward, and I saw the shadow of his burpgun swinging loose from his body. But I couldn't move. My heart thundered against my chest, my body was drained of any further physical resistance, and I kept my face pressed into the wetness of my coat sleeves.

'You lucky. All go to hole now. Another time we have class.'

I heard Joe Bob, Bertie and O.J. crunch past me, but I still couldn't lift my head. The other two guards picked me up from the grave by my coat and threw me headlong into the snow. The crystals of ice burned on my face and in my eyes. I got to my feet slowly and stood in a bent position, the compound and the hills shrinking away in the distance and then leaping towards me out of the sunlight. I tried to stand erect, and an electric pain burst through the small of my back and rushed upward into my head. Excrement dripped down my calves into the snow. I looked over at the half-covered body of the Turk in his shallow grave. One glaring eye was exposed through the snow, and his curled fingers extended upward as though he wanted to touch his toes. In seconds it seemed that the others were already far ahead of me, crunching silently between the guards towards the far end of the compound. Kwong pushed me forward between the shoulder blades with his hand, and I stumbled along in the slick, wet tracks of the others, tripping on my bootlaces, to the square of barbed wire and row of holes and sewer grates where Ding put the reactionaries.

One of the guards opened the gate and used an ice hook to pull the grates off four holes. Three occupied holes were still covered with tarpaulins from the night before, the creased canvas heavy and stiff with new snow. Ding pushed me forward with his burpgun at port arms into the first hole and kicked a GI helmet in on top of me, then slid the grate back in place. He squatted down and leaned his face in silhouette over me.

'You can play with prick when you get cold tonight,' he said.

The hole was eight feet deep and four feet wide, and the mud walls were covered with a dirty film of ice. The inside of the steel helmet was encrusted and foul from the other men who had used it, and the sour smell of urine had soaked into the floor. I heard the grates dropped heavily into place on the other three holes, then the guards moved away in the snow and chained the wire gate shut.

I spent the next six weeks there, although I lost any concept of time after the first three days. We were each given two blankets, and at night the guards marched a progressive into the wire square, and he emptied out our helmets and handed down our food pans before they covered the grates with the tarpaulins. We had to sleep in a sitting position or with our feet propped up against the wall, and there was always a hard pain in my spine, and sometimes at night I dreamed that I was in a chair car on a train and if I could just stretch my legs out in the right direction the pain would go away. Then I would wake with the blankets twisted around me, the small of my back burning, and I would stand in the darkness until my knees went weak.

During the day we would talk to each other by speaking upwards through the iron slits, then our necks would become tired or there wouldn't be anything else to say, and each of us would fall back into his silent fantasies on the floor of the hole. The wounds in my legs had festered and small pieces of lead rose with the pus to the surface of the skin, and many times I slipped off into feverish, distorted scenes that lasted until I heard the ice hook strike the grate at nightfall. Sometimes my eyes stayed fixed on the pattern of iron over my head and the distant, checkered clouds, as though I were staring upwards out of a tunnel, and then I would be fifteen years old again in a winter cornfield, the sun bright on the withered stalks, with the single-shot twelve-gauge against my shoulder and a cottontail racing across the dry rows. I aimed just in front of his head and squeezed off the trigger, and when the gun roared in my ears I knew that I had hit him clean, without destroying any of the meat, and that night Cap would deep-fry him in egg batter and flour for supper. Then I would be back in the Shooting Gallery, and I'd feel the heavy weight of the stretcher in both palms while the potato mashers exploded in our wire and the BAR man searched frantically in the bottom of the ditch for another clip. The wounded Marine on the stretcher stared up at me, his eyes full of terror, as I stumbled forward with his weight over the empty ammunition boxes, then the burpguns raked the ditch and knocked men like piles of rags into the walls, and I dropped him and ran. But in one heart-rushing second I saw the expression of helplessness and betrayal in his eyes, and in my feverish dream I wanted to go back and close his eyes with my fingers and tell him that we were all going to buy it, they had already overrun us, and there was nowhere I could have taken him.

Each day I saw the Shooting Gallery again, sometimes in an entirely different way from previously, and the faces of the men in the ditch became confused; their screams when they were hit and their death cries often sounded like a distant band out of tune with itself, and I tried to go back to the winter cornfield and the smell of oak wood burning in the smokehouse and the rabbit racing towards the blackjack thicket. I knew that if I just held that field in the centre of my mind, or the smokehouse with a shallow depression in the ground under one wall where my father used to push in the oak logs, I could keep everything intact and in its proper place and I wouldn't let Ding or Kwong make me admit that I was guilty of a wounded Marine's death.

Then on a bright, sun-spangled day I would look up through the slits at the drifting clouds and briefly realize, with a sick feeling in my chest, that they didn't care about the Marine, they only wanted me to inform on Ramos and the Negro sergeant, and eventually I might begin to cry in my sleep, as Bertie sometimes did, and one morning ask Kwong to take me into Ding's office. I heard the voices of other men from our shack farther down the row of holes, and Joe Bob whispered hoarsely up through his grate one day that the World War II paratrooper had been machine-gunned and buried next to the Turk. The temperature began to go above freezing in the mid-afternoon, the melted snow ticked into the bottom of the hole, and the reek from the helmet and my own body often made me sick when I tried to eat my bean cakes. My hair and beard were matted with mud and the thick residue of fish heads that I licked from the bottom of my food pan, and my yellow fingernails had grown out like a dead person's. My ribs felt like strips of wood to my touch, and although I had masturbated my first week in the hole, creating geisha girls under me, with their toy, pale faces and sloe eyes, I couldn't hold the image of a woman in my mind more than a few seconds. Then on a wet morning, with the fog lying close against the ground, I heard the ice hook click against the sewer grates and the hushed voices of O.J. and Bertie as the guards helped them out of their holes.

A day later I was still hoping that they would return. It was too easy now to bang on the grate with my food pan and shout for Kwong to pull me out. Whatever I told Ding now wouldn't have any effect on Ramos and the sergeant, I thought, and it was insane to die for men who possibly were already dead themselves. As the fog rolled over me and drifted through the iron slits I went through all the ethical arguments about surrender, and I discovered that there were dozens of ways to justify any human act, even dishonour. I thought of my grandfather, who had fought the most dangerous man in Texas, and I wondered what he would do if he were here now instead of me. I saw the flashes of Wes Hardin's revolver, and his murderous, drunken eyes, and my grandfather standing in the open barn door with the Winchester in his hands. Then Hardin wheeled his horse and charged, his fingers tangled in the mane, the shotgun banging against the saddle, and Old Hack leaped forward and swung his rifle barrel down with both hands into the side of Hardin's head. But his wars had been fought in a different time, between equally armed men, under hot skies and in dusty Texas streets, and death or victory came in a matter of seconds. He hadn't lived in an age when lunatics locked men in filthy holes and turned them into self-hating creatures that were sickened with their own smell.

So that night, at feed time, I knew that Old Hack would understand when I held up my hand silently to the progressive and he pulled me over the edge of the hole on my stomach.

I was the eighth man to inform. The Australian died in the hole, and it took another week for Ding to break the three remaining men from our shack. Then on a dripping, grey morning we all stood at the wire and watched Ramos and the Negro sergeant executed and their bodies thrown into an open latrine.

NINE

It was dark as Rie and I drove through the sloping hills towards the Valley. Her face was soft in the glow of the dashboard, and she rubbed one hand on my shoulder.

'You've kept all that inside you for fifteen years?' she said quietly.

'There aren't a lot of other places to put it.'

'You weren't to blame for their deaths. The others had already informed.'

'That's the strange thing about a certain type of guilt. When you try to confess it and draw the whips across your own back, there's always someone there to tell you that you're really not guilty of anything. Dixon came back from China a year after the war, and I testified against him at his court-martial. But I didn't care what happened to him any more. I only wanted to confess before some type of authority and be exposed publicly for cowardice. Each time that I tried to tell them I had informed, I was told to answer the questions directly and they disregarded anything else I had to say. After they gave Dixon five years, officers shook my hand and wished me luck in law school.'

'What happened to the others?'

'Bertie died of beriberi before the truce. O.J. married an Indian girl and was swelling like a balloon with beer fat, and Joe Bob bought a pool hall in Baton Rouge. Four others from the shack testified against Dixon, and the afternoon that he got his five years we all got drunk together, but we found that we didn't have many good things to talk about.'

She slipped her arm across my chest and kissed me behind the ear, and I felt her wet eyelashes against my skin. I wanted her again, more strongly than I had ever wanted a woman in my life, and I pressed the accelerator down and the rolling highway raced towards me in the headlights. We dropped down into the Valley, and I saw the Rio Grande under the moon and the candlelit windows of the adobe houses on the far side. She pressed her breasts close to me, rubbing her curly hair against my cheek, and I turned on to the main highway towards my motel.

I woke early the next morning and leaned over her and kissed her lightly on the mouth. Her sunburned hair was spread on the pillow, and without opening her eyes she put her arms around my neck and pulled me down on top of her. Her body was warm with sleep, and she widened her thighs and ran her hands down my back and moved her lips across my cheek. She breathed softly in my ear, touching the lobe with her tongue, and each time she pressed her stomach into me I felt my skin burn. Then my eyes were closed and I felt my body go weak, the heat gathering like a flame in my loins, and I tried to rise on my elbows and hold it back, but she held her breasts tight against my chest and put her legs in mine and ran her fingers up my neck into my hair.

'Do it now, Hack, and then we'll do it again and again and again.'

She stretched out her legs and flattened her stomach, and then the flame grew more intense and went out of me in a long heart-beating rush.

It had been years since I had slept with a woman whom I really loved, and the experience now was as strange and wonderful as the first time I had made love to a girl in high school. The times of need with Verisa, which she and I had both grown to accept, with our feigned affection in the dark, and the indifference towards one another when it was over, seemed like a sophisticated imitation of a Tijuana film that we had seen so many times we were no longer embarrassed by it.

Rie lay against me with her arm across my chest and her face close to my cheek, and I felt her large breasts and the heat in her thighs, and she told me about the strange world of revolution and political rage that she came from: her father, the University of Madrid professor, who was marked for execution by the Guardia Civil during the Civil War and walked barefoot across the mountains into France before the border was closed; her Irish mother, a member of the IWW, who worked years for the release of the Scottsboro Boys during the 1930s, went to jail during World War II in protest against the treatment of the Nisei Japanese, and was blacklisted as a schoolteacher in California during the McCarthy era. Rie joined CORE and the Mississippi Freedom Project when she was nineteen and rode across the country to McComb in an old school bus with a boiling radiator and freedom signs painted in white letters on the sides. They were going to integrate lunch counters, bus depots and water fountains and sit in front of segregated hotels with their arms locked in a chain and sing 'We Shall Not Be Moved'. Instead, their bus was burned, they were knocked off lunch-counter stools and beaten senseless by clean-cut high school kids, dragged by their hair along pavements and thrown into police vans, shocked with cattle prods, spat on by housewives, hit with nightsticks and crowded into filthy drunk tanks, and some of them ended up on Parchman Farm.

'Most of the people on our bus were middle-class kids who believed southern cops were a creation out of a Paul Muni movie,' she said. 'We were taught how to roll up in a ball with our hands over our heads when they started swinging the clubs, but nobody really thought they would do it. It was just something to talk about on the bus, and everyone was sure that if it really got tight Mr Clean would appear from somewhere with the Constitution in his hand. After it was all over I was able to accept the cops and what they did and the housewives who were having trouble with their period, but there was one scene I couldn't get out of my head for a long time. The first day in McComb we tried to integrate the lunch counter in Penny's, and a thug hit the black guy next to me in the head with a sugar shaker and split his skin. The black guy tried to look straight ahead and hold his head up level, and a blonde chick of about seventeen took the cap off a salt shaker and poured it into the cut.'

I felt her breast rise under my hand, and I pulled her close against me and pressed her face into my neck and kissed her hair. The smooth curve of her back felt like the graceful line of a statue, and when she looked up from the pillow to be kissed again her almond eyes and the slight separation of her lips made my head swim and then the fire began to build inside me again.

Later, we had breakfast in a wood-frame café filled with farm and ranch families that had come into town for church, then we drove down the highway under the early sun towards Pueblo Verde. There was still dew on the pastures, and the light breaking across the hills cast a purple haze over the sage and short grass. The air was heavy with the smell of morning and the oak thickets and the churned mud around the windmill troughs, and when the breeze changed direction I could smell the horses and cattle in the fields and the burning hickory in a smokehouse. A few clouds were drifting in from the Gulf, and great areas of shadow passed briefly over the cattle and moved across the crest of the hills. For just a moment I thought I could taste rain in the air, and then the sky was clear again and the blacktop highway began to gather pools of light.

There was a union strike meeting and barbecue planned at the Catholic church in the Mexican district that afternoon, and Rie was supposed to provide transportation for the families in the migrant worker camps who didn't have cars. Many of them had been brought in on buses from New Jersey, South Carolina and Florida, and their crew leaders, who contracted the harvest, would do nothing to help the union, and sometimes they refused to take migrants to the next job if they were seen talking with strike organizers. So we waited on the front porch of the union headquarters for a dozen battered cars and pickup trucks to arrive, and then we rolled in a long rattling caravan down a dusty county road to the first of three labour camps.

The land was flat here, without trees, and the weeds in the ditches along the road were covered with dust. The camp was surrounded with a barbed-wire fence, and crude hand-lettered signs were nailed to the cedar posts: NO TRESPASSING, BEWARE OF DOG, TRAILERS FOR COLORED, UNAUTHORIZED PEOPLE STAY OUT. The buildings were made of wood and covered on the sides with red tar paper. The windows didn't have glass or screens, and the wooden shutters were propped open with boards. The corrugated tin roofs reflected brightly in the sun, and I could hear the hum of flies around the community toilets. The yards were bare of grass, and boxes of rubbish stood along the dirt lane that ran through the camp. At intervals between every third cabin there was an iron water spigot where the women washed out nappies and cleaned their dishes, but Rie said the handles were often removed by the camp owner because the children left the water running. The showers were located in a grey concrete enclosure without doors or a roof in the centre of the camp, and when you passed close to it you could smell the wet reek of the walls and the mould and the sour stench of stagnant water in the bottom of the stalls.

Men and women with towels over their shoulders and tooth-brushes went inside together, barefoot brown children in frayed and wash-faded clothes played in the dirt yards, and emaciated

373

dogs with bent spines and mange on their bodies slunk about in the lane. Four dilapidated school buses with broken windows and licence plates from several states on them were parked by a tin trailer with an air-conditioning unit in the window and OFFICE painted above the door. Rie walked up on the porch of a cabin and knocked while I leaned against the car and smoked a cigar. Mexican men walking towards the shower building looked at me and the Cadillac, and I dropped my eyes to the ground and concentrated on the end of my cigar. I felt the same way that I had when I drove into the penitentiary to see Art. I had intruded into a place where even a courteous nod from me and the world I represented was a form of patronization.

Several children stood ten feet from me and stared at my face and the interior of the car. Their black hair was full of nicks and uneven scissor cuts, and their knees and elbows were covered with dirt. A small girl carried a kitten on her shoulder, and one little boy in cut-off overalls had a broken cap pistol in his hand. I smiled at them, but their faces showed no expression in return. I reached inside and turned on the radio, and the insane, blaring voice of some Baptist preacher roared out of the dashboard.

'Do you kids go to school?' I said. Now that's cool, Holland. Come up with another good one like that.

They looked at me with their silent, black eyes.

'We're going to a barbecue this afternoon. Why don't you ask your folks if you can come along?'

The little girl set the kitten down in the dust and pushed at him with her bare foot. The others continued to stare at the strange man who had just dropped from the stratosphere right on his head. I switched off the radio, closed the car door, stuck my hands in the back pockets of my khakis, and looked off into any direction where I wouldn't have to answer those questioning brown faces. Behind me I heard Rie talking with a woman on the front porch of the cabin, and then a man in a dirty T-shirt, with a swollen stomach, as though he had a hernia, stepped out of the tin trailer and walked towards us.

His blue jeans were bursting just below his navel, his crewcut head was beaded with sunlight in the centre, and his fly was only partly zipped. His shoulders were too small for his head, and the blue jeans sagged in the rear. There was a line of sunburn and dandruff where he wore a hat, and his grey eyes went from me to the Cadillac and back again. I took the cigar out of my mouth and nodded at him.

'How do, sir,' he said.

'Pretty fine. How are you today?'

'It's a right nice day, all right.' He ran one hand over his fat hip and looked at a spot over my shoulder. 'I keep the office here, and I'm supposed to take anybody around the camp that wants to see the workers. Sometimes people can't find who they're looking for, and I got all the cabin numbers up in my trailer.'

'Thank you. We're just giving some people a lift to the church.'

He pulled a dead cigar butt from his pocket and put it in his mouth. He lowered his crewcut head and scraped his foot in the dust and rolled the frayed end of the cigar wetly between his lips.

'You see, the soda-pop people that own this land don't like just anybody coming on it. It don't matter to me, but sometimes them union agitators come down here and try to fire up the Mexicans and nigras and shut down the harvest, and I'm supposed to see that nobody like that gets a free run around here. Now, like that Mexican woman up there on the porch. Her husband run off two weeks ago and she's got five kids in there. She can't afford to miss a day's work because some union man won't let her get into the field.'

We talked politely, on and on, while Rie loaded the Cadillac full of children and two huge Negro women. Well, we have a barbecue planned at the church today. I don't think that would bother the soda-pop people. Why don't you have a fresh cigar? Like I don't have nothing against any religion or group of people, but there's a priest down there that's preaching commonism or something at the Mexicans, and it's going to come to a lot of broken heads and people without no paycheques. I can tell you that for a fact, by God. It ain't any skin off my ass, I got that trailer and a salary whether they work or not, but I don't like to see them lose their jobs and get kicked out of their cabins because they listen to people that steals their money in union dues while the citrus burns on the vine. Now, that ain't right. I have a little Jack Daniel's in a flask. Would you like a ditch and another cigar before we leave? . . . No, sir, I'm working right now, but tonight when you come back, drop up to the trailer and I'll buy you a shot with a couple of cold ones behind it . . . Thank you. I'm looking forward to it . . . Yes, sir. You come back, hear?

I drove back out of the barbed-wire gate and headed down the road past the rows of identical cabins with their shimmering tin roofs. The dust rolled away behind me.

'You ought to do public relations for us, you con man,' Rie said, and smiled at me over the heads of the children sitting between us.

The Catholic church was made of white stucco and surrounded by oak and chinaberry trees. Pickup trucks and junker cars were parked in the side yard, and Negro, Mexican and a few white families sat on folding metal chairs with paper plates of barbecued chicken in their laps. Their clothes were sun-faded and starched by hand, and many of the women wore flower-patterned dresses that were sewn from feed sacks. A priest in shirt sleeves was turning chickens on the barbecue grill while the Negro from the union headquarters pulled bottles of beer out of a rubbish bin filled with cracked ice. I parked the car in the shade of a post oak, and the children raced off across the lawn and started throwing chinaberries at each other. In minutes their washed overalls and checkered shirts were stained with the white, sticky milk from the berries.

'Come on. I want you to meet this wild priest,' Rie said.

'I never got along with the clergy.'

'Wait till you catch this guy. He's no ordinary priest.'

'Let's pass.'

'Hack, your prejudices are burning through your face.'

'It's my Baptist background. You can never tell when the Antichrist from Rome is going to sail his submarine across the Atlantic and dock in DeWitt County.'

'Good God,' she said.

'You never went to church in a large tent with a sawdust floor.'

'With a box of snakes at the front of the aisle.'

'There you go,' I said.

'Wow. What an out-of-sight place to come from.' She took my

hand and walked with me across the lawn towards the barbecue pit.

Two Mexican men sat on a table behind the priest and the Negro, playing mariachi guitars with steel picks on their fingers. They looked like brothers with their flat, Indian faces and straw hats slanted over their eyes. The steel picks glinted in the sun as their fingers rolled across the strings.

'What do you say, whiskey brother?' the Negro said. His eyes were red with either a hangover or the beginnings of a new drunk, and his breath was heavy with alcohol and snuff. He popped the cap off a sweating bottle of Lone Star and handed it to me. The foam slipped down the side over my hand.

'I guess I have a couple of shots in the car if the smoke gets too much for you,' I said. Then it struck me, as I looked at his cannonball head and remembered the humiliation I had seen in his face the other night, that I had never learned his name.

'I'm cool today, brother,' he said. 'Saturday's for drinking, and Sunday you catch all kinds of sunshine with these church people.'

The priest looked like a longshoreman. His thick arms were covered with black hair, and he had a broad Irish face with a nose like Babe Ruth and a wide neck and powerful shoulders under his white shirt. His black eyes were quick, and when Rie introduced us I had the feeling that he had done many other things before he had become a priest.

'You handled Art's appeal, didn't you?' he said.

'Yes, I did.' I took a cigar from my pocket and peeled off the wrapper.

'His family appreciated it a great deal. The rest of us did, too.'

'I knew him in the service,' I said.

'He told me. I saw him before he was sent to prison.'

I chewed off the tip of my cigar and looked away at the line of battered cars and trucks gleaming in the sunlight. Overhead, two bluejays were fighting in the chinaberry tree. Every clergyman has to be so goddamn frank, I thought.

'Have you been here very long, Father?'

'Three months, but I'm being transferred to Salt Lake in September.'

'He's the church's favourite ping-pong ball,' Rie said, and laughed. 'He's had five parishes in six years. Kicked out of New Orleans, Compton, California, the Pima reservation in Arizona, and now he's going to turn the Mormons on. I bet those boys will be a real riot.'

'You're not improving my image, Rie.'

'Listen. This was the guy that took black children through those lines of screaming women and thugs when the elementary schools were integrated in New Orleans. He dumped a cop on his ass in the school doorway and said mass in a Negro church the same day in Plaquemines Parish while the Klan burned crosses on the front lawn.'

'Rie's given to hyperbole sometimes, Mr Holland.'

'No, I'm afraid she's pretty exact most of the time, Father,' I said.

'Well, at least it wasn't that dramatic. A little pushing and shoving and a few truck drivers sitting on the kerb with more Irish in them than they deserve.'

He filled two paper plates with chicken, rice dressing and garlic bread, and handed them to us. There were small scars around his knuckles, and his wrists and forearms were as thick and hard as cordwood. He smelled of hickory smoke from the fire, and his balding head glistened with perspiration in the broken shade. Rie was right – he wasn't an ordinary man. I remembered the television newsreels about the priest and ex-paratrooper chaplain who had led terrified Negro children from the buses through the spittle and curses in front of an elementary school in New Orleans in 1961. I also recalled the one short film clip that showed him backing down four large men who had poured beer on the children as they walked up the school steps.

We sat in the shade and ate from our paper plates and drank bottles of Lone Star while the guitar players picked and sang their songs about infidelity, their love for peasant girls in hot Mexican villages, and Villa's raid on a train loaded with *federales* and machine-guns mounted on flatcars. The children had established forts behind two lines of folding chairs and chinaberries flew back and forth and pinged against the metal, and because it was somebody's birthday the Negro climbed up an oak tree, grabbing the trunk with his knees, and hung a *piñata* stuffed with candy from a piece of cloth clothesline. Then he formed all the children into a line, in stair-step fashion, with a foaming beer in his hand, and gave the first child a sawed-off broom handle to swing against the cardboard-crêpe-paper horse turning dizzily in the dappled light. The children flailed the *piñata*, and twists of candy showered out over their heads. I borrowed a guitar from one of the musicians and ran my fingers over the strings. The sound hole was inlaid with an Indian design, and there were deep scratches on the face from the steel picks that the owner used.

'Go ahead and boil them cabbages down,' Rie said.

I couldn't be profane in front of the priest.

'I never play too well sober. Wrong mental atmosphere for hillbilly guitar pickers,' I said.

'Will you go ahead?' she said. Her eyes took on that wonderful brightness they had when she was extremely happy.

I tuned the guitar into D and ran a Jimmie Rodgers progression all the way down the neck, then bridged into an old Woody Guthrie and Cisco Houston song while the Negro opened more bottles of Lone Star and the children rolled over one another in the grass after the candy.

> Ezekiel saw that wheel a-whirling
> Way up in the middle of the air
> Tell you what a bootlegger he will do
> Sell you liquor and mix it with brew
> Way in the middle of the air.

Later, the men on the strike committee pulled two long tables and several benches together in the sun. They sat in the glaring heat, sweat dripping from inside their straw hats over their faces, their browned forearms on the hot wood, as though the sunlight were no different from the shade a few feet away. The warm beer bottles in their hands were bursting with amber light, and their faces were all of one calm and intent expression while Rie spoke to them in Spanish. Her voice was even and flat while she looked quietly back and forth at the two rows of men, and although my

Tex-Mex was good enough so that I could understand most of what she said, I realized she was speaking in a frame of reference that had always belonged in the wretched Mexican hovels on the other side of my property line. As I leaned against an oak trunk, watching them through my sunglasses and sipping a beer, I thought about Art's description of the anglo roaring down the highway in his Cadillac towards the next Holiday Inn, unaware of anything beyond the billboards that flashed by him like a kaleidoscopic vision. So have another beer on that one, Holland, I thought. And polish your goddamn Spanish.

It was late afternoon and hot when the barbecue ended. A dry wind was blowing from the Gulf, and dust devils spun out of the dirt road and whirled away in the fields. We loaded the children and the two Negro women into the car and drove back to the migrant camp. The tarpaper shacks seemed to glow with the heat, and my friend the camp manager was sprinkling the dirt lane in front of his trailer with a garden hose. His clothes were even filthier than they had been that morning, and his face had a red, whiskey flush. He turned off the water and walked over to the car. The fat in his pot stomach bulged against his T-shirt, and his odour was so strong that I opened the door part way to keep him a few feet from me.

'There was a deputy sheriff down here this afternoon, and he says you're working with them union people.'

'Must be somebody else.' I watched Rie on the front porch of one of the cabins.

'He knowed this car, and he described you exactly. Even them cigars.'

'What else did he have to say?'

'He says he's going to lock your ass in jail. And I'll tell you something else, buddy. You come down here and give me a lot of shit about taking them people to a church barbecue. I don't like nobody lying to me when they come on the property, and I got a ball bat up there in the trailer to handle anybody that tries to make my job harder than it is.'

I bit into the soft wetness of my cigar and closed the door carefully. I felt the anger draw tight across my chest, the blood swelling in my temples, and I looked straight ahead at the sunlight beating down on his silver trailer. I coughed on my cigar smoke and picked a piece of tobacco off my lip.

'Well, sir, we should be gone in a few minutes,' I said.

'You better get your luck off that porch and haul it down the road a lot faster than that.'

I opened the door again, hard, so that it hit him sharply in the knees and stomach, and looked into his face.

'You're about two remarks ahead of the game right now, podner,' I said. 'Say anything more and you're going to have problems that you never thought about. Also, if you have any plans about using that baseball bat, you'd better find an apple box to stand on first.'

His red face was caught between angry insult and fear, and the sweat glistened in his brows over his lead-grey eyes.

'You're trespassing, and I'm putting in a call to the sheriff's office,' he said, and walked away in the dust towards his trailer.

Rie got back in the car, and I closed the windows, turned on the air conditioner as high as it would go, and we rolled out of the front gate and headed down the county road towards town. There were buzzards drifting high in the sky on the wind stream, and the sun burned white as a chemical flame. The rocks and alkali dust on the road roared away under the Cadillac.

'Say, take it easy, Lone Ranger,' Rie said.

'I've been easy all my life. One of these days I'm going to blow all my Kool-Aid and rearrange a guy like that for a long time.'

She put her hand on my arm. 'That's not your kind of scene, Hack.'

'I'm up to my eyes with rednecks that come on with baseball bats.'

'Hey, man, you're not acting like a good con man at all. What did he say?'

'Nothing. He's defending the soda-pop people.'

'He clicked a couple of bad tumblers over in your brain about something.'

'I burn out a tube once in a while with the chewing-tobacco account. Forget it.'

'I heard him say something about getting your luck off the porch. Was that it?'

'Look, Rie, I was raised by a strange southern man who believed that any kind of anger was a violation of some aristocratic principle. So I turn the burner down every time it starts to flare, and sometimes I get left with a broken handle in my hand.'

'What did he mean?'

The air conditioning was dripping moisture.

'A guy like that doesn't mean anything,' I said. 'The words just spill out of a junk box in his head.'

'Talk straight, Hack.'

'It's a racial remark.'

'Is it important to you?'

I felt my heart quicken, because we both knew now why he had got inside me.

'All right, I lived around that shit all my life, and maybe I'm not as far removed from it as I thought. If I was a cool city attorney with *liberal* tattooed on my forehead I would have yawned and rolled up the window on him. But I never could deal with people abstractly, and he stuck his finger in the wrong place.'

The perspiration on my face felt cold in the jet of air from the dashboard. I looked straight ahead at the white road and waited for her to speak. Instead, she slipped close to me and kissed me behind the ear.

'You great goddamn woman,' I said, and hit the road shoulder in a spray of rocks when I pulled her to me.

'Let's go back to the house,' she said, and put her hand under my shirt and rubbed her fingers along my belt line.

'What about those college kids and the Negro?'

'I already asked them to do something else this afternoon.'

She looked up at me with her bright, happy eyes, and I wondered when I would stop discovering things about her.

I bought a bottle of Cold Duck in town, and we drove down the corrugated road through the Mexican district to the union headquarters. The beer tavern was roaring with noise, and fat women sat on the front porches of their paint-blistered houses, fanning themselves in the heat. Rie walked up the path in front of me, lifting her shirt off her breasts with her fingertips. The rusted Dr Pepper thermometer nailed to the porch just read 106 degrees, and the sky was so hot and blue that a cloud would have looked like an ugly scratch on it. Rie opened the screen door and a yellow envelope fell down from the jamb at her feet.

'Hey, buddy, somebody found you,' she said.

I set the heavy bottle of Cold Duck on the porch railing and tore open the telegram with my finger. Flies hummed in the shade of the building.

WHERE THE HELL ARE YOU ANYWAY. HAD TO CANCEL SPEECH LAST NITE IN SAN ANTONIO. SENATOR HAS CALLED THREE TIMES. VERISA QUITE WORRIED. HACK DO YOU WANT IN OR OUT. BAILEY.

Rie looked at me quietly with her back against the screen.

'It's just my goddamn brother with his peptic ulcer,' I said.

'What is it?'

'I was supposed to make a speech to the Lions or Rotary or one of those good-guy bunches last night.'

'Is that all of it?' Her quiet eyes watched my face.

'Bailey thinks an offence against the business community has the historical importance of World War III.' I folded the telegram and put it in my shirt pocket. 'He's probably swallowing pills by the bottle right now. Do you have a telephone?'

'There's one down in the beer joint.'

'I'll be back in a few minutes. Put the wine in the ice box.'

'All right, Hack.'

'I mean, I don't want the poor bastard to rupture his ulcer on a Sunday.'

'Go on. I'll be here.'

I walked down the road in the hot light to the tavern. Inside, the bar was crowded with Mexican field hands and cedar-cutters, dancers bumped against the plastic jukebox, and billiard balls clattered across the torn, green covering of an old pool table. Cigarette smoke drifted in clouds against the ceiling. I called the house collect from the pay phone on the wall, bending into the receiver away from the noise, then I heard Bailey's voice on the other end of the line.

'Where are you?' he said.

'In a bowling alley. What's it sound like?'

'I mean, where?'

'In Pueblo Verde, where you sent your telegram. What the hell are you doing at the house, anyway?'

'Verisa's pretty upset. You'd better get back home.'

'What is this shit, Bailey? You knew why I had to leave Friday.'

'The Senator wasn't very pleasant with her when he called here, and maybe all of us are just a little tired of you not showing up when you're supposed to. They waited the banquet an hour for you before they called our answering service, and I had to drive to San Antonio at ten o'clock and offer an apology for you.'

'Look, you arranged that crap without asking me first, and you knew when I left Austin that I wouldn't be back this weekend. So you hang that bag of shit on the right pair of horns, buddy. And if the Senator wants to be unpleasant with someone, I'll give you this number or the one at the motel.'

'Why do you want to behave like this, Hack? You've got all the easy things right in your hand.'

A pair of drunken dancers knocked against me, and then waved their hands at me, smiling, as they danced back on to the floor in the roar of noise.

'I just want a goddamn weekend free of migraine headaches and Kiwanians and telegrams,' I said. 'I'll be back at the office in a couple of days. In the meantime you can schedule yourself for the next round of speeches with the civic club account.'

But he was already off the phone.

'Hack?' Verisa said.

'Yeah.' I closed my eyes against her voice.

'I'm not going to say much to you. I warned you in Houston what I'd do if you blew this for us. I've got enough to go into court and win almost all of it. I'll take the house, the land, and the controlling share of the wells, and you can start over again with your alcoholic law practice.'

I took a breath and waited a moment on that one.

'I should have called you, but I didn't have time,' I said, evenly. 'I thought Bailey would tell you why I had to leave.'

'Oh, my God.'

I started to answer, and instead looked out at the dancers on the floor.

'Why should he have to tell me anything?' she said. 'You seem to have a strange idea that Bailey should take care of all your unpleasant marital obligations. He was embarrassed enough apologizing for you last night.'

'Well, I'm a little worn out with people selling me by the pound and then telling me how embarrassed they are for me. And it also strikes me that nobody was ever concerned if I was called out of town by a paying client. Maybe some people wouldn't get their ovaries so dilated if I was on another case besides a Mexican farm worker's.'

I heard her breath in the phone, and then, 'You bastard.'

I hung up the receiver softly and walked back outside into the sunlight. The road was blinding in the heat, and the noise from the jukebox and Verisa's voice were still loud in my head. I lit a cigar, sweating, and imagined the stunted rage she was now in. Poor old Bailey, I thought. He would stay at the house the rest of the evening, talking quietly to her while her eyes burned at the wall, and then he would begin to consider all the side streets they could use for my election in November, regardless of what I did in the meantime. He would drink cups of caffeine-free coffee with his ulcer pills, flicking over the alternatives in his mind, and soon he would forget that Verisa was in the room. Or maybe the Senator would phone again, and both of their faces would focus anxiously, their eyes reflecting into one another across the kitchen table, while Bailey's voice measured out his assurances about my sincerity in the campaign and my deep regret that I wasn't able to be with the Kiwanians (or whatever) last night. Then they would both wonder if we would ever get to that marble and green island of power where you carried a small, stamped gold key in your watch pocket.

Rie was sitting on the front steps with her back against the porch railing and one leg drawn up before her. She had changed into a pair of faded Navy ducks, with the laces on the back, and a rose-flowered silk shirt, and in the shade she looked as cool and beautiful as a piece of dark sculpture. There was an unopened can of Lone Star and a tall, cone glass by her foot. My shirt stuck wetly to my shoulders, and my sunglasses were filmed with perspiration.

'You look like Tom Joad beating his way out of the Dust Bowl,' she said. 'You'd better have one of these.'

I sat down beside her and opened the can of beer. The tin was cold against my hand, and the foam rushed up in the glass and streamed over the lip. I took my glasses off and wiped the perspiration and dust out of my eyes, but I avoided looking at her face. There was a broken anthill by the edge of the path, with a deep boot print in one side, and thousands of ants were moving over one another in a hot swarm.

'Was everything cool back there?' she said.

'Yeah.' I drank out of the beer – and squinted my eyes into the bright light. 'I'm going to give Bailey a frontal lobotomy team for Christmas. Or a can of alum to drink. He has a remarkable talent for calling up everything bad in a person within seconds.'

I heard her take her cigarettes out of her shirt pocket and rip back the cover.

'He's not a bad guy. He's just so goddamn obtuse sometimes.'

'Hack, I'm not pressing you.'

'Then who the hell is?'

'I don't care what you belong to outside of here.'

I looked at her quiet, beautiful face in the shade.

'I love to be a part of your Saturday morning fishing world and your crazy Indian graves,' she said. 'I'd never ask you about anything back there in Austin.'

I took the cigarette from her hand and drew in on the smoke. The trees in the dirt yards along the street were still and green in the heat.

'I put the wine on a block of ice,' she said.

'Maybe we had better drink that, then,' I said. 'What do you think, good-looking?'

She smiled at me with her eyes full of light again, and we walked into the back of the house and opened the tall, dark bottle of Cold Duck. I chipped off a bowl full of ice from the block in the top of the cooler and set it in front of the fan in the bedroom so the wind stream would blow cool across the bed. The sun burned yellow against the window shade, and across the river in Mexico a calf stuck in the mudflat was bawling for its mother. Rie undressed in the half light and put her arms around my shoulders, and I pressed my face into her neck and felt her smooth stomach and breasts curve against me.

That evening we drove over to the Gulf in the fading, lilac twilight, and just before the highway turned out of the citrus fields on to the coast we could smell the salt in the air and the dead seaweed at the edge of the surf. The water was slate-green, and the whitecaps crashed against the sand and boiled in deep pools, and then sucked out again with the undertow. Brown pelicans and seagulls, like fat white cigars, dipped out of the sky over the water, picking small fish from the crest of the waves with their beaks, and in the distance we could see the gas flares and strings of lights on offshore oil rigs and quarter boats. The red sun was as big as a planet on the horizon, and the light broke across the water in long bands of scarlet. The stretch of brown beach and the palm trees were covered with a dark, crimson glow, and then the sun moved deeper into the Gulf, with a strip of black cloud across its flaming edge, and the moon began to rise behind us over the land.

I bought another bottle of Cold Duck and some chicken sandwiches in a restaurant, and a Mexican family camped on the beach sold us two salt-water cane poles with treble hooks and a carton of live shrimp. The sand was still warm from the sun, and we sat behind a dune out of the wind and ate the sandwiches and drank half the bottle of wine, then I baited the three-pronged hooks with the shrimp, slipped the lead sinkers close to the bottom of the line, and we waded into the surf to fish the bottom for channel cat and flounder. The tide began to come in, and the waves broke across the rotted wooden pilings in the jetties, and when the wind shifted across the water we could smell the dead shellfish and baked scales and salt in the pilings. Rie held her cane pole under her arm, with both hands raised in front of her, while the waves swelled against her breasts. The water was splintered with moonlight, and the salt spray in her hair looked like drops of crystal. Then the tip of her pole arched into the water and went all the way to the bottom.

'What do I do now, Lone Ranger?' she shouted.

'Keep his head up or he'll break it.'

She leaned backwards and strained with both hands, and a cloud of sand rose in the swell at the end of her pole. Then the line pulled out at an angle, quivering, and the pole went down again. She looked at me helplessly, her face shining with water and moonlight.

'Walk him into the shore,' I said.

A large wave crested in front of her and broke across her shoulders.

'Hack, you bastard.'

'You have to learn these things to overcome your Yankee childhood,' I said.

She tried to slip the pole back under her arm and raise it again, but the fish had turned into the waves and was pulling hard for the bottom. I waded over to her and picked up the line with both hands at the water and walked backwards with it towards the beach. The line tightened around my knuckles and cut into the skin, and when I reached the shallows I could see the long blue outline of the channel cat shaking his head against the three hooks caught in his mouth. I dragged him up on the sand and placed my fingers carefully around his spiked ventral fins and made one cut with my pocket knife through his gill and across the spine. He flipped quietly in the sand and then lay still.

'God, the things you Southerners do for kicks,' she said.

But I could see the excitement in her face at having caught a large and beautiful blue-black fish under the moon in waves up to her shoulders.

'It's against Texas law to keep this kind,' I said. 'Maybe we'd better flip him back in.'

She stepped down on the top of my bare foot and pinched my arm with her fingernails. I held her close to me and kissed her wet hair and dried her face against my shirt. I could taste the salt on her skin and smell the Gulf wind in her hair, and she put her arms inside my shirt and ran her hands over my back.

We gave the channel cat, the poles and the remaining shrimp to the Mexican family, and built a fire on the sand out of dried wood and dead palm fronds. The wind caught the flames and sent sparks twisting into the sky, and the fronds, coated with sand, and the polished twists of wood snapped in the fire and burst apart in a yellow blaze. We drank the rest of the wine and sat inside the heat with our clothes steaming. On the southern horizon dark storm clouds were building over the water. The moon was high, and I could see the clouds rolling in a heavy wind off the Mexican coast, and a few large whitecaps were hitting the pilings around the oil derricks. The air had become cooler, and there was a wet smell of electricity in the air. I lit a cigar, stuck the cork in the wine bottle, and threw it end over end into the surf.

'We really get it on tomorrow, don't we, babe?' I said.

She ticked the top of my hand with her finger and looked into the fire.

The wind was blowing in gusts the next morning when we arrived at the cannery and loading platform where the union was setting up its main picket. The sun was brown in the swirling clouds of dust from the fields, and I could still smell the wet electric odour of a storm. Dozens of junker cars and pickup trucks with crude wood shelters on the back were parked along the railway tracks, and Negro and Mexican field workers had formed a long line in front of the platform where the harvest trucks would unload. Their picket signs flopped and bent in the wind, and the sand blew in their faces, while a man in slacks and a tie walked back and forth above them, waving his arms, and told them to get off the company's property. His tie was blown over his shoulder and his glasses were filmed with grit, and after he was ignored by everyone on the picket he went into his office and came back with a camera and began taking pictures. Two Texas Rangers in sunglasses and Stetson hats leaned against a state car, watching with their tanned, expressionless faces. Their uniforms were ironed as stiff as tin. The priest, in Roman collar, stood in the back of a stake truck, with his sleeves rolled over his thick arms, handing out picket signs to the people who had just arrived, and I saw one of the Rangers raise his finger, aim at the priest, and say something to his partner.

'I didn't think this was your kind of scene, whiskey brother.'

It was the Negro from the union headquarters, and he was still drunk. His slick face was covered with dust, and he had a wad of snuff under his lip.

'What the hell is your name, anyway?' I said.

'What's a name, man?' He took a bottle of port wine from his back pocket and unscrewed the cap. 'Sam, Tom, You. People give me a lot of them. But I like Mojo Hand the best. That's a name with shine. It feels good in your mouth just like all these sweet grapes.'

'Put the wine away till later,' Rie said.

'Those dicks ain't going to bother me. They know a nigger can't change nothing around here. They want to strum some white heads.' He drank from the bottle and coughed on the tobacco juice in his mouth.,

'They'll use anything they can for the newspapers,' Rie said.

'You know it don't make any difference what we do out here today. It's going to read the same way tomorrow morning. Ain't that right, whiskey brother? They could bust up Jesus with them billy clubs and the people would find out how He started a riot.'

'Let's hang a good one on later,' I said.

'Where you been, man? There ain't going to be no later. These dudes have just been practising so far.'

'Everything is cool now, isn't it?' I said.

He pulled on the bottle again and laughed, spilling the wine over his lips. 'Out of sight. But you're right. You got to keep thinking cool, cousin. You got to keep a little shine in your name.'

'We don't want a bust this early,' Rie said. 'Stay in the car until the rest of our people get here.'

But he wasn't looking at us any longer. His red eyes stared over my shoulder in the direction of the county road, and I turned around and saw the two black and white sheriff's cars, followed by three carloads of townspeople, rolling towards us in the dust. The whip aerials sprang back and forth on their springs, and muscular, shirt-sleeved arms hung out of the windows of the other cars, beating against the door sides. The wind flattened the clouds of dust across the road, and a moment later two Texas Ranger cars closed the distance with the rest of the caravan.

'It ain't cool no more, whiskey brother,' the Negro said.

The line of cars pulled into the gravel bedding along the railway track, and the Rangers and deputy sheriffs walked casually towards the two Rangers in sunglasses who were leaning against their car and looking at the priest. The other men stayed behind and formed in a group by a freight car, their hands in their back pockets, their faces tight, spitting tobacco juice into the rocks, and glaring at the Mexicans and the Negroes. They had crewcuts and faces put together out of shingles, and they wore T-shirts or blue-jean jackets with the sleeves cut off at the armpits. There were tattoos of Confederate flags and Easter crosses, Mother and the United States Marine Corps, inscriptions to Billy Sue and Norma Jean, and even the young ones had pot stomachs. They looked like everyone who was ever kicked out of a rural Texas high school.

Then I saw my friend from the sheriff's office. He walked from behind the freight car with a filter-tipped cigar between his teeth, his khaki trousers tucked inside his half-top boots, and his wide leather cartridge belt pulled tight across his flat stomach. He spoke quietly to the men in T-shirts and denim jackets, smiling, his hands on his hips, and then he and the others turned their faces towards me at one time. His green, yellow-flecked eyes were filled with an intense delight, and his lips pressed down softly on the cigar tip.

'Let's get into the picket before it starts,' Rie said.

I walked with her to the back of the stake truck, where the priest was still handing down signs. The wind whipped the dust in our faces, and swollen rain clouds were rolling over the horizon. The air was becoming cooler, and I heard the first dull rip of thunder in the distance. The priest wiped his face on his shirt sleeve and grinned at us.

'How are you, Mr Holland? We can use a good man from the establishment,' he said.

'I know a two-word reply to that, Father,' I said.

'I believe I've heard it.'

'Mojo's drunk. Try to get him into the truck,' Rie said.

'He's not fond of listening to church people,' the priest said.

'There's some badass types back by the freight car, and he's been in a winehead mood since some kids tried to get it on with him the other night,' she said.

'I'll watch him,' he said.

'Watch that bunch of assholes, too. One of the dicks was winding them up.'

The priest looked over at one of the Rangers who was talking into the microphone of his mobile radio.

'Get into the line. They're going to start moving in a few minutes,' he said.

Rie picked up two cardboard signs tacked on laths and handed me one of them. A single, large drop of rain splattered on the black eagle over the word HUELGA.

'Come on,' she said.

'Can I get a cigar lit first, for God's sake?' I said.

'We don't want anybody arrested outside the picket, Hack.'

'All right, goddamn. Just a minute.'

For some reason I hadn't yet accepted the fact that I would be walking on a picket line that Monday morning, or any morning, for that matter. The sign bent backwards in my hands against the wind, flopping loudly, and my knees felt disjointed as I followed her into the slow line of Mexicans and Negroes in their faded work clothes, battered straw hats, and dresses splitting at the hips. Drops of rain made puckered dimples in the dust, and the wind blew cool inside my shirt, but I was perspiring under my arms, and my face was burning as though I had just done something obscene in public. I saw the eyes of the sheriff's deputies, the Rangers and the pool-room account watching me, and my head became light and my cigar tasted bitter and dry in my mouth. I felt as though I had walked naked in front of a comic audience. A fat Negro woman behind me held her child, in cut-off overalls, with one hand and her picket sign in the other. She wore a pair of rippled stockings over the varicose veins in her legs.

'You don't worry about these children. They ain't going to bother them,' she said.

I looked away from her brown eyes at the man in slacks and tie on the platform. He was still taking pictures, and his face was quivering at the outrage he had seen that day against the principle of private property. Storm clouds covered the sun, and the fields were suddenly darkened and the shadows leaped across the cannery, the freight cars and the county road. The men in T-shirts and denim jackets were now pulling the caps on hot cans of beer and spilling the foam down their necks and chests.

'How you doing?' Rie said.

'I think my respect for the demonstrator just went up a couple of points.'

'Look, if those bastards move in on us, you have to take it. OK?'

'That doesn't sound cool.'

'No shit, Hack. They're waiting for reasons to split heads.'

'All right, but when do we finish this caper?'

'We've only been on the picket ten minutes, babe.'

Then I saw a television news car pull into the gravel bedding by the railway track. Two young men got out with cameras attached to half-moon braces that fitted against the shoulder. They walked over to the group of law officers by the squad cars, their faces full of confident foreknowledge about their story, and for the first time it struck me that I had never seen a newsman begin a story any differently; without thinking, they went first to the official source before they considered the people on the other end of the equation.

One of them walked towards the picket and did a sweeping, random shot with his camera, the brace pulled tight against his shoulder. Then he lowered the camera and looked at me steadily, his face as bland and unembarrassed as a dough pan. I threw my cigar away and looked back at him with my meanest, southpaw ninth-innings expression. He walked back to his friend and began talking, and the two of them stared in my direction.

'I believe a couple of kids just earned a pay rise,' I said.

'I bet you're handsome on film,' Rie said.

'Well, here they come. You want to do my PR work?'

One of them already had his camera whirring before they were close enough to speak. They had forgotten the cops and the long line of migrant workers; they were both concentrated on the little piece of entrail they might carry back to the station.

'Are you widening your district, Mr Holland?' His voice was good-natured, and he smiled at me in his best college fraternity fashion.

'No, no,' I said, in my best humorous fashion.

Isn't this a delightful game we're about to play, I thought.

'Do you think your support of the union will affect your

election?' He held the microphone towards me, but his eyes were looking at Rie.

'I couldn't tell you that, buddy.'

'The farm corporations consider this an illegal strike. Do you have a comment on that?'

'I don't know how it can be illegal to ask for a higher wage.'

'Does the union plan a strike in your area?' He was cocking the rifle now, but his face looked as sincerely inquisitive as a reverent schoolboy's.

'Not that I know of.'

'Does that mean the conditions of the migrant farm workers are better in your area?'

'No, it doesn't,' I said. 'But I tell you what, buddy. I need a cigar real bad right now, and it's hell lighting up in this wind with one hand. So how about holding this sign for a minute, and I can get one of these awful things lit and we can talk all day. That's right, just take it in your hand and fold your fingers around the stick.'

His face went blank, the lath straining in his palm, and his eyes flicked at his partner and the cops by the railway track. I used three matches to light my cigar while he blinked against the raindrops and shifted his feet in the dust.

'I appreciate that,' I said. 'Say, did you interview any of those fellows over by the freight car? I bet that bunch of boys would give you some deathless lines.'

'We just do a job, Mr Holland.'

'I bet you'll get there with it, too,' I said.

'Would you like to say something else, sir?' His face was mean now, the eyes dirty.

'You've got a whole reel of good stuff there, pal.'

He turned away from me and put the microphone in front of Rie. The sky was almost completely dark, except for the thin line of yellow light on the distant hills. His partner moved around behind him so the lens would catch me in the same shot with Rie.

'Do you think the families in the farm camps will suffer because of the strike?'

'Why don't you fuck off, man?' Rie said.

Then one of the men by the freight car threw an empty beer

can at the picket line. It missed a Negro woman's head and clattered across the loading platform. The two newsmen backed away from us with their cameras turning. A moment later three more carloads of townspeople arrived and swelled into the group by the freight car, and then one man stepped out from them and started walking towards us, and the rest followed. He wore a tin construction hat back on his shaved head, steel-toed work boots, and denim clothes that were splattered with drilling mud from an oil rig. His eyes had a wet, yellow cast to them, and his front teeth were brown with chewing tobacco. His scrotum bulged in his blue jeans between his heavy thighs, and he stretched out his huge arms, his hands in fists, as though he were just awakening from sleep, and spat a stream of tobacco juice in the dirt.

'Hey, buddy,' he said to me. 'Do you eat Mexican pussy?'

I looked straight ahead, my face burning.

'You better get that chili off your mouth, then,' he said.

'Leave that man alone, J.R. You know a lawyer don't have to eat pussy,' another said.

'This one does. You get your nose right in it, don't you?'

The looming outline of the cannery and the rusted freight cars in silhouette against the light rain seemed to shrink and expand before my eyes. My knuckles whitened on the sign lath, and my breath caught in my throat.

'He might beat you to death with that cardboard, J.R.'

'Do you get to try some of these nigger girls?' the oilfield worker said.

My eyes watered and I felt myself leaping towards him before I had even moved or changed my line of vision, but several men behind him shouted and laughed at one time in a phlegmy roar, and he turned his wide back to me. Mojo had been sitting in the cab of the stake truck with his wine bottle until it was empty, and then had decided to join the picket. His shirt was unbuttoned to the waist, his socks were pulled down over his heels, and he walked towards the line as though his knees were connected with broken hinges. There was a patch of snuff on the corner of his lip, and the drops of rain slid over his cannonball head like streaks of black ivory. An unopened can of beer flew out of the crowd and hit him above the eye. He reeled backwards, still standing, and pressed his hand like a fielder's glove against his head, the blood dripping down from his dark palm. His uncovered eye was wide and rolling with pain and shock.

'Goddamn,' I said.

'Don't, Hack,' Rie said.

'They hurt him bad.'

'Stay in the line,' she said.

Mojo bent forward and let the blood run down his forearm on to the ground, then he started walking towards us again as though he were holding a cracked flowerpot delicately in place. A man in khaki clothes with a green cloth cap on and a Lima watch fob in his pocket stepped into his path and kicked his feet out from under him. Mojo struck the ground headlong, and his face was covered with strings of dust and blood.

'This is too goddamn much, Rie,' I said.

'Don't get out of the line. They'll kill him if you do,' she said.

He pushed himself up from the ground and stood erect, the ragged cut on his head already swelling like a baseball. The wind blew his shirt straight out from his body, and his chest heaved and his nostrils dilated when he breathed.

'You can bust me 'cause I'm winehead now, but you ain't going to beat all these people,' he said. 'They too many for you, and they're going to stand all over this place when you all are long gone.'

The oilfield worker moved towards him, his buttocks flexing inside his blue jeans, but two deputy sheriffs walked up behind Mojo and led him away by each arm towards their car. Before they put handcuffs on him, they stripped off his shirt and wrapped it in a twisted knot around his head.

The car rolled off down the road, with Mojo in the back behind the wire screen, his blood-soaked shirt like a dark smear against the closed glass.

The priest was next, and they had a special dislike for him as a Catholic clergyman. The man in the khaki clothes shook up a hot beer and sprayed it on him, and the oilfield worker put his hot breath in the priest's face and insulted him with every whorehouse statement he could make. Several women had joined the crowd, and they rasped at him with their contorted faces, their eyes shrunken inward at some terrible anger, and then one spat on him. She was small and stunted, her thin arms were puckered and wrinkled at the armpits, and her electric hair was scraped back in a tangle over the thinning places in her head, but she gathered all the energy and juice in her wasted body and spat it in an ugly string over his chest.

He blinked his eyes against the spittle and obscenities, but he kept his face straight ahead, his big hands folded around the sign lath, and never broke his step in the line. His composure enraged the women to the point that they were shouting at him incoherently, their heads bent forward like snakes, the veins in their throats bursting against the skin. Then the deputy sheriff who had arrested me walked to the back of the crowd, put his hand on the oilfield worker's shoulder, and motioned in my direction. Across the railway track I saw two large police vans with cage doors on the back turn off the county road into the cannery gate, and then the crowd came towards me.

Their faces were tight with anger, the lips dry, the eyes hot and receded in the head, as though their own rage had dried out all the fluids in their bodies. In the gloom and swirling patterns of rain their skin looked white and stretched over the bone. Lightning struck against the hills, and the wind was beginning to strip the cotton in the fields.

'We ain't got a lot of time for you, lawyer. So you know what I'm going to do?' the oilfield worker said, and put a half plug of tobacco in his mouth. He pushed it into his jaw with his tongue and chewed it into pulp, then cleaned the juice off his lip with his finger. 'I ain't going to touch you with my hand. I'm just going to show you how we treat dip shit around here. Now, when you get tired of it, all you got to do is tear that sign up and walk to your car. There won't nobody hurt you.'

'I'll tell you something, motherfucker,' I said. 'You spit on me and I'll take your head off.'

The man in the khaki clothes with the green cap reached out with his fist, off balance, as though he were leaping at a departing train, and struck me in a downward swing across the nose. His ring peeled back the skin, and I felt the blood swell to the surface. I stared at them all stupidly, with the sign in my hands, while my eyes filmed and burned. The oil worker was grinning at me.

'You want to cut bait, dip shit?' he said.

The woman who had spat on the priest flicked a lighted cigarette at my face, then I was hit again, this time across the side of the head with something round and wooden. I felt it clack into the bone, and I tumbled sideways, the ocean roaring in my ears, and struck the ground on one knee and an elbow. My ear and the side of my head were on fire, and I looked up through the unshaved legs and denims stained with grease and cow manure and saw a thin, muscular boy of about nineteen with a freight-door pin in his hand. Somebody pulled my shirt loose from my trousers and poured beer down my spine. I felt a cigar burn into my neck, and a woman slapped wildly at my head with a shoe. I tried to raise my arms in front of me, but someone stepped on my hand and the man in khakis tripped in the crowd and fell across my back. I heard Rie's voice shouting outside the circle of people around me, then the deputy sheriff pulled my head up by the shirt collar and started to raise me to my feet, but before he did he flicked out his knee, in a quick, deft motion, and caught me in the eye. Half my vision exploded in dark red and purple circles, and I pressed my hand into the socket as though I had a piece of sandpaper under the lid. But in the swimming distortion I could see his khaki trousers stuffed inside his low-topped boots, and his cartridge belt and holster welded against his flat stomach and narrow hips. I rose on one knee and put all my strength into a left-handed swing from the ground and hit him in the stomach an inch above the belt. I felt the muscles collapse under my fist, just like you kick open a door unexpectedly. He bent double, his face white and his mouth open in a wide O, and his breath clicked dryly in his throat. His eyes were drowning, and when he fell forward on his knees in the mud, a line of spittle on his cheek, the crowd stepped backwards in silence as though someone had thrown an unacceptable icon at their feet.

Then the Rangers, the city police, and the sheriff's department went to work. They arrested everybody in sight. They handcuffed my arms behind me while the television cameras whirred, gave artificial respiration to the deputy and strapped an oxygen mask to his face, pushed scores of people into the vans with nightsticks until there was no more room, commandeered the stake truck, and arrested the man with the camera on the loading platform by mistake. Two deputies led me by each arm to the van, squeezing tightly into my torn shirt, their faces like hard wax, and the television newsmen were still hard at work with their lenses zooming across my manacled hands and swollen face. The rain was coming down harder now, and the gravel road was covered with wet boles of cotton and leaves stripped from the citrus orchards. The wind was rattling the tin roof on top of the cannery, and the ditches by the road were slick and brown on the sides with the run-off from the fields. I was the last man put in the second van. The deputies took the handcuffs off me, pushed me inside against the crowd of Mexicans and Negroes, and locked the wire-cage doors. The engine started, and we bounced across the railway track and turned through the cannery gate on to the county road.

The men in the van balanced themselves against the walls and each other and rolled cigarettes, or poured Bull Durham tobacco from the pouch between their lip and gums. Somewhere in the back a child was crying. I leaned against the cage door and watched the road shift in direction behind the van, while the wind shook the barbed wire on the fences and bent the weeds flat along the irrigation ditches, and then I heard Rie's voice way back in the crush of people. She pressed her way out between several Mexican men, who raised their arms in the air in order to let her pass, and her face and eyes made my heart drop. She put her arm in mine and touched her fingers lightly against the swollen place on my head, then pulled my arm close against her breast and kissed me on the cheek.

'I was very proud of you, Hack,' she said.

'I'm afraid I screwed up your picket. That was an assault and battery caper I pulled off back there.'

She hugged my arm tighter against her breast, and the rain poured down on the fields and began to flatten the long, ploughed rows even with the rest of the land, and in the distance I could see the citrus trees whipping and shredding in the dark wind.

TEN

The streets in town were half-filled with water when the vans arrived at the courthouse. Beer cans and rubbish floated along next to the kerb, and the lawn was strewn with broken branches and leaves from the oaks. The deputies, now wearing oilskins and plastic covers on their hats, formed us into a long line, two abreast, while the rain beat in our faces, and marched us into the courthouse. The booking room was small, and it took them three hours to fingerprint everyone and sort out the shoelaces, belts, pocket change and wallets into brown envelopes. Most of the charges were for trespassing or failure to keep fifty feet apart on a picket line, but after the deputy had rolled my fingers on the ink pad the sheriff filled out my charge sheet personally and he wrote for five minutes. I dripped water on to the floor and looked at his steel-rimmed glasses and the red knots and bumps on his face. His fingers were pinched white on the pencil, and towards the bottom of the page he pressed down so hard that he punctured the paper.

Then he picked up a cigarette from the desk and lit it.

'You want to hear them?' he said.

'I bet you have a whole bunch,' I said.

'Assault and battery on a law officer, obstructing an officer in the line of duty, resisting arrest, inciting to riot, and I'm holding a couple of charges open. You ain't going to get this shifted to no federal court, either. You're going to be tried right here in this county, and maybe you'll find out a lawyer's shit stinks like everybody else's.'

'I have a phone call coming.'

'It's out of order.'

'It rang five minutes ago.'

'Take him downstairs,' he said to the trusty.

I was locked in the drunk tank at the end of the stone corridor in the basement. The room was crowded with men, wringing out their clothes on the concrete floor. Their dark bodies shone in the dim light. There were two toilets crusted with filth, without seats, in the corner, and the drunks who had been arrested during the weekend still reeked of sour beer and muscatel. Through the bars I could see the screened cage where I had talked with Art, and the row of cells with the food slits in the iron doors. The stone walls glistened with moisture, and the smoke from hand-rolled cigarettes gathered in a thick haze on the ceiling. An old man in jockey undershorts, with shrivelled skin like lined putty, walked to the toilet and began retching.

Rie had been put with the other women into a second holding room on the other side of the wall. Someone had drilled a small hole in the mortar between the stones, and a Mexican man had his face pressed tightly against the wall, talking to his wife, while a line of other men waited their turn behind him. I wanted to talk with Rie badly, but the line grew longer, and often in the confusion of names and voices the two right people could never get on the opposite sides of the hole at the same time. Twice during the afternoon a deputy, dripping water from his oilskin, brought in another prisoner, and each time the door clanged open a tough, bare-chested kid, who was waiting to do a six-year jolt in Huntsville, shouted out from the back of the room, 'Fresh meat!' At five o'clock the trusty wheeled in the food cart with our tin plates of spaghetti, string beans, bread and cups of Kool-Aid, and after the group of men had thinned away from the wall I tried to talk through the hole to a Mexican woman on the other side, but she couldn't understand English or my bad Spanish, and I gave up.

That night I dragged my tick mattress against the door and lay with my face turned towards the bars to breathe as much air as I could out of the corridor and avoid the odour of the open toilets and the sweet, heavy smell of perspiration. I had one damp cigar left, and I smoked it on my side and looked at the row of grey, iron doors set in the rock. Mojo was in lockdown behind one of them, and once I thought I saw the flash of his black face through a food slit. I had never been more tired. I was used up physically the way you are after you've thrown every pitch you have in a ten-innings game. There was a raised water blister on my neck from the cigar burn, and a swollen ridge across the side of my head, like a strip of bone, where the boy had caught me with the freight pin. I fell asleep with the dead cigar in my hand, and I slept through until morning without having one dream or even a half-conscious, nocturnal awareness of where I was, as though I had been lowered through the stone into some dark underground river.

I heard the trusty click the food cart against the bars and throw the big lock on the door. The fried bologna, grits and coffee streamed from the stainless-steel containers, and the men were rising from their tick mattresses, hawking, spitting and relieving themselves in the toilets, or washing their spoons under the water tap before they formed into line. I had to move my mattress for the trusty to push the cart inside, and when I stood up I realized that I felt as rested and solid as a man in his prime. But it took me a moment to believe the man I saw walking down the stone corridor with the sheriff by his side. He wore yellow, waxed cowboy boots, a dark, striped western suit, with a watchchain hooked on his handtooled belt, a bolo tie, a cowboy shirt with snap buttons on the pockets, and a short-brim Stetson hat on the back of his head. He didn't have a vest on, and I could see the hair on his swollen stomach above his belt buckle, and his round face was as powdered and smooth as a baby's. There wasn't another man in Texas who dressed like that. It was R. C. Richardson, all right.

'Hack, have you lost your goddamn mind? What the hell are you doing in here?' he said, in his flat, east Texas, Piney Woods accent.

'R.C., you old sonofabitch,' I said.

'I was down here buying leases, and I come back to the motel last night and turned on the television, and I couldn't believe it. What you trying to do to yourself, boy?'

'Get a bondsman, R.C.'

'I already done that. I got his ass out of bed at midnight, but he wouldn't come till this morning. Do you know the bail they set on you? Ten thousand dollars. I swear to God if you ain't a pistol, Hack.'

'I tell you, Mr Richardson,' the sheriff said, 'if you go this man's bond, you're also going to be responsible for him, because I don't want to see him again.'

'Well, I guarantee you he won't be no trouble,' R.C. said. 'We might shoot on across the border this afternoon and try the chili, then go on back to DeWitt.'

'R.C., are you going to turn the key on me or just drip water on the floor?' I said.

'Hold on, son. That man will be here in a minute,' he said. 'I told him I'd put a boot up his ass if he wasn't here five minutes after I walked through that door.'

'Bail the rest of them out, too,' I said.

'You know that brother of yours is right. The whiskey's getting up in your brain.'

'R.C., how many years have I kept you out of prison?'

'Goddamn, how much money do you think I carry around with me?'

'Enough to buy this county and a couple of others.'

'Hack, I can't do that. There must be fifty people in there.'

'There's more in the next room,' I said.

'And they'll be spread all over Mexico when they're supposed to be in court.'

'Will you stop screwing around and just do it?'

'If you ain't a pistol, the craziest goddamn man I ever met. All right, but I'm going to send your brother a bill for a change, and it's going to bust his eyeballs.'

'Good, and give me a cigar while you're at it.'

The bondsman arrived, and R.C. wrote out a cheque on the stone wall for the whole amount. The bondsman, a small man with greed and suspicion stamped in his face, thought he was either drunk or insane. He held the cheque between his fingers with the ink still drying and looked at R.C. incredulously.

'Call the First National Bank in Dallas collect and use my name,' R.C. said, 'or I'll find me another man right fast.'

We had to wait ten minutes, then the sheriff opened the doors to both holding rooms and the corridor was filled with people, laughing and talking in Spanish. A deputy unlocked one of the cells set back in the wall, and Mojo stepped out barefoot in the light, blinking his red eyes, with his stringless shoes in his hands.

'What happened?' he said. 'The Man get tired of us already?'

A Mexican man put his arm around Mojo's shoulders and

pulled him into the crowd walking towards the stairwell. The Mexican spoke no English, but he pointed his thumb into his mouth in a drinking motion.

'There you go, brother,' Mojo said.

The sheriff glared at us all, the red knots on his face tight against the skin.

I came up behind Rie and slipped my arm around her waist, and kissed the cool smoothness of her cheek. She turned her face up to me and I kissed her again and ran my hand through her hair.

'How did you do it, babe?' she said.

'I want you to meet R. C. Richardson,' I said.

R.C. lifted off his Stetson with a slow, exact motion and let it rest against his trouser leg, and bent forward with a slight bow and his best look of southern deference to womanhood on his face. He pulled in his stomach and stiffened his shoulders, and for just a moment you didn't notice the bolo tie and the yellow cowboy boots.

'I'm proud to meet you, miss,' he said.

'Rie Velasquez,' she said, and her eyes smiled at him.

'I was just telling Hack I didn't have time to eat breakfast this morning, so why don't we go across the street to the café and see if we can get a steak?'

His eyes were looking over Rie's face, and I knew that it took everything in him to prevent them from going further. He stepped aside and let us walk in front of him as we followed the crowd upstairs. R.C. was about to begin one of his performances. He had several roles, and he did each of them well: good-natured oilman when he was buying leases; humble Kiwanian and patriot; friend-of-the-boys with a wallet full of unlisted telephone numbers. But now he was a gentleman rancher, somebody's father, an older friend with his fingers on all the right buttons when you were in trouble. We had to wait for the deputy to find the brown envelopes with our wallets, change and belts in them. He was young and evidently new to his job, and he had difficulty reading the handwriting of the people who had booked us.

'Snap it up, boy,' R.C. said. 'We don't want to grow no older in this place.'

'R.C., we still have about seventy-five feet to go to the door,' I said.

'You either do a job or you don't,' he said. 'That's what's wrong all over this country. Like that little bondsman back there. He don't spit without sitting down and thinking about it first.'

We signed for our possessions, and R.C. slipped his mac over Rie's shoulders. It was still raining hard outside. It came down in curving sheets that swept across the flooded courthouse lawn. Some of the oaks were almost bare, and the leaves floated up against the trunks in islands. Cars and trucks were stalled in the street, the headlight beams weak in the driving rain, and somewhere a horn was stuck and blowing. The neon sign over the café and tavern looked like coloured smoke in the wet, diffused light.

R.C. opened up a big umbrella over our heads and we splashed down the pavement towards the café. The air smelled clean and cool, and even the rain, slanting under the umbrella and burning against the skin, felt like an absolution after the day and night in jail. There's no smell exactly like that of a jail, and when you can leave it behind you and walk out into a rain storm you feel that the other experience was never really there.

The water in the street was up to our knees, and R.C. held Rie by one arm and covered our heads with the umbrella while exposing his own. The rain sluiced off the brim of his pearl-grey Stetson, his western suit was drenched, his shirt had popped open more above his belt and his stomach winked out like a roll of wet dough. He was an old crook and a lecher, but I liked him in a strange way – maybe because he had no malice towards anyone, and even in his dishonesty he was faithful to the corrupt system that he served, and his buffoonery lent a little humour to it. Possibly that's an odd reason to like someone, but I had known much worse men in the oil business than R. C. Richardson.

He opened the door for us, and we went inside with the rain swirling through the screen. Men in cowboy boots and blue jeans were drinking bottles of Pearl and Jax at the counter, a Negro was racking pool balls in the back under an electric bulb with a tin shade around it, and the jukebox, with cracks all over the plastic casing, was playing a lament about lost women and the wild side of life. R.C. took off Rie's mac and held the chair for her at one of the tables with oilcloth covers tacked around the sides. In his politeness he was awkward, like a man who had been put together with bad hinges, but it was seldom that he was called upon to show manners above those practised in the Dallas Petroleum Club.

'R.C., you're not a sonofabitch, after all,' I said.

He looked at me strangely, his thick hands on the table top.

'Well, I hope your brother was wearing his brown britches when he watched the late news last night,' he said, then blinked at Rie, his smooth face uncertain. 'Excuse me. I forget I ain't in the oilfield sometimes.'

She smiled at him, and he took in his breath and opened his fingers. We hadn't eaten at the jail that morning, and I could smell the pork chops and slices of ham frying on the stove. We ordered steaks and scrambled eggs, with side orders of hash-browns and tomatoes.

'You must have put your fist plumb up to the elbow in that man's stomach,' R.C. said. 'I've never seen a man dump over that hard. I thought he was going to strangle right there on the ground.'

'The local news boys must have done a good job,' I said.

'They sure as hell did. They got it all. You smiling with handcuffs on and them two cops holding you by each arm. I bet Bailey needed a respirator if he seen that.' R.C. laughed and lit a cigar. 'Goddamn, if I wouldn't mark off all that bail money just to see him trying to get to the phone.'

The waiter brought our steaks and eggs, and set a pot of coffee on a napkin in the centre of the table. I cut a piece of steak and ate it with a slice of peppered tomato. R.C. was still laughing with the cigar in his mouth.

'You reckon he's already called the mental ward in Austin?' he said.

'I think it's been a good morning for you,' I said.

'Hack, you and him have been giving me hell all these years, and by God I don't get many chances to bail my lawyer out of jail.'

'How bad is it going to be, Hack?' Rie said.

'I don't know.'

The door opened and the rain swept across the floor. I felt the cool air against my neck.

'Miz Rie, don't worry about Hack losing in court, because he don't.'

'It might be a little more difficult this time,' I said.

'I remember once I was almost chopping cotton on Sugarland farm, and you had the case dismissed in a week.'

I remembered it also – painfully. Four years ago R.C. had drilled into a state-owned oil pool and had bribed three state officials, one of whom went to the penitentiary.

'He walks into court with that white suit, and it don't take him five minutes to have everybody in the jury box watching him.'

Rie looked at me, and I dropped my eyes.

'Once he got a coloured man off for raping a white woman, and I swear to God the jury never even knew why they let him go.'

'It's almost noon. Let's have a beer,' I said.

'You know you ain't going to get any time. Why you let this girl worry?'

'Order some beers.'

'You really think they're going to put somebody from your family in the penitentiary?'

'Would you shut up, R.C.?'

His face was hurt and embarrassed, and Rie touched my hand under the table.

'You're giving away all his secrets,' she said. 'He hates to admit that he's anything but a left-handed country lawyer.'

He looked at her eyes, and his face mended as though a breeze had blown across it. He was in love with her, and if I hadn't been at the table his performance would have grown to absurd proportions.

We finished eating, and R.C. paid the bill and left a three-dollar tip on the table. We walked across the flooded street in the rain to his Mercedes, and he opened the car door for Rie and held the umbrella over her head while she got in. The inside panels were covered with yellow, rolled leather, and the black seats were stitched with a gold longhorn design, and on top of the dashboard there was an empty whiskey glass and a compass inside a plastic

bubble. We drove slowly out of town while the water washed back
in waves over the kerbs, and R.C. pulled a pint of Four Roses
from his coat pocket and offered it to us.

'Well, that's the first time I ever seen you turn one down,' he
said, and he drank from the bottle as though it contained soda
water.

The county road that led to the cannery had collapsed in
places along the edges from the overflow of ditch water, and the
rows in the fields had been beaten almost flat by the rain or
washed into humps of mud. The gusts of wind covered the brown
water with curls and lines like puckered skin, and the torn cotton
and leaves turned in eddies around the cedar fence posts. In the
distance I saw a cow trying to lift her flanks out of the mud.

A great section of the cannery roof had been blown away in
the storm. The metal was ripped upwards in a ragged slash, like
a row of twisted knives, and there was a huge black hole where
the rest of the roof had been. Picket signs were strewn over the
ground by my car, and the rain drummed down in a roar on the
tin building, the loading platform and the freight cars. R.C.
parked as close as he could to the Cadillac and went around to
Rie's side with the umbrella. His western slacks were splattered
with mud up to the knees, and drops of water ran down his soft
face. He closed the door after her and walked around to the
driver's side with me, the rain thudding on the umbrella.

'Look, Hack, it's going to take some money to beat this thing,'
he said. 'I know you got plenty of it, but if you need any more
you only got to call. Another thing. You take care of that girl,
hear?'

'All right, R.C.'

'One more thing, by God. I think you flushed your political
career down the hole, but I felt right proud of you out there. That
boy looked like he had muscles in his shit till you come off the
ground. I always told Bailey you was crazy but you're still a
goddamn good man.'

He slammed the door and splashed through the mud to his
car, his face bent downwards against the rain. We followed him
out through the cannery gate on to the county road, and I saw
the empty whiskey bottle sail from his window into the irrigation

ditch. Then he floored the Mercedes and sped away from us in a shower of mud and brown water.

'He's a wonderful man,' Rie said.

'I believe he liked you a little bit, too.'

'Where's he going?'

'Back to his motel room and get sentimentally drunk in his underwear. Then about dark he'll drive across the border and try to buy a whole brothel.'

'Couldn't we ask him over?'

'He'd feel better with the morning intact the way it is. In fact, it would hurt him if he had to continue.'

The collapsed places along the edges of the road were beaded with gravel, and cut back into deepening sink holes in the centre. I could feel the soft ground break under my wheels.

'Was he straight about nobody from your family going to the penitentiary?' she said.

'The deputy already has my civil rights charge against him, and if those camera boys were any good they filmed his knee in my eye, and I can make a hard case against the cops. But there's a good chance I'll get disbarred.'

'Oh, Hack.'

I put my arm around her wet shoulders and pulled her close to me.

'Stop worrying about it, babe. My grandfather knocked John Wesley Hardin on his ass with a rifle stock, and Hardin was a lot tougher than the Texas Bar Association.'

'I kept making fun of you about picket lines and the union, and now you might get burned worse than any of us.'

Her back was cold under my arm. I kissed the corner of her eye and squeezed her into me.

'Don't you know that real gunfighters never lose?' I said.

She put her hand on my chest, and I could feel my heart beat against her palm. She looked up at me once, then pressed her cheek against my shoulder the rest of the way back to town.

The dirt yards in the poor district were covered with water up to the front porches, and the waves from my car washed through the chicken-wire fences and rolled against the houses. Tin cans, rubbish and half-submerged tree limbs floated in the ditches, and a dead dog, his skin scalded pink by the rain, lay entangled in an island of trash around the base of a telephone pole. Some of the shingles had been stripped by the wind from the union head-quarters roof, and the building itself leaned at an angle on the foundation. I took off my boots, and we waded through the water to the porch.

Mojo and a Mexican man were sitting at the table in the front room with a half-gallon bottle of yellow wine between them. They had melted a candle to the table, and Mojo was heating his glass of wine over the flame. The smoke curled in a black scorch around the glass. His eyes were small and red in the light.

'My brother here is teaching me how to put some fire in the spodiodi,' he said. 'You can see it climb up right inside the colour. That's what I been doing wrong all these years. Drinking without no style.'

He drank the glass down slowly, and poured it full again. I could smell the wine all the way across the room.

'This telegram was in the door when I got back from the jail, and a man come by in a taxicab looking for you,' he said. 'He didn't leave no name, but he looked just like you. Except for a minute I thought he had to go to the bathroom real bad.'

I tore open the envelope and read the telegram, dated late last night.

I DON'T KNOW IF YOU WILL RECEIVE THIS. I GUESS I DON'T CARE WHETHER YOU DO OR NOT. CALL VERISA IF YOU FEEL LIKE IT. OR SIMPLY TEAR THIS UP.

Bailey didn't bother to sign his name.

'What did the man say?' I said.

'He was going up to the café, and then he was coming back,' Mojo said. 'He give me a dollar so I'd be sure to tell you.'

Good old perceptive Bailey, I thought.

'I think we ought to buy that man a glass of this mellow heat when he comes back. He needs it,' Mojo said.

'He needs a new mind,' I said.

Rie went into the back to change clothes. I looked in the icebox for a beer, and then drove the Cadillac down to the tavern and bought a dozen bottles of Jax and a block of ice. I found a tin bucket in the kitchen, and chipped the ice over the bottles. Rie came out of the bedroom dressed in a pair of white ducks, sandals and a flowered shirt. She had brushed back her gold-tipped hair and had put on her hoop earrings and an Indian bead necklace.

'Hey, good-looking,' I said, and put my arms around her. She pressed her whole body against me, with her arms around my neck, and I kissed her on the mouth, then along her cheek and ear. I could smell the rain in her hair.

'Do you have to leave with him?' she said.

'No.'

'Are you sure, Hack?'

'We'll give him some of Mojo's sneaky pete. That's all he needs.'

She ran her fingertips over the back of my neck and pressed her head hard against my chest.

'Don't feel that way, babe,' I said. 'I just have to talk to him.'

She breathed through her mouth and held me tightly against her. I kissed her hair and turned her face up towards me. Her soldier's discipline was gone.

'I couldn't ever leave you, Rie,' I said. 'Bailey is down here out of his own compulsion. That's all there is to it.'

I hadn't lied to her before, and it didn't feel good. I picked up the bucket of beer and cracked ice by the bail, and we walked on to the porch and sat in two wicker chairs away from the rain slanting under the eaves. The solid grey of the sky had broken into drifting clouds, and I could see the faint, brown outline of the hills in the distance. The Rio Grande was high and swirling with mud, the surface dimpled with rain, and the tall bank on the Mexican side of the river had started to crumble into the water. I opened two beers and raked the ice off the bottles with my palm.

It had been a long time since I had enjoyed the rain so much. The wind was cool and smelled of the wet land and the dripping trees, and I remembered the times as a boy when I used to sit on the back porch and watch the rain fall on the short cotton. In the distance I could see Cappie's grey cabin framed in the mist by the river, and even though I couldn't see the river itself I knew the bass were rising to the surface to feed on the caterpillars that had been washed out of the willows.

'Is he really like you describe him?' Rie said.

'I don't know. Maybe I'm unfair to him. After our father died he had to take care of the practical things while I played baseball at Baylor, and then I quit college to join the Navy, and he had to finish law school and run the ranch at the same time. He can't think in any terms now except finances and safe people, and he usually makes bad choices with both of them. Sometimes I'm afraid that if he ever finds out where he's invested most of his life he'll shoot himself.'

I drank out of the beer and leaned my chair back against the porch wall. Inside, I could hear Mojo singing, 'Hey, hey, baby, take a whiff on me.'

'Do you think that's why people shoot themselves?' she said.

'I never thought there was anything so bad that it could make a man take his life in seconds. But I do know there are other ways to do it to yourself over long periods of time.'

'Bailey sounds like a sad man.'

'He gets some satisfaction from his tragic view. His comparison of himself with me lets him feel correct all the time.'

'Hey, hey, everybody take a whiff on me,' Mojo sang inside.

I saw a taxicab turn into the flooded street and drive towards us, the yellow sides splattered with mud. The floating rubbish and tin cans rolled in the car's wake.

'Do you want me to go for a drive?' she said.

'No. I want you to meet him. It will be the best thing that's happened to him in a long time.'

'I feel like I shouldn't be here, Hack.'

'Who the hell lives here, anyway? He doesn't, and I sure didn't ask him down.'

I squeezed her hand, but I saw it made her uncomfortable. The waves from the taxi washed up through the yard and hit against the porch steps. Bailey paid the driver and stepped out of the back door into the water. His brown windbreaker was spotted with rain, and the lines in his brow and around his eye had deepened with lack of sleep. The rims of his eyes were red. In fact, his whole face looked middle-aged, as though he had worked hard to make it that way. He walked up through the water with his head lowered slightly and his mouth in a tight line.

'How you doing, brother?' I said, and took a sip out of the beer.

'I have a plane at the county airport,' he said. He looked straight at me and never turned his head towards Rie.

'Get out of the rain and meet someone and have a beer.'

'We'll leave your car there. You can fly back and get it later,' he said. His voice had a quiet and determined righteousness to it, the kind of tone which he reserved for particularly tragic occasions, and it had always infuriated me. But I was resolved this time.

'It's bad weather for a flight, Bailey. You should have waited a day or so,' I said. I was surprised that he had flown at all, because he was terrified of planes.

'Do you have anything inside?' he said.

'Not a thing.'

'Then we can be going.'

He was making it hard.

'Would you sit down a minute, for God's sake?' I said. 'Or at least not stand under the eave with rain dripping on your head.'

He stepped up on the porch and wiped his forehead with his palm. He still refused to recognize Rie. I carried a chair over from the other side of the porch and pulled another beer from the ice bucket.

'There. Sit,' I said. 'This is Rie Velasquez. She's the coordinator for the union.'

'How do you do, ma'am?' He looked at her for the first time, and his eyes lingered longer on her face than he had probably wanted them to. She smiled at him, and momentarily he forgot that he was supposed to be a sombre man with a purpose.

I opened the bottle of beer and handed it to him. The chips of ice slid down the neck. He started to put the bottle on the porch railing.

'Drink the beer, Bailey. If you had some more of that stuff, you wouldn't have ulcers.'

'The Senator and John Williams are at the house.'

'John Williams. What's that bastard doing in my home?'

'He was spending the weekend with the Senator, and he drove down with him this morning.'

'You know the old man wouldn't let an asshole like that in our back door.'

'He told me he would still like to contribute money to the campaign.'

'You'd better get him out of my house.'

'Why don't you take care of it yourself? This is my last errand.'

'Do you think we could get that in writing?' I said.

'You don't know the lengths other people go to for your benefit. The Senator is going to stay with you, and so is Verisa, and I wouldn't be here if I didn't feel an obligation to her.'

'What obligation is that, Bailey?' I said.

'I'm going to fix lunch,' Rie said.

'No, stay. I want to hear about this feeling of obligation. What is it exactly, brother?'

His eyes looked quickly at Rie, and he drank out of the beer.

'Don't worry about decorum or people's feelings,' I said. 'Dump it out on the porch and let's look at it. You're doing a swell job so far.'

'I'll be inside, Hack,' Rie said.

'No, goddamn. Let Bailey finish. He's saved this up in his head through every airpocket between here and Austin.'

'All right,' he said. 'For the seven years of disappointment you've given her and the alcoholism and the apologies she's had to make to people all over the state. A lesser woman would have taken you into court years ago and pulled out your fingernails. Right now she's under sedation, but that will probably slide past you like everything else in your life does.'

'What do you mean, sedation?' I said.

'She called me up drunk an hour after the television broadcast, and I had to go over to the house with a doctor from Yoakum.'

Rie lit a cigarette and looked out into the rain. Her suntanned cheeks were pale and her eyes bright. I didn't know why I had forced her to sit through it, and it was too late to change anything now. The wind blew the rain against the bottom of Bailey's chair.

'How is she now?' I said.

'What do you think? She drank a half bottle of your whiskey, and the doctor had to give her an injection to get her in bed.'

The bottle of beer felt thick in my hand. I wondered what doctor would give anyone an intravenous sedative on top of alcohol.

'She threw away her pills this morning and tried to fix breakfast for the Senator and Williams,' Bailey said. 'She almost fell down in the kitchen and I put her to bed again and refilled her prescription.'

'Don't you know better than to give drugs to people with alcohol in their system?' I said. But he didn't. His face was a confession of moral earnestness with no awareness of its consequence.

'Go back with him, Hack,' Rie said.

'Bailey, why in the bloody hell do you bring on things like this?' I said.

'Don't you have it confused?' he said.

'No. You have this talent for turning the simple into a derelict's hangover.'

'I think you're shouting at the wrong person.'

'You've always got all kinds of cool when you do it, too. Think about it. Isn't it in moments like these that you're happiest?'

'I don't need to listen to this.'

'Hell, no, you don't. You just dump the hand grenades out on the porch and let other people kick them around.'

'I told you I'm through with this crap, Hack.'

'You've been peddling my ass by the chunk to all buyers and bitching about it at the same time, and now you're through. Is that right, buddy? Frankly, you make me so goddamn mad I could knock you flat out into the yard.'

'Stop it, Hack. Go on back with him,' Rie said. Her face was flushed, and her fingers were trembling on the arm of the wicker chair.

'Should I run a foot race with him down to the airport? Or maybe Bailey can import the whole bunch down here and we can sit on the porch and find out what a sonofabitch I am.'

Rie put her fingers on her brow and dropped her eyes, but I could see the wetness on her eyelashes. None of us spoke. The rain drummed flatly on the shingled roof and ran off the eaves, swinging into the wind. My face was perspiring, and I wiped my forehead on my sleeve and drank the foam out of the bottle. I looked at her again and I felt miserable.

'I'm sorry, babe,' I said.

She turned her head away from Bailey and put an unlit cigarette in her mouth.

'Call me tonight at the beer joint. Somebody will come down for me,' she said.

The wind blew the curls on the back of her neck, and I could see her shoulders shaking. But there was nothing to do or say with Bailey there, and I went inside the screen and asked Mojo to stay with her until I called. When I came back out Bailey was still on the porch.

'I didn't get out the back door on you,' I said.

But he didn't understand; he stood against the railing, with the rain blowing across his slacks, as though his physical proximity was necessary to draw me into the car. I started to tell him to get in and read a road map and not raise his eyes until he heard me open the door, but he would have had something to say about that and we would start back into it all over again. When we drove away Rie was still looking out into the rain with the unlit cigarette in her fingers.

We didn't speak on the way to the airport. The air conditioner stopped working, and the windows fogged with humidity and the sweat rolled down my face and neck into my shirt. I felt a black anger towards Bailey that you can only feel towards someone you grew up with, and as the heat became more intense in the car I resented every motion that he made. He opened the window and let the rain blow across the leather seats, then he closed it and tried to pull off his windbreaker by the cuffs and hit me against the arm. I turned on the radio and we both listened to a Christian crusade evangelist rant about the communist Antichrist in Viet Nam.

The two-engine plane was parked at the end of the runway in three inches of water. The rain beat against the silver, riveted plates of the fuselage, and the wind out of the hills was still strong enough to push the plane's weight against the anchor blocks around the wheels. In the distance the hills looked as brown and smooth as clay.

The cabin had three metal seats in it, spot-welded to the bulkhead, with old military safety straps, and when the pilot turned the ignition, the electric starter on the port engine wouldn't take hold. Then the propeller flipped over stiffly several times, black exhaust blew back across the wing, and the whole plane vibrated with the engines' roar. The backwash from the propellers blew the concrete dry around the plane, and the pilot taxied out slowly on the runway with the nose into the wind. Bailey kept wiping the rain water and perspiration back through his hair, and his other hand was clenched tightly on his thigh.

'I'm going to jump it up fast,' the pilot said over his shoulder. 'There's bad down draughts over those hills.'

Bailey reached under his seat and took out a half-pint bottle of sloe gin in a paper sack. He didn't look at me while he drank. The plane gained speed, the brown water blowing off the sides of the runway, and the wet fields and the few silver hangars flashed by the windows, then we lifted off abruptly into the grey light, the plane shaking against the wind and the strain of its own engines. The crest of the hills swept by below us, and in moments I could see the whole Rio Grande Valley flatten out through the window. The fields were divided into great, brown squares of water, the orchards that hadn't been destroyed by the storm were dark green against the land, and the river had almost covered the willow trees along its banks. There were dead cattle and horses in the fields, their stiff legs turned out of the water, and the barbed-wire fences had been bent down even with the road. Milking barns had been crushed over sideways, and some farmhouses had lost their roofs, and from the air I felt that I was looking down into something private, an arrangement of kitchens and bedrooms and family eating tables, which I had been unfairly allowed to see.

Bailey's face was white, and he pulled on the bottle again and coughed. He hated for me to see him drink, but his terror of the plane was greater than any feeling he had about personal image or even his ulcerated stomach.

'We'll be there in an hour,' I said. 'He's above any bad currents now.'

Bailey was rigid in the metal seat, the safety belt strapped across his stomach. His fingers were pressed tight across the flat side of the bottle, and the perspiration was still rolling down his face.

'I don't know what kind of agreement you'll come to with Verisa and the Senator, but you and I are going to have one with our practice,' he said. His voice was dry, and his accent had deepened with his fear.

'Why do I have to come to an agreement with anyone?' I knew all the answers he had, but he wanted to talk or do anything to forget the plane and the distance from the ground.

'Because you're holding a big IOU to other people,' he said.

'Did it ever strike you that the Senator is a bad man who never did anything for anyone unless his own ass was buttered first? That for thirty years he's served every bad cause in this country? Or maybe that he needs me much more than I needed him?'

He sipped out of the sloe gin, and the cap rattled on the bottle neck when he tried to screw it back on.

'I've already told you, you say it to him,' he said. 'I don't give a goddamn where your paranoia takes you this time, because tomorrow I'm going to write a cheque for your half of the practice.'

'OK, Bailey,' I said, and watched him hold in all his anger and bent ideas about a correct world and the correct people who should live in it.

I had thought we would land at one of the small airstrips in Yoakum or Cuero, but Bailey had told the pilot to put the plane down in the empty pasture behind my house. The land was flat and cleared of stones, and ten feet above the riverbed, but even from the air I could see the pools of water that had collected in the Bermuda grass. We circled over the ranch once, the wings tilting in the wind currents, and I tapped the pilot's shoulder and leaned against the back of his seat.

'There's armadillo sinkholes and a lot of soft dirt in that field,' I shouted over the noise of the engines.

He turned sideways briefly and nodded, then began his approach over the river. The fields of corn, tomatoes and cotton rushed towards us, the stalks and green plants pressed into the earth by the wind, and I saw the natural gas wells pumping up and down and the windmill ginning like a flash of light in the thin rain, the grey roof of the stable and the weathered smokehouse leaning into the depression where we put the oak logs, and then the white house itself with the latticework verandah and the rose bushes and poplar trees along the front lane. We dipped suddenly over the post oaks by Cappie's cabin and hit the pasture in a spray of mud and grass across the front windows. The wheels went deep into the wet ground, the tail lifted momentarily into the air, and the pilot gunned the engines to keep us in a straight line across the pasture, although he couldn't see anything in front of him. Water and mud streaked across the side windows, then one wheel sank in a soft spot and we spun in a sliding half circle, with one engine feathered, against the white fence that separated my side lawn and the pasture.

The pilot feathered the other engine and wiped his face on his sleeve. Bailey had spilled the bottle of sloe gin over his slacks.

'Do you have a hard drink inside?' the pilot said.

'If you drink Jack Daniel's,' I said.

I opened the cabin door, and the rain blew into our faces. We climbed over the white fence and ran across the lawn through the oak trees to the front porch. The Senator's limousine with the tinted windows was parked on the gravel lane. The poplar trees were arched in the wind, and magnolia leaves and rose petals were scattered across the grass. One of Verisa's large earthen flowerpots had fallen from the upstairs verandah, and the soft dirt and cracked pottery lay in a pile on the front steps. It seemed a long time since I had been home; maybe the house looked strange to me because the Senator's car was parked in front, but even the worn vertical line of bullet holes in the porch column seemed new, as though Wes Hardin had drilled them there only yesterday.

I took the pilot through the front hall into my library and opened a bottle of bourbon for him and filled a silver bucket with ice cubes. He sat in my leather chair, his wet cigarette still in his mouth, and poured the glass half full without water.

'I usually stay on a formal basis with my passengers,' he said, his face fatigued over the raised glass, 'but are you guys on a kamikaze mission or something?'

I closed the door behind me without answering, and walked into the living room. The Senator was sitting in the deer-hide chair by the bar, dressed in blue slacks and a grey golf shirt with a highball balanced on his crossed knee (the whiskey was just enough to colour the water). His tan was darker than when I had seen him last, and his mowed, white hair moved slightly in the soft current from the air conditioner. John Williams leaned against the bar with his sunglasses on, tall, the face pale and as unnatural-looking as smooth rubber, and his tan suit hung on him without a line or crease on it. Verisa sat on the couch in a sundress she had bought three weeks ago at Neiman-Marcus, and if she had a hangover from the alcohol or the sedation she had done a wonderful job of burying it inside her. Her auburn hair was brushed back against her shoulders, the make-up on her face made her look fresh and cool, and she lay back comfortably against the cushions with the stem of her wineglass between her fingers as though she were at a DAR cocktail party. But there was also a quick glint in her eyes when I walked into the room, and I knew she was looking forward to a painful retribution on my part.

The Senator rose from his chair and shook hands with me. His blue eyes wrinkled at the corners when he smiled, and his hand was as square and hard as a bricklayer's.

'You've had an eventful weekend,' he said.

'It was probably exaggerated by the television boys,' I said.

'I don't believe there was any camera distortion there. Do you?' The acetylene-blue eyes wrinkled again so that it was impossible to read them. 'But, anyway, you know John Williams.'

'Mr Holland,' Williams said, and raised his glass.

'Hi.'

'I'm enjoying your taste in bourbon.'

'Help yourself to a bucket of it,' I said.

'Thank you. I think I will,' he said, and smiled somewhere behind his sunglasses.

'In fact, take a case with you. I have a crate of limes on the back porch to go with it.'

The room was silent a moment. Bailey looked at the floor, his brown windbreaker dark with rain, then went behind the bar and raked a mint julep glass through the ice bin.

'You want water in it, Hack?' he said.

'Give it to Mr Williams. I'm changing my taste in bourbon.'

'Maybe I had better wait on the porch,' Williams said.

'There's no need for that,' the Senator said, and his blue eyes moved on to my face again.

'Hell, no,' I said. 'That's a real storm out there, Mr Williams. Enough to short out all the electric circuits on an ICBM.'

I despised him and what he represented, and I let him have a good look at the anger I felt towards his presence in my home. He finished his drink and clicked his glass on the bar.

'I think it's better, Allen,' he said.

'Fix John another drink,' the Senator said to Bailey.

'Get some limes, too, Bailey,' I said.

'For one afternoon would you talk without your histrionics?' Verisa said.

'I haven't had much chance to talk today. Bailey has spent the last two hours giving me the south Texas sonofabitch award.'

'This doesn't have to be unpleasant, Hack,' the Senator said.

'Talking reasonably is beyond him,' Verisa said. 'It violates some confirmed principle he has about offending other people.'

'Give Mr Williams a drink, Bailey,' I said. 'See about the pilot, too. I think he's getting ploughed.'

'Well, we won't drag it out then, Hack,' the Senator said. 'The state committee called last night and asked me if we should drop you and run a boy from Gonzales. I told them that we would still carry the district no matter who runs, and I want you in the House in January.'

'That's good of you, Senator, but I wonder why we all have this intense commitment to my career,' and I looked right through the wrinkled light in his eyes.

'Because I feel an obligation to your father, who was a good friend to me. I think what you've done is irresponsible, but with time you'll probably make a fine congressman.'

'I'm afraid that I'm through with political fortunes.'

'That's a lovely attitude at this point,' Verisa said.

'I believe Hack is still a little angry with Rio Grande policemen,' the Senator said. 'Actually, we may have picked up more of the union vote, and your arrest won't hurt you with the Negroes and the Mexicans. The important factor is that we make use of it before the Republican gentleman does.'

'Sorry. I think that boy from Gonzales would be a better bet.'

'You're everything I expected today,' Verisa said.

'How about the car planted against the fence?'

'You're lovely just as you are. It couldn't have been more anticipated,' she said.

'I want to finish this, Hack,' the Senator said. 'I plan to talk to the committee this afternoon and give them your assurance about the rest of the campaign.'

'I don't think you should do that, Senator.'

'The assault charge can be taken care of,' he said. 'It will probably involve a small appointment in Austin, but it's a simple matter.'

He had still chosen not to hear me, and I felt the anger rising inside me.

'Don't you realize what's being done for you?' Bailey said from behind the bar. 'Try to think about it a minute. You committed a felony yesterday that could get you disbarred or even sent to jail.'

'No, I don't realize a damn thing, because I have an idea that all this investment in me isn't out of good will and old friendships. What do you think, Mr Williams?'

He sipped from his fresh drink with a sprig of mint leaves in it, rested his arm on the bar, and looked at me from behind his sunglasses. The texture of his skin was the most unnatural I had ever seen on a human being.

'I think it would save time if the case were explained to you a little more candidly,' he said.

The Senator looked at Williams, and momentarily I saw the same uncomfortable flicker in his eyes that I had seen on the trip to Washington when I had realized that predators came in various sizes. He paused a moment, then turned back to me before Williams could speak again, his fingers pressed on the highball glass.

'Possibly your alternatives aren't as clear or easy as you might believe, Hack,' he said. 'I've made some commitments in this election that I intend to see honoured.'

'It's a matter of votes on a House bill to rescind the oil-depletion allowance, Mr Holland. Although Mr Allen doesn't run again for two years, it's been necessary to promise several oil companies that the right people will be on a committee to prevent anyone from lowering the twenty-seven-and-a-half-per-cent allowance that we now have. As you know, it involves a great deal, and so a few people have pressed Allen rather hard on winning support.'

Williams was enjoying the Senator's discomfort, but I didn't care about either of them then. I felt light inside, like a high school athlete who had been told he was needed to pick up the towels in the locker room.

'Did you know about this shit, Bailey?' I said.

'No.'

'You sold my ass all over the state and you never guessed what it was about.'

'I didn't know, Hack.'

'Well, you saw me coming, Senator,' I said.

'Are we going to enjoy a melodrama about it now?' Verisa said.

'No, I think I just finished the ninth innings, and you can have the whole goddamn ball park.'

'I believe you're being overly serious about this. The oil-depletion allowance is in the interest of the state,' the Senator said. 'Also, every holder of office pays some kind of personal price to represent his constituency.'

'I'd call that boy in Gonzales. Let me have a beer, Bailey.'

'Maybe you should tell Mr Holland about the rest of his alternative now,' Williams said. He raised his drink slowly to his mouth.

'I thought you'd been saving something special,' I said. Bailey handed me the beer in a glass, and I took a cigar from the oakwood box on the coffee table. The Senator sat down in the deer-hide chair and crossed his legs with his highball in his hand, but his eyes didn't look at me.

'I don't like to do this, but there's a man named Lester Dixon in Kansas City and he's made a deposition about the time he

423

spent with you in a North Korean prison camp,' he said. His eyes looked at the end of his shoe, thoughtful, as though he were considering a delicate premise before he spoke again.

Verisa took a cigarette from her pack and put it in her mouth. Her arm lay back against the couch, and her breasts swelled against her sundress when she breathed.

I lit my cigar and stared into the Senator's face.

'What did Airman First Class Dixon have to say?' I said.

'I don't believe we have to talk about all of it here,' he said.

'I think you should, Senator. I imagine that Lester's deposition was very expensive.'

'Two men from your shack were executed after they were informed upon.' He raised his eyes into my face and tried to hold them there, but I stared back hard at him and he took a drink from his glass.

'Did he tell you how it was done?' I said.

'I never met him.'

'He's an interesting person. I helped send him to prison for five years.'

'The statement is twenty pages long, and it's witnessed by two attorneys,' he said. 'It's been compared for accuracy with the transcript from his court-martial, and I don't think you'll be able to contest what he says about your complicity in the deaths of two defenceless men.'

'The telephone is in the hall, Senator. Next to it is a list of numbers, one of which is *The Austin American*. No, instead finish your drink and let Verisa get the city desk for you.'

'It will be done more subtly than that. Possibly a leak from someone on the state committee, a small rumour at first, and then a reporter will be given the whole thing.'

'You probably have ways I've never dreamed about.'

'That's true, but the outcome will be the same in this case.'

'Then I guess we can all say good-day to each other.'

'No, there's one more thing,' he said, and his eyes took on the same expression they had before he drove the tennis ball into my nose. 'Right now, you're enjoying your virtue. With an impetuous decision you've become a Spartan lying on his shield, and I'm sure you'll need this image for yourself during the next few weeks.

But I want to correct a couple of your ideas about integrity in political office. Negotiation and compromise are part of any politician's career, and your father learned that lesson his first term in Congress.'

'What do you mean?'

'He accepted a fifteen-thousand-dollar contribution to sponsor the sale of public land to a wildcat company in Dallas. The land sold for fifty dollars an acre.'

'Bailey, do you want to tell these men to get out, or you want to wait on me?'

He looked down at the bar, his forehead white.

'Bailey,' I said.

The balding spot on his head was perspiring, and I could see the raised veins in the back of his hands.

'Just look at me,' I said.

'I'm sorry, Hack. I didn't know they were going to do this.'

'Then you tell them to get out.'

He leaned on his arms, his face still turned downwards, and I felt my head begin to grow light, as though there were no oxygen in my blood.

'Goddamn it, you're not going to bring these men into my home to do this, and then stare at the bar,' I said.

'He was going to lose the ranch, Hack. He knew heart disease was killing him, and he was afraid he'd die and leave us nothing.'

The rain blew against the windows, and I could hear the oak branches sweeping heavily back and forth on the roof. Outside, the light was grey in the trees, and the stripped leaves stuck wetly against the trunks. My dead cigar felt like a stick between my fingers.

'You and this man will leave now, Senator,' I said.

'Thank you for the drink, Mr Holland,' Williams said, and set his glass on the bar. 'You have a nice home here.'

'Thank you, too, Verisa,' the Senator said. 'I'm sorry if we've made the day a little hard for you.'

The three of them rose and walked together to the front hall. They could have been people saying good-bye after a Sunday dinner. Verisa's sundress fit tightly against her smooth back, and she had a way of holding herself at a door that made her look like a little girl. Williams raised his hand once to me, backwards, the way a European would, and smiled again somewhere behind those black-green glasses.

'Good-bye, Hack,' the Senator said.

I lit my cigar and didn't look back at him, then I heard the door click shut as I stared down into the flame.

'I'm sorry,' Bailey said.

'Forget it and give me one hard one.'

'I wouldn't have brought you back for this.'

'I know that. Just make it about three inches and a little water.'

He poured into a tall shot glass and let the whiskey run over the edge. He started to wipe off the counter with a towel, and then knocked the glass into the sink.

'Christ, Hack,' he said.

'I'm all right,' I said, and poured the shot glass full myself and drank it down neat.

'You goddamn fool,' Verisa said.

'Leave him alone,' Bailey said.

'You're going to pay for it with every stick and nail in this house,' she said.

I walked away from them towards the hall. The hum of the air conditioners and the heavy sweep of the oaks against the eaves were loud in my head, and the boards in the floor seemed to bend under my boots. I could feel something important begin to roll loose inside, in the way that you pull out a brick from the bottom of a wall. I opened the door to my library and took the cigar out of my mouth. The pilot still sat in my leather chair with the half-empty bottle of Jack Daniels in his lap. His face was colourless, and he had dropped a lighted cigarette on the rug.

'Do you think you can get it up again today?' I said.

'Yeah, buddy, if you don't mind flying drunk,' he said.

We walked out into the rain, crossed the lawn, and climbed over the fence to the plane. The air was sweet with the smell of the wet land and the dripping trees and the ruined tomatoes that had been pounded into the furrows. The chain on the windmill had broken and the water was spilling white over the lips of the trough into the horse lot. I could see the willows on the river bank bending against the sky, and the deep cut of the drainages on the distant hills and the thin line of sunlight on the horizon's edge. My two oil wells glistened blackly in the rain, pumping up and down with their obscene motion, and the weathered shacks of the Negro and Mexican farm workers stood out against the washed land like matchboxes that had been dropped from the sky at an odd angle.

The pilot wiped the plane's windows clean of mud and grass with his windbreaker, and we took off across the pasture in a shower of water from the backdraught of the propellers. Just before we reached the river the pilot pulled back on the stick and gave the engines everything they would take, and we lifted over the trees into the sky and turned into the wind. The river, the willows, the post oaks and Cappie's cabin dropped away below us, and then the house and the deep tyre imprints of the Senator's limousine on my gravel lane, and finally the small whitewashed markers in the Holland family cemetery.

EPILOGUE

No one won the strike, not the growers or the farm companies or
the field workers, because the storm didn't leave anything to win.
After the water had drained from the fields, the ruined citrus lay
on the ground and rotted under the humid sun until the air was
heavy with the smell of the cantaloupe, water melon and grapefruit that dried into cysts and then burst apart. The cotton rows
were washed flat and the sweep of mud through the fields baked
out hard and smooth in the late August heat as though nothing
had ever been planted there.

I withdrew from the election, and one of the Senator's aides
released Lester Dixon's deposition to a state news service, but no
one was particularly interested in it. A reporter from *The Austin
American* telephoned me and asked if I had seen it, would I like
him to read it to me over the phone, and I answered that I
wouldn't and would he do several things with it of his choosing,
and I never heard about it again. Since then I've come to believe
that one's crimes and private guilt, those obsessions that we hide
like that ugly black diamond in the soft tissue of the mind, are
really not very important to other people.

Bailey acted as my defence lawyer at my hearing in Pueblo
Verde, and had the assault charge dropped after he promised the
district attorney we would file our own charges against the
sheriff's department (there were several lovely frames in the news
film that showed the deputy's khaki knee bending upwards into
my eye). I was even proud of Bailey. He was a better criminal
lawyer than I had thought, or at least he was that day, and even
though the court was hostile to us and the judge stared hotly at
Bailey when he addressed the bench, he was determined that I

wouldn't get any time and he made the county prosecutor stumble in his wording and contradict himself. I was given a year's probation for resisting arrest and disturbing the peace, and we went across the street to an outdoor barbecue stand and drank beer for three hours in the warm shade of an oak tree. Two weeks later I received a letter of reprimand from someone in the Texas Bar Association, and I refolded it in the envelope and returned it with a pass to the Houston livestock show.

Verisa divorced me and took the Cadillac, eighty acres I owned up in Comal County, and the two natural gas wells, but I held on to the ranch and the house and my thoroughbred horses. She went to Europe for six months, and occasionally her name was mentioned on the society pages of *The New York Times* (a reception at the American embassy in London, dancing with a member of the Kennedy entourage in a Paris night-club), then she returned to Dallas, where she had been born, and bought a penthouse apartment overlooking the city's skyline and the green hills beyond. She entertained everyone, and from time to time I heard stories about what a radiant hostess she was and how many unusual and interesting people she managed to have at her parties. She sent me an invitation to her wedding, and at first I didn't recognize the groom's name, then I remembered meeting him once at a Democratic cocktail party in San Antonio. He had inherited the controlling stock in a newspaper, and he had turned the paper's editorial page into a right-wing invective against everything liberal in the state. But I remembered him most for the fact that he didn't drink and his cleancut chin was always at an upward angle when he turned his profile to you. I sent them a silver service with a one-line note of best wishes on a card inside. Four months later he was killed with another woman in a car accident on the Fort Worth highway. Verisa inherited the news-paper, and after a period of mourning the parties began again at the penthouse and her picture appeared regularly on the society pages with a young district attorney who rumour said might run for governor in two years.

Rie and I were married right after the divorce, and the next autumn we had twin boys. They were both big for twins, and I named one Sam for my father and the other Hackberry, since I felt there should always be one gunfighter in the Holland family. Bailey bought out my half of the law practice, although he argued against it in his emotional way and wanted to continue the partnership, but I was through with the R. C. Richardson account and dealing with oil company executives. I didn't practise for seven months, and spent the winter and early spring working on the ranch. I dug fence holes and strung new wire on the pasture, reshingled the barn roof that had been stripped by the storm, put a new water well down, and ploughed and seeded sixty-five acres of corn and tomatoes. And each time I twisted the posthole digger in the ground or drove a sixpenny nail down flat in the wood, I could feel the last drops of Jack Daniel's sweat out through my pores and dry in the wind, and a new resilience in my body that I hadn't felt since I pitched at Baylor. I worked hard each morning, with the sun low over the willows on the river bank, and through the day until late evening when the shadow from the tractor fell out across the rows and the purple light drew away over the horizon. And when I had pulled the seed drill over the last furrows against the back fence I could already smell the land beginning to take hold of new life, and after the next shower small green plants would bud one morning in long, even lines.

Rie and I took my best three-year-old up to Lexington that spring and raced him at Keeneland. Each afternoon we sat in the sun with mint juleps and watched the horses break from the starting gate on the far side of the field, with the jockeys like toy men on their backs, and move in a tight formation down the back stretch, the lead horses pushing hard for the rail, then into the far turn as the roar of their hooves grew louder, their bodies glistening with sweat, and Rie would be on her feet with her arms wrapped tightly in mine, the quirts whipping down into the horses' flanks and the sod flying into the air, and then there was that heart-beating rush when they came down the home stretch with the jockeys pouring it into them, and the thunder against the turf was louder than the shouting of the crowd. We won a thirty-five-hundred-dollar purse in one race, and placed in two others, and the evening before we left for Texas I took Rie on a long drive through the bluegrass and the Cumberland Mountains. The limestone cliffs rose straight up out of the hollows, and the tops of the white oaks and beech trees were covered with the sun's last light. I was tired and quiet inside after the two weeks of racing, and the rolling hills stretched away towards Virginia in a violet haze, but a sense of time and its ephemeral quality began to weigh on me, as when you give yourself too long a period of restoring things that you hurt through indifference or cynicism in the first place.

Two days after we returned home I drove to San Antonio and became a trial lawyer for the ACLU.

It's summer again now, and the corn is green against the brown rows in the fields, and I irrigated my cotton acreage from the water well I put down and the bolls have started to come out white in the leaves. In the evening I can smell the dampness of the earth in the breeze off the river, and the wet sweetness of the Bermuda grass in the horse pasture, and just before dusk the wind flattens out the smoke from Cappie's cabin and there's just a hint in the warm air of oak logs burning in a wood stove. I built a large, circular playpen around a chinaberry tree in the side yard for the boys to play in, and every afternoon while I sit on the verandah and try to outline a defence for impossible cases, I'm distracted by the spangle of sunlight and shade on their tan bodies. They're both strong boys and they don't like being inside the pen, and they show me their disapproval by throwing their stuffed animals out on the grass. Sometimes after their nap they shake the side of the pen so violently that Rie has to bring them up on the verandah and let them play in all the wadded paper at my feet. When I look at them I can see my father and Old Hack in their faces, and I try not to look over at the white markers in the cemetery or I would have to grieve just a little on that old problem of time and loss and the failure of history to atone in its own sequence.

THE LOST
GET-BACK BOOGIE

Chapter One appeared in slightly different form as 'Discharge Day' in *Cutbank II* (Fall/Winter, 1978), published by the Associated Students of the University of Montana.

You know, the blues is something that's hard to get acquainted with. It's just like death. Now, I tell you about the blues. The blues dwells with you every day and everywhere. See, you can have the blues about that you're broke. You can have the blues about your girl is gone. The blues come so many different ways until it's kind of hard to explain. But whenever you get a sad feeling, you can tell the whole round world you got nothing but the blues.

—Sam 'Lightning' Hopkins

For John and Judy Holbrook
Frank and Linda Loweree
and Dexter Roberts

ONE

The captain was silhouetted on horseback like a piece of burnt iron against the sun. The brim of his straw hat was pulled low to shade his sun-darkened face, and he held the sawn-off double-barrel shotgun with the stock propped against his thigh to avoid touching the metal. We swung our axes into the roots of tree stumps, our backs glistening and brown and arched with vertebrae, while the chain saws whined into the felled trees and lopped them off into segments. Our Clorox-faded, green-and-white-pinstripe trousers were stained at the knees with sweat and the sandy dirt from the river bottom, and the insects that boiled out of the grass stuck to our skin and burrowed into the wet creases of our necks. No one spoke, not even to caution a man to step back from the swing of an axe or the roaring band of a McCulloch saw ripping in a white spray of splinters through a stump. The work was understood and accomplished with the smoothness and certitude and rhythm that come from years of learning that it will never have a variation. Each time we hooked the trace chains on a stump, slapped the reins across the mules' flanks, and pulled it free in one snapping burst of roots and loam, we moved closer to the wide bend of the Mississippi and the line of willow trees and dappled shade along the bank.

'OK, water and piss it,' the captain said.

We dropped the axes, prising bars and shovels, and followed behind the switching tail of the captain's horse down to the willows and the water can that sat in the tall grass with the dipper hung on the side by its ladle. The wide, brown expanse of the river shimmered flatly in the sun, and on the far bank, where the world of the free people began, white egrets were nesting in the sand. The Mississippi was almost half a mile across at that point, and there was a story among the Negro convicts that during the forties a one-legged trusty named Wooden Unc had whipped a mule into the river before the bell count on Camp H and had held on to his tail across the current to the other side. But the free people said Wooden Unc was a nigger's myth; he was just a syphilitic old man who had had his leg amputated at the charity hospital at New Orleans and who later went blind on julep (a mixture of molasses, shelled corn, water, yeast and lighter fluid that the Negroes would boil in a can on the radiator overnight) and fell into the river and drowned under the weight of the artificial leg given him by the state. And I believed the free people, because I never knew or heard of anyone who beat Angola.

We rolled cigarettes from our state issue of Bugler and Virginia Extra tobacco and wheat-straw papers, and those who had sent off for the dollar-fifty rolling machines sold by a mail-order house in Memphis took out their Prince Albert cans of neatly glued and clipped cigarettes that were as good as tailor-mades. There was still a mineral-streaked piece of ice floating in the water can, and we spilled the dipper over our mouths and chests and let the coldness of the water run down inside our trousers. The captain gave his horse to one of the Negroes to take into the shallows, and sat against a tree trunk with the bowl of his pipe cupped in his hand, which rested on the huge bulge of his abdomen below his cartridge belt. He wore no socks under his half-topped boots, and the area above his ankles was hairless and chafed a dead, shaling colour.

He lived in a small frame cottage by the front gate with the other free people, and each twilight he returned home to a cancer-ridden, hard-shell Baptist wife from Mississippi who taught Bible lessons to the Sunday school class in the Block. In the time I was on his gang, I saw him kill one convict, a half-wit Negro kid who had been sent up from the mental hospital at Mandeville. We were breaking a field down by the Red Hat House, and the boy dropped the plough loops off his wrists and began to walk across the rows towards the river. The captain shouted at him twice from the saddle, then raised forward on the pommel, aimed, and let off the first barrel. The boy's shirt jumped at the shoulder, as though the breeze had caught it, and he kept walking across the rows with his unlaced boots flopping on his feet like galoshes. The captain held the stock tight into his shoulder and fired again, and the boy tripped forward across the rows with a single jet of scarlet bursting out just below his kinky, uncut hairline.

A pickup truck driven by one of the young hacks rolled in a cloud of dust down the meandering road through the fields towards me. The rocks banged under the bumpers, and the dust coated the stunted cattails in the irrigation ditches. I put out my Virginia Extra cigarette against the sole of my boot and stripped the paper down the glued seam and let the tobacco blow apart in the wind.

'I reckon that's your walking ticket, Iry,' the captain said.

The hack slowed the truck to a stop next to the Red Hat House and blew his horn. I took my shirt off the willow branch where I had left it at eight-o'clock field count that morning.

'How much money you got coming on discharge?' the captain said.

'About forty-three dollars.'

'You take this five and send it to me, and you keep your ass out of here.'

'That's all right, boss.'

'Hell it is. You'll be sleeping in the Sally after you run your money out your pecker on beer and women.'

I watched him play his old self-deluding game, with the green tip of a five-dollar bill showing above the laced edge of his convict-made wallet. He splayed over the bill section of the wallet with his thick thumb and held it out momentarily, then folded it again in his palm. It was his favourite ritual of generosity when a convict earned good time on his gang and went back on the street.

'Well, just don't do anything to get violated back to the farm, Iry,' he said.

I shook hands with him and walked across the field to the pickup truck. The hack turned the truck around, and we rolled down the baked and corrugated road through the bottom section of the farm toward the Block. I looked through the back window and watched the ugly, squat white building called the Red Hat

House grow smaller against the line of willows on the river. It was named during the thirties when the big stripes (the violent and the insane) were kept there. In those days, before the Block with its lock-down section was built, the dangerous ones wore black-and-white-striped jumpers and straw hats that were painted red. When they went in at night from the fields, they had to strip naked for a body search and their clothes were thrown into the building after them. Later, the building came to house the electric chair, and someone had painted in broken letters on one wall: THIS IS WHERE THEY KNOCK THE FIRE OUT OF YOUR ASS.

We drove through the acres of new corn, sugar cane and sweet potatoes, the squared sections and weedless rows mathematically perfect, each thing in its ordered and predesigned place, past Camp H and its roofless and crumbling stone buildings left over from the Civil War, past the one-storey rows of barracks on Camp I, then the shattered and weed-grown block of concrete slab in an empty field by Camp A where the two iron sweatboxes had been bulldozed out in the early fifties. I closed off the hot stream of air through the wind vane and rolled a cigarette.

'What are you going to do outside?' the hack said. He chewed gum, and his lean sun-tanned face and washed-out blue eyes looked at me flatly with his question. His starched khaki short sleeves were folded in a neat cuff above his biceps. As a new guard he had the same status among us as a fish, a convict just beginning his first fall.

'I haven't thought about it yet,' I said.

'There's plenty of work if a man wants to do it.' His eyes were young and mean, and there was just enough of that north Louisiana Baptist righteousness in his voice to make you pause before you spoke again.

'I've heard that.'

'It don't take long to get your ass put back in here if you ain't working,' he said.

I licked the glued seam of the cigarette paper, folded it down under my thumb, and crimped the ends.

'You got a match, boss?'

His eyes looked over my face, trying to peel through the skin and reach inside the insult of being called a title that was given only to the old hacks who had been on the farm for years. He took a kitchen match from his shirt pocket and handed it to me.

I popped the match on my fingernail and drew in on the suck of flame and glue and the strong black taste of Virginia Extra. We passed the prison cemetery with its faded wooden markers and tin cans of withered flowers and the grave of Alton Bienvenu. He did thirty-three years in Angola and had the record for time spent in the sweatbox on Camp A (twenty-two days in July with space only large enough for the knees and buttocks to collapse against the sides and still hold a man in an upright position, a slop bucket sat between the ankles and one air hole the diameter of a cigar drilled in the iron door). He died in 1957, three years before I went in, but even when I was in the fish tank (the thirty days of processing and classification in lock-down you go through before you enter the main population), I heard about the man who broke out twice when he was a young bindle stiff, took the beatings in solitary and the anthill treatment on the levee gang, and later as an old man worked paroles through an uncle in the state legislature for other convicts when he had none coming himself, taught reading to illiterates, had morphine tablets smuggled back from the prison section of the charity hospital in New Orleans for a junkie who was going to fry, and testified before a governor's board in Baton Rouge about the reasons that convicts on Angola farm slashed the tendons in their ankles. After his death he was canonized in the prison's group legend with a saint's aura rivalled only by a Peter, crucified upside down in a Roman arena with his shackles still stretched between his legs.

The mound of Alton Bienvenu's grave was covered with a cross of flowers, a thick purple, white and gold-tinted shower of violets, petunias, cowslips and buttercups from the fields. A trusty was cutting away the St Augustine grass from the edge of the mound with a gardener's trowel.

'What do you think about that?' the hack said.

'I guess it's hard to keep a grave clean,' I said, and I pinched the hot ash of my cigarette against the paint on the outside of the car door.

'That's some shit, ain't it? Putting flowers on a man's grave that's already gone to hell.' He spit his chewing gum into the wind and drove the truck with one hand over the ruts as though he were aiming between his tightened knuckles at the distant green square of enclosure by the front gate called the Block.

The wind was cool through the concrete, shaded breezeway as we walked towards my dormitory. The trusties were watering the recreation yard, and the grass and weight-lifting sets glistened in the sun. We reached the first lock and waited for the hack to pull the combination of levers that would slide the gate. The Saturday-morning cleaning crews were washing down the walls and floor in my dormitory with buckets of soap and water and an astringent antiseptic that burned the inside of your head when you breathed it. The dirt shaled off my boots on the wet floor, but no sign of protest or irritation showed on a man's face. Because the hack was there with me, there was some vague reason for them to redo part of their work, and they squeezed out their mops in the buckets, the ashes dropping from their cigarettes, and went about mopping my muddy tracks with their eyes as flat as glass.

'You can keep your underwear and your shoes,' the hack said. 'Throw your other clothes and sheets in a pile outside. Roll your mattress and don't leave nothing behind. I'll pick you up in the rec room when you get finished and take you over to Possessions.'

I pulled off my work uniform, put on my clack sandals, and walked down the corridor to the showers. I let the cold water boil over my head and face until my breath came short in my chest. One man on the cleaning detail had stopped mopping and was watching me through the doorless opening in the shower partition. He was a queen in Magnolia section who was finishing his second jolt for child molesting. His buttocks swelled out like a pear, and he always kept his shirt buttoned at the throat and never bathed.

'Take off, Morton. No show today, babe,' I said.

'I don't want nothing off you,' he said, and rinsed his mop in the bucket, his soft stomach hanging over his belt.

'You guys watch the goddamn floor,' I heard somebody yell down the corridor; then came the noise of the first crews who had been knocked off from the fields. 'We done cleaned it twice already. You take your goddamn shoes off.'

When I got back to my cell, the corridor was striped with the dry imprints of bare feet, and my cell partner, W.J. Posey, was sitting shirtless on his bunk, with his knees drawn up before him, smoking the wet end of a hand-rolled cigarette between his lips without removing it. His balding pate was sunburned and flecked with pieces of dead skin, and the knobs of his elbows and shoulders and the areas of bone in his chest were the colour of a dead carp. He was working on five to fifteen, a three-time loser for hanging paper, and in the year we had celled together, warrants had been filed for him in three other states. His withered arms were covered with faded tattoos done in Lewisburg and Parchman, and his thick, nicotine-stained fingernails looked like claws.

I put on the shiny suit and the off-colour brown shoes that had been brought to my cell the night before by the count man. I threw my sheets, blanket and the rest of my prison uniforms and denims into the corridor, and put my underwear, work boots and three new shirts and pairs of socks into the box the suit had come in.

'You want the purses and wallets, W.J.?'

'Yeah, give them to me. I can trade them to that punk in Ash for a couple of decks.'

'Take care, babe. Don't hang out any more on the wash line.'

'Yeah. Write me a card when you make your first million,' he said. He dropped his cigarette stub into the butt can by his bunk and picked at his toenails.

I walked down the corridor past the row of open cells and the men with bath towels around their waists clacking in their wooden sandals towards the roar of water and shouting in the shower stalls. The wind through the breezeway was cool against my face and wet collar. I waited at the second lock for the hack to open up.

'You know the rec don't open till twelve-thirty, Paret,' he said.

'Mr Benson said he wanted me to wait for him there, boss.'

'Well, you ain't supposed to be there.'

'Let him through, Frank,' the other hack on the lock said.

The gate slid back with its quiet rush of hydraulically released pressure. I waited in the dead space between the first and second gates for the hack to pull the combination of levers again.

Our recreation room had several folding card tables, a canteen where you could buy Koolaid and soda pop, and a small library filled with worthless books donated by the Salvation Army. Anything that was either vaguely pornographic or violent or, especially, racial was somehow eaten up in a censoring process that must have begun at the time of donation and ended at the front gate. But anyway, it was thorough, because there wasn't a plot in one of those books that wouldn't bore the most moronic among us. I sat at a card table that was covered with burns like melted plastic insects, and rolled a cigarette from the last tobacco in my package of Virginia Extra.

I heard the lock hiss, then the noise of the first men walking through the dead space, their voices echoing briefly off the stone walls, into the recreation room, where they would wait until the dining hall opened at 12:45. They all wore clean denims and pinstripes, their hair wet and slicked back over the ears, combs clipped in their shirt pockets, pomade and aftershave lotion, glistening in their pompadours and sideburns, and names like Popcorn, Snowbird and Git-It-and-Go were Cloroxed into their trousers.

'Hey, Willard, get out them guitars,' one man said.

Each Saturday afternoon our country band played on the green stretch of lawn between the first two buildings in the Block. We had one steel guitar and pickups and amplifiers for the two flattops, and our fiddle and mandolin players held their instruments right into the microphone so we could reach out with 'Orange Blossom Special' and 'Please Release Me, Darling' all the way across the cane field to Camp I.

Willard, the trusty, opened the closet where the instruments were kept and handed out the two Kay flattops. The one I used had a capo fashioned from a pencil and a piece of inner-tube on the second fret of the neck. West Finley, whose brother named East was also in Angola, handed the guitar to me in his clumsy fashion, with his huge hand squeezed tight on the strings and his bad teeth grinning around his cigar.

'I mean you look slick, cotton. Them free-people clothes is fierce. I thought you was a damn movie star,' he said.

'You've been sniffing gas tanks again, West.'

'No shit, man. Threads like that is going to cause some kind of female riot in the bus depot.' His lean, hillbilly face was full of good humour, his mouth wide and brown with tobacco juice. 'Break down my song for me, babe, because I ain't going to be able to hear it played right for a long time.'

The others formed around us, grinning, their arms folded in front of them, with cigarettes held up casually to their mouths, waiting for West to enter the best part of his performance.

'No pick,' I said.

'Shit,' and he said it with that singular two-syllable pronunciation of the Mississippi delta: *shee-it*. He took an empty match cover from the ashtray, folded it in half, and handed it to me between his callused fingers. 'Now let's get it on, Iry. The boss man is going to be ladling them peas in a minute.'

Our band's rhythm-guitar man sat across from me with the other big Kay propped on his folded thigh. I clicked the match cover once across the open strings, sharped the B and A, and turned the face of the guitar towards him so he could see my E-chord configuration of the neck. The song was an old Jimmie Rodgers piece that began, 'If you don't like my peaches, don't shake my tree', and then the lyrics became worse. But West was beautiful. He bopped on the waxed floor, the shined points of the alligator shoes his girl had sent him flashing above his own scuff marks, bumping and grinding as he went into the dirty boogie, his oiled, ducktailed hair collapsed in a black web over his face. One man took a small harmonica from his shirt pocket and blew a deep, train-moaning bass behind us, and West caught it and pumped the air with his loins, his arms stretched out beside him, while the other men whistled and clapped and grabbed themselves. Through a crack of shoulders I saw the young hack come through the lock into the recreation room, and I slid back down the neck to E again and bled it off quietly on the treble strings.

West's face was perspiring and his eyes were bright. He took his cigar from the table's edge, and his breath came short when he spoke. 'When you get up to Nashville with all them sweet things on the Opry, tell them the big bopper from Bogalusa is primed and ready and will be taking requests in six more months.

Tell them I quit charging, too. I done give up my selfish ways about sharing my body. They ain't got to be Marilyn Monroe either. I ain't a snob, cotton.'

Everyone laughed, their mouths full of empty spaces and gold and lead fillings. Then the outside bell rang, and the third lock, which controlled the next section of the breezeway, hissed back in a suck of air.

'Got to scarf it down and put some protein in the pecker. Do something good for me tonight,' West said, and popped two fingers off his thumbnail into my arm as he walked past me towards the lock with the other men.

'Just leave the guitar on the table,' the hack said. 'The state car is leaving at one.'

I picked up my box and followed him back through the lock. He held up my discharge slip to the hack by the levers, which was unnecessary, since the lock was already opened and all the old bosses along the breezeway knew that I was going out that day anyway. But as I watched him walk in front of me, with his starched khaki shirt shaping and reshaping across his back like iron, I realized that he would be holding up papers of denial or permission with a whitened click of knuckles for the rest of his life.

'You better move unless you want to walk down to the highway,' he said halfway over his shoulder.

We went to Possessions, and he waited while the trusty looked through the rows of alphabetized manila envelopes that were stuffed into the tiers of shelves and hung with stringed, circular tags. The trusty flipped his stiffened fingers down a row in a rattling of glue and paper and shook out one flattened envelope and brushed the dust off the top with his palm. The hack bit on a matchstick and looked at his watch.

'Check it and sign for it,' the trusty said. 'You got forty-three dollars coming in discharge money and fifty-eight in your commissary fund. I can't give you nothing but fives and ones and some silver. They done cleaned me out this morning.'

'That's all right,' I said.

I opened the manila envelope and took out the things that I had entered the Calcasieu Parish jail with two years and three months before, after I had killed a man: a blunted minié ball perforated with a hole that I had used as a weight when I fished as a boy on Bayou Teche and Spanish Lake; the gold pocket watch my father gave me when I graduated from high school; a Swiss army knife with a can opener, screwdriver and a saw that could build a cabin; one die from a pair of dice, the only thing I brought back from thirteen months in Korea because they had separated me from sixteen others who went up Heart Break Ridge and stayed there in that pile of wasted ash; and a notecase with all the celluloid-enclosed pieces of identification that are so important to us, now outdated and worthless in their cracked description of who the bearer was.

We walked out of the Block into the brilliant sunlight, and the hack drove us down the front road past the small clapboard cottages where the free people lived. The washing on the lines straightened and dropped in the wind, the tiny gardens were planted with chrysanthemums and rosebushes, and housewives in print dresses appeared quickly in open screen doors to shout at the children in the yard. It could have been a scene surgically removed from a working-class neighbourhood, except for the presence of the Negro trusties watering the grass or weeding a vegetable patch.

Then there was the front gate, with three strands of barbed wire leaned inwards on top and the wooden gun tower to one side. The oiled road on the other side bounced and shimmered with heat waves and stretched off through the green border of trees and second growth on the edge of the ditches. I got out of the car with my cardboard box under my arm.

'Paret coming out,' the hack said.

I knew he was going to try to shake hands while the gate was being swung back over the cattle guard, and I kept my attention fixed on the road and used my free hand to look for a cigarette in my shirt pocket. The hack shook a Camel loose from his pack and held it up to me.

'Well, thanks, Mr Benson,' I said.

'Keep the rest of them. I got some more in the cage.' So I had to shake hands with him after all. He got back in the truck with a pinch of light in his iron face, his role a little more secure.

I walked across the cattle guard and heard the gate rattle and lock behind me. Four other men with cardboard boxes and suits similar to mine (we had a choice of three styles upon discharge) sat on the wooden waiting bench by the fence. The shade of the gun tower broke in an oblong square across their bodies.

'The state car ought to be up in a minute, Paret,' the gateman said. He was one of the old ones, left over from the thirties, and he had probably killed and buried more men in the levee than any other hack on the farm. Now he was almost seventy, covered with the kind of obscene white fat that comes from years of drinking corn whiskey, and there wasn't a town in Louisiana or Mississippi where he could retire in safety from the convicts whom he had put on anthills or run double-time with wheelbarrows up and down the levee until they collapsed on their hands and knees.

'I think I need to hoof this one,' I said.

'It's twenty miles out to that highway, boy.' And he didn't say it unkindly. The word came to him as automatically as anything else that he raised up out of thirty-five years of doing almost the same type of time that the rest of us pulled.

'I know that, boss. But I got to stretch it out.' I didn't turn to look at him, but I knew that his slate-green eyes were staring into my back with a mixture of resentment and impotence at seeing a piece of personal property moved across a line into a world in which he himself could not function.

The dead water in the ditches along the road was covered with lily pads, and dragonflies flicked with their purple wings above the newly opened flowers. The leaves on the trees were coated with dust, and the red-black soil at the roots was lined with the tracings of night crawlers. I was perspiring under my coat, and I pulled it off with one hand and stuck it through the twine wrapped around the cardboard box. A mile up the road I heard the tyres of the state car whining hotly down the oiled surface. They slowed in second gear alongside me, the hack bent forward into the steering wheel so he could speak past his passenger.

'That's a hot son of a bitch to walk, and you probably ain't going to hitch no ride on the highway.'

I smiled and shook the palm of my hand at them, and after the car had accelerated away in a bright-yellow cloud of gravel and dust and oil, someone shot the finger out of the back window.

I threw the cardboard box into the ditch and walked three more miles to a beer tavern and café set off by the side of the road in a circle of gravel. The faded wooden sides of the building were covered with rotted election posters (DON'T GET CAUGHT SHORT — VOTE LONG — SPEEDY O. LONG, A SLAVE TO NO MAN AND A SERVANT TO ALL), flaking and rusted tin signs advertising Hadacol and Carry-On, and stickers for Brown Mule, Calumet baking powder and Doctor Tichner's Painless Laxative. A huge live-oak tree, covered with Spanish moss, grew by one side of the building, and its roots had swelled under the wall with enough strength to bend the window jamb.

It was dark and cool inside, with a wooden ceiling fan turning overhead, and the bar shined with the dull light of the neon beer signs and the emptiness of the room. It felt strange to pull out the chair from the bar and scrape it into position and sit down. The bartender was in the kitchen talking with a Negro girl. His arms were covered with tattoos and a heavy growth of white hair. He wore a folded butcher's apron tied around his great girth of stomach.

'Hey, podna, how about a Jax down here?' I said.

He leaned into the service window, his heavy arms folded in front of him and his head extended under the enclosure.

'Just get it out of the cooler, mister, and I'll be with you in a minute.'

I went behind the bar and stuck my hand into the deep, ice-filled cooler and pulled out a bottle of Jax and snapped off the cap in the opener box. My wrist and arm ached with the cold and shale of ice against my skin. The foam boiled over the lip and ran down on my hand in a way that was as strange, at that moment, as the bar chair, the dull, neon beer signs and the Negro girl scraping a spatula vacantly across the flat surface of the stove. I drank another Jax before the man came out of the kitchen, then ate a poor-boy sandwich with shrimp, oysters, lettuce and sauce hanging out the sides of the French bread.

'You just getting out?' the man said. He said it in the flat, casual tone that most free people use toward convicts, that same quality of voice behind the Xeroxed letters from Boston asking for the donation of our eyes.

I put three dollar bills on the bar and walked towards the square of sunlight against the front door.

'Say, buddy, it don't matter to me what you're getting out of. I was just saying my cousin will give you a ride up to the highway in a few minutes.'

I walked down the oiled road a quarter of a mile, and his cousin picked me up in a stake truck and drove me all the way to the train depot in Baton Rouge.

TWO

I could have taken a bus home or hitchhiked, because it was only a three-hour trip to the coast, but I always loved trains, their rows of quiet, angular seats and the suck and rattle of the vestibule opening, and also, there is no dignity in hitchhiking when you are thirty years old. The clapboard general stores and taverns and oaks clicked by the window, and beyond the highway the grey trees of the marsh began. Negroes in flop straw hats cane-fished along the canal, and white cranes rose with their wings gilded in the sunlight above the dead cypress. The butcher boy swayed down the aisle with the roll of the train, his basket loaded with magazines, newspapers, cans of grape drink, and paper cones of plums. I bought a *Times-Picayune* from him and walked to the dining car.

The porter brought me a Jax, and after I tired of the front page and its serious treatment of something the state legislature was doing, I sipped the beer and watched the fields of new sugar cane and black Angus roll past. But as we neared New Orleans, the country began to change. Somebody had been busy in the last two years; it was no longer a rural section of the delta. Land-development signs stood along the highway, replacing the old ads for patent medicine and Purina feed, and great areas of marsh had been bulldozed out and covered with landfill for subdivision tracts. Mobile-home offices strung with coloured flags sat on cinder blocks in the mud, with acres of waste in the background that were already marked into housing plots with surveyors' stakes. The shopping-centre boys had been hard at work, too. Pecan orchards and dairy barns had become Food City, Winn-Dixie and Cash Discount.

I had to change trains in New Orleans for the rest of the trip home. The train was an old one, with dusty seats and yellowed windows cracked on the outside of the double glass with bb holes. We crossed the Mississippi, and my head reeled when I looked down from the window at the wide expanse of water far below. The tugboats and Standard Oil barges and the brown scratches of wake off their hulls looked as miniature and flat as painted pieces on a map. The train clicked slowly across the bridge and the long stretch of elevated track above the levee and mud flats and willow trees, then began to gain speed and bend through the bayou country and the achingly beautiful dark green of the cypress and oak trees, covered with moss and bursting at the roots with mushrooms and cowslips.

Most of the passengers in my car were French people, with cardboard suitcases and boxes tied with string in the luggage rack. An old man in overalls and a suit jacket was speaking French to his wife in the seat behind me, and I listened to them with a violation of privacy that normally I would have walked away from. But in Angola the hacks, who came primarily from north Louisiana and Mississippi, never allowed anyone to speak French in their presence, and even back in the Block it wasn't used unless there was no non-French-speaking person within earshot, because it was considered to have the same clandestine quality as a private whisper between two snitches.

The train crossed Bayou Lafourche, and I leaned into the window and looked at the men in pirogues floating motionlessly against the cypress roots, their cane poles arched and beaten with light against the pull of a bull bream below the lily pads. Before the train moved back into that long corridor of trees through the swamp, I saw one man rip a large goggle-eye perch through a torn leaf and dip one hand quickly into the water with the cane bending in his other hand, the boat almost tilted into the shallows, and catch the line in his fingers and pull the fish slowly away from the lily pads.

Then we were back into the long span of track through the trees and the dead water in the irrigation canals and the occasional farmhouses that you could see beyond the railway right of way. I walked up to the dining car and had a bourbon and water while the train slowed into my hometown. The X signs and LOUISIANA LAW STOP warnings on the crossings moved by gradually with the decreased speed of the train, and then the uplifted faces of the people on the platform stared suddenly at mine, then turned with a quick brightness of recognition at someone stepping off the vestibule.

There was an ice wagon on the loading ramp with a tarpaulin stretched across the ice blocks, and the evaporated coldness steamed on top of the canvas in the sun. Two taxicabs were parked in the shade of an oak that grew through the pavement in the front of the depot.

'Do you know how to get to Robert Paret's place?' I said.

'Who?' The taxi driver's breath was full of beer through the window, and he smoked a filter-tipped cigarette in a gap between his teeth.

'It's up Joe's Shipyard road. You reckon you can take me there?'

'That's fifteen miles, podna. I'll turn the meter off for you, but it'll still cost you ten dollars and maybe some for the tyres I bust on that board road up there.'

The town was changed. Or maybe it had been changing for a long time and I hadn't noticed it. Many of the old brick and wood-front stores had gone out of business, the hotel had a FOR LEASE sign in its dusty main window, and only a few cars were parked in front of the beer tavern and pool hall on the corner. The dime store, which used to be crowded with Negroes on Saturday afternoon, was almost empty. We passed the courthouse square and the lines of oak trees shading the wide pavements and wooden benches where the old men used to sit, but it looked like a discarded movie set. The Confederate monument, inscribed at the base with the words THEY DIED IN DEFENSE OF A HOLY CAUSE,

was spotted with pigeon droppings, and someone had stuffed
trash paper in the barrel of the Civil War cannon next to it. Only
one or two offices besides the bail bondsman's were open, and the
corner bar that used to have a card game upstairs was now
boarded over.

'Where did the town go?' I said.

'It just dried up after they put in that new highway,' the driver
said. 'People ain't going to drive into town when you can get
everything you need out there. You just getting out of the service
or something?'

'I've been away awhile.'

'Well, there's lots of money to be made here. Like, I could be
making twice what I'm getting today if that dispatcher didn't put
me on call at the depot.' He belched down in his throat and
loosened a can of beer from a six-pack on the seat. He pulled the
ring, and the foam slid over his thumb. 'You can pick up fares at
the airport and run them a half mile down to the motel, and what
you get on tips is more money than I make all afternoon at the
depot. Take one of them beers if you like.'

'Thank you,' I said. The can was hot, but I drank it anyway.

We drove out into the parish, crossed the wooden bridge over
the bayou at the end of the blacktop, and bounced along the
yellow, rutted road by the edge of Joe's Shipyard. Shrimp boats,
rusted oil barges and quarter boats used by seismograph companies were moored along the docks in the dead water, and Negro
children were fishing with cane poles for bullheads and gars
among the cattails. The driver was out of beer, and we stopped at
a tavern filled with deckhands, fishermen, and doodlebuggers
(seismograph workers), and I bought him a round at the bar and
a carton of Jax to go.

The road followed along the edge of the bayou and the cypress
trees that hung out over the water. The expanded swell of the
trunks at the waterline was dark from the wake of passing boats,
and white egrets were nesting in the sand, their delicate wings
quivering as they enlarged the depression around them. I had
fished for bream, sacalait and mud cat under every cypress on
that bank, because they always came into the shade to feed in the
hottest part of a summer afternoon, and there was one tree that

had rusted mooring chains nailed into the trunk with iron stakes that the bark had overgrown in stages until the chain looped in and out of the tree like a deformity. My grandfather said that Jean Laffite used to tie his boat there when he was blackbirding and that he had buried a treasure between two oaks on the back of our property. The ground around the two oaks was pitted with depressions and ragged holes that cut through the roots, and as boys my older brother and I had dug six feet down and scraped away the clay from around the lid of a huge iron caldron, hollowing out the hole like sculptors, to prize up the lid with our shovels and finally discover the bones of a hog that had been boiled into tallow.

We hit the section of board road that Shell Oil had put in three years before when the road had washed out again and the parish refused to maintain it any longer, since the only people who used it were my father and the two or three doodlebug companies that were shooting in that part of the parish. The boards twisted under the tyres and slammed upwards into the oil pan, and then I saw the mailbox by the short wooden bridge over the coulee.

I paid the driver and walked up the gravel lane through the oak trees. The house had been built by my great-grandfather in 1857, in the Creole architectural style of that period, with brick chimneys on each side and brick columns supporting the lattice-work verandah on the second storey. The peaked roof was now covered with tin, and the foundation had sunk on one side so that the brick columns had cracked and started to shale. The decayed outlines of the slaves' quarters were still visible in the grass down by the bayou, and the original stone well, now filled with dirt and overgrown with vines, protruded from the ground at an angle by the smokehouse. My father had held on to forty-three acres since the depression, when we lost most of the farm, and he had refused to lease the mineral rights to the oil companies (he called them Texas sharpers who destroyed your land, cut your fences, and gave you a duster in return), but in the last few years the only sugar cane had been grown by Negroes who worked on shares. His Ford pickup truck with last year's number plate was parked in the shed, and there was an old Buick pulled on to the grass at the end of the lane.

The swing on the porch twisted slightly against the chains in the breeze. I tapped on the screen door and tried to see inside into the gloom.

'Hello!'

I heard someone at the back of the upstairs hallway, and I went inside with a strange feeling of impropriety. The house smelled of dust and a lack of sunlight. For some reason the only detail that caught in my eye was his guns in the deer-antler rack above the mantelpiece. The .30–.40 Kraig with the box magazine on the side, the lever-action Winchester and the double-barrel twelve were flecked with rust and coated with cobwebs in the trigger guards and barrels.

'What you want here?'

I looked up the stairs at a big Negro woman in a starched nurse's uniform. Her rolled white hose seemed to be bursting around her black thighs.

'I'm Mr Paret's son.'

She walked down the stairs, her hand on the banister to support her weight. There were tangles of grey hair above her forehead, and I knew that she was much older than she looked.

'You Mr Iry?'

'Yes.'

'He figured you'd be home this week. I just give him his sedative, so he won't be able to talk with you too long. After he takes his nap and has his supper, he can talk a lot better to you.'

'How bad is he?'

'He ain't good. But maybe you better wait on the doctor. He's coming out tonight with your sister. She stays with him on my night off.'

'Thank you.'

'Mr Iry, he talks funny because of that medicine. He's all right after his supper.'

I walked up the stairs into his room. It was dark, and the only light came from the yellow glow of sun against the window shade. Small bottles of urine were lined on the dresser, and there was a shiny bedpan on a stool at the head of the tester bed. His curved pipe and tobacco pouch rested against the armadillo-shell lamp on the nightstand. I didn't know that his face could look so white and wasted. The sheet was pulled up to his chin, and the knobs of his hands looked like bone against the skin. He ticked a finger on his stomach and squinted into the glare of light from the open door with one watery blue eye, and I saw that he couldn't recognize me in the silhouette. I eased the door closed behind me. He smiled, and his lips were purple like an old woman's. He moved his hand off his stomach and tapped it softly on the side of the bed.

'How'd they treat you, Son?'

'It wasn't bad.'

'I thought you might be in yesterday from your letter. I had that nigra nurse make up your room for you. Your guitars are on the bed.' His voice clicked when he spoke, as though he had a fishhook in his throat.

'How they been treating you, Daddy?'

'They like my urine. The doctor takes it away every two days after the nurse puts stickers all over it.' He laughed down in his chest, and a bubble of saliva formed on the corner of his mouth. 'They must not have much to do down at the Charity except look at somebody's piss.'

'Daddy, did Rita and Ace put you in at Charity?'

'They got families of their own, Iry. It costs fifteen dollars a day to keep that nigra woman out here. They ain't got money like that.'

I had to clench my fingers between my legs and look away from him. My sister and brother had married into enough money to bring in the best of everything for him.

'Look at me, Son, and don't start letting those razor blades work around inside you. The one thing I regret is that my children never held together after your mother died. I don't know what they done to you in the penitentiary, but don't take your anger out on them.'

His watery blue eyes were starting to fade with the sedation, and he had to force his words past that obstacle in his throat. I looked at his white hair on the pillow and his thin arms stretched down the top of the sheet, and wondered at what disease and age could do to men, particularly this one, who had gone over the top in a scream of whistles at Belleau Wood and had covered a canister of mustard gas with his own body.

'Why don't you go to sleep and I'll see you later,' I said.

'I want you to do one thing for me this evening. Cut some azaleas by the porch and take them down by your mother's grave.'

'All right, Daddy.'

'I know you don't like to go down there.' The light in his eyes was fading away like a quick blue spark.

'I was going down there anyway,' I said.

His eyes closed, and the lids were red against the paper whiteness of his face.

I had heard stories about the effects of intestinal cancer and how fast it could consume a man and his life's energy, in spite of radiation treatments and the morphine shots to take away the pain, but you had to look at it to make it become real.

I walked down the hall to my room, which he had kept as it was the day I went on the road again with the band and ended up in the penitentiary. My over-and-under, with the .22 magnum and .410 barrels, was propped in one corner, my clothes hung limply in the closet, the creases on the hangers stained with dust, and my double guitar case that held the Martin flattop and the dobro sat on top of the bed, with the gold-embossed inscription THE GREAT SPECKLED BIRD across the leather surface. I opened the case, which had cost me two hundred dollars to have custom-made in Dallas, and for a moment in the crinkled flash of the Confederate flag that lined the inside and the waxed shine off the guitars, I was back in the bar-room with the scream of voices around me and the knife wet and shaking in my hand.

I stripped naked and dressed in a pair of khakis and a denim shirt and slipped on a pair of old loafers. I put everything from Angola inside the suit coat, tied the sleeves into a hard knot, and pushed it down in the wastebasket.

Downstairs, I found the bottle of Ancient Age that my father always kept under the draining-board. I poured a good drink into a tin cup and sipped it slowly while I looked out of the window through the oak trees in the garden and at the sun starting to fade over the marsh. Purple rain clouds lay against the horizon, and shafts of sunlight cut like bands of crimson across the cypress tops. I had another drink, this time with water in the cup, and took a butcher knife and the bottle outside with me to the azalea bushes by the side of the house.

I snipped the knife through a dozen branches covered with red flowers and walked down the slope towards the graveyard. It was close to the bayou, and ten years before, we had had to put sacks of cement against the bank and push an old car body into the water to prevent the widening bend of current from eroding the iron fence at the graveyard's edge. There were twenty-three graves in all, from the four generations of my family who were buried on the original land, and the oldest were raised brick-and-mortar crypts that were now cracked with weeds and covered with the scale of dead vines. The graves of my mother and sister were next to each other with a common headstone that was divided by a thin chiselled line. It was brutally simple in its words.

CLAIRE PARET AND FRAN

NOVEMBER 7, 1945

There was a tin can full of rusty water and dead stems on the grave, and I picked it up and threw it back in the trees, then laid the azaleas against the headstone in the half-light. It had been seventeen years, but I still had dreams about the fire and the moment when I raced around the back of the house and tried to break open the bolted door with my fists. Through the window I could see my mother's face convulsed like an epileptic's in the flames, the can of cleaning fluid still in her hand, while Fran stood with a halo of fire rising over her pinafore. Alcide, the Negro who worked for us, threw me backwards off the porch and drove a pickaxe up to the helve into the doorjamb. But the wind blew the inside of the house into a furnace, and Fran plunged out of the flames, her clothes and hair dissolving and streaming away behind her.

I took a drink from the bottle and walked down the mud flat and skipped a stone across the bayou's quiet surface. The stone hit in the lily pads on the far side, and the water suddenly became dimpled with small bream. The light was almost gone from the trees now, and as I sat back against a cypress and pulled again on the bottle, I had to wonder what I was doing there at all.

When I neared the top of the slope by the smokehouse, I saw a Cadillac parked by the front porch where the nurse's car had been. It must be Ace, I thought. Rita's preference would lean towards smaller expensive cars, something conservative enough not to make the wives of her husband's law partners competitive. Or maybe both of them at once, I thought, which was more than I was ready for at that moment.

I walked around the side of the front porch just as Ace was holding open the screen door for her. Ace's face had the formality of an undertaker's, with his mouth turned downwards in some type of expression that he had learned for all occasions at a chamber of commerce meeting, and his wilted tie seemed almost glued to his throat. Rita saw me before he did, and she turned in the half-opened screen with her mouth still parted in the middle of a sentence and looked steadily at me as though her eyes wouldn't focus. She was pregnant, and she had gained a good deal of weight since I had seen her last. She had always been a pretty, auburn-haired girl, with small breasts and hips that were only slightly too large for the rest of her, but now her face was oval, her thighs wide, and her maternity dress was stretched tight over her swollen buttocks.

It wasn't going to be pleasant. Their genuine ex-convict was home, the family's one failure, the bad-conduct dischargee from the army, the hillbilly guitar picker who embarrassed both of them just by his presence in the area.

But at least Ace tried. He walked down the steps with his hand outstretched, as though he had been set in motion by a trip switch in the back of his head. He must have sold hundreds of ad accounts with the same papier-mâché smile.

Rita wasn't as generous. Her face looked like she had morning sickness.

We went inside and stood in the hall with the awkwardness of people who might have just met at a bus stop.

'How about a drink?' I said.

'I could go for that,' Ace said.

I took three glasses from the cupboard and poured into the bottom of them.

'I'm not having any,' Rita said. She was looking in her handbag for a cigarette when she spoke.

'Take one. We don't get the old boy home much,' Ace said, and then pressed his lips together.

'I'll go look in on Daddy,' she said, putting the cigarette in her mouth as though it had to be screwed in.

'Have a drink, Reet. The nurse gave him sedation about a half hour ago,' I said.

'I know that.'

'So have one with us.' It was hard, and maybe there was just a little bit of bile behind my teeth.

She lit her cigarette without answering and dropped the match in the sink. Sometimes, without even trying, you can step in a pile of pig flop right up to your kneecaps, I thought.

'Do you have a finger on a job?' Ace said.

'Not a thing.'

'There's a lot of money being made now.'

'The taxicab driver told me.'

'I'm selling more accounts than I can handle. I might get into some real estate on the side, because that's where it's going to be in the next five years.'

'Do you know if any of the band is still around?' I said.

His face went blank, and his eyes searched in the air.

'No, I didn't know any of them, really.'

'We went to high school with most of them,' I said.

Rita put out her cigarette in the sink and went upstairs. I finished my drink and had another. The whiskey was starting to rise in my face.

'Between the two of us, you think you might want to get in on something solid?' Ace said. He could never drink very well, and his eyes were taking on a shine.

'I think I'm just going to roll, Ace.'

'I'm not telling you what to do, but isn't that how you got into trouble before?'

'I finished all my trouble as of noon today.' I poured another shot in his glass.

'What I'm saying is you can make it. I've got kids working for me that are bringing in ten thousand a year.'

'You're not offering me a public-relations job, are you?'

He started to smile, and then looked again at my face. Rita came back in the kitchen and opened the oven to check on the warmed plate of mashed potatoes and gruel that the nurse had left for my father. I shouldn't have started what came next, but they were drumming their nails on a weak nerve, and the whiskey had already broken down that polite line of restraint.

'Y'all really took care of the old man, didn't you?'

Rita turned from the oven, holding the plate in a hot pad, and looked at me directly for the first time. Her eyes were awful. Ace started to nod at what he thought was an automatic expression of errant-brother gratitude, but then that toggle switch in the back of his head clicked again and his face stretched tight.

'What do you mean, Iry?' The bourbon in his glass tilted back and forth.

'Like maybe Lourdes wants too much gelt to handle him, since they have the best doctors in southwest Louisiana.'

'I don't think you understand everything that was involved,' Ace said. His face was as flat as a dough pan.

'The emergency ward at Charity looks like a butcher shop on Saturday afternoon. I mean, just check out that scene. They deliver babies in the hallways, and the smell that comes off that incinerator is enough to make your eyeballs fall out. For Christ's sake, Ace, you could write a cheque to pay the old man's way a year at Lourdes.'

'That's very fine of you,' Rita said. 'Maybe there are some other things we've done wrong that you can tell us about. It was also good of you to contribute so much while you were in Angola.'

'All right, but you didn't have to put him into Charity.'

'You're really off base, Iry,' Ace said.

'Where did you learn that one? At an ad meeting?'

'Ridiculous,' Rita said.

'How do you think he feels being shovelled in with every reject from the parish? He even defended you this afternoon.'

'If you think so much of his welfare, why don't you lower your voice?' Rita said.

463

And then Ace, the PR man for all occasions, filled my glass and handed it to me. I set it back on the draining-board, my head tingling with anger and the bourbon's heat and the strange movements of the day.

'It was a rotten thing to do,' I said. 'You both know it.'

I walked out the house into the twilight. I felt foolish and light-headed in the wind off the bayou, and there was a line of sweat down the front of my shirt. Through the kitchen window I heard them start to purge their anger on each other.

The trees were filled with a mauve glow from the sun's last light, and I went down to the shed where the pickup was parked, my legs loose under me and a bright flash of caution already clicking on and off in one sober part of my mind.

But the old reckless impulses had more sway, and I scooped some mud out of the drive and smeared it thickly over the expired plate. I turned the truck around and banged over the wooden bridge and roared in second gear down the board road, the ditches on each side of me whipping by the mudguards like a drunken challenge.

I stopped at the beer joint by Joe's Shipyard, which contained about fifteen outlaw motor cyclists and their women. They wore grease-stained blue jeans, half-topped boots with chains on the side, and sleeveless denim jackets with a sewed inscription on the back that read:

DEVILS DISCIPLES
NEW ORLEANS

Their arms were covered with tattoos of snakes' heads, skulls, and hearts impaled on bleeding knives. I didn't know what they were doing in this area, far from their usual concrete turf, but I found out later that they had come to bust up some civil-rights workers at a demonstration.

The bar had divided in half, with the doodlebuggers, deck-hands, and oilfield roughnecks on one side and the motor cyclists on the other, their voices deliberately loud, their beards dripping with beer, and their girls flashing their stuff at the enemy.

I bought three six-packs of Jax and a carton of cigarettes at the bar and walked through the tables towards the door. Someone had turned the jukebox up to full tilt, and Little Richard screamed out all his rage about Long Tall Sally left in the alley. I was almost home free when one of them leaned his chair back into my stomach.

His blond hair hung in curls on his denim jacket, and a pachuco cross was tattooed between his eyebrows. There was beer foam all over his moustache and beard, and his eyes were swimming with a jaundiced, malevolent light at the prospect of a new piece of meat.

'Why don't you just watch it, buddy?' he said. His breath was heavy with the smell of marijuana.

I lifted my elbow and the sack of beer over his head and tried to squeeze by the chair, which was now pressing into a corner of my groin.

'Hey, citizen, you didn't hear the word,' he said.

Two of the girls at the table were grinning at him with a knowing expression over their cigarettes. A real stomp was at hand. One of the straights was going to get his butt kicked up between his ears. Or maybe, even better, he would shake a little bit and then run for the door.

The one advantage that an ex-con has in this kind of situation is that you have seen every one of them before, which is a very strong credential, and as physical people they are always predictable if you turn their own totems and frame of reference against them. In fact, sometimes you look forward to it with anticipation.

I pulled a beer loose from the top of the sack and set it down before him; then I leaned casually into his ear, the gold earring just a breath away from my lips, and whispered: 'Don't turn your head now, but a couple of those oilfield roughnecks are narcs, and they know your girlfriends are holding for you. One of them was talking in the head about stiffing you with a dealing charge. That's a sure fifteen in Angola, podna.'

He turned in his chair and stared at me with his yellow, blood-flecked eyes, and I walked out the door and got into the pickup before he could glue it all together in his brain.

The Point was thirty miles south of town, down a blacktop that wound through rows of flooded cypress and fishing shacks set up on stilts. The brackish water was black in the trees, and pirogues and flat-bottomed outboards piled with conical nets were tied to the banks. I drank one beer after another and pitched the cans out of the window into the back of the truck while the salt wind cut into my face and the great cypress limbs hung with moss swept by overhead.

The Point extended into the bay like a long, flat sandspit, and the jetties and the collapsed fishing pier looked like neatly etched black lines against the greyness of the water and the sun's last red spark boiling into the horizon. The tide was out, and seagulls dipped down into the rim of white foam along the sand, and in the distance I could see the gas flares burning off the offshore oil rigs. There was a seafood place and dance pavilion by the dock where you could sit on the screened porch and drink draught beer in mugs thick with ice and feel the wind blow across the flat water. I ordered a tray of boiled crawfish and bluepoint crabs with a half bottle of wine and sucked the hot juice out of the shells and dipped the meat in a tomato sauce mixed with horseradish.

The pavilion was almost empty except for a few fishermen and some kids who had come in early for the Saturday night dance. The food had helped a little, but I was pretty drunk now, past the point of worrying about a DWI bust and what that would mean to the parole officer on my first day out of the bag, and I ordered another beer. There was only a thin band of purple light on the horizon, and I looked hard at the distant buoy that marked where a German submarine had gone down in 1943. Once, years ago, when a hurricane depression had drawn the tide far out over the flats, you could see just the tip of the bow breaking the water. The Coast Guard had tried to blow it up, but they managed only to dislodge it from the sand and send it deeper down the shelf.

Once I worked a doodlebug job out in the bay, and we would ping it occasionally on the recorder's instrument, but it was never in the same place twice. It moved a mile either way in an easterly or westerly direction, and no one knew how far it went south into the Gulf before it returned again. And as I sat there on the screened porch, with my head in a beer fog, I felt for just a moment that old fear about all the madness everywhere. The crew was still in that crusted and flattened hull, those Nazis who had committed themselves to making the whole earth a place of concertina wire and guard towers, their empty eye sockets now strung with seaweed, and they were still sailing nineteen years after they had gone down in a scream of sirens and bombs.

The first musicians came in and set up their instruments on the bandstand. The Negro waiter took away my tray and brought me another beer, and I listened to the band tuning their guitars and adjusting the amplifiers. Bugs swam against the screen, trying to reach the light inside the porch, and as I ticked my fingernails against the glass and heard the musicians talking among themselves in their French accents, like on a hundred gigs I had played from Biloxi to Port Arthur, my mind began to fade through that bright drunken corridor to the one spot of insanity in my life, a return to the dream with all its strange distortions and awful questions that left me sweating in the middle of the night for two years at Angola.

We had picked up two weeks' work at a club by the air base in Lake Charles. It was like most roadhouses along that part of Highway 90, a flat, low-ceilinged, ramshackle place built of clapboard and Montgomery Ward brick with a pink façade on the front and blue neons that advertised entertainment like Johnny and his Harmonicats. By ten o'clock the smoke always hung thickly against the ceiling, and the smell of the rest rooms reached out to the edge of the dance floor. The crowd was made up of airmen from the base, tough kids with ducktail and boogie haircuts, oilfield workers, people from a trailer court across the road, and sometimes the dangerous ones, who sat at the bar with their short sleeves turned up at the cuffs over their muscular arms, waiting to roll a homosexual or bust up anybody who would like to take his glance into the parking lot.

It was Saturday night, and because we didn't play Sundays, we were getting loaded on the bandstand and blowing up weed behind the building between sets. By two in the morning our lead singer couldn't remember the words to some of the songs, and he was faking it by putting his lips against the microphone and roaring out unintelligible sounds across the dance floor. I had my dobro hung in a flat position like a steel across my stomach, with the strap pulled down tight against my arm, but when I slipped the bar up and down the frets, the marijuana singing in my head, I hit the nut and soundboard like a piece of loud slate and my finger picks were catching under the strings. One of the bad ones, who was sitting with a couple of prostitutes at the bar, kept returning to the bandstand to ask for 'The Wild Side of Life'. His hands were large and square, the kind you see on pipeline fitters; the fingers on one hand were tattooed with the word LOVE, the fingers of the other with the word HATE. His shirt was bursting with a cruel, animal strength, and a line of sweat dripped out of his hairline and glistened brightly on his jawbone.

Our singer, Rafe Arceneaux, our one real tea head, nodded at him a couple of times when he came back for his song, but on the third time the man put his hand around Rafe's ankle and squeezed just hard enough to show what he could do if he was serious.

'Hey, get fucked, man,' Rafe said. He kicked against the man's grip and fell backward into the drums.

The people on the floor stopped dancing and stared at us through the smoke. Rafe's electric Gibson was cracked across the face, and the wire had been torn loose from the electronic jack. He got up in a rumble of drums and a clash of cymbals with his guitar twisted around his throat. He wasn't a big man, and he had always been frightened of bullies in high school, and there was sweat and humiliation all over his face.

'Get your ass out of here, you bastard,' he said.

Tables and chairs were already scraping and toppling across the floor, and the tattooed man had an audience that he would probably never get again. I heard some glass break in the front of the building; then the man raised himself in an easy muscular step, with one hand on the rail, on to the bandstand and threw Rafe headlong into the bar.

Rafe struck like a child thrown from a car. There was a deep triangular cut on his forehead, sunken in as though someone had pushed an angry thumb into the soft bone. He lay on the floor with one of his arms caught in the legs of an overturned barstool.

The bad man was still on the stand with us, and he had had just enough of somebody's blood in his nostrils to want some more.

He came for my Martin next, his face grinning and stupid with victory and the knowledge that there was nothing in his way.

'That's your ass if you touch it, podna.'

He got his hand around the neck and I hit him with my fist against the temple. He reeled backwards from the guitar case with his eyes out of focus and put one elbow through the back window. I aimed for the throat with the second punch, but he brought his chin down and I hit him squarely in the mouth. His bottom lip broke against his teeth, and while I stood there motionlessly, looking at the blood and saliva run off his chin, he reached behind him in the windowsill and came up with a beer bottle in my face.

It was very fast after that. I had the Italian stiletto in my pocket, and it leaped in my hand with the hard thrust of the spring before I knew it was there. It had waving ripples on each side of the blade, and just as he brought the bottle down on my forearm, I went in under him and put all six inches right up to the bone handle in his heart.

When I would wake from the dream in my cell, with the screams still in my head, I would go through all the equations that would justify killing a man in those circumstances. I would almost be free of the guilt, but then I would have to face the one inalterable premise that flawed all my syllogisms: *I already had the knife in my pocket. I already had the knife in my pocket.*

THREE

My father died two weeks after the day I returned home. We buried him during a sun-spangled rain shower in the family cemetery by the bayou. The aunts and uncles were there in their print-cotton dresses and brushed blue suits, the old men from town who had grown up with him, and the few Negroes who lived on the back of our property. Rita and Ace kept their children in the car because of the shower, and an old French priest read the prayers for the dead while an altar boy held an umbrella over his head.

My relatives nodded at me, and two of the old men shook hands, but I could have been a stranger among them. After they were all gone and the last car had rumbled over the wooden bridge, I stood under an oak tree and watched the two grave-diggers from the mortuary service spade the dirt over the coffin. Their wet denims were wrapped tight across their muscles as they worked. One of them became impatient to get out of the rain, and he started to push the dirt off the mound into the hole with his boot.

'Do it right, buddy,' I said.

I walked back to the house, and the grass on the lawn was shining with water and light. I sat on the porch swing a while and smoked cigarettes with a glass of bourbon and listened to the tree frogs begin to sing in the swamp. The air was cool from the rain, and the wind was blowing off the gulf, but it was all outside me and the whiskey didn't do any good and one cigarette burned up between my fingers. I went upstairs and tried to sleep. The house was dark, and the tree frogs became louder in the twilight's stillness. I woke sometime in the middle of the night and thought I heard the count man click his stick on the bars at the same time a shovel scraped deep into a pile of dirt.

I had to roll, stretch it out, shake it down the road. I had put in for interstate parole to Montana with my parole officer two days after I got out of Angola, but it was very hard for an ex-convict with three years' time still ahead of him, particularly one who had been sent up for manslaughter (which had been a reduction from second-degree murder), to be accepted by the parole and probation office in another state. First, there had to be reason for the transfer, such as the presence of family, social reformers, psychologists, good guys of any description, who would aid the state in the rehabilitation of their product. Second, there was the problem of employment, which meant that you would hold a regular job sanctified by a machine-stamped payroll cheque each week, one that would not lead you into association with other ex-cons, boost artists and the like. And in Louisiana, as in many other states, an ex-convict could violate his parole by quitting a job without due cause. Finally, a good part of your case depended on the whim of the parole officer.

Mine was a middle-aged man who had transferred from the welfare agency. He wore dark J. C. Higgins suits even in the summertime, and there were blue and red lines all over his cheeks and nose. His blunt hands were too large for the fountain pen and papers that he tried to handle, and his stomach pressed the flap of his fly outward as though he had a hernia. I had known him around town most of my life, in an indirect way, because he belonged to almost every civic organization in the parish, or at least you could always find him on the edge of newspaper photographs showing the sponsors of civic drives to promote American Legion baseball or a new park that would include areas for coloured citizens.

My file perplexed him. He said he couldn't fully understand how a man who had been decorated with two Purple Hearts and a Bronze Star could also receive a bad-conduct discharge. Also, he didn't think it was a good plan for me to go to Montana. My family was in south Louisiana, and both my brother and sister could help me get started in business or whatever I would choose, since I had two years' college education at Southwestern Louisiana Institute. His thick thumb dented and creased the papers in my folder, and his eyes wandered over my face in his abstraction as he talked about the inadvisability of leaving home roots and the possibilities of working with my brother. He ignored my open smile at the thought of an ex-convict in the employ of a public-relations and advertising company.

I had put on a pair of slacks and a sport shirt and had got a shine at the newsstand before coming into his office, but as I looked at his well-meaning face and clear blue eyes that didn't fit in the dark suit, and listened to the recommendations for my future, I wished that one of the bosses from Angola were there in his place, someone who had felt the same miserable touch of the prison farm that left a salty cut in the edge of your eye. Or at least someone whom you didn't have to con.

Because that was what he wanted. I had already talked with a state supreme court judge, a friend of my father's, who said he would push all the paper through Baton Rouge to get me an out-of-state parole. Also, Buddy Riordan, who had pulled time with me, had got his father to sponsor me with the Office of Parole and Probation in Missoula. But we still had to go through with the con.

The strange thing about conning a man who deliberately opens his vest to a series of lies is the fact that both of you have to protect him from knowledge of his own dishonesty. In this case my parole officer recorded every insult to his intelligence without an eyelid faltering over the movement of his pen, but occasionally the hand would pause and an eyebrow would lift off the paper to register some abstract discrepancy in my account, a small warning that would keep us both honest tomorrow.

So we went through it. I would like to do ranch work up in Montana, dig postholes in frozen ground, shave sheep with electric barber clippers, dehorn cows, wring the necks of chickens and shuck their feathers in pots of scalding water, shovel freight-car loads of green horse manure in one-hundred-degree heat.

Actually, most of what I told him was true. I did want to go to Montana and live on a ranch in the mountains with Buddy and buck bales on a new morning. But I couldn't tell him that most of all I just needed to roll, to flee the last two years of my life, to exorcise from my sleep the iron smell of jail and the clack of the count man's baton against my cell door.

I knew that the parole transfer might take weeks or longer to be approved in Baton Rouge, and I had only thirty-five dollars left from my discharge money. My father had left each of the children one-third of the farm, but he had borrowed against it twice, and an oil company was claiming that four acres of it was somehow part of a royalty pool. Which meant, in effect, that there was a legal cloud over the house and land title, and before the estate could be divided, we would have to settle in or out of court with Texaco as well as deal with the bank. Ace was the only one of us who had the combination of what it took to wait it through: money, a disregard for time, and an ambitious energy for the profits to be made in land development.

And Ace stayed right on top of it. Two days after my father was buried, he had his agency's lawyer draft a quitclaim settlement on the inheritance for Rita and me to sign. He drove his Cadillac up the front lane one afternoon while I was on the porch steps tuning my dobro, and began explaining in his serious way the advantages of settling the estate now. I didn't feel like talking with him or listening to his practical statements of figures and legality. And his self-deluded attitude of magnanimity was more than I could stand at the moment.

He offered me five thousand dollars in exchange for the quitclaim and power of attorney. I drank out of my beer and set the can down on the step.

'I tell you what, Ace. Get your lawyer to draw up another one, and give me the old man's truck and four of the back acres by the bayou. You can have the rest of it, and I'll sign the oil rights over to you, too. But don't put any of your tract homes near my property.'

'You're cutting yourself short,' he said.

'That's all I need, Bro'.'

I had cut myself short, but I couldn't take any money from him, and I felt better at evening off any debt I owed for my father's care. And inside he was very happy because he had gone through his act of generosity and fairness and later would realize a fortune in the subdivision of the land.

So in a moment's irritation I had become an equal member of the family at a large cost: I was still broke and had taken to buying sardines and soda crackers with my six-packs of beer at the little store down the dirt road.

Sunday morning I drove to New Iberia and looked up Rafe Arceneaux, the tea-head singer in our band. He was married now, with twin boys, and working ten days on and five off as a radio man on an offshore oil rig. We sat on the wooden porch of his small house and drank chicory coffee in the clang of church bells and the screams of his kids and the loud voice of his wife in the back of their house. The triangular scar from the bar-room fight was raised like an inner-tube patch on his forehead.

'I wish I could say something helpful, man, but it's bad right now,' he said. 'Most of the old guys are gone. Bernard's wife got him locked up for non-support, Archie got busted for possession in Pascagoula, and the rest of us catch a gig when we can. They only want rock 'n' roll bands now, and they can get the coloured guys to play cheaper than we do.'

'How about the Victory Club?'

'Some of the local punks burned it down while you were gone.'

His wife came through the screen door and put one of his nappied boys in his lap without speaking to either of us. The screen slammed shut after her. Rafe directed his embarrassed eyes at the line of dilapidated storefronts across the street. 'She's mad because I wouldn't take her to her mother's last night. It's one of those things you have to live with when you play it straight.'

I finished my coffee and started to leave, because his wife's anger hadn't been directed at him but me, the ex-convict and bad influence out of his past.

'Hey, don't cut out yet, Iry. Look, I'm sorry about all this. It's just that things aren't the same any more. I mean, ten years ago we all thought we'd be playing Nashville by this time. Sometimes it just doesn't work out. Let's face it, man – we're getting to be history.'

I finally found a job working four nights a week at a roadhouse outside Thibodaux. They didn't really need a lead-guitar man, but when I opened my case and took out the dobro, I had the job. A dobro is a bluegrass instrument, inlaid in the sound box with a metal resonator and played flat with a bar like a steel guitar, and you don't see many of them outside the southern mountains. I had bought mine on order from El Monte, California, for four hundred dollars, and the thin neck and gleaming wood of the box was as light as an envelope of air in my hands.

I made twenty-five dollars a night and my share of the tips from the money jar on the bandstand. I worked in well with the band, which was made up of hillbillies who played only country and juke-joint music. My first night I played and sang six Hank Williams songs in a row, then went into 'Poison Love' by Johnny and Jack and 'Detour' and 'I'll Sail My Ship Along', and the place went wild. They jitterbugged and did the dirty boogie, yelled from their tables, roared with some type of nostalgic confirmation when they recognized an old song, and dropped change and dollar bills into the money jar. Oilfield roughnecks with tin hats and beery faces and drilling mud on their clothes looked up at me with moist, serious eyes when I sang 'The Lost Highway'. I was good at imitating Hank Williams, and I could make the dobro sound just like the steel that he had used behind him.

> I was just a lad, nearly twenty-two
> Neither good nor bad, just a kid like you.
> Now when I pass by, all the people say
> Just another guy on the lost highway.

I played there three weeks and picked up an afternoon job on Sundays at a club in St Martinville, which got me into trouble with the parole office. The St Martinville band had a thirty-minute television show on Sunday mornings, and as an aside into the microphone the singer decided that he would mention that their dobro man, Iry Paret, would be at the club with them that afternoon.

So when I went in for my visit with the parole officer that week, I noticed first the stiffness of his handshake and then the rigidity of his elbows on the desk and the folded hands under his chin while he talked. We had to go around three corners before he got to it, but he did. And like most people who ask to be conned, he now felt that he had stepped too far over a line into a large hole.

'You didn't report that you were working in a nightclub,' he said.

'It's not much of a job. I'm just sitting in temporarily.'

It was an easy offering if he wanted to continue the con, but I could see the struggle in his face to turn the compromise around, and I knew that it was going to be at my expense.

'Your parole agreement stipulates that you won't return to any of the past associations that contributed to your crime. I know that's vague on a piece of paper, but in your case it means playing in beer joints and driving home drunk at four in the morning.'

'It's the only living I have, and I was flat broke.'

'Maybe we could have worked that out, but you should have

reported in before you took the job. It would have cost you one telephone call.'

'Let's get the rest of it out of the way, too,' I said. 'I've got a gig over in Thibodaux for twenty-five bucks a night. There's no fights and the cop at the door doesn't let hookers in and I leave there sober after we finish.'

I felt like a child explaining his conduct to an adult.

'Why did you do that? Why did you decide that you couldn't trust me?'

'Mr Mouton, it wasn't a matter of trust. I was simply broke.'

'But you think the parole office is something to use evasion on.'

I had to catch my anger and humiliation in my throat before I spoke again. My unlit cigarette trembled in my fingers, and the other ex-convicts on metal waiting chairs and parole officers and secretaries in the room were listening to our conversation with an oblique, withdrawn enjoyment.

'I can't do anything else except hustle jugs on a doodlebug crew or carry hod, and they're not hot to hire ex-cons in the union,' I said.

He stroked lines with a ballpoint pen on his note pad.

'I don't know,' he said. He was taking out every ounce of blood that he could. 'I talked with your brother yesterday. He said he could get you a job on a well test in Opelousas.'

A well-test job in the oilfield meant stringing flange pipe through a filthy sump hole for seventy-five cents an hour, and the job usually entailed only the day of the well's completion, which meant that it was no job at all.

'He didn't tell me about it,' I said.

'It's there if you want it.'

I lit the cigarette and leaned closer to him on my elbow with the butt touching against my brow. He didn't like the directness of the position, and he opened a side drawer in his desk as though he had forgotten a form or part of my file.

'Do I get violated back to Angola, or do we just play badminton awhile?' I said.

He wasn't good at that kind of encounter, and after he had pushed back the desk drawer with a slow, flat hand and ticked his thumbnail along the edge of my file, he said: 'Your transfer will probably come through in a week. Everything I sent into Baton Rouge was positive, and I made a case for your war record. But you don't play in any more bars until you leave Louisiana, and then you're somebody else's responsibility.'

I looked at him blankly and sat back in the chair.

'That's it, Iry. You're cut loose,' he said.

The letter came from Baton Rouge three days later. I had four weeks to settle my affairs and report in to the parole and probation office in Missoula. Ace had transferred the title of the pickup to me, and I had $275 saved from my two jobs. I pushed my sleeping bag and tent with the wooden supports wrapped inside the canvas behind the front seat and loaded a big box of canned stew meat, corned beef, bread, sardines and soda crackers in the truck bed and stretched a tarpaulin over the sides.

The next morning I was rolling through the piney woods of east Texas, with the mist still in the trees and the red clay banked on each side of the road. By Dallas the radiator was blowing steam from under the hood, and a kid in a filling station had to knock the cap off with a broomstick. I pushed it on through the scorching afternoon to Wichita Falls, where the water pump went out and I had to spend five hours in a tin garage that enclosed the heat and humidity like a stove. I ate a can of stew meat cold and started chewing on No-Doze south of Amarillo. I should have pulled into a roadside park to sleep, but I was hooked on the highway and the combination of beer and No-Doze now, and I knew that I could roll it all the way to Denver.

The accents began to change in the filling stations and the truck stops, and then in the early dawn I saw the first mesa in the Panhandle. It rose out of the flat country like a geological accident, its edges lighted with a pink glow, the eroded gullies filled with purple shadow. The cotton and cornfields were behind me now, and also the patent medicine and MARTHA WHITE'S SELF RISING FLOUR signs, the vegetables and water melons sold off the backs of trucks along the roadsides, the revival tents set back in empty pastures, the South itself. It simply slipped past me over some invisible boundary that had nothing to do with geographical designation, and then it was Dalhart and Texline, where the grain silos stood grey against the hot sky and clouds of dust, and finally Raton, New Mexico.

I was in a stupor from the No-Doze and case of beer that I had drunk in the last twenty-four hours, and my eyes burned with the shimmer of heat off the blacktop. I put my head under a filling-station hose and let the water sluice down my neck and face and then ate a steak in the café. But I was finished. My hands, lined with the black imprint of the steering wheel, were shaking, my back ached when I walked, and I could still feel the truck's engine vibrating up through my legs.

The filling-station operator said I could park my truck behind the building overnight, and I unrolled my sleeping bag in the bed and used the tarpaulin and my shirt as a pillow. For a while in the softness of the sleeping bag I was aware of the semis hissing air on the highway and shifting down for the long pull up Raton Pass; then I felt myself drop down into the smell of the canvas and the cool air against my face and a quietness inside me.

The next morning was like an infusion into the soul, a feeling that you can only have after you dissipate all the mental and physical energy in yourself, to the point that you know you will never return from it. And on this morning it was really the West. The town lay flat against the mountains, which climbed steadily out of brown hills into the high, green timber of the Rocky Mountain range. The broken streets of the town were lined with stucco and adobe houses, outbuildings, chicken yards, and junker cars with weeds growing up through the frames. Mexican kids roared along the pavements in roller-skate wagons, Indians with creased faces like withered apples waited in front of the state labour office for the doors to open, and the sky was alive with a green-blue magic that was so hard and beautiful that I had to blink a little when I looked at it.

But it was the mountains and the early light in the pines more than anything else. As I shifted down to second for the two-mile grade up Raton Pass, the mountains seemed to tumble one upon another ahead of me, bluer in the distance, spread across the sky in a broken monolith that should have cracked the earth's edges. The needle on the temperature gauge was almost beyond the dash, and the gearshift was knocking in my palm when I crossed the Colorado state line at the top and rolled into the old town of Trinidad.

I bought two six-packs of Coors and pushed the cans deep into a sack of crushed ice on the floor, and highballed down the four-lane through Pueblo, a decaying, soot-covered town with plumes of ugly smoke rising from tin buildings, on up the steady incline towards Denver, with the mountains always blue and tumbling higher into the clouds on my left. Denver looked wonderful, filled with fir and spruce trees, green lawns and parks with tulip gardens. I ate Mexican food in a café north of town. Then it was Fort Collins and Cheyenne and a straight roll into the late red sun across the cinnamon-coloured land of Wyoming towards the Montana line.

Deer grazed in the sparse grass, their summer coats almost indistinguishable in the fading purple light, and after dark I almost hit a doe and fawn that stood transfixed in my headlights by the side of the road. I picked up two drunk Indian hitchhikers, who both wore blue-jean jackets with two shirts underneath and sat pressed together in the cab in some type of isolation from me, passing a bottle of dago red back and forth. After we had driven fifty miles, they bothered to ask me how far I was going, and I told them I hoped to make it to Billings before I stopped. I saw their wine-stained teeth grin in the dashboard light.

'You better stay at my place tonight. You ain't going to make it to Billings,' one of them said, and he took a cigarette off the dash without asking.

'Why can't I make it to Billings?'

'Because you can't. You ought to know that, man,' he said.

I looked at him, but he had already lost attention and was staring into the cigarette smoke with his flat, obsidian eyes.

The sound of the engine hummed in my head, and the headlights briefly illuminated the names chiselled into the concrete faces of the bridges over dried-out riverbeds, MEDICINE BOW, PLATTE, SHOSHONI, each a part of something old and thundering with war ponies.

I stayed at the Indian man's place that night, on the edge of the Big Horn Mountains. He had ten acres on the reservation and a Montgomery Ward brick house with a chicken yard and a few dozen rabbit hutches and the most beautiful Indian wife I had ever seen. They put blankets on the sofa for me and went to bed, but I couldn't sleep. The highway was spinning in my head, and I couldn't close my hands. I walked across the chicken yard to the outhouse and then sat on the edge of the sofa and smoked cigarettes in the dark. The solitary electric bulb screwed into the ceiling clicked on, and the Indian stood above me in his socks and jockey shorts, with a line of black hair running up out of the elastic over his metallic stomach.

'You can't sleep good, man?' he said.

'I just need to wind it down a little bit. I didn't mean to wake you up.'

'We'll go to the tavern and find you a girlfriend. Then we'll drink some beer together and you'll be all right.'

'I wouldn't be good company for anybody right now.'

'You got some snakes crawling around? That ain't no big thing. Lots of people on the reservation is like that. Come down to the tavern. You'll see.'

'I'd better pass. But I appreciate it. I really do.'

'You got a race thing about Indian girls?'

'No, I'm not like that.'

'You're a nice-looking guy. You ain't a queer, either. You shouldn't be travelling around without no woman.'

Then I didn't know what to say. I put out my cigarette in an empty beer can and pushed my hand back through my hair, hoping that he would turn off the light and let it end there.

'I ain't one to poke in your business, but I think your insides is all stove in,' he said. 'I recognize it. Indians get like that before they kill themselves.'

'I was in the Louisiana pen. I guess I haven't got used to rolling around loose yet. They say it takes a while.'

'Get up, Irene,' he said through the curtain that hung from the bedroom door.

'You don't need to do that.'

'No, it's all right, man. We'll drink together and then you can sleep. I was in jail over in Deer Lodge. I got myself put in the hole so's I could sleep. People was always yelling and banging iron doors all night.'

His wife came out in a robe and sat silently at the table while he pulled out the beer from the icebox. Her eyes were brown and quiet, the dark skin of one cheek still lined with the creases of the pillow, and I could see the tops of her olive breasts below the V of her robe. While we drank beer and rolled cigarettes out of a large Half and Half can, she looked flatly through the back window as though she were at the table as a feminine duty. On the third six-pack I began to perspire, and the control in my conversation and mind started to slip away in the yellow electric light, the match blisters on my fingers, and the confused sentences and beer cans covered with cigarette stubs.

I popped a pill to stay alive. But instead all the wrong tubes lighted up, and I went in and out of the conversation and all the half-formed lingering and unspoken ideas and finally over the edge into the memory of that Indian girl's face. Her darkly beautiful eyes and the swirl of her black hair piled on her head flicked my mind, like the snap of a beer top, across the mountains and over the ocean to the soft clicking of bamboo shades and the dusky scent of a small Kabuki theatre with the bottles of Nippon beer iced down in a bucket between me and the geisha waitress who dipped shrimp into a horseradish sauce with chopsticks and placed them in my mouth. I had been drinking for two days, my money was almost all gone, and I had three hours to report back to the hospital, but in my mind I had already resigned from the army, the war, and all the complexities that made it important for me to go back on the firing line. I finished the Nippon in the ice bucket, the mamasan sent the boy across the street for more, and the geisha girl heated sake for me in a cup over a candle flame while I watched the actresses in their white pancake make-up and red-painted eyes move across the stage in a whisper of flowered silk as though they were an extension of a drunken dream.

Then I realized that I hadn't yet accomplished what I had set out to do. The bamboo shades clicked in the breeze through the windows, and I could hear the MPs rousting someone at the street corner. I snapped the cap off a Nippon with my pocketknife, got to my feet, and almost fell through a paper partition.

'You no drink more now,' the mamasan said. Her teeth were rotted, and she held her hand over her mouth when she talked. 'You go back to hospital now.'

I ripped the shade off its fastening and leaned out the window. Two MPs had a drunk soldier pushed back against a wall on the corner with their sticks.

'No do that,' the mamasan said. 'This not whorehouse. No bring Mike and Pat in here.'

I lobbed the bottle at them and watched it burst into foam and brown glass all over their spitshines and bleached leggings. They forgot about the soldier and looked around with their sticks clenched in their hands.

'Over here, girls,' I said, and I let another one fly, except this time I curled it in an arc along the wall so that it hit directly between them in a fountain of foam that splattered their trousers.

'You son a bitch,' the mamasan yelled at me.

'Come on, you candy-ass shiteaters,' I said through the window. 'Get your balls fried in a skillet. We'll give you a bayonet right up the ass that you can haul all the way back to the stockade.'

I pitched the other full bottles one after another into the street while the mamasan and the geisha girls pulled at my belt and slapped at me with rolled pillow mats and their hands.

The first MP into the room parted the reed curtain with his stick and held up a pair of handcuffs on his index finger. In the half-light through the door they looked like a piece of chain mail spangled around his fist.

'You have a telephone call outside,' he said.

'Hey, man, you better not drink no more,' the Indian said.

'What?' I raised my head from my forearms in the weak yellow light.

'You was making some terrible sounds.'

'I'm sorry.' His wife's chair was empty, and the curtain to

their bedroom was still swinging lightly back and forth. 'What did—'

'She just ain't used to white people. It ain't important.' He grinned at me and exposed a gold tooth next to an empty black space in his teeth. 'You got a long drive tomorrow.'

'Tell me what I did.'

'You was holding on to her hands. She couldn't make you turn loose.' His smooth leather face and obsidian eyes were both kind and faintly embarrassed.

I picked up my can of beer and tried to walk out the back door to my truck. I hit the doorjamb with my shoulder, and the can fell out of my hand on the porch. I felt the Indian touch me gently on the back and direct me towards the couch. Then while I sweated in my drunken pill-and-booze delirium on the edge of the cushions, with the sun turning the chicken yard and rabbit hutches purple in the new light, I heard the bugles blowing on a distant hill way beyond our concertina wire, and I knew that it was going to be a safe dawn because I was sitting out this dance and all the rest to follow.

FOUR

I highballed the pickup all the way from the Little Bighorn River to Missoula, with stops only for gas and hamburgers in between. Montana was so beautiful that it made something drop inside me. At first there were only plains with slow, wide rivers and cottonwoods along the banks and the sawtooth edge of mountains in the distance; then I started to climb towards the Continental Divide and the Douglas fir and ponderosa pine country with chasms off the edge of the road that made my head reel. There was still snow banked deep in the trees at the top of the divide, and deer spooked out of my headlights in a flick of dirt and pine needles. I coasted down the other side of the grade and picked up the Clark Fork River the rest of the way into Missoula. The runoff from the snow in the high country was still heavy, and the river swelled out through the cottonwoods in the moonlight. The rick fences and long stretches of barbed wire and small ranch houses back against the foot of the mountains rolled by me in the whine of the pickup's treadless tyres against the cement. Then I was in Hellgate Canyon, and Missoula suddenly burst open before me in a shower of lights among the elm and maple and fir trees and quiet streets, with a ring of mountains silhouetted like iron all around the town.

I turned south into the Bitterroot Valley and followed Buddy's map to his father's ranch. The pasture land on each side of the road extended only a short distance into the mountains, which rose high and black into clouds torn with moonlight, and the Bitterroot River gleamed like a piece of broken mirror across the long sandbars and islands of willow trees. I got lost twice on rural roads, looking at names on letterboxes with a flashlight; then I found the right wire-hooped gate and cattle guard and rutted road up to his father's place.

Buddy Riordan was working on a five-to-fifteen for possession of marijuana when I met him in Angola. He was a good jazz pianist, floating high on weed and the Gulf breeze and steady gigs at Joe Burton's place in New Orleans, and then he got nailed in a men's room with two reefers in his coat pocket. As a Yankee, he was prosecuted under a felony rather than a misdemeanour law, and the judge dropped the whole jailhouse on his head. He pulled five years on the farm, and he was one of the few there who was considered an outsider, a man who didn't belong, by the rest of us who knew in the angry part of our souls that we had bought every inch of our time.

Buddy had strange Bird Parker rhythms in his head, and sometimes I couldn't tell whether he was flying on Benzedrex inhalers or just high on a lot of wild riffs stripping off inside him. The hacks put him in lockdown for three days when they found a tube of aircraft glue in his pocket on a routine shakedown, but he was still clicking to his own beat when they sent him back to the dormitory, and after that they simply dismissed him as crazy. What they didn't understand about Buddy was that he had turned in his resignation a long time ago: an 'I casually resign' letter written sometime in his teens when he started bumming freights across the Pacific Northwest. He didn't have a beef or an issue; he just started clicking to his own rhythm and stepped over some kind of invisible line.

And I guess that's the thing I sensed in him, like a flash of private electricity, when I first met him in the exercise yard after I got out of the fish tank. The wind was cold and wet, and I was trying to roll a cigarette out of the few grains left in my package of state-issue tobacco. He was leaning against the wall, one foot propped up behind him, with his chafed wrists stuck down deep in his pockets. His pinstripe trousers hung low on his slender hips, and he had his denim jacket buttoned at the collar. The sharp bones of his face were red in the cold, and the short cigarette between his lips was wet with saliva.

'Take a tailor-made out of my coat pocket, Zeno,' he said.

I pulled the pack of Camels out and put one in my mouth.

'Take a couple extra. You won't get any more issue until Saturday,' he said.

'Thanks.'

'Is this your first jolt?'

'I spent some time in an army stockade.'

'That don't count in here, Zeno. Come on over to my bunk in Ash after chow. I can give you some machine-made butts to tide you over.'

I had already started to regret accepting the cigarettes. I turned my face towards the wall and struck a match in my cupped hands.

'Look, man, I'm not a wolf,' he said. 'I read your file in records, and we need a guy to play electric bass in our jazz band. It's not a bad deal. We play over in the women's prison sometimes, and Saturdays we just wax the recreation room instead of scrubbing out toilets. Besides, somebody ought to teach you how to split matches. Those are worth almost as much as cigarettes in here.'

The ranch ran back to the face of a canyon, and the main house was a sprawling two-storey place made of logs with a wide front porch and side rooms that had been built with clapboard.

Every room in the house was lighted, and the cliffs of the canyon rose up steep and black in the back under a full moon. When I got out of the truck, the cold air cut into me, even though it was only early August, and I put on my army-surplus jacket that I had used for duck hunting in Louisiana. A girl stepped through the lighted screen on to the front porch and held her hand over her brow to shield her eyes against the glare of my headlights.

'I'm looking for Buddy Riordan, ma'am. I don't know if I have the right place. I got lost a couple of times.'

'He lives in the cabin where the road dead-ends by the trees. You'll see his porch light.' Her voice was thin in the wind, and her silhouette seemed to shrink when she stepped back from the screen.

I drove to the end of the road, where there was a flat log building on the edge of the pines with a porch and swing and a brick chimney. The smoke from the chimney flattened out under the trees and turned in the wind off the canyon, and two fly rods were leaned against the porch with the lines pulled tight into the cork handles. Buddy came through the door barefoot, with a sleeveless nylon hunting jacket on and a can of beer and a wooden spoon in his hand.

'Hey, Zeno, where the hell you been? I thought you'd be in yesterday.' He hit me on the shoulder with the flat of his hand like a lumberjack.

'I picked up some Indian guys in Wyoming and got sidetracked a while.'

'Those Indians are crazy people. Hey, you old son of a bitch, you pulled that last year OK. Not a dent on you.'

'I made an ass of myself in this Indian guy's home. I got a little saccharine with his wife.'

'We all do funny things when we make the street. Forget it. Come on in. I've had a rack of venison in the pot since yesterday.'

He had a wood stove in a small kitchen at the back of the cabin, and the iron lids glowed around the edges with the heat of the burning sap and resin in the sawn pine limbs. He took a beer from the icebox and put it in my hand. I sat at the table in the warm smell of the venison and felt the fatigue drain through my body. He finished slicing some wild mushrooms on a chopping board and scraped them into the pot with the knife.

'A few mushrooms and some wine and wow. You got a nickel and I got a dime – let's get together and buy some wine. And that's what we got to do. Bop it down to the tavern and get some vino for the pot and some more brew, and then we'll have dinner on the porch. No kidding, Iry, you look solid.'

'I feel like somebody kicked that highway up my butt.'

'Did you have any trouble your last year?'

'I made half-trusty six months before my hearing, so I was pretty sure on getting my good time. It wasn't a sweat. Just scratching off days and staying out of the boss man's eye.'

'I was sorry to hear about your father.'

I finished the can of Great Falls and lit a cigarette on one of the stove's glowing lids.

'Let's go get the brew,' I said. 'I don't think I'll be able to sleep tonight unless I put a case down.'

'You'll be able to sleep here, partner. We have the best damn air in the United States. It blows down the canyon every night, and you won't hear a sound except the creek behind the cabin and the pine cones hitting the roof. Look, it's too late for you to meet the family, but tomorrow we'll go up to the house for breakfast, and you can talk to the old man about work. You can make ten bucks a day bucking bales, and that's not bad money around here. We got the rent free, and I catch fish every day up Bass Creek or in the Bitterroot, and with the little truck garden I have and the game out of the freezer, it's a pretty cool way to live. I should have caught on to this when I was a kid, and I never would have built that five down there with you southern primitives. And speaking of that, man, you didn't bring any of that red-dirt Louisiana weed with you, did you?'

'What do you think, Buddy?'

'Well, it was just a question, Zeno. The kids up at the university in Missoula have got some new shit around called LSD, and it takes your brain apart in minutes and glues it back together one broken piece at a time. I mean you actually hear colours blowing sounds at you. I'm sorry, man. I didn't mean to run on about my obsessions. Let's travel for the brew and put some spotiotti in the pot.'

I rubbed my palm into my eye, and a red circle of light receded back into my head.

'Yeah, I guess I was fading out,' I said. 'I still feel the truck shaking under me.'

'A little brew and a little food and you'll be cool. Come on, I'll introduce you to a Montana tavern. Meet the shitkickers. Pick up a little colour your first night here. Something to expand that jaded southern gourd of yours. You know, I read an article once that said all you southern guys are sexual nightmares. That's why your rest rooms are always filthy and full of rubber machines.'

'Are we going to get the beer, Buddy?'

'Right. Let's take your truck, since I parked my car against a tree in the middle of the creek last night.'

We banged over the ruts in the corrugated road, with the truck rattling at every metal joint, until we bounced across the cattle guard on to the smooth gravel-spread lane that led back to the main highway through the Bitterroots. The moon had moved farther to the south, and I could see the dark water of the river cutting in silver rivulets around the willow trees on the edge of the sandbars. The mountains on each side of the valley were so large now in the moonlight that I felt they were crashing down upon me. The snow on the distant peaks was burning with moonlight beyond the jagged silhouette of the pines, and each time we crossed a bridge over a small creek, I could see the white tumble of water over the rocks and then the quiet pools hammered with metal dollars at the end of the riffle.

We pulled into the parking lot of a clapboard tavern next to a general store with two petrol pumps in front. Pickup trucks with rifles and shotguns set in racks against the rear windows were parked in the lot, and the stickers on their bumpers were a sudden click of the eye back into the rural South: I FIGHT POVERTY – I WORK; PUT THE BIBLE BACK IN OUR SCHOOLS; DON'T WORRY, THEY'RE ONLY NINETY MILES AWAY.

Buddy and I went inside and had a beer at the bar and asked for a cold case to go and a small bottle of Sauterne. A stone fireplace was roaring with logs at the far end of the pool table, and there were elk and moose racks on the walls and rusted frontier rifles laid across deer hooves. Most of the men in the bar wore faded blue jeans, Levi or nylon jackets, scuffed cowboy and work boots, shirts with the colour washed out, and beat-up cowboy hats stained with sweat around the band. They all looked big, physical, with large, rough hands and wind-cut faces. The men at the pool table stamped down the rubber ends of their cues each time they missed a shot, and slammed the rack hard around the balls for a new game, and two cowboys next to me were shaking the poker dice violently in the leather cup and banging it loudly on the bar.

I didn't notice it at first, or I dismissed it as my natural ex-con's paranoia, but soon I started to catch a glance from a table or a man at the bar's elbow. Then, as I looked back momentarily to assure myself that there was nothing there, I saw a flick of blue meanness or challenge in those eyes, and I knew that I was sitting on top of something. I waited in silence for Buddy to finish his beer so we could go, but he ordered two more before I could touch him on the arm.

I felt the open stares become harder now, and I looked intently at the punchboard in front of me. At that moment I thought how strange it was that, even though I was a grown man, eyes could feel like a wandering deadness on the side of my face. I tried to compensate with a silly commitment to my cigarette and the details in the ashtray, and then I walked to the rest room with the instinctive con's slink across the yard, hands low in the pockets, cool, the shoulders bent just a little, the knees loose and easy.

But when I got back to the bar, the stares were still there. No one seemed to realize that I was a Louisiana badass. And Buddy was on his third beer.

'Hey, what the hell is going on?' I said quietly.

'Don't pay any attention to those guys.'

'What is it?'

'It's copacetic, Zeno. By the way, you looked very cool bopping into the pisser.'

'Shit on this, Buddy. Let's get out of here.'

'Take it easy, man. We can't let a few hot faces run us off.'

'I don't know what it is, but I don't like fooling in somebody else's trouble.'

'OK, let me finish and we'll split.'

Outside, I put the cardboard case of Great Falls in the back of the truck and turned around in the gravel parking lot. I shot the transmission into second gear and wound it up on the blacktop. One jagged piece of mountain cut into the moon.

'So what was that stuff about?'

'The old man has been pissing people off around here for years, and right now he's got them all on low boil.'

'What for?'

'He's trying to get the new pulp mill shut down, which means that about four hundred guys will lose their jobs. But forget it, man. It don't have anything to do with you. Those guys back there just like to snort with their virility when they have a chance.'

We crossed the cattle guard and passed the darkened main house on the ranch. The canyon walls behind the house were sheer and grey in the moon's reflection off the clouds.

'Tomorrow you got to meet my family,' Buddy said. 'They're unusual people. Sometimes I wish I hadn't burned them so bad.'

Then I realized that Buddy was drunk, because in the time I had known him, he had never indulged himself in private confession unless he was floating on Benzedrex inhalers or the occasional weed we got from the Negroes.

He poured the Sauterne into the pot of venison and sprinkled black pepper and parsley on top of it, then replaced the iron lid and let it marinate for half an hour while we drank beer and I tried to retune my dobro with fingers as thick and dull as a ruptured ear.

'I never did figure why you stayed with that hillbilly shot,' he said, 'but you do it beautiful, man. Did you ever finish that song you were working on?'

The blood had gone out of his face, and his cigarette had burned down close between his fingers.

'No, I've still got it running around in pieces.'

'Do "Jolie Blonde", man.'

I picked it out on the dobro and sang in my bad Cajun French while Buddy turned the venison in the pot with a wooden spoon. His white face glowed in the heat of the stove, and for a moment he looked as preoccupied and solitary as the man I had met over two years before in the yard at Angola.

We dragged the kitchen table on to the porch and ate the venison out of tin plates with garlic bread and an onion-and-beet salad that Buddy had chopped into a wooden bowl. I hadn't had venison in a long time, and the mushroom and wine sauce was fine with the taste of the game, and as I watched the wind blowing snow off the top of the canyon, I knew that everything was going to be all right.

But I should have recognized it at the bar. Or at least part of it. It was there, and all I had to do was look at it.

In the morning the sun broke across the blue ridge of mountains, and the wet, green meadows shimmered in the light. The shadows at the base of the mountains were purple like a cold bruise, and as the morning warmed and the dew burned away on the grass, the cattle moved slowly into the shade of the cottonwoods along the river. Buddy and I fished with wet flies in the creek behind his cabin and caught a dozen cutthroat trout out of the deep pools that turned in eddies behind the rocks. I would crouch down on my haunches so as not to silhouette against the spangle of sunlight through the trees, and then I'd let the fly sink slowly to the bottom of the pool; a cutthroat would rise suddenly off the gravel, his brilliant rim of fire around the gills flashing in the sun, and the fly rod would arch down to the water with a steady, throbbing pull.

We cleaned the fish and took them up to the main house for breakfast. Piles of wood cut in round chunks with a chainsaw were stacked high next to the barn wall, and in the side lot there was the rusted-out skeleton of an old steam tractor with dark pigweed growing through the wheels. In the back were at least fifty bird pens made with chicken wire and wooden frames, and ducks, geese and breeds of grouse and pheasant that I had never seen before wandered around the feed pens and watering pools located all over the yard.

'That's the old man's aviary,' Buddy said. 'It's probably the biggest in the state. He's got birds in there from all over the world, which is one reason why I live in the cabin. You ought to hear those sons of bitches when they crank up at four in the morning.'

We browned the trout in butter, and Buddy's mother cooked a huge platter of scrambled eggs and pork chops with sliced tomatoes on the side. The dining table was covered with an oil cloth thumbtacked to the sides, and Buddy's father sat at the head, waiting quietly until each member of the family was seated before he picked up the first plate and started it around the table. Buddy's three younger brothers, all in high school, sat opposite me, their faces eagerly curious and yet polite about their brother's ex-convict friend. Their skin was tan, and there wasn't an ounce of fat on their bodies, and in their blue jeans and faded print shirts rolled over their young, strong arms, they looked like everything that's healthy in America.

Buddy's sister and her husband, an instructor at the university, sat at the far end of the table, and for some reason they made me uncomfortable. I had the teacher made for a part-time agrarian romanticist or an eastern college man on a brief excursion into the life of his wife's family. The smile and the handshake were too easy and open – and dismissing. She favoured her mother, a well-shaped woman with clear skin and blue eyes that had a quick light in them, but none of the same cheerfulness was in the daughter's face. The daughter was pretty, with sun-bleached curly hair and beautiful hands, but there was a darkness inside her that marred the rest of it, and I could sense a resentment in her because I was someone whom Buddy had known in prison and had brought to their home.

But Buddy's father was the one who I realized instinctively was no ordinary person. His shoulders were square and hard, his neck coarse with sunburn and wind, and the edges of his palms were thick with callus and there were half-moon carpenter's bruises on his fingernails. He was a good-looking man for his age. He combed his thin, brown hair straight back over a wide forehead, and his grey eyes looked directly at you without blinking. He didn't have that soft quality to the edge of the bone structure in the face that most Irish have, and his back stayed straight in the chair and never quite rested against the wood. He took the silver watch on its chain from his blue-jeans pocket and looked at it a moment as though seeing it for the first time.

'I guess we ought to start getting the bales up on the wagon. You ready, boys?' he said.

The three younger brothers got up from the table and started to follow him through the kitchen; then he turned, almost as an afterthought, and looked back at me with those grey, unblinking eyes.

'I think I have something out in the lot that you might be interested in seeing, Mr Paret,' he said.

Buddy grinned at me over his coffee cup.

I walked with Mr Riordan and the three boys into the backyard. The whole expanse of the valley was covered with sunshine now, and the bales of green hay in the fields and the click of light on the Bitterroot River through the trees and the heavy shadows down the canyon walls were so heart-sinking that I had to stop and fold my arms across my chest in a large breath.

'Have you ever seen one of these fellows before?' Mr Riordan said.

He had opened a cage and picked up a large nutria. Its red eyes looked like hot bbs behind the fur, and its yellow buck teeth protruded from the mouth. The body was exactly like a rat's, except much bigger and covered with long fur that grew like a porcupine's quills, and the feet were almost webbed.

'I've never seen one outside of southern Louisiana,' I said. 'I didn't think they could live in a cold climate.'

'That's what most people say. However, no one has advised the nutria of that fact. How much do you know about them?'

I shook a cigarette out of my pack and put it in my mouth. I had the feeling that I was about to be taught the rules of a new game.

'The McIlhenny tabasco family brought them from South America about 1900,' I said. 'Supposedly, they were in cages on Marsh Island about twelve miles off the Louisiana coast, and after a storm smashed up their cages, they swam through waves all the way to land. Now they're in every bayou and canal in south Louisiana. They'll kill your dog if he gets in the water with them, and they can fill up a whole string of muskrat traps in a day.'

'I hope to eventually introduce them in the area. Do you think you'd like to help raise them?'

'At home they're a pest, Mr Riordan. They destroy the irrigation canals for the rice farms, and they breed like minks in heat.'

'Well, we'll see how they do in colder climates.' Then, without a change in the voice, he said, 'You murdered a man, did you?'

I had to wait a moment.

'That's probably a matter of legal definition,' I said. 'I went to prison for manslaughter.'

'I suppose those points are pretty fine sometimes,' he said.

'Yes, sir, they can be.'

'I signed for your parole transfer because Buddy asked me to. Normally, I stay as removed as I can from the dealings of the state and federal government, but he wanted you to come here. And so I've made some kind of contract with the authorities in Louisiana as well as in my own state. That involves a considerable bit on both of our parts. Do you understand me, Mr Paret?'

I drew in on my cigarette and flipped it towards the fence. I could feel the blood start to ring in my palms.

'I have three years' parole time to do, Mr Riordan. That means that on a whim a parole officer can violate me back to the farm for an overdrawn cheque, no job, or just not checking in on the right date. Maybe he's got a little gas on his stomach, half a bag on from the night before, or maybe his wife cut him off that morning. All he's got to do is get his ballpoint moving and I'm on my way back to Angola in handcuffs. In Louisiana a P.V. means one year before you come in for a hearing again.'

'Did you ever do farm work outside of the penitentiary?' he said.

'My father was a sugar grower.'

'I pay ten dollars a day for bucking bales, and you eat up at the house for the noon meal. There's a lot of work in the fall, too, if you care to drive nails and butcher hogs.'

He walked away from me on the worn-out heels of his cowboy

boots towards the flatbed wagon, where his three boys were waiting for him. I wanted to be angry at him for his abruptness and his sudden cut into a private area of my soul, but I couldn't, because he was simply honest and brief in a way that I wasn't prepared for.

I drove to Missoula that afternoon and checked in with the parole office. My new parole officer seemed to be an ordinary fellow who didn't think of me as a particular problem in his case load, and after fifteen minutes I was back on the street in the sunshine, with my hands in my pockets and a whole new town and a blue-gold afternoon to explore. Missoula was a wonderful town. The mountains rose into the sky in every direction, the Clark Fork River cut right thought the business district, and college kids in inner-tubes and on rubber rafts floated down the strips of white water with cans of beer in their hands, shouting and waving at the fishermen on the banks. The town was covered with elm and maple trees, the lawns were green and dug with flower beds, and men in shirtsleeves sprinkled the grass with garden hoses like a little piece of memory out of the 1940s.

I walked down the street with a sense of freedom that I hadn't felt since I went to the penitentiary. Even at my father's house the reminders were there, the darkness of the house, the ancestral death in the walls, the graveyard being eaten away a foot at a time by the bayou, that black vegetable growth across the brain that puts out new roots whenever you come home. But here there was sun all over the footpaths, some of which still had tethering rings set in them.

I went into places that had names like the Oxford, Eddie's Club and Stockman's Bar, and it was like walking through a door and losing a century. Cowboys, mill workers, lumberjacks, bindle stiffs and professional gamblers played cards at felt tables in the back; there was a bar without stools for men who were serious about their drinking, a counter for steaks and spuds and draught beer, the click of billiard balls in a corner, and occasionally a loud voice, a scraping of chairs, and a punch-out that sent a man reeling into the plasterboard partition of the rest rooms.

I was eating a steak fried in onions in the Oxford when a man without legs tried to raise himself on to a stool next to me. He had pushed himself along the street and into the bar on a small wooden platform that had roller-skate wheels nailed under it, and the two wood blocks sticking out from the pockets of his pea jacket looked like someone's beaten ears. One of the buckle straps on his stump had caught, and I tried to raise him towards the stool. His tongue clicked out across his bad teeth like a lizard's.

'He don't want you to help him, mister,' the bartender said.

'I'm sorry.'

'He can't hear or talk. He got all blowed up in the war,' the bartender said. He filled a bowl with lima-bean soup and placed it on a saucer with some crackers in front of the crippled man.

I listened to him gurgle at the soup, and I had to look at the far end of the counter while I ate. The bartender slid another draught in front of me.

'It's on the house,' he said, and then, with a matchstick in the corner of his mouth and his eyes flat, he added, 'You visiting the town?'

'I'm staying in the Bitterroot with a friend and looking around for work. I guess right now I'm going to be bucking bales for the Riordans awhile.' I couldn't resist mentioning the name, just like you put your foot in lightly to test the water.

The reaction was casual and slowly curious, but it was there.

'You know Frank Riordan pretty good?'

'I know his son.'

'What the hell is Frank up to with this pulp mill, anyway?'

'He's up to putting a lot of men out of work,' a man farther down the counter said, without looking up from his plate.

Oh shit, I thought.

'I don't know anything about it,' I said.

'He don't know anything about it,' the same man said. He wore a tin hat and a checkered shirt with long-sleeved underwear.

The bartender suddenly became a diplomat and disinterested neutral.

'I ain't seen Frank in a long time,' he said. 'He used to come in here sometimes on Saturday and play cards.'

'He's got no time for that now,' a man eating next to the cripple said. 'He's too busy sitting on thirteen hundred acres of cows and making sure a dollar-fifty-an-hour man gets his pink slip. That's Frank Riordan for you.'

The bartender wiped the rag over the counter in front of me as though he were rubbing out a piece of personal guilt. 'Some people say that smokestack stinks like shit, but it smells like bread and butter to me,' he said, and laughed with a gastric click in the back of his throat, exposing his line of yellowed teeth.

I could feel the anger of the two men on each side of me, like someone caught between bookends. I put the fork and knife in my plate and lit a cigarette and smoked long enough to keep personal honour intact, then walked back into the sunshine. No more testing of reactions to names, I decided, and maybe I should have a more serious talk with Buddy.

Earlier in the afternoon a gyppo logger had told me in a bar that I might get on with a country band in Bonner. I drove out of Missoula through Hellgate Canyon, a huge split in the mountains where the Salish Indians used to follow the Clark Fork and annually get massacred by the Crows and the Blackfeet (whence the name, because the canyon floor was strewn with skeletons when the first Jesuits passed through). I followed along the river through the deep cut of the mountains and the thin second growth of pine on the slopes until I reached the meeting of the Blackfoot and Clark Fork rivers, which made a wide swirl of dark water that spilled white and iridescent over a concrete dam.

Bonner was the Anaconda Company, a huge mill on the edge of the river that blew plumes of smoke that hung in the air for miles down the Blackfoot canyon. The town itself was made up of one street, lined with neat yards and shade trees and identical wood-frame houses. I hadn't seen a company town outside Louisiana and Mississippi, and though there was no stench of the sugar mill in the air or vision through a car window of Negroes walking from the sugar press to their wood porches in the twilight with lunch pails in their hands, Bonner could have been snipped out of Iberia Parish and glued down in the middle of the Rocky Mountains.

I pulled into the parking lot of a weathered grey building by the railway crossing that had a neon sign on the roof that read:

MILLTOWN UNION BAR, CAFE AND LAUNDROMAT. There were electric slot machines inside the bar, winking with yellow horseshoes, bunches of cherries and gold bars. Over the front door was the head of a mountain sheep covered with a plexiglass dome, and mounted on the wall over the jukebox was an elk's head with a huge, sweeping rack. I talked with the owner at the bar about a lead-guitar job on the weekends, and while he pushed his coffee cup around in his saucer with a thick finger, I went to the truck and brought back my double case with the dobro inside and the Confederate flag sewn into the lining. The metal resonator set in the sound hole swam with the silvery purple reflection of the lights behind the counter, and I pulled the steel picks across the strings and floated the bar down the neck into the beginning of Hank's 'Love-Sick Blues'.

The dobro did it every time. It had paid for itself several times over in turning jobs for me. He said he would pay thirty-five dollars for Friday and Saturday nights and a three-hour session on Sunday afternoons, and I drove back through the Hellgate with the engine humming under the hood and the late sun red on the walls of the canyon and the deep current in the river.

The next day I went to work with Buddy bucking bales, digging postholes and opening up irrigation ditches. The sky was immense over our heads, and the mountains were blue and sharp in the sunlight, and pieces of cloud hung in the pines on the far peaks. By midday our bare chests were running with sweat and covered with bits of green hay, and the muscles in my stomach ached from driving the posthole digger into the ground and spreading the wooden handles outward. Buddy's sister, Pearl, brought out a pitcher of sun tea with mint leaves and cracked ice in it and poured some into two deep paper cups, and we drank it while we sat on the back of the flatbed wagon and ate ham sandwiches. Her curly hair was bright on the tips in the sunlight, and the sun halter she wore with her blue jeans showed enough that I had to keep my attention on the sandwich to be polite. She didn't like me, and I wished that Buddy had not tried to ignore that obvious fact.

'I'm going to visit the wife-o and kids Sunday, Jimmie's

birthday scene, and why don't you and Melvin come along and we'll watch the hippy-dippy from Mississippi here do his Ernest Tubb act up at the beer joint in Bonner,' Buddy said.

She put the top on the iced-tea pitcher and set it carefully on the tailgate. Her eyes went flat.

'I'll have to ask Mel.'

'He's always good for Sunday afternoon boozing,' Buddy said. 'In fact, the only time he gets drunk is the night before he has to work. He goes roaring out of here to the college in the morning with a hangover that must fill up a whole classroom.'

I looked away at the cottonwoods on the river and put a cigarette in my mouth. I had a feeling that anything said next would be wrong. It was.

'You ought to hear this shitkicker, anyway,' Buddy said. 'Plays like Charlie Christian when he wants to, but for some reason my coonass pal is fascinated with the hillbillies and Okies. Loves Jimmie Rodgers and Woody Guthrie, imitates Hank Williams, yodels and picks like Bill Monroe. It's gooder than grits.'

'Let's get on it, Buddy,' I said.

'He's also sensitive about his sounds.'

I folded the remaining half of my ham sandwich in the wax paper and put it back in the lunch pail.

'Your father said he wanted those holes dug up to the slough before we quit,' I said.

'He's loyal to employers, too. A very good man, this one,' Buddy said, hitting the wet slickness of my shoulder with his palm. I wanted to dump him off the tailgate.

'Hey, Pearl, wait a minute,' he said. 'Ask Melvin, and maybe Beth can come along with us.'

She nodded without replying and walked across the hayfield, graceful and cool, her sun halter flashing a white line below her tan.

Buddy and I walked out to where the posts were laid at regular intervals on the ground along the fence line. I thudded the posthole digger in the hard dirt while he poured water out of a bucket into the hole.

'Man, I wish you wouldn't do that,' I said.

He tilted the bucket downward, sluicing water over the wooden handle and the mud impacted between the blades, as though he were preoccupied with a large engineering problem.

'No shit, Buddy,' I said.

'There were other things there, Zeno. You just didn't see them. I didn't mean to piss in your shoe with Pearl. She married this university instructor, and he's an all-right guy, but he's got an eggbeater in his head most of the time, and she's trying to keep up with whatever mood he's in next. That means pack off to Alaska on snowshoes, join some sit-in deal in Alabama, or turn up Beethoven so loud on the hi-fi three nights in a row that it blows the old man out of his bedroom.'

I pulled the posthole digger out of the ground and knocked the mud from the blades.

'Well, that ain't exactly what was really going on there,' he said. 'You see, I'm trying to get back with the wife-o, which might seem like a bad scene, but the boys are nine and eleven now, and they're not doing worth a darn in school, and Beth is taking them to some kind of psychologist in Missoula. That's the only outside thing that bothered me in the joint. I cut out on them after the old lady got me locked up one night, and I kept on going all the way to New Orleans.'

I laid aside the digger and placed the fence post in the hole while Buddy shovelled in dirt and rocks on top of it. His thin back was glistening, and it rippled with bone and muscle when he spaded in each shovel-load.

'Maybe this is a bad time to ask you,' I said, 'but yesterday I was in a place called the Oxford, and I had the feeling that your father has declared war on everybody in this county.'

'Most of those guys have a log up their ass. You can't take that kind of bar-room stuff too seriously.'

'I think they were pretty serious.'

'Here's the scene on that caper. They built this pulp mill on the river west of town, and some days the smell in the valley is so bad that you think an elephant cut a fart in your face. They make toilet paper or something up there. That's right, man. All those beautiful ponderosa pines eventually get flushed down somebody's commode in Des Moines. Anyway, the old man has got them in state court now, and if he wins his injunction, they shut down the whole damn thing. I guess I can't blame most of those guys for being pissed. They don't earn diddly-squat there, anyway, their union don't do anything for them, and the only other work around here is seasonal. Sometimes I even wonder if the old man sees the other end of what he's doing.'

He lit a cigarette while I started on the next hole. The leaves of the cottonwoods by the river flickered with sunlight in the breeze.

'But this is an old scene with him. He fought the Anaconda Company when they started polluting the Clark, and he helped stop a bunch over in east Montana that were catching wild horses and selling them to a dog-food company.' Buddy squatted down with the water can by the hole and puffed a minute on his cigarette. 'He's always got the right thing in mind, but he's one of these guys that draws a line in the dirt, and then that's it. He doesn't see anything in between.'

We dug the last hole by the slough in the late afternoon, and I looked back at the long straight line of fence posts, rigid and thick in the ground, and felt a pride in their geometric progression from the front of the ranch to the mud bottom we were standing in. The grass bent in the wind off the river, and the sun already had a black piece cut out of it by a mountain peak. We threw the tools into the wagon bed and walked back through the fields to the cabin. I felt physically tired and satisfied in the way you do when you have bent yourself to a right task. The shadows of the mountains were moving across the valley, over the log houses, the hay bales in the fields, the stone walls, and the cords of wood piled by the barns, as the light receded and gathered in the trees on the far side of the river.

We fished with worms in the creek behind the cabin during the twilight, then fired the wood stove and broiled the cutthroat trout in butter and garlic salt. I took a can of beer and the Martin out on the front porch while Buddy turned the fish in the pan. I dropped the tuning into D, clicked my thumb pick across the bass strings, and went up the neck into a diminished blues chording that I had learned from Robert Pete Williams in Angola. The strings rang with moonlight, and I felt the deep notes reverberate through my fingers and forearm as though the wood itself had caught the beat of my blood. I bridged over into 'The Wreck of the Ole 97,' hammering on and pulling off like A. P. Carter, the strings trembling with light and their own metallic sympathy.

He was going down the grade making ninety miles an hour
When his whistle broke into a scream.
They found him in the wreck with his hand upon the throttle
He was scalded to death in the steam.

Buddy walked out on the porch with a piece of trout between his fingers and drank out of my beer can on the railing.

'That sounded fine, babe,' he said. He sat on the railing, and the moonlight broke around his shoulders. I took the cigarette from between his fingers and put it in my mouth. The mountains were like a glacial blackness against the sky.

'I know what you're thinking about,' he said. 'You don't have to, man. It's going to be cool.'

That was Thursday.

FIVE

On Sunday morning, Buddy, his sister, her husband and I went into Missoula. It was a fine day for a birthday party in a green backyard, and Buddy had bought a claw mitt and spinning reel for his eleven-year-old boy, and a Swiss army knife full of can openers and screwdrivers for his younger son. I was surprised at how close Buddy was to his children. After we cracked away the rock salt and ice from the hand-crank ice-cream freezer, Buddy served each plate at the table under the maple tree, lit the candles in a glow of pink light and icing, and walked on his hands in the grass while the children squealed in delight.

He wasn't as successful with his wife, Beth. Her manner was quiet and friendly towards him, one of a shared intimate knowledge or perhaps an acceptance out of necessity. But I felt that if he had not been the father of her children, he wouldn't occupy even this small space in her life. I sat against the tree trunk and drank a can of beer, and as I watched Buddy talking to her, his arms sometimes flying in the air, his face smiling and his slacks and sports shirt ironed with sharp creases (and her eyes fading with a lack of attention and then quickening when one of the children spilled ice-cream into his lap), I felt like an intruder in something that I shouldn't see, particularly with Buddy. He had always had a crapshooter's eye for any situation, but this time he was all freight cars, deuces and treys.

She was certainly good to look at. Her hair was black with a light shine in it, and her white skin didn't have a wrinkle or freckle on it. She was a little overweight, but in a soft way, and she stood with her knees close together like a school girl, and the smooth curve of her stomach and her large breasts brought back all my stunted sexual dreams and sleepless midnight frustration.

Later, Buddy insisted that she go with us to the bar in Milltown. She began clearing the table of paper plates and talking in an oblique way about the children's supper, and Buddy walked away to the neighbour's porch, knocked loudly on the jamb, then crossed the lawn again, his face set in a purpose, and started knocking on the other neighbour's door. I saw the anger in his wife's eyes for a moment; then her lips pressed together, and she patted the two boys softly on the shoulders and told them to finish cleaning the table.

She sat between us in the pickup, and Buddy's sister and her husband followed us through Hellgate Canyon along the river to Milltown. Because it was Sunday, yellow life rafts full of beer drinkers in swimming suits, their bodies glistening with tan, roared down through the riffle in a spray of water and sunlight and happy screams of terror against the canyon walls. One raft struck against a boulder, the rubber bow bending upwards while the white water boiled over the stern; then it swung sideways into the current like a carnival ride out of control while the people inside tumbled over one another and sent ropes of beer foam into the air.

I looked into the rearview mirror and saw Melvin, Buddy's

brother-in-law, driving with both arms folded on top of the wheel and a beer bottle in his hand while the car drifted back and forth towards the shoulder. He had started drinking early at the birthday party, and before we left, he had poured a boilermaker in the kitchen.

'I'd better pull off and let you take that fellow's wheel,' I said.

'Don't do that, man,' Buddy said. 'He'll want to fight. He's a real Irish drunk.'

'He's about to put himself and your sister all over those rocks.'

'You'd have to pull him from behind that steering wheel with a chain,' Buddy said. 'Right now he's probably talking about joining a revolution in Bolivia. You know, right after I got out of the joint—' Buddy stopped momentarily and touched a piece of tobacco on his lip, his eyes uncertain in front of his wife's stare through the windscreen—'I hadn't met the guy and he asked me how you burn a safe, because he had some friends who were going to peel one in California for the revolution and he didn't know if they could do it right. I mean he didn't blink when he said it.'

In the mirror I saw the car rip a shower of gravel out of the shoulder and float back towards the centre stripe.

'Let's get some coffee and a sandwich at the truck stop,' I said.

'Go ahead. He'll be all right,' Beth said.

I glanced at her calm, lovely face in the cab, and for just a second I felt the touch of her thigh against mine and realized that I hadn't ridden close to a woman in a vehicle for over two years and had forgotten how pleasant it could be.

'Yeah, don't stop there, man,' Buddy said. 'They don't sell booze, and he'll make up for it by trying to get it on with the lumberjacks. Even the old man thinks he's got a lightning bolt in his head. He came into the house one night blowing some green weed and turned up his hi-fi until the plates were shaking in the cupboard. The birds were flapping in the pens, and the old man came up the stairs like a hurricane.'

I put the truck into second gear and slowed for the turn across the railroad embankment into the white shale parking lot in front of the bar. There was already a large afternoon crowd in the bar, and somebody was tuning an electric bass and blowing into the microphone over the roar of noise. Melvin bounced across the tracks, fishtailed on the back springs, and slid with his brakes in a scour of earth three inches from my front bumper. His face was almost totally white, and he had a filter-tipped cigar in the middle of his mouth. He leaned towards the passenger's window to speak, and his wife averted her face from his breath.

'A little Roy Acuff this afternoon, cousin,' he said.

I nodded at him and rolled up the window.

'Say, Buddy, I've only played twice with these guys,' I said. 'It's a good gig and I want to keep it.'

'It's solid, babe. Just go in there and do the Ernest Tubb shot. We'll take care of this guy.'

'I'm not putting you on,' I said.

'Go inside. It'll be all right,' Beth said.

She was a princess inside the bar. After I began the first number on the bandstand, Melvin stood below the platform with a shot glass in one hand and a draught beer in the other, his face happily drunk. He swayed on his feet, talking with a fractured smile into the amplified sound; then she took him by the elbow and led him away to the dance floor.

I did the lead with my Martin on our second song, 'I'm Moving On', and the bar became quiet while I held the sound box up to my chin and played directly into the microphone. I ran Hank Snow's chord progressions up and down the frets, thumping the deep bass notes of a train highballing through Dixie while I picked out the notes of the melody on the treble strings with my fingernail. I heard the steel try to get in behind me before I realized that I had been riding too long, and I moved back down the neck into the standard G chord on the second fret and tapered off into the rest of the band with a bass roll. The crowd applauded and whistled, and a man at the bar shouted out, 'Give 'em hell, reb.'

I saw Buddy in the rest room at the end of the set. He was leaning over the urinal with one hand propped against the wall, and his eyes looked like whorls of colour with cinders for pupils.

'I scored some acid from a guy out in the parking lot,' he said. 'You want to try some of this crazy mixture on your neurotic southern chemistry?'

'I got to work this afternoon, babe.'

'How you like my old lady? She's quite a gal, ain't she?'

'Yeah, she is.'

'I was catching your radiations in the truck there, Zeno,' he said. 'A little pulsing of the blood behind the steering wheel.'

'You better leave that college dope alone,' I said.

'Hey, don't walk out. After you get finished, we're going to Eddie's Club, and then I'm bringing a whole crew down to the place for a barbecue. Some bear steaks soaked overnight in milk. It's the best barbecue in the world. Puts meat in your brain and black hair all over your toenails.'

'OK, Buddy.'

He drew in on his cigarette, the smoke and hot ash curling between his yellowed fingers, and squinted at me with a radiant smile on his face.

Eddie's Club was a place full of hard yellow light, smoke, winos, drunk Salish Indians, the clatter of pool balls, a hillbilly jukebox, college students and some teachers from the university. One wall was lined with large framed photographs of the old men who drank in there, their mouths toothless and collapsed, their slouch hats and cloth caps pulled at an angle over the alcoholic lines and bright eyes of their faces.

'Boyd Valentine, the bartender, did all that,' Buddy said, his forehead perspiring in the smoke. 'You got to meet this guy. He's a Michelangelo with a camera. A real wild man. Your kind of people.'

Before I could stop him, Buddy had walked away into the confusion of noise and people, who were two-deep at the bar. I was left at the table with Beth, Pearl and Melvin, who couldn't find the end of his cigarette with his lighter, and a half-dozen other people whose elbows rested in spilled beer without their taking notice of it.

'Try a Montana busthead highball,' Melvin said. 'Don't try to stay sober in this crowd. It's useless.'

He lowered a full whiskey jigger into a beer schooner with two fingers and pushed it towards me.

'I'd better pass,' I said.

He picked up the schooner with both hands and drank it to the bottom, the whiskey jigger rolling against the glass. I had to shudder while I watched him.

In the back two men began fighting over the pool table. A couple of chairs were overturned, a pool cue shattered across the table, and one man was knocked to the floor, then helped up and pushed out of the back door. Few people paid any attention.

'What's on your mind?' Beth said, smiling.

'I wonder what I'm doing here.'

'It's part of Buddy and Mel's guided tour of Missoula,' Pearl said. She wasn't happy with any of it.

'You're a better man than I, Gunga Din,' Melvin said, toasting me in some private irony.

'We'll be leaving in a few minutes,' Beth said.

'Don't worry about me. I'll probably shoot on across the street to the Oxford and get something to eat.' Although I wouldn't admit the impulse to myself then, I was hoping that she would ask to go along.

'Hey,' Buddy shouted behind me. 'This is Boyd Valentine. Used to hang around New Orleans when I was making my cool sounds there. Got a '55 Chevy and blows engines out at a hundred and ten on the Bitterroot road. Outruns cops, ambulances and fire trucks. Best photographer in the Northwest.'

Buddy held the bartender by one arm, a man with fierce black eyes and an electric energy in his face. One of his thumbs was missing, and the black hair on his chest grew out of his shirt.

'What's happening?' he said, and shook hands. There was good humour in his voice and smile, and a current in his hand.

'My man here is going to load up his hot rod with good people, and we're going to burn on down to the place and juice under the stars while I barbecue steaks that will bring you to your knees in reverence,' Buddy said. 'Then my other man will crank out his Martin and sing songs of Dixie and molasses and ham hocks cooked with grits in his mammy's shoe.'

We finally left the bar after Melvin turned over a pitcher of beer in an Indian woman's lap. She raised her dress over her waist and squeezed it out over her thighs and kneecaps, her husband tore Melvin's shirt, the bartender then brought three more pitchers to the table, and that was the end of that.

Buddy and I dropped Beth off at her house. He tried to convince her to come out to the ranch, but in her quiet woman's way she mentioned the children, their supper, school tomorrow, those arguments that know no refutation. We drove down through the Bitterroots with the river black and winding beyond the cottonwoods. Rain clouds had started to move across the mountain peaks, and there was a dry rumble of thunder on the far side of the valley. In the distance, heat lightning wavered and flickered over the rolling hills of pines. I opened the wind vane and let the cool air, with just the hint of rain in it, blow into my face.

Buddy took a reefer stub from his pocket and lit it, holding the smoke down deep, his teeth tight together. He let out the smoke slowly and took another hit.

'Where did you get that?' I said.

'An Indian girl at Eddie's. You want a snort?' He pushed in the cigarette lighter on the dashboard.

'Buddy, you've got enough shit in you now to make a time bomb out of your head.'

'Forget that crap, man. The only thing I could never pull down right was coke.' He placed the stub on the hot lighter and held it under his nose, sniffing the curl of smoke deeply into his head. 'Look, I struck out with her back there, didn't I?'

'I don't know.'

'Hell yes, you know.'

'I never met your wife before. She said she had to take care of the kids.'

'That's not what I mean, man, and you know it. Don't give a con the con.'

'I was on the bandstand. I don't know what went on between you.'

'But you *know*.'

'Come on, Buddy. You're pulling me into your own stuff.'

'That's right, Zeno. But you got an eye for looking into people. You tool around the yard, throwing the handball up against the wall, cool walk under the gun hack, but you're clicking right into somebody's pulsebeat.'

He knocked the lighter clean against the wind vane and rubbed it clean again on his shoe. There were red flecks in the corners of his eyes. This was the first time I had seen a bit of meanness come out in Buddy when he was high.

'Hell, Iry, I read your action when you first came in. All that southern-country-boy jive works cool on old ladies, but you *know*, man, and you're digging everything I say.'

I was in that position where there is nothing to say, with no words that wouldn't increase an unpleasant situation, and silence was equally bad. Then the bartender's 1955 Chevrolet passed us in a roar of twin exhausts, a quick brilliance of headlights, and a scorch of black rubber as he shifted up and accelerated in front of us. The backdraught and vacuum pushed my truck towards the shoulder of the road.

'Damn,' I said. 'Does that fellow drive in demolition derbies or something?'

'That's just Boyd Valentine airing out his gourd.'

'You have another stick?' I thought it was better that I smoke it and dump it if he had any more.

'That was the last of the souvenirs from the reservation. It was green, anyway. Think they must grow it in hog shit. Makes you talk with forked brain. Pull into the bar up there and I'll buy a little brew for our crowd.'

The neon sign reflected a dull purple and red on the gravel and the cars and pickups in the parking lot. It was the same bar where we had gone my first night in Montana.

'Let's pass, man,' I said. 'We have some in the icebox, and I can go down the road later.'

'Pull in, pull in, pull in. You got to stop worrying about all these things.'

'I don't think it's too cool, Buddy.'

'Because you've got your head in the parole office all the time. Wait just a minute and I'll bop on out with the brew.'

I parked the truck on the edge of the lot by the road, and Buddy walked inside, his balance deliberate like a sailor's on a ship. I smoked a cigarette and watched a few raindrops strike against the windscreen. A long streak of lightning quivered in the blackness off a distant mountain, and I flicked my cigarette out into the moist, sulphurous air. *Well, to hell with it*, I thought, and went inside after him.

It was crowded, and the barstools were filled with cowboys and mill workers bent over into the poker dice, punchboards and rows of beer bottles. Buddy was standing in front of a table with a beer in his hand, talking with three rawboned men and their wives, who were as bovine and burned with wind and sun as their husbands. They had empty steak plates in front of them, streaked with gravy and blood, and while Buddy talked, they tipped their cigarette ashes into the plates with a kind of patient anger that they kept in with only the greatest stoicism. Buddy must have played the Ray Charles number on the jukebox, because I didn't think anyone else in the place would have, and his speech was already full of hip language that raised up and down with the song while his hand tapped against the loose change in his slacks. He was on the outer edge of his high, and Bird Parker rhythms were working in his head, and it couldn't have come at a worse time.

'Well, that's your scene, man, and that's copacetic,' he said. 'And the old man has got his scene, too. And that's cool. He just turns over his action a little different. It's a matter of understanding what kind of scene you want to build and which kind of cats you want in on it—'

I went to the bar and asked if Buddy had put in an order to carry out.

'That's it waiting on the end of the counter when you're ready to leave, mister,' the bartender said.

I picked up the cardboard case of beer from the bar and walked over to Buddy with it.

'My meter's running overtime,' I said.

'Just a minute. There's a delicate metaphysical point involved here.'

'What's involved is our ass.'

'Set it down. Let's clear this question up. Now, if that stink plant down there invested some money in a purification system, the valley wouldn't smell like it just had an enema, and they could supply all kinds of copacetic toilet paper all over the world.'

One man, with a bull neck, iron eyebrows, and his shirt lapels pressed and starched flat, looked at Buddy with a stare that I would never want to have turned on me. The thick veins in his neck and brow were like twisted pieces of cord. He breathed deeply in his chest, almost clicking with a stunted anger, and his thumb knuckle rubbed back and forth on the oil cover of the table. He blinked and looked at a far spot on the wall.

'You better tell your old man that four hundred working men are going to lose their jobs because he thinks there's a little bit of smell in the air,' he said.

'Well, that's the way the toilet flushes sometimes, Zeno,' Buddy said.

I picked up the case of beer and headed for the door. I had to wait for a drunk cowboy to kiss his girl good night and stumble out ahead of me; then I walked across the parking lot in the light rain and threw the beer in the back of the truck. Buddy followed me in the frame of yellow light from the open door.

'Get in,' I said.

'Why the fire drill, man?'

'The next time, you charge your own hill. Collect Purple Hearts when I'm not around.'

'You're really pissed.'

'Just get in. I'm burning it down the road in about five seconds.'

We pulled on to the blacktop, and I revved it up all the way in first and slammed the gearbox into second. The oil smoke billowed out of the truck's tail pipe.

'What the hell are you doing?' he said. He still had the beer bottle in his hand, and he drank the foam out of the bottle.

'Don't you know what you're fooling with back there? Those people have blood in their eye. For a minute that man wanted to ice you.'

'Iry, you don't know the scene around here. It's not like rednecks opening up a shank in your face. This kind of crap goes on all the time. Besides, I can't stand the righteousness of those bastards. They bitch about the federal government, the Indians, farm control, niggers, college kids, anything that's not like them. You get pretty tired of it.'

'Haven't you learned to leave people like that alone?'

'You're really coming on like Gangbusters tonight.'

'Yeah, well, quick lesson you taught me my first week in the population: walk around the quiet ones that look harmless.'

'OK, Zeno.'

I put a cigarette in my mouth and popped a kitchen match on my thumbnail. The rain turned in the headlights, and I breathed in on the cigarette and let the smoke out slowly.

'Buddy, I just don't like to see you fade the wrong kind of action,' I said.

'I know all that, man.'

'You got to ease up sometimes and let people alone.'

'Forget about it. I'm cool. Do I look like I'm worried? I'm extremely cool on these matters.'

I looked into the rearview mirror as I slowed to turn into the side road that led to the ranch. A pair of headlights was gaining on me through the rain as though the driver couldn't see that I was slowing. I shifted into second and accelerated into the gravel turn off, the truck body bouncing hard against the springs. The trees were black by the side of the road, and the rocks pinged and rattled under the frame. The headlights turned in after us, and I pushed the accelerator to the floor.

'Hey, you trying out for the hot-rod circuit or something?' Buddy said. 'Come on, you're going to rip a tyre on these rocks.'

I didn't answer him. The driver behind us had on his brights, and they reflected in my eyes like a shattered white flame. I wound the truck up in second, shot it into third, with the gas all the way down, and popped the clutch. It slipped momentarily until it could grab, the speedometer needle quivered in a stationary place like part of a bad dream, and the headlights suddenly loomed up close enough to the tailgate so that I could see the hood and outline of a large yellow truck.

'Pull over and let those drunk sons of bitches pass,' Buddy said.

Then they hit us. The back end of my pickup fishtailed towards the ditch, and I spun the steering wheel in my hands and heard the metal tear like someone was ripping strips out of a tin roof. The headlights beat against the dark line of trees and wavered up into the sky, and I couldn't pull the pickup to the centre of the

road again because either a bumper had been crumpled against a
tyre or the frame had been bent. Buddy was looking backwards
through the cab window, his face brilliant in the headlights'
illumination.

'Another mile, man,' he said. 'I'm going to get the old man's
shotgun and blow these assholes all over the road.'

They closed on us and caught my back bumper as a snow-
plough might, with a heavy superior thrust of engine and weight
that pushed the pickup forward as though it had no momentum
of its own, the transmission shearing into filings, the wheels locked
sideways and scouring ruts out of the rock road. I held on to the
steering wheel with one hand and tried to put an arm in front of
Buddy as the edge of the ditch cut under the front tyre and we
went over. The pine saplings slashed against the windscreen, and
the bottom of the ditch came up blackly and smashed the radiator
into the fan. Buddy's head spider-webbed the glass, and he
recoiled backwards into the seat, a brilliant jet of blood shooting
from a small raised split like a crucifix in the skin. My stomach
had gone hard into the steering wheel, my breath rushed out of a
long collapsing place in my throat, and I fought to bring the air
back in my lungs.

Then I heard their truck stop and back up on the road. Their
doors slammed, and three big men skidded down the side of the
ditch through the underbrush, their boots digging for balance in
the wet dirt. I pulled the tyre iron from under the seat and opened
the door just before the first one got his hand on it. Before I could
turn into him and swing, he brought a nightstick down on my
arm. It was the type used by policemen and bar-room bouncers,
drilled out on the end and filled with lead, and I felt the bone
crack like a piece of plate. My hand opened as though the tendons
were severed, and the tyre iron fell foolishly to the ground.

'That other one's Riordan,' a second man said. They were all
dressed in blue jeans, work boots and wash-faded flannel shirts,
and their large bodies were bursting with a confident physical
power.

They pulled Buddy from the cab and knocked him to the
ground, then held him up against the tyre well and drove their
fists into his face. They discounted my presence as they might

have a stray limb that was in their way. The blood was already swelling up in a blue knot under the skin on my arm, and my fingers were quivering uncontrollably. Buddy's hair was matted against the split in his forehead, and his face had gone white from the blows. I picked up the tyre iron with my left hand and stumbled around the front of the truck in the brush, the headlights bright in my eyes, and threw it as hard as I could into a man's back. His shoulders straightened abruptly, and his arm flickered in the air behind his spine, his body frozen as though some awful pain was working its way into his groin.

They didn't take long after that. They had finished beating Buddy, streaking his clothes with blood, and now they turned their attention to me. The man I had hit leaned against my truck with one arm, arching his back and kneading his fist into the vertebrae. I could see the pain in his eyes.

'Give that son of a bitch his buckwheats,' he said.

The first punch caught me in the eye. I felt the man's whole weight lift into it, and I spun backwards off the bumper with a corridor of purple light receding into my brain. I must have held on to the bumper, because the second blow came downward across my nose, and for just an instant I knew that he had a ring on. There was mud all over my hands and knees, the rain ticked in my hair, and I heard one man say, 'You ought to know when to stay in Louisiana, bud.' Then he kicked me between the buttocks, and I thought I was going to urinate.

I heard their truck doors slam, and as they turned around in the road, the headlight beams reflected off the tree trunks, and I saw the words on the side of the cab: WEST MONTANA LUMBER COMPANY. I got to my feet and started over towards Buddy, who was bent on his knees in the undergrowth. My back felt cold and wet, and I realized that half my shirt had been torn away from one shoulder. Then I saw the thin ribbon of fire curling up the twisted strip of cloth into the open gas tank. I ran to Buddy and grabbed him under the arm with my good hand, and we tripped along the bottom of the ditch with the pine branches whipping back across our faces and arms.

A red finger of light leaped down the gas hole, and there was a whoosh and a brilliant illumination like strobe lights in the ditch.

The truck body steamed and constricted, and the paint burst into blisters; then the fire suddenly welled up through the wooden bed and shot into the air in an exploding yellow scorch against the pine boughs high overhead. The heat burned my face and made my eyes water. The tyres became ringed with fire, and the grease in the rear axle boiled and hissed through the seals, and the hood sprang open from its latch as though it were part of some isolated comic act. I heard the Martin and dobro start to come apart in the cab. The mahogany and spruce wood, the tapered necks and German silver in the frets, gathered into a dark flame cracking through the windscreen, and the strings on the dobro tightened and popped one by one against the metal resonator, ringing out through the woods as though they were being pulled loose by a discordant pair of pliers.

I heard the rain on the windowsill and pulled the sheet up over my eyes. It was cool under the sheet, and I rolled back into that strange, comfortable world between sleep and wakefulness. On the edge of my mind I heard my father moving around downstairs in the early dawn, breaking open the shotguns to see that they were empty and dropping the decoys with their lead-anchor weights into the canvas duffel bag. I knew that it was going to be a fine day for duck hunting, with an overcast sky and enough rain to bring them sailing in low, denting the water with their feet and wings before they landed. It had been a good year for mallard and teal, and on a grey day like this one they always came in right above our blind on their way to feed in the rice field.

'*Allons aller*,' I heard my father call up the staircase.

And I could already feel the excitement of the outboard ride across the swamp to the blind, with the shotgun and the shells under my raincoat, knowing that we could take all the ducks we wanted simply because that part of the swamp was ours – we had earned it, the two of us. They would dip suddenly out of the sky when they saw our decoys while we sat motionlessly in the reeds, our faces pointed towards the ground, our camouflaged caps pulled down on our foreheads; then, as they winnowed over the bayou, we would rise together and the sixteen-gauge would roar in my ears and recoil into my shoulder, and before the first mallard had folded in the air and toppled towards the water, even before the dogs had splashed through the reeds after him, I was already firing again with the empty shell casings smoking at our feet.

But the swamp and my father's happy voice over the piled ducks in the blind didn't hold in my mind. I felt the gun go off again against my shoulder, but this time I was looking through the peep sight on my M-1 at a concrete bunker on the edge of a frozen rice field. The bunker was covered with holes, as though it had been beaten with a ball peen hammer, and the firing slit was scoured and chipped with ricochets. I let off the whole clip at the slit, the concrete shaling and powdering away like wisps of smoke in the grey air, and then I pulled back into the ditch and pressed in another clip with my thumb. The bottom of the ditch was filmed with ice and covered with empty shell casings. My hands were shaking with the cold inside my mittens, and my fingers felt like sticks on the bolt. I raised up and let off three rounds across the crusted snow on the edge of the ditch. Then I heard the sergeant behind me.

'All right, he's dead in there. Save what you got.'

The other seven stopped firing and pulled away from the top of the ditch. The moisture in their nostrils was frozen, and their faces were discoloured from the wind and the crystals of snow on their skin.

'So here's the deal,' the sergeant said. 'We got about one hour to get around that hill or there ain't going to be anybody to meet us there.'

'He's under a mattress in there. They put a whole pile of them in every one of them things,' another man said.

'Well, we can take our choices, and it's a finger any way you look at it,' the sergeant said. He had a knitted sweater tied around his ears under his helmet, and two fingers of his left hand had started to swell with frostbite. 'We can sit on our ass here and shoot everything we got on one gook, and in the meantime we're going to get left, because those other fuckers aren't going to wait on us, and we ain't going to have nothing except a frozen pecker to stick out of his hole when they send their patrols through here tonight.'

There was no answer, but each of us was thinking of that hundred yards of wind-polished snow that at least four of us would have to cross before we would be beyond the angle of the machine-gunner behind the slit in the bunker.

'OK, it's Paret, Simpson and Belcher,' the sergeant said. 'Paret, you stay on my ass. We're going around behind him and blow that iron door open. What you got left in the Browning, Roth?'

'A half clip and four in the bag.'

'Put it in his face until we get all the way across the field.'

The BAR man started firing, and we went over the top of the ditch in a run, our shoulders crouched, our boots like lead weights in the snow. The two other men headed towards the left side of the bunker, their breath labouring out in a fog before them. I followed hard on the sergeant, as though I were trying to run in a dream, and then the sun broke through the overcast and turned the snowfield into a brilliant white mirror. Our tracks looked sculptured, like a dark violation of the field's whiteness.

The snow became deeper and softer, and the sergeant and I pushed for that safe imaginary angle beyond the range of a machine-gun's swivel. Then the slit burst open with flame, and I saw the bullets clip in a straight pattern towards me in the snow. For a moment I saw the sergeant's face turn and stare at me over his shoulder, as though he had been disturbed in an angry mood. I fell forward on my elbows, my boots still locked in their deep sculptured depressions, and heard the snow hiss and spit around me.

The whiteness of the snow ached like a flame inside my eyelids.

Where are you hit?

I don't know.

Jesus Christ, his back is coming off.

Get up over the rise and tell them to wait. Shoot out their tyres if you have to.

They better have plasma. Look at the snow.

I felt the nurse rub salve with a piece of cotton over my back and pull the gauze back into place. The rain broke on the windowsill in dimples of light, and I could see the dark green of the elms and maples waving in front of the old brick buildings across the street. I raised up on my elbows and felt the skin burn on my back. The plaster cast on my forearm was like a thick, obscene weight.

'Don't turn over. You have some pretty bad blisters there,' a man's voice said.

Buddy's father was bent forward in a leather chair at the foot of the bed, his square, callused hands folded between his legs. His gold watch chain glinted against his faded Levi's, and his wide forehead looked pale in the room's half-light. His grey eyes were staring straight into mine.

'They put you under before they set your arm. The doctor said it might hang on a while after you woke up.'

My arms and bare chest were damp against the sheet, and I wiped my face with the pillow. The pressure sent a sudden touch of pain along my eyebrow and the bridge of my nose. I heard him pull his chair to the side of the bed.

'They really did a job on us,' I said.

He nodded with his eyes squinted, and I saw that he was looking over my face rather than at me. I propped myself on one elbow and softly touched the hard row of stitches under the strip of gauze bandage on my eyebrow. There were flecks of dried blood on my fingertips. When I moved, my back burned as though it had been scalded.

'How's Buddy?'

'He's asleep in the next room.'

'His head hit the glass when we went over in the ditch. Then they really hit him,' I said.

'He'll be all right. He was awake earlier and we talked, and then he wanted to sleep for a while.'

'How bad is he?'

'He has a concussion, and they put twenty stitches in his forehead.'

Outside, the rain was dripping from the trees, and I could hear someone punting a football in a front yard.

'I tried to stop it,' I said. 'I got one of them with the tyre iron, but they had already broken my arm.'

He rubbed his coarse palms over his knuckles and looked momentarily at the floor, then at me. There was a thin parting-line in his greying brown hair, and his eyelids blinked as though he were keeping some idea down inside himself.

'I didn't press Buddy this morning, but I want to know what happened. Was it something that grew out of an argument in a saloon, or was it more involved than that?'

I reached over to the nightstand where someone had placed my package of Lucky Strikes beside my notecase, and put one in my mouth. He took a book of matches from his denim shirt and lit it. I wanted to avoid his face and the private question that was there beyond the wind-burned skin, the short growth of whiskers, and those intense grey eyes.

'It started with Buddy at the bar, Mr Riordan. I was outside most of the time. You'd better ask him about it later,' I said.

'And what was it exactly about?'

'Maybe too many drunk men in a bar on Sunday night.'

'What was said?'

I drew in on the cigarette and placed it in the ashtray. The wind blew the rain off the windowsill into the room. His big hands were pressed on his knees, and the veins stood up like twists of blue cord under the skin.

'You've got me in a hard place, and I think you know that,' I said.

'Yes, I guess I do. But I'd like to have it now.'

'Buddy was talking with some people at a table about the pulp mill. I don't know who the men were who followed us out. Buddy thought they were just drunks until they smashed into the back of my truck.'

'I see,' he said.

I heard the wet slap of the football again and then the heavy rattle of leaves in a tree.

'It looks like we've gotten you into some of our family's trouble, Mr Paret,' he said.

'No, sir, that's not true. I usually make a point of finding my own.'

He took a package of tobacco from his shirt pocket and rolled a cigarette, wet the glue neatly, and pinched the ends down.

'What did you kill that man for?' he said.

'I don't know.'

'It never came to you in those two years?'

'No.'

'I shot at a man once. I would have hit him and maybe killed him if he hadn't jumped from the cab of a combine when he did. I shot at him because I'd thought for a long time about something he had done.'

'I formally resigned from my war a long time ago, Mr Riordan.'

He cleared his throat quickly, as though there were a piece of bad air in it, and put out the rolled cigarette in the ashtray. This is one that's hard to read, I thought.

'I'll be back this evening,' he said. 'The doctor said you two should be able to leave in the morning. Do you want anything?'

'I'd like a half pint of bourbon.'

'All right.'

'Wait,' I said, and gave him three dollars from my notecase.

After he had gone, I tried to sleep in the cool sound of the rain and fall back into the dream about the duck hunt with my father, but the perspiration rolled off my back on to the sheets, and when I kept my eyes closed too long, I saw the headlights roaring up out of the dark road into my tailgate. I turned on my side, with the ooze of salve thick against my skin, and stared at the wooden crucifix on the wall with two withered palms stuck behind it. I got up from the bed and found my slacks and shoes in the closet, but no shirt, and then I remembered the curl of flame climbing into the gas tank. It took me ten minutes to get my trousers on with one hand, and even with my buttocks against the bed the room kept tilting sideways from the square of pale light through the window. Sweat dripped out of my hair on to the cast, and my good hand was shaking as I tried to pop a match with my thumb and light a cigarette.

After I rang for the nurse, I looked across the room at my image in the dresser mirror. *Oh, man*, I thought.

A nun in white pushed open the door softly, and then her quiet, cosmetic-free face dilated with a red hue.

'Oh, no, you shouldn't do that,' she said. 'Please don't do that. You mustn't.'

'I think I should leave this evening, Sister, but I need a shirt. I'd appreciate it if you could find any old one you have around here.'

'Please, Mr Paret.'

'I have to check out, and I guess I'm going to. I just hate to ride the bus in a pajama shirt. You'd be doing me a great favour, Sister.'

Just then the nurse came in, and she could have been a matron in a women's reformatory. Her face was at first a simple bright piece of cardboard and irritation at an annoyance on her floor; then after a few sentences were exchanged between us, the anger clicked in her eyes, and I was sure that she would have enjoyed seeing me collapse on the floor in a spasm that would require heart surgery with a pocketknife.

The nun came through the door again with a folded checked shirt in her hands, brushed past the nurse in a swirl of white cloth over her small, polished black shoes, and put the shirt next to me, quickly, with just a flash of her concerned pretty face into mine.

I buttoned the shirt so I could rest my limp hand and the weight of the cast inside it and walked down the corridor to the desk in the waiting room. I could hear the leather soles and etched voice of the nurse echo behind me, and evidently she had enough command in the hospital to make the interns and the resident doctor look around wall-eyed and full of question marks at the strange man walking towards them a little off-balance.

I told the lady at the desk my name and asked for the bill.

'You ought to go back to your room, fella,' the resident said.

'Got to catch air, doc, and stretch it out a little bit tonight.'

He looked at me steadily for a moment.

'All right, that's fine,' he said, and motioned the nurse away. 'But we're going to give you a sling and some pills for infection and pain. You come back in tomorrow to have your bandages changed.'

I sat down in a metal chair while another nurse tied a sling around my neck and placed my elbow carefully into the cloth and clipped safety pins into the folds. She stuck a brown envelope full of pills into the pocket of the checked shirt, and I stood up to walk to the desk again. I could feel the stitches drawing tight against my eye, and I felt that there was a large blood blister swelling up on the bridge of my nose. My eyes couldn't focus on the grey dimpling of rain on the concrete outside.

I asked again for my bill and was told that Mr Riordan had asked that it be sent to him. I took out twenty-five dollars from my notecase and said that I would be back in to pay the rest.

I walked through the wet streets under the overhang of trees towards the bus depot. The wind swept the rain in gusts into my face. Clouds hung like soft smoke on the peaks of the mountains, and the neon signs over the bars were hazy red and green in the diminishing grey light.

So you showed everybody at the hospital you're a stand-up guy, I thought. Isn't that fine? Then I had to think about the rest of it. My truck and my Martin and dobro burned up, a broken arm that put me out of work, and living at a strange family's place as a bandage case because there wasn't another damn thing I could do. And deeper than any of it was just a sick feeling, a humiliation at being beaten up by men who had done it with a lazy form of physical contempt. I'd had the same feeling only once before, when a bully in the eighth grade had caught me after school and pinned my arms into the dust with his knees and slapped my face casually back and forth, then spat on his finger and put it in my ear.

SIX

In the morning the sun was all over the Bitterroot Valley, the grass had become a darker green from the rain, and the irrigation ditches were flowing high and muddy through the pigweed along the banks. I fired the wood stove and set the coffeepot to boil on an iron lid with the grounds in the water and went out the back to see if I could start Buddy's old Plymouth. He had driven it through the creek and smashed one headlight and bumper into a cottonwood when he was drunk, and white water had boiled over the front axle into the wires and distributor. But I finally turned it over on three cylinders and left it knocking and drying in neutral in front of the cabin while I drank coffee out of the pot and ate some smoked trout from the icebox.

Buddy's father and his younger brothers looked up at me from their work in the hayfield as I drove slowly with one arm up the dirt road towards the cattle guard. The ignition wires I had tied together swung under the dashboard and sparked whenever they clicked against the metal. Out of my side vision I saw Mr Riordan raise his checkered arm in the sunlight, but I slipped the transmission into third and thumped across the cattle guard on to the gravel road. I passed the burned wreck of my truck and the large area of blackened grass around it. The windows hung out on the scorched metal in folded sheets, and the boards in the bed were collapsed in charcoal over the rear axle. Through the broken eye of one window I thought I could see the silver wink of the twisted resonator from my dobro.

I drove into Hamilton, the Ravalli County seat, and parked in front of the jail. As I walked up the path towards the building, a man behind the wire screen and bars of a cell window blew cigarette smoke out into the sunlight, then turned away into the gloom when I looked into his face.

I talked to the dispatcher in the sheriff's office, then waited for thirty minutes on a wooden bench with the salve oozing out of my bandages into my shirt before the sheriff opened the door to his office and nodded his head at me.

His brown sleeves were rolled back over his elbows, and there was a faded army tattoo under the sun-bleached hair on one forearm and a navy tattoo on the other. His fingers on top of the desk pad were as thick as sausages, the nails broken down to the quick and lined with dirt, and there was a rim of dandruff around the bald spot in the centre of his head. He didn't ask me to sit down or even look at me directly. He simply clicked his fingernail against a paper spindle, as though he were involved in an abstract thought, and said:

'Yes, sir?'

'My name is Iry Paret. Buddy Riordan and I got run off the road by Florence the other night, and I got my truck burnt up.'

'You're Mr Paret, are you?' he said.

'That's right.'

He clicked his finger against the spindle again.

'I sent one of my deputies up to the hospital in Missoula after I heard about it. You fellows sure put it in the ditch, didn't you?'

'I had two guitars in that cab that were worth around seven hundred dollars,' I said.

'What would you like us to do?' He looked up at me from his finger game with the spindle. There was a blue touch in his eyes like something off an archer's bow.

'I want to get the three men that burned my truck.'

'I talked with a few people in the tavern later that night. They said you and Buddy Riordan were drunk.'

'We weren't drunk. We were knocked off the road, and somebody used my shirt to set fire to the gas tank.'

'I looked at your truck, too. There's one pair of skid marks going off into the ditch.'

I took a cigarette from my shirt pocket and tried to light a match from the folder with one hand.

'Look, Sheriff, a yellow truck with a West Montana Lumber Company sign on the door ran right over my tailgate, and then they really went to work. I don't know who those guys are, but they owe me for a 1949 pickup and two guitars and a broken arm.'

'Well, I guess you're saying you just got the shit beat out of you,' he said, and popped his thick index finger loose from his thumb on the desk blotter. He opened his desk drawer and pulled out a folder with three sheets clipped together inside. He turned over to the second page and folded it back and looked hard at one paragraph.

'Was it a coloured man you killed down there?' he said.

I lit the cigarette and looked beyond him through the open window at the soft blue roll of the mountains.

'I mean, you got off with two years for murdering a man. In Montana, you'd get ten in Deer Lodge, even if it was an Indian.'

In that moment I hated him and his wry smile and the private blue glint in his eye.

'I got three years' good time, Sheriff. I imagine that's in your folder, too.'

'Yes, sir, it is. It also says you could get violated back to that place in Louisiana without too much trouble.'

I drove back to the ranch with my hands tight on the steering wheel. I had wanted to say something final to him when I left the office, something that would crack into that blue glint in his eyes, but I had simply walked out like someone who had been told his bus was gone.

Buddy was sitting on the front porch of the cabin with a cup of tea in one hand and a cigarette in the other. His face was puffed with yellow and purple bruises, and a thick band of gauze was wrapped around his head. He tried to grin, but I could see the pain in his mouth.

'I didn't know when you'd be back, so I wired it up,' I said.

'I'm just going to guess, Zeno. The sheriff's office,' he said.

'Do you import these bastards out of the South?'

'A couple of quick lessons from Uncle Zeno. Around here the law won't do anything about bar-room brawls or any variety of Saturday night cuttings or swinging of pool cues. It don't matter if it's one guy against the whole Russian army – he's on his own. Number two, the name Riordan is like the stink on shit down there at Hamilton.'

'In the meantime we got stomped, partner,' I said. 'I'm out my truck and my guitars, and I don't know when I can work again.'

'We got this place, man. You don't have to worry about money.'

His acceptance made me even angrier than I had been in the sheriff's office.

'That's not my kind of caper.'

'Maybe you don't like to hear this, but you got to mark it off.'

'Damn, Buddy, those guys are out there somewhere.'

'Yeah, man, and maybe you'll recognize them somewhere, but what are you going to do then? Call the same dick that just threw you out of his office? Get a beer out of the icebox and sit down. I'm going to go fishing in a little while.'

'That's real Koolaid, babe. I have to give it to you,' I said.

'You haven't taken the wood plugs out of your ears yet. You talk like a fish with part of his brain still outside. You know better.'

I walked out of the sun's glare into the shade of the porch and went inside. My suitcase was opened beside my bunk bed, and I wanted to throw my clothes into it and hitch on down the road, but I was broke and stuck here with my parole. I opened a can of beer and leaned back against the wooden ceiling post and drank it. I could hear the creek through the back window.

'Come on out here, Iry,' he called through the screen door.

I drank the bottom of the can slowly, and then I felt my throat and chest begin to relax and the blood slow in my temples. I took another can from the icebox and went back outside. The ridge of mountains behind the main house was dark blue and honed like a knife against the sky.

'You see what I mean, don't you?' Buddy said. 'I know you got brass cymbals going off in your head all the time. What's the name of that guy you celled with, the one with all the whorehouse stories? He told me how you used to sweat all over the bunk at night and sometimes just sit up till morning bell. But, man, on a deal like this we just lose. That's all. You just draw a line through it and flush it on down.'

'All right, Buddy, no therapy. I'll watch you fish for a while, and then I want to borrow your car again.'

'Like what kind of action do you have planned, Zeno?'

'I need to call my brother in Louisiana, and I'm supposed to stop by the hospital.'

'There's a phone up at the house.'

'Can I use the car?'

He took the keys from his pocket and dropped them in my palm. I followed him into the woods with my can of beer and watched him fish with wet flies for cutthroat in the turning pools behind the boulders. After he had moved farther up the stream into the deeper shade of the trees' overhang, I finished my beer against a pine trunk, whistled at him softly and waved, and walked back to the cabin.

I had one good suit, a grey one that I wore when I played at good clubs, and I put it on with my half-topped black boots and a blue-and-white, small-checked cowboy shirt with pearl snap buttons. It took me almost half an hour to dress with one arm, and it was impossible to get the necktie into a knot.

I drove the thirty miles to Missoula and stopped at a beer joint with no cars in front to phone Ace. I got change for five dollars at the bar. Then it struck me what type of conversation I was about to have, and I ordered a vodka and ice to take to the telephone.

After his secretary whispered something hurriedly, like 'I think it's your brother, Mr Paret,' Ace was on the line, and I could almost see his stomach swell up in satisfaction in that reclining leather chair. 'Hello, Iry,' he said, 'how do you like it up there with the Eskimos? Just a minute. I've got about three people on hold . . . Go ahead . . . Well, I don't know if I want to buy just the two acres. Your four run all the way back to the bayou, and that's going to leave a strip that anybody can move in on later . . . I mean, if you decide later on to sell to a boat yard or let that oil company build a dock there, what I've got invested in the development isn't going to be worth spit on the sidewalk. That's the way it is, Bro' . . . What the hell went wrong up there? I thought you had a job with that friend of yours . . . Well, I don't want to be the one that told you about latching the gate too quick behind you, but that's the deal. All four acres or I can't use it.'

So I took it at $250 an acre and gave up any mineral rights or future land-lease agreements for oil exploration, and Ace said he would have the deed transfer and cheque in the morning's mail.

I walked back to the bar and finished the vodka. For a thousand dollars I had quit claim for ever to any of the Paret land, and if I knew Ace, I would not want to see the farm or the bamboo and cypress and oaks along the bayou ever again, even in memory.

I drove west of town through the green, sloping hills along the Clark. The sun was bright on the green riffles in the water, and insects were turning in hot swarms over the boulders that stood exposed in the current. Ahead I could see the huge plume of smoke that curled up against the sky from the pulp mill, and then I caught the first raw odour in the air. It smelled like sewage, and the wind flattened the smoke across the valley and left a dull white haze low on the meadows. I cleared my throat and spat outside the window, but my eyes started to water and I tried to breathe quietly through my mouth. The only thing I had ever smelled like it, on a scale that could cover a whole rural area, was the sugar mill back home in winter, which produced a thick, sick-sweet odour that seemed to permeate the inside of your skull.

I turned through the gate and parked in the employees' lot. A new shift was going in, and men in Levi's clothes and work boots and tin hats with lunch pails were walking into the side of the building. Log trucks piled with ponderosa pines, the booming chains notched tightly into the bark, were lined up in the back to unload, the tractor engines hammering under the bonnets. Someone told me later that the leather boots the men wore eventually turned black and rotted from the air inside the mill and the chemicals on the floor, and I thought their lungs must have looked like a pathologist's dream.

I asked a foreman where the management was, and he looked at me with a sweaty, questioning eye from under his tin hat.

'There's no jobs right now,' he said.

'I just want to see the timekeeper or somebody in personnel.'

His eyes moved over my face; then he pointed at a door.

'Over there. There's some glass doors at the end of the hall,' he said.

The hallway was dark and hot, and it smelled much worse than the outside of the mill. Someone had painted the walls green at one time, but the paint was blistered and peeling in flakes on the baseboards. Behind the glass doors I could see an air-conditioning unit with streamers blowing off the vents, a big-breasted secretary who sat in her chair as though she had an arrow in her back, and three men in business suits behind their glass-topped desks, each of them concerned with typed papers that brought on knitted brows, a sweep of the hand to the telephone, a quick concentration on some piece of thunder hidden in a figure.

The secretary wanted to know who it was exactly that I would like to see or if I could explain exactly what I wanted.

'It's about an accident, actually,' I said. 'I haven't talked with a lawyer yet. I thought I'd come down here and see what y'all could tell me.'

Her eyelashes blinked, and she looked sideways briefly at the man behind the next desk. There was a pause, and then the man glanced up from his papers and nodded to her.

'Mr Overstreet can talk with you. Just have a seat,' she said. (All of this in a room where each of us was within five feet of the other.)

I sat in the chair in front of Mr Overstreet's desk for possibly two minutes before he decided that I was there. He looked like a working man who had got off the green chain years ago, worked his way up to yard foreman, and finally slipped through a side door into a necktie and a place in front of an air-conditioning unit. There were still freckles on the backs of his hands, and thin pinch scars on his fingers that come from working with boomer chains, and he had the rigidity and habitual frown of a man who was afraid of his own position every day. He pushed the papers to the side of the glass desk top, then looked up flatly into my eyes.

'Sunday night my pickup was knocked off the road by one of your trucks down by Florence,' I said. 'There were three men in it, and they burned my pickup and musical instruments and left me and another guy a hospital bill to pay. I'm not after your company. I just want those three guys.'

He stared at me, and then his eyes flicked angrily at the secretary. He rubbed the back of one hand into his palm.

'What are you saying?'

'There's a truck out in your lot that probably has red paint all over the front bumper. Also, you must know who drives a company truck out of here at night.'

The other two men behind the desks had stopped work and were looking blankly at us. I could hear the secretary squeak the rollers of her chair across the rug.

'That doesn't have anything to do with the mill,' he said. 'You take that up with the sheriff's department in Ravalli County.'

'It was your truck. That makes you liable. If you protect them, that makes you criminally liable.'

'You watch what you say, fella.'

'All you've got to tell me is you'll come up with the men in that truck.'

'Who the hell you think you are talking to me about criminal charges?'

'I'm not asking you for anything that's unreasonable.'

'Yeah? I think you stopped using your reason when you walked in here. So now you turn around and walk back out.'

'Why don't you flick on your brain a minute? Do you want guys like this beating up people out of one of your trucks?'

'You don't understand me. You're leaving here. Now.'

'You ass.'

'That's it.' He picked up the telephone and dialled an inner office number. His free hand was spread tightly on the glass desk top while he waited for an answer.

'All right, bubba,' I said. 'Go back to your papers.'

But he wasn't listening. 'Send Lloyd and Jack down here,' he said.

I walked out of the office and down the dark hallway; then the outer door opened in a flash of sunlight and two big men in tin hats moved towards me in silhouette. One of them had a cigar pushed back like a stick in his jaw, and he wiped tobacco juice off his mouth with a flat thumb and looked hard at me.

'Better get in that office,' I said. 'Some crazy man is in there raising hell.'

They went past me, walking fast, their brows wrinkled intently. I was across the parking lot when I heard the door open again behind me. The man with the cigar leaned out, his tin hat bright in the sun, and shouted: 'You keep going. Don't ever come around here again.'

I drove back to Missoula and stopped at the tavern where I had called Ace earlier. I started drinking beer. Then from among the many wet rings on the bar I lifted up a boilermaker, and I guess it was then that an odd tumbler clicked over in my brain and it started.

In the darkness of the tavern, with the soft glow of the

mountain twilight through the blinds, I began to think about my boyhood South and the song I never finished in Angola. I had all the music in my mind and the runs that bled into each chord, but the lyrics were always wooden, and I couldn't get all of the collective memory into a sliding blues. I called it 'The Lost Get-Back Boogie', and I wanted it to contain all those private, inviolate things that a young boy saw and knew about while growing up in southern Louisiana in a more uncomplicated time: the bottle trees (during the depression people used to stick empty milk of magnesia bottles on the winter branches of a hackberry until the whole tree rang with blue glass), the late evening sun boiling into the green horizon of the Gulf, the dinners of crawfish and bluepoint crabs under the cypress trees on Bayou Teche, and freight cars slamming together in the Southern Pacific yard, and through the mist the distant locomotive whistle that spoke of journeys across the wetlands to cities like New Orleans and Mobile.

There was much more to it, like the Negro juke joint by the sugar mill and Loup-garous Row, the string of shacks by the rail yard where the whores sat on the wood porches on Saturday afternoons and dipped their beer out of a bucket. But maybe that was why I didn't finish it. There was too much of it for one song or maybe even for a book.

I kept looking at the clock above the neon GRAIN BELT sign, and I was sure that I had my thumb right on the pulse of the day, but each time I focused again on the hour hand, I realized that some terrible obstruction had prevented me from seeing that another thirty or forty minutes or hour and a half had passed. When I walked to the rest room, my cast scratched along the wall with my weight, and when I came back out, the tables, the row of stools, and the people all seemed rearranged in place.

'You want another one, buddy?' the bartender said.

'Yeah. This time give me a draught and a double Beam on the side.'

He brought the schooner dripping with foam and ice and set a shot jigger beside it.

'You want to throw for the washline?' he said.

'What do I do?'

He picked up the leather cup of poker dice and set it down in front of me with his palm over the top.

'You roll me double or nothing for the drinks. If you roll five of a kind, you get everything up there on the line.'

There was a long string of wire above the bar with one-dollar bills clipped to it with clothespegs.

'What are my chances?' I said.

'Outside of the drinks, bad.'

'All right.' The whiskey was hot in my face, and I could feel the perspiration start to run out of my hair. There was a dead hum in my head, and behind me I heard Kitty Wells's nasal falsetto from the jukebox: 'It wasn't God who made honky-tonk angels'.

I rattled the dice once in the leather cup with my hand tight over the top and threw them along the bar.

'I'll be damned,' the bartender said.

I had to look again myself, in the red glow of the neon beer sign, at the five aces glinting up from the mahogany bar top.

The bartender pulled twenty one-dollar bills from the clothespegs and put them in front of me, then took away my beer glass and jigger and brought them back filled. He chewed on the flattened end of a match and shook his head as though some type of mathematical principle in the universe had just been proved untrue.

'You ought to shoot craps at one of them joints over in Idaho, buddy,' he said.

'I've shot lots of craps. They keep you off night patrol.'

He looked at me with a flat pause in his face, the matchstick motionless in a gap between his teeth.

'You can throw the bones for high point right down at the end of the blanket and the other guy has got to go up through their wire. Him and fifteen others.' Then I knew that I was drunk, because the words had already freed themselves from behind all those locks and hasps and welded doors that you keep sealed in the back of your mind.

'Well, I guess you got good luck, buddy,' he said, and wiped the rag over the bar in front of me before he walked down to a cowboy who had just come in.

I drank the whiskey neat and chased it with the beer, then smoked a cigarette and called him back again.

'Give me a pint of Beam's Choice and a six-pack. While you're getting it, give me a ditch.'

'Mister, I ain't telling you nothing, but you ain't going to be able to drive.'

Outside, the stars were bright above the dark ring of mountains around Missoula, and the plume of smoke from the pulp mill floated high above the Clark Fork in the moonlight. My broken arm itched as though ants were crawling in the sweat inside my cast. I fell heavily behind the steering wheel of Buddy's Plymouth, and for just a second I saw my guitars snapping apart in the truck fire and heard that level, hot voice: *Give that son of a bitch his buckwheats.*

As I drove back down the blacktop towards Lolo, with the bright lights of semis flashing over me and the air brakes hissing when I swerved across the centre line, I remembered again the bully putting spittle in my ear, re-enacted in my mind being thrown out of a pulp mill that manufactured toilet paper, and studied hard upon the sale of my inheritance to the cement-truck and shopping-centre interests.

Bugs swam around the light on the front porch of Buddy's cabin and his fly rod was leaned against the screen door, but he must have been up at his father's house. I walked unsteadily to the back room, where he kept the '03 Springfield rifle with the Mauser action on two deer-antler racks. I put the sling over my shoulder and filled the big flap pockets of my army jacket with shells from a box on the floor. Even as drunk as I was, even as I caught my balance against the doorjamb, I knew that it was insane, that every self-protective instinct and light in my head was blinking red, but I was already in motion in the same way I had been my first day out of prison when I covered the licence plate of the pickup with mud and went banging down the road drunk into a possible parole violation.

I put the rifle on the back floor with my field jacket over it and drove back towards the cattle guard. The wind off the river bent the grass in the pasture under the moon, and the cattle bunched in a dark shadow by the cottonwoods. I saw a

bobbing across the field towards me and heard Buddy's voice call out in the dark. I stopped and let the engine idle while the sweat rolled down my face and my own whiskey breath came back sharp in my throat. He jumped across the irrigation ditch on one foot, and one of his younger brothers jumped in a rattle of cattails behind him.

'Where are you going, man?'

An answer wouldn't come, and I just flicked an index finger off the steering wheel towards the road.

'What have you been drinking?' he said.

'Made a stop down the highway.'

'You really look boiled, Zeno. Turn it around and go fishing with us. We're going to try some worms in a hole on the river.'

I got a cigarette out of my shirt pocket and pushed it in my mouth. It seemed that minutes passed before I completed the motion.

'I got lucky at craps today. There's a lady in a beer joint that wants to help me drink my money.'

'Where?'

'Eddie's, or one of those places of yours.'

'I'll go with you,' he said, and clicked off the flashlight. 'Joe, go down to the river with the old man, and I'll try to meet you later.'

'That's no good, Buddy. She's a one-guy chick, and I'm the guy that faded all the bread this afternoon.'

'I don't give a shit about the car,' he said, 'but you're going to get your ass in jail tonight.'

'Never had a ticket, babe.'

'That's because those coonass cops don't know how to write. Move it over and let's go down and investigate it together.'

'You want the car back?'

'No, I want to keep you from going back on PV.'

'I got to catch air. If you want the car, I'll thumb.'

He stepped back from the door and bowed like a butler, sweeping his arm out into the darkness.

'It's your caper, Zeno,' he said. 'I ain't got money for bond, so you take this fall on your own.'

I thumped across the cattle guard, and in the rearview mirror

I saw Buddy and his brother swing the gate closed and pull the loop wire over the fence post.

The drive back to the pulp mill was a long blacktop stretch of angry headlights, horns blowing in a diminishing echo behind me, gravel showering up under the fender when I hit the shoulder, and a highway-patrol car that kept evenly behind me for two miles and then turned off indifferently into a truck stop. I opened a can of beer and set it beside me on the seat and sipped off the bottle of Beam's Choice. I picked up a radio station in Salt Lake that was advertising tulip bulbs and baby chicks sent directly to your house, COD, in one order, and this announcer's voice rose to the fervour of a southern evangelist's when he said: 'And remember, friends and neighbours, just write "Bulb". B-U-L-B. That's "Bulb".'

There was a wooden bridge over the Clark Fork just below the pulp mill, and then a climbing log road against the mountain that overlooked the river, the sour, mud-banked ponds where they kept their chemicals before they seeped out into the current, and the lighted parking lot full of washed and waxed yellow trucks. The Plymouth slammed against the springs and dug rocks out of the road with the oil pan as I pushed it in second gear up the grade, and the dense overhang from the trees slapped across the windscreen and top like dry scratches on a blackboard. When I reached the top of the grade and drove along the smooth yellow strip of road among the pines, the heat indicator was quivering past the red mark on the dash, and I could hear the steam hissing under the radiator cap. I pulled the car into a turnaround at the base of a curve on the mountain and slipped the sling of the Springfield over my shoulder and picked up the field jacket with my good hand.

I walked down through the timber, with the brown pine needles thick under my feet, and found a clear place where I could lean back against a pine trunk and cover the whole parking lot with the iron sights. There were white lights strung up the sides of both smokestacks, against the dark blue of the far mountain, and the parking lot ached with a brilliant electric glow off the asphalt.

I opened the breech of the Springfield and laid it across my lap, then counted out the shells on a handkerchief and cut a deep X with my pocketknife across each soft-nose. I pushed the shells into the magazine with my thumb until the spring came tight, then slid the bolt home and locked it down. I re-adjusted the sling and worked it past the cast so I could fire comfortably from a sitting position and aim across my knee without canting the sights.

The first round broke through a front windscreen and spider-webbed the glass with cracks, and I drove two more shots through the top of the cab. The bullets against the metal sounded like a distant metallic slap. I couldn't see the damage inside, but I figured that the flattened and splintered lead would tear holes like baseballs in the dashboard. I shifted my knee and swung the iron sights on the next truck and let off three rounds in a row without taking my check from the stock. The first bullet scoured across the hood and ripped the metal like an axe had hit it, and I tore the grill and radiator into a wet grin with the other two.

I suppose that in some drunken compartment of my mind I had only planned to pay back in kind, on an equal basis, what had been done to me, but now I couldn't stop firing. My ears rang with a heady exhilaration with each shot, the empty casings leaped from the thrown bolt and smoked in the pine needles, and then there was that whaaappp of the bullet flattening out into another truck. I took a long drink from the pint of Beam's Choice, then reloaded and fired the whole clip all over the parking lot without aiming. I was now concentrated on how fast I could let off a round, recover from the recoil and throw the bolt, then lock another shell in the chamber and squeeze again.

On the last clip I must have bit into something electrical on an engine, either the battery or the ignition wiring, because the sparks leaped in a shower from under the hood. Then I could see the yellow-and-blue flame wavering under the oil pan and the paint starting to blister and pop in front of the windscreen.

I slipped the sling off my shoulder and began to pick up the shell casings with one hand while I watched it. The casings were hot in my hand, and I put them clinking into the flap pocket of my field jacket. The fire sucked up through the truck cab, then caught the leather seat over the gas tank in earnest, and then it blew. The flame leaped upwards into one cracking red handker-chief against the dark, and the truck body collapsed on the frame and the tyres roared with circles of light.

I drank again from the bottle and watched it with fascination. The heat had already cracked the glass on the next truck, and the fire was whipping inside the cab. The red light reflected off the river at the foot of the hill, and the dark trunks of the pines were filled with shadows. Out on the highway beyond the mill, I saw the blue bubblegum light of a police car turning furiously in the darkness. I put the bottle in my pocket and felt around for any shells that I hadn't picked up, then shoved my hand under the pine needles and swept it across a half circle on my right side. The whiskey was throbbing behind my eyes, and I lost my balance when I tried to get to my feet with the sling across my chest.

For the first time that night I became genuinely aware that I was in trouble. My mind couldn't function, I didn't know anything about the back roads, and I stood a good chance of being picked up on the highway for drunk driving. My heart was beating with the exertion of climbing to the top of the rise with the Springfield slung on my shoulder, and sweat ran in rivulets out of my hair into my eyes. I sat behind the wheel of the Plymouth and tried to think. I could take the log road over the mountain and possibly drive off the edge of a wash into five hundred feet of canyon (provided that the road went anywhere) or return across the log bridge into a good chance of a jolt in Deer Lodge plus an automatic violation back to Angola. I started the engine but kept the lights off and let the car roll down the road in neutral, braking heavily all the way down the grade. The pines began to thin towards the bottom of the hill, and then I saw the brown sweep of the river with the thick eddies of sawdust along the banks. The bridge stood out flat and hard in the reflection of lights from the mill, and there was a police car parked at the other side with the airplane headlights turned on and the bubble-gum machine swinging on the roof.

I cut on my lights and eased the Plymouth into second as I came off the incline; then I remembered the Springfield propped like an iron salute against the passenger's door. It was too late to dump it or even throw it over into the back seat. The sheriff's deputy was already by the wooden bridge rail, winking his flashlight at me.

Oh boy. And you rolled right into it, babe.

I slowed the car and looked over at the bright flame in the parking lot and the two men who were spraying it with fire extinguishers in silhouette. Then the deputy began to sweep his flashlight impatiently, and it took a second, like a beat out of my heart, to realize that he was waving me past. I rattled across the board planks, and the headlights suddenly illuminated his brown uniform, the wide gun belt and cartridges, and the Stetson pushed low over his eyes. I nodded at him and slowly depressed the accelerator.

I hit the highway and opened up the Plymouth with the rods knocking, the frame shaking, and the moon rising over the mountain like a song. I opened the wind vane into my face and felt the sweat turn cold and dry in my hair, and then I drank the last of the whiskey in a long swallow and sailed the bottle over the roof. I had walked right out of it with the kind of con luck that drops on your head when you're sure that this time they're going to weld the cell door shut.

I bought a six-pack of Great Falls to drink on the way back to the ranch, and I felt a light-headed, heart-beating sense of victory and omniscience that I had known only in the infantry after moving all the way to the top of a Chinese hill without being hit. The fact that I weaved across the white centre line or ran through an intersection at seventy seemed unimportant; I was flying with magic all over me, and the alcohol and adrenalin worked in my heart with a mean new energy.

The next morning I felt the sun hot and white in my eyes through the window. There was an overturned can of beer by the bed, and my shirt was half off and tangled around my cast. I walked into the back room where Buddy was sleeping and saw the Springfield back on the rack, though I had no memory of having put it there. I could still taste the mixture of beer, whiskey and cigarettes in my mouth, and I worked the pump on the sink and cupped the water up in my hand. When the coldness hit my stomach, I thought I was going to be sick. My hands were shaking, the blood veins in my head had started to draw tight with hangover, and my eyes ached when I looked through the window into the bright light and the dew shimmering on the hay bales.

I tried to light the kindling in the wood stove to make coffee, but the paper matches flared against my thumbnail, and as I stared at the split chunks of white wood, the whole task suddenly seemed enormous. I took a beer out of the icebox and sat on the edge of the bed while I drank it. The sickening taste of the whiskey began to dissipate, and I felt the quivering wire in the middle of my breast start to dull and quieten. I finished the beer and had another, and by the bottom of the second can that handkerchief of flame in the parking lot became removed enough to think about. Then I saw Buddy leaning against the doorjamb, naked to the waist, his blue jeans low on his flat stomach, grinning at me.

'Are you getting in or getting up, Zeno? Either way, you look like shit,' he said.

'What's up?' I said. My voice sounded strange, distant and apart from me, a piece of colour in the ears.

'Did you get bred last night?'

'Get me a can out of the icebox.'

'Man, I can hear those hyenas beating on their cages in your head.'

'Just get the goddamn beer, Buddy.'

'My car ain't in the pound, is it?'

I hadn't thought yet about the car or what condition it might be in. My last memory of the Plymouth was winding it up out of Lolo after some drunk discussion in a bar about steelhead fishing over in Idaho. Then I remembered the tack-hammer rattle out of the crankcase that meant a burnt bearing and maybe a flattened crankshaft.

I heard Buddy click off the cap from a bottle of beer and the foam drip flatly on the floor. He pushed the bottle inside my hand.

'What did you get into last night?' he said.

He struck a match on the stove. Then I smelled the flame touch the reefer.

'It's a real bag of shit, man.'

He pulled a chair out from the table and sat down, his eyes focused and serious over the joint in his mouth.

'Like what?'

'I really went over the edge and hung one out.'

'What did you do?'

'I took your Springfield and shot the hell out of the parking lot in that pulp mill.'

'Oh man.'

I couldn't look at him. I felt miserable, and the absurdity of what I had done ached inside my hangover like an unacceptable dream.

'How bad?'

'I left about three trucks burning and probably blew the engine blocks out of a half-dozen others.'

'Wow. You don't fool around, do you?'

It was silent for a moment, and I heard him take a long inhale on the reefer and let it out of his lungs slowly.

'Iry, what's in your head? They're going to pour your ass in Deer Lodge.'

'I got out of it. There was a dick at the log bridge, but he must have thought the damage was done inside the lot.'

'Forget that. You were in the sheriff's office yesterday, and maybe these cowboys ain't too bright, but they're going to put the dice together and waltz you right into the bag. And believe me, buddy, they hand out time to outsiders like there's no calendar.'

He set the reefer on the edge of the table and walked back to the bedroom.

'What are you doing?' I said.

He unlocked the bolt of the Springfield, and an unfired cartridge sprang from the magazine.

'Really cool, man. What do you think I'm going to do?'

He walked out of the screen door, and then I heard a shovel crunching in the earth behind the cabin. I wanted to argue with him about his rifle, but I knew he was right. I wet a towel under the pump and held it to my face and neck. I couldn't stop sweating. Buddy dropped the shovel on the porch and came back through the door with grains of dirt in the perspiration on his arms. He was grinning again, with that crazy light in his eyes that used to get him into isolation at Angola.

'You're sure a dumb son of a bitch,' he said.

'That's the smartest thing you've said since I got out here.'

'But we're in a real hardball game now, partner.'

Fifteen minutes later we heard a car rumble over the cattle guard. Buddy looked through the window, then back at me.

'That's your taxi, Zeno,' he said. 'Don't say anything. Little Orphan Annie with empty circles for eyes. You were juicing in the saloon at Lolo, and you were too drunk even to drive into Missoula.'

'Get rid of the roach.'

He went to the sink and peeled the reefer, then pumped water over it.

'This is a crock, ain't it?' he said.

'Give me all the cigarettes you have.'

'Look at that pair of geeks. They love making a bust on the old man's place.'

He handed me two packs of Lucky Strikes and a paper book of matches.

'I ain't got the bread for a bondsman, so you're going to have to sit it out, Zeno,' he said.

'I should have a cheque by tomorrow or the next day. Bring it down to the jail and I'll endorse it.'

The deputy didn't knock. He opened the screen door and pointed one thick finger at me.

'All right, Paret. Move it up against the car,' he said.

He held the screen open while I walked past him to the car. The other deputy leaned against the mudguard with his palm resting on the butt of his .357. Both of them were over six feet, and their wide shoulders were stiff and angular against their starched shirts.

'Lean on it,' the first deputy said.

I spread my legs and propped my hands against the roof of the car while his hands moved inside my thighs, then dug inside my pockets and turned them inside out. He pulled my arms behind me and snipped on the handcuffs, and the other deputy held open the door into the wire-mesh segregated back seat.

'Are you going to give us any trouble on the way back, or do you want me to sit with you?' the first deputy said.

I didn't answer, and he locked both back doors from the outside. As the car rolled along the rutted lane, I leaned back against the handcuffs and felt the metal bite into the skin. I tried to raise myself forward to keep the pressure off my wrists, but each chuckhole in the road sent me back into the seat and another dig into my skin. The mountains had taken on a deeper blue and green from the rains, and the boulders in the creeks under the bridges were wet and shining and steaming in the sunlight at the same time. But at that moment, in my comical effort to sit rigid in the back of a sheriff's car, I remembered a Negro kid at Angola who was handcuffed and taken down to the hole and beaten with a garden hose for stealing a peanut-butter sandwich. He spat on a hack, and so they sweated him five more days and took away his good time.

At that time, what bothered me was meeting him out on the yard after he got out of lockdown. There were still blue gashes on the insides of his lips, and while he smoked a cigarette, he told me he didn't mind pulling the extra three years because he knew that eventually he would fall again anyway.

SEVEN

The holding cell was dull yellow with a crisscrossed door of flat iron strips that were coated with thick white paint. Names had been burned on the walls and ceiling with cigarette lighters, and there was a small, round drain in the centre of the floor to urinate in. I sat on the concrete against the wall and smoked cigarettes and listened in my preoccupation with my own troubles to all the jailhouse complaints, stories of bum arrests, wives who should have had their teeth kicked in, and advice about how to deal with each screw on the day and night shifts. The area around the drain was covered with wet cigarette butts and reeked with a stench that made your eyes water when you had to stand over it. Two Flathead Indians were still drunk and waiting for the reservation police to pick them up, a cheque-writer who was already wanted in Idaho kept calling the sergeant back to the cell to ask about his wife, who was in the lock upstairs; a deranged old man, whose toothless gums were purple with snuff, sat by the drain, hawking and spitting through his knees; and then the one dangerous man, a twenty-five-year-old tar roofer, with square, callused hands that had no fingernails and were dark with cinders, leaned against the wall on a flexed arm, waiting for his wife to bring the bondsman down to the jail.

He asked me for a cigarette; then he wanted to know if I had ever pulled time. He paused a minute, lighting the cigarette with his thick, dark fingers, then asked what for.

After I told him, his muddy eyes looked at me for a moment, then stared off into the smoke. He sat down beside me and pulled his knees up before him. His white athletic socks were grimed with dirt. I said nothing to him, made no enquiry about his crime, and I could feel the sense of insult start to rise in him.

'What they got you for, podna?' I said.

'This guy give me some shit at Stockman's last night. Like he was going to whip my ass with a pool cue. I put him once through the bathroom door. Then he learned what real shit smells like. And he ain't going to press no charges, either, believe me.'

An hour later his wife, a vacuous and pathetic-looking blonde girl in a waitress's uniform, was at the jail with the bondsman. As I watched them through the grated door, holding hands in front of the property desk, I could see the humiliation in her face and the fear of another night and all the others to follow. They would pay out their lives in instalments to bondsmen, guilty courts, finance companies and collection agencies.

At seven that evening a deputy sheriff stood in front of the door with a pair of handcuffs hung over his index finger and waited for the sergeant to turn the lock.

'Get rid of the cigarette and put them behind you,' he said.

I flicked the butt towards the drain and waited for him to snip the cuffs around my wrists. He ran his hands under my armpits and down both sides of my trousers, then caught me under the arm with his hand. The cell door clanged behind us, and we walked down a corridor with spittoons on the floor towards the back of the building. Our shoes sucked against the damp mopping on the wooden floor, and a frosted yellow square of light shone from an office by the exit sign.

'Before we go in, tell me what the hell you thought you were going to get out of it,' he said.

'What?'

'Your parole officer said you were straight and probably wouldn't do time again. You must have had some real ingrown hairs in your asshole, buddy.'

Inside the office the deputy took off the cuffs, and I sat down in a wooden chair in front of the sheriff's desk. The room was poorly lighted and smelled of cigars, and the desk lamp shone upward into the red corpulence of the sheriff's round face. There was a tangle of grey hair above the V of his shirt, and the roll of fat on his stomach hung heavily on his gun belt. The red stone on his Mason's ring glinted when he moved the wet stub of his cigar in the ashtray.

'It looks like you can't stay out of a sheriff's office,' he said. 'Yesterday you tried to file a complaint down in Ravalli County, and today I get to meet you after you did some target practice at the mill.'

I looked him back in the eyes, but because of the lamp's glare, I couldn't tell yet how hard he was ready to turn it on. He took a sandwich out of his drawer and unfolded the wax paper.

'Go down to the cooler for me, John,' he said.

While the deputy was gone, he ate the sandwich and didn't speak, and I thought, Watch out for this one. The deputy returned with a beaded can of beer and set it on the blotter. The sheriff sucked out half of it with one quick upward turn of the hand, the sandwich bread thick and white in his mouth.

'Now,' he said, 'this shouldn't take either one of us long. You know all the rules, so we don't have to explain a lot of things.

We'll take a statement from you, you can look over it and add or change anything, and I'll get you into court within a week and then off to Deer Lodge.'

'I don't even know what you're charging me with, Sheriff.'

'Son, you weren't listening too good. I don't have time for a game. I can charge you with any one or all of half a dozen things. I guess about the worst one down on your sheet might be arson.'

'I don't know what we're talking about.' Our eyes locked together and held until he picked up his cigar.

'I see,' he said, and turned his swivel chair partly into the shadow, obscuring his face. 'Well, tell us what you were up to last night.'

'I was boozing in a couple of beer joints in Lolo and another place just south of Missoula.'

'Did you meet any interesting people who might remember you?'

'Ask them. I don't remember. I was drunk.'

'Maybe you had a little trouble with a cowboy or knocked over some chairs.'

'Don't recall a thing.'

He turned his big, oval face abruptly back into the light.

'You're lying, son. Yesterday you were out at the mill raising hell about your pickup and your guitars, and last night you had Buddy Riordan's Plymouth up on that mountain, and you drilled holes in those trucks like an infantry marksman. Some of my men ain't the brightest in the world, or you wouldn't have got back across that bridge. But the deputy made you, and that's going to get you at least a two-spot. Now, if you want to piss around with us, we'll see how much time we can add on to it.'

My con's antennae quivered for the first time with a sense of hope. His eyes stared confidently into mine, but he had come on too strong and too soon. Also, I hadn't been booked yet, and I realized that I might still have another season to run.

'I was at the mill yesterday afternoon, and I was driving Buddy's car last night, but I don't know a thing about your deputy or a bridge.'

'Why don't you use your head a minute? You're still a young man. You can be out with good time in nine months, and maybe

Louisiana will waive on you if you get a strong recommendation from here.'

'Number one, I'm not going to take the fall for some local crap with that toilet-paper factory. Number two, you know the parole authority doesn't work that way, Sheriff. They'll send me straight back to the joint.'

He looked at me steadily and held the flattened wet end of his cigar to his mouth. Then his gaze broke, and he finished the rest of his beer.

'I don't know what to tell you, then, son. It looks like you have things pretty well figured out for yourself.'

Without thinking, I put my fingers in my shirt pocket for a cigarette. The deputy behind me put his hand on my arm.

'That's all right, John,' the sheriff said. 'Tell me, what's your connection with Frank Riordan?'

'I did time with his boy.'

'That's right. Buddy was in the Louisiana pen, wasn't he?'

He lit his cigar again, and the red stone on his ring glowed with fire. 'Tell me another thing, since you got it all tucked in your watch pocket. How far away from this jail do you think your life's going to be?'

I kept my face expressionless and looked at his massive weight leaning into the desk.

'I mean, do you believe you're just going to walk out of it? That you can come into this county as a parolee and destroy fifteen thousand dollars' worth of machinery and go back to your guitar?'

'You don't have anything, Sheriff.'

'Before you go back to the tank, let me give you something to roll around. How do you think you got five the first time? And believe me, son, you're just about to become a two-time loser.'

The deputy walked me in the handcuffs back to the front of the building, then pointed me towards a spiral metal stairs.

'My coat's in the holding cell,' I said.

'You'll get it later.'

'Do I get booked?'

'Don't worry about it.'

He locked me in a four-man cell upstairs with a wire-mesh and barred window that looked out on a brick alley. I could hear heat thunder and dry lightning out in the mountains, and momentarily the alley walls would flicker with a white light. There was a rolled tick mattress and a blanket on one empty iron bunk, and I sat down and rested the weight of my cast on my thigh and began to take off my shoes with one hand. Then a large black head, glistening like shoe polish in the gloom, leaned over the bunk above me, and before I could even look into the wine-red eyes, the odour of muscatel and snuff and jailhouse funk washed over me.

'Hey, blood,' the man said, 'do you got a cigarette for a brother? I been up here a whole day with this white whale that's got money stuck up his ass but won't give the screw two bits for some cigarettes.'

I handed up the pack, but the Negro dropped off the bunk with one arm, and then I saw the black, puckered stump on his other shoulder. He picked a cigarette out with his fingernails and pulled down his white boxer undershorts and squatted on the seatless toilet. I unrolled the mattress and lay down with my head pointed towards the door and the draft of the corridor, then looked across the cell at the white whale. He lay on his back with his trousers and shoes on, and his stomach rose up like a mountain under his dirty white shirt. The fat in his cheeks hung back against his bones, and his eyes stared like burnt glass into the bottom of the bunk overhead.

I heard the Negro cracking wind into the toilet, and I turned on my stomach and lit a cigarette.

'Now catch this,' the Negro said. 'They grabbed this cat on a morals charge. Eleven-year-old boy in a hotel room. The screw says all he's got to do is pick up the phone and he's out. But he just lays there and says "Jesus, forgive me."'

'You shut up,' the white man said quietly.

'He says that, too,' the Negro said. 'Every time I tell him to loosen up with some change. You ain't crazy, too, are you, brother?'

'I don't think so,' I said. Then I wondered, *Good Lord, am I?*

'He won't eat his food, and now they don't even bring him none.'

The cell was hot from the heat rising in the building, but I folded the blanket over my head and tried to close the sickening odours, the Negro and the sad man out of my consciousness. The thunder echoed across the mountains like rows of distant cannon, and as I lay with my forehead damp against my wrist and the mothball smell of the blanket enveloping me, I slipped away through the concrete floor and the resonating clang of iron through jail corridors, melting with the softness of a morphine dream into yesterday when I could still turn the dial a degree in either direction and reshape the day into sunlight on trout streams, blue shadows on the pines in the canyons, or just a glass of iced tea on a lazy porch.

I awoke sometime in the middle of the night to the rain falling on the windowsill. The drops sprayed inside on the concrete floor, and I could smell the cool wetness blowing through the air shaft. I felt a sick ache in my heart, and I lay on my back and smoked, waiting for it to pass, but it wouldn't. In the darkness I felt the beginnings of a new awareness about myself, one that I had always denied before. When I was in Angola, I never thought of myself as a real con, a professional loser who would always be up before some kind of authority. I was just a juke-joint country musician who had acted by chance or accident in a beer and marijuana fog without thinking. But I realized now that I killed that man because I *wanted* to. I had shot people in Korea, and when I put my hand in my pocket for the knife, I knew exactly what I was doing.

Now I had run right back to jail, just like every recidivist who is always sure he will stay on the street but works full time at falling again. And maybe you got your whole ticket punched this time, I thought. Yes, maybe this is the whole shot, and you never saw it during those two years you waited for that cosmic mistake in time and place to correct itself.

'Put the board up in the window, blood,' the Negro said.

I got off the bunk and picked up the piece of shaped plywood that fitted into the frame against the bars. The mist blew into my face, and I looked at the glistening brick of the alley wall and heard a train whistle blow in the distance.

'Come on, man. I feel like somebody pissed on my mattress,' the Negro said.

In the morning an Indian trusty and a deputy opened the cell and handed us two tin plates of cold scrambled eggs and bread and black coffee in paper cups.

'Is he going to eat today?' the Indian said.

The Negro touched the white whale on the knee. He lay in the bunk with his face towards the wall, and the black hair on his buttocks showed above his trousers.

'Better eat now. The man don't bring it back again till two o'clock,' the Negro said.

The whale didn't answer, and the Negro held his palm up in a gesture of failure in trying to reason with a lunatic.

'If you want any candy or cigarettes from the machine, give me the money and I'll bring it back to you this afternoon,' the Indian said.

I reached in my pocket and felt a wadded dollar bill with a quarter inside.

'Forget about him,' the deputy said, and locked the cell door.

'Hey, man, what these cats got down on you?' the Negro said.

'I don't know. I haven't been booked yet.'

'I mean, you got in the man's face last night or something?'

'I didn't read it like that. Maybe I did.'

'Let me have a smoke.'

There were two cigarettes left, and I gave him one and lit the other. He sat on the floor in his white undershorts, his knees splayed, and ate the eggs with one hand and held the cigarette in the back of his knuckles. His skin was absolutely black.

'I got a hundred and eighty to do,' he said. 'But I don't do nothing except wash cars. The judge says he'd send me to the joint, but you can't cowboy with one arm.'

He laughed, and the dried eggs fell from his bad teeth back into the plate. 'I'll tell you why they ain't put me in Deer Lodge, brother. Because they won't take no niggers up there. That's right. There ain't a coloured man in that whole joint.'

I sat on my bunk and drank the coffee from the paper cup. It tasted like iodine.

549

'You a paperhanger?' he said.

'No.'

'I ax you this because, you see, this is my living place, and they bring in this white whale that moans at night and makes gas every fifteen minutes. I don't like jailing with no queer, either.'

'His family will come for him eventually,' I said.

'Which means me and you, brother.'

'OK, let me give it to you. Five in Louisiana for manslaughter. Maybe another jolt here for shooting up some people who leaned on me.'

He pressed the scrambled eggs into the spoon with his thumb and dropped them into his mouth, then took a puff off his cigarette and laughed again.

'What they putting you badasses in with me for?'

'I think the man wants to talk with me,' I said.

I heard the deputy's keys and leather soles in the corridor.

'They ain't bad guys,' the Negro said. 'Most of them work another job in town. Just don't stick your finger in the wrong place.'

The deputy who had brought breakfast with the Indian trusty turned the key and opened the cell door.

'Let's get it, Paret,' he said.

He didn't have the handcuffs out, nor did he catch me under the arm, which I waited automatically for him to do.

'Down the stairs,' he said.

'What's going on?'

'Just walk.'

We went down the spiral metal staircase to the first floor, and I had to squint at the sudden light off the yellow walls. I looked over at the door to the booking room, the box camera on its tripod, and the ink pad, rollers and cleansing cream on the counter.

'Sign for your stuff at the property desk,' he said.

I turned and stared at him, but his attention was already locked on the holding cell, where a man in a suit was shaking the door against the jamb.

I walked to the property desk and gave my name. A woman in

a brown uniform smiled pleasantly at me, pulled a manila envelope from a pigeonhole and placed it, my folded coat with one wet sleeve, and a release card in front of me. I slipped on my watch, put my notecase in my pocket, and in a signature I was back on the street, in the sunlight, into a cool morning with a hard blue sky and the brilliant whip of Indian summer in the air.

I didn't have enough money to ride the bus back to the ranch, and I didn't feel like hitchhiking, so I walked towards the Garden District by the university, where Buddy's wife lived. It didn't seem an unreasonable thing to do, and I didn't allow myself to think deeply on it, anyway. The air was so clear and bright from the rains and the touch of autumn that I could see college kids hiking high up on the brown mountain behind the university and the line of green trees that began on the top slope. I crossed the bridge over the Clark and looked down at the deep pools where large rainbow hung behind the boulders, waiting for food to float downstream. The paths in the Garden District were shaded by maple and elm trees, and overnight the leaves had started to turn red and gold.

Buddy's boys were playing catch in the front yard, burning each other out with the baseball. I started to walk up on the porch, and then I felt a sense of guilt and awkwardness at being there. I paused on the walk and felt even more stupid as the two boys looked at me.

'Did your old man ever show you how to throw an in-shoot?' I said. 'It's the meanest pitch in baseball. It leaves them looking every time.'

I wet two of my fingers, held the ball over the stitches, and whipped it out sidearm at the older boy's claw mitt. He leaped upward at it, but it sailed away into the trees.

'I've been having trouble with my arm since I threw against Marty Marion,' I said.

'That's all right. I'll get it,' the boy said, and raced across the lawn through the leaves.

You're really great with kids, Paret, I thought. I heard the screen door squeak on the spring.

'Come in,' Beth said. She wore white shorts and a denim shirt, and she had a blue bandana tied around her black hair.

'I was trying to get back to the ranch, and I thought Buddy might be around,' I said.

'I haven't seen him, but Mel ought to be by later. Come on in the kitchen.'

I followed her through the house, which was darkened and furnished with old stuffed chairs and a broken couch and mismatched things that were bought at intervals in a second-hand store. She pulled a pair of dripping blue jeans from the soapy water in the sink and then rubbed the knees against one another. Her thighs and stomach were tight against her white shorts, and when she leaned over the sink, her breasts hung heavily against her denim shirt.

'What are you doing in town?' she said.

'I managed to get put in the bag yesterday.'

'What?'

'I just got out of the slam.'

'What for?' She turned around and looked at me.

'Some trucks were shot up down at that pulp mill.'

She went back to her washing in silence, then stopped and dried her hands on a towel.

'Do you want a beer?'

'All right.'

She took two bottles from the icebox and sat down at the unpainted wooden table with me.

'Do they want Buddy?'

'They were just interested in me because I'd been out there about my pickup being burned.'

The younger boy came in perspiring and out of breath for a glass of water from the sink. She waited until he finished and had slammed the screen behind him.

'Buddy can't go to jail again. Not here,' she said.

'It doesn't have anything to do with him.'

'There're many people here who would like to destroy Frank Riordan, and they'll take Buddy as a second choice. I had five years of explanation to his children about where he was, and we're not up to it again.'

I wanted to explain that he wasn't involved, that it was my own drunken barrel of snakes and southern bar-room anger that had put me up on the mountain with a rifle. But I had stepped across a line with a heavy, dirty shoe into her and her children's lives, and I felt like an intrusive outsider who had just presented someone with a handful of spiders. I drank down the bottle and set it lightly on the tabletop.

'I guess I'd better catch air,' I said. 'I can probably hitch a ride pretty easy out by the highway.'

'Wait for Mel. He comes by after class for coffee.'

'Buddy's probably junking his Plymouth for bond, and I have to go by the hospital anyway.'

She got up from her chair and took another beer from the icebox. The V in the tail of her denim shirt exposed the white skin above her shorts. She clicked the cap off into a paper bag and put the bottle in front of me.

'Buddy says you could make it as a jazz musician if you wanted to. Why do you play in country bands?'

'Because I'm good at what I do, and I have the feeling for it.'

'Do you like the people you play for?' She said it in a soft voice, her eyes interested, and I wondered why Buddy had ever left her.

'I think I understand them.'

'The type of men who beat you up and burned your truck?'

'Not everybody in a beer joint is a gangster. We wouldn't have had that scene if Buddy—'

'I know. Buddy's favourite expression: "That's the way the toilet flushes sometimes, Zeno." He has a way of saying it when somebody is already thinking about killing him.'

'Well, it was something like that. But when you cruise into it with your signs on, somebody is going to try to cancel you out.'

'I read the story in the paper. Did you really do that much damage from across the river?' Her dark eyes were dancing into mine.

'What do you think, kiddo?'

'That you don't understand the sheriff you're dealing with or Frank Riordan either.'

'Ever since I came here, people have been telling me I don't understand something. Does that happen to everybody who wanders into Montana?'

'Pat Floyd might look like a fat Louisiana redneck behind his desk, but he's been sheriff for fifteen years, and he doesn't let people out of his jail for something like this unless he has a reason. I think you're going to find, also, that Buddy's father can be a strange man to deal with.' She went to the sink and pulled the rubber plug in the drain, then began squeezing water out of the jeans and T-shirts. 'Excuse me. Take another beer. I have to get this on the line before it rains again.'

I took a Grain Belt from the icebox and looked at the motion of her shoulders while she twisted the water out of her boys' clothes. I was never very good with women, possibly because I had always thought of them simply as women, but this one could reach out with an intelligent fingernail and tick the edge of your soul and walk away into a question mark.

I waited three minutes in the silence, drinking the beer and looking out through the screen at the green trees in the backyard.

'So why is Mr Riordan a strange man to deal with?' I said.

'He doesn't recognize anything outside his idea of the world and the people who should live in it. He might be a good person, but he's always determined to do what he calls right, regardless of the cost to other people. You might not have thought about it yet, but to his mind you probably created something very large for him when you shot up those trucks.'

'I don't create anything for anybody. I've tried to announce in capital letters that somebody's fight with the pulp mill or the lumberjacks isn't part of my act. So far I've got my arm broken and lost my job just for being around. So I don't figure I owe anybody.'

'Why did you come here?'

'Sometimes you got to roll and stretch it out.'

'You should have stayed in Louisiana.'

'Do I get a bill for that?' I smiled at her, but her face stayed expressionless.

'If the pulp mill shuts down because of Frank Riordan, you won't want to see what the people in this town will be like.'

'I've met some of them.'

'No, you haven't. Not when they're out of work and there's no food in the house except what they get from the federal surplus centre. There's nothing worse than a lumber town when the mill closes down.'

'Why don't you leave?' Then I felt stupid for my question.

'I could probably wait tables at the bus depot in Billings or a truck stop in Spokane. Do you recommend that as a large change?'

'I'm sorry. Too much beer in the morning.'

She dried her hands and pushed her hair back under her blue scarf.

'Tell me another thing,' she said. 'Do you believe Buddy is going to stay out of jail?'

'Sure.'

'You don't think that someday he'll go back to prison for one thing or another? For dope or a drunk accident or a bottle thrown across a bar or any of the things that he does regularly and casually dismisses?'

'Buddy's not a criminal. He fell in Louisiana because he was holding some weed at the wrong time. If he wasn't a Yankee and had had some money, he could have walked out of it.'

'That wasn't the first time he was in jail.'

'He told me about that.'

'What?' she said.

I felt uncomfortable again under her eyes, and I took a sip from the beer.

'He said you had him locked up once.'

'That's wonderful. He drove his car through the lawns all the way down the block and ran over the front steps, then stuck a matchstick in the horn. Every neighbour in the block called the police, and the next day we were evicted from the house. While he spent ninety days in jail, we lived in a trailer without heat in East Missoula.'

I heard the front screen slam back on the spring. Melvin walked through the hallway into the kitchen, chalk dust on the back of his brown suit coat, his face bright and handsome, and poured a cup of coffee off the stove. He began talking immediately. He didn't know it, but at that moment I would have enjoyed buying him a tall, cool drink.

He talked without stopping for almost fifteen minutes. Then

he set down the empty coffeepot on the stove and said, 'You ready to roll, ace?'

'Yeah, let's get it,' I said.

'Jesus Christ, you blew the hell out of that place, didn't you?'

'No.'

'Well, all right. But I drove past the mill last night, and they were still scraping up a melted truck from the asphalt. Partner, that was a real job.'

'Let's hit it if you're going.'

We walked through the hallway to the front with Beth behind us. I paused at the screen door.

'I should have a cheque in the mail today if you and the kids would like to go on a barbecue or something,' I said. 'Maybe Melvin and his wife would like to come, and Buddy can take along his little brothers, and we'll find a lake someplace.'

She smiled at me, her blue-black hair soft on her forehead. Her dark eyes took on a deeper colour in the sunlight through the trees.

'I used to make the second-best sauce piquante in southern Louisiana,' I said.

'Ask the others and give me a call,' she said.

I winked at her and walked across the shady lawn to the car.

Winking, I thought. Boy, are you a cool operator.

'You want to stop at Eddie's Club for a beer?' Melvin said.

'I'd like to get this jailhouse smell off me, and I'll buy you one this afternoon.'

We rolled across the bridge over the river, and I looked at the deep flashes of sunlight in the current.

'Did you use Buddy's Springfield?' he said.

'I was pretty drunk that night, and I don't remember much of anything.'

'OK. But you ought to throw it in the river.'

'That's a good idea,' I said.

The wind was blowing up the Bitterroot Valley, and the leaves of the cottonwoods trembled with silver in the bright air. I watched the fields of hay and cattle move by, and the log ranch houses chinked with mortar, and the drift of smoke from a small forest fire high on a blue mountain. The creek beds that crossed under the road were alive with hatching insects, and the pebbles along the sandy banks glistened wet and brown in the sun. Damn, Montana was a beautiful part of the country, I thought. It reached out with its enormous sky and mountains and blue-green land and hit you in the heart. You simply became lost in looking at it.

Buddy got up from his chair on the porch of the cabin and spread his arms in the air when he saw the car. Melvin let me down and drove up the rutted road towards the main house, and I saw Buddy flip away a hand-rolled cigarette into the wind. His shirttail was pulled out, and his stitched and bruised face was grinning like a scarecrow's as he walked disjointedly across the lawn.

'One night in the bag and Zeno has made the street,' he said. 'That's what I call accelerated.'

I could smell the marijuana on his clothes when I was five feet from him.

'I can see you've been sweating out your podna's poor ass being in jail.'

'I knew you were going to walk late last night. I did a ding-a-ling on the ring-a-ling after the old man said he would go a property bond. But they said there was no bail because Zeno hadn't been charged, and you would be sent home safely in the morning.'

'What time was this?'

'About midnight.'

'That's great, Buddy. So I spent the night with one of your local homosexuals and a one-armed Negro psychotic while everything was cool on the farm. I'm relieved as hell to know that I didn't have anything to worry about.'

'I couldn't get you out that late. They don't hire a night jailer, and I don't think they liked you down there too much anyway. Look, man, I got something for you inside. Also, you got to see the rainbow I took this morning.'

We walked up on the porch, and Buddy went through the screen door in front of me.

'I got it on credit, so don't worry about it. I got credit out my winky hole, and I just send them a hubcap from the Plymouth when they threaten to take my property.'

On my bunk was a new Gibson guitar with a Confederate flag wrapped around the sound box. The blond, waxed wood in the face and the dark, tapered neck and silver frets shone in the light through the window.

'They ain't got dobros in Montana, and I couldn't find a Martin,' he said.

'Well, hell, man.'

'But this has got a lifetime guarantee, and the guy says he'll sell us a case for it at cost.'

'Well, you dumb bastard.'

He folded a torn match cover around a roach and lit it, already grinning into the smoke before he spoke.

'I tried to get you a Buck Owens instruction book, but they didn't have it,' he said.

I sat down on the bed and clicked my thumbnail over the guitar strings. They reverberated and trembled in the deep echo from the box. I tried to make an awkward E chord, but I couldn't work my cast around the neck.

'Can you figure that scene down at the jail?' I said.

'You got me. I thought they had you nailed flat.'

'What do you know about the sheriff?'

'Look out for him. He's an old fox.'

'Yeah, Beth told me.' Then I regretted my words.

'What were you doing over there?' he said.

'I didn't have any bread to catch the bus, and I thought you might be around.'

He looked at me curiously. I took a flat pick out of my pocket and began tuning the first string on the guitar. The room was silent a moment.

Then he said, 'Take a look at the rainbow I got on a worm this morning,' and lifted a twenty-inch trout out of the sink by the gill. The iridescent band of blue and pink and sunlight was still bright along the sides. 'I had the drag screwed all the way down, and I still couldn't horse him out. I had to wade him up on a sandbar.

If you can keep your ass out of jail today, we'll go out again this evening.'

'My cheque ought to be here today. What if I pick up the tab for a beerbust and a picnic this afternoon?'

'That sounds commendable, Zeno. But I already went to the letterbox, and your cheque ain't here. Also, before we slide into anything else, the old man wants to talk with you.'

He opened up the trout's stomach with a fish knife and scooped out the entrails with his hand.

'How involved is that going to be?' I said.

'It's just his way. He wants to talk a few minutes.'

'Say, I know I'm getting free rent here, and maybe becoming an instant sniper is pretty stupid, but like you said, it's my fall.'

'You are the most paranoid bastard I've ever met. Look, he was going to go a property bond for you. I mean put the whole place on the line. OK, big deal. But give him his innings. He's all right.'

This was the first time I had seen Buddy become defensive about his father.

'OK,' I said.

Buddy worked the iron pump over the trout and scraped out the blood from the ridge of bone on the inside with his thumbnail.

'All root, all reet,' he said, and lit the kindling in the stove. 'A few lemon rings and slices of onion, and we'll dine on the porch and do up some of this fine Mexican laughing grass.'

'Your father came to my room while we were in the hospital and said he tried to shoot someone once.'

'I'm surprised he would tell you about that.'

'He was pretty intent on making a point.'

'That's something he keeps filed away in a dark place. But by God, he tried to do it, all right. When I was a kid, we used to live over by Livingston, and every day I climbed over this guy's barbed wire to fish in his slough. I climbed over it enough until it was broken down on the ground, and thirty of his cows got out on the highway. The next morning he caught me at the slough with a horse quirt. It only took him about a dozen licks, but he cut through the seat of my overalls with it. I had blood in my shoes

when I walked into the house, and that's the only time I've ever
seen the old man look the way he did then.'

The trout broiled in the butter inside the pan, and Buddy
squeezed a lemon along the delicate white-and-pink meat.

'So do I march up to talk with your father or wait around?' I
said.

'No, you take a beer out of the icebox, and then we eat. If you
want to boogie down the road then, and not blow five minutes
with the old man, that's OK. We'll catch a couple of brews and
worm fish along the river. Don't fret your bowels about it.
Everything's cool.'

We ate out on the front porch, with the breeze blowing up
through the pines from the river. It was almost cold in the shade
of the porch, and Mr Riordan's four Appaloosas and his one
thoroughbred and Arabian stood like pieces of sunlit stone in the
lot next to the barn. Beyond the house, the edges of the canyon
and the cliffs were razor blue against the sky.

I was eating the last piece of trout with a slice of onion when I
heard Mr Riordan step up to the side of the porch. He had
slipped his overalls straps down over his shoulders so that they
hung below his waist, and the red handkerchief tied around his
neck was wet with perspiration. He reached into the bib of his
overalls and took out a small cigar that was burned at the tip.
Buddy's face became vacant while he cleaned off the tin plates.

'I guess you get pretty serious when you decide to do something,' he said.

He lit his cigar, and his grey eyes looked through the smoke
and lighted match without blinking.

'I thought we had an understanding back there at the hospital,'
he said.

'It wasn't something I planned. I just have a bad way of letting
the burner get too hot until something starts to melt at the wrong
moment.'

He took a piece of tobacco off his lip and made a sound in his
throat. There were drops of perspiration in his eyebrows. Buddy
took the plates inside, and I heard him work the iron pump in the
sink.

'I guess I had you called wrong. I didn't have you figured for this,' he said.

I looked away from him, took a cigarette out of my pack, and thought, Jesus Christ, what is this?

'Then, I never figured that my own boy would spend five years in a penitentiary,' he said.

'Sometimes you can't call what people will do,' I said.

'Is that the kind of observation you make on human conduct after you're in jail?'

'I don't know if I learned it in jail or not, but my own feeling is that people will do what's inside them and there's not much way to change that.'

'That must be a strange philosophy to live with, especially if what you do ruins most of your life.'

'I thought I had my dues paid, Mr Riordan, and I was going to live cool for as long as I could after that. But maybe you have to keep paying dues all the way down the line and there's no such thing as living cool.'

'I won't try to argue with your experience and what you've shaped out of it. But the world isn't a jail. We just make our own sometimes. Does that make any sense to you?'

I drew in on my cigarette and looked off at the green-yellow haze on the meadow. The field hands were bucking bales on the back of a wagon, and the short pines at the base of the mountain were bent at the tops in the wind.

'I'm sorry I dragged some trouble on your place,' I said, 'and I appreciate your willingness to go bond for me. Otherwise, I'm not sure what to tell you. I'll probably be moving into town in a day or so.'

'I didn't ask you to do that. I just ask you to think a little bit about what I said.'

'You want a beer, Frank?' Buddy called from inside.

'Bring two out, Son.' Then to me, 'You probably can't do much with that arm around the place, but I'll pay you to help me with the nutrias. I'm going to introduce them into a couple of beaver ponds up Lost Horse Creek this weekend.'

'You shouldn't ever let those things loose in Montana,' I said.

'I'm afraid you're more conservative than you think, Iry.'

My cheque from Ace was in the mail the next day, and I treated everyone to a beerbust and picnic at Flathead Lake. We loaded up in two cars, with children's heads sticking out of the windows, goggle masks already strapped on their faces, and I bought two cases of Great Falls with cracked ice spread among the bottles and a wicker basket of sausage, cheese, smoked ham and French bread. It was my first trip up to the Flathead country, and I realized that I hadn't yet seen the most beautiful part of Montana. We began to climb higher north of Missoula, the mountains blue on each side of us, the air thin and cool, and then we were rolling through the Salish Indian reservation, across the Jocko River that was now low and flowing a clear, jello green over the smooth bed of rocks with the short grass waving in the current along the banks. Buddy had the Plymouth screwed down to the floor, and he was drinking a beer with one hand, his shoulder against the door like a 1950s hood, and laughing into the wind and talking about the three-point-two weed that grows wild in Montana, while Beth kept one frightened eye on the speedometer and a nervous cigarette between her fingers.

'Look at those buffalo,' he said. 'You know those cats can run at forty-five miles an hour? A chain fence doesn't even slow them down. They got gristle and hair on their chests like armour plate. And they stay in rut like rabbits. So I asked this park ranger once why the government didn't just turn them out and let them reproduce all over the country. And he says, now dig this, man, just imagine some Nebraska wheat farmer going to bed dreaming of a thousand acres of cereal out there, and then he hears this long rumble and looks out of the window in the morning and there's nothing but torn ground and thousands of buffalo turds.'

When we stopped for petrol, Beth asked me to drive, and Buddy sat against the passenger's door and lit a reefer. The Mission Mountains were the most beautiful range I had ever seen. They were jagged and snow-covered against the sky, with long, white waterfalls running from under the snowpack, and Kicking Horse Lake lay at the bottom like a great blue teardrop. My head was reeling with the thin air and the two beers that I had drunk, the wind and the shouts of the children in the back seat, and I felt Beth's thigh against mine and I wondered if a person could ever hold on permanently to an experience like this.

I slowed the car as we neared Polson, and then I saw Flathead Lake, with the cherry trees along the shores, the huge expanse of blue water, the ring of mountains around it, the cliffs of stone that rose from the middle of its brilliant, quiet surface. It looked like the Pacific Ocean; it was so large that you simply lost conception of your geographical place. Boats with red sails tacked in the thin breeze, their bows white and glistening with sunlight, and the sandy stretches of beach were shaded by pine trees. We drove along the shores towards Big Fork, the water winking through the trees, and I watched the cherry pickers on their stepladders lean heavily into the leaves, their hands working methodically, while the cherries rained like blood drops into their baskets.

It was a wonderful day. We ate poor-boy sandwiches on the beach, drank beer in the sun until our eyes became weak in the glare, then dived into the water and swam out breathlessly into the cold. I rented a small outboard, and we took turns taking the kids out to an island that was covered with Indian cuttings in the rock. Then Melvin bought some large cutthroat trout from a fisherman, and we barbecued them inside foil with tomato sauce. We were all tired and happy when we drove back towards Missoula. Before we got to town, Buddy went to sleep in the back seat with the children, and Beth laid her head against my shoulder and put her hand on my knee. I couldn't tell if it was deliberate or if she was just in that type of dreamy exhaustion that gives women an aura in their sleep. But it made me ache a little, that and the absence of a wife and family at age thirty-one and the probability that I would never have either one.

The next week went by, and each morning I could see the Indian summer steal more heavily across the mountains. The trees were turning more rapidly, flashes of red and yellow among the leaves where there had been none yesterday, and the sky became a harder blue, and there was more pine smoke from the chimneys in the false dawn before the sun broke across the top of the Bitterroots. I helped Mr Riordan introduce his nutrias into

Lost Horse Creek and worked a couple of afternoons in the aviary, but I spent most of each day sitting on the front porch, either drinking beer and playing the Gibson with an open tuning (which can be done with one hand if you use a bottle neck along the frets as you would use a bar on a steel or a dobro) or trying to forget the awful itch and stench of medicine and sweat inside my cast. On some days when I drank too much beer and fell into an afternoon delirium on top of my bed, I imagined that white ants that had never seen light were eating their way into my blood veins.

But altogether I felt quiet inside, and I had a strange notion that if I stayed in one place for a while and didn't do anything extravagant, my scene at the pulp mill would disappear, and my personal war with the locals would be filed away in a can somewhere.

I was cleaning some brook trout in a pan of water on the porch when I saw the sheriff's car turn through the cattle guard and roll along the road in a cloud of dust. I put my hands in the red water and wiped them on my blue jeans and lit a cigarette before he stopped in front of the cabin. He saw that I wasn't going to get up from the porch, so he turned his wheel towards the steps and drove to within four feet parallel of me. There was a bead in his corpulent face, and his arm on the window looked like a fat bread roll. He took his cigar out of the ashtray, puffed on its splayed end, with the red stone of his Mason's ring glinting in the sunlight, and then opened the door part way to release his weight from under the steering wheel.

'You should have been a little more careful, son,' he said.

'How's that, Sheriff?'

'I told you that some of my men are a little dumb and it takes us a while to get there. It took me a while to figure out where you were shooting from, too. You picked them all up from that clip except this one. It was under the pine needles right beside the tree you sat against.'

He held up a small plastic bag, wrapped at the top with a rubber band. Inside was a spent brass cartridge.

'I understand that a print will burn right into a shell after it's fired,' he said. 'You can't scrub it off with sandpaper.'

'I couldn't tell you.'

'Well, you hang around here. I'll let you know what I find after I take it over to the FBI man in Helena.'

EIGHT

I couldn't sleep that night. I smoked cigarettes in bed, then went out on the porch with half a glass of Four Roses, sat in the chill, and watched a herd of deer graze their way across the meadow towards the canyon. They were sculptured in the moonlight and the wet grass, and when a car passed out on the highway, I could see a brown glass eye flash at me from the darkness. Through the pines the wide expanse of the Bitterroot River was dripping with a blue shimmer. I drank the whiskey and tried to keep the shell casing in the plastic bag out of my mind, but I couldn't. I was angry at my carelessness, my failure to count the hulls as they had ejected from the chamber, and the fact that an inconsequential thing, a spent cartridge, could put me back in prison for years.

I don't know when I fell asleep in the chair, but I smelled the smoke just before the false dawn. In my whiskey dream I thought it was pine wood burning from a chimney, but then I heard the horses whinnying and rearing and crashing inside the stalls. The flames were already up one side of the barn, the sparks whipping across the shingled roof, and the loft was framed in a bright square of yellow light from inside. On the dirt road I heard a truck clank hard into gear and thunder across the cattle guard. I ran barefoot into the cabin and shook Buddy by the shoulders in bed.

'What the hell's going on, man?'

'Your barn's on fire.'

We started running across the field just as a single flame cut through the roof and caught the air and sucked a large hole downward in a shower of sparks. Lights were going on all over

the main house, and I saw Mr Riordan run off the front porch
without a shirt on. The hay bales that had been stacked against
one wall of the barn were turning into boxes of flame, and the
aviary was filled with flickering yellow light and shadows and the
wild beating of birds' wings in the cages.

'The horses,' Mr Riordan shouted.

Their screams were terrible. I could hear their hooves slashing
into the wood, and even in the smoke and the heated absence of
air I could smell the singed hair.

The rope pulley on the loft caught fire from the heat alone and
burned away like a solitary thread of flame. Buddy's three
younger brothers ran into the lot behind their father in their
pajamas, their eyes wide with fear and uncertainty, the skin of
their faces red with the glowing heat.

'Soak blankets and bring them running, boys,' Mr Riordan
said, then started through the barn door.

'Get out of there, Frank,' Buddy yelled.

The cinders and ash fell across Mr Riordan's bare shoulders
and back as he walked towards the stalls with his forearm held
across his eyes.

'That crazy old son of a bitch,' Buddy said.

I don't know why – maybe because I didn't think about it—
but I went in behind him. The heat was like the inside of a
furnace. The loft door was dripping fire through the cracks, and
all the tack was popping in black leathery blisters. The air was so
hot it scalded my lungs, and before I had gone five feet, I could
feel the smoke getting to my brain. Mr Riordan had opened two
of the stalls of the Appaloosas, and one bolted through the door
to the outside, but the other had pitched his forelegs over the stall
wall and was rearing and cutting his head against an upright
post.

'Let him go. You won't get him out,' I said.

'The Arabian,' he said.

The stall was at the back of the barn, which hadn't yet caught
fire but was smoking at every joint and crack and seam. The
Arabian had kicked half the stall down, and one of his shoes hung
twisted off a broken hoof. His eyes stuck out with fright, and he
had used his nose to try to break the latch on his door. I threw

the bolt and he started out towards the main door, then reared and crashed sideways into a row of stalls that were etched with fire. He rose on his knees, with sparks in his mane and tail, and pawed at the flames that had already consumed the first Appaloosa's stall. The front of the barn was starting to sink, and burning shingles were raining across the doorway, and the smoke was now so thick that I could no longer see Mr Riordan or the other horses. I worked my shirt off my shoulders with one hand and waited for the Arabian to back away from the flames and turn in another circle. Then I hit him running and jumped with my stomach across his back and pulled both knees high up into his shoulders. He kicked backward into a post and some tack, and I hit him behind the ear with my cast and got my shirt around his eyes. Then I gave it to him with both heels close under the flanks and bent low on his neck with the shirt pulled tight in both hands, and we bolted through the flames and exploding bales of green hay into the sudden coolness of the blue dawn outside.

His head went up when he smelled the air and the river, and he cut sideways and threw me on my back in the middle of the lot. Then I saw Mr Riordan come out of the huge collapsing square of fire with a soaked blanket wrapped around the thoroughbred's nose and eyes and a trouser belt pulled tight around his neck.

The boards in the walls snapped and curled as the wind blew the flames up through the roof and burst the remaining support timbers apart in arching cascades of sparks. The dark pines at the base of the canyon behind the house wavered in the light from the fire, and the birds in the aviary stood out in the reflection like ugly phoenixes with their wings extended. There were red welts all over my feet, and I could feel small holes on my shoulders like deep cigarette burns. The gauze bandages around my back were black and smelled of the boiled ointment inside, and when I pushed my hand through my hair, it felt as stiff and sharp as wire.

'Hey, man, are you all right?' Buddy said. He stood above me, looking down out of the dawn. Then his father and three brothers were beside him.

'Hey, Iry,' he said. He was kneeling beside me, and he rubbed his hand back and forth over my hair. 'Hey, get out of it, man. We got them all out except one.'

Then Mr Riordan's face was close into mine. He was squatted on his haunches with his hand around my arm. The matted grey hair on his shoulders was burned down to the skin like pig bristles. There was a long red burn along his cheek and through part of his lip that was already swelling into water.

'Let's go up to the house, son,' he said.

'Where in the hell are your neighbours?' I said.

'They'll be here. It just takes them a while.'

Half an hour later the volunteer fire truck from Stevensville came up the front lane, followed by two pickup trucks from neighbouring ranches. The early sun had climbed above the lip of the mountains, and there were long, cool shadows across the porch, where we sat and watched the firemen spray the burnt timbers and piles of ash. I wore one of Mr Riordan's soft wool shirts over the butter that his wife had spread on my shoulders.

'How fast do these guys get out here when your house is burning down?' I said.

'It ain't what you're thinking,' Buddy said. 'They have to come twenty miles, and before they can do anything else, they have to drag people out of bed all over the valley. They don't like us, but they won't turn away from you in an emergency.'

'Somehow you don't convince me, Zeno.'

'You don't understand Montana people. They'll hate your ass and treat you like sheep dirt, but they come through when you're in trouble. Wait and see what happens if you bust an axle back on a log road or get lost deer hunting.'

I lit a cigarette and poured another cup of coffee from the pot Mrs Riordan had brought out on the porch. The tops of my bare feet looked like they had been boiled in water.

'I don't know if you want to see this, Frank, but you better look at it,' one of the firemen said. He had a scorched petrol can impaled on the end of his fire axe. 'It was against the south wall, and there's a long burn back through the grass where somebody strung out the petrol.'

'Just put it there,' Mr Riordan said.

The fireman shook the can off the hook and looked away at the smoking timbers. Water dripped off his yellow waterproof, and his face was powdered with ash.

'How many did you lose in there?' he said, squinting his eyes without looking back at us.

'One Appaloosa.'

'I'm sorry about this, Frank. You know it just takes a few sons of bitches to make you think that everybody is one.'

'Tell the others to come on up for coffee,' Mr Riordan said. 'Joe, go into the cabinet for me.'

Buddy's little brother went into the house and came back with a quart of Jack Daniel's while Mrs Riordan poured out cups of coffee with both hands from a huge pot. The firemen and the neighbours in the pickup trucks sat on the steps and the porch railing, mixing whiskey in their cups and smoking hand rolled cigarettes. Their politeness and quiet manner and the cool blue morning reminded me of scenes in Louisiana on our back porch before we went hunting in the autumn, but there was an unrelieved tension here in the averted eyes, the concentration on rolling a cigarette, or the casual sip of whiskey from the bottom of a cup.

The bottle went around a second time, and Mrs Riordan brought out a tray of biscuits that she had heated from the night before.

'When the hell are you going to lay off it, Frank?' It was one of the neighbours, a big man in a blue-jean jacket with patched corduroy trousers pulled over his long underwear, and work boots that laced halfway up his thick calves. He didn't look at Mr Riordan, but took a bite off a plug of Brown Mule and worked it against his cheekbone.

'When I close it down, just like we all should have done when they first came in here,' Mr Riordan said.

'I'll be go-to-hell if I should have done any such thing,' the neighbour said. He spat off the porch and put the tobacco plug in his jacket. 'What they do up in Missoula ain't my business. Maybe it smells like a hog farm, but we ain't breathing it and that's them people's jobs up there. If they want to shut it down, let them do it.'

'Do you remember what Missoula was like when you could drive down the Clark without that smoke plume hanging over the water?' Mr Riordan said. 'Do you ever fish that stretch of river today? What are you going to do when you have something like it right here in the Bitterroot?'

'Nobody's going to argue that with you, Frank,' the fireman said. 'But, damn, those people can't go anywhere else for work. Anaconda ain't going to hire them, and that don't even count the gyppos that are going to be losing their tractors and everything else.'

'All they have to do is put in a purification system,' Mr Riordan said. 'Don't they realize that they didn't come here as a favour to us? They're here for profit, and they destroy the air and make you like them for it.'

It was silent a moment; then one of the firemen set his cup in the saucer, nodded, and walked back to the truck. The other men smoked their cigarettes, deliberately looking out across the fields and up the canyon, where the sun was now breaking against the cliff walls and tops of the pines. Then one by one they casually stripped their cigarettes along the seam and let the tobacco blow away dryly in the breeze, or placed their cups and saucers quietly on the steps, and walked back across the lawn, pulling their gloves from their backpockets and slapping them across their palms, yawning and arching their backs as though they were thinking profoundly of the day's work ahead of them.

'I'm going to report this to the sheriff's office as arson,' the fireman who had found the petrol can said. 'That won't put anybody in jail, but he can scare two or three sons of bitches out of trying to come back here again.'

'They won't be back.'

'Frank, this is a hell of a thing, and I want you to know what I think.'

'OK, Bob.'

The fireman got up in the seat of the volunteer truck and drove down the lane towards the cattle guard with the other firemen sitting against the coiled hoses in a lazy euphoria of sunlight and early-morning whiskey.

'You want another drink, Iry?' Mr Riordan said.

'Sure.'

Then we went inside and had a breakfast of pork chops and

eggs. They were a tough family. There was no mention of the fire at the table, though I knew the image of the burned Appaloosa under the collapsed roof was like a piece of metal behind Mr Riordan's brow. Buddy ate his breakfast quietly and left the table first. Through the window I saw him pick up the bottle from the porch and walk back towards the cabin.

When I got back to the cabin, he was sitting at the kitchen table with a tin cup of whiskey and water in his hand. The bottle was almost down to the bottom.

'Pour a shot,' he said.

'I hate to get drunk before nine in the morning.'

'You were belting it pretty heavy on the porch.'

'I don't get fried every day of the week.'

He drank down the cup and picked up a cigarette butt from the ashtray. I threw my pack of Lucky Strikes on the table, but he ignored the gesture and puffed on a match held close to his lips.

'How'd you know the barn was on fire?' he said.

'I couldn't sleep last night. That fat cop put my *cojònes* in a skillet when he showed me that spent cartridge.'

'Don't worry about it. He's just sweating you.'

'You got it figured out, do you?'

'What do you think? If he had you nailed, he would have busted you right there. He could have got that shell anywhere.'

'I wish I could be that damn sure, considering it's my ass that's on the line.'

'You talk like a fish. Use your gourd a minute. He wants you to jump your parole.'

There was a touch of irritation and meanness in Buddy's voice that I didn't like.

'Maybe I didn't read him right, then,' I said.

'Besides, even if he picked that shell up, he still don't have crap. You could have been target shooting up there two weeks ago. So forget it.' Buddy poured the rest of the bottle into the tin cup.

I sat on the edge of my bunk and rubbed Vaseline over the tops of my blistered feet, then put on a pair of white socks with my loafers.

'What did the old man talk about after I left?' Buddy said.

'Nothing, except finishing the fence line down by the slough.'

'That's all. Nothing about the weather or the goddamn cows or cleaning out the birdcages?'

'He didn't say anything.'

'You all just sat in silence and chewed on your pork-chop bones.'

'I don't know what you're pushing at, Buddy.'

'Not a thing, Zeno. Open a beer. Let's get high.'

'I told you I've had it.'

'You look great.' He went to the icebox and came back with an opened can.

'I have to go to the hospital this morning to get my arm checked,' I said.

'That's cool, because you can drive me somewhere else afterwards.'

I sipped off the beer and looked at him. His eyes were red, and he rubbed the nicotine-stained ends of his fingers together. I knew Buddy too well to intrude on whatever strange things were beating inside his crazy head, but something bad was loose and it was ugly as well.

'What do you have to do at the hospital?' he asked.

'I want to find out when I get this cast off so I can start playing again. I feel like worms are crawling inside the plaster.'

He wasn't listening to me. He knocked the chair over in getting up from the table and went in the back room to change clothes. He came back out dressed in a pair of sharkskin slacks, a blue sports shirt, half-topped boots and a grey windbreaker. He pumped some water in the sink and washed his face and combed his hair back in ducktails on the sides.

'What are we doing?' I said.

'Getting your arm back into gear, Zeno. Don't worry about it.' He opened the icebox and took out a saucer that had the torn corner of an ink blotter on it.

'Hey, man, let that stuff slide today,' I said.

'There's enough for two. You ought to get up after charging the flames and doing that Korean War–Bronze Star scene.'

'Come on, Buddy.'

He put the blotter in his mouth and bit down easily on it.

'I was talking with this guy in Missoula who's been sending acid into Deer Lodge under postage stamps,' he said. 'All a guy has to do is take one lick and he's flying for the rest of the day.'

We drove through the Bitterroot towards Missoula, and Buddy was snapping to the music on the radio and lighting one cigarette off another while he kept a can of beer between his thighs. I couldn't tell exactly when the acid took him, because he already had enough whiskey in his system to make him irrational and feverish in the eyes. But by the time we reached Lolo he was talking incoherently and punching me on the shoulder with two fingers to illustrate something, and each time he touched me a ripple of pain danced across my blistered skin. I shouldn't have left the cabin with him. I looked up the highway that led off the junction at Lolo over the pass into Idaho and thought of driving up somewhere high in the lodgepole pines to let him get his head straight again, but he read me.

'Keep it straight into Missoula, Zeno. We want to get your arm flattened out so you can get into the shitkicker scene again. Then we'll go over to Idaho later.'

I went through the light at the junction and took the can of beer from between his legs.

'That's what you don't understand about acid, Iry,' he said. 'You can look into people's thoughts with it. Right on down into their ovaries.'

I parked the car in the shade of some elm trees by Saint Patrick's Hospital and left Buddy outside. As I walked up towards the entrance in the bright autumn air and spangle of sunshine, I turned around and saw Buddy's half-topped boots resting casually over the edge of the driver's window. The Irish nun who had been a friend to me before changed the dressings on my back with her cool fingers and then took me over to the X-ray room, where I was told that the crack in my arm had knitted well and I probably could have the cast sawed off in another week.

When I got back to the car, Buddy was sitting behind the wheel, drinking a hot beer and listening to a hillbilly radio station. His eyes were swimming with colour.

'The heat came around and told me to get my feet out of the

window,' he said. 'They said it don't look good around the hospital.'

'Let's go to the Oxford. I'll buy you a steak,' I said.

'They must have told you something good in there.'

'I get my cast off next week.'

He slipped across the seat when I opened the car door. I pulled out on to the street and started to drive towards the Oxford. We crossed the bridge over the Clark Fork, and I looked away at the wide curve of green water and the white rocks engraved with the skeletons of dead insects along the banks. It was going to be a good day after all, with no thoughts of cops or parole violation or FBI fingerprint men in Helena. Buddy was probably right, I thought. The sheriff just wanted to spook me into jumping my parole so he could have me violated back to Angola, and if I kept my head on straight, I could probably walk out of the thing at the mill.

'Let's get the steak later,' Buddy said.

'I'm flush and I don't do this often,' I said. 'A couple of T-bones and then we'll have a few drinks with your photographer friend over at Eddie's.'

'Just head on down the highway and I'll give you the directions. You ain't seen Idaho yet.'

'Why don't we keep it solid today, Buddy, and just booze around a little bit this afternoon and fish the river tonight?'

'It's my car, ain't it? Head it down the road, and I'll tell you when to stop at this 1860 bar with bullet holes in the walls.'

'I don't think this is cool. The rods knock on the highway like somebody put glass in the crankcase.'

'Turn left at the light or let me drive.'

We drove west along the river through the high canyons towards the Idaho line. When we climbed a grade towards a long span of bridge and looked down, the river shone blue and full of light, and the moss waved on the smooth boulders below the current. Just before the state line there was an old bar set back from the road against the base of a mountain. The rambling back part of the building was half collapsed, the windows were boarded, and a section of tin roof was torn up from the eave. But the bar itself was made of mahogany and scarred in a half-dozen places by pistol balls, with a long brass rail and a huge, yellow-stained baroque mirror that covered the entire wall.

Buddy ordered two whiskey sours before I could stop him, then dropped a quarter into the jukebox, which was located right next to a table where three working men were playing cards. They were annoyed, and they looked at him briefly before they moved to a table in the back.

'They built this place when the railroad came through,' Buddy said. 'The back of the building was all cribs. Up on the side of the mountain there's about twenty graves of men that were shot right here.'

One of the cardplayers got up and turned the jukebox down.

'Hey, Zeno, you're messing with my song,' Buddy called out.

I asked the bartender for two paper cups, poured our whiskey sours into them, and walked towards the door. Buddy had to follow me or drink by himself.

'What are you doing, man?' he said outside. 'You can't walk away every time some guy puts his thumb in your eye.'

'You want to bet?' I said.

The light was hard and bright, and the blue and green of the trees seemed to recede infinitely across the roll of mountains against the sky. Without looking at Buddy, I casually turned the car around the gas pump towards Missoula. His hand went out and caught the wheel, his forearm as stiff and determined as a piece of pipe.

'No, man, I got to deliver you to this other scene,' he said.

'All right, what kind of caper are we on to?'

'We're going to a cathouse.'

'I don't believe this.'

'Does that rub against some Catholic corner of your soul?'

'Aren't we over the hill for that kind of stuff? I mean, don't you feel a little silly sitting in a hot-pillow joint with a bunch of college boys and drunk loggers?'

'Well, you righteous son of a bitch. You eyeball everything that looks vaguely female, you get drunk and try to make out with some Indian guy's wife, and then you got moral statements to make about your partner's sex life. Some people might just call you a big bullshitter, Zeno.'

We crossed the state line and began to drop down into the mining area of eastern Idaho, a torn and gouged section of the state where everything that hadn't been ruined by stripping had been blighted and stunted by the yellow haze that drifted off the smokestacks of the smelter plants. It was Indian summer in the rest of the northern Rockies, but here the acrid smoke made your head ache and your eyes wince, and the second growth on top of the destroyed mountains was the colour of urine. At the bottom of the grade was Wallace, and beyond that, Smelterville, towns that were put together in the nineteenth century out of board, tin, crushed rock for streets, and some type of design on making the earth a gravel pit. The buildings in Wallace looked caved in, grimed with dirt and smoke from the smelters, and their windows were cracked and yellowed. Even the pavements sagged in the middle of the streets as though some oppressive weight were on top of them.

'You can really pick them, Buddy,' I said.

'Drive on up the hill to that big two-storey wooden house.'

The house sat up on a high, weed-filled lawn, with a wide sagging front porch and a blue light bulb over the door. The white paint was dirty and peeling, and crushed beer cans were strewn along the path to the steps.

'I'll wait for you,' I said.

'None of that stuff. You're not going to pull your Catholic action on your old partner.'

'I'm going to pass. This isn't my scene.'

'You see that car at the bottom of the hill? That's the deputy sheriff who watches this place, and if we keep fooling around he's going to be up here and you can talk to him.'

'I'm telling you, Buddy, you better not get our ass worked over again.'

'Have a beer in the living room. Talk to the bouncer. He's a real interesting guy. He has an iron bolt through both temples.'

'I'll listen to the radio till you come out,' I said. I smiled at him and lit a cigarette, but there was nothing pleasant in his face.

He walked up the path and knocked on the torn screen door. A girl in blue jeans and a halter opened it, her face expressionless, the eyes indifferent except for a momentary glance, almost like curiosity, in my direction; then she latched the screen again without any show of recognition that a human being had walked past her.

Fifteen minutes later I heard people yelling inside, and then I heard Buddy's voice: 'You go for that sap and you're going to be pulling a shank out of your throat with your fingernails.'

I walked quickly up the path, focused my eyes through the screen, and saw him facing an enormous, bull-necked man in the middle of the living room. The braided leather tip of a blackjack stuck out of the big man's back pocket. Buddy's face was white from drinking, his shirt was ripped and pulled down on one shoulder, and a full whiskey bottle hung from his right hand.

'Turn around and walk out the door and you're out of Indian country,' the bouncer said.

I put my hand through the torn screen, unlatched the door, and stepped inside. All the windows were drawn with yellow roll shades that must have been left over from the 1940s. An old jukebox with a cracked plastic casing stood against one wall, the coloured lights inside rippling up and down against the gloom. A hallway separated by a curtain led back from the living room, and there was a rubbish bin in one corner that was filled with beer cans and whiskey bottles. In the half-light, mill workers and drunks left over from last night's bars sat with the whores on stuffed couches and chairs that seemed to exude a mixture of dust, age and stale beer. Their faces were pinched with a mean dislike for Buddy, for me, and even for each other. I wondered at my own passivity in allowing Buddy to lead us into this dirty little corner of the universe.

The bouncer's face was as round as a skillet. He smiled with a look of pleasant anticipation.

'Well, I guess it's guys like you that keep me honest and make me earn my pay,' he said. 'But I'm afraid it's a bad day at Black Rock for you boys.'

'Wait a minute, mister. We're leaving,' I said.

'So leave. But if you bring your pet asshole back here again, we'll have to whip some big bumps on him. Give him some real mean hurt. Take his mind off his tallywhacker so he don't have to come here no more.'

'You notice how these guys have a quick turn for everything?' Buddy said. 'They memorize all kinds of hep phrases for every life situation. But they put rock 'n' roll on their jukeboxes and pay their money to the cops and hand out blow jobs to the Kiwanis Club. Look at Mad Man Muntz here. He got his brains at the junkyard, he probably makes a buck an hour, but he comes on like the poet laureate of the brooder house.'

I walked over to Buddy and took him by the arm.

'Our bus is leaving,' I said.

'So long, you lovely people, and remember the reason you're here,' he said. 'You're losers, you got one gear and it's in neutral, and you hire this big clown to keep you safe from all your failures.'

I pulled hard on his arm and pushed him towards the door. The bouncer lifted his finger at him.

'You ought to go to church, boy. You got somebody looking over you,' he said.

The screen slammed behind us, and we walked down the path in the sunlight. The sharpness of the afternoon seemed disjointed and strange after the gloom and anger and bilious view of humanity in the whorehouse.

'I bought a bottle at the bar and was drinking a shot out of it when I saw the guy next to me buying drinks for him and his girl out of my change,' Buddy said as we drove down the hill towards the highway out of town. 'I couldn't believe it. Then he called me a pimp and put his cigarette ashes in my glass. The next thing I knew, his girl was trying to tear my shirt off my back. Man, I thought I saw people do some wild action in the joint, but that's the bottom of the bucket, ain't it?'

I drove without answering and wondered what had really taken place. We passed the town limits, and I stepped on the accelerator as we began the climb up the slope towards the blue tumble of mountains on the Montana line. In the rearview mirror the ugly sprawl of that devastated mining area and stunted town disappeared behind us.

'Yeah, that was a real geek show,' he said.

'Well, how the hell did you get there?' I said righteously, but I was angry at his irresponsibility and the physical danger he had put both of us in again. 'They didn't send out invitations to

Florence, Montana. That's their action every day back there, and you go on their rules when you walk through the door.'

I could feel his eyes on the side of my face; then I heard him take a drink out of the whiskey bottle. He didn't speak for another five minutes, and the whistle of air through the window and my cigarette ashes flaking on my trousers began to feel more and more uncomfortable in the silence. I just couldn't stay mad at Buddy for very long.

'How much did they hook you for the bottle?' I said.

'Twelve bucks. You want a shot?'

I drank out of the neck and handed it back to him. The warm bourbon made me wince and my arms tingle.

'Look, Zeno, what's this lecture crap about?' he said.

'Jesus Christ, I just don't want to get busted up again.'

'You could have cancelled out early. You didn't have to drive us up there.'

I didn't have an answer for that one.

'You knew what type of scene we were floating into,' he said. 'You better run the film backwards in your own gourd. You were clicking around about maybe improving your love life yourself.'

We dropped over the Montana line, and I really opened up the Plymouth. The front end was badly out of alignment, at least two bearings were tapping like tack-hammers, and the oil smoke was blowing out of the frayed exhaust in a long black spiral. The car frame shook and rattled, the doors vibrated on the jambs, and when I had to shift into second to pull a grade, the heat needle moved into the red area on the gauge and the radiator began to sing. Buddy pulled on the bottle and lit a cigarette. But before he did, he split a paper match with his thumbnail, as fast as anyone could pull one from a cover, and flipped the other half on the dashboard in front of me.

'That's pretty good, ain't it, Zeno?' he said. 'I once beat a guy out of a whole deck of cigarettes by splitting thirty in fifty seconds.'

'Why don't you forget all that prison shit?'

'Why don't you forget about destroying my car because you're pissed off?'

I let the Plymouth slow, and I heard Buddy drag off the bottle again. The sun had moved behind the edge of the mountains, and the yellow leaves on the cottonwoods along the river looked like hammered brass over the flow of the current. The blue shadows fell out in front of us on the highway, and the short pines at the base of the hills were already turning dark against the white slide of rocks behind them. The air became cool in minutes, the wind off the river in the canyon seemed sharper, and the banks of clouds on the mountains ahead took on the pink glow of a new rose above the trees.

Buddy pulled steadily on the bottle until he sank back against the door and the seat with an opened can of hot beer between his thighs.

It was almost dark when I saw the lights of Missoula in the distance. The last purple twilight hung on the high, brown hills above the valley, and a solitary plane with its landing lights on moved coldly above the city towards the airport. The city seemed so quiet and well ordered in its soft glow and neat pattern of streets and homes and lines of elm and maple trees that I wondered how any community of people could organize anything that secure against the coming of the night and the morrow. For just a moment I let it get away inside me, and I wondered, with a little sense of envy and loss, about all the straight people in those homes: the men with families and ordinary jobs and ordinary lives, the men who pulled the green chain at the mill and carried lunch boxes and never sweated parole officers, cops, jail tanks, the dirty knowledge of the criminal world that sometimes you would like to cut out with a knife, all the ten years' roaring memory of bleeding hangovers, whorehouses, and beer-glass brawls.

But this type of reflection was one that I couldn't afford. Otherwise I would have to put an X through a decade and admit that my brother Ace was right, and the parole office, the psychologist in the joint, the army, everybody who had told me that I had a little screw in the back of my head turned a few degrees off centre.

Buddy came out of his whiskey-acid stupor just before we reached the edge of town. His glazed eyes stared at the lights for a moment, then focused on me and brightened in a way that I didn't like. He popped the hot beer open, and the foam showered against the windscreen.

'Man, I feel like a dragon,' he said. 'I think I'll go see the wife-o.'

'I think you better not,' I said.

'Just save your counselling and tool on down by the university, Zeno.'

'You're not serious?'

He drank out of the whiskey bottle, chased it with the beer, and then hit it again.

'That's a little better,' he said. 'I could just feel the first snakes getting out of the basket.'

I drove without speaking until I got to the turnoff that would take us back into the Bitterroots.

'Where the hell are you going? I said I wanted to go to Beth's.'

'Let it slide, Buddy.'

'She's my old lady, man.'

'That's the last thing you want to do now.'

'Let Professor Riordan worry about that. Just get it on over there.'

'Where's your head? How do you think she's going to feel when you waltz up to the door like a liquor truck?'

'You should have gone into the priesthood, Iry. You can really deliver the advice about somebody else's life.'

'All right, you've been telling me you want to go back with her. Pull a scene like this and you'll disconnect from her permanently.'

'I guess all this crap comes out of the new Bronze Star you won this morning.'

'What are you talking about?' I said.

'You charged the hill again, didn't you? Shot the heads off all them sixteen-year-old gooks in the trench. Went through the barn door after my old man when I couldn't move.'

'Don't drink any more.'

'You told me about it, right? You went up the hill when everybody else froze and dumped a BAR in their faces, and when you turned them over, you said they looked like children.'

'Put your bag of needles back in your pocket, Buddy. I'm not up to it.'

'No, man. It was the same scene. You saw I was froze, and

you followed the old man into the fire. You didn't do it because of him. You knew I was nailed, and your heart started beating. Because you're scared shitless of fire, baby, but you had a chance to make me look like a piece of shit.'

I could feel the anger tighten across my chest and swell into my throat and head until I wanted to hit Buddy as hard as I could with my fist. I took a cigarette off the dashboard and lit it and drew in deeply on the smoke.

'You want to go to Beth's?' I said.

'I told you that, Zeno.'

OK, son of a bitch, I thought, and drove towards the university district through the dark, tree-lined streets and past the quiet lawns of all those ordinary people I had wondered about with a sense of envy just a few minutes before.

Later, reflecting on the events that were to follow, I would sometimes feel that a human being's life is not shaped so much by what he is or what he pretends to be or even by the compulsions that he tries to root out and burn away; instead it can be just a matter of a wrong turn in an angry moment and a disregard for its consequences. But I didn't know then that I would betray a friend and once more become involved in someone's death.

NINE

I parked in the dark shadow of the maple tree in front of Beth's house.

'You want me to wait or catch air?' I said.

'Come on in. She's got some beer in the icebox.'

'This is your caper, daddy-o. I'm going to rain-check this one.'

He walked across the lawn and the dead leaves on to the wood porch. Under the door light, his body looked small and white. He had to lean against the wall for balance when he knocked again.

I guess I wanted to see Buddy ruin himself with Beth, but as I looked at him there, dissipated, his head crawling with snakes, the unfulfilled rut still in his loins, I wished I could get him back in the car and home again.

Beth opened the door, and I heard Buddy's voice in its strained and careful attempt to sound sober. But the words came too fast, as though they had been rehearsed and pulled out like a piece of tape.

'Somebody burned out the old man's barn this morning, and we were cruising around and decided to drop by.'

She didn't open the screen, and there was a quiet moment while she said something to him, and then his arms went up in the air and he started to rock on both feet in the shadowy light.

'They're my boys, too, ain't they?' he said, and his voice became louder after a few seconds of silence. 'I mean what the hell they have to go to bed so early for, anyway?' Then another pause while Beth spoke.

'You keep listening to that goddamn psychologist and they're going to grow up in Warm Springs.' Another pause.

'I'll roll out the whole fucking neighbourhood if I want to. We'll give all these straight cats something to talk about over their breakfast cereal for a week.'

I saw Beth open the screen, then latch it and turn off the porch light. I waited fifteen minutes in the darkness of the maple tree and listened to a hillbilly radio station in Spokane, then decided to go to the Oxford for a chicken-fried steak and a cup of coffee and leave Buddy to his self-flagellation.

But then the light came on again, and Beth stepped out on the porch in a pair of blue jeans and a denim shirt bleached amost white with Clorox. Her blue-black hair hung in a tangle on her shoulders, and her bare feet looked as cold as ivory in the light. She motioned at me, a gentle gesture of the fingers as though she were saying good-bye to someone, and I walked across the dry, stiff grass and dead leaves towards her with a quickening in my heart and emptiness in my legs that confirmed altogether too quickly what had been in my mind all day while I had let Buddy tear his chemistry apart with whiskey and guilt.

'Help me put him upstairs. I don't want the children to see him,' she said.

Buddy was leaned back against the couch in the lamplight, his knees wide apart; his head rolled about on his shoulders like a balloon that wanted to break its string. He was talking at the far wall as though there were someone standing in front of him.

I tried to lift him by one arm, and he slapped at me with his hand, his hair over his eyes and ears.

'What the shit you doing, man?' he said. 'You trying to get me kicked out of two places in one day?'

'We got to go to bed. Your old man wants us to finish the fence line by the slough tomorrow,' I said, though I should have known better than to patronize a drunk, particularly Buddy.

'Well, cool. Louisiana Zeno is looking out for the old man's Angus after he went through the flames.' He tried to raise his head and focus on my face, but the effort was too much.

'What did he take today?' Beth said.

'Just a lot of booze.'

'No, he's been using dope again, hasn't he?'

I heard the boys' voices shouting in the backyard. Beth shook him again by the shoulder.

'Get up,' she said. 'Straighten up your head and stand.'

Buddy fell sideways against the arm of the couch, with one wrist bent back against his thigh. His face was as bloodless and empty as a child's. The back screen slammed, and Beth walked hurriedly into the kitchen and told the children to stay outside. She returned with a wet towel in her hand and pressed it into Buddy's face.

'Goddamn,' he said, his head rolling back.

'Walk to the stairs,' she said. 'Lean forward and hold on to my arm. Damn you, Buddy, they're not going to see you like this.'

'Come on, partner, let's get up,' I said, and wondered at my pretence towards friendship.

We stood him up between us, like a collapsing gargoyle, and walked him towards the staircase. His head hit the banister once, his knees knocked like wood into the steps, and I had to grab his belt and pull with all my weight to keep him from rolling backwards down to the first floor.

As I got him over the last step on to the safety of the carpet, my lungs breathless and my good arm weak with strain, I had a quick lesson about the way we as sane and sober people treat the drunk and hopelessly deranged. Considering the amount of acid and booze in his system, and the pathetic behaviour in front of his wife on the couch, I had believed that his brain, at that moment, was as soft as yesterday's ice-cream, and as a result I had helped drag him upstairs with the care and dignity that you would show a bag of dirty laundry. But when I stood up for a breath before the last haul into the bedroom, he fixed one dilated, bloodshot eye on me from the floor, the other closed in the angry squint of a prizefighter who has just received a murderous leathery shot, and said:

'You really go for the balls when you win, Zeno.'

I put him down on the bed with his head slightly over the edge so the blood would stay in his brain and he wouldn't become sick. Downstairs, a moment later, I heard him hit the floor.

'There's nothing you can do for him,' Beth said.

'I'll get him back on the bed.'

'If he wakes up, he'll wake up fighting. I know Buddy when he's like this. He chooses the people closest to him to help him destroy himself. Take a beer out of the icebox while I get the boys ready for bed.'

'I'd better go.'

'Stay. I want to talk with you.'

The boys came in from the backyard, their faces flushed with cold and play, and drank glasses of powdered milk at the kitchen table. Then they went up the stairs with their eyes fixed curiously on me.

'I'll bet you still don't believe I used to pitch against Marty Marion,' I said.

'My daddy says you're a guitar player that was in jail with him,' the younger boy said over the banister.

Learn one day not to try to con kids, Paret, I thought.

'Upstairs, and I don't want to hear any feet walking around,' Beth said.

The boys trudged up to their room as though they were being sent to a firing squad.

'What's this about Frank's barn?' Beth said.

'Somebody set fire to it this morning and burned it to the ground.'

'Was anyone hurt?'

'We couldn't get one of the Appaloosas out.'

'Does Frank know who it was?'

'He might, but I don't think he would tell anyone if he does. He seems to play a pretty solitary game.'

'Yes, and it's the type that eventually damages everybody around him.'

'That hasn't been my impression about him.'

'He draws an imaginary line that nobody else knows about, and when someone steps over it, you'd better watch out for Frank Riordan.'

'How long did you and Buddy live with him?'

I didn't know that they had, but at this point I simply guessed it as an obvious fact.

'Long enough for Buddy to have to make choices between his own family and his father,' she said.

I avoided the flash in her eyes and looked blankly around at the worn furniture and wondered how I got into this subject. I could think of nothing to say.

'Why did he use dope today?' she asked.

'I guess the fire set off some strange things in his head. I don't know. Sometimes people see the same thing differently.'

'What do you mean?'

'He got wiped out after I followed his old man into the barn and he stayed outside. So I guess he thinks he froze and so he's a coward. After anything like that, you go back over it in your head and try to understand what you did or didn't do, but he doesn't have the experience to see it for what it was.'

She didn't understand what I was saying, and I wished I hadn't started to explain.

'Buddy's not a coward,' I said. 'I've seen him go up against yard bullies at Angola that would have cut him to pieces in the shower if they had sensed any fear in him. He laid it on pretty heavy in the car this afternoon about the Bronze Star I got in Korea, but what he doesn't understand is that you go in one direction or the other, or just stand still, for the same reason – you're too scared to do anything else. It doesn't have anything to do with what you are.

'Look, I shouldn't have brought him here. It's not his fault. He just fried his head today. And I think I better cut.'

'No, I have more beer and some sandwiches in the icebox. Just a minute.'

She walked towards the kitchen with a cigarette in her hand, her thighs and smooth rear end tight against her jeans, and her uncombed hair tangled with light. She came back with a tray and sat on the couch next to me with one bare foot pulled under her leg.

'How did you stay sober while you were carrying around the mad man of Ravalli County?' she said, and laughed, and all the anger with Buddy and Frank Riordan was gone.

'I got some good news about my arm this morning. They're going to saw the cast off next week. I'll probably have to play finger exercises like a kid for a few days, but I ought to have my act back in gear at the beer joint if that fat sheriff doesn't nail me and get me violated in the meantime.'

'Have you run into Pat Floyd again?'

'He eased himself out to the ranch yesterday afternoon to show me a spent shell he said he picked up across the river from the pulp mill. I might have my signature burned right into it.'

Her eyes passed over mine with a gathering concern, then lowered to the ashtray, where she picked up her cigarette.

'Can you go back to prison?' she said.

'If I left that shell and my print is on it. It might not get me time here, but it could be enough for my PO to have me sent back to Louisiana.'

When I saw her expression and realized the casual tone of my voice, I also realized something about the impropriety of speaking out of one's own cynical experience to people who are not prepared for it.

'Buddy thinks he's just trying to turn on the butane and get me to jump,' I said.

'Pat Floyd will put you away,' she said.

The seriousness of her voice made something drop inside me.

'Well, you said he wasn't a hillbilly cop.' But the detachment that I wanted to show in my voice wasn't there.

'What do you plan to do?'

'Nothing. What the hell can I do? I can sweat this fat man or run, and if I run, I have another three to pull in Angola for sure. I figure I'll hang around and let Gordo Deficado do his worst.'

'He can do it, Iry.'

'I've known some bad men, too.'

She poured some of her beer into my glass and lit another cigarette from my pack.

'I've got to roll, kiddo. I've burned up too much of your evening,' I said.

'Buddy will need a ride home tomorrow. There's no point in making two trips.' She looked away from me, and I saw the nervous touch of her fingers on the cigarette.

'I don't want to cause an inconvenience.'

'Oh, shit,' she said, and stood up from the couch and turned off the lamp on the table. In the darkness, she paused momentarily, listening for a sound from upstairs, then began to undress. She unsnapped her blue jeans and pushed them to her ankles, then pulled off her denim shirt and tried to reach for the back of her bra. In her hurried movement, with the glow of the kitchen light against her white stomach, she looked like an embarrassed contortionist in front of an audience of dolts.

My heart was beating, and I felt the heat come into my face when I looked at her bare legs, her white line of swollen stomach above the elastic of her panties, and her wonderful soft breasts pressing against her bra. I looked up the stairs, where my friend was asleep after his day of dissipation, and before I could reflect on whether my quick glance was a matter of concern for Buddy or personal caution for myself, I looked back at Beth again and felt all the weak ache of two years stiffen into an erection.

I rose uncomfortably from the couch in a bent position and unfastened her bra, and she turned towards me and put her arms around my neck as though she wanted to hide her huge white breasts. I pulled her close, with my face in her hair, and kissed her ear and ran both my hands over the small of her back, down inside her panties and over her butt and thighs. I smelled her blue-black hair, her perfume, the dried perspiration on her neck, her breath, and I felt the backs of my thighs start to shake.

She took her arms away and slipped her panties down over her thighs, then stepped out of them.

'Sit on the couch,' she said.

Her body was silhouetted like a soft white sculpture in the glow of light from the kitchen. I undressed and sat back on the couch, and then she moved over me. She moaned once in her woman's fecund way, her eyes widened, and she spread her fingers across my back.

Then I felt it grow inside me, too early and beyond any attempt at control, and when it burst away in that heart-twisting moment, she leaned forward and held my head to her breasts as she might a child's.

In the morning we all had breakfast at the kitchen table, and the sky outside was blue and clear over the elm and maple trees, and the sun shone brightly through the window. The two boys were talking happily about a football game at school, and Beth turned the hashbrowns and eggs in the skillet as though she were fixing breakfast on any ordinary morning. But I could feel the tension in her whenever she looked towards me and Buddy at once. He was badly hung over, his hand shaking on his cigarette, the eyes puffed and dim and still focused inward on some barrel of snakes out of yesterday. His plate went cold in front of him, and finally he dropped his cigarette in his coffee and rested his forehead on the palm of his hand.

'Boy, I really got one this time,' he said.

I didn't want to look at him, because I not only felt an awful guilt towards him but also that sense of primitive victory in making a cuckold out of a rival, particularly one who was coming apart while you had it all intact.

'Try some tomato juice,' Beth said.

'You got any ups? Or some of those diet pills will do it,' he said.

'Don't take anything else,' she said.

He remained with his head in his palm and breathed irregularly.

'Do you have a hangover, Daddy?' the younger boy said.

Buddy got up from the table without answering and walked duckfooted to the icebox. He opened a can of beer and then began looking through the cabinets.

'Where the hell is that bottle of sherry you keep?' he said.

'Don't do it, Buddy,' she said. 'Just let it work out of your system and you'll be all right this afternoon.'

'Give me the sherry and don't tell me how to survive the morning.'

She took the bottle from under the sink, and he poured a glass half full of it and then filled the rest with beer and broke two raw eggs into it. He sipped the glass slowly at the table, with his head bent over, holding the glass with both hands. Five minutes later the colour began to come back into his face, and his hands stopped shaking.

'Man, that's a little better,' he said. 'That whiskey must have had shellac in it. I haven't had an eggbeater in my head like that since I sniffed some transmission fluid in the joint.' He looked up at Beth, then shook his head. 'OK, I know, wrong reference. But, man, somebody must have stuck an enema bag full of piss in my ear last night.'

That's great, Buddy, I thought.

Beth told the boys to put on their coats and go outside.

'All right, all right, I got a speech defect about bad language,' he said. 'But they hear all that shit at school. You don't have to put earmuffs on them when they're in the house.'

The table was silent, and Beth made a point of not looking directly at either one of us.

'How did I get upstairs last night? You must have dragged me up there by my heels.'

'You floated up there like a balloon,' I said.

'I feel like somebody worked me over with a slapjack. What did you do to me, partner?' He fixed one watery blue eye on me over his cigarette, and I flinched inside.

'I had to use force on you a little bit after you started taking off your clothes in the street. That wasn't too bad in itself, but after you threw those flowerpots through the neighbour's window, I had to do something to keep both of us out of the bag.'

His face tensed momentarily with hangover fear and disbelief. Then he drank from the sherry and beer and stared back hard at me with his cigarette between his lips.

'Son, you are a dirty bastard to put your hungover partner on like that,' he said, and I saw Beth's hand relax on her coffee cup.

But I couldn't quite forget his lingering, watery blue eye and the probe that it had made. Buddy had a way of knowing things that it was impossible for him to know, and I never was sure if the gift came from the fact that possibly he was crazy or if in his cynicism about human behaviour he simply intuited, with a great deal of accuracy, what bad things some people would do in certain circumstances.

He finished the glass and took another beer from the icebox.

'Let's get it down the road,' he said. 'Didn't you say the old man wants us to finish the fence line down to the slough?'

I blinked inside again, because he remembered exactly, almost to the word, what I had told him before we carried him up to bed.

'Well, damn, Zeno, get it in gear,' he said.

We walked out on to the front porch, and the yellow and red leaves were blowing across the grass in the sunlight, and the mountains behind the university were sharp and clear against the blue Montana sky. The crack of the autumn air was like a cool burn against my face. I wanted to say something, anything, alone to Beth before we left, but I couldn't, and so I just smiled as I would at a casual friend and said good-bye.

We drove back into the long, blue-green stretch of the Bitterroots and stopped at Lolo for a drink because Buddy's nervous system was starting to become unwired again. In the bar I drank a cup of coffee while he began on his second vodka collins. I had a hard time looking at him directly in the eyes.

'You're a quiet bastard this morning, ain't you?' he said.

'I got burnt out yesterday. No more Idaho excursions.'

'Right. Bad scene. I ain't going to let you lead me over there any more. I feel like somebody stuck thumbtacks all over my head. Come on, let's get out of here and put down those fence posts so I can stop thinking about my problems with ex-wives and kids.'

At the ranch we went back to work on the fence line, though I could do little more than unload the posts off the wagon with one arm and hold them steady in the hole while Buddy shovelled in the dirt. Then he would have to go to work on the next one with the posthole digger, the sweat and booze running off his face and neck into his flannel shirt. We spoke little. He was too hung over, and I was too preoccupied with the latest thing I had got myself into. I didn't know what to do about either Beth or Buddy, and any of the answers I could think of were bad ones. Maybe I should just drop it on him, I thought, because I was going to see her again, and eventually he would find out about it if he didn't already have his finger on the edge of it. I slept with your wife last night. What do you think about that? Oh, you don't mind? That's cool, because I thought the shit might hit the fan.

He started to clean the posthole digger in the bucket of water, his face pale with fatigue, then dropped the wood handles and let the whole thing fall to the ground. He wiped his face slick with his sleeve.

'Shit on this. We can do it this evening,' he said. 'Man, I'm going to quit that damn drinking once and for all.'

He walked away alone towards the cabin, his shoulders bent slightly and his back shaking with a cigarette cough.

Buddy slept through the rest of the morning, and I sat on the porch in the cool wind and tried to read from an old paperback copy of *The Old Man and the Sea*. I had read it once in college and again in Angola, and it was my favourite of Ernest Hemingway's books. But I couldn't concentrate on the words; my attention would slip off the page, across the meadow of grazing Angus to the pile of ash and blackened boards where the barn had been.

So where do you go now, I thought. You can move out and try to explain to him why you have to, or you can let things keep falling one on to another without any plan at all until something even worse happens. Under other circumstances I would have just checked it on down the road, maybe up to Vancouver or out to San Fran, but the parole office had a nail through my foot, and the only type of transfer I could get would be back to Louisiana, and that was like going back to first base after you had knocked the ball out of the park.

But if I thought I had great problems to resolve there in the solitude of the porch and a windy sun-filled afternoon, I realized with a glance at the sheriff's car turning in the front cattle guard that the complexities of my day were just beginning. Pat Floyd pulled the car off the dirt road on to the grass and put the gearshift in neutral with the engine still running, which meant we were going somewhere together.

I closed the paperback and set it beside me and looked at him without speaking. At first I'd had no feelings about him; he was just another dick, a member of that vast army who play out their roles and games with their sets of keys and paper forms and intricate rules of human behaviour. But I was learning to dislike this fat man. I had the feeling that he was taking a special interest in me, one that went beyond the prosecution of a drunk ex-convict who shot up the local toilet-paper factory. I was an outsider, a rounder with a corn-pone mystique, a glib troublemaker who had been kicked off his own turf and was using the locals for a doormat.

'Let's take a ride,' he said.

'You got a paper on me, Sheriff?'

'This ain't an arrest. And I wouldn't need a warrant to make one, either, son.'

'Hey, Buddy,' I called back through the screen door.

'You don't need him. Just get in, and we're going to talk a minute.'

'I just want to tell him we'll be back soon. We're going fishing shortly.'

I opened the screen and spoke into the dim shadows of the cabin. Buddy was on my bunk with the pillow and quilt over his head, his body deep in the mattress with sleep.

'I'll be out with Sheriff Floyd a few minutes. OK?'

I got in the passenger side of the car and lit a cigarette, and we started up the road towards the cattle guard.

'You're a pretty sharp boy,' he said.

'How's that, Sheriff?'

'You thought I might take you out, beat the shit out of you with a billy, and leave you in a ditch, didn't you?'

'It didn't cross my mind.'

'We don't do it that way up here. In fact, we don't hardly have any crime here to speak of. On Saturday night a few boys might try to break up each other in a bar, and I have to lock them up till Sunday morning, but that's all we get. People around here obey the law most of the time.'

We turned out on the highway, and he reached over with his huge weight and popped open the glove compartment. Inside was a half-pint of whiskey in a paper bag twisted around the neck. He unscrewed the cap with his thumb and took a drink, then set the bottle between his swollen khaki thighs.

'Actually, being a sheriff around here is easy,' he said. 'A lot of times people take care of the law by themselves. A few years ago one of those California motor-cycle gangs rode into Virginia City on a Saturday afternoon and said they were taking over the town. By that night every sheepherder and cowboy in the county was in town. They broke arms and heads and legs, beat them till they got down on their knees, and left just enough of that crowd intact to drive the others out of town. That's the way it gets done out here sometimes.'

'What's all this about?'

'Not too much. I just want to tell you a couple of things.' We passed the Sweeny Creek grocery store, a small wooden building set back from the blacktop in the trees, and turned on to a rock road that led back towards the mountains. I puffed on my cigarette and looked at him from the side of my eye. He wasn't carrying a billy on his hip, and I hadn't seen one in the glove compartment, but maybe it was under the seat or lying within a second's reach against the doorjamb.

I had never been beaten in prison, or even mistreated for that matter, but I could never forget the time I saw what a Negro could look like after he had been sweated with a garden hose three nights in isolation. He was serving peas in the chow line for the free people, and when one of the hacks told him, 'You had better start ladling out them peas a little faster, boy,' he replied, 'You ladle them out yourself, boss.' Three hacks cuffed him in the serving line and took him down to the hole. When he came out his eyes were swollen shut, and the striped bruises on his stomach and back looked like a black deformity.

The sheriff parked the car close into the shade of the pines along the creek and cut the engine. He took another drink out of the whiskey and offered the bottle to me.

'Go ahead. You ain't going to get trench mouth out of it.' He laughed and took a cigar from his pocket. 'You know, you've got a shit pot full of good luck. The FBI man couldn't find a thing on that shell casing. Either you must have wiped all them hulls clean before you put them in the magazine or a deer walked over and took a good, solid piss right on top of it.'

He bit off the tip of the cigar and spat it through the window, then wet the end as though he were rolling a stick around in his mouth.

'Do you think you got pretty good luck?' he said.

'You tell me.'

He struck a match on the horn button and lit the cigar.

'I don't think your luck is too good at all,' he said. 'But that's another matter. I wanted to drive up here today mainly because it's my day off and this is where I always come the first day of deer season. You see where that saddle begins right after the first mountain, where the meadow opens up in the trees? I get two whitetail there opening day every year. I got an elk cow there last year, too, right up the nose with this .357 magnum from forty yards. I was using a shotgun with deer slugs, and I got some snow in the barrel and blew it all apart firing at a doe. Then the elk walked into the meadow with the wind behind her and never smelled a thing. I put it in her snout and tore her ass all over the snow. Those steel jackets will go through an automobile block, and they don't even slow down when they gut an animal.'

I handed his whiskey back to him and looked out the passenger's window.

'You're not a hunter, are you?' he said.

'I gave it up in the army.'

He had started to take a drink, but he lowered the bottle and looked hard at me. I tried to keep my gaze on his face, but it was too much. His anger towards me and what I represented in some vague place in his mind or memory – some abstraction from a childhood difficulty, a sexual argument with his wife, a fear of the mayor or the town councilmen or himself – was too much to contend with in a stare contest, even though he was trying to pull my life into pieces.

'Let me tell you something before we drive back,' he said. 'I don't like you. I probably can't get you for shooting up the mill right now, but I'm going to make you as unwelcome as I can in Missoula County. I'll put you in jail for spitting on the street, throwing a cigarette wrapper down, walking in public with beer on your breath. I'll have you in jail every time I see you or any of my department does. I have the feeling that if I lock you up enough and call your parole officer each time I do it, you'll get your sack lunch and bus ticket back to Louisiana. Which means you better keep your ass out of my sight.'

'Is that it?'

'You better believe it, son.'

I opened the door and stepped out on the short grass. My head was light, and the wind blowing through the pines along the creek bed was cold against the perspiration in my hair.

'Where the hell do you think you're going?' he said.

'I'll hitch a ride back to the Riordans'.'

The sun's rays struck through his windscreen, revealing in his face all his anger, all his doubt about leaving me to find my way home (and the possible recriminations later), and the most serious question – whether he had struck the fear of God into me with a burning poker.

I walked up the rock road towards the blacktop, smoking a cigarette, and he drove along beside me in first gear with his fat arm over the window, the doubt and anger still stamped in his face, and I was glad no one could see this sad comedy of two grown men acting out a ludicrous exercise in a mountain wilderness so that one of them could go home with a piece of scalp lock to keep his pride intact.

The sheriff floored the car in front of me, fishtailing off the grass that was already turning wet with dew, and spun a shower of rocks off the back tyres when he hit second. He threw the whiskey bottle out of the window into the gravel as he turned on to the blacktop, then roared away towards Missoula with both exhausts throbbing, his arm like a ham on the window.

By the time I had hitched a ride back to the ranch, the sunlight was drawing away over the mountains in a pink haze, and Buddy was sitting on the porch steps in a sheep-lined jacket, tying tapered leader on his fly line.

'Where you been, man?' he said.

'I went for a ride with that fat dick.'

He looked up from his concentration on the leader and waited.

'That shell casing was clean, but he says he's going to make my life interesting every time he catches me in Missoula,' I said.

'Just stay out of his way. It'll be cool after a while.'

'What am I supposed to do in the meantime? Live out here like a hermit?'

'You want to go fishing?'

'Yeah.'

We took the car down to the river and fished two deep holes in the twilight with wet flies. As the moon began to rise over the mountains, they started hitting. I saw my line straighten out quickly below the surface of the pool; then there was that hard-locking tension when the brown really hung into it, and the split-bamboo rod arched towards the water and the backup line started to strip off the automatic reel. I held the rod high over my head at an angle and walked with him through the shallows until he started to weaken and I could back him into the cattails at the head of the pool. I couldn't manage the rod and the net at the same time because of my cast, and Buddy came up under him slowly with his net, the sandy bottom clouding as the dorsal and tail fins broke the water, and then he was heavy and thick and dripping inside the net, his brown-and-gold colour and red spots wet with moonlight.

We cooked the fish with lemons, onions and butter sauce, and it was warm and fine inside the cabin with the heat from the wood stove and the smell of burning pine chunks and the wind blowing through the trees on the creek. But I couldn't eat or even finish my coffee. Paret, you wrecker of dreams, I thought. How did you do it?

*

During the week I helped Buddy's father feed the birds and clean the cages in the aviary. We finished the fence line down to the slough, and much against all my instincts and previous experiences with nutrias in Louisiana, I went with him and Buddy up Lost Horse Creek to release two pairs of males and females. At the time I rationalized that it would be two or three years before the damage was felt on a large scale in the area, and I would be safely gone when a mob of commercial trappers, typpo loggers and fishermen tore the Riordan home apart board and nail.

I resolved in a vague way to leave Beth alone, but like an alcoholic who goes through one day dry and has to count all the others on the calendar, I knew it was just a matter of which day I would call her or suggest to Buddy that we drive into Missoula.

As it turned out, it was neither. I drove to town on Thursday morning with Melvin to check in with my parole officer, though my appointment wasn't until the following week. He dropped me off by the university library, since I told him that I had three hours to waste before I saw my PO, and then I walked the four blocks to Beth's house.

She was scraping leaves into huge piles in her front yard with a cane rake. She wore a pair of faded corduroy jeans and a wool shirt buttoned at the throat and rolled over her elbows. Each time she scraped the rake and flattened it across the dry grass, more leaves blew in cold eddies off the piles.

'Do you want to go eat lunch at that German restaurant?' I said.

She turned around, surprised, then stood erect with both of her hands folded on the rake handle. She blew her hair away from the corner of her mouth, her cheeks spotted with colour in the coldness of the shade, and smiled in a way that made me go weak inside.

'Let me put on another shirt and get the leaves and twigs out of my hair,' she said.

We went in her car to the Heidelhaus, which inside was like a fine German place in the Black Forest, with big wooden beams on the ceiling, check-cloth tables, candles melted in wine bottles, and a large stone fireplace over which was skewered a roasting pig. We drank Tuborg on tap and ate sausage-and-melted-cheese sandwiches, and then the waitress, in a Tyrolian dress, served us slices of the roasted pork in hot mustard. It was so pleasant inside, with the warmth of the fireplace, the buttered-rum drinks after dinner, the college kids in varsity sweaters at the bar, and the candlelight on her happy face, that the threats of the sheriff and my other problems lapsed away in a kind of autumnal euphoria. Her eyes were bright with the alcohol, and when her knee brushed mine under the table, we both felt the same recognition and expectation about the rest of the afternoon.

We went back to her house and made love in her bed upstairs for almost two hours. I heard the screen slam downstairs and jerked upward involuntarily, but she simply smiled and put her finger to my lips and opened the bedroom door slightly to tell the boys to play outside. She walked back to the bed, her body soft and white and her huge breasts almost like a memory from my prison fantasies. Then she sat on me and bit my lip softly, her hair covering my face, and I felt it rise again deep inside her until my loins were burning, and the weak light outside seemed to gather and fade from my vision in her rhythmic breathing against my cheek.

That Saturday I had my cast cut off at the hospital. The electric saw hummed along the cast and shaled off the plaster, and then the whole thing cracked free like a foul and corroded shell and exposed my puckered, hairless white arm. The skin felt dead and rubbery when I touched it, as though it wasn't a part of me, and when I closed my fist, the muscle in the forearm swelled like an obscene piece of whale fat. But it felt good to have two arms again. While I put on my shirt and buttoned it easily with two hands, I recalled something I had thought about when I was in the hospital in Japan after I had been hit: that everybody who thinks war is an interesting national excursion should give up the use of an arm, an eye or a leg for one day.

I practised chord configurations on the guitar for three days to bring back the coordination in my left hand. I had lost the calluses on my fingertips, and the strings burned the skin on the first day and raised tiny water blisters close to the nails, and the back of my hand wouldn't work properly when I ran an E chord up the neck in 'Steel Guitar Rag'. But by Tuesday I could feel the resilience and confidence back in my fingers, the easy slides and runs over the frets, and the natural movements I made without thinking.

It was twilight, and I was alone in the cabin, slightly drunk on a half-pint of Jim Beam and my own music and its memory of the rural South. The glow from the wood stove was warm against my back, and I could feel the chords in the guitar go through the sound box into my chest. A freight-train whistle blew coldly between the mountains, and though I couldn't see that train, I knew that it was covered with the last red light of the dying sun and in the cab there was an engineer named Daddy Claxton, highballing for Dixie like the Georgia Mail.

I put my thumb picks on and played every railroad song I knew, double picking like A. P. Carter and Mother Maybelle, moving on with Hank Snow, running from Lynchburg to Danville on the Ole 97, the tortoise shell picks flashing over the silver strings, the rumble and scream of mile-long legendary trains as real in that moment as when they ran with overheated fireboxes and sweating Negro coal shovellers and engineers who would give their lives just to make up lost time.

Buddy never understood why I made my living as a country musician when I probably could have worked steady with hotel dance bands in New Orleans or tried the jazz scene on the West Coast, where I might have made it at least as a rhythm guitarist. But what he didn't understand, and what most northerners don't, is that rural southern music is an attitude, a withdrawal into myths and an early agrarian dream about the promise of the new republic. And regardless of its vague quality, its false sense of romance, its restructuring of the reality of our history, it is nevertheless as true to a young boy in southern Louisiana listening to the Grand Ole Opry or the Louisiana Hayride on Saturday night as his grandfather's story, which the grandfather had heard from *his* father, about the Federals burning the courthouse in New Iberia and pulling the bonnets off white women and carrying them on their bayonets. It was true because the boy had been told it was, and he would have no more questioned the veracity of the story than he would have the fact of his birth.

I was deep into my southern reverie and the last inch of Jim Beam when Buddy walked through the door, his eyes watery with the wind.

'I heard you across the field. It sounds very good, young Zeno,' he said. 'For a minute, I thought I heard that coloured blues player on Camp A. What was his name?'

'Guitar-git-it-and-go Welch.'

'Man, he was shit on that twelve-string, wasn't he? What the hell were you doing with Beth at the Heidelhaus?'

I poured the rest of the Beam in my tin cup and picked up my cigarette from the edge of the table. The stove was hot against my back, and I felt a drop of perspiration slip down from my hairline.

'You want a drink?' I said.

'No, man. I want to know what you were doing with my old lady.'

'Having lunch. What the hell do you normally do in a restaurant?'

'What other kind of lunch did you have?'

'All right on that shit, Buddy.'

'You just happened to bop on down to the university library with Mel and take Beth out and not mention it for a week.'

'I saw my PO and had four hours to kill before I met Melvin. I didn't want to hang around town and get picked up by the sheriff again, and I didn't feel like sitting in the library any more with a bunch of college students. So I asked her to go out for lunch.'

I had done a number of things over the years that were wrong, but lying was not one of them, even in prison, and I don't know if this was because of my father's deep feeling for truth and the habit it established in me or if I had found that the truth is the best pragmatic solution for any complex situation. But I had lied to Buddy and the words burned in my cheeks. I lifted the cup and took a sip out of it, then puffed off the cigarette.

'So why don't you tell somebody about it?' he said. 'I ain't going to cut out your balls in the middle of the night.'

'I thought it wasn't a big deal.'

'Well, it ain't, Zeno. It ain't. Just drop some words on your old partner so I don't feel like a dumb asshole when Mel sends this kind of news across the mashed potatoes. I mean, that cat is all right, but my mother is serving the steak around, and he says, 'Was Beth's car still working all right when she took Iry down to the Heidelhaus?'

He took my cigarette out of my fingers and drew in on the stub.

'What was I supposed to say, Zeno?' he said. 'My sister had gloat in her eyes, and the old man took out his pocket watch like he'd never seen it before. Say, no shit, man, you ain't balling her, are you?'

'No.'

'You want to get high? I got some real good Mexican stuff today.'

'I'd better go to bed early. I want to go up to Bonner tomorrow and see if I can get back on with the band.'

I took the guitar strap off my neck and laid the sound box face down across my thighs. I pulled the picks off my fingers and dropped them in my shirt pocket.

'Come on and get loaded,' he said.

'I better look good tomorrow.'

'That's on the square? You haven't been milking through your partner's fence?'

'I already told you, Buddy.'

I wrapped the Gibson in a blanket and went to sleep on my bunk, leaving him to a large kitchen matchbox of green Mexican weed and all the paranoid nightmares he could get out of it.

Friday night I was playing lead guitar again on the platform at the Milltown Union Bar, Café and Laundromat. The barstools and the tables were filled with mill workers and loggers and their masculine women, and at nine o'clock I attached the microphone pickup to my sound hole and opened up with Hank's 'Lost Highway', a lament about a deck of cards, a jug of wine and a woman's lies. Their faces were quiet in the red-and-purple neon glow off the bar, and by the time I slipped into 'The Wild Side of Life', they were mine. Then I did a song about gyppo loggers written by our drummer ('the jimmy roaring, the big wheels rolling, the dirt and bark a-flying'), and I could see the words burn with private meaning, with affirmation of their impoverished lives, into all those work-creased faces.

It was good to be working again, to hear the applause, to sit at the bar between sets in a primitive aura and receive the free drinks and the callused handshakes. We played until two in the morning, turning our speakers higher and higher against the noise on the dance floor, the rattle of bottles, and the occasional violent scrape of chairs when a fight broke out. My voice was hoarse, my left arm throbbed, and my fingertips felt like they had been touched with acid, but that was all right. I was playing with that sense of control and quietness inside that came to me only when I was at my best. After everyone had left, I had a bowl of chilli and a cup of coffee at the bar with the drummer, both of us light-headed with alcohol, exhaustion, and the electric echoes of the last five hours. Then I walked out into a sleeting rain and drove the Plymouth back towards Missoula and Beth's house.

TEN

During the night the sleet and wind whipped the trees against the second-storey bedroom window, and when the dawn began to grow into the sky, the grass was thick with small hailstones, and the paths looked like they had been powdered with rock candy. I drove back to the ranch as the sun broke coldly over the edge of the Bitterroots, and I saw the snow in the pines high up in the mountains and the drift of white, shimmering light when the wind blew through the trunks. I should have left Beth's house earlier, but in the warmth of her bed and with her woman's heat against me and the wet rake of the maple at the window, I drifted back into sleep until the room was suddenly grey with the false dawn. Now, I worried about Buddy and the lie I would have to tell him if he was awake.

But he was asleep, face down in the bed with his clothes and shoes on, his arms spread out beside him, a dead joint stuck like a flag in a beer can on the floor. It was cold inside the cabin, and I fired the wood stove, fanned the draught until the kindling caught and snapped into the hunks of split pine, and started to undress on the edge of my bunk. Through the side window I could see the snow clouds above the mountaintops turning violet over the dark sheen of the trees. My body was thick with fatigue, and I could still hear the noise of the bar and the electronic amplifiers as though the few hours' interlude with Beth hadn't been there. Then, as I lay back on the pillow with my arm over my eyes and started to sink into the growing warmth of the wood stove and the lessening of my heartbeat, I heard Mr Riordan's boots on the porch and his quiet knock on the screen.

He said he needed one of us to go up Lost Horse Creek with him to turn loose some more nutrias, so I got in the pickup, and we headed down the highway with the wire cages bouncing in the bed. I looked around through the window at the red eyes of the nutrias and their yellow buck teeth and porcupine hair and had to laugh.

'You must find them a great source of humour,' he said. His red-check wool shirt was buttoned at the collar and wrists under his sheep-lined jacket.

'I'm sorry,' I said, still laughing. 'But I can't get over these things being introduced deliberately into an area. One time my father and I had to spend a week cleaning out the irrigation ditches in our rice field after these guys had gone to work.'

'They're that bad, are they?' he said, his face on the road.

'No, sir, they're worse.' I laughed again. It was too ridiculous.

'If these prove that they can acclimatize to the environment and be of commercial value, the beaver in the Northwest might be with us a few more years.'

He was a serious man not given to levity about his work, and I now felt awkward and a bit stupid in not having seen as much. He drove with his forearms against the steering wheel and tried to roll a cigarette between his fingers while the tobacco spilled out of both ends of the paper.

'You want a tailor-made?' I said.

'Thank you.' He crumpled the paper and tobacco grains in his palm and dropped them out of the wind vane. I had a notion that he could have rolled that cigarette into a tube as slick as spit if he had wanted, but he was a gentleman and had just erased that moment of righteousness that had led to my discomfort.

We turned on to the rock road that wound along Lost Horse Creek and started up the long gradient through the timber in second gear. As we veered on the corner of the switchbacks and the creek dropped farther below us like a cold blue flash through the tree trunks, I felt the air begin to thin, and the smell of the pines grew heavy in my head. On up the road I could see the first mountain start to crest, and then others rose higher and bluer behind it until they disappeared in the wet mist and the torn edges of snow clouds. We turned up another switchback, and again I looked down below at the creek. It was small and flecked with white water, and the remaining leaves on the cottonwoods looked like pieces of stamped Byzantine bronze. Rocks spilled off the edge of the road and dropped a hundred feet before they struck a treetop.

'We'll pick up the creek again farther on. The height doesn't bother you, does it?'

Hell no, I always light one cigarette off another like this, I thought.

'I just wonder what you might do if you blow out a tyre on one of these turns,' I said.

'We probably just wouldn't have to worry about putting the nutrias in a beaver pond today.'

The grade evened off, and the road began to straighten with thick pines on each side of it, and then I saw the creek again, this time no more than fifty yards away through the front window, a white roar of water breaking in a shower between smooth grey rocks that were as big as small houses. Mr Riordan pulled the pickup off the road at an angle into the pines and rolled a cigarette between his thumb and forefinger, licked it, seamed it down, twisted both ends, clicked a match on his thumbnail, and had it smoking in less than a minute, and there weren't three grains of tobacco on his flat palm. He opened the door and laid his sheep-lined jacket on the seat. His bib overalls and buttoned-down, red-check shirt made me think of a southern farmer. We could hear a logging truck up the road as it shifted into low gear for the slow descent down the grade.

'Are you courting Buddy's wife?' he said, the cigarette wet in the corner of his mouth.

I got out the passenger's door and walked around to the tailgate and pulled loose the chain hook. The nutrias had been frightened by the ride over the rock road and the rattle of the chain, and they started to chew against the wire cages with their yellow teeth.

He leaned with one stiff arm against the truck bed and held the cigarette between his thick fingers as he looked away at the fallen trees across the creek.

'Are you courting his wife?' he said. 'Which means, are you sleeping with her?'

'Yes, I am.'

'Have you thought about what he'll do if he decides to stop looking in the other direction?'

'I haven't got that far yet.'

'Because frankly I don't know what he'll do. I just know I don't want my boy back in prison again. I think you can understand that.'

'He's not the type to do what you're thinking about,' I said.

'You're pretty damn sure of that, are you? Let me tell you a lesson, son. The man who kills you will be the one at your throat before you ever expect it.'

The wind felt cold on my neck. The thought of Buddy as a murderous enemy seemed as incongruous and awful as a daytime nightmare.

'I won't try to explain any of it to you,' I said, 'but sometimes things just happen of their own accord and it's not easy to revise them.'

'I didn't ask you for an apology. I just want you to think about consequences. For everybody.'

'Is that why we took this ride?'

'No. I figure you already knew what I had to say. And it's probably not going to make any difference anyway.'

'You want me to pull out?'

'You're his guest. That's between you and him. I don't hold anything against you. Beth marked him off a long time ago, but he hasn't come to accept that yet. I'd just hoped that with some time he could come to see things as they are. He's not up to having another big hole dug for him.'

'Maybe he's tougher than you think.'

'It doesn't take "tough" to go to jail and do all five years because you can't stay out of trouble.'

'I don't think you know what kind of special feeling the hacks had for him in there. He was different. He didn't take them seriously, and that bothered them right down in their scrotums.'

'That's blather. Buddy was looking for that jail for years, but there's no point in arguing about it. Let's get these cages down to the pond.' He rubbed out the fire on his cigarette between his fingers and scattered the tobacco in the wind.

We heard the gears of the log truck wind down on the switchback, the air brakes hissing. Then the cab bent around the edge of the mountain with the huge flatbed behind it, and the great snow-covered ponderosa trunks boomed down with chains that cut whitely into the bark. The driver was bent over the wheel, his arm and shoulder working on the gear stick as the weight shifted on the bed; then the brakes hissed again, and he slowed to a stop where the gradient evened off. He pulled off his leather gloves and picked up a cigar stub from the dashboard.

'Hey, Riordan,' he said. 'You turning more of them rats loose?'

'What the hell does it look like?'

'Goddamn if they ain't beautiful,' the driver said, and laughed with his cigar in his teeth. 'I guess if one of them tops a beaver, we'll see animals running around with yellow teeth and porcupine quills growing out their asshole.'

'You're probably late with your load, Carl,' Mr Riordan said.

'Don't worry about that. I want to see you put them things in the creek. Do you have to club them in the head first and carry them down on the end of a shovel?' The driver giggled from the truck window with the cigar stub in the centre of his teeth.

'You have a hot dinner waiting for you at home, Carl. Don't make your wife throw it out in the backyard again.'

'You want me to help you with them things, in case they start biting your tyres all to pieces?' the driver said.

'Tell him to get fucked,' I said.

Mr Riordan looked at me with a sharp, brief expression, then picked up the two sawn-off broom handles that we used to put through the cages and carry them to the stream.

'Better put them in here, because the creek is dryer than a popcorn fart higher up,' the driver said. 'In fact, I seen a couple of them rats walking up the road carrying a canteen.'

Mr Riordan pushed the broom handles through the first cage, and we lifted it out of the pickup bed and carried it down the incline towards the beaver pond. The truck driver was still giggling behind us; then we heard him turn over his engine and shift into gear. We walked over the pine needles through the short trees, the nutrias tumbling over one another in the cage and gnawing with their buck teeth on the wood handles.

'Why do you take it off them?' I said.

'He's a harmless man. He means nothing by it.'

'I don't know how you define son of a bitch around here, but it seems to me that you have an awful lot of them.'

'They're afraid.'

'Of what, for God's sake?'

'The people who control their livelihood. All the eastern money that gives them a job and tells them at the same time that they're working for themselves and some pioneer independent spirit. They tried to organize unions here during the depression, and they got locked out until they begged to work. So they think that any change is trouble, and they've told themselves that for so long now that they've come to believe it.'

'You have more tolerance than I do.'

'I imagine that you made the same type of realizations in growing up in the South, or you would have left it a long time ago,' he said.

He set his end of the cage down by the edge of the pond and began to roll a cigarette, his grey eyes focused intently on the quiet swell of water around the pile of dead and polished cottonwoods and pines that had been cut through at the base of the trunks by beavers until they toppled into the centre of the creek. The wood had turned bone white from sun and rot, and tree worms had left their intricate designs in the smooth surface after the bark had cracked and shaled away in the current. On each side of the pile, two feet under the current, were burrowed openings where the beavers could enter and then surface into a dry, sheltered domed fortress. Behind the dam, where the gnawed stumps of the cottonwoods protruded from the water and formed a swift eddy against the surface, cutthroat trout, brookies and Dolly Vardens balanced themselves against the pebble bottom, drifting sideways momentarily when food floated downstream towards them, their colour a flash of ivory-tipped fins and gold and gills roaring with fire.

I unhooked the cage door and tilted the cage upwards into the pond. At first the nutrias clung to the wire mesh with their strange, webbed feet; then they clattered over one another and splashed into the water, their pelts beaded with light. They turned in circles, their red eyes like hot bbs, then swam towards the log pile.

'I don't think the beavers are going to like these guys,' I said.

'Then one of them will move,' Mr Riordan said.

I looked at him to see if there was a second meaning there. If there was, it didn't show in the rigid profile and the lead-grey eyes that were still focused intently on the pond.

'You see those grouse tracks on the other side?' he said. 'There haven't been grouse up this creek since I was a boy. Two years ago I turned some blues loose about fifty yards from here, and they still water at this hole.'

He dropped the cigarette stub from his fingers into the shallows, as though it were an afterthought, and we got back in the pickup and started down the gradient in second gear. Through the pines bordering the road I could see the blue immensity of the valley and the metallic sheen of the Bitterroot River winding through the cottonwoods.

'I'll buy you a steak at the Fort Owen Inn,' he said.

'You don't owe me anything.'

'You better take advantage of it. I don't do this often. Besides, I'll show you the place where the Montana vigilantes hanged old Whiskey Bill Graves.'

'I'll bet some of the locals put a monument up there.'

He cleared his throat and laughed. 'How did you know?'

'I just guessed,' I said.

It was Saturday afternoon, and the Inn was full of families from Stevensville and Corvallis and Hamilton. They sat around the check-cloth tables like pieces of scrubbed beef, stuffed in their ill-fitting clothes and chewing on celery and radishes out of the salad bowl. A few of the men nodded at Mr Riordan when we walked in, but I had the feeling that we were about as welcome there as cow flop. He slipped his sheep-lined jacket on the back of the chair and ordered two whiskies with draught chasers.

'Are you sure you want to eat here?' I said.

'Why shouldn't we?'

I saw the same type of deliberate non-recognition in his face that I used to see in my father's when he refused to accept the most obvious human situation.

'It was just an observation,' I said.

He drank the whiskey neat, his lead-grey eyes blinking only once when he swallowed. He sipped off the top of the beer and set the mug evenly on the tablecloth.

'You don't care for Jim Beam?' he said.

'I have to work tonight. Musicians can get away with almost anything except showing up high.'

His eyes went past me, into the faces of the people at the other tables; then he looked back at me again.

'You have to use that kind of caution in your work, do you?' he said.

I drank out of the beer.

'I have a habit of falling into the whole jug when I get started on bourbon,' I said. I smiled with my excuse, but he wasn't really talking to me any more.

He took his package of string-cut tobacco out of his pocket and creased a cigarette paper between his thumb and forefinger. His nails were broken back to the cuticle and purple with carpenter's bruises. But even while the tobacco was filling and shaling off the dented paper, before he wadded it all up and dropped it out of his palm into the ashtray, I already saw the dark change of mood, the vulnerable piece in his stoic armour, the brass wheels of disciplined empathy shearing against one another. At all those other tables he was at best a tolerable eccentric (since it was a Saturday afternoon family crowd that would make allowances).

'You want to drink at the bar?' I said.

'That's a good idea.'

We walked between the tables into the small bar that adjoined the dining room, and Mr Riordan told the waitress to serve our steaks in there.

'How are you, Frank?' the bartender said. I recognized him as one of the volunteer firemen who had come to the ranch when the barn burned.

'Pretty good, Slim. Give this man here a beer, and I'll take a Beam with water on the side.'

The bartender set a double-shot glass on the counter and continued to pour to the top.

'Just one,' Mr Riordan said.

'I like to give away other people's whiskey.' The bartender glanced sideways at the empty stools and into the dining room. 'Did you hear anything about who might have had that petrol can?'

'No.'

'There were some guys drunk in here the other night talking about lighting a fire to somebody's ass.'

Mr Riordan rolled the whiskey back against his throat and swallowed once, deeply, the grey eyes momentarily bright.

'Who were they?' he said.

'I think one of them drives a tractor-trailer out of Lolo.'

'Slim, why in the hell would a truck driver want to burn me out?'

'I don't know. I just told you what I heard them saying.'

'And you don't know this man's name.'

'Like I said, maybe I've seen him pulling out of Lolo a couple of times. I thought I might be of some help to you.'

Mr Riordan clicked his fingernail on the lip of the glass.

'Well, next time call me here while they're here, or ask them to leave their name and address.'

The bartender's lips were a tight line while he poured into the glass. He set the bottle down, lit a cigarette, and walked to the rounded end of the bar and leaned against it, with one foot on a beer case and his back to us. Then he squeezed his cigarette in an ashtray and took off his apron.

'I'm going on my break now,' he said. 'Pour what you want out of the bottle, and add it on to your dinner bill.' I could see the colour in his neck as he went through the doorway.

I shook my head and laughed.

'Buddy told me you had a private sense of humour,' Mr Riordan said.

'I can't get over the number of people around here who always have a fire storm inside themselves,' I said.

'Oh, Slim's not a bad fellow. Actually, his problem is his wife. Her face would make a train turn left on a dirt road.' He was into his third shot, and the blood was starting to show in his unshaved cheeks. 'One time he came in on a tear from the firemen's picnic, and she sewed his bed sheet down with a sail needle and wore him out with a quirt. He got baptized at the Baptist church the next Sunday.'

When he grinned, his teeth looked purple in the light from the neon beer sign above the bar.

'Do you believe what he said about that man in Lolo?' I said.

'No. But it's not important, anyway.'

'It's pretty damn important when they're setting fire to your home and your animals.'

It was rash, and I hated my impetuosity even before I saw his face fix mine in the mirror behind the bar. The skin was tight against the bone, the eyes even, his red-check wool shirt buttoned like a twisted rose under his neck.

'I think I know who they are,' he said, his voice low and intense. 'I don't know if I could put them in the penitentiary, but I could probably do things to them myself that would make them never want to destroy a fine horse again. But that won't stop others like them, and it won't change the minds of those people in the dining room, either.'

The waitress brought our steaks, thick and swimming in blood and gravy, a piece of butter on the charcoaled centre, surrounded with boiled carrots and Idaho potatoes. The meat was so tender and good that the steak knife clicked against the plate as soon as you cut into it.

Mr Riordan finished his bourbon, then began to cut at the steak, his back rigid and his elbows at an angle. The steak slipped sideways on the plate and knocked potatoes and gravy all over the bar.

'Well,' he said, and picked up the bartender's towel. He had a good edge on, and I could feel him deciding something inside himself. He pushed the plate away with his fingertips, rolled a cigarette slowly, and poured again from the bottle of Jim Beam. 'Go ahead and eat. Remind me in the future to stay away from morning whiskey.'

It was colder when we walked outside, and the snow clouds had covered the sun. The wind bit into my face and made my eyes water. A few early mallard ducks were winnowing low over the cottonwoods on the river. Mr Riordan walked across the gravel to the truck as though the earth was about to shift on its axis. He took the keys out of his overalls pocket and paused at the driver's door.

'I think you probably want to drive a truck again,' he said, and put the keys in my hand.

As we rolled along the blacktop towards the ranch, he looked steadily ahead through the windscreen, his shoulder sometimes slipping momentarily against the door. He started to roll another cigarette, then gave it up.

'What do you plan to do in the future?' he said, because he felt that he had to say something.

'Finish my parole. Take it easy and cool and slide with it, I guess.'

'You probably have about thirty or forty years ahead of you. Do you think about that?' The movement of the truck made his head nod, and he blinked and widened his eyes.

'I've never got around to it.'

'You should. You don't believe you'll be fifty or sixty. Or even middle-aged. But you will.'

I looked over at him, but his eyes were focused on the blacktop. His large, worn hands lay on his thighs like skillets. The back of his left hand was burned with a thick white scar, hairless and slick as a piece of rubber. He cleared his throat, blinked again, and then his eyes faded and closed. He breathed as though he were short of breath.

Buddy had told me about his old man riding for five bucks a show on the Northwestern rodeo circuit during the depression. In 1934 he couldn't make the mortgage payments for seven months on an eight-hundred-acre spread outside Billings, and a farm corporation out of Chicago bought it up at twenty dollars an acre. They knocked the two-storey wood home flat with an earth grader, bulldozed it up in a broken pile of boards, burned it and pushed it in a steaming heap into the Yellowstone River. Mr Riordan pulled his children and wife around in a homemade tin trailer on the back of a Ford pickup through Wyoming, Utah and California, working lettuce, topping carrots and onions, and picking apples at three cents a crate.

He took a job in Idaho on a horse farm by the Clearwater, breaking and training Appaloosas for a man who provided rough stock on the rodeo circuit. In a year and a half of stinting, eating welfare potatoes and listening to the wind crack off the mountain and blow through the newspaper plugged in the trailer's sides, he put away four hundred dollars in the People's Bank of Missoula. It all went down on the ranch in the Bitterroots. He had no idea of how he could make the first mortgage payment. But nevertheless it went down, and he pulled the tin trailer up to the house, stomped down the chicken-wire fence with his boot, let the kids out of the trailer door into a yard full of pigweed and cow flop, and said: 'This is it. We're going to do it right here.'

He stayed two days at the house and then left Mrs Riordan to clean, scrub and boil an entire ranch to cleanliness while he followed the circuit through Oregon and Washington and Alberta. He worked as a pickup man and hazer, then rode bulls and broncs for prize money. In Portland he drew a sorrel that had a reputation as an easy rocker, but when the sorrel came out of the chute, he slammed sideways into the gate and then started sunfishing. Mr Riordan stayed on for six seconds, and then he was twisted sideways on the horse's back with his left hand wound in the leather. The pickup men couldn't get the bucking strap off. The leather pinched Mr Riordan's hand into a shrivelled monkey's paw, and the bones snapped apart like twigs.

His rodeo career ended six months later at Calgary. He had won forty dollars that afternoon in the calf roping and had enough money for his trip back to Montana and the entry fee in another event. So that night under the lights he entered the bulldogging competition and drew a mucus-eyed, blood-flecked black bull with alabaster horns that had already taken out two riders and ground a clown into a board fence. The rope dropped, and Mr Riordan bent low over the quarter horse and raced even with the bull towards the far end of the arena, the judge's clock ticking inside him with his own heartbeat and the blood rushing in his head as he leaned out of the saddle, waiting for that right second to come down on the horns with both hands, the weight perfectly balanced, the thighs already flexed like iron for the sudden brake against the earth and the violent twist of the bull's neck against his chest. But he misjudged his distance and pushed the quarter horse too hard. When he left the saddle, one arm went out over the bull's face, the other hand grabbed a horn as though he wanted to do a gymnastic press-up, and his body folded into the horns just as the bull sat on all four legs and brought his head up. He was impaled through the lung in a way that could be equalled only by a medieval executioner. The blood roared from his nose and mouth while he was twisted and whipped like a rag doll on the boss of the horns and the pickup men and clowns tried to pull him free. The bull dipped once, knocking him into the sawdust and horseshit, then trampled over him in a shower of torn sod.

Buddy said he should have been dead three times during his first week in the hospital, and the surgeon who cut out part of his lung told Mrs Riordan that even if he lived, he would probably be an invalid the rest of his life. But four months later he got off the train in Missoula (thirty pounds lighter and as pale as milk, Mrs Riordan said) with a walking stick, a tan western suit on, a gold watch in his jacket, and an eight-hundred-dollar cashier's cheque from the Rodeo Cowboys' Association. While he was on the circuit through all those dusty shitkicker depression towns, he had put his money together with a rider named Casey Tibbs, who at that time saw the profit to be made in buying rough stock and trained horses for Hollywood films.

I had the heater on in the truck as we bounced along the corrugated road towards the main house, where I planned to let Mr Riordan off, but the cold seemed to gather and swell in all the plastic and metal of the cab, and even the windscreen looked blue against the cold sky. The grass along the irrigation ditch was dry and stiff in the wind, or a momentary sear brown when a gust out of the canyon blew it flat against the ground. Flurries of snow were starting to whirl out of the grey sun and click in broken crystals against the glass. It was a good day for pine logs burning and snapping and bursting into resinous flames in a stone hearth, with mulled buttered rum in flagons and tin plates full of venison stew and French bread.

'It's early this year,' Mr Riordan said.

'Sir?' I said, because I had thought he was still asleep.

'It's early for snow.' His eyes were squinted at the canyon behind his house. 'The deer will be down early this year. As soon as a snow pack forms on that first rise, they'll move down to feed along the drainage just the other side of my fence. The grouse move down about the same time.' He straightened himself in the seat and opened the window slightly to let the wind blow into his face. 'Where are you going?'

'To your house.'

'Let yourself off at the cabin and I'll take the truck home.'

'I can walk across the field.'

'Son, just do what I tell you. Besides, Buddy is probably wondering where we've been.' His breath was heavy with whiskey.

I backed the truck around in the centre of the road and drove back to the Y fork that divided off towards Buddy's cabin. I could see Buddy on the front porch in a red wool shirt and a pair of corduroys with a white coffee cup in his hand.

'I don't guess there's a need to take up our conversation with him, is there?' Mr Riordan said.

I didn't want to answer him or even acknowledge his presumption. But he was still drunk, his grey eyes staring as flatly at me as though he were looking down a rifle barrel.

'No, sir, I don't guess there is,' I said.

I got out of the truck, and he slipped behind the wheel, clanked the transmission into first with the clutch partially depressed, the gears shearing into one another like broken Coke bottles, then popped the pedal loose and bounced forward across the field towards his house. I heard him shift into second, and the transmission whined as though there was a file caught in it.

Buddy walked towards me off the porch with his cup of coffee in his hand. His face was pinched in the wind.

'What happened to the old man?' he said.

'He got the sun in his eyes.'

'I don't believe it. The old man really drunk? He don't get drunk.'

'He had some bad stuff working in him back there in the restaurant.'

'What?'

'He wants to believe in his friends.'

'What are you talking about, man?'

'All those shit-hog people who call themselves neighbours.'

'You smell like you put your head in the jug, too.'

'Tell me how you live around these bastards. They treat your old man like sheep-dip.'

'What set you off?'

We closed the cabin door behind us, and I felt the sudden warmth of the room in my face and hands.

'I really don't understand it,' I said. 'Your father's a decent man, and he puts up with a gyppo logger giggling on a cigar like a gargoyle, and these guys in the restaurant acted like somebody held up a bed pan to their nostrils when we walked in.'

'Are you sure you weren't into my blotter when you left here this morning?'

I pulled off my coat and took a beer out of the icebox. Two elk steaks covered with mushrooms and slices of onion were simmering in the skillet on the stove.

'Man, you're a righteous son of a bitch today,' Buddy said.

'You're genuinely pissed because people can act as bad here as where you come from. And remember, Zeno, that's where redneck and stump-jumper was first patented.'

'You're wrong there, podna. I didn't grow up around a bunch of thugs that would beat the hell out of you or burn you out because they didn't like you. They might sniff at you a little bit, but you have your own variety of sons of bitches here.'

I picked up the guitar and put the strap around my neck. I tuned the big E down and did a run from Lightning Hopkins' 'Mojo Hand'. Buddy took a cigarette out of my shirt pocket and lit it. I could feel him looking down at me. He flicked the paper match at the stove.

'Are you playing tonight?' he said quietly.

'Yeah, at nine.'

'Are you looking for company?'

'Come along. It's the same old gig. A bunch of Saturday-night drunks from the mill getting loaded enough to forget what their wives look like.'

'You've really got some strong shit in your blood today, babe,' he said. 'I'm going to walk down and fish the river for a couple of hours. Move the skillet to the edge of the fire in about thirty minutes.'

I nodded at him and began tuning my treble strings with the plectrum. I heard him open the back door and pause as the wind blew coldly against my back.

'You want to come along?' he asked.

'Go ahead. I better sleep this afternoon,' I said.

I had another beer and played the guitar in my sullen mood while the sky outside became greyer with the snow clouds that rolled slowly over the peaks of the Bitterroots. But even in my strange depression, which must have been brought on by lack of sleep and early morning booze, I felt a tranquillity and freedom in Buddy's absence, the way one would after his wife had left him temporarily.

Still, it was a dark day, and no matter how much I played on the guitar, I couldn't get rid of that heavy feeling in my breast. Normally, I could work out anything on the frets and the tinny shine of sound from my plectrum against the strings, but the blues wouldn't work for me (because you have to be a Negro or a dying Jimmie Rodgers to play them right, I thought). And I still couldn't get my song 'The Lost Get-Back Boogie' into place, and I wondered even more deeply about everything that I was doing. I was betraying a friend, living among people who were as foreign to me as if I had been born in another dimension, and constantly scraping through the junk pile of my past, which had as much meaning as my father's farm after Ace surveyed it into lots and covered it with cement. And I was thirty-one now, playing in the same beer joints for fifteen dollars a night, justifying what I did in a romantic abstraction about the music of the rural South.

The reality of that music was otherwise. The most cynical kind of exploitation of poverty, social decay, ignorance of medicine, cultural paranoia, racial hatred and, finally, hick stupidity were all involved in it. And the irony was that those who best served this vulgar, cynical world often in turn became its victims. I remembered when Hank Williams died at age twenty-nine, rejected by the Opry, his alcoholic life a nightmare. They put his body on the stage of the Montgomery city auditorium, and somebody sang 'The Great Speckled Bird' while thousands of people slobbered into their handkerchiefs.

I put the guitar down and moved the skillet of elk steaks to the edge of the fire, then lay down on my bunk with my arm across my eyes. For a few minutes I heard the wind outside and the scrape of the pines against the cabin roof, and then I dropped down into the warmth of the blanket and the grey afternoon inside my head.

I dreamed I was in Korea again. It was hot, and three of us were sitting in the shade of a burnt-out tank with our shirts off, drinking warm beer out of cans that I had punched open with my bayonet. The twisted cloth straps of the bandoliers crisscrossed over my chest were dark with perspiration, and the metal side of the tank scorched my back every time I leaned against it. A couple of miles out from the beach, in the Sea of Japan, a British destroyer was throwing it into two MIGs that banked up high into the burning sky each time they made a strafing pass. I hadn't seen Communist planes this far south before, except Bedcheck Charlie in his Piper Cub when he used to drop potato mashers on us, and it was fun to be a spectator, in the shade of the tank, with a lazy cigarette in my mouth and a wet can of beer between my thighs. The sea was flat and slate green, and the tracers from the pom-poms streaked away infinitely into the vast blueness of the sky. Then suddenly one of the MIGs burst apart in an explosion of yellow flame and flying metal that spun dizzily in trails of smoke towards the water.

The man next to me, Vern Benbow, an ex-ballplayer from the Texas bush, belched and held up his beer can in a toast. There were grains of sand in his damp hair, and his pale-blue, hillbilly eyes were red around the edges.

'May you find peace, motherfucker,' he said.

Then the scene changed. It was night, and Vern and I were in a wet hole fifteen yards behind our concertina wire, and the dark outline of a ridge loomed up into a darker sky that was occasionally violated with the falling haloes of pistol flares. I was shaking with the malaria that I had picked up in the Philippines, and I thought I could hear mosquitoes buzzing inside my head. Every time a flare ripped upward into the blackness and popped into its ghostly phosphorescence, I felt another series of chills crawl like worms through every blood vein in my body.

'I think I got it figured out why they blow those goddamn bugles,' Vern said. 'They're dumb. That's why they're here. Nobody in his right mind would fight for a piece of shit like this.'

My rifle was leaned against the side of the hole with a tin can over the end of the barrel. I tried to straighten the poncho under me to keep the water from seeping along my spine.

'What the hell do we want that hill for?' Vern said. 'Let the gooks have it. They deserve it. They can sit up there and play their bugles with their assholes. You couldn't grow weeds here if you wanted to.'

His young face and the anxiety in it about tomorrow and the barrage that came in every day at exactly three o'clock was lighted momentarily by the pale glow of a descending flare. He took his package of Red Man chewing tobacco out of his pocket, filled his fingers with the loose strands, and put them in his mouth along with the slick lump that was already in his jaw. Out in the darkness, we saw the sergeant walking along the line of holes with his Thompson held in one hand.

'I guess I'll go out tonight,' Vern said.

'You went out last night,' I said.

'You pulled mine two days ago. Besides, your teeth are clicking.'

I raised myself on one elbow, unbuttoned my shirt pocket, and took out the pair of red dice that I had carried with me since the Philippines.

'Snake eyes or boxcars?' I said.

'Texas people is always high rollers. Even you coonasses ought to know that.'

I rattled the dice once in my hand and threw them on the edge of his muddy blanket.

'Little Joe. You son of a buck,' he said. He put his pot on, picked up his rifle, slipped a bandolier over his shoulder and lifted himself out of the hole. His back and seat were caked with mud.

That was the last time I saw him. He and fifteen others were caught halfway up the hill between two machine-gun emplacements that the Chinese had established on our side of Heart Break Ridge during the night.

I heard the screen door slam on the edge of my dream and Buddy pulling off his heavy jacket. His hair was powdered with wet snow, and his trousers were damp up to the thighs from the brush along the riverbank. He rubbed his hands on his red cheeks.

'It's too damn cold to fish,' he said. 'I had one brown on and almost froze my hand when I stuck it in the water.'

'Where's the brown?'

'Very clever,' he said.

'It was just a question, since I was trying to sleep and you came in like Gangbusters.'

'Go back to sleep, then. I'm going to eat.' He unlaced the leather string on one boot and kicked it towards the wall. 'You want some elk?'

'Go ahead. I'm not hungry.'

'You're not anything these days, Zeno.'

'What am I supposed to do with that, Buddy?'

'Not a goddamn thing.'

'You want to just say it? If it's on your mind, if it's in some real bad place?'

'I don't have nothing to say. I didn't mean to piss you off because I woke you up. Or maybe you're just pissed in general about something that don't have anything to do with you and me.'

I sat up on the bunk and lit a cigarette. Outside, the snow was swirling in small flakes into the wet pines next to the cabin. The clouds had moved down low on the mountains until the timberline had disappeared. I wanted to push him into it, some final verbal recognition between the two of us about what I was doing with Beth and to him, my friend, so I wouldn't have to keep contending with that dark feeling of deceit and betrayal that caught like a nail in my throat every time I looked at him. But I couldn't push it over the edge, and he wouldn't accept it either. I blinked into the cigarette smoke and took another deep puff, as though there was something philosophical in smoking a cigarette.

'I got pretty drunk last night, and it didn't help to get half loaded again this morning,' I said. 'I think I ought to hang up my drinking act for a while.'

'When you do that, Zeno, the Salvation Army is going to pass out free booze on Bourbon Street.'

'I believe that would be a commendable way to celebrate my sobriety.'

'Man, you are a clever son of a bitch. You sound like you went to one of those coloured business colleges. You remember that psychotic preacher back in A that used to start hollering when the captain clanged the bell for evening count? His eyes were always busting out of his head after he'd been drinking julep in the cane all day, and he'd scream out all this stuff about standing up before Jesus that he'd memorized from one of those Baptist pamphlets, but he could never get all the words right. He'd stand there in the sun, still shouting, until the captain led him into the dormitory by the arm.'

In a moment Buddy had been back into our common prison experience, which I didn't care to relive any more, and I suddenly realized that maybe this was the only thing we shared: an abnormal period in our lives, since neither of us was a criminal by nature, that contained nothing but degradation, hopelessness, mindless cruelty (newborn kittens flushed down the commodes by the hacks), suicides bailing off the top tier, a shank in the spleen on the way to the dining hall, or the unbearable sexual heat that made your life a misery. I just didn't feel any more humour in it, but Buddy's face was flushed with laughter and anticipation of my own. I drew in on my cigarette and blew out the smoke without looking at him.

'What's all that noise out there?' I said.

'What noise?' he said, his face coming back to composure.

'It sounds like a fox got into somebody's hen house.'

He stood up from the kitchen chair and looked through the front window. He held the curtain in his hand a moment and then dropped it, almost flinging it at the window glass.

'What's the old man doing?' he said. 'He must have lost his mind.' He sat on the chair and pulled his wet boots back on without lacing them.

I looked out of the window and saw Mr Riordan walking off balance through the rows of birdcages in the aviary, the snow swirling softly around him in a dim halo. He had a canvas birdfeed sack looped over one shoulder, and he was pulling back the tarps on the cages, unlatching the wire doors, and slinging seed on the ground.

'I'll go with you,' I said.

'I'll take care of it.'

'I was the one that got him drunk.'

'Nobody gets the old man drunk, Zeno.'

We walked hurriedly across the wet, cold field to the main house. Mrs Riordan and Buddy's sister had come out on the front porch and were standing silently by the rail with the wind in their faces. I could see a bottle of whiskey on top of one of the cages.

Birds were everywhere, like chickens all over a roost when an egg-sucking dog gets inside: ruffed grouse, Canadian geese, green-head mallards, ground owls, gulls, bobwhites, ring-necked pheasants, an eagle, egrets, pintails, blue herons and two turkey buzzards. Most of them seemed as though they didn't know what to do, but then a mallard hen took off, circled once overhead, and winnowed towards the river. Buddy started latching the doors on the birds that hadn't yet jumped out after the seed.

'Frank, what in the hell are you doing?' Buddy said.

Mr Riordan's back was to us, his shoulders bent, as he sowed the seed from side to side like a farmer walking a fallow field.

'Don't let any more of them out,' Buddy said. 'It'll take us a week to get them back.'

Mr Riordan turned and saw us for the first time. The bill of his fur cap was pulled low over his eyes.

'Hello, boys. What are you doing here?' he said.

'Let's go inside,' Buddy said, and slipped the heavy sack of feed off his father's shoulder. The pupils in Mr Riordan's eyes had contracted until there was nothing left but a frosted greyness that seemed to look through us.

He walked with us towards the porch, then as an afterthought picked up the bottle of whiskey by the neck. I thought he was going to drink from it, but I should have known better. He was not the type of man who would be seen drinking straight out of a bottle, particularly when drunk, in front of his family.

'Put it away for today, Frank,' Buddy said.

'Go get us three cups and the coffeepot that's on the stove,' he said.

'I don't think that's good,' Buddy said.

He looked at Buddy from under the bill of his cap. There was no command in his expression, not even a hint of older authority, just the grey flatness of those eyes and maybe somewhere behind them a question mark.

'All right,' Buddy said. 'But those birds are going to be spread all over the Bitterroot by tonight.'

He went inside with his mother and sister and a moment later came back with three cups hooked on his fingers and the metal coffeepot with a napkin wrapped around the handle.

We sat on the steps and leaned against the wood railing, with the snow blowing under the eave into our faces, and drank coffee and whiskey for a half hour. Occasionally, I heard movement inside the house, and when I would turn, I would see the disappearing face of Mrs Riordan or Pearl in the window. The snow was starting to fall more heavily now, with the wind blowing from behind us out of Idaho, and I watched the mountains on the far side of the valley gradually disappear in the white haze, then the striped cottonwoods along the river, and finally our cabin across the field.

Mr Riordan was talking about his grandfather, who had owned half of a mine and the camp that went with it at Confederate Gulch during the 1870s.

'He was a part-time preacher, and he wouldn't allow a saloon or a racetrack in town unless they contributed to his church,' he said. 'He used to say there was nothing the devil hated worse than to have his own money used against him. Once, two of Henry Plummer's old gang tried to hoorah the main street when they were drunk. He locked them in a stone powder house for two days and wouldn't give them anything to drink but castor oil and busthead Indian whiskey. Then he made them wash in the creek, and took them home and fed them and gave them jobs in his mine.'

'It's starting to come in heavy, Frank,' Buddy said. 'We better get the birds back in and the tarps on.'

Mr Riordan poured the whiskey and coffee out of his cup into the saucer to cool it.

'You should take Iry to a couple of the places around here,' he said. 'There's a whole city called Granite up eight thousand feet on the mountain outside of Philipsburg. Miners were making twelve-dollars-a-day wage, seven days a week, in the 1880s. They had an opry house, a union hall, a two-storey hospital, one street filled with saloons and floozy houses, and the day the vein played out you couldn't count ten people in that town. They left their food in plates right on the table.'

He was enjoying his recounting of Montana history to me, not so much for its quality of strangeness and fascination to an outsider, but because it was a very great part of the sequence that he still saw in time.

'I told you about where they hanged Whiskey Bill Graves,' he said, rolling a cigarette out of his string tobacco, 'but before they got to him, they bounced Frank Parrish and four others off a beam in Virginia City. You can still see the rope burns on the rafter today. When they hoisted Parrish up on the ladder with the rope around his neck and asked him for his last words, he hollered out, "Hurray for Jefferson Davis! Let her rip, boys!" and he jumped right into eternity.'

'I'm going to get the canvas gloves,' Buddy said.

'What?' Mr Riordan said.

'Those damn birds.'

Buddy went inside again, knocking the heavy wooden door shut when it wouldn't close easily the first time. Mr Riordan smoked his rolled cigarette down to a thin stub between his fingers, his elbows propped on his knees, his face looking out into the blowing snow that covered the whole ranch. The bib of his overalls had come unbuttoned and hung down on his stomach like a miniature and incongruous apron. I felt sorry for him, but I didn't know why.

'I guess we'd better go inside,' I said.

'Yes, that's probably right,' he answered.

By that time Buddy had come out on the porch with the thick, canvas elbow-length gloves for handling the birds. Mr Riordan started to rise, then had to grab the banister for support. I put one hand under his arm, as innocuously as I could, and helped him turn towards the door. The whiskey and blood drained out of his face from the exertion. His weight tipped sideways away from my hand. He breathed deeply, with a phlegmy tick in his throat.

'I believe I'm going to have to leave it with you, boys,' he said.

Buddy and I walked him upstairs to bed, then went outside and set about trying to put three dozen confused birds back in their cages. After an hour of chasing them in a whir of wings and cacophony of noise, we still hadn't caught half of them.

'Shit on it,' Buddy said. There were two blood-flecked welts on one cheek. 'The ducks won't go any farther than the slough, and the rest of these assholes will put themselves back in when they're ready.'

I went inside the house with him to return the canvas gloves. His sister sat by the burning fireplace with a magazine folded back in her hands. When Buddy walked into the back of the house and left us alone, I could feel her resentment, like an aura around her, in the silence. I stood in the centre of the room with an unlit cigarette in my mouth, the melted snow dripping out of my hair.

'You really leave your mark when you stay at somebody's place, don't you?' she said, without looking up.

'How's that?' I said. I really didn't want an exchange with her, but it looked like it was inevitable, and I was damned if I was going to lose to someone's idle attempt at insult.

'Oh, I think we both know that you have a way of letting everybody know you're around.'

'Yeah, I guess I led your father into a bottle of whiskey, and I got Buddy those five years in the joint. They must be pretty susceptible to what a part-time guitar picker can do to them.'

Her curly head looked up from the magazine, the light from the fireplace bright on the sunburned ends of her hair.

'You are a bastard, aren't you?'

'A genuine southern badass.'

'It must be nice to have that awareness about yourself,' she said.

No more tilting, babe, because you're an amateur, I thought. I had got to her, but I should have known then that she was going to pull out that arrow point later and give it back to me, in a form that I wouldn't recognize until it was too late.

Buddy and I walked back to the cabin in the grey light. Most of the afternoon was gone, and there wasn't enough time to take a nap before I would have to get ready to work that night. I hadn't realized how tired I was. The lack of sleep from last night, unloading the nutrias with Mr Riordan, an hour of fighting birds that pecked and defecated all over you, and two excursions into drinking in one day all came down on me like a wooden club on the back of the neck.

I got into the tin shower and turned on the hot water, and just as I was thinking of a way to coast through the evening (no booze on the bandstand, long breaks between sets, letting the steel man do the lead and the drummer most of the vocals) until I could be back at Beth's after we closed, Buddy decided that everyone should go to Milltown with me. The water drummed against the tin sides of the shower, and I tried to think of some reasonable way to dissuade him, but I knew that Beth was in the centre of his mind, and there was nothing I could say that wouldn't sound like a door kicked shut in his face.

So while I dressed, he went back to the main house and talked to Melvin, who needed little encouragement for any kind of adventure, and half an hour later they were sitting in the front room of the cabin with a bottle of vodka that Melvin had been working on through the afternoon. Pearl evidently had argued about going, because Buddy and her husband kept making reassuring remarks to her in the way obtuse or drunk people would to a child. Actually, I couldn't believe it. Neither one of them saw how angry she was or how much she disliked herself for being in any proximity to me.

Then Buddy went one better. While I was wrapping the guitar in a blanket, he took a blotter of acid out of the icebox and convinced Melvin to eat some of it. Pearl looked out the window like an angry piece of stone.

'Take a hit, Iry,' Melvin said.

'I've got too many snakes in my head already.'

'Zeno has to do his Buck Owens progressions tonight,' Buddy said.

'Why don't you join them?' Pearl said, her face still turned towards the window.

'I'm afraid I can't handle it.'

'It's all them big slides on the guitar neck,' Buddy said. 'There's three chords in every one of those shitkicker songs, and Zeno has to stay sharp.'

Buddy's voice had a mean edge to it, and I knew that no matter what I did, we were headed into a bad one.

I drove the Plymouth to Missoula while Buddy sat beside me, giggling and passing the quart bottle of vodka to Melvin in the backseat. The wind was blowing strong off the river, and the melted snow on the highway had glazed in long, slick patches. The Plymouth's tyres were bald, and every time I hit ice, I had to shift into second and slow gradually, holding my breath, because the brakes would have sent us spinning sideways off the shoulder.

We stopped at Beth's house, and Buddy banged on the door as though there were a fire inside. The porch light went on, and I could see Beth in silhouette and the children behind her. I felt awful. I wished I could tell her in some way that this wasn't my plan, wasn't something that was born out of a day's drinking and dropped on her doorstep to contend with. But I knew that I wouldn't get to talk with her alone during the evening, and there would be no visit at her house after the bar closed, and she would be trapped four or five hours at a soiled table while Buddy and Melvin got deeper and deeper into a liquor-soaked, acid delirium.

We drove along the Clark through Hellgate Canyon to the bar, with the snow blowing out of the dark pines into the headlights. There was no easy way to coast through the evening. The building was already crowded when we got there, the steel man had cut off one of his fingers with a chain saw that afternoon, and the drummer, who I thought could take the vocal, had four opened beers sitting in a row on the rail next to his traps.

I got up on the platform, slipped the guitar strap around my neck, and tripped the purple and orange lights with my foot. In the glare of light against my eyes I saw Buddy walk with his arm around Beth's shoulders to a table by the edge of the dance floor. I put on my thumb pick, screwed the guitar into D, and kicked it off with 'Poison Love'. I didn't have a mandolin to back me up, and my fingers still felt stiff from the cold outside, but Johnny and Jack or Bill and Charlie Monroe never did it better. Then I rolled into Moon Mulligan's 'Ragged but Right' and knocked out four others in a row with no pause except for the bridge into the next key. The Cellophane-covered lights were hot against my face, and my eyes were starting to water in the drifting clouds of cigarette smoke. The dance floor and the tables were lost somewhere behind the rail of the platform and the violent glitter and rattle of bottles and glasses. I felt the sweat roll down off my face and hit on my hand, and when I went into the last song, I heard the drummer miss a beat and clatter a stick against the metal edge of the trap.

'Hey, man, save some for later,' he said.

After the set I went to the table, which was now wet with spilled beer and scorched with cigarettes that Buddy had mashed out on the cloth. Beth's face was almost white.

'Give me the keys,' he said.

'What for?' I said.

'Because they're my keys. And because it's my goddamn car, and that's my goddamn wife. You understand that's my wife, don't you?'

Everyone looked momentarily into the centre of the table.

'Don't go driving anywhere now, man,' I said.

'I ain't. And you didn't answer my question.'

'Take the keys. Get into the stock-car derby if you like,' I said.

'Just answer me. Without all that southern bullshit you put out.'

'I got to get back on the bandstand.'

'No, man, you answer something straight for the first time in your fucking insignificant life.'

'He just wants the keys to get in the boot,' Melvin said. 'He bought a couple of lids from some university kids.'

'They're right there,' I said. I rose from the chair and started back towards the platform. Out of the corner of my eye I saw Beth lean forward and place her forehead against her fingertips.

I couldn't get between two tables because a fat man had fallen over backward like a beer barrel in his chair. Up on the stand, the drummer was draining the last foam from a bottle, and our bass man was slipping his velvet glove back on his hand. I felt Melvin's arm on my shoulder and his sour liquid breath along the side of my cheek.

'Take a walk with me into the head,' he said.

I followed him inside the yellow glare of the men's room and leaned against the stall with him.

'Look, he just ate too much acid, and maybe we ought to get out of here early tonight,' he said.

I looked at him, with his tailored attempt at some romantic western ethic, and wondered if his rebellion was against a mother or father who owned a candy factory in Connecticut.

'I work here,' I said. 'If I leave, I don't get paid. Also, I probably get fired. What happened at the table with Beth?'

'What do you mean?' He looked at the garish colour of the wall in front of him, as though he had seen it for the first time.

'She looked sick.'

'Buddy was trying to feel her up under the table.'

'Man, I don't believe it,' I said.

'That's what I said. We should leave early tonight.'

I left him leaning over the trough and went back to the platform just as the rhythm guitarist was starting to fake his way through 'Folsom Prison Blues' by humping the microphone and roaring it out with enough amplification to blow the front windows into the parking lot.

I cut it short at one-thirty in the morning, and normally there would have been a protest from the crowd. But the temperature was dropping steadily, and the little plastic radio behind the bar said that a storm that had already torn through Calgary and southern Alberta would hit the Missoula area tomorrow.

The bar emptied out while we put away our instruments on the bandstand, and after I tripped off the purple and orange lights with my foot, I could see Buddy at the table with his arms folded under his head. Melvin was leaning back in the chair, his tie pulled loose and a dead cigarette in his grinning mouth, his arms hooked back over the chair's supports like a man who had been crucified by comical accident.

There were no keys to the Plymouth. No one was sure what happened to them. Buddy possibly broke one off in the boot and lost the other one while wandering around in the snow after all his reefer blew away in the wind. I said good-night to Harold, the owner, took a glass of Jim Beam with me, and while Melvin, Buddy and Pearl slept in a pile in the backseat, Beth held the flashlight for me under the dashboard, and I used a piece of chewing tobacco tinfoil to wrap together the wires behind the ignition.

She sat close to me in the drive back to Missoula, with her hand inside my coat, and each time the draught would come up through the floor board, she would press her thigh against mine and hold a little tighter with her arm. I forgot about Buddy in the backseat and what he would think later. I just wanted to be with her again upstairs in her house with the tree raking against the window. She knew it, too, as we came through the Hellgate into Missoula, with the water starting to freeze into white plates on the edge of the Clark. She leaned her breasts into my arm and kissed me with her tongue against my neck, and I knew everything was going to be all right when I came around the last curve on the mountain into Missoula.

The sheriff's car pulled out even with the Plymouth from the gravel turnaround, the bubble-gum light revolving in a lazy blue-and-orange arc. His souped-up V-8 motor gunned once when he went past us on a slick stretch of ice. He braked to the side of the road and got out with a flashlight in his hand, the collar of his mackinaw turned up into the brim of his Stetson to protect his ears. He walked back to the Plymouth against the wind, as though his own weight was more than he could bear, and opened the door with the flashlight in my face.

'Don't kick over that glass trying to hide it with your foot, son,' he said. 'You don't want to spill whiskey all over the car. Now what's those wires doing hanging under the dashboard with tinfoil around them?'

I took a cigarette from the pack inside my coat and tried to pop a damp kitchen match on my thumbnail, but it broke across my finger. He clicked off the light and pulled back the door a little wider for me to get out.

'Sometimes you get caught by the short hairs, Paret. You ought to look out for that,' he said.

ELEVEN

Fifteen days. I thought I would get out of it with a fine when I went to guilty court the next day, but the sheriff put in a few words for me with the judge to make sure that would not be the case. (He mentioned, as a casual aside, that I was an out-of-state parolee.)

They put me in a whitewashed eight-man cell on the second floor with the usual collection of county prisoners: habitual drunks, petty cheque writers, drifters, bar-room brawlers and hapless souls in for non-support. There was no window in the cell, the white walls were an insult on the eyes, and we got out only one hour a day for showers. It was going to be a long fifteen days.

I was angry with myself for getting busted on a punk charge like driving with an open container, but I realized that the particular charge didn't make any difference. That fat cop was going to nail me one way or another; it was just a choice of time and place.

Buddy came to see me during the visiting hours that afternoon. I didn't want to talk with him after the scene in the bar, and in fact I wasn't in the mood to talk with anyone. The men in that crowded cell were generally a luckless and pathetic lot, but nevertheless each of their movements (their knee bends and press-ups) and attempts at conversation to relieve their boredom were irritating, eye-crossing reminders of all the wasted nights and days and the impaired, lost people I had known in Angola.

The hack unlocked the cell door and took me downstairs to the visitors' room by the arm.

'You want some cigarettes from the machine while we're down?' he said.

I gave him some change from my pocket and sat on one side of the long board table across from Buddy. There were still grains of ice on his mackinaw, which hung on the back of his chair. His face was white with hangover, and his hand with the cigarette shook slightly on top of his folded arm.

'You have thunder in your eyes, Zeno,' he said.

'Room service was bad today.'

'I'm sorry, man. That's a bad deal. I thought they'd just lighten your wallet a little bit.'

'It could have been worse. They might have tried for drunk driving.'

He paused and looked away.

'You want a butt?' he said.

'The screw's bringing me a pack.'

'Hey, man, I didn't mean to go over the edge last night.' His eyes came back into mine.

'Everybody was drunk. That stuff's always comedy, anyway.'

'You want the guitar? The jailer said you can have it up there.'

'I better not. A couple of those characters would probably try to screw it,' I said.

'Look, I feel like a piece of shit about it.'

'Forget it. I'm going to take up yoga.'

'No, I mean getting it on about Beth.'

The guard put the package of Lucky Strikes in front of me, and I peeled away the Cellophane from the top.

'I wouldn't have brought it out like that unless my head was soaking in acid and booze. Shit, I know I can't make up back time with her. What you do is between you and her, Zeno.'

I felt my face flush, and I didn't want to look at his self-abasement.

'I haven't been thinking about any of that,' I said.

'Man, I can read you. I know what you're going to think before a spark even flashes across that guilt-ridden spot in the centre of your brain. You're going to tango out of here after your fifteen days, move out of the cabin, and start being a family man in Missoula with some bullshit guilt about old friends hung on your shirt like a Purple Heart.'

'You've got it figured a lot better than I do, then,' I said.

'Because I know you.'

'You don't know diddly-squat, Buddy. The only thing I've got in mind is living two weeks upstairs with some question about what my parole officer is going to do with this. After that scene at the pulp mill, this could be the nut that violates me back to Angola.'

'Yeah,' he said, quietly mumbling, with the backs of his fingers against his mouth. 'I hadn't thought about that. That geek would probably do it, too. I didn't tell you I went to high school with him. He has the IQ of a moth, a real pocket-pool artist. He would probably put you in the toilet just to close the file on you.'

Buddy had a fine way of making you feel better about the future.

'Maybe we can bring a little pressure to bear,' he said, his eyes still introspective. 'My sister says he hangs around with a bunch of faggots in East Missoula.'

'I'd appreciate it if you wouldn't do these things for me.' I

634

could see the colour coming back into Buddy's face as his fantasy became more intense and the memory of last night and his discomfort in front of me started to fade into an ordinary day that he could live with.

'We always have alternatives, Zeno,' he said. 'You can't sit on a bunk all that time and worry about Louisiana and moving your baggage around and all this marital crap.'

I heard the hack light a cigar behind me and scrape his chair. Buddy looked past my shoulder, then put his pack of cigarettes on the table with four books of matches.

'I better roll, babe,' he said. 'I'll bring some candy bars and magazines tomorrow.'

'You don't have to do that.'

'Become popular with your bunkies. But look, man, the cabin's yours when you get out. None of this moving into town because you think you got to do something. Besides, the old man wants you to stay there.'

'When did he say this?'

'This morning.' He answered me in a matter-of-fact way, then looked at me with a new attention. 'Why?'

'I just wondered. I thought I might have burned my welcome.' But it didn't work.

His eyes studied mine for even the hint of some private relationship between his father and me, and I was probably not good in concealing it.

'Keep the butts and the matches,' he said. 'You never did learn how to split them, did you?'

He put on his mackinaw and walked down the hall towards the front door of the courthouse, that square of brilliant natural light with the snow blowing behind it, and the trees along the street hung with ice, rattling and clicking in the wind, and the people in overcoats and scarfs, their shoes squeaking on the pavements while they walked towards homes and fireplaces and families. I put Buddy's cigarettes, along with my own and the books of matches, into my denim shirt pocket and waited for the hack to put his hand around my arm for the walk upstairs.

The days passed slowly in the cell, with the endless card games and meaningless conversation and the constant hiss of the radiator. Beth visited me every afternoon, and I almost asked her to stop coming, because I wanted her so badly each time after she left. At night I lay on the bunk and tried not to think of being in bed with her, but when I drifted into sleep, my sexual heat embraced wild erotic dreams that made my loins ache for release. Then I would awake, my mattress damp with sweat, draw up my knees before me like an adolescent child suddenly beset with puberty, and debate the morality of masturbation.

I didn't think it was going to be so hard to pull fifteen days. But after nine days I would have volunteered to pull thirty on a road gang to get away from my seven cell mates, their explosions into the toilet, their latent homosexuality (which they disguised as grab-assing), and finally a definite hum that was beginning in the centre of my brain.

I noticed it at the end of the first week when I was sitting on my bunk, with my back against the wall, and staring at nothing in particular. Then I saw a plastic Benzedrex inhaler on the concrete floor, and the hum started like a tuning fork beginning to vibrate. It was like that dream you have as a child when you pick up something small and inconsequential off the ground, and suddenly it grows in your hand until it covers the whole earth, and you know you are into a nightmare that seems to have no origin.

Somebody in the cell had got hold of some inhalers and was chewing the cotton rings from inside, which was good for a high that would knock the head off King Kong. But for some reason my glance on that split-open plastic tube brought back all the listless hours in my cell at Angola and all the visions I had there about madness in myself and madness all over the world. My mother had killed herself and my sister Fran in the house fire, even though my father always pretended that it was an accident, and as I grew up, I always wondered if she had left some terrible seed in me. But in Korea I believed truly for the first time that I was all right, because I realized that insanity was not a matter of individual illness; it was abroad in all men, and its definition was a very relative matter. I even took a perverse pride in the fact that I *knew* the lieutenant was lying when he said we couldn't take six gook prisoners back to the rear and we had to blow them all over a ditch. Four members of the patrol did it and enjoyed it, but they never admitted later that it was anything but necessary.

Even my father had the same strange dualism about war and people at their worst in the middle of an inferno, and their failure to recognize it later for what it was. He went all the way across France in the Great War, as he called it, a seventeen-year-old Marine who would be hit twice and gassed once before his next birthday. But he refused to talk about it in even the most vague or general way. I often wondered what awful thing he carried back with him from France, something that must have lain inside him like a piece of rusted barbed wire.

But he was working on an oil job at Texas City when it blew up in 1947 and killed over five hundred people, many of them roughnecks whom he had known for years. A ship carrying fertilizer was burning out in the harbour, and while people watched from the docks and a tug tried to pull it out to the Gulf, the fire dripped into the hold and then the ship exploded in a mushroom flame that rained on to the refineries and chemical plants along the shore. The town went up almost at once – the gas storage tanks, the derricks, the entire Montsanto plant – and blew out store windows as far away as Houston. The men caught in the oilfield, where blown wellheads fired geysers of flame into the sky under thousands of pounds of pressure, were burned with heat so great that their ashes or even their scorched bones couldn't be separated from the debris.

A year later my father and I were cane fishing for bream in some tanks on a stretch of bald prairie about six miles from Texas City, and we walked around a huge, scalloped hole in the earth where a sheet of twisted boiler plate, the size of a garage door, had spun out of the sky like a stray, ugly monument to all that agony back there in the flames. The hole had filled partially with water, tadpoles hovered under the lip of the rusted metal, and salt grass had begun to grow down the eroded banks.

My father rolled a cigarette from his package of Virginia Extra and looked out towards a windmill ginning in the breeze off the Gulf.

'I lost some of the best friends I ever had in that thing, Son,' he said. 'There wasn't any reason for it, either. They could have got that fertilizer ship out of there or shut them rigs down and taken everybody out. Those boys didn't have to die.'

So the madness in war was an area that was sacrosanct, not even to be recognized, and there was no correlation between that and the death of your best friends because of corporate stupidity.

But I lost my point, with that description of the hum in my head back in Angola, that distant echo of a bugle that went even farther back to a hole in Korea. The Benzedrex inhaler had conjured up my old cell in the Block, on a languid Louisiana summer afternoon, with the humidity damp on the walls and the bars, and my cell mate W. J. Posey across from me, wiping the sweat off his naked, tattooed body with a washcloth. We were both stoned on Benzedrex and the paregoric that he had stolen from the infirmary.

'So you killed the son of a bitch,' W.J. said. 'A punk like that has it coming. You iced people in Korea that didn't do nothing to you.'

'He broke the shank off in him when he went down. He bled on the bandstand like an elephant.'

'You're breaking my knob off. You got two years. Take another drag on ole Sneaky Pete.'

I got out of jail on Tuesday. Buddy was waiting for me at the possessions desk with a crazy grin on his face.

'How did you know what time I was coming out?' I said.

'They always flush you wineheads out about ten in the morning.'

I had hoped Beth would be there, and he must have seen it in my face.

'She couldn't leave the house,' he said. 'Both of the kids swoll up with mumps yesterday.'

'Are you putting me on?' I picked up the brown envelope with my belt, shoestrings and wallet inside.

'I know you never had them, Zeno. I wouldn't put you on like that.'

Damn, I thought.

'Figure it this way,' he said. 'You could have gone over there one day earlier and had your rocks swell up like a pair of basketballs.'

The woman behind the desk looked up with her mouth open.

'Let's get out of here,' I said.

'There you go, babe. Let's boogie on down the street, because your daddy is about to get into a gig again.'

We walked outside into the cold, sunlit day, and the sharp air cut into my lungs. The green trees on the mountains were heavy with snow, and the sky was so clear and deeply blue that I thought I would become lost in it.

'Let's walk to this place,' Buddy said. 'My tyres are so bald you can see the air showing through. I didn't park the car at that angle. It slid sideways through the intersection.'

'What's this gig?'

'I thought I might clean up my act and get back in the business. A guy I know runs this college joint up in the next block, and he wants to try a piano player to bring in all those fraternity cats and their sweet young girls. Somebody with class, such as myself. Someone to keep them plugged into magic sounds so they won't bust up the place every night and puke all over his crapper.'

'That sounds good, man.'

'Well, he's not real sure about me. Thinks I'm crazy. Undependable. I might show up with a hype hanging out of my forehead. Anyway, he asked me to come down this morning and play a few because his wife will be there, and she knows music. Now dig this, man. I used to know her in high school when she was in the band, and she couldn't tell the difference between a C chord and a snare drum. She was so awful that the bandleader put the tubas in front of her to blow her back into the wall. She used to wear Oxford therapeutic shoes and these glasses that looked like they were made out of the bottoms of Coke bottles. She also had gas all the time. Every two minutes you could hear her burping through her alto sax.'

I was shaking my head and laughing.

'Zeno, you don't believe anything anybody tells you,' he said.

'Because nobody in the world ever had experiences or knew people like these.'

'All right, you'll see, partner. Just be prepared to meet humanity's answer to the goldfish.'

639

I never did know why Buddy boozed and doped. He could get high in minutes on just himself.

The bar was a beer-and-pizza place with check-cloth table covers and rows of fraternity steins on the shelves. The contraceptive machine in the men's room had long since been destroyed, and young, virile Americans had punched out big, ragged holes in the fibreboard partitions. I sat at the bar and had a sandwich and a beer while Buddy played the piano for the owner and his wife, who looked exactly as Buddy had described her. (This is why I could never tell whether he was lying, fantasizing, or telling the truth.) She stared at him a few moments with those huge orbs of colour behind her glasses, then began washing glasses in a tin sink.

I watched Buddy play. I had forgotten how really good he was. He started out with 'I Found a New Baby', and he played it the way Mel Powell used to at the Lighthouse in California: a slow, delicate, almost conventional entrance into the melody, then building, the bass growing louder, his right hand working on a fine counterpoint, and finally he was way inside himself and all the wild sounds around him. He didn't even look the same when he played. A strange physical transformation took over him, the kind you see in people who are always partly out of cadence with the rest of the world until they do the one thing that they're good at. As I looked at him, with his shoulders bent, his arms working, the eyes flat and withdrawn, I would have never made him for the Buddy I knew the rest of the time.

Later the owner bought us a beer and told Buddy to come to work the next night. He wanted to hide it, but I could see he was truly happy. He hadn't worked as a musician since he went to jail, and that was six years ago.

'Let's make it,' I said.

'One more beer. I have to ease the effect of joining the work force again. It really blows my self-image.'

'One, damn it, and that's it. I'm not getting into any more of your bloody capers.'

'Oo, oo, oo, oo,' he said, his face in a feminine pout. 'Dig who's coming on about capers. The mad fire bomber of Missoula.'

'Hey, man,' I said, hoarsely.

'Anyway, I wanted to tell you this story, since it just rolled into my gourd while I was into that 1950 Lighthouse shot. I never told you about the Legend of the Gigantic Fart, did I?'

'Put the beer in a paper bag. Let's get it on the road.'

'No, man, this story became a legend and is still told in the high schools around the county. You see, it was at the junior prom, a very big deal with hoop dresses and everybody drinking sloe gin and R.C. Cola outside in the cars. Now, this is strictly a class occasion if you live in a shitkicker town. Anyway, we'd been slopping down the beer all afternoon and eating pinto-bean salad and these greasy fried fish before we got to the dance. So it was the third number, and I took Betty Hoggenback out on the floor and was doing wonderful, tilting her back like Fred Astaire doing Ginger Rogers. Then I felt this wet fart start to grow inside me. It was like a brown rat trying to get outside. I tried to leak it off one shot at a time and keep dancing away from it, but I must have left a cloud behind that would take the varnish off the gym floor. Then one guy says, "Man, I don't believe it!" People were walking off the floor, holding their noses and saying, "Pew, who cut it?" Then the saxophone player on the bandstand threw up into the piano. Later, guys were shaking my hand and buying me drinks, and a guy on the varsity came up and said that was the greatest fart he'd ever seen. It destroyed the whole prom. The saxophone player had urp all over his summer tux, and they must have had to burn the smell out of that piano with a blowtorch.'

Buddy was laughing so hard at his own story that tears ran down his cheeks. He caught his breath, drank out of the beer glass, then started laughing again. The woman behind the bar was looking at him as though a lunatic had just walked into the normality of her life.

We drove back to the ranch, and later in the afternoon I walked up the gravel road to the general store on the blacktop and used the pay phone to call Beth. I told her that I had never had the mumps and couldn't come to the house because I didn't feel like becoming sterile; then I waited with my hand tight on the receiver during a long, heart-beating pause. She said she didn't have anyone to stay with the boys and couldn't leave them for any period of time anyway, and that was the end of that. So that meant another two weeks on the shelf, I thought, as I walked back down the road in the cold air between the rows of pine trees.

During the next week I helped Mr Riordan feed the birds in the aviary and start work on a new barn, but I couldn't go to sleep at night, even though I was physically exhausted, until I had sat at the kitchen table alone for two hours with a bottle of Jim Beam. I was back with the band on the weekend, and one night I went into town with Buddy to the pizza place and called Beth again in a beer fog, hoping that she would say, *Yes yes yes. Check into the Florence. I'll be there in a few minutes.* However, like most drunken wishes, it didn't have much to do with reality. I liked to hear Buddy play, but I couldn't sit long in the middle of that college crowd.

I don't know why they bothered me. It wasn't their loud and bullish behaviour that came after three beers, or even their curiosity about my foreign presence, which was like the appearance of a dinosaur among them. They reached down and touched something else in me that I couldn't articulate. Maybe it was just the fact that they were young and still standing on first base with all the confidence and expectation of stealing second. There was no such thing as a clock in the universe, and all of them knew that they would never die. I walked down the street to the Oxford in the light snow and sat on one of the high wooden chairs in the side room and watched the strange collection of late-night characters play cards until Buddy got off.

Monday afternoon we caught part of a storm that blew over the mountains from Idaho, and my hands got so cold hammering nails into the side of the barn that I could hardly feel the blow when I missed once and came down on my thumb. My ears felt like iron inside the hood of my coat, and when the light started to fail, I waited for Mr Riordan to stick his hammer through the loop of his overalls; but instead he kicked a bunch of scrap boards into a pile, poured petrol over it, paused long enough to relight his cigarette in his cupped hands, and dropped the match into the pile. We finished the side frame in the light of the fire, which flared into a cone of flame and then flattened into a white circle of heat each time the wind sucked under the boards.

When we got back to the cabin, Buddy took off his clothes,

dropped them on the floor, and turned the hot water on in the tin shower just long enough to bring the feeling back into his body. He stood naked by the wood stove and dried himself with a towel. His ribs drew tight against his sides each time he breathed. There was a tattoo of a pair of dice showing a six and a five inside one thigh.

'Wow, I'm tired,' he said, rubbing the towel into his face and hair. 'And I'm late, and my fingers feel like balloons, and I didn't press a shirt this morning, and I don't feel like making that gig, Zeno.'

'Do it,' I said. I sat at the table, with my wet clothes dripping on the floor and a damp cigarette in my fingers. I had poured a glass of neat whiskey, but I hadn't had the strength yet to pick it up.

'That's very cool. While I entertain these college cats, you'll be sitting home by the fire digging on some whiskey dream about southern freight trains. So I have a suggestion. Why don't you zip on my Uncle Zeno suit and try filling in for me. If you think playing for a bunch of shitkickers is a zoo scene, do a shot with the junior lettermen that ask you to play "Happy Birthday" for a chick they're going to assault in the backseat that night.'

'Go to work, Buddy.'

He went into his bedroom and came back with his suit on the hanger, his underwear, and the soiled shirt that he had worn last night. He dressed by the stove, his body thin and yellow in the light of the electric bulb overhead. I took a drink out of the whiskey, and I felt the first warmth come back into my lungs.

'Where did you get that tattoo?' I said.

'Before I got nailed, I used to live with this mulatto girl that played sometimes at Pat O'Brien's. I sat down at the piano once with her, and she thought I was her Mister Cool, the best thing since Brubeck, Monk, Mel Powell, or anybody. Except she liked shooting craps better than playing jazz. She made me take her to a couple of those upstairs games on Rampart, and she'd fade every bet on the board. When we got cleaned out, she'd bust up the apartment and call up some Baptist preacher in Mississippi and promise never to hang around white musicians again.'

'How did you get the tattoo?'

'I just told you.'

'Buddy, you are a dislodged madman. I think the hacks were right. That glue got to you a long time ago.'

'That's because you got all your wiring tuned in to another radio set,' he said. 'And speaking of that, while your highrolling daddy is about to move it down the road and do his act for the sweater girls and their Howdy Doody boyfriends, let me click on the radio so we can listen to that fine jazz station in Spokane and dig on Shorty's flügelhorn.'

Buddy turned on the radio that was set in the kitchen window, his trousers unzipped, one-half of his shirt hanging off his back. The tubes warmed in the old plastic box, the static cracked, and when the sound sharpened through the speaker, Shorty Rogers and Shelly Mann were actually playing.

Buddy put his arm through the other sleeve, as though he had been in suspension, and then began jiggling all over in rhythm to the music while he buttoned his shirt in his bare feet.

'Tell me, truthfully,' he said. 'Were you ever tempted when you were inside? I mean, to just quit fighting it and let the girl have her way?'

Without rising from the chair, I reached over and turned up the radio to full volume and finished the whiskey in my glass. A few minutes later I heard Buddy grind the starter on the Plymouth outside.

After I had showered and put on a soft wool shirt and clean pair of khakis, I saw the pickup truck stop in front of the porch. I opened the door and looked through the screen at Pearl in the blowing snow. She wore a man's mackinaw with a scarf tied around her head, and her face was red with cold.

'Tell Buddy that—'

'Come in before you turn into a snowman,' I said.

'Just tell him that Frank—'

I opened the screen for her.

'Come in if you want to talk with me. You might not mind freezing, but I do,' I said.

She stepped inside, and I closed the wooden door behind her.

'Frank'll pick him up at six-thirty in the morning to go into Hamilton for some lumber,' she said.

'Oh, he'll like that.'

'You can do it for him.'

'All right. No problem in that.' I could see she had on only a light shirt under the mackinaw, and she was shaking with the sudden warmth of the room. 'You want a cup of coffee?'

'I have to get a loaf of bread up at the store before it closes.'

I took an unopened loaf from the bread box in the cupboard and set it on the table.

'Sit down. A cup of coffee won't ruin your general feelings towards me.' I washed a cup under the iron pump and filled it from the pot on the stove.

She untied her scarf and shook her hair loose. It was wet with snow on the ends. She picked up the cup with both hands and sipped at the edge.

'Put a little iron in it,' I said, and tipped a capful of whiskey into her coffee. 'Where's Mel tonight?'

'He's at a faculty meeting.'

'Is he serious about that revolution business?'

'In his way, yes, I guess he is.'

'What do you mean "in his way"?'

'You wouldn't understand,' she said.

'I've had some experience with people who are always trying to right the world by wiping out large portions of it. They all have the same idea about sacrifices, but it's always somebody else's ass that gets burned.'

'Mel's a good man,' she said, and looked at me flatly.

'I didn't say he wasn't. I didn't say anything about him. I just asked a question.'

'He believes in idealistic things. He wasn't in a war like you, and he doesn't have your cynicism about things.'

I took a good hit out of the bottle on that one.

'You know, I think you're a crazy woman and you belong in a crazy house,' I said. 'The next time I get drafted into one of Uncle Sam's shooting capers, I'll write the draft board and tell them I'd rather opt out because I don't want to come home with any cynical feelings.'

'Let me ask you a question. Do you feel anything at all about taking from everything around you no matter what it costs other people who have nothing to do with your life?'

I walked in my socks to the stove and poured some coffee and a flash of whiskey in her cup and sat back down. She had pulled back her mackinaw, and her breasts were stiff against her shirt as she breathed. Her full thighs were tight inside her blue jeans and spread open indifferently on the corner of the chair. I had to hold the anger down in my chest, and at the same time she disturbed me sexually.

'Let me hang this one on you, Pearl, and you can do with it what you want to,' I said. 'I didn't take anything from anybody, and any problem they have isn't of my making. It was already there.'

She moved herself slightly in the chair, just enough so that her thighs widened an inch and her buttocks flattened.

'That must be a convenient way to think,' she said.

'It's better than that. It's the truth. And I don't like anyone trying to make me take somebody else's fall.'

'That must be some of your prison terminology.'

'You better believe it is. I paid my dues, and straight people don't con a con.' I felt my heart beating and my words start to run away with themselves.

'Maybe all people don't behave towards one another with a frame of reference they learned in jail.'

'Well, the next time you want to talk about people's problems, come down here again and I'll help you solve a couple of yours.'

She didn't say anything. She just buttoned up her mackinaw, tied her scarf around her damp hair with the remote manner of a lady leaving a distasteful situation, and walked out of the door to the truck. She left the door open, and the wind drove the snow into the room.

I didn't even bother to shut it for ten minutes. I felt a red anger at myself for my loss of control that left me trembling. Talk about a con not being conned, I thought. You are a fish who just got conned into thinking he was a con who could not be conned. And for somebody who thought he had touched all the bases over the years, this was no mean thing to consider.

*

The two weeks finally passed, and it was a bright, cold day with the snow banked high on the lawns of Missoula when I knocked on Beth's door. The boys were at school, and we made love on the couch, in her bed, and finally, in a last heated moment, on the floor. Her soft stomach and large, white breasts seemed to burn with her blood, and when she pressed her hands into the small of my back, I felt the fifteen days in jail and the two weeks of aching early morning hours drain away as in a dream.

Each morning I helped Mr Riordan put in the stall partitions in the barn and feed the birds in the aviary; then after lunch I hitched a ride or flagged down the bus into Missoula. Beth and I whitefished in the broken ice along the banks of the Clark, a fire of driftwood roaring in the wind with the coffeepot set among the coals. We ate bleeding steaks by the stone fireplace in the German restaurant and explored ghost towns and mining camps up logging roads and drainages where the trees rang with the tangle of ice in their limbs. I had forgotten how fine it was simply to be with someone you love.

We drove up a graded log road off Rock Creek, high up the side of the mountain, to a mining camp that had been abandoned in the 1870s. The cabins were still there along the frozen creek, where they used to mine placer gold that washed down from the mother lode, and the old sluices and rocker boxes were covered with undergrowth, the rusted square nails and bits of chain encased in ice. But if you blinked for just a minute, and let your imagination have its way, you could almost see those old-timers of a century ago bent sweatily into their futile dream of a Comstock or Alder Gulch or Tombstone. They always knew that wealth and the fulfilment of American promise was in that next shovel-load of sand.

'What are you thinking so hard about?' Beth said, her face bright with the cold wind that blew down the drainage.

'Those old-timers must have really believed in it. Can you imagine what it was like to pull the winter up here in the 1870s when they had to haul everything up the side of the mountain on mules? Before they could even go to work, they had to do something minor, like build those cabins. I bet they didn't even think about it. They just did it. And I bet you couldn't tear those logs apart with a prising bar.'

She put her hands inside my arm and pressed against my coat.

'You're a strange mixture of men,' she said.

'Well, none of that analysis crap. You see that house down there with the elk droppings by the door? Think of some veteran from Cold Harbor in there, drunk every night on whiskey just to stay warm until the next day, and not sure that an Indian wouldn't set his place afire after he passed out. Those must have been pretty formidable people.'

She pulled the bill of my fur cap and laughed and squeezed herself against my arm.

'I thought you believed Montana people were barbarians,' she said.

'Only those who burn up trucks and guitars that belong to me.'

'I guess destroying half of a parking lot at the mill doesn't count,' she said, and laughed again.

I built a fire in the snow and boiled a can of stew on a piece of tin from one of the cabins, and as the snow melted away in a widening circle from the heat, I looked over at her and wanted her again. We went into her car and made love on the backseat, with the doors open and the wind blowing snow in the sunlight and the distant sound of a gyppo logger's truck grinding up the next hill.

We went grouse-hunting up Rattlesnake Creek for blues and ruffs with an old dogleg twenty-gauge that I borrowed from Buddy's little brother, and we knocked six down in a stand of pines on the lip of a huge canyon and cooked them at her house in wine sauce, onion and wild mushrooms. The next day I bought a resident deer tag, and we drove into the Swan Valley, which was so white and blinding under the sun that you had to look at the green of the timberline to keep from losing the horizon. We crossed two hills of lodge pine in deep snow, pulling her boys' sledge in blue tracks behind us, our lungs aching in the thin air, her Enfield rifle slung by its leather strap on my shoulder.

We found a place on the edge of the trees that overlooked a long valley where they would probably cross at sunset. I took the folded tarpaulin off the sledge, spread it in the snow between the pine trunks, and set down the big coffee Thermos and ham-and-turkey sandwiches. The air was clean and sharp, with the sweet scent of the pines, and the far side of the valley seemed to grow and recede in the sunlight over the mountain. I unscrewed the Thermos top, and the steam and the smell of the coffee blew around us in the wind.

I hadn't hunted for deer, or any animal for that matter, since I was discharged from the army. At home after the war, I had shot ducks and certainly fished a lot, but I wouldn't go out with my father any more after coons or shoot deer with him in east Texas. Once, he asked me why I would take the lives of fish and knock birds out of the air with a double-barrel when I wouldn't drop an animal running across the ground. I didn't have an answer for him, because I had thought until his question that it was just a general reaction to killing things, and he said: 'You don't want to bust something living on the land because it's just like you. You know it hurts him just like it does a man.'

Regardless of my father's explanation about the lack of ethical difference in taking the lives of wild things, I wasn't up to busting a deer or an elk that might work down through that snowfield in the sun's last red rays over the mountains. Also, I had hunted enough deer at home to know that anything that came out of that distant stand of pine on the far side of the valley would be either a doe or an elk cow, because the males always kicked them out into the open before they would cross themselves.

However, Beth had no such reservations. She was a real Montana girl. While I was holding an unlit cigarette and cup of coffee in my hands and thinking about striking a match (my dead army friend from Texas, Vern Benbow, used to say that a deer can see you fart from six miles), Beth slipped the sling of the Enfield up her left arm, eased the buckle tight, pushed a shell into the chamber, and lay on the tarp in a prone position. The sun had started to dip behind the line of trees on the next ridge, and the light fell out in long bands of scarlet on the valley floor.

'You know how to use iron sights at a distance like that?' I said.

649

'Be quiet. They're coming down in a minute,' she said. The hood of her coat was back on her shoulders, and her black hair was covered with snow crystals.

'You're frightening, woman.' But she wasn't listening. She was aimed into the other side of the valley, her white hands numb with cold, those wonderful breasts as hard as ice against the ground.

I leaned back against a pine trunk and drank out of the coffee and ate a ham-and-turkey sandwich. Before the last Indian wars of the 1860s and 1870s, the Blackfoot and the Salish used to pass through this valley on their way to the Clark in their timeless migrations across their sacred earth. As I set my coffee down in the snow and felt the sandwich bread turn stiff in my jaw, I looked into that dying sunset on the snowfield and thought of how those countless people who had been here for thousands of years were decimated and removed without trace in one generation. I wondered if in spring, when the snow melted and mountain flowers burst from the wet ground, there wouldn't be some scratch on them there – a rose-quartz arrowhead, a woman's broken grinding bowl, a child's foolish carving on a stone.

My reverie was broken by the explosion of the Enfield. Two doe had started down out of the pines on the opposite side of the valley, their tracks sharp and deep behind them, and Beth had fired high and popped snow into the air off a wind-polished drift. She ejected the brass casing, slammed another shell into the chamber, and fired again. I saw her cant the rifle before she squeezed off. The deer turned in a run and headed for the far end of the valley.

'You better hold it straight and lower your sights,' I said, quietly. 'We're higher than they are, and that bullet's not dropping.'

She worked the bolt and pushed it home, pulled the rifle tight against its sling, and let off another one. The doe in the rear bucked forward on her knees as though she had been struck by an invisible hammer. She struggled in the snow, the hooves tearing long scratches and divots in the incline as she tried to get to her feet. Then she stumbled forward, with a single trail of bright red drops behind her.

'Damn, you gut-shot her,' I said. 'Bust her again.'

Beth's hands were shaking, and when she pulled the bolt, it hung halfway back, and the spent shell caught in the chamber. The doe was pumping hard for the cover of the trees, the blood flying in the wind behind her flanks. I pulled the sling of the Enfield free from Beth's arm, banged the heel of my hand against the magazine until the brass casing dislodged, shoved another shell into the chamber, and locked the bolt down. I didn't have time to use the sling or get into a prone position. I steadied the Enfield against a pine trunk, aimed the iron sights just ahead of the deer, let my breath out slowly, and squeezed off. The bark shaled off the pine from the recoil, and my right ear was momentarily wooden from the explosion. I hit the doe right behind the neck, and I knew that with the downward angle the soft-nosed bullet must have torn through her heart and lungs like a lead tennis ball.

Beth sat up on the tarpaulin and shook the snow out of her hair with her hands. She tried to find a cigarette inside her coat, but it was as though all of her pockets were sewn together. I set the rifle down and handed her my pack.

'That was a wonderful shot,' she said, but her voice was uneven with an unnatural pitch to it in the quietness.

'Where did you learn to hunt deer?' I said.

Her hands were still shaking when she lit the cigarette.

'Why?'

'Because you never take a shot from a distance like that without a telescope.'

'Should I apologize?'

'Don't be defensive about it. Hell, you know you were wrong.'

She picked up my coffee cup from the snow and drank out of it, then took a deep drag on the cigarette.

'Buddy told me you could be righteous sometimes,' she said.

'Well, shit, you let off on something that you can only hit with luck, and she wanders around for two days before she dies.'

We didn't speak for a moment, and I ejected the spent shell from the Enfield and slipped out the unused cartridges from the magazine. She looked out over the valley, where the last light was starting to glow in a rim of fire on the mountain's edge.

'You didn't want to shoot anything and you did,' she said. 'You want me to walk home with my mad money?'

I pulled the hood of her coat up on her head and tied the strings under her chin. Her cheeks were red, and there was still a brush of snow in the black hair over her eyes. I pushed her hair back with my hand and stuck one stiff finger in her ribs.

'We'd better get her on the sledge before they send the search-and-rescue in after us,' I said.

She looked away, still angry and unwilling to give up, then kicked me gently in the calf with her boot and turned her fine woman's face into mine.

The snow was already starting to freeze as we pulled the sledge across the valley floor. Our boots crunched through the surface, then sank in the soft snow underneath, so that by the time we reached the doe, we were sweating inside our clothes, and the moon had come up in a clear sky and turned the whole valley into a blue-white, tree-lined place on the top of the world that made you fear time and mortality. I gutted the deer and threw the steaming entrails on the ground, and we tied down the frozen carcass on the sledge and worked our way back up towards the dark border of pines. The sleeves of my coat were splattered with blood, my head was dizzy from the thin air and the effort of pulling the sledge up the hill behind me, but I felt a quiet exhilaration in the long day and its completion. We roped the doe on the bumper of the car and drove back out of the moon-drenched mountains of the Swan Valley towards Missoula, and as I steered down that blacktop highway with those huge, dark shapes on each side of me, I understood why men like Jim Bridger, Jediah Johnson and Jim Beckworth came here. There was simply no other place better, anywhere.

The next week Frank Riordan got his way with the state of Montana, the Anaconda Company, and in fact the whole lumber industry and anybody else who had anything to do with polluting the air. He and an environmental group got a temporary injunction from the court in Helena to shut down every pulp mill and tepee burner in western Montana. It was one of those things that nobody believed. A court decided on an abstraction that had nothing to do with economics, jobs or clean air and water. It was just a matter of law. A judge's signature went on the injunction, and suddenly the plume of smoke blowing down the Clark thinned and disappeared, and the tepee burners smouldering with sawdust crumpled slowly into ash and were covered by snow.

But other things happened, too. The workers at the plywood mill got a pink slip with their next cheque, the men who planed boards and pulled the green chain at the lumber companies were told to come around again in a month or so, the Anaconda Company was shut down at Bonner, and the gyppo loggers (the independents who owned their own tractors) had to either haul pine to a market in Idaho or Washington or go out of business.

Beth had told me once what a lumber town could be like when the mills shut down and the paycheques stopped and families had to line up at the federal food-surplus centre. Except in this case there was no working man's strike involved, no collective anger directed at management or unions, no depression to be blamed on federal bureaucrats and New York sharpers. Every unemployed man in Missoula County and the Bitterroot Valley knew there was only one reason for the deprivation of his family, his humiliation at accepting welfare and food commodities, and his daily visits to the state employment office for the chance of a casual labour job with the Forest Service: Frank Riordan.

Their mood was mean and dirty. It took on different forms that ran the gamut from an insult in the face to the failure of a neighbour to wave out of his truck cab, but it was all the same thing. I can't say that they hated him, because they didn't; it was more a matter of outrage and disbelief that one of their own kind would betray them and join forces with college people and slick lawyers to cause so much trouble in their lives.

I stopped going to the Oxford in Missoula for steak dinners after I sat at the counter and heard the loud and pointed remarks from the poker table behind me, and Eddie's Club across the street was no place to have a beer in the afternoon when there were three or four drunk men against the bar who would happily bust your head open with a pool cue. One day I walked up to the small grocery store on the blacktop for a loaf of bread and a quart of milk, and the woman behind the counter looked through me like smoky glass while she counted out each hot coin in my palm.

The irony is that my job was also affected when the mills shut down. Our band was fired at the Milltown Union Bar, Café and Laundromat. On Saturday night, the first week after the injunction came down, there was a crowd of five people in the bar, and all of them were drinking on the tab. We played loyally to them until one in the morning, which was like singing into a neon-lighted cave, and the owner paid us off, gave us free bowls of chili and a fifth of Cutty Sark, and said to come back when the mills opened.

I could do without the job financially, because I had money in the bank, but our steel man and bass player got loaded on the bottle of Scotch in their truck before they drove home. Both of them had been laid off at the sawmill in Seeley Lake, and they had been cleaning furnaces three and four days a week to make enough, along with their three nights' work at the bar, to keep from going on welfare until the mills reopened.

Now I had no job, except for my work on the ranch, and no place really to go. I lived with a man whom I had made a cuckold out of. I slept with his wife every evening I could get into Missoula, and without embarrassment he and I fished each afternoon through the ice on the Bitterroot, which was shameful in itself. On the nights I couldn't be with Beth (because of her boys or her temporary job waiting tables at the bus depot) and when Buddy went off to play at the college pizza place, I stayed alone in the cabin and drank neat whiskey and looked out of the window at the fields of snow under the moon and the glistening sides of the canyon behind the Riordan house.

I worked on my song, the one I had never finished while I was in the penitentiary. The strange thing was that I could play lead on almost any country song that I had ever heard, and I could imitate Hank Williams, Jimmie Rodgers and Woody Guthrie in a way that left a southern or Okie audience banging their tables with beer bottles when I finished. But I couldn't write a song myself. As I sat there with the three tortoiseshell picks on my fingers and the Gibson across my knee, I was reminded of an old Negro preacher who did odd jobs for my father. His son had been given five years on Sugarland Farm in Texas, and when the old man was told of the sentence, he said: 'I tried to keep him out of the juke joint. But he just like a mockingbird. He know every song but his own.'

I had most of my song, but the rest wouldn't come. Maybe that was just because when you try to catch all of something, particularly something very good, it must always elude you in part so that it retains its original magic and mystery. I remembered when my cousin André and I found an Indian canoe submerged in four feet of water back in the swamp. The canoe was made of cypress and had stayed intact for over a century. The bow and sides were etched against the silt bottom with green moss, and we slid through the water quietly so as not to cloud it, our hearts tripping inside our wet shirts. We caught the canoe by each end and tried to lift it slowly, and when it wouldn't rise, we pulled harder and our hands slipped on the moss, and the silt swelled out in a black balloon from the bottom. Then I ducked under the surface again and jerked on the bow with all my strength. It ripped away like wet newspaper in my hands. I felt heartsick, and with each of our hurried, young efforts to salvage what was left, we tore the canoe into dozens of pieces until finally he had only a pile of rotted cypress wood, like any other in the swamp, to take home in the bottom of my pirogue.

I heard a shotgun go off across the meadow, and before I could set down the guitar and walk to the window, there were three more reports and then a chain of five cracks in a row that must have come from an automatic without a plug in it. I threw open the door and the snow blew in my face, but I could see the individual flashes of the guns in the aviary, a lick of flame and sparks against the darkness of the mountain beyond. There was a pause while they must have reloaded, and then another roar of noise and streaks of fire that looked like a distant night scene from the war.

Jesus God, I thought.

I could hear the birds crying in their cages and the splatter of shot against the wire and wood sides. The only gun in the cabin had been the Springfield, which Buddy had buried, and as I stood there with my coat half on, I felt suddenly impotent to do anything about the terror that was going on in the aviary. But I went anyway, running across the dry grass that protruded through the snow, my chest beating with a fear that I hadn't felt since Heartbreak Ridge. The cold air cut like a razor in the dryness of my mouth and throat, and in my feeling of nakedness in that bare field under the moon I prayed desperately that something would happen before I got there.

All the lights were on in the house now; there was a brief silence while the shots echoed away into the canyon, then one more solitary crack, and then I saw three men in silhouette running like stick figures with their guns for their truck, which they had parked on the far side of the house. They roared off with the cab doors still open, the tyre chains ripping snow and frozen mud into the air.

I saw Pearl under the porch light, wearing only a brassière and a pair of blue jeans, with a Winchester lever-action in her hands.

'You goddamn dirty bastards!' she yelled, and at the same time let off the round in the chamber. Then she worked the action and fired one round after another at the diminishing dark outline of the truck. But she got home with one, because a moment after the explosion from the barrel I heard the bullet whang into the metal like a ball peen hammer.

When I got to the porch, she was trying to pump free a spent cartridge that was crimped in the slide. Just as it ejected and she shoved another cartridge home, a pair of headlights came down the gravel road and bounced across the cattle guard, illuminating the truck that was headed out at a good fifty miles an hour.

Pearl aimed the Winchester against the porch post, her breath steaming in the air, the white skin of her shoulder already red from the recoil of the rifle. I slapped at the barrel and knocked it at a downward angle, and her face, which had been filled with murderous intent, suddenly went blank and looked at me as a surprised girl's would have.

'That's Buddy's Plymouth,' I said.

TWELVE

The three men did a thorough job in the few minutes that they unloaded on the aviary. We could see the freezing tracks of their boots where they had walked to the fence and fired, and the empty shotgun shells that had melted with their own heat deep in the snow. They had loaded with precision to take care of everything living in the yard: their shells ranged from deer slugs and buckshot to bbs. They had laid down a pattern to kill, blind or cripple every animal and bird within thirty yards. The deer slugs and buckshot had blown the cages into splinters, and the blood dripped through the floor wire in thick, congealing drops. The birds that had only been wounded twisted on their broken wings or quivered like balls of feathers in the snow. The bald eagle had been shot right through the beak, and he lay with his great reach of wings in a tangle of wire and birdseed.

The nutrias were at the far end of the yard. None of the birdshot had got through the other cages to them, but those twelve-gauge deer slugs, which were as thick as a man's thumb, had flattened against the board side of their pen and hit them like canister. Their heads were torn away, their blue entrails hung in ropes out of their stomachs, and their large, yellow teeth were bitten into their tongues.

Mr Riordan had on only his overalls and long-sleeved underwear with the bib hanging loose in front and the straps by his sides. He had put on a pair of unlaced leather boots without socks, and the snow and water squeezed over his ankles with each step as he walked back and forth through the aviary with a terrible rage on his face.

'That's unbelievable,' Buddy said.

Mr Riordan methodically knocked one huge fist against his thigh, and I was sure at that moment that he would have torn the lives out of those three men with his bare hands. His face was livid, his throat was lined with veins, and his grey eyes were so hot in the moonlight that I didn't want to look at them. He bent over and picked up one of the wounded nutrias, and the dark drain of blood ran down his forearms before he placed it back in the shattered cage.

'Go back inside, Daddy,' Pearl said.

But he didn't hear her. There was a heat inside his brain that must have made the blood roar in his ears. His chest began to swell up and down, as though his heart were palpitating, and I heard that deep rasp and click in his throat.

'It don't do any good to stay out here now, Frank,' Buddy said.

'You don't tell your father what to do,' Mr Riordan said.

We stood in the silence and looked at him standing among the scattered bodies of the birds and the wet feathers that blew in the wind and stuck against his overalls. His grey hair was like meringue in the wash of moon that shone down over the canyon.

He coughed violently in his chest and bent forward to hawk and spit in the snow, as though he had some terrible obstruction in his throat. The vein in his temple swelled like a piece of blue cord. Then he coughed until he had to lean against one of the remaining cages for support.

'You better get him inside,' I said.

Still, Buddy and his sister and the others on the porch remained motionless.

'You better listen to me unless you want to put him in a box,' I said.

'Let him be,' Buddy said.

'You're crazy. All of you are,' I said, and walked up to Mr Riordan and put my hand under his arm. His long-sleeved underwear was wet with perspiration. He turned with me towards the house, the back of one hand against his mouth and the spittle that he couldn't control. I heard Buddy walk up quickly behind us and take him by the other arm.

We led him up the steps and into the house and laid him on the couch. When Mrs Riordan pulled off his boots, his feet were blue and covered with crystals of ice. The top button on his underwear had twisted loose, and I saw the flat, white scar where a bull's horn had gone deep into his lung. He turned his head sideways on the pillow to let the phlegm drain from his mouth, and his wife pressed a towel into his hand and moved it up so he could hold it close to his face. I heard Pearl on the telephone in the kitchen, calling a doctor in Hamilton.

Buddy wiped the water out of his father's hair with his hand, then began to brush at it with a shawl that was on the back of the couch. But Buddy's hands were trembling, and his face had gone taut and pale. He took the blankets from his mother and spread them awkwardly over Mr Riordan, then took the bottle of whiskey out of the cabinet.

'Don't give him that,' I said.

'He's cold,' Buddy said.

I took the bottle gently, and he released his fingers while he stared into my eyes with an uncomprehending expression.

'Why not?' he said.

'It's just no good for him,' I said.

I looked at Mr Riordan's ashen face, his lips that had turned the purple colour of an old woman's, and his great knuckles pinched on the top of the blankets, and wondered at how time and age and events could catch a man so suddenly.

Twenty minutes later we saw the red lights on the ambulance revolving through the fields towards us, the icy trees and snow-drifts momentarily alive with scarlet until they clicked by and disappeared behind the glare of head lamps. The doctor, who was actually an intern at St Patrick's in Missoula, and the volunteer fireman who drove the ambulance strapped Mr Riordan on to a litter and carried him gingerly outside. Buddy pulled open the back door of the ambulance, and they eased the litter up on to the bed without unbuckling the straps. The doctor turned on the oxygen bottle and slipped the elastic band of the mask behind Mr Riordan's head.

'Well, what the hell is it, doc?' Buddy said. 'He got horned in the chest once—'

'I don't know what it is. Shut the door.'

Buddy closed the door, and the ambulance turned around in a wide circle in the yard, cracking over the wood stakes on the edge of Mrs Riordan's vegetable garden, and rolled solidly down the road towards the cattle guard with the red lights swirling out over the snow.

'Why not the whiskey?' Buddy said.

'You just don't give it to somebody sometimes.'

'Don't give me that candy-ass stuff. There ain't anybody else out here now.'

'He's probably had a stroke.'

'Goddamn, I knew that's what you were going to say,' he said, and pushed his snow-filled hair back over his head.

'Take it easy, Buddy.'

The sports clothes he had worn to the pizza place were soaked through. There were bird feathers all over his trousers, and his white wool socks had fallen down over his ankles. The army surplus greatcoat he wore over his sports clothes was eaten with moth rings and hung at a silly angle on his thin shoulders. His eyes were still looking at me, but his mind was far away on something very intense.

'Come on, Zeno. Hold it together,' I said.

'They took it all the way down the road this time.'

'Yeah, but, man, you got to—'

He turned away from me and went inside, then came back out with a handful of cartridges that he spilled into the pocket of his greatcoat. He picked up the lever-action Winchester that Pearl had propped beside the door, and headed for his father's pickup truck. His shoes squeaked on the snow in the silence. I caught him by the arm and turned him to face me.

'Don't do something like this,' I said.

'I know who they are. I saw the driver's face in my headlights. I won't have any doubts when I find his truck, either, because Pearl slammed one right along his door.'

'Then call the sheriff.'

'That bastard won't do anything, no more than he did when they burned the barn. They'll just say the truck got hit while they were hunting.'

'You don't know that. Give it a chance. At least until tomorrow.'

'Let go, Iry.'

'All right,' I said. 'Just talk a minute. A minute won't make any difference.'

'Tell my mother I went to the hospital.' He started for the truck again, and I stepped in front of him.

'Look, maybe I'm the last person that should tell anyone about being rational and not going out on a banzai trip to blow somebody away,' I said. 'But, damn it, *think*.'

'That's right. You are the last person that should. Old Zeno, the shank artist of Louisiana and the fire bomber of lumber mills. The saver of horses from the flames. But he's my old man, and maybe they've punched his whole ticket.'

He started around me for the truck, his mouth in a tight line, and I stepped once more in front of him.

'I ain't going to play this game any more with you, Iry.'

His hands were set on the barrel and stock of the rifle, and his right arm and shoulder were already flexed.

'What are you going to do, bust me in the teeth? You ought to save your killer's energy for those cats you're going to blow all over a bar-room wall someplace.'

But it didn't work. He glared into my face, breathing loudly through his nose, his hair wet against his forehead.

'OK, step in your own shit,' I said.

He walked past me and got in the truck, then set the Winchester in the rack against the back glass and started the engine. He turned around and drove slowly past me with his window still down. I began to walk hurriedly along beside the truck, my legs almost comical in their attempt to keep pace with it before Buddy accelerated down the lane.

'Jesus Christ, don't do this,' I said. 'I'll go after them with you in the morning. We'll put their ass in Deer Lodge for ten years—'

He rolled up the window, and his face disappeared into an empty oval behind the frosted glass; then he hit second gear and the loose tyre chains clanked and whipped along the frozen earth.

I started to go back into the house, but I didn't belong there, and there was nothing truthful that I could say to anybody inside. I walked back across the field to the cabin and poured a glass of straight whiskey at the kitchen table and tried to think. I imagined that Mrs Riordan or Pearl or Melvin had already called the sheriff's office, but that wouldn't do any good for Buddy, as none of them knew why he had left in the truck, unless someone had noticed that the Winchester was gone, which they probably hadn't. So that left few alternatives, I thought, and sipped at the whiskey and looked at the crumbling ash in the grate of the stove. I could tell his family about it and let them make their own decisions, or I could call one of the deputies aside in front of the house (and I could already see him talking into the microphone of his car radio, with the door open and one leg sticking out in the snow, telling every cop in Ravalli County to pick up dope-smoking ex-convict Buddy Riordan, who was armed and headed down the Bitterroot highway to gun somebody). Then they could call the intern back to the house to give Mrs Riordan a tranquill-izer shot, and in the meantime there would be shitkicker dicks with shotguns behind roadblocks all the way to Missoula who would urinate with pleasure in their khakis if Buddy should try to get past them.

So you can't tell his family, and you don't drop the dime on a friend, I thought, and drank the last of the whiskey from the glass and filled it with water under the pump. And that leaves us where in this Sam Spade process of deduction? Nowhere. He's simply out there someplace on the highway, driving too fast across the ice slicks, his heart beating, the Winchester vibrating in the rack behind his head, his brain a furnace.

Then I thought, That's exactly what he's doing. He's looking at every beer joint on the way back to Missoula, pulling into the gravel parking lot and cruising slowly past the line of parked cars and trucks. Because he is con wise to criminal behaviour, and he knows that anyone, except a professional, who pulls a violent job usually does not go back directly to home and normality; he stops at what he thinks is the first safe bar to toast his aberrant victory and quiet that surge of blood in his head.

I tied the ignition wires together on the Plymouth and drove down the blacktop towards Missoula. I was guessing about the direction Buddy would have taken, as well as the three men in the pickup, but I doubted that the killing of the birds was done by anyone in the south Bitterroot, since there was only one small sawmill south of us, at Darby, which was almost to Idaho, that had been affected by the injunction. I passed the bar at Florence, which would have been too close for them to stop, and looked for

Buddy's truck in the parking lots of the two bars at Lolo. The snow was coming down more heavily now, in large, wet flakes that swirled out of my headlights and banked thickly on the windscreen wipers that shuddered and scratched across the glass. As I dropped over the hill into the outskirts of Missoula and again met the river, shining with moonlight and bordered by the dark, bare shapes of the cottonwoods, the wind came up the valley and polished the ice along the road and buffeted the Plymouth from side to side.

I pulled into every bar parking lot on the highway until I reached the centre of town. No Buddy, no ambulances, no bubble-gum lights swinging around on the tops of cop cars. Strike three, babe, I thought. So I drove over to Beth's, with the ignition wires swinging and sparking under the dash and the snow piling higher on the hood against the windscreen.

The elm and maple trees in her yard were dripping with ice, and the yellow porch light fell out in shadows along the glazed pavement. She opened the door partway in her nightgown against the draught of cold air, her mouth in an oval, beginning to smile; then her eyes focused on my face. She closed the door behind me and touched my chest with her hand.

'What happened?'

I told her, in the quietest way I could, keeping the sequence intact and lowering my voice each time I saw the brightness and sudden confusion start to come into her eyes.

'Oh God,' she said.

'He'll probably just drive around until he gets the lightning bolts out of his brain.'

'You don't know him. Not when it comes to his father and all his crazy guilt about failing him.'

'Buddy?' I looked at her with the strange feeling of an outsider who would never know the private moments of confession between them in the quiet darkness of their marital bed.

'He's not a violent man,' I said. 'Even in Angola, the big stripes let him alone. He wasn't a threat to anyone. He was just Buddy, a guy with glue fumes in his head and music in his fingers.'

But I was talking to myself now. Her eyes were looking at the blackness of the window, and she held an unlit cigarette in her lap as though she had forgotten it was there.

'I don't know what else to do, Beth.'

'Call the sheriff's office.'

'You're not thinking.'

'He told you he knew who they were. He's going to kill someone.'

'You weren't listening while I was talking,' I said.

'We'll have to use the phone next door or go to the filling station.'

'Listen a minute. That fat son of a bitch you call a sheriff would love blowing Buddy all over the inside of that truck or welding the door shut on him in Deer Lodge.'

Her eyes were blinking at the darkness beyond the window.

'I'll talk,' she said. 'I'll tell them he's drunk and he tore up my house and I want him arrested.'

'That's no good, kid.'

'Why? What do you offer as an alternative, for God's sake?'

'He won't pull over for any dicks, and it'll get real bad after that.'

She sat back in the chair and rubbed the palm of her hand against her brow. I took the cigarette out of her fingers and lit it for her.

'I can't sit here,' she said.

I wished I hadn't come. It was selfish, and now I had included her in my own impotence to do anything in an impossible situation.

'Do you have anything to drink?' I asked.

'I think it's in the cabinet.'

I found the half bottle of Old Crow and brought back two glasses. I poured into a glass and put it in her hand. She raised it once to her mouth as though she were going to drink, then set it aside on the table.

'I lied to the children for five years about their father,' she said. 'They're too old to lie to now. They're not going to go through any more because of Frank Riordan and Buddy and all their insane obsessions.'

'Mr Riordan didn't choose this.'

'He's done everything he could for twenty years to leave his stamp on everybody around him. He was never content simply to live. His children always had to know that he wasn't an ordinary man.'

'He wouldn't want Buddy out with a gun. You know that.'

'I'm sorry, but you didn't learn very much living at his place.' That fine strand of wire was starting to tremble in her voice again. 'He never thought about what would happen after he did anything. If he raised children to live in the nineteenth century, and if they ended up neurotic or in jail, it was the world's fault for not recognizing that the Riordans were not only different but right.'

'You've got him down wrong,' I said. 'His ball game is pretty well over, and I think he knows it and doesn't want grief like this for Buddy or anybody else.'

She put her fingers over her eyes, and I saw the wetness began to gleam on her cheeks.

'Don't let it run away with you,' I said. 'He might have gone to the hospital by now.' I stood up behind her and put my hands on her shoulders. They were shaking, and she kept her face averted so I couldn't see it.

It was a time not to say anything more. I rubbed the back of her neck until I felt her composure start to come back and her shoulders straighten. I picked up my whiskey glass and looked out of the window while she got up and went into the bath. Behind me I could hear the water running.

The snow was frozen in broken stars around the edge of the window glass, and the shadows of the trees swept back and forth across the banked lawn. High up on the mountain behind the university I could dimly see the red beacon for the aeroplanes, pulsating against the infinite softness of the sky.

'I'm sorry,' Beth said, behind me, her face clear now.

'Do you want your drink?'

'I'd rather go to the hospital. You don't mind, do you?'

'No.'

'It'll take me just a minute to dress.'

A few moments later she came back downstairs in a pair of corduroys and a wool shirt with a mackinaw under her arm. Her blue scarf was tied under her chin, and the flush in her face and the strands of black hair on her cheeks gave her the appearance of a young girl on her way to a nighttime ice-skating party.

I closed the door on her side of the Plymouth and put the ignition wires back together to start the engine. Her breath was steaming, and I could see her breasts rise and fall under the heavy mackinaw.

'If Buddy's not at the room, that doesn't mean he hasn't been and gone back home,' I said as I drove slowly up the street.

'The head sister will know if he's been there.'

'There's another thing to think about, too. He might just talk to the doctor downstairs and go to sleep in the truck out on the street.'

'Just drive us there, Iry.'

We didn't get past the receptionist's desk. Frank Riordan was in intensive care, no one was allowed to see him, and the only persons in his family who had been at the hospital were Melvin and Pearl, and they had gone across the street to the all-night café.

'How's he doing?' I said.

'You'll have to ask the doctor when he comes down,' the receptionist said.

'When does he come down?'

'I don't know. Are you a member of the family?'

'Where's that little Irish nun that used to work here?'

'Sir?'

'There was an Irish sister that used to work on the second floor.'

'I don't know who you mean.'

I walked outside with Beth towards the car. The snow had stopped blowing, and there was just a hint of blue light beyond the mountains in the east. The thin shale of ice over the gravel in the parking lot cracked under our feet.

'You want to go back home?' I said.

'No. Call Mrs Riordan.'

'I don't think we should do that.'

'She's not sleeping tonight. One of the boys will answer the phone, anyway.'

'Beth, let it slide for tonight.'

'A phone call isn't a lot to ask, is it?'

I put her in the Plymouth, started the engine, turned on the heater, and walked across the street to the café to use the public phone outside. My fingers were stiff with cold, and I had trouble dialling the numbers and depositing the coins for a toll call. Through the lighted window of the café I could see Melvin and Pearl drinking coffee in front of their empty plates.

Buddy's little brother, Joe, answered the phone and said that Buddy hadn't got back yet from the hospital, and no, there was no light on in his cabin, and no, sir, he would have seen the headlights if the pickup had come down the road.

I walked back across the street to the car and sat down heavily behind the steering wheel.

'Where do you want to go now, kiddo?' I said.

She shook her head quietly and looked straight ahead at the dark line of mountains. Her face was drained of emotion now, and her hands lay open in her lap. I put my arm briefly around her shoulders, and we drove back in silence to her house.

She wanted the glass of whiskey now, but I took it out of her hand and walked her upstairs to bed. It was dark in her bedroom, and she turned her head on the pillow towards the opposite wall, but I could see that her eyes were still opened when I covered her.

'I'll be downstairs when you wake up,' I said, and closed the door softly behind me.

I fixed coffee in the kitchen while the blueness of the night began to fade outside and the false dawn rimmed the edge of the mountains. I poured a shot of whiskey into the coffee and smoked cigarettes until my lungs were raw and my fingers and the backs of my legs started to shake with fatigue and strain. I lay back on the couch and closed my eyes, but there were red flashes of colour in my head and that persistent hum in my blood that I had felt in jail. I touched my brow, and my fingers were covered with perspiration.

I put on my coat and walked out into the cold, early light and drove to the sheriff's office. The streets were empty, and newspapers in plastic wrappers lay upon the quiet lawns. Some of the kitchens in the houses were lighted, and occasionally I caught a glimpse of a working man bent over his breakfast.

I walked up the courthouse steps, trying to light a cigarette in the wind. I was sweating inside my clothes, and when I entered the gloom of the hallway and smelled the odour of the spittoons and dead cigars, the hum started to grow louder in my head. Three sheriff's deputies sat on wooden chairs in front of the dispatcher's cage, reading parts of the newspaper and yawning. A drunk who had just bonded out of the tank was accusing the dispatcher of taking money out of his wallet while it was in Possessions.

'You used it to go bail,' the dispatcher said. The other deputies never looked up from their paper. Their faces were tired and had the greenish cast of men who worked all night.

'I had thirty-five goddamn dollars in there,' the drunk said.

'Get the hell out of here before I take you upstairs again,' one of the deputies said from behind his paper.

The dispatcher looked at me from his radio desk.

'Yes, sir?' he said.

I started to speak, but didn't get the chance.

'What are you doing in here?' the sheriff's voice said behind me.

His khaki sleeves were rolled up over his massive fat arms, and the splayed end of his cigar was stuck in the centre of his mouth. He clicked his Mason's ring on the clipboard that he carried in one hand.

'Do you have Buddy Riordan in jail?' I said.

'Should I?'

'I don't know.'

'What's he been doing?'

'He didn't come home last night.'

His head tilted slightly, and he narrowed his eyes at me.

'What is this, Paret?'

'I want to know if he's in jail. That's not hard to understand.'

He took the cigar out of his mouth and pushed his tongue into one cheek.

'Did you book Buddy Riordan in here last night?' he said to the dispatcher.

'No, sir.'

The sheriff looked back at me.

'Is that all you want?' he said.

'Sheriff, there's something you might want to know,' the dispatcher said. 'One of the deputies at the Ravalli office called on the mobile unit and said that three guys shot the hell out of Frank Riordan's birds last night.'

The sheriff walked to the spittoon, his head bowed into position as though he were over a toilet, and spit a dripping stream into it.

'What was Buddy driving?' he said.

I wanted to get back out into the cold air again, away from the hissing radiators and the indolent, flat eyes of the men looking at me.

'Forget it,' I said. 'He's probably on a drunk over in Idaho.'

'Don't fool with me, son. I ain't up to it this morning.'

I lit my cigarette and wiped my damp hair back over my head.

'Give me that accident report that come in from Frenchtown,' the sheriff said to the dispatcher. He took his glasses out of his shirt pocket and squinted at the small writing on the paper.

'Was he driving a '55 Ford pickup?' he said, pulling his glasses off his nose.

'Yes.' I felt something drop inside me.

'Take a ride with me.'

He started walking down the hallway towards the front door, his waist like an inner-tube under his shirt. I remained motionless, the cigarette hanging in my mouth, watching his huge silhouette walk towards the square of dawn outside.

'You better go with him, mister,' the dispatcher said.

I caught up with the sheriff outside on the glazed footpath. I could feel my shoes slipping on the ice, but his very weight seemed to give him traction on the cement.

'All right, what are we playing?' I said.

'Get in.' But this time his voice was lower and more human.

I got in on the passenger's side and closed the door. The sawn-off twelve-gauge pump clipped vertically against the dashboard knocked against my knees. He flicked on the bubblegum light without the siren, and we headed west out of town. He was breathing heavily from the fast walk to the car.

'About an hour ago a '55 pickup went off the road on 263 and rolled all the way down to the river,' he said.

My head was swimming.

'So what the hell are we doing?' I said. 'You've got a junked truck in the river. You want me to identify it so you can give Buddy a citation?'

He opened the wind vane and flipped his cigar out. He waited a moment, and I saw his hands tense on the wheel before he turned to me with his pie-plate face.

'The driver's still in there, Paret. It burned.'

We drove down the highway by the side of the Clark, and the water was blue and running fast in the middle between the sheets of ice that extended from the banks. The sun came up bright in a clear sky over the mountains, and men were fishing with wet flies and maggots for whitefish on the tips of the sandbars. The thick pines on the sides of the mountains were dark green and bent with the weight of the new snow, and the sunlight on the ice-covered boulders refracted with an iridescence that made your eyes water.

The truck was scorched black, and all the windows had exploded from the heat. There was a large melted area around it in the snow, and the tyres had burned away to the rims. I could see the huge scars in the rock incline where the truck had rolled end over end and had come to rest against a cottonwood tree, as though its driver had simply wanted to park there with a high-school girl after a dance. The men from the coroner's office had already wrapped the body in a rubber sheet, covered it with canvas, and strapped it on an alpine stretcher that they worked slowly up the incline. A deputy sheriff walked to the car with the melted barrel and torn magazine of a rifle in his hand. The stock had been burned away, and the ejection lever hung down from the trigger.

'Look at this son of a bitch,' he said. 'Every shell in it blew up. He must have had a bunch of them in his clothes, too, because they went off all over him.'

We were outside the car now, standing in the snow, though I

didn't remember how we got there. Across the river the sunlight fell on the white mountain as it would on a mirror.

You don't know it's Buddy, I thought. *There are ranchers all over this county that drive pickup trucks, and they all carry a lever-action in the deer rack. Every week a drunk cowboy goes off the road in a pickup. And this one just happened to burn.*

'You don't know who he is,' I said, my voice loud even to myself.

The deputy looked at me curiously.

'Did you find anything that says who he was?' the sheriff said.

'No, sir. The tag was burned up, and so was anything in the glove. But like the coroner said, the damnedest thing is the way that guy went out. He must have caught his head inside the steering wheel when he turned over, and the top half of him was burned into a piece of cork. But there wasn't a mark on his legs, except for a tattoo inside his thigh.'

I walked away from the car, along the shoulder of the road and the glistening shine of the snow melting on the asphalt and the yellow grass that protruded through the gravel. I could hear the cottonwoods clatter dryly against one another in the wind along the river, and water was ticking somewhere in flat drops off a boulder into a crystalline pool. Then I heard the powerful engine of the sheriff's car next to me, the idle racing, and his voice straining through the half-open passenger's window.

I turned and looked at him as I might at someone from the other side of the moon. He was trying to hold the wheel with one hand and roll down the window completely with the other. His pie-plate face was filled with blood and exertion, and his words came out with a laboured wheeze in his chest.

Get in, Paret.

That's all right, Sheriff. I just got to stretch it out a little bit.

Get in, son. Then he pulled the car at an angle to me so I couldn't walk down the road farther, and popped the door handle on the passenger's side.

Take a drink out of this.

The steam on the highway sucked away under us, and then we began to pass cars full of families and ranchers in pickups and a few gyppo loggers that were still operating in western Montana.

They were all in their ordered place, driving into a yellow, wintry sun, with the confident knowledge that they would never have to correct time when there was none left.

Take another bite out of that bottle.

I felt the steady vibration of the engine under my feet, and then I saw the mountains re-form and come back into shape on the horizon, and the river was once more a blue spangle of light coursing through the sheets of ice far below.

That's better, ain't it?

Sure.

Damn right, it is. And he turned up the volume on his mobile unit and drove intently with a fresh purpose.

EPILOGUE

Frank Riordan was in the hospital four weeks, and by the time he was released, the lawyers for the lumber mills had got his injunction lifted. So when they brought him back home in the ambulance, he could look out the window and see the smoke in the valley from the pulp mill and the plumes rising in dirty strings from the tepee burners.

But he didn't seem to care now. His right side was paralysed from the stroke, his arm was frozen at a crooked angle against his rib cage, and when he talked, his mouth worked as though there was a stitch sewn on the edge of his lips. He stayed in a wheelchair the first two months at home, and then he was able to walk about the house with a stick, but he looked stricken and grey as though a light had been blown out inside him. When the weather started to warm towards the end of March, I took him fishing with me on the Bitterroot, and he could hold the rod stiffly and work the automatic reel with his atrophied hand and take up the slack line with the other. He couldn't wade the stream or false cast, and he had to stay in one position and use wet flies, but when he hooked into a rainbow, I could see a smile come back into his grey eyes again.

Beth and I were married in a Catholic church in Missoula, and I bought twenty acres off Mr Riordan by the base of that blue canyon that cuts back through the mountain into the climbing pines beyond. Twenty acres isn't much in Montana, but it's mine, and it has a small stream and apple trees on it, and at night the deer come down to feed in the grass under an ivory moon. Two of the musicians from the band helped me build a split-log house on it, with a huge stone fireplace and a chimney and a front porch that looks out towards the river, the line of cottonwoods along the banks, and the infinite roll of the mountains beyond the fields.

I finished my song. I didn't get everything into it that I had wanted; but maybe you never do, just like the time my cousin André and I tried to raise in our young vanity that dead Indian's canoe from the silt bottom of the swamp. But I got most of it – the bottle trees during the depression, the smoky green of the Gulf at sunset, the Southern Pacific blowing down the line at night towards Mobile. My parole officer gave me interstate travel privileges, and I drove up to Vancouver with Beth and our bass man and recorded it. It wasn't a big record. It was released only on the West Coast, but it played on the radio and on jukeboxes for a month, and two weeks after I thought it had been melted into slag, a recording studio in Nashville called and asked me to send a tape of anything else I had written.

It's May now, and the runoff from the snowpack on the mountain behind my house has filled the creek bed in the canyon with a torrent of white water that bursts over the boulders in a rainbow's spray, lighting the pine and fir trees along the bank with a dripping sheen, and then flattens out at the base of the mountain and runs in a brown course through the pasture towards the river. The grass is tall and humming with insects where the water has flowed out into the field, and occasionally I can see the sun flash on the red beaks of mudhens in the reeds. The river is high and yellow, the sandbars and gravel islands have disappeared under the churning surface, and the bottoms of the cottonwoods cut long, trembling Vs in the current. I can feel the spring catching harder each day, and the irrigated fields across the river are a wet, sunlit green against the far mountains and the patches of snow still melting among the pines on the crest.

In the early evening it turns suddenly cool, you can smell wood smoke in the air, and mauve shadows fall across the valley floor as the sun strikes its final spark against the ridge. From my front porch, I can see Buddy's cabin faintly in the gathering dusk. Even after it has dissolved into the darkness and black trees and the laughter of his sons playing in the yard, I can still see it in mind's eye, lighted, the wood stove lined with fire, and sometil in that moment I'm caught for ever in the sound of a blues pia and the beating of my own heart.